Also by Barbara Metzger

The Scandalous Life of a True Lady

Barbara Metzger

A SIGNET ECLIPSE BOOK

SIGNET ECLIPSE
Published by New American Library, a division of
Penguin Group (USA) Inc., 375 Hudson Street,
New York, New York 10014, USA
Penguin Group (Canada), 90 Eglinton Avenue East, Suite 700, Toronto,
Ontario M4P 2Y3, Canada (a division of Pearson Penguin Canada Inc.)
Penguin Books Ltd., 80 Strand, London WC2R 0RL, England
Penguin Ireland, 25 St. Stephen's Green, Dublin 2,
Ireland (a division of Penguin Books Ltd.)
Penguin Group (Australia), 250 Camberwell Road, Camberwell, Victoria 3124,
Australia (a division of Pearson Australia Group Pty. Ltd.)
Penguin Books India Pvt. Ltd., 11 Community Centre, Panchsheel Park,
New Delhi - 110 017, India
Penguin Group (NZ), 67 Apollo Drive, Rosedale, North Shore 0632,
New Zealand (a division of Pearson New Zealand Ltd.)
Penguin Books (South Africa) (Pty.) Ltd., 24 Sturdee Avenue,
Rosebank, Johannesburg 2196, South Africa

Penguin Books Ltd., Registered Offices:
80 Strand, London WC2R 0RL, England

First published by Signet Eclipse, an imprint of New American Library,
a division of Penguin Group (USA) Inc.

First Printing, June 2008
10 9 8 7 6 5 4 3 2 1

To Dreamers and Believers

Chapter One

Virginity was just another commodity, like coal or carrots. That's what Simone told herself, anyway. She had no coal to heat her rented attic room, no carrots—or anything else—in her tiny larder. In fact she would not have a cot to sleep on or a roof over her head at the end of the week, not without the rent money. She had no hidden skills, no new talents, nothing that could earn her a living, much less keep her young brother in school and out of the manufactories or mines.

Simone Ryland was willing to work, and had tried to do so for the last three years since her parents' deaths. She had taught languages learned from her half-French mother, and tutored in Latin, her scholar father's passion. Each position had ended in failure or flight, since each post had included dealing with the master of the house, an older son, a superior male servant, even a visiting clergyman at one residence. They all seemed to think that the red-haired governess was fair game. One so-called gentleman would bear the brand of a fireplace poker for the rest of his life as proof she was not playing. Simone almost landed in prison that time, except the baron's wife did not wish the scandal of a trial. Now Simone had no references, and thus no chance of being hired by a school as an instructress, or by a respectable household as a governess, nursemaid, companion, secretary, or parlormaid. She did not cook well enough to be considered for kitchen staff.

Shopkeepers wanted male clerks; seamstresses wanted faster sewers; theaters wanted women who could sing or dance, if they could not act. Simone had tried her hand at serving in a tavern. She'd raised her hand to two lecherous drunks, lost the pub money, and lost her job, along with her bed and board. For a peaceful person, Simone was resorting to more violence than she had seen in her life, all to protect her last valuable asset. Diamonds could be sold and recut, then sold again. Virginity, that sought-after commodity, had one sale, once. A man had no other way of knowing his children were of his own line. The loftier the title, the greater the wealth, the wider the acres, the more a chaste bride was valued. Let a stableboy's son inherit an earldom? Hell, no.

Simone's worth as a bride no longer mattered; finding her next meal did. She had nothing left to sell, no jewels or books or fancy fabrics, only herself. And time was running out. Not just the month's rent and her brother's tuition, but her looks and her youth. At twenty-two, she was growing old in a business that valued fresh-faced girls from the country; worry and hunger did nothing for her appearance. It was now or never, do or die. Then her brother, Auguste, would die with her; his chances of a better life, at least. Condemn Auguste to ignorance and poverty? She could not do that, whatever the cost.

Her half-French mother would shriek and tear at her clothes. Her English father would bluster and bellow. But they were the ones who left her—unintentionally, of course; no one could have foreseen the riding accident or the influenza epidemic, respectively, that carried them away—without a guardian, without a dowry, without a bank account. Her mother's relations had likely perished in France; her father's family had paid him an annuity to stay away after his embarrassing misalliance to tainted blood. The Ryland remittance had ended with Papa's death, with no acknowledgment except a message from the bank saying the payments would cease. The only legacies her parents left were medical bills and a little boy. Simone sold their house, then her father's books and her mother's clothes and trinkets, just to get Auggie to boarding school so he could go on to university to become something, anything. Simone hoped he'd choose the law, since she'd lost respect for the church and was afraid of his chances in the army.

Auggie would join the army in an instant, she knew. He'd stick his scrawny chest out and forbid her to take up a life of sin. Then he'd go get himself shot. Or else he'd take a job at the mills and die in the machines.

But Simone had sworn to her mother to look after him. Besides, her practical side reminded her, his sacrifice would not help her one bit. A bookish boy could never earn enough to support the both of them, not even as a clerk in some dreary office. She could, by sacrificing her honor, her hopes for marriage, her self-esteem. To be realistic—which hunger encouraged her to be—Simone knew she was lucky to have kept her maidenhead this long. Sooner or later some employer or customer or chance-met stranger was going to trap her in a dark corner, simply because she was unprotected and too weak to defend herself, despite the long hatpin that adorned her reticule. Why, even Mr. Fordyce, the first-floor boarder, crowded her on the stairs when he thought their landlady wasn't looking. Mrs. Olmstead said he was a financier of some kind, making investments and reaping the profits. Simone thought it was peculiar, if not scary, the way he never spoke or smiled, and always wore a black knitted scarf around his neck, even when the weather was mild. The thought of being his victim made Simone shudder now, even though the sun shone brightly.

No, better she sell her virginity, rather than let some dastard steal it from her. She might as well profit from its loss.

Her degradation would not last forever, either. Well, her purposeful fall from grace was irredeemable, Simone supposed, but her new occupation would last only until Auguste became a solicitor, perhaps even a barrister in time, able to keep them both from the poorhouse. He, at least, would be respectable enough to tell the Rylands to go to the devil.

Which was right where Simone was headed now, before she lost her nerve.

Luckily the path to perdition started nearby.

Mrs. Olmstead's rooming house faced a larger, more handsome establishment diagonally across the street. From her high, narrow window, Simone could see carriages coming and going all evening. Some were hired hacks, but many of the coaches had crests on their doors, liveried grooms, and highbred horses between the traces. Others were expensive sporting vehicles, with, she guessed, more-expensive horses. By the streetlamp's light she could tell that the gentlemen who stepped down were all elegantly dressed, swinging their walking sticks and top hats as if they had no concerns. They could afford a night's pleasure; their reputations were not in jeopardy for entering the premises. None appeared terribly inebriated, although Simone never stayed awake to watch the last departures. They never escorted any of the women out, unless they used a rear door.

Simone had seen the women. To her landlady's horror, the ladies of the night attended Sunday morning services at nearby St. Jerome's. Mrs. Olmstead had pulled Simone away to a farther pew, lest she be tainted. The females, some mere girls, were not all painted and rouged. Granted, some of them looked tired, and many appeared petulant at having to come out on their day off, but they did not seem all that different from the rest of the congregants. They had no horns sprouting from their heads, no marks of shame branded on their foreheads.

The madam herded them in, then preceded them out after the sermon, which always dwelled on the sins of the flesh. The abbess, as Mrs. Olmstead called her, stared straight ahead and held her chin high.

"Arrogant, that's what," Mrs. Olmstead had declared, "and if that Mrs. Lydia Burton was ever married, I'll eat my Sunday bonnet. Disrespectful, her coming to church like that, no matter what she leaves on the plate or in the poor box. Money won't buy her way into heaven."

No, but it did purchase her the finest building on the street. Mrs. Burton's house was freshly painted, her flower beds were well tended, and her kitchens always sent out enticing aromas. The girls there did not starve, it seemed. No matter; becoming one of them was not Simone's intention. Being bachelor fare in a house of accommodation would not serve her purposes. Her parents had taught her better than that, given her a higher estimation of her own worth.

The man who opened the door at Mrs. Burton's establishment did not share her opinion. He was as formidable as any starchy butler in his black coat, and as rough-hewn as a dockworker. Simone supposed he served as gatekeeper, to keep undesirables out and keep the gentlemen in order. He was large enough—that was for certain—and appeared to be built of stone, with crags and crevices. He was as immovable as granite when she asked to see Mrs. Burton about a position.

He looked her over, looking down, from her ugly bonnet to her rusty black cloak and her dull gray gown to her serviceable boots.

"We ain't hiring no schoolmarms." He started to shut the door in Simone's face, but she placed one of those sturdy boots in the opening.

"I fear your grammar could use improvement, sir. But I am well aware of the nature of Mrs. Burton's establishment."

"Then you know you ain't one of her type. Go on back to governessing, where you belong."

The primrose path might have been short, merely across the street, but Simone felt as if she'd climbed a mountain. She might as well have, for the difference in the two worlds between Mrs. Olmstead's and Mrs. Burton's. She would never have the courage to make the journey twice, so she stiffened her backbone, thought of her younger brother, and glanced around the entryway behind the majordomo. She nodded at the valuable Chinese urn holding canes and umbrellas, the silk wallpaper, and the spotless marble tiles.

"Mrs. Burton's enterprise appears to pay better than educating young minds," she said. "I wish to speak to her about becoming a . . . a . . ." She couldn't say it. She could *do* it, she hoped. She went on: "If someone is going to take what they wish, I want to be paid for it. And paid well."

"You got bottom, missy, I'll grant you that. The nobs like a wench with spirit. You might do, with some fancifying. I'll ask Lydia if she's hiring."

*   *   *

The madam found Simone's request amusing. "*You* wish to become a courtesan?"

Simone swallowed her indignation. Who knew the standards for the low life were so high? "I wish to become a rich man's *chérie amour*, yes." She had decided on that course as her best option. She would choose the man herself; one man. He had to be clean, respectful, and rich. Also generous and kind, but mostly rich. "A gentleman's mistress."

"Then why did you come here, where the arrangements are far less formal and certainly shorter? You should attend the Cyprian's Ball or some such to make a more permanent kind of arrangement." Her half smile showed what she thought of Simone's chances among the Fashionable Impures. "Not that any such, ah, liaisons are lasting."

"I do not seek permanency. And I came to you because I live across the street and I have seen you at church. I have heard that your reputation is for honesty," Simone said, "and for treating your, ah, employees well. I thought you might assist me in making that other kind of connection. For a fee, of course."

"Of course. No nob dips his wick for free. Not here."

Simone blushed. It was all well to put her foot in the waters, so to speak, but she'd been raised in a genteel household. Perhaps coming here was not such a good idea.

Mrs. Burton ignored Simone's reddened cheeks as she poured tea. "I'm not certain I want to be known as a procuress."

What else was the madam of a bordello—a matchmaker? Simone accepted a cup of tea. "I merely hoped you might know of a gentleman seeking a longer, more . . . personal relationship."

"Tell me—why not look for a husband?"

Maybe the woman was a matchmaker after all. So Simone explained how she had no dowry, no family connections, no great wealth or title. She did not mention that her father had been disowned, that her half-French mother was also half-Gypsy, or that she had a young brother to support. His existence, his innocence, his very name, did not belong here with her disgrace. She did tell Mrs. Burton about her onetime suitor in Oxford, a neighbor who was not willing to take a penniless bride after her parents' deaths.

The madam shrugged. "It's a common enough story: a girl disappointed by a cad who was less interested in her than in what she could bring him. Men are selfish swine at the best of times. Remember that. It is not enough to have a lovely mother for their sons, a willing woman in their beds, a helpmate for life. They want gold, too, the fools."

Simone nodded as if she agreed with the businesswoman who made a good living selling love. "Were you disappointed that way?"

Mrs. Burton did not take offense at Simone's personal question, thank goodness. "Hell no. I married a rich old man who did me the favor of leaving me enough brass to set myself up in business, bless him and his bad heart. I chose this trade because I thought I'd be good at it. Why did you?" she asked, just as bluntly.

Simone repeated her tale of work gone wretched, fire poker and all. "I no longer have references for"—she almost said "honest employment" before recalling her hostess's profession—"teaching positions. Other jobs I tried offered insult and injury, without decent wage. I feel the, ah, demimonde is my best course. Will you help me?"

Mrs. Burton tidied the dish of biscuits in front of her. "You say you speak several languages?"

Perhaps the madam knew of a foreign gentleman in need of a mistress. Simone counted off her qualifications. "French, Italian, and Spanish, a bit of German. I can read and translate Latin, but not Greek." Again, she made no mention of Romany, which, in her experience, led only to distrust and fear, as if she were going to steal horses or children or candlesticks, or put a curse on someone's house. She had wished she could, a few times, but no one had taught her that Gypsy magic, if it existed.

"You say you have served in homes of polite society? Yes, I can see where your manners are refined enough."

Simone had wondered why the older woman had watched so carefully as Simone handled the fragile teacup, used her serviette, and nibbled daintily at the tiny biscuits that were the only meal she'd have this day. She'd taken a second one only when Mrs. Burton did. Now she said, "One child I taught was the daughter of a member of Parliament; another was of a titled family." The so-called gentlemen at those addresses were no better than the patrons of the pub where she briefly worked. Inebriated, poorly washed, they all thought their coins entitled them to take liberties. "I learned my manners from my parents, however. My father was manor born. And my mother's mother"—who scandalously wed a Gypsy horse trader—"was descended from French nobility."

"You just might do. Take off your bonnet, if that is what you call that monstrosity, and let your hair down, please."

"Here? Now?"

"Modesty is out of place for this calling, my dear. And I need to see what your governessy garments are hiding. All cats might be alike in the dark, but a tom who's going to have a pampered kitten on his arm at the opera expects more."

"Of course." At least Simone thought she understood. She rose and set her hat down, then started pulling out pins from her straight red hair, inherited from her English father. Her nearly black eyes must have come from the Gypsies, along with her almond complexion, for both of her parents had light eyes and fair skin. Simone unbraided the coronet of curls fixed to the back of her head and spread it out with her fingers. She always wore her hair scraped back and carefully confined like this to avoid any hint of wantonness. Now it fell over her shoulders, down her back, in red-gold waves where it had been in the braid so long. Her serviceable gray gown pulled across her chest as she combed out the curls, and Mrs. Burton walked around her, clucking her tongue.

"What a shame you have wasted all this for so long. That hair, those eyes . . . but yes, you just might do, and we both might profit. I have a gentleman in mind."

"A client?"

"A patron, if you will, but more a friend. He helped me start my business, so I owe him a favor. He expressed a need for a female to accompany him to a house party at a country estate. None of my ladies is respectable enough."

"He would bring his mistress to a house party?"

"It's a bachelor gathering for the swells. They're bringing their own entertainment from Town."

Simone started to gather her hair up again. "An orgy? I will not—"

Mrs. Burton laughed. "Gracious, no. You must have been listening to your landlady, that old biddy. My, ah, friend would not take part in anything that scandalous. Not since he's come of age, anyway. Nor would some of the other guests, from what I hear. Government types and businessmen, with reputations to uphold, don't you know.

As far as the neighbors will see, this party will be as polite as a debutante ball, without chaperones, of course. Another old friend of mine will act as hostess. She's been Lord Gorham's mistress for the past ten years, at least."

"It sounds . . . lovely."

"Well, it is a few days only, and nights, naturally. But if you please my friend, who knows but he might keep you on? He is generous."

Now, that truly did sound lovely. "If he is generous, I shall make sure I please him."

"That's the ticket, dearie. Just be honest."

If Simone were honest, she'd admit her knees were knocking together at the very prospect.

Mrs. Burton went on, "If it doesn't work out, you come on back. With proper clothes and a bit of training, you could make a lot of money right here."

"I'd rather try to find a wealthy protector, ma'am. No offense. But a house, jewels I could sell, a bit of security for the future, that's what I want."

"Don't we all, dearie. Don't we all."

Chapter Two

After a few more questions, Mrs. Burton rose to cross to her cluttered desk. "Help yourself to more biscuits while I send a note to Harry," she told Simone as she pulled a sheet of paper closer. "The gentlemen like a female to have a bit of meat on her bones."

The madam filled her delicate chair and her bodice in ways Simone never hoped to. She did hope the woman's old friend approved of her, despite her lack of soft curves and billowy bosom. The house party sounded like a distinguished gathering, one that might even offer other avenues of employment. Who knew but some nobleman's mistress had a misbegotten child that needed a governess? Simone could not afford to miss the chance. Besides, Mrs. Burton's patron must be intelligent and well-mannered if he demanded the same in his companion. From what the older woman said, Simone suspected he was of middle years, no randy youth or rakish, hardened town buck. He'd know she was inexperienced from the letter being written, so his expectations could not be too high. How low was too low? Simone's education had serious gaps, especially when it came to questions of what a man expected for his money, and how much money was involved, anyway.

For that matter, Simone realized she should have come to terms with Mrs. Burton first, to agree on who got what share of the gentleman's largesse. Simone needed the coins more, and she'd inherited more than black eyes from the horse-trading grandfather she'd loved as a child. It would never do to offend the woman, though, not before the letter was sent. Mrs. Burton might decide Simone was not biddable enough for her efforts, or too mercenary for an aristocrat's mistress. Members of polite society, Simone knew, believed discussions of money matters to be crass. Which, she supposed, was why so many of them landed in dun territory or debtors' prison, and why so many of their merchants' bills went unpaid. Did such foolish conventions hold among light-skirts and their protectors? Simone could not afford such nicety in her dealings. Why, she might have to ask the gentleman for an advance on her pay, if he expected her to dress the part of a highly paid courtesan.

Simone had to laugh at herself, counting her chickens before the rooster arrived. He might decide she was too old, too plain, too unskilled, too unsophisticated to be his paramour. The doorman had not thought she had the proper—or improper—qualities. Neither did the women who peeked into the open door, then giggled. Their hair was prinked in ringlets, their breasts pushed over their low-cut bodices, and their skirts had been shortened to show a bit of lace petticoat or silk stocking. No, Simone did not look like one of them and never had, not even when her family was in funds.

Mr. Harry had not hired any of them, she reminded herself again for confidence, taking another biscuit. In case he did not like her, or like what Mrs. Burton wrote, at least her belly would be full.

Men *were* interested in her. Otherwise she would not

be in this fix, unless males commonly assaulted any female to cross their paths. No, no one had tried to take advantage of her in Oxford, under her parents' roof. Why, her own beau, the suitor she thought she'd marry when he established himself in his career, had never tried to steal a kiss. Too bad she had not aroused in him the same ardor some of her employers had shown. Then the young curate might have wed her despite her lack of dowry.

Simone could not decide if she actually wanted to be the object of this Harry's passions. If he did not hire her—or did not reply to Mrs. Burton's note—then she was not a fallen woman, unless her landlady had seen her cross the street. Surely in all of London there was an employment agency that did not require references. Or some old bat so difficult no one else would work for her. Simone could try harder to find a post. Maybe Mrs. Olmstead would let her clean the house in exchange for rent. Maybe Mr. Fordyce downstairs needed a secretary. Simone quickly dismissed that idea. But maybe Mrs. Burton would pay her to instruct the women here. After all, if none were acceptable for a genteel house party, they ought to be taught, to attract a higher class of customer. That was a far better plan.

Simone almost interrupted Mrs. Burton's pen scratching. But what if men wanted their women ignorant and silly and soft? This house obviously was a success, with just such fluffy wares for sale. There was nothing frothy about Simone, not a curl, not a frill, not a giggle.

And she had no heart for the transaction she was contemplating. She reached for her black cloak. Then she remembered her brother and sank back on her cushioned chair. The biscuits were all gone, along with her choices.

Mrs. Burton rang a little bell on her desk and the beefy doorkeeper came, as if he'd been waiting nearby to come to her aid. "See that this is delivered to Harry, George. If you bring it to McCann's Club, they'll know where to find him. I'll be waiting for an answer."

George looked at the folded sheet, then at Simone. "Harry?" Disbelief resounded in his voice.

Mrs. Burton waved him on his way with one beringed hand. "By the time our Harry arrives, he'll be pleased."

George still seemed dubious, so Simone's hopes—if hopes they were; she was still undecided—sank. "I should go back home and wait there."

Mrs. Burton brushed that aside, too. "What, would you have me bring Harry to Mrs. Olmstead's? Should we discuss your business in her front parlor, which I'd wager is dark and dreary?"

The woman was right on all counts. Mrs. Olmstead would have apoplexy to see Lydia Burton on her doorstep, much less with Simone's prospective lover in tow. She'd die of outrage; then Simone would have another sin on her head. "Heavens, no. But you could send for me. Or I could watch out of my window."

"Hm. That might be better. Then Harry and I could settle the finances right off. You wouldn't want to be haggling over pounds and pence the minute you meet him. I'll take care of that business for you."

Simone was not quite sure she trusted the gleam in Mrs. Burton's eyes, a gleam that matched the diamonds in her ears and on her wrists. Simone might sacrifice her scruples, but she meant to hold tight to her wits. Let a bawdy house madam settle her fees, and perhaps keep more than her fair share for making the introduction? Not likely. "You said Mr., ah, Harry was generous. I think we should see if we suit first, before worrying over the money."

"You'll suit. I'll see to it. One of the girls must be about your size. Come."

Simone was supposed to wear the trappings of a prostitute? Oh, dear. "I do not wish to appear too . . . too . . ."
She could not think of a word that would not offend her
hostess.

"Fast? Loose?" Mrs. Burton supplied, frowning.
"Immoral?"

The unknown Harry would know she was a fallen
woman by her presence here. Simone did not want to appear cheap or tawdry. Her intention was to command a
substantial fee. She settled on, "Unladylike."

"Of course not. Harry is particular. Otherwise any of
my girls might have done well enough. We'll find something suitable, never fear." She sniffed. "And anything
would be better than what you have on. I suppose all of
your gowns are fit for the trash bin?"

"For the schoolroom. I do have one silk gown for dinner, but it is gray." And shapeless and adorned with a single frayed ribbon.

"We wish to impress Harry, not depress him. Come on,
now. There is much to be done."

Like making a silk purse out of a cow's ear. Simone
would have thought it impossible, until she saw the results. Lydia Burton was not simply a businesswoman or a
matchmaker; she was a fairy godmother. She waved her
wand—her glittering hand, at any rate—and miracles
happened.

Watching herself being transformed, Simone worried
they were all wasting their time and efforts. "What if he
doesn't come?"

"Oh, he will. Harry knows I would not bother him
without good reason. Besides, he is not half as busy now
that the war is over."

"He works with the army, then? The government? Or
does he deal with supplies or shipping?"

Mrs. Burton bit her lip as she supervised Simone's new hairstyle. "He'll tell you what he wishes you to know. Gentlemen cherish their secrets and their privacy. You must remember that, Miss Ryland, above all in this business. What is spoken in private must stay private. Do you understand?"

"Of course." And not at all. Weren't the girls rushing to do the madam's bidding gossiping about their latest patrons? Simone assumed there were different rules for becoming a mistress.

Someone produced a gown that Mrs. Burton deemed acceptable, but it was too long for Simone, too wide around, too gaping at the collar. An older woman quickly fetched pins and needles and thread.

"I cannot pay you," Simone told her. "Or any of you, for the loan of the gown, the alterations, the help with my hair."

"Oh, we'd do anything for our Harry," one of them answered, and they all agreed.

He was a favorite of the house, it seemed. Simone was not sure if that was good or bad, either. Obviously he was a womanizer, not likely to keep a steady mistress. Just as certain, he was a friendly fellow, polite to all classes, and considerate. He'd brought this woman ribbons for her new bonnet, sent a message to that one's brother, sent a homesick girl back to the country, and delivered medicine when anyone fell ill. He always brought sweets when he came, and often read novels to the girls when they were not busy. Why, the man sounded like a veritable paragon—except that this was a brothel, not a charity home.

When Simone started to ask more about him, his age, his looks, his likes and dislikes, Lydia clapped her hands. "Privacy, ladies, privacy." She meant Harry's, not

Simone's. "Let us leave Miss Ryland to form her own opinions. It is the impression she will make on Harry that we are concerned about, not the other way about."

Soon the lovely gown was raised over her head again, and over her plain mended shift.

Mrs. Burton frowned but did not insist Simone disrobe completely. "No one will be seeing that today, thank goodness."

The gown was a dark vibrant blue watered silk. The color matched Harry's eyes, Molly swore. Harry's eyes were more like sapphires, Susie said, although she'd seen only paste copies of the gems. Nell declared Harry's eyes were prettier than any jewel, because of the dark rims around the blue, and because they sparkled so when he laughed.

Simone relaxed a bit. The man sounded charming. She might even like him, which was far more than she'd expected.

The gown's neckline was far lower than she'd expected. The borrowed corset forced her breasts higher than she was used to, but now the gown looked as if it were made for her, and she were made for a man's admiration. She did not object. No one would have listened, for one thing, and she wanted to win Harry's approval, for another.

Her hair was gathered loosely instead of in its tight braids, twirled into fashion with a curling iron, and held up with a bouquet of silk violets Meg volunteered.

"Lord Maynes couldn't keep his regular appointment. His wife was in Town, so he sent these instead."

Everyone laughed except for the madam, who chided them again. "Privacy, girls."

Then Jenny brought out a tray of cosmetics.

Face paints? "Oh, I could not use—"

The job was done before Simone finished the sentence. A blush of color on her almond skin highlighted her prominent cheekbones and made her coloring seem sun-kissed instead of swarthy; a dark line around her eyes made them look wider and mysterious, instead of just somber; an ashy substance seemed to make her lashes longer; polish disguised the rough treatment her fingernails had recently undergone. Lydia fixed a strand of pearls around Simone's neck and declared them just the proper touch for a well-bred miss. "Nothing garish, mind. Harry would not want that." Then she bade Simone stand and walk across the room.

Simone took one step before her fairy godmother cursed and clutched her heart. "By Satan's short hairs, she is wearing blasted boots!"

Five girls ran to find slippers to fit.

Then Simone walked the way her mother had taught her: back straight, chin high, in smooth, graceful steps.

"Ooh, don't she look like a lady for true?"

Lydia poured them each a glass of wine in celebration. "Let us hope so, for Harry's sake."

Chapter Three

"To Harry!" someone cheered.

"And to Miss Ryland, for luck," another woman added, so Simone raised her glass to them all. "To new friends and good fortunes."

"Especially the good fortunes," Mrs. Burton added.

George, the butler, cleared his throat at the door to the proprietress's private parlor, then entered and whispered in her ear.

"Major Harrison is coming? Drat the man. I was hoping for—" Lydia caught herself from saying more and clapped her hands to get the girls' attention. "Privacy, my dears. You know how Major Harrison feels about his personal life. I am sure you have chores to do to ready yourselves for this evening. Meg, your singing voice needs practice. Sally, your hair appears dull. Some lemon juice, perhaps?"

In minutes they were all gone, with the jars and sewing baskets and extra slippers.

Simone set down her glass. "Someone else is coming? I was quite getting used to the idea of Harry. He sounded a pleasant sort."

"Oh, he is, and that's our Harry. Major Harrison. I

wish he could cease—" She stopped herself again. "Oh, well, he is coming within the hour."

Simone wished the madam had completed the sentence. At least now she knew that Harry was a military man, an officer and a gentleman. He was well-off if he'd purchased the rank, courageous if he'd earned it on the field of battle. Like many other officers, he would most likely resign his commission now that Napoleon was finally defeated, unless he was old enough to have fought long ago or had a desk job in London. Or he might have been injured during the war and retired on half pay, which would not serve Simone's purposes at all. What if he was scarred or maimed and that was why he could not find a willing woman for himself? Oh, dear. Then there were commanding officers who were martinets, used to having their every order obeyed. Oh, dear, oh, dear.

She must have moaned aloud, for Lydia refilled her wineglass. "Don't worry," she said, mistaking the source of Simone's distress. "Harry will be pleased. I am certain of that, especially if you remember one important thing."

"I know, to respect his privacy."

"Two things, then. His privacy and his demand for honesty. Harry is the most accommodating fellow in England, but he cannot abide lies. Just tell him the truth, and you'll do fine."

Tell him the truth, that she was terrified, mortified, and unqualified? Simone groaned.

"You are not going to swoon, are you?"

"I never have before," Simone answered. Of course she'd never been a member of the frail sisterhood before, nor been on display in borrowed finery for a gentleman's approval, like a horse at Tattersall's. She swallowed the contents of her glass for courage. Her French grandmother had fled to England with her Gypsy horse trader;

her mother had eloped with a Latin scholar whose family disapproved. Simone swore to be brave like them, a woman making her own way in the world.

. . . A woman whose knees were knocking together loudly under her borrowed silk skirts.

No, that wasn't the sound of her bones rattling; it was the sound of a cane tapping down the hallway. Good grief, he was blind! No again, for Mrs. Burton would not have insisted on the face paints if Harry couldn't see.

Either a century or a second later—Simone was too addled to notice which—George opened the door, bowed, and announced, "Major Harrison, ma'am."

"Very impressive, George," came from behind him, the guest being hidden from view by George's bulk. "No one would know you were a prizefighter in an earlier life."

"Yes, sir. I mean no, sir." George tucked the proffered coin into an inner pocket and actually smiled at the bent old man who hobbled around him into the room. Lydia rushed forward and kissed his whiskered cheek. "You devil. Why have you—"

"Aren't you going to introduce me to the young lady you invited me to meet, Lyddie?" the ancient asked, turning to Simone.

She regretted not seeing his eyes through the thick tinted spectacles he wore, for the reputedly stunning blue would have been the only attractive thing about the elderly officer's appearance. His voice was pleasant, and his manners were polished as he bowed in her direction. Otherwise, he could have passed for any of her father's fellow classics scholars, half-asleep at their favorite club. He smelled like one, too, of old leather, pipe smoke, and spirits. His clothing, not a uniform, was not in fashion, either, although it was well tailored to fit his hunched shoulders and bowed legs. His brown wig belonged to the previous century, as did his silver-streaked beard and mustache. Simone grasped her chair—and her courage—with both hands as she stood to make her curtsy.

"Lovely, Lyddie," he said. "As promised. You have done well."

"So I thought. Shall we let Miss Ryland visit the downstairs parlor while we discuss particulars?"

He laughed. It was a very nice laugh, Simone decided, looking for something to like. And he was intelligent enough not to buy a pig in a poke, suggesting he and Miss Ryland ought to converse a bit first, to see if they could be comfortable together.

Lydia's eyes narrowed. "You suit. She is young and attractive, speaks several languages, and has good manners, as I told you."

"Ah, but there is more to this, ah, affair than reading a résumé."

"And I wish to be privy to whatever agreement is made," Simone put in. He wanted honesty? She would not pretend this was anything but a financial arrangement.

He laughed again. "And she's bright, Lyddie, and refreshingly straightforward. Run along, do. You know you can trust me to deal squarely with both of you."

None too pleased with either of them, Mrs. Burton left in a huff of tight red satin. Harry, Major Harrison, took a seat across from Simone. She pushed a footstool closer, the way she would have done for her papa. She thought he smiled, but it was hard to tell, under all the facial hair.

"Now that Lyddie is gone," he said, "we may speak freely. And honestly."

She had been warned. "I understand, sir. I was raised to speak truthfully."

"Good. I would know a bit more about you, if I may?"

She nodded, thinking he might ask about her health or her sickroom experience, for the gentleman looked more in need of a nursemaid than a mistress.

"I understand you came to Lydia because you have fallen on hard times, my dear," he began.

He wanted honesty? She wanted to flee. Instead she answered: "I would not say I have fallen, more like I've been pitchforked into poverty by the death of my parents. I could not keep a position because of fear of molestation, so I am becoming a Jezebel rather than starve."

He coughed. "Perhaps that is a bit more information than I asked for. But thank you. You have no other relations?"

"No."

His mouth twisted, as if he'd swallowed something sour, or was bilious. Old men suffered from wind, she knew.

"I thought we agreed on the truth. Lies leave a bitter taste in my mouth." He started to rise. "Lyddie was wrong. We cannot suit. *Ciao*."

Simone hadn't realized they were speaking French until he switched to Italian. So he was testing her, her skills and her readiness to obey orders. That nonsense about truth was an old man's idiosyncrasy—he could not have known about Auguste—but she thought she ought to humor him, to keep Mrs. Burton's favor. "My apologies. I thought you meant other relatives who might assist me. I have a young brother whose education depends on my income."

"And you would not have pursued this line of work otherwise?"

"I could have made do, I suppose." Her savings could have bought her more time to find a respectable position if she had not spent the last few coins on Auggie's books and board.

Major Harrison seemed satisfied with her answer, for he sat back and accepted the glass of wine Simone poured from Mrs. Burton's sideboard. After taking a swallow, he asked, "What if I offered to finance your brother's schooling?"

She almost choked on the sip she took. "Why would you do such a thing as that?"

"Because I can afford to, and because people were good to me when I was young. And because I would not see any woman forced into this kind of life against her will. Lyddie chose her profession, when she had no need to."

"But then I would be in your debt. I would still feel that I needed to repay you, in services if not in money. I could not accept an outright gift, not even on my brother's behalf. I would rather work, at whatever I need to do, than be beholden to charity."

"What if I did not wish a martyr in my bed?"

"I would pretend I was pleased to be there, not out of gratitude."

He grimaced at the thought. "That would be worse."

"No, for I might enjoy a house party, charming company, the chance to see a famous home where I would never be invited otherwise, a visit to the countryside, perhaps an opportunity to ride again."

"Let us begin afresh. Tell me of your family."

"Why? I swear no one is going to challenge you over my honor."

He chuckled. "Tell me, in truth. More depends on your answer than I can tell you now. And I'll have investigators checking, before I trust you with explanations."

Simone decided the old man was more than eccentric; he was touched in the head. She had no idea why else he would be so obsessed with the truth about a stranger if he was not senile. Heavens, he was hiring a ladybird for a week, not a lawyer! He was waiting, though, staring, she thought, through his green-tinted spectacles. So she repeated her background, this time not leaving out the Gypsy and French heritage that made her mother unwelcome in England. "At first my mother pretended to read fortunes to add to what my father earned as a Latin tutor. They were never well-to-pass, nor well accepted among the local society, but they were happy together, and our house was full of love."

"Could she? Tell fortunes, that is."

Now Simone was positive he had bats in his belfry, or in his wig. She did not reply to that bit of nonsense but went on to tell what she knew of the unknown Ryland relations, and about her unfortunate employment history.

He listened carefully, making no judgments, other than to ask the name of the baron who now wore the mark of her fireplace poker.

"He will not give me references, you know. Not for any kind of employment."

"He will not assault another young woman in his employ," was all the major said, sending a shiver down Simone's spine. Then he sipped at his wine, thinking.

"I have connections," he finally said, when Simone feared he'd fallen asleep. "I can find you another position, an honest one. And lend you the funds for your brother until he can earn his own way to repay me."

"But you do not know me. There is no reason for you to put yourself to that effort." An effort, she did not say, that no one, not even her father's relations in distant Cumberland, saw fit to make.

"As I said, people helped me, people who did not have to. I was not born to a life of advantage, but was given far more than I had any right to expect."

"Your parents were poorer than mine, less accepted?"

"They were not married."

"Oh." Simone knew most illegitimate children were raised as outcasts, if not abandoned. They were often ostracized worse than those with Gypsy blood. "I am sorry."

"Do not be. I was taken in by a wonderful family, the Harrisons, and made to feel like their own son. My true father smoothed my path with education and introductions, although his kindness cost him the trust of his own family. I have tried to show that same kindness to others, to live as the gentleman he is, in tribute to him. Leading a woman into the life of a demirep does not suit my notions of honor."

He might be crazy, Simone decided, but Major Harrison—Harry—was a dear. No wonder the girls at Mrs. Burton's establishment all liked him. "I thank you for caring, but I have made my own decisions. Working as a governess or companion will never give me a home of my own or any kind of future except a pension when I am retired, with luck. And you cannot guarantee my safety from employers like the baron."

"No, but this life is not without perils of its own. Would you still be willing to attend the house party as my companion if there was danger involved?"

She edged farther back in her seat. The sweet old man might be more deranged than she thought. "Danger to me?"

His bushy brows drew together. "I do not believe so, but that is possible. I would do all in my power to ensure your safety."

What would he do, hit an attacker with his cane? The whole idea was absurd. "What danger could there be at a polite house party?"

"As I said, explanations must wait, but there is more to

this gathering than a sennight's holiday in the country. I have made enemies. Threats have been made against my life."

"Truly?"

"I never lie. I do not always tell all of the truth, because a good card player never shows his full hand, but I do not lie. There will be danger. Almost certainly."

"Then I cannot go with you." Her regret surprised even herself. A week out of London, away from her worries, with an amiable old man had sounded attractive. "I could not chance leaving my brother alone in the world with no family if I were hurt, with no one to care for him."

"I understand your concern, yet you would be perfect for the position. Your skill at languages, the hint of something exotic in your appearance, the fact that you would be unknown to everyone. That is just what I need." He set his wineglass aside and steepled his fingers, which were long and graceful, not gnarled or age spotted, she noticed. After a moment he asked, "What if I arranged for a guardian for the boy, should the worst happen?"

Simone started to shake her head, but Major Harrison went on: "An earl, who I swear would see to his future."

"An earl?"

"Now that I think on it, Lord Royce is not in the best of health, nor young enough. His son Viscount Rexford would be willing to take on the responsibility."

"I think you must be dreaming, sir, or you have had too much wine. An earl? A viscount? What have they to do with a boy who is part Gypsy, part French, and entirely impoverished?"

"They are . . . friends of mine. I can have legal documents for you to sign before we leave for Richmond."

"Then you would take me?"

"I am torn. Leading a young lady into a life of debauchery and dissipation is against my principles, as is entangling an innocent in dangerous pursuits."

Simone prayed the life of a courtesan was not as degrading as he made it out to be. She was not standing on a street corner, after all, nor sharing her body with countless men each night in a brothel like Mrs. Burton's employees. "You would treat me well," she said, with conviction.

"Of course. Yet this is not how you wished to lead your life, is it?"

"No, and that is the truth." She hated the idea, in fact. She could not trust the largesse of a lunatic old man, though. His family might protest his support of an unknown student. For all she knew, his family could lock him in Bethlehem Hospital before he paid Auguste's tuition. "I require the money I can earn, however."

"And I unfortunately require just such a female as you appear to be: loyal, intelligent, able to follow instructions, honest, and brave."

"I am not brave."

He licked his lips. "Sweet. Will you come, knowing the danger, knowing you cannot go back to being a governess, knowing this is a temporary arrangement only?"

The more Major Harrison tried to convince her otherwise, the more, perversely, she was sure of her decision. "Yes, I will go with you, if you answer a question for me. Mrs. Burton warned me about not intruding on your private life, but can you at least tell me if you are married? I do not know if I can do this if I would be injuring another woman so."

"No, there is no Mrs. Harrison pining for me. I have hopes to wed in the future, but not now, with unfinished business."

Simone had to hide her own smile at the dodderer's

optimism. What in the world was he waiting for? She wondered if he could still father a child and, for that matter, why he needed a mistress. She decided she might as well ask while he was permitting such license.

"The house party requires it. Lord Gorham's mistress wishes to play hostess to a select gathering. I need to attend, to face the threats against me."

"Why not simply avoid them?"

"And let danger come at me in the dark? No, I choose to face my enemies, not take a knife in the back."

"The party could be so perilous?"

"That is not the half of it."

"Then I want twice the fee. You need me."

Chapter Four

He needed her.

No, he needed a female *like* her. Otherwise he could take one of Lyddie's girls and be done with it. He'd have a pretty bit of fluff on his arm with less effort, less money, and less on his conscience. He'd also make less of an impression as a connoisseur of women, a man with exquisite taste and deep pockets. He needed a lady-bird who was almost a lady, one who would have everyone talking, to create a stir heard back in London. For once, Harry sought the publicity, the notoriety, with everyone and his uncle knowing precisely where he was and with whom. Then Major Harrison, Harry's alternate identity, could die.

Miss Ryland was perfect; too perfect, unfortunately. No matter that every head would turn when she walked into a room—he could not turn a well-bred woman into a whore. If he didn't, though, Lyddie would, so what would his scruples and sacrifice have accomplished? Nothing. Furthermore, Miss Ryland herself seemed determined on the course. She had problems, too, and lofty principles could not outweigh bare necessity. She needed money; Harry needed a mistress. Both of them were in a hurry.

As she watched him, Harry watched her, wishing he knew what she was thinking, how she wanted him to decide. Then he recalled that he was done making decisions for others. His half brother had pummeled the fact into him that he was not always correct in what he thought best for everyone else. No matter that he thought himself omniscient, he did not have the right to play god with anyone else's life. Rex had said so while Harry lay bleeding on the canvas at Jackson's Boxing Parlour. Of course Harry had let the younger man win the match; Rex was lame in one leg, after all.

He could make provision for Miss Ryland and the brother. That was no problem. He could even leave her as chaste as he found her. That might be a problem, for the woman was exquisite. Her reputation would be destroyed, though, and he knew how precious that was to a female.

But, damn, she was stunning enough to make headlines in the gossip columns, and smart enough to listen to whispered conversations in whatever language.

Harry wanted to be done with this scheme, with all intrigue, for all times. The war was over; his days as spymaster in the Intelligence Division of the War Office were almost at an end. He wanted to retire, by Zeus, not live in shadows and disguises and under aliases for the rest of his life.

He saw how happy his half brother, Rex, was, with his lovely wife, Amanda, helping him recover from his war wounds, both mental and physical. Why, they had twins already, a boy and a girl, that Rex doted on. Harry was jealous, not just of the infants, but of the peace he felt surrounding the viscount and his wife at the christening.

Harry hadn't wanted to attend the event at all. What, the bastard brother waving his bar sinister at the church for all to see? His presence would have embarrassed everyone. But Rex had insisted, and their father, the Earl of Royce, had written his hopes of seeing all his family, sons and grandchildren, together. Even Lady Royce, his father's wife, had written a polite letter of invitation herself. The countess, Harry knew, felt guilty for keeping the half brothers apart so long. Some women would have taken their husband's by-blow into their home to raise. Not Lady Royce. She'd left the earl and her own son, instead. Now that she and Lord Royce were reconciled, secure in their own marriage at last, she could be forgiving of the boy—a man now, of over thirty years—for coming between them through no fault of his own.

Harry might still have refused the invitation to the family's ancestral home, where he would never be part of the true family, but Cousin Daniel had insisted they'd all be offended otherwise. Daniel reported that his own mother wanted to meet her new nephew, and his sister was excited when she heard he was as handsome as the other Royce males, with the same dark coloring and unique black-rimmed blue eyes. She wanted to show him off to her girlfriends, which would have been enough to keep Harry in London, except Amanda, Rex's wife and the sweetest woman he knew, had asked him to stand as godfather to the boy. He could not refuse.

Daniel was godfather to the girl. He started weeping the instant that tiny scrap of lace and love was placed in his arms. Everyone laughed except Harry, feeling the tears well up in his own eyes, to see them reflected in matching blue ones with the dark rim. A baby, born in harmony, wanting for nothing, his future assured. Oh, lucky Rex, and oh, how Harry wanted that peace, that promise, a son, for himself.

And that was the truth. It was as sweet as honey, as sweet on his tongue as nectar.

Miss Ryland coughed, and he came back from his woolgathering to wonder what her lips would taste like.

He sighed. Such thoughts were for another tomorrow. Today was for finding out the truth, the way the Royce men always had, always could. Rex saw colors, true blue for honesty. The earl heard notes of discord for lies. Poor Daniel got rashes at untruths. And he, Harry, the illegitimate son, could taste a falsehood.

The odd, unheard-of gift of truth-knowing made them all invaluable to the country. Lord Royce acted in the legal system; Rex and Daniel had been the Inquisitors on the Peninsula, interrogating prisoners to find the enemy's secrets, secrets that could keep the generals informed and the soldiers safe. Recently Rex had been a huge help to Bow Street's police force before he left London for his wife's confinement and the infants' births. He'd do more when he returned to Town. They all worked in secrecy, of course, for the talent was too close to sorcery or witchcraft or magic for the public's comfort. Or for Daniel's. He was determined to sow his wild oats in London, then become a gentleman farmer, where only nettles could make him break out in hives. He had no interest in serving the country in time of peace, only in carousing his way through the city's underworld. Harry could sympathize, but he had plans for Daniel, anyway. The gift was too important to waste on barmaids, brawls, or barley crops.

As for himself, Harry was usually tucked away in hidden offices, in wigs and disguises when he went out. He was the Aide, a state secret unto himself. Half myth, half truth, he could sift through all the gathered intelligence and recognize the truth. He had fingers in every aspect of military and political and criminal life, in everything that could threaten his country. Recently he'd dealt with smugglers, embezzlers, and spies, French sympathizers all.

Now Napoleon was gone, and the Aide could be, too. Then Harry might make a real life for himself, as himself. The house party was the key. Harry Harmon, Lord Royce's bastard son, was invited now that he was acknowledged by his powerful father. He'd go, raffish Harry, and Major Harrison would stay behind. An assistant was already fitted for the right clothes, the wig and beard and mustache. The man wouldn't be in actual danger despite the death threats—Harry would not have let another man take a bullet meant for him—but he'd die, anyway. He'd suffer a heart spasm spectacularly, loudly, visibly, right there on the steps of Whitehall for everyone to see. He'd be carried inside, physicians sent for, for naught. Harry had the obituary already written.

Farewell, Major, with all your enemies. Welcome, Harry Harmon, rakehell from the wrong side of the blanket. No one could connect the two, not when Harry was conducting a torrid affair at Lord Gorham's party in Richmond. He'd be safe and done with intrigue, ready for the rest of his life.

Of course "Harry Harmon" wasn't his real name, either, but it was close enough. The son of an unwed opera dancer, he could not carry the Royce family name, naturally, except Ivy Harmon had written "Royce" on the birth records, anyway. He was Royce Harmon, a name that would have kept the scandal of his birth on everyone's lips, and in the mud, for all time. The Earl of Royce had been too generous to Harry for such a blatant affront, and his lady wife deserved far better. The *ton* was willing to endure if not wholeheartedly accept Harry Harmon in their midst. He was not quite proper, but raised a gentleman and wealthy in his own right, with excellent connections. But Royce, son of Royce? No.

So he was Harry Harmon in public these days, a rakish young man about Town. He was the soon-to-expire Major Harrison at the War Office; middle-aged Mr. Harris at McCann's Club; Harry the footman there on occasion; Harold the coach driver; Hal the beggar. Sometimes he forgot who he was.

That was not by choice. The Crown commanded, and his loyalty to his country governed his actions. Even now, more than his own life was at stake. Harry was willing to let the Aide die with Major Harrison; the prince regent was not. So while Harry was indulging in debauchery in the countryside, he'd also be trying to recover letters from a blackmailer. Oh, and listening for rumors from dissatisfied men who had supported Bonaparte's efforts and hoped to free him from exile to retake France. That was where Miss Ryland's education came in. No one expected a courtesan to be conversant in so many languages; no one was as careful of his whispers when he was full of wine, his arms full of woman. So Harry would be serving his country even while he entertained a female of respectable past and questionable future.

All depended on if she was trustworthy, naturally, because he'd have to explain his work—and his altered identity—to enlist her cooperation. She could be invaluable to him, or she could be the worst threat of exposure he'd ever faced. Time would tell, and his truth-knowing.

Meanwhile, for the possible gains, for the risk, double her fee was fair. "How much were you earning as a governess?" he asked.

Simone assumed he'd base his offer on that, so she added ten pounds to her yearly wage, which was nothing but a pittance, anyway.

Harry stood up, too quickly for an old man, but he was too angry, yes, and too disappointed, to care. The money was of no account, nothing more than a bit of loose change. The lie was his whole life. He tasted bitter almonds, almost like arsenic in his mouth. "I will not deal with untruths. I told you. Lyddie told you. You said you understood. I am sorry you did not understand the value of honesty. Good day, Miss Ryland, and good luck to you." He reached for his purse, intending to toss the lying wench a coin to tide her over until she found some gullible pigeon to pay her rent.

She jumped up and grabbed his cane before he could reach for it, in an attempt to stop him. "No, wait. Please, Major Harrison. I am sorry. It was desperation making me exaggerate my pay. Surely you can see that? My grandfather was a horse trader. I told you, didn't I? Never leave yourself without a bargaining point, he always said. I swear I shall never lie to you again."

Now Harry tasted something like wine, sherry perhaps. She meant what she said, at least. She might not hold to her oath, but she meant it, which was something.

"I think we should take a few days to decide if this is what we both want," he said, buying time to investigate the Ryland connection, that baron's household, her landlady's impressions, and her own ability to keep a promise. He was not fool enough to take an unknown female into his confidence, no matter how pretty or how needy. He had to reveal too many secrets, not all of them his. "I can meet you here in a few days. Shall we say Friday?"

Simone's rent was due on Thursday. "I . . . I fear I cannot wait that long. I need to find employment immediately if I am to keep my lodgings. They are not much, but they are clean and safe."

That was a porridge-tasting half-truth. Harry raised a bushy eyebrow. "How safe?"

She stared at the cane in her hands. "The downstairs lodger is . . . unsettling."

Hell, another cur to bring to heel. Harry could see where dealing with every man who had designs on Miss Ryland could be a full-time occupation.

"You shall not go back there. I have a house"—he had several; Harry Harmon often stayed at one—"in Kensington where you can stay."

Simone knew gentlemen often kept their ladybirds in love nests in Kensington—close enough for quick visits, far enough from Mayfair to be discreet. "How can I stay at your house if we are not . . . not . . ."

"Well enough acquainted yet?" he politely supplied for her, taking his cane out of her hands. "I also have rooms at my club." The apartment at McCann's was private, hidden, and well guarded, but it was no place for a lady, or a woman he did not have full confidence in. "I can stay there until we come to an agreement. My secretary, Mr., ah, Harris, will not mind staying in Kensington for a few days to assist you."

"But—"

He twirled the cane in the air, stifling her protests. "If we do decide to attend the house party together, you'll need a new wardrobe, won't you? I doubt a governess's salary extended to the several ball gowns required for that elevated company. Do you possess a stylish riding habit, since you wish to ride?"

She could only shake her head. The only fashionable—nay, the only passable—gown she had was the borrowed one she wore. "I hadn't realized how complicated this would be. Or how costly."

Harry had. He knew his companion had to be elegant

and expensively dressed for this to work. Lord Royce's bastard had to be seen as an extravagant wastrel, a devil-may-care hedonist no one would suspect of having a serious thought, much less a spymaster's convoluted mind. "Harris can arrange for a seamstress to come to the house. I would not wish you out and about before we leave for Richmond, if we are to go." He would not want her gossiping with friends, mentioning his name, telling her landlady about her windfall. What he said was, "I'd fear some other man might catch your fancy. The dressmaker will know what is suitable."

"Or Mrs. Burton," she began.

They both recalled the red satin Lydia was stuffed into.

"No, I trust you and Harris and the dressmaker he'll select."

"But the money, sir. I cannot afford anything such as you suggest."

"Consider the new wardrobe my token of honorable intent. That is, my dishonorable intent, I suppose I should say. The fripperies will be yours to keep whatever we decide."

"I do not know if I can accept such a gift."

"My dear, you truly must determine once and for all if you wish to pursue this new path. Accepting gifts is precisely what a mistress does best. Well, perhaps not best, but she never turns down a bauble or an opportunity to feather her own nest. She never makes a gentleman feel that he has stepped over the line of propriety, either. That is what wives are for. Besides, have you never heard that it is better to give than to receive? I will have the pleasure of seeing a pretty woman dressed as her beauty deserves."

Simone blushed. "You are too kind."

Harry recalled he was not supposed to sound like a flirtatious mooncalf yet. He made an old man's "Harrumph" and told her that Harris would see to everything. He also offered to send a man to fetch her things from across the street. "That way you need not face the boarder, or the landlady."

In her new finery, either would have been awkward, so Simone accepted still more of the major's generosity. "There is not much. A trunk, a few gowns on hooks, my toilet articles on the nightstand. Oh, and a parcel of letters from my brother. I should not want to lose those."

And Harry would not mind reading them, to see that all was as she'd said. "Done. I'll make arrangements with Mr. Harris, then send a carriage back for you. I think it best we not leave together, don't you?"

With Mrs. Olmstead likely sitting by her parlor window? "Definitely."

He took her hand in his. "Excellent. And we shall speak again in a few days, yes?"

"I hope so, if we are to get to know each other." How else were they to decide to become roommates, bedmates, lovers? Simone doubted most liaisons were conducted from afar, but she understood that, along with accepting gifts, a kept woman kept her mouth shut. She did not disagree with her protector or tell him he was the strangest man she had ever met. She certainly did not pull away, even if his beard tickled her hand when he raised it to his lips. At the soft touch of his kiss, she pictured a younger, far more handsome man, tall and dark-haired, with startling blue eyes, the Harry of her wishful thinking. Maybe she was imagining Major Harrison in his younger days. He was definitely not young enough now for her to brush at the white hairs on his dark coat sleeve, the way she would have done for her brother. She supposed she could show concern for him, though. "You will be safe until then?"

He smiled, or she thought he did under the heavy mustache. "Now you are sounding just as a mistress ought, concerned about next week's bills."

"No, sir, I recall the danger you spoke of."

"I know, my dear. I was teasing. My, we do have a great deal to learn about each other, don't we? I promise to explain more when I see you. Rest assured you will be in no peril at the Kensington house. Mr. Harris will guarantee it. And I have not forgotten about your brother's schooling. Mr. Harris will handle that also if you give him the proper address. I shall send a messenger to Lord Rexford for that other document's signature."

"If nothing does happen to me, this viscount will not have any hold over Auguste, will he?" She could not imagine what a viscount would want with a bookish youth, but had to be certain. Auguste was her brother, and she would not let any disinterested nobleman send him off to the navy or the East India Company to be rid of the responsibility.

"Nothing will happen, to you or your kin. I promise. And I do not lie."

But Major Harrison was obviously a madman or a senile old fool. What good were his promises?

Chapter Five

Major Harrison left. Not long after, an undistinguished carriage pulled up at Mrs. Olmstead's boardinghouse. The thickset driver handed the reins to a young groom and got down, pulling his broad-brimmed hat lower over his eyes.

"Come to fetch Miss Ryland's things, I has," he explained to the scowling landlady. "She's been taken on by a connection to the Earl of Royce in a hurry."

"The Earl of Royce? Oh, my." The scowl turned to avid curiosity. Mrs. Olmstead kept up with the latest news of the polite world and knew every notable by name, if not by sight. "I wonder which. I know the earl's son was married not long ago and fathered twins. His wife is an accused murderess. Miss Ryland should have asked me before accepting a post there."

"Lady Rexford were never brought to trial," the coachman answered in a gruff tone. "They found the real killer. And the twins are mere babes. Too young for a governess."

"Quite right. I wonder which relation, then," Mrs. Olmstead hinted, waiting for information.

"Not for me to say, for sure. I just drives the coach.

Bound to be better'n her last post, from what I hear tell." Now the driver paused, waiting for information himself.

None was forthcoming except a nod of agreement. "I suppose I should be glad for her, even if it means I'll have to look for a new boarder. I'll miss the young lady, I will. Never gave me a moment's trouble."

"Nice sort, was she?"

The landlady was glad to talk as she hauled her rounded body up the stairs to the attic room. "She was a lady," Mrs. Olmstead told him, between huffs and puffs, "no matter her going into service. Didn't put on airs or nothing, but she acted proper, modest, and well-spoken. She went to church regular-like, too, which proves her decency." She looked out the tiny window of Simone's former chamber, the one that overlooked the street, and Lydia Burton's house. "Not like the females across the way, who miss more Sundays than they make. And no wonder, with the hours they keep. Why, I could tell you—"

"So this room's for rent now, eh?" Harold said, opening the shabby trunk under the eaves to load in more books, two gowns on hooks, a threadbare robe and flannel nightgown, and a small portrait. He tucked the small stack of letters into his coat pocket, but bumped his head when he stood up. "Got any other rooms to let, iffen I come across any swells lookin' for quarters? I never know who's gettin' in my coach these days."

"Why, that would be real neighborly of you, Mr., ah?"

"Harold, ma'am," he said, barely tipping his hat, keeping his eyes lowered while he rubbed at his skull and then wiped at his mouth. "Bigger rooms'n this one?"

"Well, I have the ground floor, naturally, so I can watch the comings and goings of my tenants. I permit no hanky-panky in my dwelling, you understand."

"Wouldn't of thought otherwise, ma'am."

She glared at the dark driving coat he wore. "And no pets, neither."

Harold quickly brushed at his sleeve. "I'll remember that, ma'am. What about the middle floor, then? Is that one occupied?"

"Mr. Fordyce has the whole apartment." Mrs. Olmstead pursed her thick lips. "He pays his rent on time—that's about all the good I can say of him. Never goes to church, he doesn't. Doesn't talk much, neither. Too busy counting his coins, I'd suppose. An investor, is what he calls hisself. Coldhearted heathen, is what I call him, what never shares a pint or a pastry or a bit of chitchat. But he pays on time." She sighed. "And more'n the rooms are worth. Too bad about the lass, either way. I'll miss her." She stuffed some of Miss Ryland's things into a carpetbag, things not fit for a gent's eyes, she told him.

Harold kept his own eyes on the landlady, devout Christian that she was, to make sure Miss Ryland's belongings got into the satchel. Then he closed the trunk and hoisted it to his shoulder.

"My, you are a strong one, aren't you?" Mrs. Olmstead admired. "Don't suppose you are looking for accommodations, are you?"

"No, ma'am," Harold said, hurrying down the stairs and out to the carriage, guessing the overweight widow, churchgoer or not, meant more than a room. "I'm well-set where I am." He stowed the trunk, handed the boy on the coach the satchel, and handed Mrs. Olmstead a coin for her trouble. Then he said as how he ought to go back up for one last look, to make certain they hadn't missed anything.

Mrs. Olmstead decided to wait below. "No need for us both to climb those stairs again, I suppose."

Her voice held a tinge of doubt, so Harold quickly said, "No, ma'am," and took the stairs two at a time, out of her sight. He knocked on the door of the other lodger, however, before reaching the attic room.

"Come to give you a good-bye message from Miss Ryland," he said when a short, middle-aged man with pale skin, deep-set eyes, and hanging jowls opened the door.

He frowned, at the intrusion or the information. "Leaving, is she?"

Harold heard a flicker of regret, as the boarder licked his lips, his tongue darting out like an asp's. Harold planned to deliver his message as a fist to the soft gut that overhung the man's trousers.

"Well, what is it?" the investor demanded. "I am busy."

Harold touched the brim of his brown hat and looked down in humble servitude. "Sorry to interrupt, Mr., ah . . . ?"

"Fordyce, sirrah. Malcolm Fordyce."

The coachman stepped back. He decided to withhold his lesson in manners toward defenseless women until he did a bit of investigating. Why would a surly man lie about being busy, and lie about his own name?

Simone, meanwhile, remained in Lydia Burton's private sitting room, hoping to be fetched before dark, when, she supposed, gentlemen callers would begin arriving. Mrs. Burton was all smiles, bringing her tea and small sandwiches, so Simone assumed she was satisfied, even gratified, by what Major Harrison had said on his way out. The madam appeared to know that the arrangement was not finalized, for she kept giving sly hints on how to please a gentleman.

Simone almost choked on her meal. Men do . . . that?

They want a woman to do . . . what? Surely an older chap like Major Harrison would not expect . . . ?

Gracious. All her mother had told her was that she'd enjoy it with the right man. Simone remembered asking what would happen if the man in question—her young curate—knew as little as she did. Her mother, half French and half Gypsy, had laughed and said men were born knowing how to do it. If he did not, he was not the right man. Simone tried to put thoughts of her mother out of her mind. And thoughts of Major Harrison, naked.

Lydia gave her a brief lesson on protecting herself against pregnancy, and a little pouch with a sponge. Simone doubted Major Harrison could father a child, if he did not suffer palpitations trying, but she accepted the gift and the advice. Then she let her curiosity overcome her reticence by asking, "If you are so well versed in . . . in pleasure, why did the major not invite you? That would have been less costly, less time-consuming, less chancy for him, since he knows me not at all."

Lydia laughed. "What, sleep with old Harry? Why, we're like sister and brother, nearly raised together."

Simone stared hard at the madam. No cosmetics in the world could disguise the decades between her age and that of the old officer.

Lydia must have caught her look, for she amended, "We've known each other forever, it seems. Asides, he needed a new face." She laughed again, and again Simone did not get the joke. "Everyone in Town knows my phiz and my reputation, and knows Harry and I aren't lovers. So that wouldn't fadge." She patted Simone's knee. "He wants a younger filly, to make a real splash. This is the opportunity of a lifetime, if you play your cards right. Now, listen. . . . "

And here Simone thought all she had to do was lie

quietly while a man took his pleasure. She'd heard that some women recited hymns, meanwhile, or composed shopping lists. The act never took too long, Simone gathered, having chanced upon gropings at various houses where she'd been employed. The novels she'd read spoke of fervid kisses and fevered brows, not much more. Fool, she called herself. Of course there was more to sex than that. People would not fornicate like rabbits if they did not enjoy it. So many sermons would not be preached against it.

Simone tried to ignore the reminder of church teachings, too. In fact, she wished she could ignore the whole uncomfortable subject. "Um, how many gowns do you think I'll need for the trip?"

The coachman finally came for Simone at Mrs. Burton's, but he did not apologize for the delay. He did not get down to help her into the carriage, doff his cap, or introduce himself. The boy on the driver's box beside him jumped down, grinned, and tipped his hat while he opened the door for her, which was reassuring. She was anxious enough over facing the major without facing his servants' disrespect.

Lydia had given Simone a coal-scuttle-style bonnet, so she had no fears of being recognized by Mrs. Olmstead, if the fat old gossipmonger was at her window seat as usual. She must look like just another fast woman with a knot of fake cherries on the brim of her bonnet, going to meet her latest lover. Only Simone wasn't, not yet.

Oh, Lord, what was she doing? Maybe she should jump out of the coach now, before it was too late.

No. With her luck she'd be run over by the wheels, or get so scraped and battered no man would want her, not even a half-blind relic like the major. Her last coins would go to apothecaries. For now, she was well fed, feeling almost pretty, and the coach bespoke comfort if not luxury. That was a good sign, she told herself. And her trunk rested on the opposite seat, so she could not return to Mrs. Olmstead's, not without a better story than any novelist ever conceived, and the next month's rent.

The boy handed over her carpetbag, which held Auguste's letters. So Major Harrison had not forgotten. She wanted to ask the lad about their destination, about his employer, even about the unfriendly driver, but he merely grinned, shut the door, and climbed up beside the coachman. The man knew his way, and knew his horses, for he drove quickly and competently. Simone stopped reaching for the hanging strap to balance herself as the coach feathered corners or passed wagons on the narrow roads. The major did not hire incompetents, it seemed, which gave her another scrap of confidence. He must think she had potential.

When they reached a neat town house on Morningside Drive, the boy—Judd, he told her, Jeremy Judd—opened the door and put down the steps, then took the satchel from her. "Harold"—Jeremy grinned and jerked his head toward the driver, who hadn't turned—"will bring your trunk in later. I'll introduce you to my mum. She's the cook and housekeeper. Mr. Harris, he's out and about on the governor's business right now."

Mrs. Judd was almost as closemouthed as Harold. Simone wondered if they were related, but ceased speculating as she admired her surroundings. The house was a perfect gem, small but furnished with comfortable-looking furniture that was gleaming with care. The colors were bright and inviting, and warm fires burned in every room Mrs. Judd showed her. Other doors remained as tightly closed as Mrs. Judd's lips.

Simone's own bedroom was done in soft shades of blue, with flowers embroidered on the bedstead and painted on the walls.

"The major must have had other women staying," Simone guessed out loud, from the sweet femininity of the furnishings.

Mrs. Judd sniffed. "The master's business is the master's business, I am sure, miss." She left, making Simone feel like a poor student who forgot his lesson. Privacy, she told herself. She had to remember to tell the truth and respect his privacy. And avoid the disapproving housekeeper whenever possible.

Unpacking her cloth bag took Simone no time at all; she placed Auguste's letters on the dressing table and stuffed the pouch with the sponge under her stockings in the drawer. She did not know if she was expected to return belowstairs or stay here until the secretary sent for her, or the major did. She stared out the window that overlooked a narrow walled garden to the back of the house. With its shade tree and bench, the garden looked to be a lovely place to read a book, if the house had a library. She had not seen one on her abbreviated tour, nor the master's rooms, nor the kitchens or servants' quarters. She was tempted to go exploring, but her trunk arrived before she could decide.

The heavyset coachman carried it on his shoulder like a sack of grain, and he was not even out of breath from carrying it up the steep stairs. He still wore his hat, still pulled low over his forehead, and he still did not speak. He grunted. Simone thanked him anyway, as prettily as she could, since she had too few coins to give him one. He grunted again and left. So someone else disapproved of her presence in the house and thought she was a soiled dove. Now she had someone else to avoid.

Then a young maidservant flew into the room and took Simone's few gowns out of her hands to hang in the wardrobe. Her name was Sally, Sally Judd, and she was here to wait on Miss Ryland, if it pleased. Mr. Harris said miss would need someone to look after her fancy clothes and help her dress, and Sally had ambitions of being a lady's maid, and wasn't miss the prettiest female ever with all that red hair, and what a cunning bonnet? Cherries were all the thing this Season, according to *Ackerman's Repository*, but feathers were more suitable for night, didn't miss agree?

Simone had never conversed with a whirlwind before, and never had a lady's maid of her own in her entire life. She would have dismissed the girl on both counts, but Sally was the only one in the house to smile at her. Worse, the new gown fastened down Simone's back. She could never get out of it on her own, and asking Mrs. Judd to help would have been beyond her. More importantly, Sally said she already had kettles of water on to heat for miss's bath, and did she prefer rose scent or lilac for her soap?

A bath, in a full tub young Jeremy Judd was already carrying into the room? That sounded like heaven. She smiled back at the grinning pair and decided to enjoy the wages of sin.

Sally helped wash Simone's long hair, bringing her mum's own recipe shampoo, hot towels, and chatter about her beau, a footman at the next household, but Mum thought Sally was too young to be courted at sixteen, and what did Miss Ryland think?

Simone thought she just might enjoy being treated like a lady, especially now, when she was becoming anything but.

Sally was humming, which was a good sign, Simone

thought. No one ever sang at the baron's house, not even the children. Sally was obviously happy in her work, and Simone vowed to be happy in hers. She'd try, anyway.

Sally clucked her tongue over the shabby, dreary gowns that constituted Simone's wardrobe, as if she were trying to decide which to burn first instead of which to lay out for dinner.

"Oh, I shan't need to dress," Simone told her. "I ate such a large tea I'd be content with a slice of toast here in my room later."

"Mum says you are to sup in the dining room like a proper guest, with Mr. Harris. She's fixing a special meal, she is, everything he likes. Do you fancy syllabub? Mum's is the best."

Simone did not care for the sweet dessert, but her tastes did not matter, not to the chatelaine of the house. "Your mother does not approve of me, does she? Or my reason for being here."

"Oh, it ain't you, miss. Mum was an actress herself, and she ain't one for looking down on any female what wants to better herself. You're a guest, plain and simple. It's himself she's worried about."

"Major Harrison? Then he really is in danger?" That was not gossip, Simone told herself. She needed to be prepared for protecting her protector.

"The master always finds trouble, but Mum is worried you'll bring him worse."

"Me? That is, I?" She'd gone at the baron with a fireplace poker, true, but she did not usually accost gentlemen. She looked around the lovely room. "Why would I hurt him when he has been so kind?"

"Without meaning to, I am sure, miss. It's that we were all hoping the master'd be done with his havey-cavey doings now that the war is over."

"Havey-cavey?"

"Dark, you know. Secret. For the good of the country, but that's all I can say about the master's work. He's not much out in public, which is why Mum worries about strangers. Mr. Harris'll tell you more, if he thinks you ought to know."

The secretary would tell her, if she had to threaten him with her bread knife. Simone had to know what she was getting herself into. "Then I better wear my new gown, don't you think?"

Mr. Harris was going to be late for dinner. It was taking longer than he expected to find Baron Seldon at one of the lesser gambling clubs the man was known to frequent. Once he found Miss Ryland's former employer, he quickly defeated the man at cards, soundly. He seldom played with fools like Seldon, for there was no challenge in it. Now he hurried the baron into debt without listening to the puffgut's boasting and blathering so he could savor his glass of brandy without having a sour taste in his mouth. Then he offered Seldon double or nothing, which the gudgeon accepted, and lost.

"I cannot pay right now, but you'll let me have the usual month, won't you, my good man?"

Harris was not good, not when he was on a mission. He shook his head, with its silvered hair at the temples, and pushed his tinted spectacles back up on his nose. "I have need of the brass myself."

"But I'll have the blunt as soon as I return from Gorham's house party. That affair is bound to be expensive, tricking out my doxy to compete with Gorham's hoity-toity mistress."

"You are not going to Gorham's."

"Of course I am. I wouldn't miss it for the world. The

wagering will be high. I'll win back your brass, and more."

Harris laid a stack of gambling vouchers on the table, all with Seldon's initials. That was another reason he was so long about this distasteful task. "I say you are not going."

The other man's hand started shaking as he reached for his glass, tipping it over. Harris quickly moved the IOUs out of danger. "I say you are returning to your country estate with your wife and children. And staying there."

"But why?"

"Because I bought these from your debtors, and because I do not like your face."

The baron instantly reached to the scar across his cheek.

"Exactly." Harris leaned closer, so only Seldon could hear his whispered threat. "If you stay in the country and act like a gentleman, I shall not call in your markers. If I ever hear—and I have ways of hearing, believe me—that you have accosted another female in your household, another unwilling woman anywhere, I shall claim everything you have that is not entailed. Everything."

Seldon rubbed at the ugly scar, which stood out twice as livid now that his cheeks had gone ghost white. "But how did you know? That is, I never touched the jade. Nervous female, don't you know, one of those starched-up spinsters always seeing monsters under the bed."

Now Mr. Harris was almost choking on the bitter taste on his tongue. "You better not be under anyone's bed, or in it—except your wife's, if she wants you. Is it a bargain?"

Seldon knew he had no choice. No one would let him into any gaming hells or gentlemen's clubs, not if he couldn't pay his debts of honor. He'd have to leave Town, anyway. "You say you won't call in the markers?"

"Not unless you return to London. Or if you ever mention that particular lady's name."

The baron stared at the vouchers, then at his opponent, wondering how the deuce the two were connected. "She's no lady, only some half-breed educated beyond her station, putting on airs to impress my wife. As if her prunish attitude could cover all that red hair and fire." He rubbed at the scar again. "I should have had the wench arrested instead of letting her think she was better than me."

Harris tucked the chits back in his pocket and stood. "She was, and is. Her father's father holds a title; her mother's family was French aristocracy. Even if she were a goatherd living in a shanty, an orange seller at the opera, or a whore's daughter, you have no right to take what is not offered. Do you understand?" Since he towered over the baron, and since Harris's shoulders were broader and his hands were clenched into fists, Seldon understood. The baron could not see Harris's eyes through the dark lenses of his spectacles, but he knew in his heart, in his gut, in his shriveling manhood, that his life was in peril if he did not agree to the other's terms. "I understand. My estates have been needing better supervision, anyway. My wife has been complaining I do not spend enough time with her."

"The poor woman," Harris muttered on his way out of the club.

"That poor girl." His housekeeper started her lecture the minute he came into the Morningside Drive house by the back entrance and sat at the kitchen table. "She's been sitting in the parlor awaiting her supper this age. And what you are doing with an educated, polite female, I'll never know. And that's not to say you should be bringing strange women home, neither, not that it's any of my affair."

It wasn't, but that never stopped Mrs. Judd. She'd been a friend of his mother's and he'd taken her in when her husband deserted her and the children. Now he told her not to worry. "Miss Ryland will not know anything until I am ready to tell her."

"The lass is downier than you think. Else why did she ask Sally if Major Harrison kept cats?"

"That's nothing. A lot of people keep cats. Maybe she likes them."

"And maybe she noticed the hairs on Harold's coat when he brought in her trunk? White ones, what matched what she'd seen on the major's sleeve?"

Harry stood up so fast the feline on his lap hissed at him.

Chapter Six

Major Harrison's secretary was a tall, distinguished-looking gentleman of middle years with silver in his long sideburns and well-trimmed mustache. His upright, military bearing was far unlike his employer's hunched posture, but like the major, Mr. Harris wore tinted glasses. When he bowed stiffly over Simone's hand, not bringing it anywhere near his lips, she again pictured the image of a handsome, dark-haired young man, the way both Major Harrison and his secretary might have looked in their youth. Perhaps they were related, she thought, although Mr. Harris was too young to be the major's brother and too old to be his son. He was too rigid to be as congenial as the man of her dreams, the Harry she wished to meet. Why, he almost marched her into the brightly lit dining parlor and then sat as far from her as he could and began filling his plate from the platters laid out. Obviously they were meant to serve themselves, and just as obviously, she was merely another duty he had to perform, as hurriedly as possible.

"Should I have Mrs. Judd remove some of the candles?" she asked, trying to be friendly. She looked toward the tinted spectacles. "Major Harrison also seemed to be affected by the bright light." She did not mention the similarity of their names, or the white hairs on his midnight blue superfine coat.

"We served together," was his terse answer, leading Simone to believe that either there had been an explosion or too much exposure to the Spanish sun, or it was none of her business. He spoke in the clipped tones of English public schools when he politely offered to pass this plate or pour from that bottle, but he did not say much else. He was more interested in his own meal than in Major Harrison's *chérie amour.*

Simone acknowledged his circumspection, but still took offense. Mrs. Olmstead had more conversation in one of her plump fingers than this gentleman had in his whole body. She ate more than she thought she might, partly because the meal was excellent, partly because she was afraid of offending Mrs. Judd, and partly to fill up the silence. She did refuse the syllabub, with no doubt that Mr. Harris would do justice to the bowl. He smiled at young Jeremy, who brought in the sweet, in a way he had not smiled at Simone.

Out of unworthy petulance, she admitted to herself, Simone waited until he had filled his spoon, then asked, "Have you been with the major long?"

He barely set the spoon down long enough to say, "Long enough." Then he went back to his dish.

"Will he be visiting soon?"

This time the spoon hit the edge of the bowl with a clatter. "Soon enough," was his unhelpful reply.

She waited until the spoon was almost at his mouth. "Tomorrow?"

He decided to swallow first, his tongue licking the sweet stuff from his mustache. Simone was vaguely repulsed, wondering what other crumbs and spills left remnants there. Yet she found the gesture oddly boyish, too.

"The major is a busy man," he said after quickly spooning another mouthful down his throat.

She could be as rude as he was. "Are all men in this household closemouthed and taciturn? Do you all speak in riddles?"

He stared at his bowl of congealing dessert with longing, she thought, although the dark spectacles hid a lot of his expression. The sigh he made did not. "Jeremy is an outgoing lad. He can tell you everything you wish to know about the horses."

She did not want to know anything about Major Harrison's stables, as he well knew. "But I wish to speak with him of our . . . agreement. He must have mentioned it to you."

That got her his attention at last. He leaned closer, staring across the table at her. "Are you dissatisfied with your room? Your treatment here?"

"Oh, no, everything is lovely. It's just the uncertainty of the whole arrangement." She shrugged. "I feel peculiar being a guest here without knowing where I will be tomorrow, or what is expected of me."

He sighed again and pushed his bowl aside. "The major will make other plans for you if you are not content with these. I can make inquiries among my acquaintances to see if anyone is seeking a governess."

"I have no references."

"I have friends who can supply whatever you require."

"Without meeting me? Wouldn't that be dishonest?" And what kind of friends did the secretary have, anyway, who could supply references sight unseen?

"Are you a good governess?"

"I tried."

"That would be good enough." He went back to his syllabub, evidently considering the discussion over.

Simone relented and let him have a spoonful or two before saying, "I do not know if the major discussed my difficulties."

"The major and I share everything."

If green glasses could shoot sparks, she'd be on fire. As it was, his words made her blood run cold. She almost dropped the glass of wine she'd been toying with. "You share . . . everything?"

Now he did drop his spoon, which spattered the once-frothy confection on the tablecloth. "Great gods, Miss Ryland. No, we do not share women. Whatever gave you that idea?"

Lydia Burton, of course, but Simone did not say so. "I am not sure of the rules of this, ah, business. The major and I did not discuss terms and conditions."

"I do not believe the rules, if there are any such, are written in stone. This is not like a legal contract, you know. Simply trust the major to see you are not subjected to any behavior you find offensive. He will take care of everything."

"Of course. That is what Mrs. Burton said. I am sorry I doubted his intentions. Or yours."

He grunted, then ignored her in favor of his dratted syllabub. Simone was reluctant to annoy him further, since the secretary was the one to make whatever arrangements the major decided upon. He must have become aware of her silence, or his lack of manners, for he asked, "Tell me, have you ever considered becoming an actress? Especially with your financial needs, the stage might pay more."

"But it is not very respectable."

"And prost—this path is?"

Simone took a spoonful of syllabub without thinking. No wonder the major liked it so well; the stuff must be half spirits. She had another spoonful while she considered that the former soldier—an officer, she assumed—disapproved of her, too. She wondered if the major would have hired a mistress at all, considering his staff's attitude, if he did not wish to attend the house party.

"Will you be going to Lord Gorham's gathering?"

Mr. Harris pushed his plate away again, considering his answer. A lie would ruin his dessert. The truth could jeopardize everything else. "I go where I am needed," he said, the good secretary.

Simone wished he would go to the devil. The idea of this unsmiling man watching her fall from grace, judging her performance, was more unsettling than the alcohol sinking to her stomach. She had already suffered through the most awkward meal of her life. Any more of his favorite concoction and she would suffer through the rest of the night, too. She stood, forcing him to rise also. "If you are done?"

He was not, of course, but manners forced him to invite her to take tea in the parlor, or port if she preferred.

"I think not, thank you. I am too weary. This has been an eventful day."

Eventful? She didn't know the half of it. Harry served himself another bowl of Mrs. Judd's finest cooking. He might as well have that treat, since he'd been denied anything else. Now he could not secretly admire the woman's beauty from behind his spectacles, or watch her trying to act worldly when she was shaking in her boots, or in those tiny silk slippers he'd noticed at Lydia's. He noticed everything, how the candles caught bronze highlights in her red hair, making it more auburn. How her black eyes flashed with annoyance when he ignored her, how her honey-toned cheeks flushed when she realized she'd been forward. Damn, he had barely eaten his supper, for staring at the tops of her breasts, softly edging over her gown. Thank goodness for the tinted glass, or she'd have gone at him with the fireplace poker, too. And he would have deserved it, for every lustful, lascivious thought. Hell, he should not be thinking of a woman at all, only his plans. He had never let his urges interfere with his duty, and he would not start now, no matter how tempting he found Miss Ryland. Syllabub be damned.

Mrs. Judd was right. He had to be certain.

Sally arrived to help her out of the blue gown and into her flannel bedclothes that were so worn and faded they had no color at all.

"Did you enjoy dinner, miss?"

"Very much. Please tell your mother."

"Jeremy says you hardly touched the syllabub. I told Mum she had a heavy hand with the brandy, for a lady's taste."

"Oh, no, I am sure it was perfect. I've never been partial to that dish for some reason. Mr. Harris appreciated it, I am certain."

"Well, you won't be seeing it again any time soon—my mum is that mad at him. She said he could eat digestive biscuits for all she cared."

"I suppose he was rude to her?"

Sally laughed. "Rude? He's never been rude in all my born days. No, Mum was all put out on account of he brought Miss White back with him."

So the sanctimonious prig had a lady friend of his own. What hypocrisy, to make Simone feel unclean while he was bringing Miss White to his employer's house. She wondered if Major Harrison knew, then decided he must. Why, poor Mrs. Judd must be thinking she was running a bordello, what with all the loose women about. And what a terrible example to set for Sally. Then Simone had a dreadful thought: "This isn't her bedroom, is it?"

"Lands, no. Mum would never let the likes of her abovestairs."

Simone supposed only the master's companion earned that right, along with her higher salary. The secretary's woman was relegated to the servants' quarters. She was so disturbed by the situation that she almost missed Sally's next words, coming from the dressing room, where she was hanging up the blue gown. "He took her in the same as he took us, so Mum can't really complain, now, can she?"

Nor could Simone, although she'd rather eat a bucket of syllabub instead of meeting Miss White at breakfast. She sat quietly while Sally brushed out her hair and braided it for the night. Sally did not notice, prattling about the clothes Miss Ryland would need, the colors she ought to pick, and where they might shop for ribbons and gloves and stockings. And did miss prefer chocolate in the morning or tea?

She finally left, leaving Simone alone with her thoughts, which were not good company, either. What was she doing, taking up a life no one respected, including herself? She'd face the contempt of all the Mrs. Olmsteads, all the Mr. Harrises, all the curates in all of England, for all the rest of her days, if not longer.

There in the dark, in a strange room in a peculiar household, she had second thoughts, or thirty-second. She simply did not know if she could go through with her plan.

It was one thing for a woman to fall in love, to give herself to a man who loved her in return, with the promise of marriage, or so Simone believed. The church demanded the wedding come before the bedding, but society looked the other way when so many infants were born months prematurely. No harm was done but a bit of embarrassment at the birth.

It was another thing to be so overcome with passion for a handsome, charming rogue that a woman lost her wits, and thus her virtue. Females in plays and poems and operas did that all the time, didn't they? Simone had never experienced such overpowering passion, but she supposed it was possible. Reprehensible, but possible.

Her decision, though, selling herself to a man she barely knew, was outright wrong. Sinful. Shameful. Scandalous. No matter that her need was great and her alternatives were few, offering herself as man's plaything was against her every precept and her parents' teachings. She could have done it this afternoon, acting on impulse born of desperation, but now, with a full stomach? Now she had too much time to think.

Where was Major Harrison, anyway? He should be here to help her decide. Was he as kind as he seemed? Then he should understand her trepidations. Would he treat her like a lady, or like the harlot she was becoming?

He was generous; he'd already proved that. If he paid Auguste's school fees, Simone could retire after her one venture into the demimonde. She was getting cold feet, that was all. She pulled the blankets tighter around her, then felt too warm and tossed them aside.

The secretary was a cold man. She sat up again, wondering why she was suddenly thinking of Mr. Harris at all. He'd likely hand over her wages with a sneer, then go back to his own bed, his occupied bed. Now she clenched the covers in her hands.

Bother, she was never going to fall asleep at this rate. She decided to write a letter to Auguste at school, instead of twisting her nerves and the sheets into rumpled knots. She lit another candle and found paper and ink in the desk near the window. She sat there, barefoot, and composed a note filled with so many lies that the major would dismiss her on the spot. She told her brother all about her new, well-paying position. She was on trial, she explained in case nothing came of it, but she wrote that she had great hopes of succeeding with the pleasant, well-established family in Mayfair, in their beautiful house filled with friendly servants. The children were young enough, she told Auggie, that she could have a contented place with them for years, and he must not worry about her. She would send him the address when she was certain they were keeping her on. *Wish me luck*, she concluded, *your loving sister*. Of course the teardrops made her words run together, but Auggie would suppose her letter got wet in the rain. And if he could not read all of it, well, then she had a few less lies to atone for.

She sealed the letter but knew she'd have to ask Mr. Harris to post it in the morning, dash it. She had no desire to face the secretary again, with his smirk hidden behind his mustache and his scorn hidden by dark glasses. If he were more friendly, she might have asked him if the house contained a library; then she could have had a new book to read tonight, instead of dwelling on her fears. She supposed she could read her Bible. No, not tonight, not in this house, not with her intentions.

A scratching sound came at her door and Simone was almost glad that Sally had come back with her chatter. But Sally did not come in when she called out, "Enter." Neither did Major Harrison, thank goodness. Simone was not ready for him, not by a long shot.

The sound came again, so she went to the door and opened it to find a cat in the hall, a big white cat, the fattest, fluffiest cat Simone had ever seen, which explained why everyone was covered in white hairs, except that Major Harrison said he did not live here, and he'd also said he never lied.

The cat's presence did explain Miss White. The feline's ears twitched when Simone said the name out loud, and Simone had to laugh at her own false presumptions. Mr. Harris had brought a cat home, not his doxy, and Mrs. Judd disapproved. Simone could not blame the housekeeper, given the way her own hand was quickly covered in cat fur just from stroking the overgrown animal. She fetched her own hairbrush and comb and sewing scissors and started to brush tangles and mats and leaves out of the long white coat, her own anxieties soothed with the steady motion and the cat's constant purring. "You and Sally seem to be the only friendly ones here," she told Miss White, "but I don't know who or what to believe anymore. Not even my own decisions."

The cat jumped down and left, only now she was sleek and half the size, and damp from Simone's tears.

Chapter Seven

The cat might have looked better in the morning, but Simone's prospects were as bleak as the old gray gown she put on by herself before Sally came with a breakfast tray. Hot chocolate, a sweet roll with jam, even a nosegay of violets, threatened her resolve, but no. She was not so easily tempted by luxury and a life of leisure. She'd sell the blue gown—Major Harrison said it was hers to keep, no matter what happened—and put an advertisement in the papers. She could hope Mrs. Olmstead had not rented her room yet, and hope a position arose before week's end. That was what she would do, and that's what she would tell the major. She felt that was the least she owed the man, a personal confession that she was no highflier after all. Her feet were planted too firmly on the well-trodden ground of virtue and respectability.

Instead of confronting Mr. Harris to ask for an appointment with Major Harrison, Simone decided to ask Sally to talk to the stuffy secretary for her. Sally, however, brought the message that Mr. Harris wanted to see her in the breakfast parlor at her earliest convenience.

The former soldier looked well rested, Simone thought

with a touch of rancor over her own sleepless night. He wore a corbeau-colored coat this morning, with a simple knot in his neckcloth that made him appear exactly what he was: a gentleman of dignity and means who happened to earn his own living instead of being an idle ornament of society. Too bad he was a churlish boor.

He did not speak when she entered the room, but he did rise, then stared through his spectacles at the drab governess's gown she wore, the tight coil of braids at the back of her neck, the sturdy worn boots. Sally was near tears to send her charge downstairs looking like she'd come to sweep the parlor, but Simone had insisted.

Mr. Harris did not comment on her altered appearance; he merely gestured to the coffeepot on the table and told her to ring for Jeremy if she preferred tea or chocolate. Covered dishes were on the sideboard, with eggs, kippers, kidneys, and bacon. He'd already eaten, he said as he resumed his seat, getting an early start to a day with much to accomplish.

What, did the officious oaf think she was lazy, besides a trollop? He did look busy, though, with books and newspapers and notepads stacked in front of him next to a plate of buttered toast.

Simone said that she'd had a tray in her room, and would not keep him from his important work. She wished only to request an appointment with his employer.

That was impossible, according to Mr. Harris. The major had a full schedule. So did Miss Ryland, he informed her. A modiste would arrive within the hour, a coiffeur soon after, then a boot maker to measure her foot for riding boots and shoes.

He *had* been busy. And the meddlesome creature was not finished.

"You can make a list of any other items you deem

necessary and I'll have them delivered. I will visit the jeweler's myself. Do you have any preferences?"

"Jewels? I have no need for jewels."

His lip curled under the mustache. "Every woman of fashion needs jewelry. Obviously you do not in your current mode. But Major Harrison's companion does require gems, to give weight to his standing."

"That is precisely what I wish to speak to the major about. I cannot go with him to the house party. We have not concluded the arrangement, you see. He told me to think on it, and I have. I must regretfully decline his employment." She headed toward the door and her room, to pack her few belongings back into the trunk.

"You could not have found another protector since last night."

Simone should have expected the insult, but it still hurt. She turned at the door to say, "I have decided to pursue a different line of work. I shall provide for myself, not in such rich style, of course, but with my head held high."

If her chin rose any higher, she'd fall over backward. Mr. Harris pushed a notepad aside and stroked his chin, thinking. What he thought was that he did not want her to leave. He wanted to see her dressed in satin and lace, with jewels dripping from her arms and ears and neck. No, he wanted to see her wearing nothing but a single red ruby between her breasts, breasts which she might not have had, so loose was the sack she wore. He'd wrestled with his conscience all night and decided he could not ruin a respectable woman, not even to save his life or escape to a better one. But now that she had decided the same thing, that her honor was too precious to barter, he changed his mind. Now he had to change hers. Or else he could lock her in the room and tie her to a chair, like one of the spies he'd interrogated. That might work better.

"No," he said. "You cannot leave yet. I believe you agreed to think about the position for a few days. The major cannot see you until then, anyway."

A few days? The longer Simone spent in this bachelor household, the more compromised she would be and the harder she'd find it to explain to a prospective employer where she had resided. She walked back to the table, and pounded her fist on it. "That is unacceptable."

"I think you might spare the time, considering I sent Major Harrison's bank draft to your brother's school this morning." He knew using her love for her brother was an unworthy weapon, but he had no rope or manacles handy.

Simone sat down, heavily. "You sent the check? But—but how did you know where to send it?"

By reading the brother's letters, of course. "Sally brought down a letter you'd written, to be sent with the mail. I addressed my note to the headmaster there."

"I'll have to write to him, to send it back. Dear heaven, what will the man think?"

Harris adjusted his spectacles. "I understood that the major promised the funds, no matter the outcome of your stay here."

"But I do not intend to stay."

"A promise is a promise. If not yours, then Major Harrison's. Further, the deed is done. The mail has been posted. Now, about dressmakers. Do you have a modiste that you prefer?"

"You must know I have no knowledge of such things. Lady Seldon patronized Madame Genevieve, but I—"

"No, her taste is abominable. In apparel and husbands. I took it upon myself to make inquiries as to who dresses the *ton*'s dashers."

"But I am not a dasher and I am not staying. I shan't

be going to the house party; therefore I do not need new gowns. I cannot make it any plainer."

"That is for you and the major to discuss, Miss Ryland. Meantime, the woman I selected is on her way with pattern books and sample fabrics. She has been paid in advance, to set aside her other customers' orders."

"Have you not been listening? I am not staying!"

He raised the coffee cup to his lips and smiled as if he knew something she did not, or if he'd tasted something sweet. "Who knows? You might change your mind. You already did once. And 'twould be best to have the new wardrobe begun, rather than rushed, do you not agree?"

"No, I do not agree with your overbearing organization. I'll wait to speak to the major, out of courtesy and gratitude on my brother's behalf, but I will not accept more than his hospitality until then." She would share his house, but not his bed.

"I think he might have expressed the urgency of the house party."

"He did explain, if one considers such fustian to be an explanation, that he requires an unknown female with a modicum of intelligence to accompany him. Surely he can find someone else, someone more willing."

"But I promised—that is, I swore to see his wishes carried out. The major will insist that he promised you a new wardrobe either way, in addition to your brother's schooling." He mentioned the brother again, which was more underhanded, but expedience always trumped politeness in the spy business. He'd use guilt, obligation, even sympathy, any port in a storm.

She stared at her hands, since she could read nothing in the secretary's shielded eyes. "I cannot refuse the major's largesse for my brother's sake, but I swear to repay him eventually. I will not go further into his debt."

"The money for the school is not a loan. It is a gift to a worthy student, an outright gift. We—he—makes charitable contributions to less-noble causes."

She nodded in concession. "Very well, my brother has a scholarship. But I will not accept a shilling more."

"Dratted female," she thought he muttered, but he'd bent down to pick up the cat, so she could have mistaken the secretary's words for "dratted feline." Then he exclaimed that a stray cat must have wandered in to take Miss White's place at the breakfast table.

"I brushed the cat to rid it of all the knots and mats."

"And this elegant creature is what is left? You have wrought a miracle."

His delight made Simone smile, despite knowing the secretary was manipulating her for his master's purposes and pleasures. "She ought to be brushed regularly."

"Do you think no one has tried? Miss White has drawn blood on many occasions. I have given up all attempts to groom the beast."

"I had no problem."

"You see? The major is in your debt, not the other way around. He is inordinately fond of Miss White." Who was purring loudly, in the secretary's lap.

The major was not the only cat lover, it seemed. Mr. Harris was pouring cream into a saucer and crumbling bits of toast into it while the cat purred loudly enough to be heard across the table. The sight and sounds made the secretary more human, Simone decided, more approachable. So she asked, "Major Harrison is a very caring gentleman, isn't he?"

Caring? Harry ordered assassinations, sent men to certain death, broke every law in the name of patriotism, and did nothing about half the atrocities he saw every day. Caring? He cared about his family, old and new, but the cat was closer to him than many people. "I cannot say."

"He took in Miss White, and the Judds, I understand. He helped Mrs. Burton establish her business, and aids many of her employees, from what they said. He must have a good heart."

Which had started working again only recently. "Like most of us, he cares for his own."

"Exactly. I am neither kith nor kin to him. Nor a charity case. I truly must be on my way."

Truly? As soon as the Aide's minions could return with reports of Miss Ryland's background, as much as could be discovered in so short a time, he was willing to let her go, or chance revealing what no more than a handful of people knew. He'd never reveal his family's secret, of course, only some of the government's workings. With her help he could uncover a subversive plot, if Lord Gorham's gathering truly harbored such a scheme, and expose an extortionist. Then his work would be over and he could be who he wanted to be.

"Please wait," he said. "He needs you. I am not at liberty to say why, but I think—that is, I know—he needs you a great deal."

No woman could need so many clothes.

Yes, she could, insisted Sally and the dressmaker and the two seamstresses sewing in the corner. A back parlor had been turned into a linendraper's fitting room and workshop, with Jeremy and another groom bringing in trunks of gowns, bolts of cloth, stacks of pattern books.

But it was only for a brief house party.

Among a vain crowd with deep pockets, *oui*. The women—and half the men—would change ensembles five or six times a day, to parade among the same people they saw in London. Madame Journet added another ball gown to the growing pile of dresses that needed minor alterations. Not only had the popular modiste set aside her customers' orders for Mr. Harris, it seemed, but she'd been bribed enough to make over their half-completed gowns for Simone. Some fit nearly perfectly, having been taken in or taken up just that morning, at great expense, Simone was certain. Sally had sent measurements from the blue gown before cock's crow, on the efficient Mr. Harris's orders. Madame Journet had set her needlewomen to work instantly. She'd even hired extra sewers, their wages added to the gentleman's account.

Aside from all the money she had already earned, now the Frenchwoman had a stake in Miss Ryland's debut. Whatever business from irate customers she might lose, she'd gain back threefold when the beau monde caught sight of the latest star on the demimonde's horizon, wearing Madame's designs. Miss Ryland was going to outshine them all, Madame Journet declared, and meant to make certain. Simone's success would be a feather in the modiste's cap, and a fortune in her purse. Besides, when a message from a certain gentleman arrived to call in a favor, she was only too happy to respond with her finest, most elegant creations.

She'd brought whichever would look becoming on a redhead with dusky skin. No whites or pastels—the debutantes could keep their come-out gowns. No clashing oranges or reds. Those were for females with no color of their own. But the browns, greens, golds, and antique lace, those were *magnifique* for Mademoiselle.

On a whim she'd also brought a daring froth of black silk studded with red brilliants that was meant for an entertainer who was older, far more sophisticated, and considered the most beautiful woman in all of London. Mademoiselle outshone her. They all agreed that the gown would be wasted on a jaded old hag treading the boards, when it made Simone look like a queen, the queen of the night. Her dark eyes gleamed with diamond flecks; her skin glowed warmer, her hair more vibrant. And that was before the master coiffeur arrived.

Another French émigré, he'd often acted as ears for the War Office. Ladies were known to rattle on when they were in their boudoirs with a trusted servitor. He'd been happy to pass on information that might lead to the overthrow of that usurper Bonaparte. Now he was happy to make Monsieur's *chérie amie* overshadow every other woman at the Cyprians' house party.

No, he would not cut off that glorious mane. *Quelle horreur!* Besides, he had orders from Monsieur. But he trimmed a bit here and a snip there. He used a curling iron while Sally watched and the seamstresses sewed and Madame Journet made lists for matching bonnets, gloves, stockings, fans, and undergarments. Oh, and jewels.

No jewels. Simone was insistent on that.

What, go to a marquis's house dressed as a peasant? Ruin Madame's creations? Not put a diamond tiara atop Monsieur's glorious new curls when she wore the black gown? Make her patron look miserly?

Great heavens, why was no one listening to her? Madame Journet chuckled when Simone begged her not to start any new gowns until Major Harrison returned. The master hairdresser rolled his eyes when she demanded a simpler style, one she could fix herself. The seamstresses giggled when she insisted the necklines be raised or filled in. No one paid her the least attention. She might as well have been a mannequin they were dressing, or a doll. Like children at play, they were exuberant and self-absorbed, uncaring of the cost or her debt to Major Harrison, or how hard she'd find it to refuse his offer.

Then she saw the riding habit. Someone *had* listened to her, or the longing in her voice. It was the latest style, with a divided black velvet skirt, a jacket woven of the finest wool two shades darker than her red hair, trimmed with black frogging. Black lace spilled over the high, military collar. Simone sighed just looking at it.

The gowns were all beautiful: silks and satins, with muslins for daytime, with ribbons and lace and puffed sleeves and scalloped hems. None of the women she'd worked for had owned anything half so becoming, so au courant, so luxurious. She'd never imagined even attending a function where such frocks were the norm. But the riding habit . . . ? That was a dream.

Simone thought of open fields and fresh air and riding astride, of a freedom she'd not known since girlhood, racing bareback on the pony her grandfather had given her, to her sedate father's dismay and her mother's understanding. Now she imagined riding cross-country with a handsome, dark-haired gentleman by her side. He'd ride a magnificent black stallion. And she'd be mounted on a—

". . . chair, miss. Do step up, so I can take an accurate drawing." The boot maker had arrived. Like the dressmaker, he brought a trunk filled with finished shoes to see if any fit her small foot. Now he wished to trace a pattern for the slippers he'd make to match her new gowns.

Simone held her breath to see if any of the riding boots fit. One pair was only a shade too wide, and the boot maker quickly inserted a felt lining. Perfect. The hairdresser kissed his fingertips. Sally clapped her hands.

Even the seamstresses put aside their work to circle her chair as if it were a throne. The habit's skirt's hem was only basted, the tiny black shako hat was still missing its feather, and her hair was trailing ringlets that had not been gathered into a lace snood yet—but Simone knew she'd never looked better.

Until the apothecary's assistant arrived with an assortment of lotions and face paints, brushes and colored papers. Simone did not bother demurring, not after seeing the results so far.

"Mademoiselle is *très belle, non*? She is meant for a man's admiration."

"Monsieur will be pleased, *oui*."

The coiffeur and the modiste were speaking in French, not realizing that Simone could understand. She understood all too well. They thought she was a perfect courtesan.

Chapter Eight

"You have to speak with her, Daniel. Convince her to stay."

Daniel Stamfield set his glass down and leaned back in his soft leather chair, staring at his cousin. Harry was a cousin from the wrong side of the blanket, but the right side of McCann, to have such a cozy suite of rooms above the exclusive gambling club. He was enigmatic, and the best man to have at your back, now that Daniel's other cousin, Rex, was settled down. Married and a father—who could believe it? Certainly not Daniel, who was nowhere near ready to put on leg shackles. Hell, no. But a mistress? Almost as bad, from what he could see everywhere he looked. Expensive, demanding, and only a little easier to get rid of than a wife.

"Don't see why you want to keep one woman, with so many others out there."

Harry gave him a dark look, from eyes that matched Daniel's own, deep blue with a black rim around the iris. For that matter, Harry looked a lot like Daniel, with the same wavy black hair and straight nose. They might have been twins instead of cousins, except that Daniel was taller and broader and heavier, and Harry looked far older than the four-year difference in their ages. Of course he did, Daniel reflected, with the weight of the country, if not the world, on his shoulders. Now he wanted a mistress, and an unwilling one at that. The man was a riddle, that was for certain. And not the only one. "You're saying the prettiest girl you ever saw doesn't want to become your mistress?"

"That's what I said, dammit."

"I thought they all wanted to climb into your bed."

"This one is different." Harry blew a smoke ring from his cigarillo over his head, looking like the devil with a halo.

Daniel raised his glass. "Then maybe she'd prefer my bed."

Harry knocked Daniel's bare feet off the low table, almost making him spill his cognac. "No. She is too delicate for an ox like you. And I need her at Gorham's."

"Why? If the gal ain't willing, she won't do you any good."

"She'll be perfect, if she'll go."

"Then use your charm. Rex's wife, Amanda, likes you well enough to name you godfather to her son, and you even wrapped your father's wife around your finger, eventually. Lydia Burton and all her chicks think you can walk on water."

"I've known Lydia for ages. That's different, almost like family, like the others. Besides, it's not that Miss Ryland doesn't want to be my mistress. She doesn't want to be any man's mistress."

Daniel needed another swallow of cognac for that. "Holding out for a ring, is she?"

"Holding on to her virtue, more like."

"Prigs are the worst kind, I say. Leave them to their cold comfort and find a warm, willing female to cuddle."

"This isn't about cuddling, you clod. Not everything involves sex. Gorham's party concerns national security, the regent's reputation, life and death."

"And sex."

"And sex," Harry agreed. Private matters were hard to hide in a family that knew truth from lies. "So you go talk to her, tell her what a good chap I am. Or Major Harrison, I suppose."

"You've made a muck of it this time, haven't you, with your wigs and beards and glasses? No wonder she doesn't want to bed that old goat."

"I told you, she doesn't want to bed anyone."

"So how am I supposed to convince her? You know I ain't in the petticoat line. Not with respectable females, anyway. Although if the bird flew over to Lydia's, I don't see why she's all prunes and prisms now."

"She has scruples, which, I might remind you, is an admirable trait."

"Hey, I've got scruples. Just because I don't want to work with Bow Street or the magistrate's office doesn't mean I'm some kind of villain. I don't go seducing innocent females, do I?"

"Dammit, I am not asking you to marry the woman— just go talk to her. I need her at Gorham's."

"You still haven't explained why."

"Because I like her, dammit!"

"Ah." Daniel had another drink, then grinned at his half cousin and onetime superior officer. "Caught at last, eh?"

"Nothing of the kind."

Daniel put his feet back up on the table so he could scratch his itchy toes. He grinned wider. "Top over teakettle, I'd wager. What do you want me to do?"

"She'll be bored in the house, with too much time to fret. Take her somewhere—"

"To balls and parties? Gads, you are asking a lot." Getting Harry's would-be paramour into the polite world meant he'd have to go, too. "You know I hate all that bowing and backstabbing gossip. Makes me itch, don't you know."

"I know. All those social lies give me a sour taste for days after. But that's not what I mean. I don't want her out in the public eye, not yet. She'll like museums and such."

"But I won't, deuce take it. Cousins and all, but I've got my limits. You can escort her yourself to those dry-as-dust places. Museums, faugh." He needed another drink to wash away the dust by suggestion.

Harry studied the burning tip of his cigarillo. "I cannot keep lying to her."

"But I can? Gives me a rash just thinking about it. Tell the gal the truth."

"Which truth, that lies taste like dirt in my mouth and make you scratch your arse? She'd think me insane, if she did not run as fast and as far as she could."

"Not that truth. Tell her about who you are, and why Gorham's party is so important to you."

"I'm not ready yet. I feel that I can trust her—I hope so—but my men are still checking facts. There's something about her fellow lodger that's unsettling, and the fireplace-poker incident does set a bad precedent. I need a few more days to be certain."

"Well, show her your handsome face meantime. It's not as pretty as mine, of course"—they were both spit and image of the Earl of Royce and his son Rex—"but she'll toss her cap over the windmill before you can say 'Jack Rabbit.' I don't see why you didn't meet her as Harry, anyway."

"I was too busy to change, and if she wasn't right, no harm done."

"You were testing her."

There was no sense in lying, not to Daniel. "Yes."

"You were a fool."

"Yes, but she wouldn't want to be a young bastard's mistress any more than an old one's. At least Harrison wouldn't expect too much between the sheets."

"Then make her an honest proposal."

Harry choked on a smoke ring that suddenly had him by the throat. "Marry her?"

"Why not? She's smart and pretty and has principles. And you like her. What more can you ask? It's not as if you need the money from a dowry, either. You show your good intents, she'll show you—well, she'll go along with you. Then you can back out if you want, after Gorham's do."

"Jilt her? Great gods, man, do you take me for that much a cur?"

Daniel was too busy pouring himself another drink, and laughing to himself, to answer.

Harry stabbed his cigarillo into the ashtray. "Well, I won't do it. If I ask any woman, it will be because I mean to wed her. I can't think about things like that until this other situation is resolved." So what if they both knew he'd thought of it, a lot?

Daniel stopped smiling. "You think the attempts on your life will end at Gorham's?"

"Hopefully."

"Then I better come along. Think you can get me an invite?"

"What, so you can bring one of Lydia's drabs? I doubt Gorham will be willing. You're not exactly known for good taste." Harry eyed Daniel's yellow cossack trousers, the spotted kerchief tied around his neck. "And your pockets aren't deep enough for the gambling that will go on. Maybe you can come if they hold a ball for the neighborhood."

"Neighborhood rakes, you mean. Not even Gorham would invite the gentry and his tenants to that kind of affair. But try to get me in. I hear they are going to have a contest for the queen of the courtesans, with side bets among the gents."

"Lud, I wouldn't want Miss Ryland exposed to that bit of vulgarity."

"Then don't take her."

"That's no answer. I'll send for you if there's a chance of Gorham's welcoming you, though. You can help protect her from unwanted familiarity."

"I still say you should pick another female if you have to go, one who won't be offended by the company. It's not like there are no other fish in the sea."

Harry did not want another female. He did not want Simone swimming in that milieu, either, but who knew what she'd decide to do next, without a position or an income? Hell, she might join Astley's Circus and wear tights and spangles for the men to ogle. The pay was better than a governess's. Dammit, he admitted, but only to himself, he did not want her out of his sight.

Daniel had found a tin of biscuits on the sideboard and was helping himself to a handful. "Tell me again why you can't escort the governess about Town yourself, show her the sights. Museums." He spit out the word and a biscuit. "What the deuce are these things?"

"Cat treats."

While Daniel washed his mouth out with Harry's expensive cognac, Harry explained that he planned on the element of surprise at Gorham's. "I don't want her seen until then, and certainly not with me. Harrison, either, which would be worse. But you could take her out to some quiet place, with her in her old clothes and prim hairstyle."

"Faugh, she doesn't sound like any baggage I'd want on my arm. No fun, either. I could go visit Rex's old nanny if I wanted a proper female."

"Now that I think of it," Harry said, "your language and your manners are too coarse for the lady."

"I thought you said her grandfather was a Gypsy."

"So? Mine was a blacksmith."

"But your other granddad was an earl."

"And hers is a major landholder in Cumberland. Go meet her. See for yourself."

"I just might. To see what's got you tied in knots. This could be the best fun I've had in ages. Are you sure you won't go to Lydia's tonight? How about Chatsforth's? I hear they've got a new dealer who goes home with a different chap every night. Maybe—"

"I am not in the mood. And if that is how your mind is working, I take it all back. I don't want you near Miss Ryland."

Which meant, of course, that Daniel decided to stop round in Kensington, to see what had bowled over the steadiest man he'd ever met. Damn if cold-blooded old Harry didn't have some fire in him after all.

A caller arrived during the final fitting for some of Simone's new clothes. She looked at the card Jeremy brought in to her in the back parlor that had been turned into a sewing room, but she did not recognize the name.

"Tell Mr. Stamfield that neither the major nor Mr. Harris is home," she told Jeremy, who grinned at her. She thought he liked the riding habit she was trying on. So did she. It was still her favorite of all her new wardrobe, although the glittering black lace gown stirred her imagination with visions of dancing at a ball with her dark-haired lover. Not that she'd ever wear such a scandalous garment, and not that she was going to take a lover.

"But Daniel Stamfield is nephew to the Earl of Royce and cousin to Viscount Rexford," Sally told her, checking to see that a black curling feather was firmly affixed to the riding habit's matching shako cap.

Those were the two names Major Harrison had suggested as guardian for her brother. Simone knew nothing would come of that offer when she left his household, and she was glad. She never liked the idea of leaving Auguste's future in the hands of strangers. Nor did she like leaving him with no one should anything happen to her, but she would worry about that another time. Mr. Harris refused to discuss the matter; Mr. Stamfield might. "Perhaps I should see Mr. Stamfield."

The gentleman followed Jeremy's return to the small room but stood in the doorway, staring, even after Jeremy announced him in as formal a manner as the grinning youth could manage.

"Mr. Stamfield?" Simone asked in the silence.

The visitor closed his dropped jaw. "I have got to place a bet, by Jupiter!"

"Sir?"

Her caller was too large, too casually dressed for a noble connection, but he was handsome for all that, almost like the image she had of her dancing partner. He even had uniquely attractive blue eyes. Botheration, now she was seeing the man of her dreams everywhere.

Daniel was seeing a fortune to be made, if he could get both of them—and Harry, he supposed, curse him for finding her first—to Gorham's house party and the contest. "Can you sing?"

The seamstress in the corner giggled. Sally clucked her tongue.

Simone stepped forward and held out her hand. She would *not* let this lack-witted giant have anything to do with her little brother, not when he spoke of wagering before he said hallo. She cleared her throat, which served to bring Mr. Stamfield's attention to her outstretched hand. He took it in his much larger one, and then forgot to let go.

"My apologies, miss. Harry said you were a good-looking female, but he didn't do you justice."

"You've seen Harry? That is, Major Harrison?"

"Him, too. That is, yes."

"He hasn't been around."

"Been busy, I suppose. The devil always is."

He was still staring, still holding her hand. Simone tugged it away, with effort, and said, "Mr. Harris is out, so if you've come to see him . . ."

"No, it's you I came to see. Glad for it, too, let me tell you. That is, I came about your brother. Harry said he needed a guardian."

"Thank you for your concern, but I shall make arrangements of my own." She was convinced to find a suitable person, maybe a solicitor, now more than ever.

"You won't find anyone better'n my cousin Rexford. Honest as sunshine, diligent, devoted to his family and the land. Harry thought I ought to come and send my recommendation to Rex along with his papers to sign. I mean, not even Harry can expect Rex to take on a strange boy sight unseen." That was the story he and Harry had devised, to give credence to Daniel's visit.

"The major was correct, that someone should have

Auguste's welfare at heart if I cannot. But while my brother is a stranger to you, Lord Rexford is also a stranger to me."

"Exactly. But he's in the country, with his wife and babies. And your brother is at school. So I have come for us to get acquainted. Surrogates, don't you know."

An odd kind of logic, Simone thought, but Mr. Stamfield's smile was friendly, his admiration reassuring. He was obviously a friend of the major's and known to the staff here, so Simone did not feel uncomfortable in his presence. Further, she had hardly spoken to anyone but Sally, the seamstress, and Miss White in two days. Major Harrison never visited, and Mr. Harris stayed locked behind the doors of his library, which she had never been invited to visit or use. At breakfast he stayed rapt in his papers, making it plain as day that he did not wish to be interrupted. At dinner, he made less conversation than Jeremy did as he passed the plates. They'd said everything they needed, the secretary's taciturn manner indicated, with neither budging from his or her position. He still thought she was ungrateful and foolish and dishonest; she thought he was secretive, autocratic, and pigheaded. He wanted her to stay; she was going.

So she might as well chat with Mr. Stamfield. Perhaps he could tell her a little more about the major and how soon she could expect him, to be done with this charade. She decided to offer the large gentleman tea, since he must need a great deal of sustenance. At least she thought he had a hungry expression in his startling blue eyes. A single female did not entertain an unmarried, unrelated male caller, much less a total stranger, but she'd broken so many social rules, what was one more?

Before she could send Sally to fetch a tray from the

kitchen, Mr. Stamfield said, "I say, you're dressed for riding. Care to take a turn in the park?"

Simone couldn't think of anything she'd like better; she'd been in the house so long. But she did not have a horse, naturally, and hadn't been on one in ages.

"Neither one's a problem," he said. "Can't gallop or anything in the park, so you'll get your seat back. Um, am I supposed to say 'seat'?" He went on without waiting for a reply: "And Harry's stables are bound to have something suitable, I'm sure. He'd have nothing to carry my weight, of course, but I rode my own mount."

"If you are certain the major won't mind me riding one of his horses?"

"Harry wouldn't mind if you rode his— That is, 'course not. Great chap, old Harry. Generous to a fault. Um, he did think you ought to wear a veil if we went out."

That suited Simone, too. That way no one could recognize her later if she applied at somebody's doorstep looking for a governess position. A scrap of netting was quickly pinned to the shako cap, and her hair was gathered into another net, while Mr. Stamfield visited the major's stables.

Not much conversation took place as Simone got used to the horse, a prettily behaved bay gelding, and the noise and traffic. The gelding was more used to navigating the crowded streets than Simone, so they managed. Then they were in the park, and could head down a riding path clear of carriages and strollers.

"Ready for a trot?" Mr. Stamfield asked.

Simone clucked to her horse and took off.

When they stopped to rest the horses, Simone was out of breath, but she was exhilarated, too. Mr. Stamfield was humming and smiling, enjoying the day and the ride also, Simone could tell. He seemed much more at home in the saddle than in a parlor. According to Sally, who'd rattled on the whole time she was fixing Simone's hair when Mr. Stamfield was bringing the horses around, he was a profligate, prodigal son. He was supposed to be a country squire, taking over his father's estate, but he came back from the wars wanting nothing but pleasure, no responsibility, no work. Gaming and drinking and wenching, that's what everyone said he did, among the lower orders. According to Sally, he was not accepted in polite society unless his uncle and cousin were with him.

So he was a town buck, a blood, a rakehell? That was precisely the kind of gentleman Simone never wanted her brother to meet. Still, he did not look dangerous, laughing at the ducks in a pond, humming to his horse. Simone found nothing flirtatious or suggestive about his manner, either. If he seemed a bit rough around the edges, he treated her with courtesy, almost like a friend.

Simone relaxed and felt the clean air sweeping the last cobwebs away from her mind. Only certainty remained. She could enjoy the day, wait for the major, and not regret leaving. After another short trot, she told her companion, "I doubt I'll be needing to name a guardian for my brother. Whatever peril the major might face, I shall not be with him. I know I might fall off this beautiful fellow and break my neck, or fall down the stairs at the house. But I am not going to the country."

She was not going to become the major's mistress; that was what she wanted this bluff, cheerful man to know. He didn't seem to think badly of her, but he had to know what she was doing at the Kensington hideaway. "I am not going to the house party," she repeated, hoping he would understand.

He nodded, unsurprised, but said, "Too bad, you'd win the contest. If you can sing. That's one of the competitions."

"You mentioned singing before. My voice is passable,

enough to instruct young girls, although my pianoforte is far more skillful. But what contest are you speaking of?"

"Harry didn't tell you? I suppose not, with him turning into a dry old stick. There's to be a tournament of sorts at Gorham's. The betting will be deep, and amusing because each houseguest will have to back his own lady friend, if he wants to keep the peace. No matter if she doesn't stand a chance. I hear there will be side bets behind the women's backs."

"But what is the contest?"

"Didn't I say? The women will vie against each other in various fields. I heard voice was one of them. Archery is another. Looks, of course. I don't know what else. Oh, horsemanship. You'd beat them all to flinders."

"Thank you. My grandfather taught me. He was magical with horses."

"You could have taken that event and the purse hands down."

"The purse?"

"Seems each event has a prize and points. At the end, the overall point winner gets crowned Queen of the Courtesans. And a thousand pounds."

A thousand pounds? Grandfather would be ashamed; Simone almost fell off the horse.

Chapter Nine

M ajor Harrison arrived at the end of the week, in time for dinner. Mr. Harris had a previous appointment, which suited Simone, who felt better having the major to herself. He was kinder, more understanding, more flexible than the ramrod-straight secretary. How could the major disapprove of her when he was the one wanting to hire a mistress?

While Jeremy served, the major asked about her ride with Mr. Stamfield, about her new clothes, and if she'd heard from her brother recently, or if the headmaster had replied to the bank draft. He spoke of the news of the day and the latest books, which he promised to find for her in his library. He was surprisingly knowledgeable about horses for an elderly gentleman who appeared anything but an outdoorsman. Simone should not have been surprised, recalling the quality of the gelding she'd ridden.

He complimented her gown and her new hairstyle. He cared, she felt, almost in an avuncular way. He looked like someone's eccentric relation, too, a bit messy, shaggy, and old-fashioned.

As soon as the young footman left, leaving the several

courses on the table for them to serve themselves, Simone said she had come to a decision.

"Later, my dear, later. Let us not ruin Mrs. Judd's excellent meal with such weighty matters."

She could not eat much, not with the difficult conversation looming ahead, but the major seemed unaffected. He also appeared a bit different now that she had time to notice, while he ate. Simone could have sworn his mustache had gone up at the ends when they first met. Now the ends went down like Mr. Harris's, whose lips were always in a downward scowl anyway. The major had also limped more at Mrs. Burton's, she thought, but perhaps the climb to the madam's sitting room had been tiring. Or the weather that day had made him ache. Grandfather's fingers used to swell before a rainstorm. This evening was dry and clear, for a change.

The major still leaned on his cane as they walked toward the drawing room after dinner. He'd gladly forgo his solitary smoke for her company, he told her.

She started to tell him of her decision, but he held up one hand. "I may do without my cigarillo for the pleasure of your presence, my dear, but I do enjoy my port after dinner, especially after a trying day. Helps an old man's digestion, also, you see. "

She saw he was not ready to speak yet. He told her to order tea for herself, which would have meant another delay. She chose to taste the port instead, breaking yet another law of ladylike decorum. The rule book had flown out the window days ago, and no one would know anyway, except the two of them and Miss White.

The cat wound herself around the major's feet, then leaped into his lap, ignoring Simone altogether. Strangely enough, the big cat had hissed at Mr. Stamfield, arched her back at the deliverymen, and twitched her tail at Jeremy, yet she adored both the major and his assistant.

Simone was waiting for Major Harrison to notice the difference in his pet, how well-groomed she was, and lighter in weight, but he did not say anything, just sank back in his chair and sighed with contentment, one hand stroking the now-smooth white fur, the other holding the glass.

Simone did not like her efforts being ignored, her speech put off, or the taste of the port. She walked to the door where Jeremy was waiting, to ask for a tea tray after all.

The cart was wheeled in, the tea was poured, and still the major sipped and sighed. The cat purred. Finally, almost reluctantly, the major set his glass aside.

"Now, my dear, we can have our discussion."

"Thank you." She tried to keep the "at last" under her breath. A man was entitled to relax in his own home, she supposed, although she felt as taut as a bowstring. "I have come to a decision. I—"

He interrupted her. "I beg your pardon, but so have I. So I will save you the awkwardness of refusing my offer. I withdraw it."

"I am going."

"Yes, so you told Mr. Harris, quite forcefully, too. I understand your scruples and I admire you for them. Never fear I am angry, my dear. Recall, I was the one who suggested you take this time to decide on such drastic action, wasn't I?"

"You do not understand. I am going with you to Lord Gorham's party in Richmond."

In his usual slow, deliberative way, he waited before replying, then asked, "With all that the trip entails?"

Simone could feel the color rising in her cheeks, but

she looked straight at him, cursing the dratted spectacles that hid his eyes and most of his expression. "Yes, I wish to be your . . . companion."

"No, you do not." He grimaced, then asked for a cup of tea, with extra sugar.

She prepared the cup and got up to hand it to him. "You cannot know that."

"Oh, I know." He took a deep swallow of the sweet tea, almost burning his tongue. "In addition, you told Mr. Harris."

"I changed my mind."

"So did I." He took another mouthful of tea.

"What about that nonsense you spoke of: the danger, how you required an escort, a new face, an educated woman? Furthermore, you have already spent a fortune on my clothes and my brother."

He brushed that aside, as only a wealthy man could. "Money is not as important as your self-esteem."

"It is if you are starving. Charity makes a bitter breakfast."

He chose to misinterpret her words. "Has Mrs. Judd not been feeding you well?" He slowly looked her over from head to toe, his scrutiny pausing at her hips and her bust, outlined by the thin fabric of the ecru silk gown she wore.

Simone quickly went back to her chair across from his, away from his examination. It was all she could do not to hold her hand above the gown's bodice, where the fabric did not extend far enough for her taste. Madame Journet had made the décolletage to a gentleman's taste, she said, not a governess's. Once she was seated, Simone told the major, "Mrs. Judd is an excellent housekeeper and cook, as you must know. She would never permit a guest in your home to go hungry, whether she approves of that guest or not." The housekeeper did not approve of Simone, but that was not the major's concern. Or Mrs. Judd's, Simone considered.

Harrison nodded. "So you have not gone hungry. And your brother's education is secure. As is his welfare." He pulled some papers out of his pocket. "Rexford has agreed to stand as guardian, in case of emergency only. The clothes are yours to keep. So you do not have to commit a transgression you might regret for the rest of your life."

"No, sir, I disagree. I will regret *not* going more. You have been kind and more than generous, but I intend to win Lord Gorham's contest."

"Blast! I knew I should not have let Daniel near you. Buffle-headed and cowhanded, both, the jackass. No one else would have mentioned it."

"I disagree again. You should have told me. Mr. Harris could have. Mr. Stamfield was kind enough to do so."

"Greedy, more likely. Did he also explain that the contest will be rigged so that Gorham's mistress wins?"

"Oh. No, he did not mention that. I suppose the points can be miscounted or awarded unfairly so she wins the thousand pounds, but she cannot win each event, as I understand it. A clay pigeon does not play favorites, for one."

"She used to be an opera singer."

"Very well, I concede to her at voice, but I intend to take the horsemanship prize, and make a good showing at the archery contest. Madame Journet's wardrobe is beyond anything I have ever seen, if clothing is judged. I am also proficient at the pianoforte. Mr. Stamfield was not certain what else would be judged."

"Bedroom skills."

"Oh. Oh, dear. And you would not lie, would you?"

"I told you, I cannot. Despite Gorham's probable anger, I was not going to put up the entry fee, if you did accompany me."

"You can afford it."

"Yes, but I thought to save you from that decadence by not placing your name in the running."

"You saved the Judds and Miss White, but I am no stray. I want the opportunity to rescue myself."

"You want to win the purse, or whatever part of it you can. You do not wish to become my mistress. Isn't that the truth?"

"You must know it is. It was always about the money."

"Good, because I have decided that I do not want you for my lover." He added more sugar to his tea and gulped it down.

She gasped, not at the amount of sugar he'd just swallowed, but at the insult. This old man with his shabby beard, stooped posture, and peculiar notions did not want her? Who was he to be so particular? Then she remembered his many kindnesses. "You found another companion?"

"No, I found my own conscience. I cannot lead a woman down the primrose path. Do you know what is at the other end? You can see them on the street corners outside Drury Lane. Or coughing to death like my own mother. Lord Gorham seeks to be rid of his long-term mistress, as men often do. By holding the contest, getting each gentleman to put in his stake, he can send her off with a handsome pension without reaching into his own pocket, while enjoying the spectacle. Not many kept women retire half so well, nor last so long with one lover. I know a few courtesans do wed their protectors, but the number of them is very small. Most find themselves with child, with the pox, with a handful of baubles as their entire fortune, after being passed from gentleman to gentleman. I will not send a young lady down that road."

Simone was near tears. Everything he said was true. But a governess's lot was no better unless she was fortunate in her workplace. Nor had Simone forgotten that her virtue was no safer where she'd been honorably employed. She could have ended pregnant, diseased, or in jail without even a trinket to sell for a lawyer's fees. Whereas if she won Lord Gorham's disgraceful competition . . .

"I have another proposition."

She leaned forward. "Yes?"

"I propose to hire you as an actress."

She sat back, the bubble of hope deflated. "I am no actress."

"For one hundred pounds."

"I can learn. What role shall I play?"

"Why, my mistress, of course. I told you some of my reasons for going to Gorham's. They are still true, no matter what you believe. Plans are afoot, so I have to attend the house party, which means I need a beautiful woman with me."

"But what is the difference? I will be just as ruined whether I pretend to be your mistress or if I actually am."

"Not in your heart, and not in my mind. Only your good name will suffer, which is easy enough to fix by changing it. You already look different from the Miss Ryland anyone knows or might encounter in the future. After the house party, you can return to being that woman of impeccable reputation, richer by a hundred pounds."

"And whatever else I can win."

He smiled. She saw a flash of white, not an old man's brown-stained teeth. "And whatever else you can win. I shall back you. Afterward, you'll have far more choices, your own choices, apart from the money."

"What if I choose to become Lord Gorham's next paramour?"

"Then I might have to kill him."

He spoke so grimly, Simone almost believed him. Then she laughed. "I can see I must take acting lessons from you, sir."

"There's more than pretending. We shall have to share a bedroom. I see no getting around that. The servants would talk, otherwise. Sally will come along as your lady's maid, and she would never betray us, but—"

"But she is a delightful rattlepate," Simone concluded for him. "She might let something slip."

"Exactly. So she has to think our arrangement is as it should be."

"Country houses usually have large beds. We can manage. After my cot at Mrs. Olmstead's house, I suppose I could sleep on the floor if need be. Do you snore?"

"No one has complained about that yet," he said with another smile. "We have more important matters to discuss, however. As I told you, there is more to this gathering than a foolish romp. I need you to listen, to tell me anything suspicious you hear from the women. Sally and Jeremy will do the same in the servants' hall."

"And Harold, your driver, can be on the alert in the stables."

"Um, of course. No one pays much attention to the staff. They might learn something helpful. As for you, I see no reason for anyone to know that you speak French or Spanish. You might hear other conversations that way, spoken in private."

Simone did not actually believe in the major's fustian nonsense, but if he was willing to take her to Richmond, she was willing to act as his mistress and his spy. Gracious, she'd act as his valet if that's what it took.

Heaven knew he needed one. "What is it I should be listening for?"

"Plans to overthrow the government."

If Daniel had not said what a knowing man the major was, how he worked for the army and terrified lower-ranking soldiers, she would never believe her new partner was in his right mind. "That is impossible."

"It is all too possible. Not everyone approves of our royal family, riddled with madness, extravagance, and debauchery as it is. An assassination here, a bribe there, a judgment of mental incompetence, all can accomplish as much in the right hands as incriminating letters in the wrong ones."

"But why?"

"Because not everyone who will be at Gorham's believes in the aristocracy. He has invited men of title, but other men of wealth and ambition. They want more power, more say in the governing of the country. Some might prefer a republic, like in America, to a monarchy. Some are known to wish a stronger role for the Commons. A few are suspected of wanting to bring Napoleon back from exile. I shall explain more once we are on our way to Richmond."

"You do not trust me now?"

"I am trusting you with my life. But too many things can go wrong, and you are better, safer, not knowing everything yet. Do you trust me?"

She hesitated a moment before answering yes.

He licked the tea off his ragged mustache. "You are not sure."

"Stop guessing at my mind."

"No, I only recognize the truth."

"Bosh. You cannot know what I am thinking. I could tell you my mother's name was Ermentrude—"

"Marielle. Your mother was called Marielle, and her mother, Simone, was kin to the comte du Chantrevieu. You bear her name."

"How did you . . . ? No, I do not wish to know. Yes, I trust that you will keep your promises and that you speak the truth."

"That is enough for now, so let us proceed. What do you wish to call yourself? It should be something that you will answer to with ease—perhaps something close to your real name, in case you make a mistake."

"Do you mean how 'Harrison' and 'Harris' are so similar?"

He paused and looked at her, his head cocked to one side. "Something like that. Do not forget Harold Coachman."

"How absurd."

"I agree. But back to your name, it would be best if it were not a total lie, yet the more exotic the better. 'Mona' is too plain. 'Sima'?"

" 'Noma.' That was what my brother called me when he was little, when 'Simone' was too hard for him to say."

"Ah, perfect. 'Noma' suits you, with your un-English looks. You might be from the American Plains, or the tropical Indies, or the steppes of Russia. What last name?"

"I am tempted to use 'Ryland,' to shame my father's family for not doing better by us, but it is Auguste's name also, and I would not have him connected to my scandalous actions."

"Hmm. 'Reilly' is too common. 'Roland' too close. How about 'Royal'? Noma Royal, favorite in the race for Queen of the Courtesans."

"No one will believe that is my real name. It sounds more like one you'd give a racehorse."

"But an actress often adopts a stage name, the way an author uses a pseudonym. They select a prettier name, something memorable and easier to pronounce than their own. I know, but shan't tell anyone but you, that Gorham's mistress, Claire Hope, is really Claudinia Colthopfer."

Simone laughed. "You are making that up."

The major shook his head. "I do not lie, Miss Royal."

" 'Royale,' I think, with an *e*. Miss Noma Royale."

"Lovely. Tell Sally and Jeremy so they and you can become familiar with it. And you must start calling me Harry, Noma, as intimate acquaintances would."

Somehow the notion of sleeping in the same room was easier to contemplate than the familiarity of using an older gentleman's given name. "I shall try . . . Harry."

"Capital. Now, when we leave on Wednesday, the coach will take you and Sally out of Town. I have matters to attend to along the way, but I'll meet up with you before you reach Richmond. I'll visit a barber and my tailor before then. Why, I'll be so dashing you might not recognize me."

Simone smiled politely, not speaking a lie. "Whatever is convenient, ah, Harry, as long as I do not have to arrive at Lord Gorham's estate without you."

"Have no fear, we shall make a grand entrance together. Which reminds me, you'll need to practice acting the part. You'll have to be a bit more convincing as a courtesan if we are to succeed."

"I did not put on the face paints this evening, or the most revealing gown."

"No, my dear. What I meant is about showing affection: kissing, touching, standing close, holding hands, sending smitten glances."

"In public?"

"Such displays will be common at Gorham's, even expected. A proper female would be aghast at the blatant behavior, but you must not be shocked, no matter what you see. In fact, you have to be just as forward and free with your favors—to me, naturally. Make no mistake, the house party is about sex also, not merely games and intrigue. If you do not seem loving, receptive of my attentions, no one will believe we are lovers, and then they will start asking questions neither of us wants to answer. We will not be paramours, in fact, but only the two of us must know that."

"I . . . I think I can do that."

"Then kiss me, Noma. For practice, of course."

"Of course." Simone stood and stepped toward his chair. She bent down, closed her eyes, and pressed her pursed lips to his mustache.

"Lud, sweetheart, you really are no actress, are you?"

Chapter Ten

Simone sprang back as if she'd been scalded. "You knew I was no Cyprian."

"I didn't know you'd never been kissed, dammit!"

"I have too." Before he could accuse her of a lie—had the kiss been that bad, that he could tell?—she amended her statement: "That is, the baron did, before I hit him with the poker. The son of my previous employer caught me alone in the nursery once, and kissed me until I could scream for help. And I was properly kissed by a gentleman under the mistletoe my last Christmas at home."

"By your blasted curate? None of those count. Lud, we'll be found out within an hour of our arrival. You might as well wear a chastity belt if you are going to show that much enthusiasm for lovemaking. Damn, you'll stand out like a donkey at Epsom Downs. I'll be a laughingstock, bringing a virgin to a bacchanal; you'll be banned from the foolish games. Worst of all, no one will talk to you."

"I can learn. How hard can it be?"

"It's not supposed to be hard, by all that's holy, and a lot that's not! I'm the one supposed to— Never mind. Relax and try again."

Relax, after he yelled at her loudly enough to make the cat run out of the room? This time Simone did try to soften her lips. She kept her eyes open, too, to make sure she found his mouth, not his mustache. She did manage to hit her target, after bumping his nose. His lips were firm but pliant under hers, a not unpleasant feeling, she decided. "There," she said, pulling away so fast she dislodged his spectacles. "You see, I can do it."

He did not see at all, for he kept his eyes closed while he replaced the glasses on his nose. "That was hardly a kiss. More a cold brushing of lips so quick it might have been a passing snow shower. Devil take it, couples married for thirty years manage to put more emotion into an embrace than that. Tell me, Simone, do you wish to kiss me or not?"

"That's Noma, sir, not Simone."

"That is avoiding my question. I know who you are. Yes or no?"

Simone couldn't say, "No," not and keep her job. "Yes" would be a lie, which he'd know instantly. "It's . . . it's the mustache. I do not like the feel of it."

He stroked the offending article. "I would feel naked without it. But tell me this, Noma, what if I asked you to attend the party with another man, one who was clean-shaven, young, passably good-looking?"

Simone was more indignant than if he'd said she kissed like a cow. "I will not be handed around like a flagon of wine. I made an agreement with you and no one else. Your friend might be far more demanding of my services, or far less appealing to me."

"And hell might freeze over," he muttered. Aloud he said, "I was afraid you'd say that. But what if he was Harry, too?"

"How can he be? Either you are Harry or you are not. You said you never lie."

"Aye, that's a problem."

"Which makes no sense. There can be any number of Harrys, but only one you. Harry, Harrison, Harold, a name means nothing. You said so yourself. Why, I would never kiss Mr. Harris, no matter what that dry stick calls himself."

The major started coughing, so she brought him another cup of tea.

When he was done choking, he said, "People are not always who or what they seem to be."

"If that is a riddle, you will have to solve it for me."

"I cannot, not yet. Too many lives are at stake. If you spoke to the wrong person before we leave, unknowingly whispered a doubt, plans could go awry and end badly."

"But you said you want me to listen to gossip."

"Listen, yes, but not give anything away. You'll understand later."

Now she understood that for all her pretty clothes and intentions, she seemed to remain Miss Simone Ryland at heart, a sensible woman who disliked paradoxes and puzzles. "I do not know if I can manage this after all."

"You simply have not grown into your character yet. Unfortunately we have no month to rehearse. Come, let us try again. This time I will take charge."

"Take charge?" She did not like the sound of that, but before Simone could react, the major pulled her onto his lap where the cat had been moments ago. Startled by his quick move and his strength, she still noticed his surprisingly firm thighs under her bottom. She would have expected weak and wasted muscles if she'd considered a gentleman's thighs at all, which she had not until now. He must ride his horses after all, she thought, before he tilted her chin and brought his mouth down on hers.

The mustache tickled and the beard rubbed at her chin, but now she understood about a real kiss. His lips felt warm and dry, not parched like the curate's, not slobbery like the baron's, not cold and hard like that lecherous son's. Now her lips grew warmer. They even tingled. Then his tongue flicked out and licked her lips, a butterfly's caress, not threatening, not intrusive, just . . . nice. That ought to be enough to convince any watchers. How many could there be, anyway? No matter what the major said, no one but farm animals indulged in such pastimes amid company. She certainly did not. Simone pulled back, and his hands immediately left her shoulders.

"Maybe you would enjoy this more if you imagined that younger man."

She had been enjoying his kiss, somewhat, at any rate. "Hm, tall, dark, and handsome?"

He brushed her lips with his again. "More or less."

"Blue eyes?"

"If that's what you like."

It was. And sure enough, she had the picture of him in her mind's eye, the Harry she must have dreamed about from the stories at Lydia Burton's. With her eyes closed, with the mustache forgotten, she kissed him, and Harry kissed her back. His hands stroked her back and her neck and down the sides of her ribs, and she grew heated, wanting to be nearer. She dared to raise her hand, then reconsidered. No, she did not want to touch his old-fashioned wig and ruin her dream.

Feeling disloyal for thinking of an imaginary hero while kissing her feeble old patron, she spread her hands on his chest and his shoulders. They felt hard and strong, muscular like his legs, far more suited to the man in her mind than the man in her future. Then she forgot about everything but him, Major Harrison, the Harry who held her. Now her own body told her what to do, what it wanted, what he most likely wanted back. Those were her only thoughts, while shooting stars danced across her sky. She'd never . . . no wonder . . . his tongue could do that? There was more?

Eventually they both needed to breathe. Simone pulled away and grinned. "I can do this!"

"Oh, lady, you certainly can." Harry pushed her farther onto his knees and straightened his coat over his lap. He was panting, so she worried that kissing, kissing his way, was too much exertion for a frail man. But he was smiling. His wig was askew, his neckcloth was unknotted—had she done that?—and now one end of his mustache tilted up, the other down.

She was going to Richmond.

Harry was going to burn in hell if they did not stop. He sent her to bed—her own bed—and poured himself another glass of port. Then he sat back, readjusted his clothing, his privates, and his thinking.

This new plan would work perfectly, he told himself. She'd keep her virtue; he'd keep his reputation as a rake.

She'd be acting; he'd be the perfect gentleman, not the bastard he was born to be.

Keeping her chaste would be easy; he didn't want the woman anyway.

Then he set the port aside and ate three sugar cubes from the tea tray.

Harry had his spies, his ears to the ground, throughout London, his cadre of intelligence officers. He had paid informants in the highest levels of society and the lowest dregs of humanity. Nothing of his, however, compared to the servants' grapevine.

Everyone, it seemed, knew about the courtesan competition. Why, Sally could tell Simone the names of half the women supposedly attending Lord Gorham's house party, plus their special talents, favorite dressmakers, and scruples when it came to cheating. She had to watch out for one who hated all women, another who liked women all too well. One was known to be desperate for money to settle gambling debts her protector refused to pay. A viscount was about to marry and leave Town, so his mistress needed funds until she found a new financier. The desperate ones were the most competition, Sally warned, after Miss Claire Hope, of course, Lord Gorham's constant companion when his wife wasn't looking. Simone had to hide her chuckle behind a cough, knowing of the woman's true name.

Sally understood entirely about using aliases. Why, she was going to be Sarah Boyle, from her own given name and her mother's maiden name. It would not do, she said, begging miss's pardon, for Sally Judd to be known as a ladybird's dresser, not if she wished to find a position with a proper lady of fashion afterward. And thanks be to Miss Royale for all the training she'd be getting. She was that thrilled to be going to the highfliers' gathering, but, begging miss's pardon again, 'twould be a poor reflection on both her mother and the Kensington household for a connection between them to become known.

"Mum's gone right respectable, I swear, and doesn't intend me to follow in her shoes. Not that I'd throw my bonnet over the windmill for the first handsome face and pretty talk, of course."

Her brother, Jeremy, would be Jem Boyle, for the same reasons. Besides, the major had asked both siblings to use a different name, and no one refused Master Harry, or asked for explanations.

Likely because they never got answers to their questions, Simone thought, but she listened carefully to everything Sally could tell her.

She made a mental list until the information grew too complicated. Then she had to write it down. With over twenty couples invited, according to the rumor mill, the pages of her notebook quickly filled.

Sally—Sarah—was happy to report all the news she could gather from nearby households and the scandal sheets she adored; Jem did his research at the taverns where footmen took their ale; Mrs. Judd herself took to visiting her old friends at the theaters. She listened to the greenroom gossip for Harry's sake, Simone knew, not Simone's. Even the surly driver Harold, who she supposed did not need a new name since he never spoke his old one, or anything to anyone but Mrs. Judd, passed on scraps of knowledge about Lord Gorham's stables and the surrounding countryside. What surprised Simone most was Mr. Harris's cooperation.

Everyone was fairly certain that one of the contest events would involve the maze at Richmond, close to Lord Gorham's estate of Griffin Woods. The maze was notoriously complicated, with a groundskeeper seated on a high ladder to direct lost trekkers back out. Everyone was also certain that Lord Gorham would provide his mistress with a map of the paths. All the other gentlemen were scrambling to purchase or purloin one for their own partners. Viscount Martindale was known to have sent a groom to Richmond last week to figure it out and make a diagram. The man had not returned.

The secretary took dinner with Simone, but he appeared more dour and disapproving than ever. He most likely believed she had sold her soul to the devil for a chance at the thousand pounds, and that after spouting her pious drivel about honor and self-respect. So Harry had not taken his assistant into his confidence about their new arrangement, which gave Simone a small sense of satisfaction. Mr. High-and-Mighty Harris did not know everything after all. He took his seat at the table without holding her chair, then paid more attention to his food than to her. He hurried through the meal as if he could not wait to be rid of her company.

The devil take the secretary, Simone told herself. She had enough to worry about without his scowls and his silence. Why, she was glad he was not going with them, according to Sally.

Yet before she left the room, leaving him to his solitary coffee or port or poison, for all she knew or cared, Mr. Harris handed her a folded sheet of paper. On it was a replica of the Richmond Maze, with the center clearly marked, and the proper path to it drawn with red ink. Now she stood a chance!

"Why, thank you. That is too kind of you, sir."

He grunted and waved her away before she could ask how he came upon a key to the maze or why he was helping her.

Likely the man was wagering on the outcome, she decided, or he'd never have bothered.

More assistance came from Daniel Stamfield, who admitted he was betting on her. She wanted to ride again the next morning, but he thought they should go somewhere quiet, so they could talk. "Harry suggested a museum. No one I know goes there."

"I do, taking all my students to them when I was a governess. The children adored getting out of the classroom, and I thought they might learn history better seeing it in person rather than merely in books."

Daniel did not look happy, so Simone mentioned that she had never been to the gardens at Kew. They were near enough to walk, if Daniel could secure them admission.

"I can't. Stuffiest old board of directors in charge, I

swear, but old Harry can do anything. I'll have the pass by noon. Oh, and maybe you ought to wear the veil again. I wouldn't want anyone thinking I was poaching on Harry's preserves or anything."

So they went to Kew in the afternoon. Simone wore a new walking gown of figured muslin, with a matching spencer that was trimmed in fur, against the slight chill. She wore a cottage bonnet with a veil and carried a parasol to hide more of her appearance.

Daniel shocked her by knowing the names of many of the plants and shrubs in the extensive gardens. "I'm a countryman, don't you know?"

No, all she'd heard of him was how he was a wastrel, a gambler, a drinker, and a sometime brawler. None of that showed today, as he treated her as carefully as the tender flowers he admired. For such a big man, with such a bad reputation, he was remarkably gentle, guiding her across muddy spots and away from curious gardeners. Mr. Stamfield was yet another riddle, a thankfully well-informed one.

"Made an effort, don't you know, to scout the terrain for you."

"You went to Richmond? I already have a map of the maze."

"I didn't mean literally. That's just army talk for gathering information."

Simone knew about his former career, but not any specifics. "Were you on the Peninsula? Did you serve with Mr. Harris or the major?"

Daniel stumbled, almost walking into her parasol. She closed it now that they were out of view of the workmen.

"We need to talk about the competition," he said when he recovered, "not boring old history."

He added pages to her store of data, gathered from the

betting books at the gentlemen's clubs. Anyone with two shillings in his pocket—or with good enough credit—was making wagers on the ladies' chances. Simone—Noma, that is—was a dark horse, an unknown. Her name was not even mentioned. He himself had placed his money on Harry's companion.

"I wouldn't tell 'em a thing about you, not even your nom de guerre. That's for going to war, you know. We'll keep the odds high that way, for a bigger payoff. They all think I'm backing Harry because we're cou—close. I'll wait until the day you all leave, then increase my bets. If we win big, I'll buy you a bracelet."

"If we win big, I won't need you to buy me a gift. But I do hope you do not wager more than you can afford to lose. The contest is not going to be a legitimate one, from what I understand."

"Oh, Harry won't let much cheating get by him. A matter of honesty, don't you know."

She knew the major had an obsession with the truth, but she did not see how that could translate into keeping the contest fair.

Daniel said, "Well, you don't need to worry about the equestrian event. The only competition is Madeline Harbough. She used to be Maddy Hogg, a bareback rider at Astley's before she became what they call a Pretty Horse-breaker. Pretty gals on horseback exercising Thorough-breds in the park until they catch a gent's notice. She's Ellsworth's mistress now, and as fat as he is. She might know a few tricks, but you can outrace her."

"Doesn't that depend on the horse I am riding? Again, Lord Gorham can mount his lady friend on the fastest goer in his stable and leave the plodders to the rest of us."

"Hm. That's a good point. I'll talk to Harry about bringing a few of his own mounts down."

Simone did not know if the handsome bay gelding was fast or not. She knew a few tricks, too.

Daniel went over some of the other events, as he knew them. The singing contest would be no contest, everyone agreed. Not one bet got placed against Claire Hope in that category, but Sir Chauncey Phipps's *chérie amour* was with the Royal Ballet, so she was getting good odds for the dancing.

Dancing? Simone had no ballet training, and could not possibly perform in front of an audience.

"Oh, I doubt Gorham will let Claire lose that one so quickly," Daniel told her as they inspected the medicinal-herb garden. "He'll pick a quadrille or a waltz, or something with partners. He and Claire have been dancing together for years. I saw them once at the Cyprian's Ball."

Simone's heart sank. She knew all the steps, but Major Harrison on the dance floor? With his hunch and his hobble and his cane? Good Lord, they'd finish last at that.

"I heard," Daniel went on, "that Gorham is considering billiards as one of the trials. Claire is said to be a dab hand at it."

"I have never played." Simone was reconsidering her enthusiasm for the competition altogether.

"Well, you mentioned archery. There's sure to be a round of that."

"I'm quite good at that." Then she recalled how long it had been since she'd practiced. "Or I used to be."

"Target shooting?" There was hope in Daniel's voice.

She had used her grandfather's old pistol only a few times before her scholarly father confiscated it.

She sank down on a nearby bench, not concerned about soiling her gown on the mossy seat. "I haven't got a chance."

Daniel sat beside her and patted her hand. "Of course

you do. You'd get my vote for most beautiful." He blushed, but she leaned over and kissed his cheek anyway. "Thank you."

"And best dressed. From what I hear, some of the females are complaining that their gowns won't be ready on time."

"Mine will." They shared a smile.

"Well, there might be poetry reading. I heard half the women can't read, so you're bound to outshine them there, too, or if Gorham chooses a game of Questions and Quotes. Claire considers herself a literary type, don't you know. She holds salons and that kind of rot. You're bound to have all the answers. A governess ought to know her Shakespeare, I figure."

She sighed. "Yes, but I understand that two of the women are actresses. They'll know the plays, too."

"What about cards?"

"I can play chess." She'd beaten her father. Twice. She sighed again, louder.

"Well, you'll just have to make a good showing at the other events. They're all worth points, don't you know. The prize goes to the overall winner, but the betting is for second and third place, too."

"No one thinks Claire Hope can lose, do they?"

"Of course they do. Of course she can."

Then Daniel, who shared Harry's talent—or the family curse—scratched his neck, where a rash had suddenly appeared. "Must be from one of the plants."

Chapter Eleven

The carriage arrived to take Simone and Sally to Richmond precisely at eleven, as Mr. Harris had said it would. Not a moment earlier, not a moment later, fiend seize the punctilious prig. He did not even come to see them off.

Simone wasted time, checking the baggage, running back inside to make sure nothing was left behind, looking into the hamper Mrs. Judd had handed them—filled with enough food for a week's journey, not the short trip to Richmond—then leaving directions for the grooming of the cat, to the housekeeper's disgust and the coachman's impatience.

Well, the housekeeper was always annoyed with the cat and Simone, and the coachman was always crotchety. Harold sat on the driver's bench, his hat pulled low, his muffler tied high around his neck, the reins in his hands, ready to go. The coach was different from the one that had carried her to Kensington, and the chestnuts pulling it had matching white socks, while the other team had none. This carriage was still well appointed, but larger, darker, more undistinguished; the horses were still well bred, and looked to Simone's critical eye to be equally as sweet-going as the others.

Jeremy and Sally looked different now, too, with darker hair instead of their towheads, and no more freckles. They appeared older, more sophisticated, except for their grins at each other and Simone in their excitement about the trip. Harold squelched that with a bang of his whip handle down on the footrest.

"T'horses," he growled.

At least he cared about something, Simone thought, finally taking her seat inside the carriage.

Jem shut the door behind her and scrambled up to sit beside the driver while Sarah, which name suited her better than "Sally" now, helped arrange the hamper, the blankets, and the warm bricks. She was as merry as a mayfly to be going to a grand house, seeing all the Fashionable Impures and their fancy dressers, practicing her skills. They'd have a wonderful time, Sarah was sure, what with all the surprises.

Simone hated surprises. They often ruined plans, and seldom turned out to be what a person wanted or needed.

"Oh, you'll be happy with some of these, I'd warrant," Sarah told her, grinning to show where one tooth had been darkened.

Simone had delayed as long as she could, especially since she did not wish to keep the major waiting for them along the route. She told Sarah to open the communicating window and tell Harold they were settled, ready to leave. She thought she heard a muttered "About time, b'gad" under the crack of the whip, and they were off.

So she never got to bid the secretary farewell. Nor did he bother to wish them luck, the dastard.

The last she'd seen of Mr. Harris had been last evening when he handed her a heavy silk purse. The coins were for vails along the way, for her personal use, for emergencies, he said. He might have been handing the major's precious gold to a leper, the way he half tossed it at her without letting their hands touch. He must think the money was payment for services about to be rendered, the wages of her sin.

Let him think what he would, Simone told herself. She'd earn her pay by using her skills and her wits, not her body. She'd help the major with whatever hugger-mugger he imagined, and she'd try to add to the promised hundred pounds with the courtesans' contest. She knew she could not win the thousand-pound prize, but she'd do her deuced best at the preliminary rounds.

The young maid chattered about Simone's new wardrobe and exclaimed about the passing countryside, while Simone studied her notes. She'd learned just this morning in a note from the major that two of the women expected to attend were French, but she was not supposed to speak that language with them. Mimi Granceaux was known to be Maisy Grant, born in Seven Dials instead of along the Seine, so she was not liable to converse *en français*. Joseph Gollup's convenient was also French. He was a wealthy shipowner; his wife was breeding. So, the rumor went, was Lord Comden's mistress. She'd be no competition at riding or dancing, but betting was heavy over whether the bachelor baron would marry her or not. And so it went. Simone fretted over the competition and Sarah babbled about everything and nothing. The miles flew by under the horses' hooves.

All too soon for Simone's jittery nerves, they reached the inn where they were to meet up with Major Harrison. She and Sarah stepped down for refreshment, while Harold took the coach around back, to rest and water the horses.

Sarah clucked her tongue over the innyard dirt on Miss Royale's hems, and brushed at them as best she could while they waited in the bespoken private parlor. "We both need to make a good first impression, that's what Mum said."

We need to see if Major Harrison did anything about his appearance as he promised, Simone told herself. If he had not trimmed his beard or found more-fashionable garments, all Sarah's efforts were in vain. Miss Noma Royale would look like his nursemaid or his granddaughter. No, her sapphire carriage dress was too fine for the first; too low-cut and clinging for the second. They'd look exactly what they were, May and December, an affair of interest. Bank interest, that was.

Many of the women she'd meet were younger than she was. She doubted few of the men would be older than the major. The first impression they'd make? That of a foolish old frump and his avaricious doxy.

What was she doing?

The same as all the rest of the ladybirds were doing. Only for more money, she thought, and for slightly less-shameful work.

Perhaps she could walk back to London.

Jem knocked on the door to the private parlor before she could bolt. Whenever they were done with their cider and scones, he told them, they could leave. Simone forced herself to her feet, thanked the innkeeper, and slowly headed to where Major Harrison waited. She raised her chin and stepped out the door. She was going to make her fortune, hers and Auguste's, see if she didn't.

The carriage was out front, but not the major. Another coach was nearby, with trunks lashed to the back. Sarah headed toward that coach and the familiar bay gelding tied behind alongside a huge, restless stallion. "The master will ride with you from here on. Jem's to see about the horses while I go ahead with his valet and start unpacking."

Major Harrison had a valet? That enormous brute was

the former-officer's mount? "I would feel better with you with me," were the words out of Simone's mouth. "In case my hair comes out of its pins or something."

"Oh, I am sure Master Harry can repair any damage," Sarah answered with a wide grin. Jem laughed as he mounted the bay and gathered up the stallion's lead. "And you need time to get acquainted."

She already knew the major and his peculiar ways. She supposed he wanted to give her last-minute directions, or more instruction in the art of flirting for the audience they'd soon have. His kisses were not half as bad as she'd thought they would be, and his cuddles were pleasant. She'd manage, as long as he did not ask more of her. And she'd smile, as if she were enjoying every minute of it.

The other coach pulled away, and still she sat alone, growing more nervous and vaguely nauseous. Now, wouldn't that make a good first impression on the gathered swells and their strumpets?

She leaned out the window for fresh air, and to call to Harold to ask if he knew how long before they could leave. He did not bother to turn around. Somehow he loomed larger. All her troubles did.

Then a strange man opened the door to her coach. Not the innkeeper bringing a hot brick, not the major, not anyone she had ever seen before. She'd remember this fellow, who looked more like the man of her dreams—of any maiden's dreams—than any footman or messenger. He had pitch-black hair cut in short waves, a square chin with a cleft in it, broad shoulders in a caped riding coat, formfitting deerskin breeches, and high boots. Good grief, he was a highwayman! Then why wasn't Harold whipping the horses up? Or the landlord running with his blunderbuss?

Simone clutched her reticule and its valuable store of

coins to her chest. "I am sorry, sir. You must have the wrong carriage. The one with the baggage and valuables just left."

He grinned at her, a white-toothed smile with dimples. "Oh, no, sweetings. This is right where I want to be." He bounded into the carriage and slammed the door behind him.

A rake. Worse and worse. The major would be coming, and heavens, what would he think? That she was being unfaithful before they arrived, or that her virtue needed defending? Either idea was appalling.

"You must go."

Instead he rapped on the roof and called up to the driver, "Move on."

"No!" she shouted. She wished she'd thought to see if the major carried a pistol in his carriage as some travelers did, to guard against thieves. Gracious, a robber was in her carriage, across from her, grinning. Then he was reaching out, as if to take her purse. Simone might not have a pistol, but she was not entirely defenseless. Ever since the first libertine had tried to take advantage of her, she'd fixed a long hatpin with a beaded head to the front of her reticule, like a decoration. Now that pretty weapon was decorating the hand that was reaching for her money, and who knew what else.

She hadn't meant to sink the hatpin entirely through his thumb, but the carriage lurched forward just then. Harold must have had more than a pint of ale while he rested the horses. He'd be no help, trying to get control of the horses.

"Eeeow!" the intruder yelled, pulling the hatpin out and sticking the wounded thumb in his mouth. "Dash it, woman, don't you know me?"

Now that he seemed cowed, like a little boy sucking on

his finger, Simone took a better look. He was still devastatingly handsome, of course, but she finally noticed that his dark-rimmed eyes were a brilliant blue, blue the exact color of her carriage gown that Sally had insisted she wear. He seemed a bit familiar, although she could not imagine how or where. Yes, she could. "I dreamed you up, from the stories, that's all." And the inn's cider must have been tainted.

"Harry." That was all he said, his thumb still in his mouth, but he pulled a ragged false mustache from his pocket.

"Harry?"

He made a half bow, there in the carriage, and handed back her hatpin. "At your service, Miss Royale."

She ignored the proffered weapon, reached over, and slapped him.

Now he rubbed his cheek, where a handprint was forming. "Lud, woman, you are a hazard. I thought you'd be happy I'm not a weak old man."

She'd been betrayed. "Sally knew, and Jem. And Mr. Ha— There is no Mr. Harris, either, is there?"

"Are you going to attack me again?"

"I just might. Is there a Mr. Harris?"

"Uh, that depends."

"Do you mean your answer depends on who you are lying to? You, who demands the truth from everyone else? You bastard."

"I told you I was a bastard the day we met. That was the truth."

"Well, I never liked Harris anyway. And now I do not like you, whoever you are. I want Major Harrison back." She knew her words sounded absurd. Worse, she could hear the quiver in her voice.

He almost reached out to pat her shoulder, then

thought better of it. "I'm sorry, but that's impossible. You see, that's what the whole charade is about, so people know we are two different people. The major is still in London, or someone who looks a lot like him is going about his business."

"While you create a stir in Richmond."

"Precisely. And continue investigations for the government in secret, do not forget that."

She took the hatpin and skewered it through the fabric of her reticule again, not looking at him. "Is your name Harry?"

"It's what I have been called since I was born."

"Not Harrison?"

"No, but I lived with that family for many years after my mother died. I was their son in all but blood and name. I bear my mother's name, Harmon, and her shame, I suppose. Between 'Harmon' and 'Harrison,' 'Harry' was an easy step."

"But that is not your true name."

"I never use my given name."

She moved to open the little window to the driver's box. "And I never deal with people I do not trust, or who do not trust me."

He grabbed her hand before she could touch the communications window and order the driver to halt. "I could not. Surely you see that. Lives are at stake. Mine, for one. I'd like to live the rest of it in peace, as Harry Harmon."

"What would happen if I made Harold st—? That's not Harold, is it?"

"I am afraid not, my dear. And he will not obey any orders but mine."

She toyed with the hatpin, but he was watching her closely with eyes that saw too much and revealed too little. "What if I told Lord Gorham of all your disguises when we arrive?"

Now his eyelids drooped and he brushed a speck of mud off his boot. "Do you think you would enjoy Canada?"

"What do you mean?"

"I mean, my dear, that no one can be permitted to destroy the government's plans, no matter how it would pain me. First I would convince our host and his guests that you were a revolting drunk." He removed a flask from an inside pocket and held it up, as if he'd pour it down her throat, or over her gown. "Then I'd have you on a ship out of England so fast your new shoes would not get dirty. You'd be drugged, of course, in case you tried to natter on to someone else. I cannot afford to have my secrets made public." He took a swallow of whatever was in the flask, without offering her any.

She might have accepted, anything to deaden her shock.

Harry tucked the flask away. "Will you tell?"

"Why would you believe me, no matter what I say? I hardly believe anything you tell me." Except, perhaps, his threats.

"If you promise to hold your tongue until after the house party, I will believe you. After that, no one else will believe your far-fetched gibberings."

"What is your real name?"

"Harmon, as I told you. My mother was Ivy Harmon, an opera dancer. A rich man's mistress. I did not lie about that. In fact, I may have misled you, and I certainly did not reveal all the truth, but an outright lie? I try not to. It tastes bad."

"Botheration, enough of your obfuscation. Lies taste bad, hah! Either you trust me with your first name, or I do not trust you. I'll run off to find the local magistrate and ask his protection. I am not afraid of you."

"You are lying, but it is 'Royce.' "

"Royce, as in the earl?"

"An earl who would be embarrassed by the revelation. His undeserving lady wife would be mortified, my half brother and cousin made uncomfortable. We rub along well now, and I am accepted in all but the highest circles, but there's no need to rub everyone's nose in my bastardy. The *ton* accepts only what it can ignore."

Simone was thinking about what she'd heard. "If Lord Royce is your father, Viscount Rexford is your half brother, and your cousin would be . . . Mr. Daniel Stamfield. I'll murder him."

"Not until we reach Gorham's place, please. It's not good for the horses."

"He's driving? Harold?" She tried not to scream, or cry, which would ruin the coloring on her eyelashes. "Daniel is Harold?"

"Only for a while. He wanted to come and he's a handy fellow to have around."

"You are both insane. You and your whole household. Why, Lydia Burton knows, too, doesn't she?"

"She lived next door to the Harrisons."

Oh, Lord. "Who else knows?"

"My family, of course, both of them. The Judds, naturally. My personal staff and perhaps two or three of my superiors at the War Office. The Duke of Wellington, the prime minister, Prinny."

"Prinny? The prince regent?"

He smiled at her, almost in sympathy. "Well, the future king ought to know who is working for him, oughtn't he?"

She shook her head, when she really wished to bang it against the side of the carriage. Then maybe her scrambled wits could find their feet. If wits had feet. Heaven help her. "No one would believe this."

"I am hoping the man who is trying to kill Major Harrison does not."

"There really is such a person? Not another of your machinations?"

"There have been several attempts on my life. The major's, that is. Harrison is an important figure, if seldom spoken of, rarely seen. He and his office have accomplished much for England, and destroyed many of those who would see it brought down."

"I am in the middle of a nightmare."

"No, you are in Griffin Woods. We entered Gorham's gate while you were shrieking."

"I was not shrieking. I am merely understandably upset."

"You are right. You have every reason to be upset. I thought you knew."

"I suspected something, but my conclusions were so outlandish that I ignored my doubts."

"I really am sorry."

Simone wasn't ready to accept an apology from a blue-eyed snake. "Hmph."

"Should we kiss and make up? After all, this is our first lovers' spat."

"We are not lovers, we are not having a spat, and I do not kiss strangers."

"Should I put on the fake mustache?"

"If I ever see it again, I will—"

He placed his fingers over her lips. "Come, pet. We must act like lovers for our grand entrance. You look stunning, if no one has told you, or if everyone has told you. I've never known a more beautiful woman, and I'll be the proudest man in the kingdom to have you on my arm. I did place bets on you, you know. On Harry Harmon's companion. All over London."

"Who placed the wagers? Which one of you?"

He grinned. "Everyone I could think of."

Simone ignored the smile, dimples and all. She was thinking ahead to the house party, the days, but especially the nights. Harry, this Harry, was not a feeble old man. Not by half. "Does our agreement still hold?"

Harry did not pretend to misunderstand. "It might kill me, but I will not go back on my word. Your honor is safe with me. Will you keep your promise?"

"Which one?"

"To help me. To keep my secrets. To act like you worship the ground I walk on."

"That's three."

"I am not such a bad chap."

"That's what everyone says. I'll reserve judgment."

"There's no time, sweetheart." He reached over and pulled her into his lap—as if she were as light as thistledown—and kissed her soundly. Then softly. Then as if he were sharing his soul along with his life's breath. "Trust me, Noma."

She kissed him back, which he took as an answer and encouragement to continue. His hands stroked her back, and hers wove through his short wavy hair. She lost herself in the kiss and caresses and sighs of pleasure—or were those low murmurs hers? This was far better than their first kiss, with no scratchy beard or coarse mustache, no worries that Harry would have a heart spasm, not this Corinthian, this nonesuch, this . . . this fork-tongued viper. She pulled away.

"Ah, now you have stars in your eyes."

"And you have lip rouge on your mouth."

He wiped at his face but not very thoroughly. "That will make our act all the more convincing. Come, love, the curtain rises."

Chapter Twelve

Almack's never glittered so brightly. Of course Simone had never attended the hallowed assembly rooms where the beau monde gathered to dance and converse and arrange marriages, but this was how she imagined it. Mrs. Olmstead had read her enough gossip-column reports to build a fair picture in her mind. Beautiful young women wore elegant gowns of silk and lace, while the gentlemen appeared courtly, attentive, and handsome. The men raised their quizzing glasses and wineglasses; the women flashed bright smiles and brighter jewels, from head to gem-studded sandals.

The Almack's patronesses would have apoplexy here.

The jewels may have been real; the smiles were not. A few of the men were already unsteady on their feet, and a few of the women, too. The couples at Griffin Woods stood too close together, hands where no hands politely rested, and some actually disappeared into dark corners and draped alcoves. The women's gowns revealed more of their charms than they hid, and the men did not bother to hide their stares. Worse, this was midafternoon, not close to midnight.

The biggest difference, of course, between society's

assemblies and this one was that a young lady went to Almack's to find a match. Men came here to avoid one, or ignore the ones they already had. "Marriage" was a word never spoken among the demimonde. That was as hard and fast a rule as any that held sway at King Street.

Simone almost wished she hadn't come. Then she wished she hadn't been so adamant about refusing jewels. The firework displays of gemstones on bare skin looked garish and cheap to her, but she might have felt more comfortable among the women if she were better armored. Still, Harry's hand at her waist, a gesture that was altogether too familiar for polite society, was reassuring. If nothing else, a quick glance told Simone that she had the handsomest escort in the room. Too bad there was no prize for that.

Lord Gorham welcomed them effusively. Harry whispered that the marquis wished to curry favor with Lord Royce, but the tickle of his voice in her ear, the ruffle of her hair as he leaned down, the scent of his spice cologne and soap—all drew her attention to him, not the florid host.

Lord Gorham's mistress welcomed them as if she were the lady of the fine old house. She not so subtly kicked her lord in the ankle when he held Simone's hand too long. Claire Hope was as beautiful as her reputation claimed, with a deep, opera diva's bust that could have doubled as a sheet music rest.

The marquis seemed to be admiring Simone's lesser endowments, for his eyes never reached hers. "I can see where the betting is going to get interesting, my love," his lordship said to his mistress when she kicked him again. He quickly added, "Not that I have any doubts about your winning."

Simone could not understand why the marquis was discarding his beautiful, longtime lover, for the pair acted like an old married couple. Then she remembered that the aristocrat was already married. Perhaps it was Claire who was leaving, with hopes of a more permanent relationship with a different gentleman. She was certainly smiling at Harry with the eyes of a predator. Simone stepped closer to him.

Claire led them around to make introductions like a proper hostess. Simone smiled to the women, curtsied to the men, and wished she had her notebooks to consult. She was never going to put names to so many faces. They were nearly twenty couples, with a few of them taking rooms at the nearby inn rather than at the crowded manor, according to Claire. The men welcomed Harry warmly, the women more warmly. Simone kept her hand on his arm; he placed his other hand over hers. Either he understood or he did not like the way the men were ogling her, almost licking their lips.

Simone did not like to be so scrutinized, not after facing that same hungry look from her former employers. So she was pleased when Claire invited the women into a drawing room done in Egyptian style while the gentlemen discussed the coming competition in Lord Gorham's library. She ought to have been less eager to leave Harry's protection.

The ugly crocodile-footed furniture was more friendly than the inquisition she faced.

How long had she known Harry, how did they meet, and where was she from? Oh, dear. She and Harry had never discussed details—not that Simone ever intended to tell the truth; she'd join the mummy in the sarcophagus first—so she did not know what Banbury tales he'd concocted for the gentlemen. She gave a vague answer, "Oh, I have been here and there, and met Harry on one of my travels," which satisfied no one.

Why didn't she have any jewelry if Harry Harmon was supposed to be so generous?

Simone wanted to hiss at the cat who'd made that observation, the dark-haired woman with a ruby as large as a roof tile hanging at her neck. Maybe it was paste.

"Oh, my Harry is generous with other . . . gifts."

The ruby wearer gave an affected titter. "Is he as good a lover as they say, then?"

Simone sipped at the tea Claire offered, rather than tossing it at the rude woman. The tea might be good quality, and the china cups as delicate as any in the best houses, but this was not polite company, no matter how they pretended to act like ladies. Simone would not stoop to their level. She batted her darkened eyelashes and smiled coyly. "Do I look dissatisfied? More than that, a lady never tells."

Her reply earned a shout of laughter.

"I do."

"Me, too."

"What do you want to know about Anthony?"

Claire offered more tea, then wine, then said, "We have to look out for each other, don't we?"

Not when it came to the contest, it seemed. No one was going to compete against Claire at singing, so they thought she ought to withdraw and be a judge. Professional that she was, she refused not to perform. After that, the women started to make side bets among themselves. Could Noma dance? Did she play billiards? What about cards?

She smiled and repeated her words: "A lady never tells." Neither did a gambler show her hand.

Soon the women dispersed to dress for dinner, to Simone's relief.

"Country hours, you know," Claire announced, disdaining the manor's staff for not being up to London standards.

At least they'd have a late-night supper after the evening's entertainment.

The men's conversation was not much different. Everyone wanted to know where Harry'd found such a diamond.

"A mutual friend introduced us," he answered, which was not a lie. Then they asked how long he'd had Miss Royale in keeping, and why was he hiding her away from their eager eyes, when any number of them might have made her a better offer?

They all laughed when he said, "You answered your own question. Why should I parade my doe-eyed lass in front of a herd of stags in rut? And I haven't had her under my protection nearly long enough," which was a definite warning to all of them to keep their distance.

"I don't know, Harmon," a wealthy banker who did not know Harry's reputation with a sword or a pistol said. "Maybe the gal would prefer a nabob who can keep her in diamonds?"

"I believe Miss Royale prefers sapphires."

The banker stepped outside the library door to the gardens with his cigar. If Harry's tone of voice hadn't convinced him to make himself scarce, Lord Gorham's whispered caution did.

A knight too deep in his cups to know he was drowning asked, "Is the wench as good a lover as she looks? You know what they always say about redheads: hot temper, hot blood."

If Harry had a sword in his hand, the knight would be a head shorter. He thought of reaching for the knife in his boot, or the small pistol in the back of his waist. He could not ruin the party so soon, though. Instead he fixed his black-rimmed gaze on the hapless drunk and calmly, deliberately said, "A gentleman never asks. A gentleman never tells." Then he looked away, effectively changing the subject. "Who wants to place a bet?"

A few of the men thought of withdrawing their paramours' names from the contest, knowing their ladybirds could never fly so high as Harry Harmon's newest dove, but they laid their stakes on the table anyway. Gorham marked down the entries with a sympathetic laugh, knowing there'd be hell to pay if any of the females got wind of the traitorous thoughts.

He stopped laughing when they discussed the various choices for competition, and he was forced to make some changes in his plans. The men wanted independent judges and more inclusive events, sabotaging Claire's sure win of the singing match. Lord Gorham was not happy, particularly not with Harry, who refused to have a best-lover category.

"Let us maintain our dignity, gentlemen," he said, well aware that he was a bastard in the midst of wellborn, titled, wealthy men, and they all knew it. "And remember the courtesy owed a lady. Let us simply assume that each of our partners is well versed in pleasing a man. There is no objective way of awarding grades."

Captain Entwhistle, late of His Majesty's Navy, said, "I'd say by your smile, Harmon, that there is a way. Cat in the cream pot, if you asked me."

Harry laughed. "Noma is far more delectable than the sweetest cream, but I will still not wager on bed play."

The captain knew when he was defeated. "What kind of name is 'Noma' anyway? I've not heard its like."

"It is an interesting one, isn't it? Part foreign, I believe, and part Gypsy." He was glad to be telling the truth, which suited his purposes of making Simone sound like anything but an English governess.

"Gypsy, you say? Damn, trust you to find a diamond in the dust heap. You are a lucky man."

"I am, at that." Which was also true.

Upstairs, Simone met Harry's valet, a small man bustling about between the large bedroom and the adjoining dressing rooms. Metlock was a former actor, Sarah informed her as she laid out Simone's clothes, to see if any needed pressing. He was a dab hand at costumes and wigs and makeup.

Simone glared at the older man. She'd bet he was. Then she frowned at Sarah. "You could have told me."

The maid laughed and held up the gown she'd chosen for the first dinner here. "I did tell you there'd be a fine surprise."

"I thought we were friends."

"And right proud I am to be considered a friend to a real lady like yourself, Miss Royale, but Master Harry, he does pay our wages. Not Mum nor Jem nor me could be disloyal, now, could we, not after what he's done for us? Asides, we knew you'd be happier this way. What female wouldn't be?"

Sarah was not the one to blame, so Simone had to forgive her. Especially when the maid showed off the bathing room across the hall, with running hot water from cisterns and heaters on the roof.

"Master Harry says the marquis wants some land Lord Royce owns near his family seat. Lord Gorham's hoping Master Harry will convince the earl to sell, or Harry will do it iffen he inherits the property on account of it not being entailed. That's why you have such fine accommodations, almost as good as the duke's second son what brought the Indian woman who used to be a slave. You didn't meet her, on account of she took sick on the carriage ride. Metlock heard she wears pantaloons, like a man."

"Did you meet any of the other maids yet?"

"Hoity-toity, some of them, if you ask me. As if their mistresses aren't mistresses. And some of them are no better than they ought to be themselves. Why, the servants' hall is more like a hiring fair for dolly-mops."

"Heavens, you must not let any of the footmen or valets lead you astray, no matter what they promise. That would be disastrous, and sinful. You are too young, and not meant for—" For the life that Simone was supposedly leading. Now she'd have young Sally's morals to worry about, too. "That is, your mother would be upset to have you exposed to such debauchery. Perhaps you should sleep here, on a cot in the dressing room. Yes, that would be better." For everyone.

"Gracious, no, Miss Noma. You and Master Harry won't want the company, not even as close as next door." Her knowing smile convinced Simone that the girl's experience was already more extensive than it should be, far greater than her own. "Asides, I'll be fine. My brother'll be nearby. He's staying at the stables, on account of Harold going into the village, where there's more room, what with all the grooms and extra servants here."

Simone vowed she'd find that oversized muckworm later, with her hatpin. She'd find another one to give to Sarah for protection. Meanwhile, she had to dress for dinner. Some of the women, according to Sarah, took all afternoon to get ready. Simone wished she could take another week.

The gown they decided on—"they" being Sarah and Metlock—was of blue silk, with a blond lace overskirt tied at the high waist with matching blue ribbons. Sarah wove another through Simone's fiery hair, then let one long, ribbon-entwined braid of it fall over Simone's shoulder. She fussed with the puffed sleeves and pulled down the bodice that Simone kept yanking higher.

"The others will be showing off their jewels, Miss Noma. If you want to outshine them, you'd best be showing more bosom."

"Compared to Claire Hope, I have none. Hope or bosom."

Sarah clucked her tongue. "You have natural beauty, that's what, and no one can say different."

The maid's prejudiced opinion did not reassure Simone. Harry's low whistle of admiration did, especially when it was joined to a crooked grin showing dimples. He came in from the dressing room, his hair wet from his own bath. He was dressed in formal evening clothes, white satin knee breeches, midnight blue coat, a white marcella waistcoat, and a large sapphire in his high, intricately tied neckcloth. He had a velvet box in his hand. He paused in the doorway to watch Sarah hand Simone a lace fan with forget-me-nots painted on it.

"I doubt anyone will ever forget how you look tonight, my dear. I know I won't." He handed her the box. "Only this could make your ensemble complete. I hope you will wear it, for me."

Simone raised the lid to find a gold chain with a filigreed pendant, set with a sapphire to match the one he wore, the ribbons on her gown, and his eyes. He'd planned the whole outfit with Madame Journet, she realized, disregarding her wishes. "Tell me this is paste," she begged.

"And ruin my dinner with the lie? That is, I would not give you false compliments or false gems. I am afraid it is quite real."

"But we agreed that—"

He looked at Sarah and nodded toward the door to the hall. "Your lady is dressed. You have done well. Go on now to your own supper. And stay close to Metlock and Jem. I promised your mother you'd be safe."

"I'll be as safe as I want to be, thank you. Mum sent me to learn a bit about the world, didn't she?"

"Saucy minx. Get on with you."

When Sarah was gone, Harry took the necklace from its box and told Simone to turn around. He lifted the trailing braid of red hair and blue ribbon, then kissed the back of her neck.

"No one is watching," Simone told him. "You do not have to do that."

"Oh yes, I do. I've been wanting to do so since I first saw you with your prim bun at the back of your neck." He kissed her again.

"Your necktie."

"Hmm. Who cares about the damn thing around my throat when I can finally taste yours?" He was taking tiny nips on her bare skin, tiny licks.

Simone stepped away before he noticed she was trembling. "You'll muss it and Metlock will be furious and we will be late for dinner."

He smiled. "We cannot have that, can we?" He fastened the chain around her neck, then turned her around to adjust the large pendant to rest in the valley between her breasts. He kissed there, too. Simone gasped.

"Is it cold against your skin?"

No, it was on fire.

Their hostess was sulking after dinner. The men, after much argument and a few bottles, had convinced Gorham to change the singing portion of the tourney to a talent show. The ballet dancer could compete against the trick horse rider. One of the actresses could perform after Miss Althorp, who fancied herself a poetess, and so on. A few of the women would provide the entertainment each evening, with all of the men, not merely their host, voting for the winner.

No one wanted to be first, not without practice and preparation, so this night was declared a holiday from the competition. Claire refused to sing, saving her voice for her actual performance, but someone suggested music anyway. Two of the women sang country tunes while Noma and a few of the others took turns at the pianoforte. Several gentlemen joined in the choruses, and soon the drawing room was resounding with rollicking tavern songs.

"Would you care for cards?" Harry asked Simone when the verses turned risqué and the wine turned to potent punch. "They are getting up tables in another room."

Two couples seemed to be playing for articles of clothing, instead of points, to bystanders' inebriated hilarity. Harry led Simone to a quieter corner, facing away from the outrageous exhibition. They played piquet, and after three games, Harry warned her not to count on winning that round of the competition.

She hadn't been counting on anything—not the cards in her hand or the points on the score sheet—only the number of garments tossed onto the floor with each raucous outburst. She knew her face must be scarlet enough to clash with her hair.

"Shall we call it a night, my dear?" Harry asked, gallantly coming to her rescue. "It's been a long day."

It was going to be a longer night, sharing a bedroom with a man who'd betrayed her trust, and whose kisses turned her mind to mush. "How about a chess match?"

Chapter Thirteen

"Y ou are still angry at me, aren't you?" Harry asked later that night.

"What gives you that idea?" Simone answered from within the tightly drawn curtains of the canopied bed.

Harry looked at the closed hangings surrounding the bed, then at the stack of pillows and blankets on the floor near the hearth. A familiar velvet box rested on top of the pile. "Oh, a lucky guess, I suppose." He sighed loudly enough to be heard from within Simone's draped cocoon. "The floor covering is not very thick, you know."

"Your skin cannot be all that thin, not with the barbs that bounced off you tonight. Harry the Heartbreaker, humph. There are extra blankets in the dressing room. Put another down over the rug."

He sighed again. "I'll wake up with a stiff neck and a sore back."

The silence from the direction of the bed told how much Simone cared about his comfort.

"What if Metlock or Sarah comes into the room early and sees me sleeping on the floor? Worse, what if one of Gorham's servants enters to rekindle the fire and trips over me? How will we explain that?"

"We won't need to explain anything if you simply lock the door. I'd suppose, in this household, the servants are used to waiting until they are called."

He didn't bother sighing another time, realizing he'd get no sympathy. "You are a hard woman, Miss Noma Royale. And a cheat. I think you moved your king while I helped pick Sir Chauncey Phipps off the floor."

"I won."

"Too bad we were not playing for kisses like some of the others."

"I would not do such a thing!"

"I know, and I apologize for exposing you to the unseemly behavior, but it's part and parcel of this affair."

A loud sniff was the only answer.

He kicked at the pile of blankets, muttering about how far a man had to crawl for a decent night's sleep. He tried flattery this time. "You looked magnificent tonight and played your part well. Not overacting, not overreacting to my loverlike attentions. Those little cooing sounds you made were just the right touch."

He'd heard them? Simone groaned, but tried to hide the sound in the bedcovers.

Harry went on, "No one would know that you are a respectable female."

"I am not a proper lady. I'm here, aren't I? I am an actress, or worse." The worst was how she enjoyed it, his hand on her shoulder, his arm brushing her breast as if by accident, the whispers in her ear. "I am not respectable at all."

Harry thought he heard a fist pound a pillow. So much for flattery. "You are performing a role, remember that, not living a life of moral turpitude. We need to talk about that role before we go any further. We have to get our stories straight, before anyone catches us in a discrepancy. I brushed the questions aside with vague answers tonight, but a few of the worst gossips are persistent. So were two wantwits thinking to take my place in the middle of the house party. I do not want them looking for answers on their own."

Simone had to agree, since she'd met with more questions over sherry in the drawing room, then pointed queries from the gentlemen on either side of her during dinner, and the women again afterward. "We should have talked days ago."

"You are right, but that was impossible. May I come closer to the bed, so we can converse now? I'd hate to have to shout, not knowing how thick Gorham's walls are."

"I do not trust you."

Rightfully. He was already opening the hanging bed-curtains. Simone pulled the covers closer to her chin because the night rail she wore covered her as well as a spiderweb might have.

Sarah had not bothered to pack her old flannel gown or robe, claiming they were fit for the fire—not even good enough for the poor box. The new garments, ones Simone had never selected—she prayed Harry had not, either—were all equally as sheer, silky, and sirenlike. Simone was not letting anyone, least of all the handsome man at the foot of her bed, think she was acting the seductress in her own chambers. The role stopped at the bedroom door. That was the deal they'd made.

She had not bargained on Harry by candlelight, by all the saints and stars. He looked magnificent in his brocade robe, with the sash tied low enough to reveal the vee of his bare chest, with the faintest covering of dark hair. His shoulders were broad; his waist was narrow. His lower legs were muscular, well formed, and also bare. So were his feet, which was worse. "You are not wearing a nightshirt or slippers," she accused, pointing to the opening in the draperies. "Go. I cannot talk to a half-naked man."

"I am sorry, but I could not find where Metlock hid my slippers, and I wear a nightshirt only in the dead of winter, to avoid chills."

The chill emanating from the bed right now ought to have sent him back to the fireplace. Instead he asked if he could lie next to her on the mattress, the better to converse. "I promise not to remove my robe."

Simone reached for the fireplace poker she'd stuck under the top blanket.

"Right, I'll just sit at the foot of the bed. And keep my feet on the floor and my eyes averted." He'd try, anyway. Between the firelight let into the cavernous bed and the candle on the nightstand, her hair gleamed like molten lava, flowing down her shoulders. Her bare shoulders, he noticed when she reached for the weapon. He took a deep breath and turned to stare at the embers in the fireplace. "I promised your virtue was safe from me."

But was it safe from her own wayward thoughts? Simone ignored the traitorous little voice in the back of her mind. She pulled her feet to one side, giving him more room, and more distance. "I am not worried about my own virtue, which I firmly intend to protect, promises or not. But I worry about young Sally. Sarah, that is. I do not wish this kind of life for myself, or for her. After one night, I am more certain than ever."

"As I am certain you do not belong among the birds of paradise." Simone's quick gasp gave him pause. "No, not that you are not as beautiful or accomplished as they are, but that you are made of finer stuff. Bringing you here was like setting a Thoroughbred among cart horses, serving champagne in an earthen jug. You should not have heard half the conversations tonight."

Simone was so pleased by his comments, his estimation of her worth, that she decided to be generous. "Oh, proper ladies can be just as scandalous. At my last place of employment, the baroness entertained her friends in a sitting room directly below my bedchamber. The sounds carried up the chimney."

"And you listened? My, my. A cheat at chess and an eavesdropper. I am disappointed, madam."

She knew he was teasing, but still defended herself. "I could not avoid hearing them. They did not simply gossip about others like Mrs. Olmstead did, but they recounted their own affairs and immoral intentions. I accidentally heard of this one's cicisbeo, that one's new underbutler. Thank goodness the children did not hear them, except for when the baroness requested their presence in the drawing room during tea. Those titled ladies did not cease discussing one wife's plans to leave her husband because of his lack of . . . of . . ."

"Vitality?" Harry supplied, flashing a wicked grin that signified he'd never suffer such a deficiency.

Simone ignored him. "And other improper conversations. I prayed the children did not understand, and hustled them out of there. So, no, I was not shocked by the women's talk tonight. Their actions were more lewd, perhaps, but allowances must be made because of their desperate situations."

"Desperate? They are some of the highest-paid courtesans in all of England."

"But for how long before their lord tires of them? They are all as beautiful as you said. Of course they are. No man chooses a homely mistress, does he? Well, he might if he liked her, but he would not bring her to this gathering."

"No, a less attractive female would only feel inferior."

"Precisely. What happens when the *jeunes filles*, the

filles du jour, grow into matrons of middle years? Their complexions less rosy, their figures less firm? How well paid will they be then? I believe every female here feels the sands of time running out, so they all strive to keep their beaux happy as long as they can. Mostly, they all want to win some of the prize money from the contest. They fight for their futures, the same way I do."

"You do not blame them for choosing the demimonde? For breaking every law of society?"

"Many of them had no choice. I would be in their shoes right now—and in some gentleman's bed—except for your kindness."

"You are in some gentleman's bed," Harry pointed out, disgruntled that his feet were getting cold. "Mine."

"But we have a different arrangement from Claire or Mimi or Madeline. Becoming a harlot for hire was their only choice. Did you know that Captain Entwhistle's lady friend Daisy came to London to find work to support her family in the country? An abbess met her at the posting house and offered her a room until she found a seamstress position. The room was in a brothel!"

"That is all too common a story. Country girls have always been duped into prostitution. The government does not do enough to protect them from unscrupulous procurers. And no, Lyddie would never resort to waylaying innocents."

Simone nodded. "Mrs. Burton's employees appeared content. Daisy was not. If the captain had not found her and been charmed into buying her contract, she'd be there still. She says she might be forced back into that business when he moves on to another pretty girl. And Miss Morrow is breeding. What happens to her and her child if Lord Comden does not support her? He gave her a diamond ring when what she needs is a gold band. And the

Indian woman who'd been a slave? She knows no one in London and barely speaks the language. What happens to her if her protector gambles his new fortune away and cannot win another, as was whispered tonight? The women doubt Lord James Danforth will permit her to keep any of the money if she wins the contests."

"The duke's son? I did not know his pockets were empty, or recently filled. I will have to look into his finances to see how he can afford a concubine and this house party. That is just the hint I hoped to gather, a lead to follow."

"Then at least some good will come from this wretched house party. I regret thinking I could be content with this kind of life."

"I regret the necessity of bringing you here."

"It was my choice."

"I could have found another way, another woman."

"No, for you are giving me the chance to better my prospects. Why should you regret anything? This is the life you live, by your own choice also."

"I live many lives, not all of them by my wishes or preferences. I do what I have to. Soon enough I hope to put all that behind me. I've been thinking of asking Lord Royce to sell me that land. I don't want him leaving me anything in his will that should go to Rexford and his son. Thanks to him and his advice, I have the funds to invest."

"I cannot picture you as a country squire."

"A horse breeder, maybe. I have not decided. Perhaps I'll travel now that it is possible, but a place to come home to sounds appealing. A house that is all my own, where I do not have to hide my identity."

"With a wife and children?"

"For one such as I? That is harder to imagine."

Not for Simone. She could almost see three children

scampering across a wide lawn while young colts frol-
icked on a hill in the distance. The children were two
dark-haired boys and one redheaded girl who chased her
brothers while the proud parents held hands in a gazebo.

Harry's hand? Simone was holding Harry's hand?
She dropped it quickly. Gads, when had he climbed up
beside her to rest against the pillows? "I knew I could
not trust you!"

"I haven't done anything! We're only talking, aren't
we? I was getting a cramp in my leg, that's all. And, look,
you are under the covers and I am not. I'll fetch those
blankets so my toes don't turn blue, all right?"

He did it before she could say no, or send him to find
stockings for his bare feet. She placed the fireplace poker
down the center of the bed, dividing it.

He stayed on his side, spreading the blankets out.
"Would you be happier if I fetched my sword and placed
it between us?"

Simone ignored how he seemed to be settling in for the
night, not just for their talk. "You brought a sword?"

"Of course. I am hoping for a fencing match or two, to
keep in condition."

Simone had seen nothing wrong with the devil's condition. "Who else fences?"

"Metlock is too small and slow and not much of a
challenge, although he tries when no one else is available.
Daniel is too big and clumsy. But Gorham trains at
Antonio's. Sir Chauncey has won a duel or two."

"He does not seem sober enough, or physically fit."

"Looks can be deceiving, as we both know. Forget
about Sir Chauncey. Tell me what talent you are going to
perform for the company and the contest. Do you need
music, an accompanist? An instrument or a certain
book?"

"I cannot decide. Miss Hanson plays the pianoforte far better than I do, and Miss Smythe, Lord Martindale's friend, is said to be proficient at the harp."

Harry groaned. "We have to listen to that?"

"She intends to wear white lace, to appear angelic."

"That woman has no halo, I swear. She was Dunley's before Martindale's, and Chadwick's before that. Lord knows when she has time to practice."

Simone did not want to know any more. "I'm sure Mary Connors can portray Lady Macbeth far more convincingly than I. She was with a traveling troupe of actors before accepting Sir John Foley's carte blanche. I do not write poetry like Miss Althorp, or whistle like Mademoiselle Granceaux. Yes, the self-styled Frenchwoman is going to whistle for her supper, or for the prize."

"Heaven help us all."

"My thoughts exactly. I'd never dare try singing, although I have not heard Miss Hope perform. Her reputation is far too intimidating. Miss Harbough is sending for her trained horse from the circus, and Sir Chauncey's partner from the Royal Ballet will undoubtedly dance. The woman who wore the large ruby intends to cut silhouettes for the company, but from the salacious laughter, I doubt she is going to trace facial profiles. I have not seen a cat that needs brushing here, which appears to be my only talent."

"The men won't mind if they watch you brush your own hair, but I am certain you'll think of something, and you'll do admirably at it. You can delay your performance, saying you need to send to London for some trifle first, like Maddy's horse. Not that a horse is a trifle, but you understand."

He propped another pillow behind his head, a bit closer to Simone's side. She did not protest, not wishing to argue over an inch or two, now that he was on the bed. Then he stretched, reaching his arm over his head, over her head. She frowned; he gave her an innocent look and yawned. "Sorry, it has been a long day and we still have to decide what to tell the snoops and scandalmongers. They'll repeat it to the servants, who are liable to sell the information to the gossip columns. I would not be surprised if there are reporters in the village even now, waiting for morsels to send on to London. You and I will be the favorite topic, I'd wager."

"Why? I'd think the presence of a former harem concubine would be more interesting."

"Ah, but no one wants to be reminded of slavery. Besides, my very name is scandalous, remember? And I have never been known to have a woman in my keeping before."

"What, never?"

"No, my life has been complicated enough without chancing my identity on a more lasting liaison."

"Well, I've never had a man in my bed before." Was she imagining things, or had he inched closer?

Harry stared up at the canopy over them. "Oh, I used to sleep with several of the Harrison boys, all in one big bed. I learned to defend my territory early."

And to take up as much space as possible, Simone thought, pulling her own blankets closer. "What about girls?"

"Hell yes, three of them. The Harrison chits were proper little ladies. They shared a room down the corridor and squealed on us constantly. Two of them are married with families of their own."

"That's not what I meant, and you know it."

"I do know. I have known many women, Noma. That was part of the persona I wanted to create, part of who Harry Harmon had to be, as dissimilar from Major

Harrison as possible. And why not? The earl's by-blow was not going to be respectable, no matter what I did, so why not enjoy myself?"

"Did you?"

"At first. Now? Not as much. My father and half brother wish me to join them at proper affairs, government functions, business meetings, respectable doings, where I'd have to play the gentleman, but I am not certain. That seems too tame."

"I see."

"Do you, little governess? Have you ever wished for more excitement in your so-proper life?"

"This week will be quite enough of an adventure, thank you. I'll have something to tell my children, if I dare."

"Oh, you are going to have children to listen to your tales of dissipation?"

"Yes, three: two boys and a— That is, I have no idea. Harry, do you believe in fortune-telling?"

He turned on his side, to study her face. "Why?"

"Because I thought I'd seen you before, when I met Mr. Harris and Major Harrison, but of course I had not. And sometimes my mind creates detailed pictures of things I cannot have known. They are not dreams, but happen while I am wide-awake."

"You said your mother made extra money telling fortunes."

"Yes, but Grandfather taught her how to tell foolish maids what they wanted to hear. I never believed she could actually do it."

"Stranger things have happened. Lord knows that's the truth." He gently touched her cheek, so she looked at him. "Your mother was half Gypsy. You are only a quarter Rom, but if the talent is in the blood . . ."

She shook her head. "No, that's too silly to consider. I suppose I simply have a vivid imagination."

"We can use that now, to make up a past for you, when we cannot avoid direct questions or give vague answers. Try to stick to the truth. That's always the best."

"Like you did?"

"I tried, sweetheart. I really did."

"Then tell me truly, why was Mr. Harris so mean to me?"

He kissed her then, on the forehead. "Because that was what his role demanded."

On her eyelids. "Because he could not trust himself to keep his hands off you."

On her lips. "Because you were mine."

Chapter Fourteen

Mine? What did he mean by that? She wasn't the mistress kind. He wasn't the marrying kind. What was left? Simone would have asked him, but she was too busy trying to decide whether she should kiss him back or slap him. Maybe both, but the kiss first.

Middecision, or midkiss, he rolled away, said good night, and went to sleep, on his side of the bed, atop the covers.

Mine? In his dreams, maybe, because he reached out for her later when she'd doused the candle. She was trying to get comfortable with a fireplace poker beside her, a strange man's breath near her pillow, and unanswered questions buzzing like angry bees in her mind. He put his arm across her chest in his sleep, to stop her restless tossing. That worked, because she was afraid to move, to have his hand so close to her breast, even on top of the covers. She felt anchored, which was not a bad way to feel with the storm of emotions swirling around her.

She placed her hand over his, for the warmth, the strength. Mine.

No matter what happened after this week, she'd have her hundred pounds, the new clothes, and memories. She wouldn't keep the necklace, but the shadow of his smile in her heart, that was hers forever.

Harry was gone when she awoke, along with any evidence of his makeshift bed. The fireplace poker was back where it belonged, too, and his robe was draped over the foot of the bed. Was that a studied effect for any servant who might enter, or had Harry taken it off in the night? That naked image was not conducive to her falling back asleep, despite the early hour, the silence in the halls.

Simone pulled the robe up to touch its fabric, to rub it against her cheek, to sniff for his scent. She held it close. Hers for this week, anyway. She'd collect more memories of being Noma Royale, royalty among the princesses of pleasure, with Harry as her consort. She jumped out of bed to find him.

Ladies of the night, it seemed, were expected to sleep most of the morning, for no one came with fresh coals or hot wash water or a cup of chocolate. Simone was used to rising early, breakfasting with the servants, to have time to herself before dealing with the children in her care, but she was not sure of the protocol of a house party for philanderers. Besides, her new garments fastened in the back, over corsets that required a maid to pull on the strings. Nor could she manage a hairstyle elegant enough for this company, not without Sarah's deft fingers and hot curling irons.

The young maid finally answered the bellpull, coming with a jug of hot water and rubbing her eyes. She was quiet for once, with no new hints about the competition or the plans for the day. She answered Simone's questions in monosyllables, between yawns, until Simone gave up trying. She only hoped the girl wasn't exhausted from a strenuous night, but it was not her place to lecture, not with the indentation of Harry's head still on the pillows.

Only a handful of gentlemen were having breakfast when Simone finally followed the smell of coffee and bacon to the morning room. Harry was not one of them, so Simone would have withdrawn, but five men of various ages, social standings, and sobriety leaped to their feet. They all offered to fill her plate, her cup, her morning hours.

Harry? You don't need that paltry fellow, one told her.

Another had a mistress and a wife. He had enough females, the cad.

A third would-be Lothario kept his lover in an unheated garret. He could not afford Simone, were she for sale.

The fourth, Lord Comden, whose *chérie amour* was *très enceinte*, cheerfully announced that since Alice was up and suffering morning sickness, he was at Miss Royale's convenience.

Simone lost her appetite. She did accept a buttered sweet roll for herself and a few sugar cubes for the horses, thinking she would walk around to the stables to see if Harry was there. She wanted to have a few words with Daniel, too, if he was back from the village. She also wanted to get a better look at Harry's stallion.

Before she left the morning room, she asked, "Does anyone know what activity is planned for today?"

"We were supposed to have the maze competition, but it's been raining off and on. The women won't want to dirty their hems." The banking magnate raised his quizzing glass to inspect Simone's skirts, or her ankles.

Simone hadn't noticed the weather. She did notice the leers.

"Nearly everyone has a map of the place anyway," Lord Martindale whined, since he'd paid double what everyone else had, and all for nothing. "Claire and Gorham will come up with something else."

Simone took one look out the front door of Griffin Woods Manor and decided not to walk to the stables after all. She could barely see the woods the estate was named for, through the heavy downpour. She'd take a tour of the old building's public rooms instead, in hopes of finding Harry and some hidden talent for her evening performance.

She wondered who had furnished Griffin Woods, the marquis, his wife, or Claire Hope, who seemed at home here. The Egyptian Room must have been Claire's, with its ornate, dramatic colors that set off the raven-haired woman perfectly. A sewing room that overlooked the rear gardens was definitely the marchioness's. The worn, comfortable furniture, the faded brocades, the many windows to let in the light, were not Claire's style at all. Nor was it her portrait hanging over the mantel. A maid polishing the doorknobs informed Simone that the brown-haired woman in the painting was Lady Gorham herself, as she used to look. She had not been to this house in years, and no wonder why, the servant added in a low mutter.

Lady Gorham looked familiar to Simone, which was impossible. She knew few titled ladies from her years of employment, and this one had to be somewhat older now, different-looking. She was neither a handsome woman nor a happy one, judging by the frown lines around her thin mouth. Or perhaps the artist had not done her justice. He'd done well capturing her interests, with a tambour frame by her side and a kitten playing with some yarn at her feet. Lady Gorham was undoubtedly an excellent needlewoman. Simone could tell by the embroidered doilies on every surface, the flower-stitched seat covers, the framed tapestries throughout the room. She doubted Claire ever used the chamber, not with her lover's wife's portrait and fancywork still in it.

Simone continued on her tour until she found the billiards room, where Sir John Foley and Captain Entwhistle were playing. And drinking, although the clocks had not chimed ten yet. Both offered to teach Simone to play. She knew enough about the game to understand that instruction involved the tutor's arms around the pupil, which was totally improper. That was also most likely the reason the two men almost came to blows over who got to show Simone the proper grip.

"Oh, Harry said he'd teach me," she told them before leaving the room. She realized she shouldn't be wandering around by herself, not in a nest of hornets, but she did not want to go back to her room. A glance told her the rain continued, so that eliminated a walk, a ride, a tour of the gardens. She peeked back into the breakfast room to see if any women had come down, but they must all be taking trays in their rooms, if they were awake. A different set of men rose at the sight of her, but they expressed the same interest, the same innuendos. A footman did suggest she try the ballroom for Mr. Harmon.

What in the world could Harry be doing in the ballroom in the morning? If he wanted to practice for the dancing, he should have waited for her.

She had to ask two more servants for directions to the vast chamber in a far wing, with closed doors and family portraits along the corridors. She could hear the noise before reaching the ballroom, and it was not music. Swords were clashing; men were grunting, others cheering.

Harry and Gorham were fencing while several others, including the valet Metlock, watched at a distance. They wore masks to protect their faces, but Simone would know Harry anywhere. She could not believe he could compress his lean, muscular body into Major Harrison's bent frame, or that she had not seen through his pretense.

He was a master at disguise, though, and a master at sword work, it appeared.

Lord Gorham was older than Harry and less well formed, but even Simone could tell he was well trained. He was also graceful and patient, although his breath was more labored than Harry's. Harry was far more agile and active, quicker on his feet, more aggressive in his moves.

They had buttons on the swords, but fought with the intensity of a duel to the death. Attack, feint, parry, advance, retreat. The spectators called out encouragement and, as their number increased, wagers. Simone felt faint. She knew the masks and the padded canvas jackets offered some protection, but she also knew a slip, a miscalculation, an accidental loss of the sword's cap, could be catastrophic.

And Harry suddenly seemed to be doing more retreating than advancing.

"Don't fret, Miss Royale. Harry's just toying with Gorham now, wearing him down."

She had not noticed Sir Chauncey taking a position at her side, and would not take her eyes off the duelists to acknowledge his presence. He patted her hand. "He's one of the finest fencers in the land, our Harry."

Now he did get her attention. "Oh, have you known him long?"

"Schoolmates, you know. Excellent fellow. Not good enough for you, my dear. I, on the other hand—" One of his hands snaked around her waist.

Harry flipped the sword out of Gorham's grip and had his own blade at Sir Chauncey's throat before Simone could step away from the bosky knight.

"I heard that," Harry said, glaring at his onetime friend.

"I forgot what excellent hearing you have, old chap. No harm meant. Shall we drink on it?"

"We'll have a match. You used to be good with a blade.

You're younger than Gorham"—who was wiping sweat off his face and panting—"so you'll be a better challenge."

"Me? I mean, I? Sorry, Harry, but I am out of practice. Too-thirsty work for me, you know."

"I know you are drinking yourself to death and I won't have it. Here." He picked up Gorham's sword and tossed it. Sir Chauncey had to catch it or have the thing slice his pantaloons, if not his foot.

"I'll be damned," Sir Chauncey said, fastening on the mask Metlock handed him.

"Not on my watch. *En garde*."

Surprisingly, it turned out to be another good match, almost even. Gorham shouted encouragement to Sir Chauncey, and put his money on him. Simone wondered if it was good form for her to place a wager, too. Here was a way to earn extra money, since she had no chance at the talent contest or the billiards games. She had a few of Major Harrison's coins in her pocket.

Three men offered to take her bet. They'd match her coins if Harry won, but they wanted her to stake a kiss, an address in London, a walk in the woods when the weather cleared, if he lost.

Harry knocked Sir Chauncey's sword aside, set the buttoned point to the man's throat, then walked to Simone's side. "I heard that, too." He tossed the mask and sword to Metlock and put his arm around her. "Mine," although he did not have to say it in words. "The next time, bare swords."

The men disappeared. Harry kissed her, his lips tasting a bit salty from his exertion, but his tongue thrusting and parrying in a different challenge. Simone knew he was simply performing for the lingering servants and any gentlemen with second thoughts. Act or not, her knees went weak. Who knew fencing could be so arousing?

Metlock cleared his throat and Harry released her. "Your coat, sir," the valet reminded both of them, holding out Harry's superfine. "And you'll be wanting breakfast after the, ah, exercise."

Simone blushed, but Harry winked as he let the valet fit him into his coat. "Old fussbudget," he whispered in her ear as they left the ballroom. "But I am hungry. Care for a tray in our room?"

That was too dangerous, and not for show. Simone looked around to make sure they were alone, then said, "Lord James Danforth was making outrageous wagers, tossing money around as if he had no cares in the world."

"I already sent a message to London. We know his father, the duke, is not well-to-pass, and refused to pay the fool's gaming debts. Lord James grows more interesting as a suspect. Keep listening. What else did you learn this morning?"

That his kisses were like a drug she wanted more of? No, he must have meant about the company. "I discovered that not a one of the men is faithful to the female he brought with him."

"I am not surprised," he said when they entered the breakfast room. "They are not faithful to their wives or betrotheds, either. That doesn't mean they are disloyal to their country."

Simone waited until he pulled a seat out for her at the far end of the table, where no one could overhear, or interfere. "Do you think that is right?"

Harry took a cup of coffee from a servant, and waited until the man left to bring toast and eggs and ham slices. "The light-skirts understand. They'd be just as disloyal if someone offered more money, a bigger house, a fancier carriage."

"No, I meant, is it right for a man to take a vow and then break it?"

"Hell, no," Harry said around a forkful of kippers. "No lies, remember."

"You came close to breaking your promise last night."

"Not nearly,˜sweetheart. I was too tired."

Chapter Fifteen

Lord Gorham's mistress was disgruntled. In fact, her compressed lips looked like Gorham's wife's in the portrait. Not only was Claire denied her guaranteed singing prize, but her plans for winning the maze event this afternoon were washed away by the incessant rain. On top of that, the former slave girl made an appearance at luncheon. Sandaree was younger than Claire and exquisite, a shimmering houri, a creature of myth in baggy saffron trousers and a gilt-embroidered gossamer vest. She was as graceful as the tiny bells that chimed in her ears, as exotic as the henna-dyed patterns on her hands, as sultry as the kohl-rimmed eyes she kept modestly lowered.

Lord James Danforth preened beside her. The other men forgot to eat, watching her delicate movements. Gorham watched her, too, until Claire stuck her fork in his leg under the table.

Worst of all in Claire's eyes, Gorham declared the afternoon competition to be a sewing contest to spite his wife, who was bound to hear of it in the gossip columns. Claire wished she'd used her knife.

The men intended to spend the afternoon settling details of the competition and their wagers, and inspecting Gorham's wine cellars. Which meant they'd be too cast-away to enjoy the lavish dinner she'd planned.

The women gathered in the marchioness's sewing room, where stacks of linen squares were set out, along with needles, scissors, and thread. The female who hemmed the most handkerchiefs before dinner would be declared the winner, if the stitches were neat and the knots secure enough for use by the parish poor.

Simone was surprised by such a worthwhile venture among pleasure-seekers not known for charity or caring for the less fortunate.

Once the women were assembled with the proper supplies, it was obvious that Captain Entwhistle's Daisy was a sure winner. She'd come to London to be a seamstress, after all, and would have earned a decent wage at it if she had not fallen into bad company. Five of the other courtesans set their needles aside, choosing to work at their coming performances, their wardrobes, or their beauty sleep, rather than expend a futile effort among females. Claire stood, too, although she wasn't conceding defeat.

"I refuse to sit in this room with that woman." She pointed to Lady Gorham's portrait. "If not for her, I'd be set here for life, where I belong. The old cow insists he set me aside. After twelve years! I'll take my sewing to my chambers, instead of sitting in this shabby place that's nothing but a monument to the ugly witch."

Simone loved the old-fashioned room that reminded her of her old home, her mother's constant mending and sewing to keep them all well dressed if not up to the current fashions. She picked up another square to hem. She could not give the needy much money; the least she could do was produce handkerchiefs for them.

Sandaree started to leave. In newly learned English,

she explained that women in her calling were never taught to sew.

Simone invited her to stay, to tell them about her country, her customs. "That will make our task go faster."

The foreign girl did, sensing Simone's honest interest. She haltingly explained how she was born to a concubine and reared in a palace, with no other goal or function than to please whichever man bought her, or was given her as a gift. She had studied the pillow books, learned to sing and dance and prepare tempting tidbits and scented massage oils, how to make herself beautiful, and how to make any man feel like a prince.

Her training worked well, too well. The rajah preferred her to his first wife, second wife, and head concubine. As in Claire's situation, they demanded her banished. The rajah had to listen if he wanted peace in his harem, and not his favorite's outright murder. So he sold her to a British nabob who was returning to England.

"But there is no such thing as slavery here."

"They call it indenture, I think. But it is the same. I still have no home, no funds, no saying when I dance or when I sit in the garden. Here I have no friends, no future, either. At the palace, I would have been retired to train young girls or help with the prince's children. Here? I did not please my owner. I was traded to Lord James Danforth, but he is not easy to please, either, not like the rajah. English gentlemen do not appreciate my training. They have no—how is it said?—no subtlety. No time. Sex is for the dark, for the relief, for the man."

"Isn't it always?" Daisy looked up from her stitching to ask.

Simone did not wish to hear the answer. She said, "Then leave."

"I cannot. Lord James repaid my master the price of my passage."

"But he cannot own you!"

"I have nothing of my own. Not my clothes or jewels. I am like one of your English wives. Is that not how it is in your country?"

Husbands did have omnipotence over their wives, their money, their children. Being a beloved concubine in a palace might be better than being a rich man's wife, yet the latter was still the dream of every woman in the room.

Sandaree shook her head. "Married women are slaves by another name: chattel."

"Not all marriages are like that," Simone insisted. "Not all men hold themselves so superior. My mother was happy. My father gave up his world for her."

Four of the women never knew their fathers. Two others ran away from theirs. Daisy's mother worked harder than any servant to keep her family fed and her house clean, going without so her husband could visit the pub. No one but Simone knew of a marriage where the partners were equal, where a woman did not trade her independence for security, respectability, permanence. And children.

Pregnant Alice Morrow wiped her eyes on one of the new handkerchiefs.

They all concluded that life was hard for a woman, no matter her station.

"À vrai dire," Mr. Gallop's French mistress said, then translated for the other women, including Mimi Granceaux, who wasn't French at all. "To tell the truth."

That women suffered was no secret to any of them, but Sandaree's situation was worse than most. The needles paused while the sewers contemplated solutions for her.

Mimi forgot her accent to insist: "If you win, that

Danforth lordling cannot keep your winnings. You take them right to a bank to hold for you."

"Maybe you can win some of the other contests," suggested Alice, who could afford to be generous, since her condition kept her from competing at most. "What skills have you? Besides pleasing a man. Can you sing?"

"Not in your language."

"Claire never sings in English, either, but she'd have conniptions if you rivaled her performance."

"Dance? Play an instrument? Tell stories like that Scheherazade female?"

Sandaree lowered her eyes. "I dance a little, not in your style."

That did not sound promising to the others, who considered a way for Sandaree to make money of her own, although that was what they were all trying to do.

"We could wager among ourselves, like the men are doing."

"How would that help? We could lose." Which did not stop some of them from wagering at cards, Simone knew.

Someone suggested they all cheat and lose to a designated winner who would promise to divide the prize.

Harry would hate Simone's doing something so dishonest. Besides, Claire Hope would never agree to lose, or to share. And no one actually volunteered to give up her own winnings.

"Gorham has a great deal of influence," Daisy said, finishing the last square of linen. "Claire can ask him to speak with Danforth. Or maybe Claire has another idea."

Claire had many ideas, reading a book of philosophy on her chaise longue when Simone entered her sitting room. Her maid was sitting nearby amid a stack of finished handkerchiefs. She tried to hide the needle and thread under the pile.

"I thought you were the maid with tea," Claire said, after using a word Simone had never heard from a woman's lips.

"You're going to cheat?" Simone asked the obvious.

"I am going to win."

"But others need the money, too."

"Not as much as I do. I am too old to find a new protector, too used to the luxuries of life to give them up. Gorham owes me."

"Then he should pay, not count on your winning."

"His wife would find out. She has her man of affairs look at his books. Her dowry paid for everything—that's why he married her—but her brass came with conditions."

"But you cannot cheat! Daisy deserves this round. She needs it badly to help support her family in the country."

Claire tossed her book to the floor. "Let them find jobs like all the other poor farmers. They do not send me mutton and I'll be damned if I send them money."

"Surely you saved money from all your years with Gorham? Your music career?"

"Surely what I do with my funds is none of your concern."

A duchess could not have delivered a more imperious setdown, but Simone did not retreat. "I cannot let you do it."

"What will you do, Miss Righteous? Tell Gorham? He'll never take your word over mine. He loves me."

"Then think of him. If he calls me a liar, then Harry will have to call him out." Harry never would, not to ruin his own plans, but Simone could think of no other threat.

Claire waved a manicured hand in the air. "Pish tosh. Gorham is one of the best swordsmen in England."

"Harry defeated him this very morning. If you love Lord Gorham so much, you would not want to see him wounded, would you?"

Claire looked at the pile of handkerchiefs, then back at Simone with sorrow in her eyes. "I will lose him either way. I need to win."

"She is going to lie, I know she is," Simone told Harry while they got dressed for dinner, where the women would produce their handkerchiefs for counting. "If I accuse her, she will only deny it. Her maid will, too, of course, for her position is at stake."

"What do you want me to do?" Harry asked, his chin in the air as Metlock tied his starched neckcloth. Politely respecting her modesty, they'd waited until she was dressed to enter the bedroom. Now she watched, fascinated, as Metlock put the finishing touches to the complicated knot.

She had to gather her thoughts back from the breadth of Harry's shoulders, the cleft in his freshly shaved chin, the blue of his eyes that matched the sapphire pendant she wore again tonight with another blue gown. "I don't know what you can do, but someone ought to speak against the injustice of it all. You are the one who admires the truth so much."

"It matters to you?"

"Of course it does! I doubt the other women are being paid as well as I am, so they deserve to have a fair chance at winning."

"I thought *you* wanted to win."

"I do, but not at someone else's expense. All of the women are in dire straits—Alice and her baby, Daisy, and even Claire is losing everything she holds dear. They all need to have an even chance."

He dismissed Metlock and took Simone's hand in his. "Did you ever think you would be arguing for the rights of fallen women?" He did not wait for an answer, but kissed her hand, then said, "I'll think about it."

"And think about doing something for all the others like poor lost Sandaree."

"You want me to change the ways of the world?"

She took her hand back. "You say you have influence and power. I want you to use them, instead of using women like other men do."

They walked without speaking toward the drawing room where sherry was served before dinner. The piles of handkerchiefs were on display, all tied with ribbons with calling cards affixed to them. Claire's stack was taller than Daisy's; Simone's was inches shorter. Gorham's mistress would win this round.

Harry left Simone's side and accepted two glasses of sherry from the waiter. He brought one to Claire, bowed, complimented her gown, then pointed to the pile of handkerchiefs with her name on it and bluntly asked, "Did you sew all of those?"

"Of course."

He upended the second glass of sherry into his mouth. "No, you did not."

"You cannot prove it."

"No, but I can prove your name is not Claire Hope, Miss Colthopfer."

"You wouldn't."

Unfortunately he had no more of the sweet wine to take away the taste of that untruth. "I would. By the way, how is your daughter?"

Claire almost dropped her own glass, so he took that one from her. "You bastard."

He bowed again, and sipped at her sherry. "Does Gorham know?"

She looked around to make certain the marquis was not nearby, which was answer enough. "I went on tour. But why do you care about the sewing anyway? Noma cannot win."

"But she can see justice done."

"Bosh. Since when does a rogue like you care about justice? In a just world, you'd be heir to an earldom."

"Even bastards care about the truth. I have since I was born, I suppose."

Half of Claire's pile was removed. Her maid, the singer said with a laugh, must have misunderstood, adding her own sewing for the poor to Claire's. Simone still came in third, but Daisy was declared winner.

Everyone at the lavish dinner was merry, except for Lord Gorham at one end of the table and his mistress at the other. Wine flowed among the guests; glares passed between the host and hostess.

They all trooped into the music room after the meal for the start of the entertainment competition. Miss Smythe, currently in Lord Martindale's keeping, went first. Several gentlemen went elsewhere as soon as the delicate blonde sat at the harp. She wore a flowing white gown, her hair in ringlets, and she played as divinely as she looked. Unfortunately, the harp was a bit too high-toned for many of the women who were more used to fiddles and foot stompings. They started chatting back and forth across the aisles, flirting with their beaux, the ones who had not decamped or fallen asleep. Miss Smythe played on, but with a less cherubic expression on her lovely face.

The applause at the end of her performance was heart-felt, until the audience realized Miss Smythe was merely resting between pieces. Couples tiptoed out of the room; bankers and baronets sank lower in their seats.

Simone sat upright on a gilt chair next to Harry, ignoring his sighs of discontent. "How did you do it?" she whispered. "Make Claire change her count?"

He draped his arm around the back of her chair and wrapped one red curl around his finger. "Blackmail, extortion, threats, misuse of power and information. Everything I try to combat in this world." He tugged at the curl. "I did it for you."

Miss Smythe launched into her next piece, over the whispers and the scuffling, with a few giggles mixed in. Then Lord Martindale snored. Loudly.

The angel turned into a she-devil right before their eyes. She stood up, hefted the music stand, and tried to bash in her lover's head. Harry and Mr. Anthony, the East India Trading Company partner, jumped up to grab her. Martindale tossed a leather purse her way, then ran out of the room.

"Now he knows why she's had such a long string of lovers," Harry told Simone after the woman was led out by the servants.

Miss Elizabeth Althorp, who was the daughter of a vicar and mistress of a viscount, hesitated before stepping to the front of the room when Lord Gorham introduced her, and her original poetry.

More seats emptied, which, Simone considered, was the loss for the deserters. The poems were moving, especially the one about love choosing its course like the river.

"The river doesn't choose where it goes," Harry whispered, a shade too loudly. "What the deuce is she talking about?"

Simone hushed him by laying her hand on his thigh, so close to hers.

"Right, the river. Choices. Lovely."

When Elizabeth was done, the viscount stood and applauded with vigor. So did those whose partners were still to perform, knowing they could defeat the first two. Simone knew she couldn't.

Then Claire Hope stood and sang as if she were in front of the Italian Opera House with kings and princes come to see her. Gorham shocked everyone by accompanying her on the pianoforte. Claire sang of one tragic love after another, leaning toward him.

"Twelve years," Harry whispered in Simone's ear. "That's a lot of practice together."

That was a lot of love, Simone thought.

Claire was stunning in looks, with a voice to pierce the hardest heart. Simone's eyes grew damp, until she remembered she was not supposed to understand the words. Others simply thrilled at the magnificent sounds, without knowing Italian. The missing members of the audience hurried back into the room, with servants standing at the back and filling the hall. When Claire finished, the shouts for encores shook the chandeliers. She sang again, and again, until her voice grew weak.

She had to win.

No one wanted to perform after Claire, so Gorham declared the competition over for the night, with a supper set out in the dining room, cards in the Egyptian Room, and dancing to be here in the music room, with a hired trio to provide the music. No, he was not going to sit at the pianoforte while everyone else got to dance as soon as the servants rolled back the carpets and shoved the chairs to the sides. He was going to see about a drink, after playing his best to match his lover.

"Are you hungry?" Harry asked Simone.

"I think we should practice dancing first, if we are to compete at that. I understand Claire is inviting the countryside to a grand ball and I would not wish to embarrass you."

"You never could, my dear," he said, for the benefit of another couple walking near, waiting for the music to start.

As soon as the others passed, Simone confessed that she had never performed the waltz, although she thought she knew the steps from observing her students' dance classes. Whatever dances the young ladies were taught, however, they were never like this.

There were no country dances. No studied minuets or complicated quadrilles, either. First the trio played a fast-paced polka, which Simone had never seen. Then came a reel, with much skipping and clapping and laughing. Finally they played a waltz.

Simone and Harry danced awkwardly at first, with not much room to maneuver among the twirling couples. Mrs. Olmstead would be scandalized if she could see the partners touching, leaning into each other, against each other, even kissing while they swayed.

"Relax, sweetheart. You are too stiff."

"You are holding me too close."

"Not half as close as I'd wish." He spun her around, the silk of her skirts flowing against her legs, his thighs against hers, his arm firm at her waist, their gloved hands entwined—the dance of the devil, indeed. Simone felt like a soap bubble, floating effortlessly on the breeze of Harry's nearness. She refused to think about how he was such an expert dancer that he could make any partner appear graceful.

Maura Doyle shouted for an Irish jig, and she kicked up her skirts, showing ankle, knee, and a bit of white thigh, while her partner clapped the beat. A few of the other women tried to emulate Maura's acrobatics, after glasses of punch, but one fell flat on her bum, amid much loud laughter.

"I think it is time we left the music room," Harry decided, once more trying to shield Simone from the ribald jokes and rum-inspired revelry. "Danforth set out for the cardrooms earlier, and I should follow. I haven't found anything about a seditious plot or a blackmail attempt, but I might hear something later, when they're all too foxed to mind their tongues."

"You are still searching for treason?" She looked around at the drunken dancers, lurching into one another and shattering the gilt chairs at the sidelines, or entwined in the corners. "These men have no thoughts but how to spend money and sate their appetites, no matter who is watching."

She went up to bed, wishing Harry were not cut from the same shoddy cloth.

Chapter Sixteen

Sarah had laid out another nearly transparent night-gown. The blue gauze had white ribbons for straps instead of sleeves, and a matching see-through robe with a white satin collar. Simone wore both to bed, and still pulled the covers up to her chin. Then she tried to stay awake with a book she'd borrowed from Sandaree. She could not read the words, but the pictures . . .

No, that was impossible. No, a lady would never do that. Were those two ladies? No body could bend that way, could it? No, no, no! Except for one or two maybe's, and a few oh-my's. She hid the book under her pillow when she heard Harry speaking to Metlock in the dressing room, before he came into the bedchamber in his robe.

He sighed when he saw the blankets on top of the bed, on one side. "At least it's not the floor again."

"Did you learn anything?" she asked. She certainly had.

He yawned. "Nothing out of the usual. This fast crowd always gambles too high, whether they have funds or not. I heard no whispers, saw no groups holding private conversations. I'm hoping Daniel has better luck in the village, or Jeremy and Sarah among the servants."

Harry should be gathering information, too, instead of adding more disturbing images to those already in Simone's head, with his smile and his bare feet. "Maybe some of the men are staying up later, after the house is quiet." And maybe he'd stay away long enough for her to fall asleep.

"I waited until they all went to their bedrooms with their partners. Except Caldwell and Bowman, who must have changed horses midstream, so to speak."

"They switched partners?"

"Why not? You must know by now that loyalty is not valued here."

"Would you . . . ? That is . . . ?"

"Choose a different lady?" He pulled her over to his side of the bed. "No." He pressed her against his chest, cursing about the blankets in the way, which was not exactly a love poem like Miss Althorp's verses, or a romantic aria like Claire's, but he'd said no. How could she not kiss him? How could she stop kissing him?

Harry did not seem inclined to stop on his own, either, moving from her lips to her neck to her shoulders, and then to her breasts, over the sheer fabric of her negligee. The bedcovers were pushed aside, and so, it seemed, were both their good intentions. If not for a coal tumbling in the fireplace, who knew where the kisses would lead, except the illustrators of Sandaree's book?

At the noise, Harry pushed her back to her side of the bed. "Maybe I ought to put my sword between us after all. You are too damned hard to resist."

Now a corner of her heart felt as warm as the skin he'd touched. She reached for his hand.

He brought hers to his lips, then held it against his cheek, before rolling farther away from temptation. "I did have an interesting conversation, though," he said. "Gorham asked if I would consider trading a property near his country seat—buying it from Lord Royce myself or getting him to sell it to Gorham—in exchange for a Jamaican plantation he owns. He needs a manager there immediately, but would be glad enough to be rid of the headaches of being an absentee landlord outright. According to Gorham, society in the British colonies is not as strict, and a man's birth is not as important as his wealth and his power."

"Why doesn't he go, then? He and Claire could live happily together."

"Unwed? No society is that forgiving. And he has responsibilities here: tenants, dependents, investments, Parliament. And sons in school."

"Then I do not see why Claire cannot stay here. She adores being hostess, and they seem perfect together."

"His wife has suffered a great deal of scandal over the years. I suppose she is tired of being the discarded female, when it is she who holds the purse strings. Or perhaps she worries about when her sons are old enough to be out on the town. Or she may simply be a woman scorned, getting revenge. If she is not happy, why should Gorham be?"

"After twelve years? I'd think she'd be happy to see him in Jamaica, or Hades."

"Yes, but he won't go, to Jamaica, that is. I doubt Claire would, either, to give up her singing career. He wants me to consider taking over the plantation instead. A man could go far there, according to him. In the government, in shipping, in agriculture."

"Is that what you would like to do? For that matter, would your family give up their land to see you go?"

"Hell, no. They don't want to be rid of me at all, it seems. Lord Royce is hoping I'll go into the law. Or stand for one of the seats in the Commons he controls. Rex believes I ought to help establish a nationwide police investigative force. Daniel—well, Daniel sees nothing wrong with my being a wastrel, watching his back in fights, going bail for him."

"That is no way to live, for either of you!"

"No, but in Jamaica, I could accomplish much. They are still struggling with the slavery issues, repatriation, reparations. There is a lot of intermingling between the British and the natives whether the starchiest swells approve or not."

She knew what he was saying: A bastard could wed a half-caste more easily there. She could never leave England, though, or her brother. Trying to sound encouraging, she said, "It sounds like an opportunity you'd enjoy."

He still held her hand, absently rubbing his thumb over her palm. "An adventure without subterfuge or danger or disguise. It has been a long time since I have known such tranquillity." Life was hard for a baseborn child, even if he was loved and cared for. He was always a bastard in British eyes, except when he was someone else.

Simone tried to picture Harry in the tropics, surrounded by brilliantly colored birds and bright flowers hanging from vines. She couldn't put him in the landscape. The man she saw in her mind was short and square and sweating, a lot like Lord Comden, with whom she'd danced a waltz tonight, since pregnant Alice wasn't feeling up to the activity. Still, that was her imagination. Harry could decide to leave England. She shivered.

"Feeling cold?"

"No." Except in that same corner of her heart.

"I am," he said. He shoved aside his coverings and slid beneath the blankets, her blankets, with her. He pulled her close into his arms. "Ah, that is much better."

He had his robe on; she had a gown and a robe. He was

honorable. That's what Simone told herself as she returned the embrace, as if her arms could keep him from leaving the country. She knew she could not hold him after this week, but somehow London would be a lonelier, emptier place without so much as a chance of seeing him. She rested her head against his chest. His arms enclosed her, like a waltz, with the beat of their hearts as music. He caressed her back, her neck, the side of her ribs. "Much better. What was it I promised?"

"That my virtue would be intact, even if my reputation was blown to smithereens."

He kissed her, with a smile. "Intact is intact, but there are vast ranges of virtue, you know."

She did, from the illustrations in the book.

"May I show you?" One of his hands was already caressing her breast, with the other one reaching for the hem of her nightgown.

"Yes, please."

A picture might be worth a thousand words, but Harry's touch was worth a thousand broken hearts.

Simone was trapped. A hot, heavy burden lay across her legs. She could never escape the heat or the weight! She jerked awake, only to realize the weight was Harry's leg—his bare leg—over hers. His arm—his bare arm—was across her chest, pinning her to the bed. He hadn't . . . ? She hadn't . . . ? She'd wanted to, for certain, and thought she might have begged. Why, she was no better than the other courtesans—maybe worse because she knew he hadn't gotten his money's worth. Except that wasn't what he was paying her for. Maybe she ought to be paying him for last night. What a muddle, and, blast, could he feel that her nipples were tightening at the scandalous thoughts? She shoved him away.

"You cheated!"

He was awake and smiling, watching her as if he knew the thoughts going through her mind, the guilt and the remembered glory. "I did not. Your maidenhood is as intact as ever. You can go to your husband without a qualm."

"You took off your robe."

"Zeus, Noma, you are concerned about that, after I made you moan with a woman's pleasure?"

She blushed as only a redhead could, like a tomato. She was mortified at what she'd done, at what she'd let a practiced seducer do.

Harry explained, "I got too warm in my robe, so I took it off."

No apology, no regrets? "Put. It. On."

He started to pull the covers down, exposing his chest and every muscle that rippled when he moved. Then he put a foot out.

"Not now!"

He grinned at her. "When?"

"After I leave." She got out of bed and marched toward the door to her dressing room. She'd forgotten her apparel was entirely transparent until he said, "Thank you."

Harry knew he ought to feel guilty. Damn, he was playing with fire, and semantics. She'd been an innocent, by Jupiter, and she sure as hell wasn't anymore, except technically. It was her clothes, he told himself, a doxy's wardrobe. No, her hair, a siren's beacon. Her dark chocolate eyes that burned so sweetly, her breasts that begged to be cradled in his hands, her caring, her mind, her breasts. Lud, he was getting aroused just thinking about her breasts. Guilty? He felt like a king for giving her plea-sure, like a beggar for wanting more, but he did not suffer a shred of regret. Hell, this was government business. And he was only a man. He'd do it again right now if she hadn't scampered out of the room. He'd pleasure her again tonight if she let him, even if his unsatisfied condition almost killed him.

Since none of the others would be up for hours, Harry suggested they ride into the village for breakfast with Daniel. His stallion needed exercise. Lud knew he did, too. He also wanted her to become more familiar with the bay gelding before the coming race. And he had to hear Daniel's news.

Simone decided to enjoy the sunny morning, the horses, and Harry's company. That way she would not have to think about the night. Last night, this night, all the nights to come.

The ride to the village was short, but fast and glorious. The grooms who watched them take off decided to make side bets of their own. The bay could never catch Harry's black Fidus, of course, but Miss Royale rode like the wind, and didn't she look a treat in her red and black habit? Harry almost fell behind watching her, wishing her hair was undone and flowing behind her. Hell, he wished she were riding him with that look of ecstasy on her face. Damn, now he was jealous of a horse!

Daniel was not happy to be awakened so early. He was done with his disguise, he said when Simone asked, after she threatened him with her riding crop for deceiving her. "A bunch of other chaps have come down from Town to see the race and watch the scramble in the maze. I'm here to support my cousin, don't you know, nothing untoward about my being in Richmond."

He was annoyed the maze event had been canceled, because his money had been on Miss Royale.

Harry was annoyed when Daniel sat close beside her

at the breakfast table in the private parlor Harry'd paid for. First a horse, now his hulking cousin, damn. He decided he had to get his mind back on business. "Has Danforth's apartment been searched?"

Daniel stopped filling his plate with enough food to serve the entire inn. "They didn't find any letters or journals."

"Who went?"

"Inspector Dimm and two of Bow Street's reformed burglars. One to pick the lock, the other to help search, and Dimm to make sure they didn't take anything else."

"Dimm wouldn't miss anything. Damn, then either Danforth is not our man or he has the evidence with him."

Simone stopped marveling at how much food the cousins could consume to ask, "You think Lord James Danforth is a blackmailer? A duke's son?"

Harry answered while Daniel kept eating. "He's the black sheep of the family, and he's come into too much money for anything honest. He was already on my list, having, ah, visited the house where the documents went missing."

"Lots of chaps visited her, I'd wager," Daniel said between mouthfuls. "She's a popular woman, that one. Too bad she's too old now, or I'd pay her a call myself. I like spring better'n summer. And autumn—ouch. Why'd you kick me? Oh. Sorry, Miss Royale. I forget you aren't family."

"Just don't forget she's a lady," Harry said with a growl. "As for that other female, it's too bad she didn't burn her lovers' letters and her journals, instead of letting them get stolen."

Simone thought of how openly the gentlemen at Griffin Woods showed off their mistresses. "Would it be so terrible if people discovered the gentlemen were her lovers? Most of the wives must know by now, no matter what the husbands think or hope. We all know how fast gossip travels, and how far."

"With those wives, yes, it matters. With those men, so high in the government, yes. And it's not just the written proof; the woman's journals recount how much her lovers spent on jewels and horses and furs for her."

"Royal-exchequer money, maybe, or army funds," Daniel added, reaching for the last slice of beefsteak. "There'd be hell to pay if that got out."

"There ought to be," Simone said in indignation. "That's misappropriation of funds if I ever heard it."

"True, but Prinny and his brothers are unpopular enough as is. And she might have exaggerated."

"Are you certain she isn't the one collecting the black-mail money?"

"She swears not," Harry said.

"And you believe her, an immoral woman who has had that many lovers? A whore?" Simone forgot for an instant that a whore was precisely the role she was playing.

The cousins looked at each other, blue eyes to blue eyes.

"Tasted right to me," Harry said.

"No prickles," Daniel said.

Simone looked from one to the other, wondering where she had lost the thread of the conversation, or if the Royce men were all lunatics. "Not the beefsteak or the tongue. Did you believe her?"

They both said yes and went back to their meals.

When they were done, Harry said, "I'll have to search his rooms. Lud, what a row there'd be if Danforth caught me near his concubine, and it's not like we are friends, visiting back and forth. He's always been a snob about my birth."

"He's a jackass."

"And he treats Sandaree poorly."

When Daniel volunteered to conduct the search, Harry turned him down. "You're too big to skulk in corners, and you don't belong in the house, not as Harold, not as yourself."

"Sure I do, at the ball, leastways. I've been invited, don't you know. I can trot upstairs while everyone's dancing."

"The servants will know you don't belong anywhere but the ballroom or the refreshments room."

"They'll be too busy serving. And I could say one of the ladies invited me up. That's not too far-fetched at Gorham's party."

Harry looked at his large cousin's rumpled shirt, shaggy hair, and spotted kerchief. "You'll throw spots, telling that tale."

"I could do it," Simone offered, ignoring the nonsense she supposed was cousinly banter. "I can say I am calling on Sandaree to return her book if anyone catches me."

Daniel wanted to know what book.

"Just a picture book from her country."

Harry dipped his finger in the honey jar and licked it. Daniel rubbed his ear. They both said no, she could not become a thief.

"It is too dangerous and not your job."

"I am supposed to be helping, aren't I? All I've done so far is ruffle Claire's feathers. I still haven't decided on a performance, either."

"Your role is to be noticed, and you've done it in aces. Metlock can come up with something for me. He always does."

"Lud, I'd give anything to see you dressed as a housemaid!" Daniel laughed so hard tears came to the big man's eyes. Then he decided to ride back to the manor house with them to scout out the lay of the land.

That almost made Harry weep. He'd had plans to lay Simone down in a secluded glen he'd found. He'd even tied a blanket behind his saddle. Maybe he'd use it to smother his cousin.

Chapter Seventeen

Claire announced over another ample spread at luncheon that the afternoon's contest was watercolor painting on the lawn. Several of the women groaned. Claire frowned them into silence and explained that they could not hold the archery or billiards contests, the card matches, or the horse race, not without the gentlemen's presence. Most of the men were riding out in search of a rabid dog seen in the neighborhood.

Two women—who could not draw at all—feigned horror at the thought of being outdoors with a mad animal and no one to protect them.

"The servants will be nearby, and those gentlemen who do not wish to ride." Claire looked down her nose as if such a man was beneath contempt, ensuring that anyone who could would aid Gorham in ridding the countryside of the danger. "We will all paint Griffin Manor from the front of the house, but affix our initials to the back. The paintings will be displayed in the drawing room before dinner, and the gentlemen will vote for the best. Do you deem that fair, Miss Royale?"

"Exceedingly," Simone replied to the snide question,

unsurprised. Besides being a vocalist of professional caliber, Claire must obviously be a superb artist.

She was. Not many of the other women were, however, so the competition was not fair at all. Only a handful of the ladybirds had been reared in gentility, with the training and education of a lady. Drawing lessons were hard to come by in Seven Dials, or on the farm. Sketching maybe, but watercolors in the poorhouse? Not likely. The females who plied this trade were lucky if they could read and write, although they all could add their incomes and knew the value of their jewels to the last shilling.

The crude curses that met Claire's announcement proved it: These might be the cream of the courtesans, the highest paid, most in demand of the demimondaines, but they were no ladies.

As Lord Gorham had quietly said to Harry before they left, "You can take a wench off the streets, but you cannot take the streets off the wench."

Some of the women chose to withdraw from the artistic event they had no chance of winning. They'd play lawn tennis or pall-mall instead, both of which Claire considered beneath her dignity, so they were not included in the tournament. The unartistic Fashionable Impures could also laze about the house, seeing to their looks and apparel, their two favorite entertainments. No one wished to stroll the gardens or sightsee, not without their escorts to admire them, not with the sun out to destroy their complexions, not with a mad dog on the loose.

Ellsworth's mistress, Madeline Harbough, declared she had to practice dressage, which was not, she told the less well informed, putting on a corset by herself. She was going to perform her circus act this evening.

Other strumpets gave up on the whole contest altogether. They hadn't the looks, the clothes, the talent, or the cleverness of Claire, so why let their gents see that? London had more to offer than this rubbishing house party where one had to watch one's manners and watch Claire or Miss Royale to see which fork to use. There was more fun at the gaming clubs, the theater, the shops, and the daily drives in Hyde Park to be seen and to see if perhaps a nob with deeper pockets showed any interest. Their companions agreed. Wagering on a losing prospect held no appeal, nor did endangering themselves going after a rabid beast. Besides, some of them had to get back to their wives or their businesses. They'd return for the ball, of course, and the final judging, to pay their debts and negotiate for the favors of the winning women.

As a result, only seven artists sat at portable easels or with lap desks on the north lawn, looking up at the sprawling brick manor house. Four others sat watching from beneath a large awning, where servants served iced lemonade and biscuits, tea and tiny sandwiches, even though luncheon was just past. Sandaree sat on a cushion on the ground, midway between the painters and the gossipers, shivering in her thin garments despite the spring sunshine.

Simone sent Sarah back to her room for a shawl for the poor girl. Sandaree thanked her, then confessed she was more disconsolate than cold. Lord James was going to be angry at her again, because she was not going to win. She'd never used watercolors or drawn a landscape.

"Then you should paint the wonderful designs you have on your hands. That is a real skill, too."

Sandaree smiled and took up a brush, but she soon grew frustrated at the drips and smears she produced. Instead she politely inquired of the females under the awning if they would like her to paint on them, not with her henna dye, but using these bright colors. The bored nonpainters were delighted, especially knowing the vines and chains would wash off. One wanted a butterfly on her cheek, another a heart on her shoulder. Soon they were all laughing except for Claire, who was painting with dark intensity.

Miss Althorp, the poetess, was also ignoring the happy chatter, so Simone decided she'd better get to work. Both of their paintings were starting well with the bright blue sky, she saw as she passed behind their positions. They knew what they were doing and had command of the flowing medium. The other artistes were not as proficient, or as fast.

Simone knew she could never match Claire's skill, but she'd always loved painting, and rejoiced when her students were old enough or interested enough to pursue one of Simone's favorite pastimes. Without a governess post, she could not afford paints for her own pleasure. Or a horse, naturally. Just think, today she'd enjoy both of her best-loved pleasures. And last night—no, she was not going to think of last night, pleasure, love, or Harry. Which meant she saw him, his bare chest and devilish smile, instead of the landscape. She thought of painting him, for her own enjoyment, her own keepsake, instead of trying to compete with Claire and Elizabeth Althorp. Then she thought of her brother and her own future. Even third place was worth points in the overall contest. She'd paint Harry another time, in private. Perhaps he'd pose. As the rugged sportsman he'd appeared after lunch? In evening wear, the perfect gentleman? In his robe? Bare-chested in her bed?

Simone stood to fetch a lemonade to cool her suddenly heated cheeks rather than calling for a servant. She walked behind Claire, not to disturb the opera singer's view or concentration. Claire never noticed her presence, or Simone's sigh when she saw the lovely picture coming to life on her paper.

Then she stepped behind Miss Althorp, who hunched over her easel, hiding her work. The Frenchwoman, the real Parisian, was muttering French blasphemies as her brush dripped a muddy streak and she had to start over. Miss Hanson, the banker's convenient, had more paint on her apron than on her paper; Miss Mary Connors, the actress who shared a love of the theater and a flat in Kensington with Sir John Foley, laughed and admitted she'd painted only backdrops before. Her sketch looked like it.

Simone sipped her lemonade and studied the manor; then she studied the nearby flower gardens, the stream, the beginning of the forest that gave Griffin Woods its name. Then she looked at her blank paper again and knew what she wanted to paint.

She made a hasty mental sketch, then quickly began adding shape and color to the real page. She used a dry brush on top, to keep the bright hues from bleeding into one another, and then a thinner brush for detail work. She wondered if Harry would like it or, like Sandaree's Lord James, he'd be disappointed she could not measure up to Gorham's mistress. Harry certainly surpassed Gorham and Lord James, in any contest she could think of.

The devil take him, she felt heated again, despite the wide straw bonnet that shielded her from the sun. And her mouth was dry. Sarah was not in sight, and the others had wandered over to watch the lawn games, so Simone simply walked around the circle of painters again. This time she could see Miss Althorp's painting, and was surprised. The landscape's sky was now overcast, while the afternoon was a clear one. How odd.

Claire stood to stretch, too, smiling contentedly. Her painting must be perfect, Simone thought in despair. Then Claire started screaming like a fishwife, losing all semblance of polite manners. She snatched up Miss Althorp's painting and shook it under the blond-haired poetess's nose.

"This is my painting, you cheating bitch! I did it last month. I know my own work." She waved the painting for Simone and the others to see. "I wished to catch the heaviness in the air just before a rainstorm. Gorham and I had to run back to the house with it. See? There's a smudge on the corner. And look, here is her painting still on the easel, as ugly as she is with her long nose and her fancy airs. You stole my work, you sneak. And your poetry reeks, too!"

"Mon Dieu," the Frenchwoman exclaimed.

Simone whispered another blasphemy, but to herself. The vicar's daughter? The one who held literary salons? Simone looked, and sure enough, another painting was on the easel, this one not half as well executed. But the sun was shining in it, and the flowers were the same ones in bloom today.

"I did it in my bedroom," Miss Althorp claimed.

"You found it, more like," Claire screeched. "Lud knows what you do in your bedroom with that chinless viscount of yours."

The other lady shrieked right back. "You cheat at everything else. And you don't need blunt like the rest of us do."

"Ha! Your viscount has deep pockets."

"And he needs to marry, for the succession, a lady with a dowry. He's too honorable to keep a mistress while he goes courting this Season, unlike Gorham."

"How dare you pick on my lord when you stole my painting!"

"You called my lover chinless!"

"And witless to take up with a pretentious, priggish female like you."

Miss Althorp grabbed for the disputed drawing. Claire swiped at the blonde's bonnet. Miss Althorp kicked grass on Claire's skirts, and Claire picked up the jug of dirty water filled with used paintbrushes. She would have tossed it, but Simone held her arm. "Ladies, the gentlemen are returning."

That stopped the argument before it turned into a melee among mistresses. Simone felt as if she were back in the classroom with the petulant, spoiled children of her employers. She was happier to see Harry than she thought possible, and ran to meet him and the other men on foot before they got to the easels.

He raised a dark eyebrow, but followed her lead and folded her into a hug, kissing the top of her head. "What, were you worried about me, sweetheart?"

She was worried she'd have to referee dueling paintbrushes at twenty paces. "Of course, darling. Did you find the dog?"

Now he raised two eyebrows at the endearment, but said, "Yes, we started at the farm where he'd been spotted, and the poor beast was still there. Gorham and Caldwell had their rifles on him, but we wanted to keep our distance, not jeopardizing the horses. There's no telling what a rabid animal will do."

Gorham took up the story. "The cur was slobbering at the mouth, all right, skinny and trembling, unsteady on its feet. Sick. We knew we had to put it out of its misery before it bit another dog, or one of my tenants' children."

"Then he wagged his tail," Harry added.

Gorham shook his head. "Who would have thought Harry Harmon had such a soft heart? We had the beast cornered, and damn if Harry didn't dismount and approach the cur, right in the line of fire."

"You didn't!" Simone cried, knowing that was just what he would do.

"I thought I saw something, and I was right."

"A fishhook, by damn," Sir Chauncey Phipps said. "The mongrel's mouth was all swollen. Not rabid a'tall, just starving and in pain."

Another of the riders said, "Harry proved it to us by offering the dog water. A rabid animal won't touch it, you know."

Sir Chauncey pretended to shudder. "Water? I won't drink the stuff, either."

Simone hadn't recovered from the thought of Harry on foot facing a deadly threat. "So you put it down humanely?"

He brushed at his sleeve, where she now saw black hair. "Not exactly."

"He dragged the blasted creature back to my stable, dash it!" Gorham took a lemonade from a servant who appeared with a tray. "Harry insisted, and carried it in front of him on that brute he rides."

"Fidus did not mind," Harry said, "nor did I. Jem and the head groom are doctoring the dog now, after we removed the fishhook so he could eat. He appears to be some kind of sheepdog, but he's all matted and filthy. There's no telling how long he was out there on his own. I was hoping you'd look in on him, since you had such success cleaning up Miss White."

"Of course. Um, he doesn't bite, does he?"

Gorham snorted. "I wouldn't have let the gudgeon bring it home if it was vicious. Claire doesn't like dogs, do you, dearest?" he called over to where his mistress was still standing.

"Calmed right down, it did, as if it knew Harry was a

friend," Sir Chauncey added. "He's got the touch, old Harry does, doesn't he?"

Harry winked at Simone. She blushed, thinking of his touch, knowing that he was thinking of it, too.

She quickly agreed to go with him right away. "I'm done with my painting. We all are." She said it loudly enough for the women to understand the argument and the competition were both over. "But you cannot see it, or any of them, to keep the judging fair." She went back to the easels and took hers, Claire's, the one Miss Althorp had actually done, and the three others. She left Claire clutching the rainstorm painting, looking like thunderclouds herself.

Simone handed the paintings to Sarah, Sandaree, and the servants, keeping them separate in case they needed more drying time. "Give them to the butler, please. I understand they are to be displayed in the drawing room before dinner." She only prayed the ladies displayed better behavior.

Simone spent the rest of the afternoon trying to rid the dog of knots, burrs, and vermin while Harry held him and talked softly. While she worked, he kept stroking the dog's head and back, getting hair and drool all over him. Simone still wore her painting apron, so her clothes were safe, but Metlock was going to be furious, she warned Harry.

He did not care, too concerned with the animal's condition after Simone cut away enough of the matted mess to show its bare ribs. "We can't feed him too much at once, you know. And only broth and a bit of boiled beef at first." Except he was breaking one of the tea sandwiches into tiny bits for the dog to swallow.

"I think the dog values your attention more than food

right now. He must know you saved his life. What shall you name him?"

"A better question is, what I am going to do with him? Gorham won't keep him. He'll likely shut down the manor house after the party, when Claire leaves. I'm thinking the animal might make an excellent gift for my godson."

"I thought the boy was only an infant."

"You can see how gentle he is."

Simone saw how big the dog still was, without the mass of hair. "Maybe you should ask your sister-in-law first."

"I'm not worried about Amanda. It's Verity, Rex's mastiff, who might not take to a strange animal in the house."

"Why don't you keep him, then?"

Because he never knew who he was going to be, or where. Because a dog could give away any disguise he might put on. Because he had enough responsibilities in his damned life. "No."

"Mr. Black."

"You know someone who'd want him?"

"No, that is what you should call him," Simone said, ignoring his refusal. "Miss White can learn to live with him. So can Mrs. Judd."

"Blackie? Black boy?" The dog's ears perked up. "I never had a dog of my own, you know." The dog rolled over for his belly to be scratched, moaning with joy.

"You do now."

And now Simone was jealous.

Chapter Eighteen

Simone took a second glass of sherry before dinner that night, to settle her nerves. Three would not be enough, not during the exhibition of the watercolors. She also held on tightly to Harry's hand at the side of the drawing room where all the houseguests were gathered for the judging. She was used to such familiarity in public now. Goodness, hand-holding was nothing compared with the blatantly sexual displays of affection—or lust—she had seen at this party. Lord Gorham had his arm around Claire's shoulder, and Lord Caldwell had his hand in Maura Doyle's bodice. Before dinner? Simone turned away. Hand-holding was sufficient for her needs right now.

She *did* need Harry's support, whether it was merely for show or not.

Six paintings were framed and displayed on gilt stands along the mantelpiece in the drawing room, with six glass bowls in front of them. Each of the fourteen remaining gentlemen, whether his inamorata had entered or not, was given a single new guinea to place in the bowl in front of his favorite entry. The three paintings with the highest amount of coins would win points for their artists, who also got to keep the money. Some of the men were making a great show of judging, raising their quizzing glasses to inspect the artwork, viewing the collection from different angles, talking about brushstrokes, the painter's "eye," lyricism, and perspective.

Hogwash, Simone decided, from self-important peacocks trying to show better taste and more intelligence than the next fellow. Connoisseurs, ha! The banker likely bought whatever masterpieces his man of business recommended as good investments, and Sir Chauncey Phipps, who had already had three glasses of sherry and heaven knew what else, admitted he preferred nudes to houses.

In addition, everyone knew that only four of the six paintings were truly in contention, since two were muddy blurs that looked like landslides instead of landscapes. Everyone—even the jug-bitten Sir Chauncey and the surly Lord James Danforth, disinterested because his harem-bred mistress had not bothered to enter—had to know which was best. They also had to recognize it as Claire's. Not only was that one a perfect rendering of Griffin Woods Manor, but it was painted with skill and affection. Besides, watercolors exactly like it except for seasonal differences, the sky, and the flowers hung in nearly every bedchamber.

Six gentlemen placed their coins in that bowl.

The two unfortunately brown entries each received one coin, from the artists' loyal beaux, even though no one was supposed to know who painted which.

That left six votes, six coins, and three paintings: Simone's, Elizabeth Althorp's unfinished original, and the Frenchwoman's. Madame Lecroix had chosen to depict the manor house in the distance, with the gardens in the forefront as splashes of color in a more modern style than Claire's painting. Joseph Gollup, her shipping-magnate lover, put his coin there, and so did Mr. Anthony of the East India Company because, he said, the flowers reminded him of home. Miss Althorp's viscount almost placed his money there, too, until she hissed at him to drop it in the correct bowl, hers.

Three gentlemen had still not cast their votes. Simone clutched Harry's hand so tightly he couldn't leave to study the paintings or place his coin. The other men were standing in front of the mantel, so he could barely see to choose.

"I have to go vote, my love."

She let go of his hand before he had to pry her fingers loose. "I won't tell you which picture is mine, for I want you to pick your favorite because it is the best, not out of misplaced loyalty or fear of reprisal if you do not."

"I couldn't lie," was all he said as he joined the other men studying the paintings. Then he started laughing, and Simone wished the floor would open up and swallow her, or a servant would come by with another glass of sherry. She'd made a fool out of herself. Worse, her poor efforts had made a joke out of Harry, who was making the best of things. She hear the clink of a coin, but she couldn't look. Then she heard two others. The voting was done. She studied the view out the window.

Harry touched her on the shoulder, then kissed her hand when she turned. He smiled and held out a bowl with three coins.

"Three? I got three votes?" Simone did a hasty calculation. She had second place! She threw her arms around Harry's neck and kissed him, right there for everyone to see. Metlock would be angry she'd ruined the creases of his starched cravat, but Simone did not care. "You voted for me?"

"I voted for my favorite, in all honesty. I knew it had

to be yours, because who else had the daring, the imagination, the wit, to paint a griffin in Gorham's garden, lion's tail and eagle's head and all? You did get the house in, too, so Claire couldn't disqualify you, although I'd wager she tried. You are brilliant, Noma."

So she kissed him again, to applause from their audience.

Claire was miffed again, that she, the winner, was not receiving the accolades. Worse, she'd won only six of the guineas when she deserved them all. Lord Gorham kept patting her hand and telling her she was the best artist, with the best technique, the finest eye. And he needed another picture of the manor for his own bedroom.

"He wants this one," Harry whispered to Simone, "but I told him he'd have to fight me for it."

Miss Althorp's viscount was also aggravated. He'd gotten wind of her attempted swindle and took that as a poor reflection on his own taste. Conscious of his elevated station, he'd picked the least scandalous mistress he could find, the most educated and upright, when she wasn't lying in his bed, of course. Now her artistic light had dimmed, and his own honor was damaged by her heinous actions. They were discussing the situation rationally, he thought, as mature adults of intelligence and manners. Then she called him a twit.

"And Claire was right—you are a coldhearted, chinless clunch." She kicked him in the shin for good measure before stomping off to pack.

The viscount looked more embarrassed by the scene she'd caused than affronted by her insults. He also appeared more relieved than upset. He went up to the mantel, retrieved his coin, and handed it to Simone.

That didn't make her the winner, but it did make Claire angrier. "When are you going to perform for us, anyway, Miss Royale? Have you decided on your entertainment?"

Simone tried to be diplomatic. "I would not dare sing, not after your thrilling concert. I beg you for a few more days to decide."

"Hmph. You are running out of time. And I am running out of patience with your airs and graces. You pretend to be so mannerly, butter wouldn't melt in your mouth, but I don't trust you. You, Miss Royale, who appeared out of nowhere to snabble a top-of-the-trees protector, are not what you seem."

Gorham stepped in and led Claire away. "Come, my pet, announce your surprise for tonight."

Simone mangled Harry's sleeve. "She knows."

"No, she is guessing. Don't worry. You are the most enchanting female here. Five rakes have asked my intentions, to see if they have a chance. I expect to hear from the chinless viscount before the night is over."

Simone didn't care about other libertines or other indecent proposals. She wanted only to know Harry's intentions, too. But Claire was clapping her hands to silence the guests to hear her surprise.

Simone's last surprise had turned her world upside down. She could not imagine Claire's announcement to be anything heartwarming, either, unless Gorham's mistress was going to tell them she was withdrawing from the competition. The chances of that happening were as slim as Simone's chances of receiving an honorable offer from anyone.

"I called you down early for the judging and because I have planned a special dinner this evening, before we view the performances of the ladies who are going to display their talents tonight." She shot Simone a nasty look. "Since it is such a lovely evening, we are dining alfresco, in a tent set up near the stables. It is a short walk, but the ladies might wish a warmer wrap."

They might wish boots and heavier skirts, too. Claire received a lot of scowls herself. She was wearing a red woolen gown with long sleeves and a high collar that would have appeared modest on anyone with a lesser bosom, or less-formfitting seams. She looked like a ripe strawberry. She looked warm.

The other women were in silk and lace and as little of both as possible. They wore silk slippers that would be ruined walking through grass, face paint that would not show in the dark, jewels that already felt cold on their necks. They grumbled on their way to find shawls and spencers to cover what they had spent hours adorning.

Simone did not see Sandaree in the crowd, but she decided to bring down an extra wrap in case the Indian girl needed more warmth than Lord James Danforth seemed to have provided. Sarah handed Simone her new brown velvet cape, and excitedly told her the servants were permitted to watch tonight, those not waiting on tables or helping in the kitchens. A real treat for the visiting maids and valets, she went on, and she was going to wear her own new shawl, but she'd bring one for Miss Sandaree—weren't her clothes peculiar? And did Miss Royale think she needed her bonnet?

Simone was excited, too. Now that the art judging was over, and she was not the one performing tonight, she could enjoy herself. And Harry's company. In the dark.

He was waiting in the hallway for her, and tenderly draped the cape over her shoulders, pulling the hood up. "Brown velvet," he murmured as he tied the bow at her neck before she could do it herself. "Just like your eyes. I used to think they were black, but tonight they look soft and inviting. Like velvet." His hands were still on her shoulders, stroking the soft fabric, stoking her anticipation. He lowered his head to hers and she raised her mouth for his kiss.

The butler at the front door coughed. "The others have gone on, sir."

"Quite right. Dinner. In a tent." The butler, the footman waiting with a lantern, and Simone all knew he'd rather go back upstairs and go hungry. "Dammit." He took her arm and followed the footman out into the dusk.

Whatever Claire's other faults, she was a good hostess. Colorful Chinese lanterns lit the way toward the stables, swaying on branches in the light breeze. Bells hung there, too, giving the path an enchanted feel, as if magic waited in the tent they approached. More bells chimed, silk banners fluttered, and garlands of flowers on every post and support scented the air.

The dinner guests were serving themselves from long tables filled with scores of platters and tureens, while servants kept filling glasses with wine. Simone did not spot Sandaree in the jovial crowd, but she did see Danforth standing by himself, drinking.

"Too bad," Harry said when she pointed Lord James out to him. "This would have been a good opportunity to search his room. The personal servants are all coming to watch, I understand, after their own meals."

Simone was glad. She wanted Harry at her side tonight, away from danger, thinking about her, not an unlikely blackmail scheme.

They ate another sumptuous meal on monogrammed china, with linen tablecloths, floral centerpieces, and scented candles, which almost masked the odors from the nearby stables.

"What the deuce are we doing in the paddocks?" Sir Chauncey wanted to know, almost staggering into one of the uprights on his way out of the tent. His companion, a dancer at the Royal Ballet, was gracefully picking her way between evidence of the equines. Miss

Susan Baylor would dance another time, inside, thank goodness.

Simone tucked her cape more closely around her now that they had left the tent. "I believe Miss Harbough is going to perform tonight. Claire would not let her bring the horse into the ballroom at the manor, so this is her stage."

Sir Chauncey was appeased. "Always liked a circus rider. They don't wear much besides rhinestones, don't you know."

The ballet dancer attached herself to Danforth, who was still by himself with Sandaree absent. Sir Chauncey shrugged, then grabbed on to a fence post for balance. "Tired of her anyway."

The area next to the stable had been fenced off, ringed with flambeaux, decorated with more flowers and streamers. Benches were placed to one end, with servants already gathering to stand at the other end.

Gorham assisted Claire up onto one of the benches so she could introduce the performers. In a voice used to filling concert halls, she announced that Miss Harbough would ride Majesto. Since they required musical accompaniment, but the pianoforte could not be brought outdoors, other arrangements had been made. Simone knew that Miss Hanson was willing to play here, but Claire refused to subject the instrument to the night air, the dampness being good enough for the women, not the pianoforte.

Claire went on to explain that their two French guests had kindly offered to share their talents at the same time. Madame Eloise Lecroix, the shipping magnate's diversion while his wife was breeding, and who had taken third place in the painting contest, would play the violin. Mademoiselle Mimi Granceaux—Claire coughed for the onetime Maisy Grant—would grant—cough, cough— them the pleasure—cough—of her talent: whistling.

Several gentlemen applauded the prospect. This had to be better than opera and poetry and the harrowing harp. Some laughed.

First, Madame Lecroix stepped out to another circle of lantern light, holding her violin. The shipowner cleared his throat and all laughter died. The women took seats on the benches. Many of the men stood closer to the fence.

Eloise shook off the shawl she was wearing and blew on her fingers. Then she plucked at the instrument's strings before beginning a classical piece. Simone was almost reminded of her grandfather and his fiddle, how he played outdoors because it reminded him of his youth and Gypsy campfires. Sometimes Simone's mother had let her stay up to listen under the starlight.

Madame's playing was excellent as far as Simone could tell, but held none of Grandpapa's haunting chords of love and loss.

Then more flambeaux were lit by the footmen. Eloise took up a sprightly tune, and Madeline Harbough, née Maddy Hogg, rode into the ring atop a gleaming white steed. The horse had red ribbons entwined in its mane and tail. Maddy had the same color ribbons holding her improbably yellow hair in a braid. Equally as improbable, she had somehow squeezed herself into her old red satin riding costume. One of the men clapped, until Maddy's stout Lord Ellsworth tapped him on the shoulder with his cane. This was serious art.

While Madame Lecroix played, Maddy put the horse through its paces. Silent, unmoving, perfectly posed on her sidesaddle atop the large animal, Maddy got her mount to change gaits to the music, to circle the ring one way, then the other. With no words, no reins, and no riding crop, she directed Majesto into figure eights, then a prancing high step, then a sideways sidle, and finally a bow to the audience. Now Ellsworth cheered along with the rest of the party and the servants across the way.

Maddy rode off, but Eloise played one more complicated violin concerto to show off her skill. Then she too curtsied and stepped aside when Mimi Granceaux, mistress to the East India Company's Mr. Anthony, stepped forward. Mimi waited until Majesto trotted into the ring, building tension in the audience. This time Miss Harbough wore white tights, a lace overskirt covered in red spangles, and a short, tight red blouse. She had gained more than a bit of weight since her performing days, and more during the house party with its lavish spreads. So her ample bottom spread across the horse's broad back as she rode astride, sans saddle. The horse was in better condition.

Madame Lecroix set her violin to her chin, Mimi took a deep breath, and Maddy leaped to her feet atop the white horse's wide back.

Everyone cheered as they did a circle of the ring, almost drowning out the violin and the whistling. Maddy did a handstand—wobbly, but she did it. The crowd grew quiet, waiting for her next trick. Now they could hear the whistle of "Greensleeves."

So could the dog in the stables. Mr. Black started howling.

Maddy and her accompanists ignored the noise, and the snickers from the audience at the rail. Maddy did a pirouette atop the horse, bouncing a bit. Then she tried a one-footed pose, while Majesto gathered into a canter around the ring.

That's when Mr. Black escaped his stall in the stable. Maddy was performing her best trick, a sideways half dismount, then a tremendous leap back onto the horse's back, then onto her feet. The violin started to build to a crescendo; the whistle rose in volume.

The dog ran onto the ring.

The horse was used to circus dogs, small terrier types who wore tutus and jumped through rings and respected the other performers. It was not used to shaved sheepdogs, yapping and baying despite a swollen jaw. It jumped right over the skinny mongrel. Madeline Harbough landed on the other side of her horse, on the ground, on her arse, cursing at the horse, the dog, and the hard ground. Mimi laughed so hard she couldn't whistle, especially after Maddy got up and slapped her. The Frenchwoman cried, *"Mon Dieu,"* and started batting at both of them with her violin, which shattered.

Lord Ellsworth tried to catch the horse he'd paid a pretty penny to hire for the week, but the animal had no trailing reins, so he looked like a fool chasing around the circle. Now that the whistling had stopped, so did the dog's yowls, but Mr. Black ran after Ellsworth, trying to help.

Majesto did figure eights, reversed direction, did dance steps and caprioles, staying out of Ellsworth's reach and jumping over the dog, just like the act where the clowns were chasing him.

Madame Lecroix's shipowner walked off, not wanting to be associated with such a debacle. His pregnant wife was sure to hear of tonight's goings-on. A discreet affair was one thing; this was a horse of quite a different color. White, to be exact, which the scandal sheets were certain to mention.

Mr. Anthony, Mimi's East India trader, was not amused, either. He had no wife, but he did have his pride. A whistling doxy was a joke, but he was not laughing.

Neither was Claire. Once more her plans had failed. She blamed it on Simone, naturally, since Harry had brought the dog to Griffin Woods. She pointed a red-lacquered fingernail at Simone's nose and ordered: "Stop it!"

Harry was already in the ring to catch the dog, while two grooms ran after Ellsworth and the horse. The audience cheered the best entertainment so far, and wagered on the horse, the dog, or Ellsworth and Harry. Stop it? How? Then Simone spotted waiters bringing wine and cheese. She grabbed a handful of cheese and leaped into the ring, calling the dog, who, naturally, did not recognize his new name.

"Get out of here," Harry shouted. "The horse is out of control and unpredictable."

The only one who might have managed Majesto was crying, knowing she'd lost her protector, and knowing she couldn't go back to trick riding for the circus, either.

Majesto did not seem frenzied or malicious to Simone. The horse seemed to be enjoying itself, as a matter of fact, feet picked high, ears pricked forward, performing the best it could without a rider.

She was tempted to call to Majesto, to approach him, since he was used to women riders. But her skirts were too tight for that, and if she was wrong and had to climb over the fence in a hurry, her slippers were too flimsy. She'd help Harry with the dog instead. She held out her hand with the cheese and stayed quiet, so as not to disturb the horse further. Mr. Black was exhausted anyway, and hungry, and the horse did not seem to be one to herd. The dog came to Simone. Or to the food she held out. She broke off small pieces for his sore mouth and to keep him nearby until Sir Chauncey threw his neckcloth over the fence for her to knot around Blackie.

Ellsworth had stalked off, leaving the horse to the

grooms, when he realized the beast was playing with him. The stablemen were in a huddle, deciding on their next best move.

Majesto hadn't heard his exit music yet, so he kept circling and cavorting. Harry, seeing Simone and the dog safe and the horse heading his way, stepped to the side and leaped onto its back. He used his knees and leg position—and a hand firmly in the braided mane—to bring the horse to a halt, and a bow. Harry waved to the applause as he turned Majesto toward the stable.

The men went wild. "Stand on its back, Harry," they shouted, wanting more.

The women simply wanted Harry.

Chapter Nineteen

Who needed more entertainment? Claire announced the rest of the evening would be devoted to the ladies' card match. The gentlemen could play among themselves, of course, or watch and cheer on their favorites. There was to be no advice given, no hints. No cheating, in other words.

Which Simone knew meant that Claire was confident of her own skills.

Each woman was to be given ten red markers. Matches were for markers, not points. The best two out of three hands won a marker. Each woman had to play at least ten matches before play ended at the twelve o'clock supper. The three with the most markers won points toward the overall total, but all players could cash in their winnings for guineas. It was not a huge sum by gentlemen's wagering standards, but no one complained. Playing with house money, no one could lose.

Lord Ellsworth volunteered to monitor the competition. His now-former mistress, Maddy Harbough, was in their room, nursing her bruised body and her bruised pride. Ellsworth would find another bed to sleep in tonight, and for the rest of the house party.

The match was to begin as soon as the women changed out of their wet shoes and dirty hems. Claire's red gown showed nary a smudge. Simone's was covered in mud, dog hair, grass, and other questionable spots and stains from the riding ring.

Harry had not accompanied her back to the house. He said he needed to find better accommodations for Mr. Black, who had worn out his welcome in the stables. Harry also, she guessed, wanted to talk to the grooms, checking their loyalties and hearing Jem's news, if any.

Sir Chauncey and Lord Ellsworth had each taken one of Simone's arms, as if she were too delicate to follow the lantern-bearing servants on her own. Of course Lord Ellsworth leaned on his cane, and Sir Chauncey leaned on her, breathing brandy fumes in her face.

Simone thought about not returning to the parlor, not till she spoke to Harry, at least. She was merely adequate at piquet, Claire's game of choice. Since losing to Harry, Simone doubted she could defeat the favorite, especially without using some of her grandfather's tricks. Like Miss Althorp's viscount, Harry would be furious at the dishonesty. Simone had thought she might take second or third place, but Alice Morrow, Lord Comden's pregnant mistress, was crowing that she was raised in a gaming hall. She could spot a cheat anywhere, she said, and could take on the best.

Alice needed the win, and the money, since she couldn't compete in many other events, not in her condition. She was going to sing country tunes for her entertainment, but what was the use, after Claire's performance?

Alice might have been raised in a gaming hall, but Ruby Dow's last position was as a dealer in one. With her signature ruby at her throat, she admitted that her silhouettes might draw laughs, but she'd never win the talent contest. This and the billiards event were her best chances to accrue points and coins.

Any of them could best Simone, even the ballet dancer or the actress. They'd spent more time at it, while Simone had not played in years, not since becoming a governess. Luck might have something to do with the outcome, but the others might keep better counts in their heads, especially the actress, who was used to memorizing roles.

She'd lose, but maybe not every round, she convinced herself. She had to play ten times or surrender her markers by default, but she might get to keep one or two, which could be one or two more guineas than she had yesterday. Besides, she had too much pride to let Claire Hope defeat her. Or show her up as a poor loser.

Before she went down, she decided to call on Sandaree, to make sure the Indian girl was all right. She wondered if she should mention that Danforth had gone off in the dark with Sir Chauncey's ballet dancer after the trick riding, but, no, that was none of her affair. If she were Sandaree, she'd be glad, anyway.

She took up Sandaree's pillow book as an excuse to visit Lord James's chambers, after another quick look through the pages once Sarah left to hurry her soiled gown to the laundry room. Simone was going to take the opportunity to snoop a bit, too. She couldn't see how else she was helping Harry with whatever he hoped to discover.

Sandaree called a soft "Come in," but she stayed in the shadows.

"Are you well? I looked for you at the riding ring and at dinner."

"Yes, I am well, thank you, but it is too cold for me outside."

"We are playing cards tonight, for points."

"Yes, my lord's valet told me. I do not know this piquet. It is too late to learn. Lord James is disappointed."

He must be easing his disappointment with the ballet dancer again. Simone did not think Sandaree needed to hear that, not from her. "I returned your book."

"I hope it was helpful," Sandaree said, coming out of the shadows to take it.

Simone saw the discoloration on the other girl's cheek. "He struck you?"

"No, Miss Noma. I fell."

"On your face, you, the most graceful creature I have ever seen? I do not believe you."

Sandaree looked away. "My lord was angry."

"That is no excuse! That maggot had no right to hit you."

"In my country, he could kill me if he wished."

"Well, this is England, and he cannot." He could, and get away with it. They both knew it. "You have to leave the worm. Maybe Harry—"

"Would take me on when you separate, pay my debt to Lord James? But that will not be for a long time, I think, from the way he looks at you."

"He does? That is, I was hoping he'd know of a way, or someone to help. What would you like to do if you had a choice, and funds to do it?"

"I would go home to my country. There I could open a pleasure house for wealthy men and earn a fortune. Then I could purchase my mother's freedom."

Simone did not know if Harry had that kind of money or connections, or if he'd approve of setting up a private seraglio. She was thinking that Sandaree might be happier at Lydia Burton's establishment meanwhile, where her exotic looks and erotic knowledge could draw a fancy price. She'd have the company of the other women, which she was used to, and protection from scum like Lord James Danforth. "I'll talk to Harry. We'll find you a better situation, I promise. Until then, you might need this, so hide it somewhere safe." She handed Sandaree the coin from Miss Althorp's viscount at the painting judging.

The coin disappeared down the scanty bodice of Sandaree's bedgown; then she bowed, almost to the ground. "You are too good, my friend."

Simone felt her cheeks grow warm. "Not at all. I did not earn that one. But now you must come down with me. I know you can cover your cheek with cosmetics, and I can teach you how to play piquet."

They both knew she could never learn enough in time, but Simone had another idea. "I say, do you know how to play *vingt-et-un*?"

"Oh yes, the captain of the ship I sailed on taught me. The rules were simple, but the strategy was more complicated."

"Hurry, then. We'll have our chance."

While Sandaree left to change her clothes, Simone walked around, noting that a duke's son rated better accommodations than an earl's by-blow. This suite had its own small sitting room with a desk and bookshelves. She opened drawers and moved a few books, looking behind them, touching this and that. Then she joined Sandaree in the bedroom to watch her apply her face paints.

"I am curious. Does Danforth keep a journal?"

"A journal? Like a diary?"

Simone was looking around, but saw nothing suspicious. "A book he might write in, or read sometimes? Something he keeps private, like old letters? I ask because Harry has many private interests, and I wondered if all gentlemen did."

"I know of no letters or journals."

Simone could not search the dressing room, she knew, or look under the mattress. "He keeps nothing hidden?"

"I will keep my coin with me. The servants would find anything otherwise."

That was too bad. Simone still knelt and peeked under the bed, pretending to look for another coin she said she dropped. The servants hadn't found the dust there.

Claire had defeated three of the women by the time they returned to the Egyptian Room, where card tables had been set out. Now they were eleven players altogether, after Simone and Sandaree collected their ten red markers from Lord Gorham. The three losers, plus several of the others who had lost to Ruby and Alice, thought Simone's plan was an excellent one.

She went back to Lord Gorham, behind Claire's chair. "The competition is for cards, my lord, so we have decided to play twenty-one. After we each lose at least three rounds of piquet."

Claire turned worse colors than Sandaree's cheek before she'd covered it. "No! We must all play piquet until all the money has changed hands, that is, until twelve."

"That was not in the rules."

Claire was losing her first hand against Alice, so she threw her cards down. "I make the rules."

"Come now, my pet," Gorham said, "you already have a tidy sum to get you that cottage in Cornwall. Why you want to go to that godforsaken place is beyond me, but you can win a goodly sum playing each of the other ladies once."

Claire looked around for Harry, but he hadn't returned yet. She might have throttled him if he had. But, no, Gorham was looking confused at her search of the room, so he did not know her secret. But Miss Royale might, and she might reveal Claire's past to the room if she did not get her way.

Claire ground her teeth. "Very well. But I wish a different dealer than one of the players." She did not trust any of them.

Mr. Anthony hadn't departed yet, although his former mistress had left in the shipowner's carriage with Madame Lecroix. He volunteered to deal for the other game.

Simone quickly lost her first piquet match to Ruby, who was a fast, daring player. She won the first of three hands with Claire, who was so angry she was not concentrating on her cards. After that, Simone lost the final two hands and decided Claire was memorizing the deck, since Simone could not spot any rough edges on the cards or extra markings. She lost all three hands to Alice, one on purpose. The baby needed that guinea more than Simone did.

Alice defeated Ruby, raising her odds with the gentlemen placing side bets on each game, and raising her confidence. Lord Comden stood at her back the entire time, bringing her tea and wine. Claire won over Ruby, but not easily. She said she wanted to play others before taking on poor Alice again, who should rest. Or go to bed, although Claire did not quite say that.

Alice had rested through the afternoon and was wide-awake. She smiled at Claire, who was at least ten years older. "I am quite ready, but if you need a nap, I can wait."

Claire turned another shade of purple, which truly clashed with her red gown.

Ruby found a few more partners for piquet after she admitted losing her last two matches. She won two and lost two, to the actress and the pianoforte player. "It's not so easy when you don't have your own deck," she confessed.

Sandaree lost all three of her piquet matches, even to

Daisy, who had just learned the game that week. The others were even, markers passing back and forth.

While the piquet matches were conducted in silence except for murmurings from the gentlemen who watched and wagered, the *vingt-et-un* games proceeded with shouts and laughs, moans and hurrahs. The gentlemen yelled "stay" or "take," sometimes both at once. Some of the women placed two markers when they thought they had a good hand. The ballet dancer placed all six of her remaining markers on one bet, so she could go up to bed. She was performing tomorrow, she claimed, and needed her rest. More likely she was tired after her tryst with Danforth, Simone assumed, looking to see if Sir Chauncey had noticed his mistress's defection. He was keeping company with a decanter of cognac.

That pot was split between Sandaree and Simone.

Simone did not know Harry had returned until someone placed his fingers on the nape of her neck. She thought she'd know his scent and his touch anywhere, even if she forgot that nine and eight made seventeen. She lost that deal and he laughed. Then he shook his head to her silent question: No, he had not learned anything. He raised his eyebrow at the stack of red markers in front of her. She shook her head. No, she had not cheated.

They played on, until some of the women were down to their last markers. A few tossed those in, choosing to lose sooner rather than later. Mr. Anthony seemed to be giving better cards to Sandaree, Simone thought, but couldn't believe a gentleman with his fortune would cheat. Danforth, who would, she was sure, was staying close to Sandaree now, showing more interest in his mistress—or in getting his hands on her markers—than he had shown since the first day.

Finally only five players remained: Ruby, Alice,

Simone, Sandaree, and Claire. Twenty minutes remained on the mantel clock. Claire had yet to replay Alice at piquet, and a large crowd gathered to watch the two best players. The other three women played another round of *vingt-et-un*, which Sandaree won. They went to watch the piquet match, too.

Claire took the first hand.

Alice took the second.

The only sound in the room was Sir Chauncey's snoring. Then the clock struck twelve.

"Damn," someone said. "It's a draw. All bets are off."

Lord Comden helped Alice to her feet while Claire smiled graciously at all the congratulations and patted her pile of markers. She, Alice, and Sandaree obviously had the most. Ruby had sixteen and Simone nine. Lord Ellsworth and Mr. Anthony counted the others. To no one's surprise, Claire won.

Simone was happy that Alice came in second with thirty-six and Sandaree third with twenty-eight. She was happier still when Sandaree asked Mr. Anthony to hold the guineas for her, after Lord Gorham exchanged them.

But Simone was doing calculations in her head, and something was not right. "There were eleven of us," she told Harry. "So there should be one hundred and ten red markers. But I count one hundred and fourteen."

The two gentlemen checked their score sheets. Then Miss Hanson's banker came over to study the results. Then they called for Lord Gorham, who announced in funereal tones that there seemed to be a discrepancy.

When everyone gathered around, the banker stood by Simone, telling her that he admired a gal with a quick mind. He admired her bosom, too, never taking his eyes off it. Harry stepped between them.

Lord Gorham looked five years older than he had five

minutes ago. "Somehow the servants must have miscounted when they handed the markers out."

Harry reached into his pocket for a peppermint drop. No one else believed Gorham, either.

"It seems Miss Alice Morrow and my dear Claire are tied for first place. I suggest a final play-off round."

"I think someone ought to be disqualified," Alice's Lord Comden said, but Gorham glared at him.

"It was an unintentional error, easily resolved."

Harry pulled another peppermint from his pocket. "For a, um, an upset stomach, don't you know," he told Simone when she gave him a quizzical look.

Sir Chauncey was awake and too hungry to wait for three hands. "I say let them cut the cards. No chance of miscounting, eh?" he asked, with a snicker. Claire worried she'd lose to the peagoose who let herself get pregnant, her own history aside, so she readily agreed. Simone thought Alice should demand the game she could win, but the young woman hastily agreed to the simpler solution, rather than offend their scowling hosts.

Lord Ellsworth called for a new deck. Alice cut first, a king. Lord Gorham groaned. The betting among the men grew louder.

For the first time in anyone's memory, except perhaps Gorham's, a bead of sweat formed on Claire's forehead. Her card was a six.

"Supper is waiting in the dining room," the marquis quickly announced, leading his lady off in that direction before she threw the deck, the clock, or the Egyptian mummy in the corner.

As usual, Simone went up to bed first, while Harry stayed behind with some of the hard-drinking, hard-gambling men who were not, it seemed, hardened

Romeos. Mr. Anthony, Lord Ellsworth, and Sir Chauncey sat in Gorham's library, along with a few others whose ladybirds were on their way back to London, were too tired, or had a headache. That was not what they were paying the females for, but at least the brandy was good.

Danforth did not join them, either because he preferred his mistress—or Sir Chauncey's—or disdained the company of bankers or bastards.

No one grumbled about the government, the condition of Europe, or the defeat of Napoleon. They discussed nothing but the cards, the coming horse race, and what a good cook Gorham employed, dammit.

Harry was thoroughly frustrated, and more so when he went up to his bedchamber and saw his beautiful governess propped up in bed with a book in her hands. A scrap of pink lace showed at her shoulders over the covers, and a long flame-colored braid lay atop the blankets. Lud, she was gorgeous. And she'd done exactly what he'd asked of her, created a stir. No one was going to forget they were here at the house party. He was never going to forget it, either.

He headed toward the dressing room to find his robe, which he intended to discard as soon as possible. Then he spotted Mr. Black and a pile of blankets on the floor by the hearth. "Ah, it was kind of you to bring the dog in here before Metlock carved him up. I feared he'd resign rather than share his bedchamber in the attic. And you've made Blackie a comfortable bed, too."

"That's not for the dog; it's for you."

"Me? What did I do? I thought we were beyond such—"

"We have gone beyond the line, that's where we've gone. And we are not going any further."

He could taste the sweet truth of that—and his own

bitter disappointment. Not one to give up easily, he set out to change her mind. "Very well, my dear, we shall go back to sleeping on separate sides of the bed. Shall I fetch the fireplace poker?"

"That did no good before, did it? No, you are too much of a rake for me to trust in the same room, much less the same bed. I'd feel safer sleeping with Mr. Black than with such a hardened seducer."

"Me?" he asked again. "A seducer? I did not hear you complain or tell me to stop last night."

Simone nodded. "Exactly. You are very good at what you do."

He couldn't find a spy or a blackmailer. "What was it I did? I kept my word. You kept your virginity."

Now she put the book down and crossed her arms in front of her chest, denying him even that glimpse of pink paradise. "I did not keep my self-esteem. I am not blaming you entirely, you must understand. I do not trust myself any more than I trust you. To be completely truthful, I wanted you to make love to me."

"And now you do not?"

"Now I want more, more than I could live with later. You prize honesty, Mr. Harry Harmon. Well, here is the truth: You make me feel things I ought not. Your touch stirs my blood. Your kisses steal my wits."

"You are saying the devil made you kiss me back?"

"You are the devil, you know, for making me want you."

"I suppose that is a compliment, but it sure as hell is cold comfort."

She threw him another blanket.

Chapter Twenty

D amn, she was right. He was the one who had taken advantage of her innocence and inexperience. Hell, he was older and wiser, and should have used his head, as much as any man could use his senses with his nethers in a knot. He should have left her alone in her virginal purity, in her governess primness, in her big, soft, warm bed.

Damn, he'd do it again, make her moan with pleasure, cry out in passion, fall asleep in his arms. He'd take all she let him, give everything he had. He wouldn't chance creating a child—the world had enough bastards, lud knew—but he'd teach her and coax her and . . . and damn, he was aroused just thinking about making love to her. Something about the woman set him on fire and burned his good intentions to a crisp. Burned his loins—hell, he never understood where his loins were until she smiled at him. Burned his brains.

What brains? Here he was sighing, his manhood stirring, over a hired female. She was at Gorham's to make money; he was here to solve problems, not cause them for her or for himself. He did not have a place for her in his life, not now, not ever. She wanted a respectable future for her and her brother. He was never going to have one.

She would hate his world, hate him for dragging her into danger she did not understand, could never understand. He was a freak of nature as much as a two-headed chicken or an albino cow, only rarer. Only three other men shared his oddity: his father, his legitimate half brother, Rex, and his cousin Daniel. That was all, in the entire universe, as far as he knew. It was far too soon to know about Rex's infant son.

If the boy bred true, he could blame luck and the Royce blood for making him recognize lies on someone's lips. Maybe the babe could hear the truth like his grandfather, or see it in colors like Rex. Harry hoped the babe would be spared his own bad tastes of dishonesty, and, lud, Daniel's rashes.

Simone would be horrified, the same as the Countess of Royce had been. His father's legal wife had left the earl and her son, because she could not live with their difference from the rest of the world.

Not so long ago the truth of Harry's birth—not his bastardy but his talent—would have seen him burned at the stake, accused of wizardry or dealing with the devil. Even in this modern age, he'd be shunned, ostracized, or imprisoned, locked in an asylum, feared by the innocent and guilty alike. No one wanted to believe he could see behind their words to the truth. Or taste it, which had to be more strange, more unbelievable.

He could hide the knack, hide the bitter taste with rum balls and peppermint drops, except the power of truthseeing went with the responsibility to use it for the good of mankind. Almost as much a burden as the Royce gift, that altruism meant all the Royce men had a need to put their special skill to use. They were destined to serve the country that had given them a title, great wealth, influence, and, in Harry's case, purpose and a way to repay the world for the opportunities he'd had.

He did not blame Lord Royce for his bastardy; rather he thanked the earl for providing for him, educating him, showing him what a gentleman was made of, and giving him the gift of the truth.

He was born to serve his country. All the Royce men were. National treasures, that's what Lord Wellington had called them. Daniel might fight it, but he'd find a way to be of use, now that the army was finished with him. England was not finished with Harry yet. He had a job to do right now.

A national treasure? Hell, he'd be a national disgrace if he couldn't get his ballocks farther than a governess's bed.

So Harry did what he should have done the first night they'd arrived at Griffin Woods Manor. He went back to Gorham's library, where almost a dozen men were smoking and drinking and boasting of their successes, in business and the bedchamber. And he asked questions.

No more subtlety for him. No more waiting to hear a misspoken word or sending his servants to listen at keyholes. He stood in the center of the library, with its smoke and old books and old leather and men showing a day's beard. He looked at each of them in turn and asked: "Anyone here know about a plot to overthrow the government or help Napoleon escape?"

He couldn't be more blunt, and the others couldn't be more surprised. Sir Chauncey even set his glass aside long enough to say, "The war's over at last, thanks be. We've had enough of that argle-bargle."

True.

Gorham said he'd have heard if anyone in the neighborhood was stirring up unrest or bad feelings.

True.

Lords Comden, Ellsworth, and Caldwell said they knew nothing of any such rumors.

True.

Mr. Bowman and the baronet shook their heads.

"Yes or no," Harry demanded. Everyone stared at him, but both gentlemen said no, they knew nothing of any subversive plots, thank goodness.

Captain Entwhistle cursed at the idea of going back to war. "The country's had enough."

The banker said such talk was bad for business. He did not like speaking of it.

True and true.

Harry turned to the last gentleman in the room, Mr. Anthony of the Trading Company. The nabob was older than most of the others, with lined cheeks and tanned skin from the Indian sun. He had one gouty foot up on a hassock, and he swirled the cognac he should not have been drinking around in his glass. He looked at Harry and said, "Madame Lecroix."

"Eloise, who played the violin tonight?"

"Two of her brothers died fighting the English. So did her father, Jacques Casselle, a gun dealer. She hates Britain."

"How do you know?" Harry asked, furious no one had known about the brothers or the Frenchwoman's maiden name. He knew all about Jacques Casselle, and had personally ordered his execution.

"She and Mimi became friends," Anthony said, naming the mistress he'd sent back to London. "Even after Eloise realized Mimi was no more French than a French poodle in Hyde Park. They practiced together for tonight's performance. They talked. I listened, but I didn't think anything much of it. Women's chatter, you know. If anyone was going to start trouble, though, she'd be my bet."

"Did Gollup know?" The shipbuilder was English born and bred; Harry's sources had told him that much.

"Eloise's father was Gollup's partner. I suspected Gollup was running guns in his trading ships, along with other contraband. That's how he became so rich."

Anthony's words tasted true, dammit, and none of them were in the information Harry had. "Were they really lovers, the Frenchwoman and the merchant?"

Anthony shrugged. "His wife is pregnant. I know that much."

So did Harry, but that didn't mean they hadn't come here to plot and plan, or to trade information or pass notes to others. Or to find him, for revenge.

"Didn't you think you ought to tell someone your suspicions?"

"As I said, women cluck like hens. I put about as much stock in their gabble as I'd do in a chicken's. I did send a note to a chap at Whitehall called Major Harrison. I heard he could get a message to a shadowy figure they call the Aide, who's in charge of cloak-and-dagger stuff for the government. Secret, don't you know."

Now everyone knew. Anthony's note was likely on Harry's desk right now, while Eloise and Gollup were on their way to London.

Damn, damn, damn.

Harry accepted a glass of brandy while he thought.

They had to be intercepted. There was no choice, unless he wanted to chance losing Eloise and her plans on one of Gollup's sailing ships. He could have Gorham call out the stables and mount these swells to go after them. They couldn't be all that far away, not with the women needing to pack, the coach traveling in the dark, a stop for supper if he was lucky. He looked around the room, at

Anthony with his foot propped up, Ellsworth with his cane, Sir Chauncey in his cups as usual.

Rather than count on the rest of the useless aristocrats in the room, he could roust up the magistrate and the local sheriff to go halt the carriage in the name of the Crown, but on whose authority? Major Harrison's? The Aide's? Harry Harmon had none. He'd be giving up his identity, his other plans, his future.

No, he'd do better to get word to Whitehall immediately and let his trusted staff handle this. They could wait at Gollup's house and Eloise's. Or Mimi's, when they dropped her off. The problem was, Gorham's servants couldn't be trusted with such a message. Jeremy Judd couldn't get to the right people. Daniel, who could, was in the village, but likely in a stupor or some barmaid's bed. And no one could get there fast enough, or with such effect as he could himself.

Before he left the library, feigning a yawn, he asked one more question: "Does anyone know anything about blackmail letters?"

No one knew anything, and Danforth was not in the room.

"Traitors, spies, extortionists? Lud, what's next on your list of gossip, Harry?" Gorham asked. "Assassinations?"

Exactly.

At the stables, he told a drowsy groom that he was going into the village to spend time with his cousin Mr. Stamfield. He waved the boy off, saying he'd saddle his own horse.

He put the saddle on the bay gelding, not his stallion, who was too well-known and easily recognized. Neither Harry Harmon nor his horse could be seen on the road to London or at an arrest in the city. The bay was not as fast, but had stamina and a good heart. He wouldn't be such a handful as Fidus, besides.

He stopped in the village, as he'd told the groom he would, but only long enough to drag Daniel out of a card game and tell him what happened.

"Watch after Noma if I don't return by morning."

"What about searching Danforth's rooms at the manor?"

"No, we have time. The next demand is not due until after the house party. You stay out of trouble. Make sure the woman does, too."

He rode like the wind, in the wind and occasional rain. He kept his hat pulled low, his muffler high, but wore no beard or mustache. The dark was his disguise tonight.

Gollup's coach was big and ornate, easily recognized by hostlers along the way, especially with few other travelers out on so moonless a night. He was lucky to spot the inn where they'd stopped to change horses and stayed for a late supper. He kept pace with them afterward, then passed them on the outskirts of London, waiting to be certain they were not headed toward the docks. Why should they be, when they had no idea they were being followed or even under suspicion? Then he watched to see if they took Mimi home first. They did.

He knew the address of the love nest on Clarges Street where Gollup kept Madame Lecroix. That, at least, was in the dossier of house-party attendees. He also knew the shipowner would not take Eloise home to his own place on Russell Square, not to meet his pregnant wife, who was not expecting him for a few more days.

Harry raced through Town to McCann's Club, to a secret back door hidden down an alley under a fallen shed that was big enough to hide a horse. Inside he found the manager, Frank Harrison, one of his adopted brothers, and issued a string of orders. He watched in the shadows of Frank's office as trusted employees ran out to army barracks, Whitehall, and various members of the intelligence department.

When the coded messages were sent off, Harry shook Frank's hand and said, "It's almost over."

"We'll all pray it is."

Harry headed the bay gelding toward Clarges Street.

The Horse Guard was already there. Whitehall was there. Bow Street was there. Harry Harmon wasn't, not that anyone saw. No one saw him, but he saw the Frenchwoman taken out in manacles, screaming about death to Englishmen. Oh, she was guilty all right, but of what? She'd be kept in confinement until he sent Daniel back to question her, to find the truth. Gollup was babbling, also in handcuffs. The greedy fool sold guns to his country's enemy, slept with his dead partner's daughter, and left his own pregnant wife behind. He ought to hang, but most likely his fortune could buy him exile instead. Harry wondered what the wife would do.

The gelding had rested while he watched, so Harry headed back, but without the urgent speed. He dared not stop at his place in Kensington because he had to be at Gorham's before anyone missed him except Simone, but he stopped at Daniel's room at the inn first.

His knock on the door sent a half-dressed wench rushing past him.

"Idiot, you are going to end with the pox."

Daniel wore a towel and a grin. "No, they are good clean girls."

Harry peered around the room to make sure it was empty. "They? You had more than one tonight?"

Daniel's grin grew wider.

"Then you'll litter the countryside with bastards. I'll

have you drawn and quartered, I swear, if you get one of your doxies with child."

"That won't happen. Sponges, don't you know."

Harry knew how fallible such preventatives were. He was proof. "You're not leaving a babe without a name, damn you. I'll make you marry her, whether she's a tavern bawd or a royal princess."

"You and who else, little cousin?"

"Me and my sword, you lummox. Now get dressed. I need you in London."

"I'm here for the party, remember."

So Harry told him about the arrests in London. Then he told Daniel that he had to go interrogate the woman so they got the rest of the conspirators.

"Hell, no. I'm not in the army anymore. I'm not one of your Inquisitors anymore, either. I'm not going, by Hades."

Daniel and his cousin Rexford had saved countless soldiers' lives by getting the truth from French prisoners. They were commended by the generals, and feared by everyone else. "I am not asking you to intimidate the female. Just listen, find out if she's naming all her coconspirators, admitting to the real plans they had."

"I don't care if she is or not. The war is over. Whitehall has her. They'll get to the bottom of the mess without your help or mine."

"That's not good enough, and you know it. How can anyone else know if she's lying?" Harry tossed a shirt from the floor at Daniel. "Get dressed."

Daniel tossed the shirt onto the bed. "I can't go. I've got too much money on the horse race. Have to cheer on Miss Ryland—Miss Royale."

Harry'd forgotten the race was today. "What time is it set for?"

"Eleven. That's not many hours away, so let me get my rest. Now that you've scared away my bed warmer, the least you can do is leave me in peace."

"Very well, you can go up to London after the race. Madame Lecroix will keep. She might even be more amenable to talking after a few hours of solitude. I'll send messages that you are coming."

"Deuce take it, I said no, Harry."

Daniel started to turn toward the bed, but he stopped when he felt a knife at his throat. "You wouldn't."

"Do you dare to find out? If I have to go back to London, the rest of my life will be spent looking over my shoulder, and it will be a damned short life at that. If Harry Harmon is not at Gorham's while Major Harrison is in London, this whole mare's nest"—he gestured with the knife to indicate Richmond, hiring a mistress, acting like a rake—"would be for nothing." Except Simone was something. "You might be willing to throw away your gifts, but I am not willing to let you."

"But the Lecroix female will lie. Criminals always do. I'll get such a rash it won't go away by the time of the ball. I was invited, you know. Looking forward to it, too."

"Why, so you can step on more females' toes? That's not for two more days anyway. You'll be back. Metlock can cover your rash."

"Your valet can't take away the itch, can he?"

Harry was tired of arguing. "I'll let you dance with Noma."

"She already promised me a waltz. How about if you sell me Fidus? Your stallion is big enough to carry my weight."

"He's big enough, but you're not rider enough to handle him." He stepped out of range of Daniel's fists after that insult. "But I will give you one of his colts. Rex has a mare we want to—"

"Done."

Harry put the gelding away himself, rewarding the bay for a job well-done.

He went into the manor through the kitchen, where the cook was just taking bread out of the ovens for the servants' breakfast. He tossed her a coin and took one with him.

The night footman in the hall handed him several sealed messages that had just been brought by riders.

"Sick relative," he explained when the footman looked curious enough to ask questions, or mention the notes to his fellow servants. "More will be coming. Bring them up to my room, there's a good fellow." Harry tossed another coin into another eager hand before carrying his letters up the stairs. He read by a candle left burning in the corridor where his room was, where Simone was sleeping, he hoped.

The shipowner was the one doing all the talking, the Aide's assistant wrote; Gollup was blaming Eloise Lecroix for everything, naming others involved. The Home Secretary was pleased.

So was Harry. He was also exhausted. He'd stayed up the whole night before, loving Simone, then watching her as she slept. The night before that, he'd been up planning, laying his trap. Now it was almost dawn and all he wanted was his bed. And Simone. He'd want her from the grave, he thought.

Just to hold her would be enough. Just to sleep next to her, to hear her breathing, that's all he wanted.

He ate a chunk of warm bread to get rid of the bad taste. He never could lie to himself, but he told himself he was a realistic man and a decent one. He might want her, but knowing he could not have her, he could control his baser instincts. He would.

Until he saw the shape on the bed next to her. In his spot. The knife was back in his hand in an instant. He never thought he could kill a man in peacetime.

Or a dog. Mr. Black woofed a sleepy welcome and wagged his tail.

Hell, no. If he couldn't sleep next to Simone, neither could the dog. Harry might give up the soft bed to save his honor, not to save a flea hound from the floor. He ordered the dog down. "And not on my blankets near the fireplace, either." He sat on the mattress to take off his boots, wishing for Metlock, who would be bringing his shaving water all too soon. The effort was too much. Harry leaned back and fell asleep, next to Simone. He didn't even awaken when the dog jumped back up and ate the rest of the bread.

Chapter Twenty-one

Simone awoke to feel hot breath on her neck, and a weight against her right side. "I told you, dogs do not belong on the bed, Blackie. They don't even belong in the house, but you're not welcome anywhere else."

Mr. Black licked her cheek—on her left side. Simone rolled over with a start. She hadn't heard Harry come back in, or change his clothes.

He hadn't. He'd fallen asleep on top of the covers, in his shirt and breeches and boots. He'd come to her bed in boots? He'd also come unshaven and unwashed, smelling of horse and spirits and sweat. He looked like a libertine who had stayed out all night, which was what he was and what he had done, the lizard. She sniffed the air for the scent of perfume, but detected only damp wool and dog. Good. Her honorable Harry would not shame her by going to another woman after she'd refused him her bed. Would he?

The very idea of him tomcatting like some of the other men made her shake him harder than she'd intended. "Where were you?"

He rolled over, proving why he was better at managing the Intelligence Division from an office than he would have been as a spy in the field. He'd be shot his first morning.

Simone shook him again. "Get up. We have a busy day."

He made a gurgling sound—or was that the dog, wanting to go out?—but he did not move.

"Harry, it's the race day. And you promised to teach me billiards this morning before anyone else is up. That contest is scheduled for tonight after the entertainment."

"Mm. Start without me."

"I can't, you dunce. I do not know how." When she got no response, she tried to arouse his jealousy. After all, it worked on her. "Maybe I'll get one of the other gentlemen to teach me."

"Fine. You do that, sweetings."

She put her hand to his forehead. "Are you sick?"

Harry pulled a pillow over his head, sending a cloud of bread crumbs over the sheets. That showed Simone how much he cared about her concerns and her comfort. Why should he, anyway? He'd hired her only to impress his friends. She ignored all his blather about national security and personal danger as more weapons in a rake's arsenal. The silver-tongued devil could get a gullible female like Simone to believe anything he said, and permit any liberties he chose to take. She tossed her own pillow atop his head. "Take that, you dastard."

She didn't ring for Sarah, not wanting the girl to see her master so . . . so sunk in dissipation. She didn't want anyone to know he'd spent the night elsewhere, either. She had her pride. She found a morning gown she could fasten for herself.

Many of the gentlemen must have stayed up late, too, for few of them were in the breakfast room when Simone went in. Claire was, for the first time since Simone had arrived. She must be thinking about the race also, Simone decided, to be up so early. Claire was dressed perfectly, every black hair in place, unlike Simone's hastily coiled braid. Simone decided not to stay to watch Lord Ellsworth and Mr. Anthony fawn over their hostess. She selected a sweet roll to take with her when she went out to the stable to speak with Jem.

Claire set her coffee cup down before she could leave. "Where is Harry?"

Simone dipped her head. "Good morning to you, too."

"I need to speak to him."

Simone couldn't keep the rancor from her voice. "So do I."

"Trouble?" Claire sounded delighted.

"Of course not. He's merely sleeping in this morning. I believe he stayed up with the gentlemen last night."

"No, he went to the village. His cousin Stamfield— half cousin, I suppose—has been making the acquaintance of every serving girl at the inn, I understand. My maid's sister's husband tends bar there."

Simone knew what Claire was implying, that Harry'd sought a soft bed to sleep in, and a soft woman to sleep beside. "Harry and Mr. Stamfield are very close friends."

Claire sank her teeth into an apple when she didn't get a rise out of Simone. "Are you ready for the race?"

"I will be."

"What about the entertainment? Have you decided what you will perform?"

"Not yet."

"Perhaps you should consider withdrawing from that event if you do not have confidence in any of your, ah, talents."

"Not yet," Simone repeated, putting an apple in her pocket to bring to the gelding. "But what did you wish to speak to Harry about? Perhaps I can help."

A shutter came down over Claire's face. She gestured that Simone should come closer so none of the gentlemen or servants could overhear. "Did he tell you?"

Tell her what, that he was going to the village? That was none of Claire's affair. "I do not know what you are speaking of."

Claire looked around to be certain they were private. "Did your lover tell you about my past?"

Ah, now Simone understood: Claudinia Colthopfer. "Yes, he mentioned something most people do not know. Do not concern yourself. I am no gossip."

"I need to know who else he told and how he found out."

Simone started to reassure the other woman that Harry was as close as a clam, but then she had an idea. "We have an hour or more before getting ready for the race. I'll tell you what Harry told me, if you teach me to play billiards."

"We are rivals. Why would I do such a thing?"

"Because you must know that I cannot learn enough in an hour to defeat you. I merely wish not to look like a fool. I might even find a game with one of the others who is worse. Sandaree never played, I'd wager."

"That poor girl," Claire said, the first kind words Simone had heard her utter. "Get her. I'll show both of you at the same time."

Simone couldn't tell if Claire was sabotaging the lessons by giving them the wrong rules or bad advice, but she and Sandaree had fun, with no male acting superior or making suggestive remarks when they leaned over the table. Sandaree was a natural at holding the stick, while Simone was better at figuring angles. Together they might have a chance. Claire actually laughed with them.

Before they left the billiards room to change into their riding habits, Claire held Simone back instead of letting her follow Sandaree. "Inform Harry that if he tells anyone else about my daughter, I will see every door in London shut to him and to you, Royce connection or not."

"You have a daughter?" Simone gasped. "Harry never told me."

Claire slammed the cue stick down so hard it shattered.

Simone drew her own conclusions. "I suppose Gorham does not know. And I also guess that is why you need the money so badly. I sympathize; I truly do. I have a young brother to support, so I understand. I would never tell anyone your secret. Neither would Harry. He's better at keeping secrets than anyone I have ever met."

She could tell, from the hard wooden ball that went sailing past her head into a painting of one of Gorham's ancestors, that Claire was not appeased. Claire would have used the information against a competitor; she obviously thought Simone would, too.

"I am not your enemy," Simone said before Claire could pick up another billiard ball to toss, although she did consider letting her hostess destroy the room so the contest could be canceled. "And Harry is trustworthy."

She repeated that to herself on her way to the bedchamber, where the trustworthy toad was still sleeping. She could hear Sarah in the dressing room, but Metlock must have taken the dog out. He must also have pulled Harry's boots off and covered him with a blanket so he did not appear quite as debauched. He still smelled of brandy, though, and Simone hoped he'd have the devil's own headache when he finally woke up. Which had to be now if he was to be any help to her at all.

"Harry, the race."

He succeeded in opening an eyelid, with great effort. "You don't have to ride. It's almost over."

"No, the race won't begin for another hour."

He yawned. "Not the race, the other."

"What other?"

"I can't tell you, not yet."

She watched him stretch, pulling his shirt taut over hard muscles, then remembered her grievances and Claire's daughter. "There is a great deal you do not tell me. But you can tell me about Gorham's racetrack. You said you were going to look it over yesterday. And you can tell me anything I need to know about pacing the gelding."

He rubbed at his eyes, then said, "You can't ride the bay. Too tired."

"I realize you are tired, but you have no one to blame but yourself, and you might try to help for my sake. Or for the bets you've placed, at the very least."

He put one foot out of the bed. "Not me. It's Lodestar who's spent. I had to ride him last night."

"You rode my horse?" The bay gelding was his, of course, but Simone could not bother with minor details right now.

"Gorham's bound to have something suitable. Ask him for a mount. Lud, I need a bath."

Simone almost gave him one with her dirty wash water.

In her elegant new habit, Simone should have felt confident, eager for the race. Instead, she was dreading it, with good cause. The male houseguests were all at the stables, along with many London bucks who had come for the race and the ball, plus a score of local residents. Simone could see Daniel Stamfield over the crowd; he was so much bigger than anyone else.

The females who were to ride were either flirting with the newcomers or listening to their protectors giving last-minute instructions. Not many of the original twenty courtesans were left to race.

Of the women still at Gorham's, Mary Connors, the actress, had never learned to ride, although, she told everyone, she could drive a high-perch phaeton to the inch. Pregnant Alice was suffering from morning sickness again, and Sandaree had ridden only elephants. Madeline Harbough, the circus rider, was departing for London as soon as she found enough cushions to put under her sore derriere, and the banker's companion, Miss Hanson, was going to practice the pianoforte for her evening's performance. That left Simone, Maura Doyle, Daisy, Ruby, in a ruby-colored habit, of course, and Sir Chauncey's—or Danforth's—ballerina, who was also going to perform tonight, but insisted on riding anyway. And Claire Hope.

Simone did not see Claire yet, but she knew there'd be no race if their hostess wasn't sure she could win.

Jem agreed that Lodestar was sluggish this morning. The bay could be ridden, and the gelding would give his all, but Miss Noma wouldn't have a chance to win and might injure the horse. Daniel agreed and went off to ask Gorham's head groom to find her a mount. His own horse was a slow, lumbering beast that suited him perfectly but would never win any race.

Daniel and the head groom brought out a pretty chestnut mare. She looked sound, Jem told her after inspecting her legs and back and neck. The stableman called her a sweet goer, Miss Hope's second-favorite mount.

Then Simone saw a groom lead out Claire's first favorite, and her dreams turned to horse droppings. A snow-white, part-Arabian mare pranced past her, looking like visiting royalty. Shouts of changing odds went up from the spectators.

Simone saw Claire now, looking as stunning as her

horse in a stark black habit to match her black hair, a white feather in her jockey-cap-type bonnet, and a ruffle of white lace at her throat. She and her horse were a matched set of rare, high-priced, and exquisite works of art.

Simone looked at the dainty mare she was to ride. Then she looked at Claire's long-necked, thin-legged beauty that was built for speed. She marched young Jem back into the stable.

"Saddle Fidus for me."

Daniel was leading the chestnut mare after Simone. He laughed. "You can't ride Harry's horse. He'll kill you. Harry, that is, or the horse might, too. No, Harry'll kill me. Fidus will toss you before you reach the starting line."

Simone put all her courage and confidence in four words: "I can ride him."

Jem said, "Pardon, Miss Noma, but Fidus has never carried a lady. He'd never take to a sidesaddle."

Simone raised one leg to show her split skirt. "Then it is a good thing I am prepared to ride astride."

The boy stood his ground. "You can't take the horse out, not without the governor's permission."

"I have it," Simone lied.

Daniel stepped behind the mare to scratch his groin. "No, you don't."

She crossed her arms over her chest. "I say I do. You did not speak to Harry an hour ago. I did."

"He wouldn't let you ride Fidus. Hell, he won't let me ride him."

"It is my word against yours."

Daniel couldn't say how he knew she was lying. He couldn't scratch his privates and tie her up on the borrowed mare at the same time, either. She was already striding down the long stable corridor to Fidus's stall at the end.

"Get the saddle now," she ordered. "Or I'll ride bare-back."

Daniel stopped itching. She was telling the truth, by Jupiter.

"Harry won't want me breaking my neck, will he?"

"He just might," Daniel told her, and that was the truth, too. No matter, the woman was as thickheaded and stubborn as the horse. Daniel knew he was defeated either way, which was why he usually avoided independent women. "I'll go get Harry."

"Fine. He ought to be in his bath by now." She was crooning to the big stallion, ordering another groom to take the mare away because she was distracting Fidus. The black liked the apple she'd brought for the bay gelding, and didn't put up any fuss when Jem tightened his girth on a lighter, smaller saddle he'd found. The boy warned her that Fidus didn't like the whip. Simone set hers aside and took the reins to lead him out, still talking quietly, telling Fidus how handsome he was, how he was going to help her win a new life, how proud Harry would be. "You believe me, don't you?"

A hush fell over the crowd; then there was a mad scramble to record new bets. The ballet dancer tried to reach Lord Gorham, to withdraw from the race, but Claire blocked her way as she pushed forward to confront Simone.

"You cannot ride that horse."

"Oh, yes, I can. I can ride anything. My grandfather was a horse trader and trainer. He taught me."

Danforth went to put his money on Claire. "No filthy Gypsy ought to be allowed among decent people," Simone heard him mutter. Simone glared and Claire curled her lip at the duke's wastrel son who kept poor Sandaree a near slave.

Then Claire recalled the issue at hand. "You cannot sit astride in a manner unsuitable to a female. This was supposed to be a test of ladylike accomplishments."

"Then you should have invited ladies. But you did not, knowing they would not have come. I did. I am in the contest. I shall ride."

Fidus did not like the commotion. According to Daniel, he did not like anything or anyone but Harry. Simone spoke softly to him again, stroking his ear, and had Jem give her a leg up. The poor boy looked to be near tears, but he did his job, holding the horse by the halter in case Fidus tried to get rid of the new burden on his back before she was settled in the saddle.

"I'll just take him around the paddock a bit, to shake the fidgets out."

"The race is due to start in ten minutes." Claire pointed to the nearby track Gorham had built. "If you are not there, you are disqualified."

"Of course." Simone gave Fidus his head, and he almost took off a nearby gambler's. Fidus sailed over the fence of the paddock where the trick riding had been held. He kicked up dirt there, knocked over one of the flambeaux, did as many acrobatic moves as Maddy's horse, but without Simone's direction or decision. She stayed on his back by luck and skill and sheer determination. When her hat sailed off, she laughed and shook out her red hair to flow behind her. She fought Fidus for control, and won enough that she could turn him. Someone ran to open the paddock gate for her. This time the stallion went through it, instead of over.

"Good boy." He wasn't even breathing hard by the time they reached the starting line. Claire was.

The ballet dancer had pretended to swoon when she thought Simone would be thrown, so she could collapse into Danforth's arms rather than race. Sandaree bowed low to Simone from outside the oval ring. Jem was as white as a ghost. Harry hadn't come.

Harry dressed, looked at the clock, and knew he had a few minutes. From a window at the end of the hall he could see the large crowd around the stables, Gorham's servants, villagers, and guests. He could not see Simone over the heads of the men, and hoped she had not lost the opportunity to ride. He regretted her disappointment, but that couldn't be helped. He did see the Indian girl in her distinctive dress standing alone, then spotted Danforth placing bets with a badly dressed man in a straw hat. So he went and searched Danforth's rooms.

He did not have time to be as thorough as he wished, but he found nothing, no hiding places, no journals or letters. Damn. Then he heard a loud cheer from outside, so he left and loped off around the house, past the stables, and to the track just in time to see Gorham raise his pistol.

Oh, hell.

He couldn't get there fast enough to stop them. Couldn't watch. Couldn't not watch. Couldn't breathe. Bloody, bloody hell.

Daniel hurried over to him. "I tried. I swear, I tried. Then I looked everywhere for you."

Gorham fired in the air. The horses kicked up so much dust, no one could see the start, only a white streak shooting ahead, Claire's Arabian. Then four other horses set out to chase them twice around the oval. Simone and Fidus were left at the starting line, with the black stallion trying to leave the ring altogether. Fidus was circling, crow-hopping, rearing. The crowd groaned. Harry tasted blood in his mouth from where he'd bitten his lip.

Harry watched Simone lean over his horse's shoulder

and talk to him. Whatever she said must have worked because Fidus gathered himself, took one mighty leap, then set off at a gallop on the right course. In seconds he flew past the slower horses, past the spectators for the first lap; then he slowed down. He did not seem to notice Simone's heels dig in any more than he would have noticed a gnat. The watchers shouted, as if to urge Fidus on. Or was that Harry yelling? His tongue was too numb to tell.

Claire was half the track ahead of them, on her final lap. She turned to look back to check her position, and then she held up her whip and waved it at Simone in triumph.

Fidus did not like whips.

He increased his speed a notch. Simone leaned forward, her weight on her legs, not his back, as if that mattered to the massive stallion. They gained ground.

Claire started using her whip on the Arabian. Fidus lengthened his stride. They were almost at the mare's tail.

"Don't you go getting ideas now," Simone warned when his ears pricked forward. "You are racing, not courting. And that is a lady. You have to ask permission. Now go impress her!"

He went. And defeated the mare by two lengths. Of course Simone couldn't bring him to a halt for another half of the oval, until Harry stepped onto the track in front of them.

Simone was afraid he'd be trampled. Then she saw the look on his face and was afraid he wouldn't be.

Chapter Twenty-two

"A ren't you going to kiss me for congratulations? Everyone is watching."

Harry recalled the rest of the world, not just Simone and the horse and the dust and the pounding of his heart. He pulled her off the horse and into his arms. Then he kissed her, hard and fast, without tenderness. She tasted of track dirt and still he felt aroused.

"You're alive."

For now. Simone was glad he held her, because her bones were like butter. She'd never ridden so hard or so fast. Or so close to death. Between the race and his kiss, she'd never felt so exhilarated, so sure she was right where she belonged: in his arms, in the winner's circle. "I won!"

"We'll talk about that later," Harry said when well-wishers came toward them. He put his arm around her in case she thought to escape, and tried to put a smile on his face for the spectators. When Jeremy came to take Fidus, Harry stopped trying to look delighted that his hired companion had stolen his horse from right under his servant's nose. "I'll talk to you later also."

"She told me and Mr. Stamfield that you gave permission."

"And you believed her?" He turned to where Daniel was taking Fidus's other side, but not even the stallion's great size could hide Daniel from Harry's piercing blue eyes. "*You* believed her?"

"Hell, no, but what could I say? Asides, you should have been there to stop her. Your horse, your lady and all."

Harry was already annoyed with himself for letting the female out of his sight, especially when he knew she was counting on the race to add to her nest egg. "Aren't you expected somewhere?" he asked Daniel. "That family business we spoke of last night?"

With one more look at his furious cousin, Daniel decided it was time for him to leave as soon as he collected his winnings, and hers.

"You bet on the gelding?" Harry asked her.

"I bet on myself."

Daniel returned with a fistful of brass that he poured into Simone's hat, which someone had recovered for her. The black bonnet couldn't be worn again and its feather was missing altogether, but Simone thought it looked far more beautiful as a money pouch than it did on her head.

Daniel claimed an appointment in London, made a hasty bow in light of his cousin's blue-dagger glance, and promised to be back for the ball.

Lord Gorham brought Simone the winner's heavy leather purse and kissed the air above her smelly riding glove. "Good race, Miss Royale, even if it cost me a fortune and Claire's goodwill." He sighed. "Not for the first time, or the last, I suppose. My darling is not a good loser, I fear. Harry, I'll be speaking to you about using your stallion as stud. Both of you owe me that for cutting up my peace."

Harry did not say yes or no, but Simone whispered to Gorham: "I promised Fidus the mare. That's why he ran so fast."

Gorham went away laughing, determined to avoid his not-so-darling, smoldering mistress for the rest of the day.

Three men handed Harry his winnings; then the straw-hatted oddsmaker brought him more.

"You wagered on me?"

"I thought I was betting on my gelding." He checked to see the count was right, then added it to the pile in Simone's bonnet. She kept one hand beneath the hat, in case the stitching gave way under the weight of all the pound notes and gold and silver coins. She had no idea how much money was in her hands, but she was rich!

"You're giving your winnings to me?"

"No, I am paying in advance for flowers for your funeral if you ever do anything that crazy again. Devil take it, Si—sweetheart, I thought you were going to be killed any second."

"You care?"

Now that Harry was a little calmer—and had a glass of wine in his hand from the victory toast—he admitted he cared. "A broken neck could ruin all my plans. I'd have no excuse for staying on till the end of the party next week."

"No, you care." Simone stood on her toes and kissed him again, softly, slowly. "Say it."

"I care." The words tasted as sweet as her lips, without the track dirt.

Luncheon was a delight for everyone. Claire did not attend. Without the hostess to maintain the manners of polite society, the company relaxed. They talked across the table, used their fingers to pass rolls, and speculated on plans for the afternoon.

Alice thought they ought to hold the billiards tournament without Claire, so someone else had a chance to win. Since she'd spent half her life in a gaming hell, Alice was confident of her skill, if the baby did not get in the way. Ruby was all for the archery contest. She'd been practicing.

Simone felt she had to discourage them. Holding either event would not be fair to Miss Hope. Everyone laughed to think of Claire and fairness in the same breath, even Lord Gorham at the head of the table.

He raised his glass to her: "A real lady." Since she won, he said, she ought to decide the afternoon's activity.

Simone wanted nothing more than to spend the time with Harry. She thought about getting lost in the famous maze with him, but knew the others had no desire to tromp through high hedges for no prize. Besides, Miss Susan Baylor announced that she had to practice her ballet routine, with Miss Hanson at the pianoforte. Maura Doyle giggled and said she was also going to dance that evening, an Irish jig, to her own singing. She supposed, she said with another giggle directed to her lover, Lord Caldwell, that she ought to practice.

If those two practiced the jig that afternoon, pigs would sprout wings. Simone ignored the smirks and titters and her own desire to be with Harry. "Does anyone play chess?"

That received more hoots of laughter. What did she think this was, a club for retired generals? Only Gorham and Harry and Captain Entwhistle were willing to play. Simone's next suggestion was a drive to the nearby village. She'd heard it was market day, with farmers and peddlers bringing their wares to the little town. She wanted to speak to Harry first, but she finally had an idea for her performance and needed to make a few purchases. For the first time in her life, she had more than pennies to spend on herself without worrying about rent or food or Auggie's education. In fact, she'd send him a pound note that very day, as an early birthday gift.

The women were happy at the chance to shop for fripperies. The quality of the goods could never match that in
London shops, they all agreed, but they might as well
look for a new ribbon or a bit of lace trimming, perhaps
a bonnet if one of the local women was talented. Alice
said she needed to start buying fabric for baby clothes,
and Daisy offered to help with the sewing. Sandaree
really needed a warmer cloak, so she asked Lord Gorham
for some of her money that he was holding. She did not
wish to get further in debt to Lord James Danforth. Miss
Baylor decided she needed no practice; she needed a new
feather for her costume more. Miss Hanson had already
memorized the ballet piece, and thought she could get her
banker to fund a new pair of gloves, at the least. Six pairs
of eyes lit up at the prospect of finding a local jewelry
store.

The gentlemen were not as enthusiastic about the proposed jaunt, once they heard the ladies' eagerness to
spend their blunt. Lord Gorham urged them on with hints
of the excellence of the local pub's ale, and the chance of
prime horseflesh for sale.

Lord Gorham was going to stay behind to help Claire
get over her headache—someone cleared his throat;
Maura giggled—but he sent for carriages to transport his
guests, and a wagon for their purchases.

Harry regretted that he had too much correspondence
to deal with, so could not go along.

"Are you still angry at me?" Simone wanted to know.
She'd thought they could speak about last night, the race,
and her performance while walking through the village.

"Not at all," he said, but his mouth was twisted in the
way Simone recognized as evidence of his displeasure.
"In fact, buy yourself something from me." He reached
into his pocket.

She stopped him with a hand on his arm and for a moment she could see the old Harry of her imagination, laughing and holding her hand. She hoped she had not lost that dream altogether with her daring, and her lie. "No, I am well-to-pass, remember. And you have done so much already. I shall buy you a present. Do you need anything?"

"Peppermint drops."

"For your digestion?"

"For my sanity."

Before she left, Simone handed him her spare reticule that was full of her winnings, minus what she thought she might need that afternoon. "Not that I do not trust the servants, but I cannot feel right leaving such a sum lying about."

He took the heavy bag and watched her go, regretting not being at her side. He'd like to purchase her a new riding hat, a new necklace, a horse of her own, a pair of silk stockings he could ease down her shapely legs. The reticule fell to the floor.

"A lovely woman," Gorham noted while Harry recovered the purse and his composure.

"Very."

"A cut above your usual companion at Lydia Burton's, eh?"

"I am beginning to think Miss Noma Royale is a cut above everyone's companion, Miss Hope excepted, of course."

"Too bad she's damaged goods," Gorham said, speaking more to himself than to Harry, thinking more of Claire than Simone. "She'd make a deuced good wife."

"Ah, but would I make her—that is, any woman—a good husband? I doubt it. Nor do I consider Miss Royale in any way imperfect."

"No gentleman would marry her."

Harry set the reticule on a table. Gorham was blunt, but correct; no gentleman would wed Miss Royale. Scores of them would leap at the chance to marry Miss Simone Ryland, now that she was bringing a modest dowry with her. Money-grubbing maggots, all of them. Damn their eyes . . . and their married mothers.

He must have made some kind of angry noise, because Gorham said, "Love is a headache, isn't it?"

Harry fixed the older man in his sharp gaze. "Were we speaking of love?"

"Of course not." Gorham looked away and changed the subject. "I say, my staff tells me a flurry of messengers arrived for you during the race."

"A bit of business I need to tend to. Otherwise I would have gone into the village and helped the ladies spend their money."

"I thought you mentioned a sick relative."

"I believe my relation will recover." Daniel might come back from London with a rash, but he'd get the job done.

"The butler said one of the messengers looking for you was in uniform."

Harry toyed with the strings on Simone's bag. "Perhaps he meant the fellow was wearing Royce livery."

"No, he specifically said it was a military uniform."

"One of Rex's friends might have carried a note from him, I suppose." Rex might have known the lieutenant, so that was not entirely a lie. "Viscount Rexford was with the army not too long ago, you know." Harry did not wish to be rude to his host, but neither did he want to pursue that avenue of conversation. Gorham was too curious, too suspicious for Harry's comfort. Until Daniel got back, telling who Madame Lecroix named as coconspirators, Harry could not rule out anyone.

"I did write to the earl concerning that piece of property you are interested in," he said now, distracting Gorham. "But I have not heard yet. Perhaps his answer is in one of the posts." He patted his inside pocket, where papers rustled.

"Good, good. Be sure to let me know. Nice acreage, near my country seat. If nothing comes of that, however, I still need a manager for my Jamaica estate. Or I'll sell it to the right man, on good terms. To be honest, I could use the money."

Harry raised an eyebrow. He saw no sign of financial difficulties here, not in the number of servants, the quantity and quality of the food, the immaculate grounds and well-filled stables.

Gorham understood Harry's skepticism. "My wife's money pays for everything, don't you know. That other property would be all mine, to give away if I wish. I will not leave Claire empty-handed. Nor can I bear the idea of her living so far away in Cornwall, if she could afford it now that the contest is not going as planned. She has . . . responsibilities of her own."

Harry wondered how much Gorham knew about Claire's daughter. "Does she have a family to support like Miss Royale? Noma has a brother in school."

Gorham stared at a painting on the wall, one of Claire's watercolors of Griffin Manor on a stormy day. "I am not quite sure. Women like to keep their secrets, you know."

So did spies, and secrets far more important than Claire's right now. "Is there a place I could go to be private with my messages? More might be coming and I would not wish to disturb your household."

Gorham recommended the sewing room. Claire never used the small parlor, but it was comfortable and quiet.

"Thank you, that will be perfect. In the meantime, do

you think I could put this purse"—Simone's money—"in your safe? I cannot very well walk around with a lady's reticule, can I? And it is too large to stuff in my coat. My valet would give notice if I did. The dog is straining Metlock's patience enough as is."

Gorham sympathized with Harry at the demands of old retainers. "Of course. A lot of the chaps have put things there, the females, too. Their jewels and such. With so many strangers and their servants in the halls, no one can be too careful."

Harry followed Gorham into his library, then watched as the marquis pushed on a wall of books. He politely turned his back as the other man opened the safe. He put Simone's winnings in, and a smaller velvet pouch from his own pocket.

"A necklace," he told Gorham. "I am saving it to give Noma for the ball."

"Lud, that means I better find something spectacular for Claire." They both laughed; then the marquis said, "Dash it, it's obvious you are fond of the chit. You really ought to think of making your arrangement more permanent. Miss Royale is beautiful and smart and kind. And great with horses and dogs. What more do you want? It's not like she'd have to produce the next earl."

"That job belongs to Rexford's lady wife, and Amanda has succeeded with admirable speed."

"Dash it, you know what I am saying. Don't let such a rare opportunity pass you by. I know what I'm talking about. You're not getting any younger, and happiness is far more elusive than the next card game or horse race."

If Gorham could speak so personally, so could Harry. "Yet you are ready to give up Claire."

"No, I will never be ready. It is my wife who demands her gone. I married Harriet for money, you know, and for her family's bloodlines. I owe her some respect. My sons are at school, but they are old enough to understand now, old enough to hear the gossip. If Claire could wait a few years at that cottage of Lord Royce's until they are older still, then Harriet might not care."

"Why don't you simply find her a place in Town so you can still see her? It's no more adulterous than having her here for twelve years, or tucked away in the country."

"Harriet says she'll have her father ruin me. Like a fool I invested Harriet's dowry with the old skint, what he didn't keep in trust. My estate is in poor condition due to my ancestors' gambling, so my own income does not meet my expenses."

"You should speak with Lord Royce's man of business. He has helped make me a comfortable living."

"Maybe I will. Maybe I will."

Before Gorham closed the safe, Harry noticed a stack of letters and papers tied with a string.

"Love letters?"

"I have no idea. On the first night of the house party, everyone asked to put their valuables here. I can only suppose they did not trust each other."

"The letters are not yours?"

"No. Claire and I have seldom been apart long enough. And I wouldn't keep anything Harriet wrote except a check."

"Then whose letters are they?"

Gorham shrugged. "I suppose I should have kept a list. If I were better at these details, I mightn't find myself in such a tight corner."

"I'll give you the name of my solicitor before I leave."

Simone found just what she needed in the village and at the market square. The apothecary was her first stop, for Harry's sweets. After that, she left the other women at the emporium, poring over trimmings and yard goods, while she went on to the stalls of produce and handcrafts. She wished she'd had time to consult with Harry about her plan for her performance, in case he hated it, but she had no other ideas. And now she had an excuse to shop.

One peddler had the colorful fringed scarves she needed, and a tinsmith had a whole tray of inexpensive trinkets. She found a booth of pieced quilts, another of embroidered blouses. Her favorite purchase was a bright red petticoat a farm wife was selling. She'd never worn a red garment in her life, not with her hair, but the petticoat delighted her so much that she bought another for Sarah. What pleased Simone most was that she could afford to buy whatever she fancied.

She purchased a carved wood chess set for Auguste, a china teapot painted with flowers for Mrs. Judd, a set of sable paintbrushes for Claire, and a length of braided leather for a dog collar. The last wagon in the market square displayed soft homespun wool dyed in pastel colors that would be perfect for baby blankets and a shawl for Sandaree.

Her arms were full and the string wrappings were digging through her fingers, but she still hadn't found the right gift for Harry. The gloves were not supple enough, the watch fobs too tawdry. She did not know if he smoked a pipe, or what cologne he preferred. She had only a few minutes before she had to meet the others at the inn for the return to the manor house, so she went back to the apothecary. Now her shopping was complete.

She couldn't find Harry when they arrived at the house, but a great flood of news awaited them. The London papers had been delivered, with stories of Madame Lecroix's arrest. Claire was appalled; the servants were agog; the courtesans were stunned. Spies and traitors in their midst? Zounds, they hadn't had this much excitement since Katherine Bottswick castrated her unfaithful lover at the Cyprians' Ball.

At dinner, Lord Gorham asked Harry if he knew anything about it. "You were speaking of sedition just yesterday."

All the chatter around the table stopped while everyone listened, footmen as well as guests.

Harry set down his fork and said, "It appears that the government took Mr. Anthony's suspicions before it was too late." He raised his glass in a toast to the East India Company man and they all followed suit, asking Mr. Anthony what he knew and how he heard.

Simone was too shocked to listen. She looked at Harry, smiling and sipping his wine. She looked at everyone praising Mr. Anthony. Great gods, there really was a plot against England.

Chapter Twenty-three

Simone needed to speak with Harry more than ever, but Claire herded them all back into the music room. No port and cigars for the men tonight; she knew they'd never cease speculating on what little facts they had. She had too much to accomplish this evening for them to dally over bothersome politics.

First came the night's trio of entertainers. Claire introduced Miss Hanson, who curtsied prettily to the audience, smiled at her banker, then sat at the pianoforte and played Handel. She played far better than Simone could, although her performance was not as professional as Claire's singing.

Claire was all smiles again, nearly overflowing the bodice of her green silk gown in her exuberance. A set of emeralds bounced on her lush bosom as she applauded. She was still the best, and everyone knew it.

Then Miss Hanson started into the overture of a popular new musical drama, *The Lament of the Phoenix*. Simone had heard of it, but she'd never seen it performed, the ballet being beyond her means in London, and her students too young to claim an educational outing. No matter, for Sir Chauncey Phipps staggered forward with a sheaf of papers in his hand and started to read the story, like a libretto. He had to lean on the pianoforte for balance, after trying to lean on Miss Hanson's shoulder. She batted his hand away and he told her to play lower, so the audience could understand what he was saying. Of course he slurred his words, dropped a page, skipped lines, and ended: "Oh, hell. The damned bird dies of a broken heart, only to come alive again—no one says how or why—falls in love, gets rejected again. She's a burning torch, for God's sake, so what did she expect? And farking dies again. Here's my own true love to dance for you, Miss, ah, Miss—"

Miss Hanson at the pianoforte hissed a name at him. "Of course, Miss Susan Baylor, of the Royal Ballet."

Susan leaped onto the makeshift stage, where the rugs had been pulled back. She tossed a concealing cape away—directly at Sir Chauncey's head—and pirouetted in a costume consisting of a tight, long-sleeved bodice that was entirely covered in red and gold feathers; a short, feather-strewn red tulle tutu; glittering gold tights; and a headpiece that was cut to look like a flaming crown. The men were applauding already and she'd hardly begun to dance.

She was on her toes, doing grand jetés, spiral twirls, leaps, and dying. She did arabesques, pliés, and more dying. She tossed a handful of red feathers in the air to simulate the fire; then she died again. This time she stayed in a graceful heap on the floor, while the audience leaped to their feet, cheering.

"Encore, encore."

Sir Chauncey was pulling feathers out of his hair, but he did ask if Miss Butler could die once more. Claire pushed him aside. "That's Baylor, you sot. And we do not have time for an encore." Claire's smile had slipped a bit. Her complexion was now as green as her gown and jewels. She introduced Maura Doyle, Lord Caldwell's mistress.

Maura was laughing when she stepped to the front of the music room, wearing a short tartan gown that showed her knees. "How can a poor Irish lass compete with a flaming Bird of Paradise? Mimi was going to whistle for me, but since she's gone—lud, I hope she's not in jail like those others—I'll be a-singing whilst I dance. But I'll be asking you to clap to help me keep the beat. Come on, all you fine gents, hands together, now."

Maura danced a jig, clicking her heels together with her hands over her head, turning, then tapping her hand to her heel, spinning with her feet moving so fast she might have been on ice skates. Soon she was too out of breath to sing, but she kept to the beat of the clapping, the soles of her shoes tapping time on the wooden floor. Faster and faster, around and around. Her bosom was jigging, too.

The clapping grew louder. So did the cheers and whistles and foot stomping in the audience.

Lord Gorham cheered and clapped and ogled along with the rest, which was not what Claire had in mind for the decorous evening of culture, or for her lover. She stuck her elbow in his ribs.

The marquis stood and announced the billiards tourney, with cards, chess, and charades for those waiting their turns at the billiards table. Supper was at twelve.

Claire won the billiards match as expected, handily defeating every single one of the other women. Alice came in second and Ruby third. Simone lost to all of them and refused to try against anyone else, including Sandaree. She blamed Harry for not teaching her, which drew ribald comments about balls and shafts from some of the men who were making up for their missed port with

Gorham's cognac. Lord Bowman offered to instruct her, on the spare billiards table in the greenhouse.

Harry pulled her out of the room, but not before sending a sour look in Bowman's direction. There was no spare table, of course.

Simone defeated Gorham, Captain Entwhistle, and Mr. Anthony at chess. Too bad they were not playing for money or points in the contest. Sandaree watched, trying to learn the game, until Mr. Anthony set out another board to let her practice. The captain went to join Daisy at charades, and Gorham went to cheer on Claire, not that she needed it.

Simone lost to Harry. Too bad she could not concentrate with him so close. "We must talk," she tried to tell him when their next match ended in a draw.

"Not here, not now," was all he said.

They played chess until the midnight supper, neither wishing to take part in the risqué games that had supplanted charades in the parlor. The talk around the Egyptian Room, where the cold collation was set out, centered on the talent contest at first. Much of the debate was about which had been better, the ballet or the pianoforte tonight. Maura's jig was an audience pleaser, but no one thought it measured up. Besides, Maura's ankles were a bit thick.

No one dared suggest either of the others was better than Claire's performance. Of the earlier entertainments—the harp, violin, poetry, whistling, and trick horseback riding—none were in contention. Not one of those women was even part of the house party any longer.

Claire took the opportunity of having everyone's attention to once more ask Simone about her performance. This time she did not ask what Simone intended, only if she had any talent at all, other than displaying her legs atop an unmannered horse.

Simone was relieved she could say, "Yes, I think I do have a talent my friends might find entertaining. I prefer it to stay a surprise for now."

Harry looked surprised, too, as if he could not imagine what new skill Simone had discovered overnight. "Can you win?"

"I can try," Simone told him, making him smile. Which made her stomach flutter.

Claire consulted the notes she constantly carried. "Well, tomorrow Miss Mary Connors is going to enact Shakespeare for us, and Miss Sandaree is going to perform a dance from her native country. Both very edifying, I am certain, suitable for a Sunday. I believe Miss Alice Morrow is also planning a surprise. I pray it is not delivering her by-blow in my parlor."

Gorham cleared his throat.

"Why are you looking at me so disapprovingly? In polite society, a lady would not show her face in public with her condition so evident." Claire quickly looked over to where Harry was shaking his head, reminding her that not every pregnant female could afford to go on tour. "Yes, well, I am sure we all wish her and the infant well." She went back to her lists. "The following day, Monday, is the night of our grand ball, of course. Also the judging for best dressed and best dancer. Which leaves Tuesday, the last night of the house party, for Ruby to cut her silhouettes, Daisy to find some talent other than milking cows and sewing hems, and you." Claire's scathing tone of voice said she had no fears that any of them could surpass her own artistry. "I thought I might sing a bit afterward if there is time, in case anyone forgot my earlier presentation."

As if anyone could forget hearing what was once the finest voice in England, Simone thought, or as if Claire would let them. "I'm sure we will all be delighted to hear you sing again before we leave."

"And I do need to keep my voice exercised." She slapped a lobster patty onto Gorham's plate. "In case I have to resume my career."

"Your fans will be pleased."

Claire would not be. She slammed another lobster cake on her lover's dish. Gorham hated lobster. It made his eyes swell shut.

"Wednesday the final category will be judged," she continued. "What Gorham and I have decided to call Quality. That includes appearance, demeanor, everything a woman should have to bear the title of Queen of the Courtesans. After that, the points will be counted and tallied, to be followed by an early dinner and celebration. Then everyone can set out for London before dark." And Claire could start her packing. She popped a forkful of lobster in Gorham's mouth.

Simone finally went up to her bedchamber. Harry said he would follow soon, so she quickly washed and changed into yet another new, nearly nude nightgown. Then she dismissed Sarah, who'd been sewing on what Simone had bought that afternoon.

Once her maid was gone, Simone gathered blankets again for another bed on the floor. She did not get into her own, not yet.

When Harry entered through the dressing room door, he stayed rooted in one spot, staring at her in the firelight. Simone knew her every curve showed through the thin fabric, her darker nipples, her red lower curls. For once she was glad to own such immodest apparel, seeing him speechless, knowing she'd addled his wits, the same as he did to her.

"My God, you are beautiful," he finally managed to say.

He was, too, with his untied neckcloth draped around

his neck, his black hair curling over his forehead, looking as if a woman had already run her hands through it. A woman soon would, Simone vowed.

She handed him a large paper sack from the shopping excursion. Inside were paper twists filled with the peppermint drops he wanted, but also rum balls, taffy, marchpane, boiled honey, licorice, and tiny sugar mice.

"What, did you empty the apothecary shop?"

"I didn't know your favorites, so I bought some of everything."

"Trying to turn me up sweet, are you?" He put the sack on the mantel, out of the dog's reach.

"I wanted to apologize to you for lying to Jem and Daniel. And for taking your horse without permission. But I really had to win that race. Can you forgive me?"

While she was standing in front of the hearth wearing what amounted to a shadow and a smile, Harry knew he'd forgive her anything. Damn, his mouth was watering, and not for a peppermint drop or a rum ball. He wanted to take her in his arms—hell, he wanted to take her to that bed behind them—but knew they had to talk. Which meant he had to keep his distance. "I'll forgive you because you did not break your neck, or Fidus's. Now that I know you can manage him, I can forget my horror at seeing you on the brute."

"You do not have to worry that I'll try again. Fidus is as willful as a demon, and twice as strong. But tell me, are you angry at Jem? None of it was his fault, you know, and I cannot let him take the blame for my actions."

"I doubt any man could stand up to you, and Jem is just a boy, really. It's Daniel who should have stopped you. He knew I did not give permission."

"How could he know, when he had not spoken to you?"

"Because I never would give you leave to ride Fidus,

that's how. And because Daniel is big enough to carry you away if you did not listen to his reasonable arguments. He could have stopped you from killing yourself. He should have."

"But I did not injure myself or the horse. And I won."

"That doesn't make it right. Promise me you won't take chances like that again."

"But, Harry, what if you were in danger, or my brother was? I'd have to chance my own safety. What if someone's life depended on me?"

What could he say? "My life depends on you."

She sat on the bed, as if waiting for him to join her. He did not. He bent to pet the dog instead.

Simone drew her feet up. "Now, tell me about Madame Lecroix. Was she truly the spy you were looking for?"

"I am waiting to hear."

"But, Harry, if you did not know who was involved, how did you know to look here, at Lord Gorham's party, for a plot against the country?"

"I heard rumors that tasted true."

She smiled. "Tasted? Don't you mean sounded?"

"That also." He rubbed behind Blackie's ears without looking at her. "What if I said I could taste the difference between the truth·or a lie?"

Simone stared at him and the dog, trying to gauge whether he was teasing her or testing her somehow. "I'd say you were speaking nonsense, of course. What you described is impossible."

"Of course it is." He reached for the sack of sweets.

She wanted to shake him for spinning tales when she wanted answers. "Are you really involved in espionage?"

"Did you doubt my word?"

"I didn't know what to think. Your explanations were so fantastical, when you gave any at all. So are you a spy?"

"No, I never do the actual gathering of information. I mostly organize it, decide if rumors are worth pursuing, then send someone else to act on the ones that are. I am— I was, that is—a glorified clerk, that's all."

Simone knew he had to be more than that, or why would he need so many disguises, and why would he think people were trying to kill him? The more she mulled over what she knew, the more questions she had. "Harry, how is it that you trust me with your secrets if they are so important to the country's welfare?"

"Because soon it won't matter. I did try to tell you my involvement with the intelligence department will be over after this week. I cannot explain more yet, not with so much at stake. As for the other, my appearing as the major, that was unfortunate and I instantly regretted putting you in jeopardy. But I was short on time and had to know if you could be trusted. If I decided you could not, then you would have been placed in a governess position in the country where you could not interfere with our plans."

"You could simply conjure up a governess job when I'd been looking for months? No, do not answer that. I don't want to know. But what about now? Do you have no fear that I will betray you?"

He came closer and sat on the bed. "You said you would not."

"You believed me? Just like that?"

"Just like nectar."

"Drat, Harry, you are back to making no sense. Sometimes I think you are uncommonly clever, but then you speak of nectar, and I worry that your brain is stuffed with cotton wool."

"Sometimes I am not sure myself." He smoothed the covers on the bed. "If I tried to explain, you'd be convinced my attics were to let. More importantly, yes, I believed you. Shouldn't I?"

"Of course you should. I would never tell anyone about Mr. Harris or Harold the driver. But what if we argue and I change my mind? What if you turn brutish like Danforth or flirt with one of the real Cyprians? I might seek revenge like Lady Gorham."

"That will not happen."

Which, his cruelty or his disloyalty? She knew her heart would break if he cast her off, and everyone knew about a woman spurned. "Who can say what a woman feels, what she will do?"

"No man, for certain. But if my plan succeeds, then no one will believe you. Enough of that. Tell me about this secret performance of yours."

Simone pulled the covers up over herself because the silly nightgown offered no warmth; Harry's words and quick change of topic were chilling.

He took her hand in his, seeming to understand. "Tell me."

So she did, and asked for his help because she had no other choice. She did not want him to compromise his honor or betray friendships, just share a little of the information she knew he had.

Harry thought about it for less than a minute while he rubbed his thumb over the sensitive palm of her hand. "You are brilliant, my dear! That is just what I need to trap our blackmailer. I'll do it. I'll even wear a gold hoop in my ear."

"I thought you should sport a fake mustache."

"Hell, no. That is, I hate the things. So do you. And a mustache might remind people of Mr. Harris or the major. I don't intend to put one on again, not ever. Or spectacles. I'll wear them when I am seventy, not before."

"What about a sash around your waist?"

"Am I supposed to look like a pirate or a Gypsy?"

"You are supposed to look like Harry, my lover."

Now every inch of his body became sensitive, straining toward hers, half-naked on the white sheets, her red hair in a night braid already coming loose. Oh, Lord, he wanted her more than he wanted to see the end of Major Harrison. He didn't need any strange powers or complicated plotting or a wealth of information, only Simone. She pulled the sheets down and patted the space beside her. She wanted him.

He was ready to rip his clothes off and join her under the covers. Hell, he was ready to burst. That was the problem. He knew she'd never leave that bed a virgin if they shared it. No one could ask him to spend another night lying beside her, giving her pleasure, and taking none, not even himself. He wasn't that much of a saint. No red-blooded male was. He stood up. "I cannot do it."

"You can't? Lydia and her girls said—"

"I won't," he amended. "I gave you my word."

"I am giving it back."

"No, I cannot be so unfair to you. You want a better life than you had. This is not it. You've seen what happens: The men go back to their wives or they find a respectable debutante to wed, if she is rich enough. Or else they simply move on to another woman like bees flitting from flower to flower. You do not want to travel that road—you've always said so—and I cannot let myself walk down that path with you."

"I have reconsidered. Yes, I have seen what happens to affairs between a man and his mistress. I've also seen how some couples find unending love."

He was a man. How could he speak of love? How could he promise forever when next week was so uncertain?

"You could change your mind tomorrow, too late. No, my dear, we shall keep to our original terms."

"You do not want me?"

"Now who is attics-to-let, sweetheart?" He shifted uncomfortably. "A blind man could see how much I want you. I dare not pass any of the servants in this state. I almost regret Gorham's hot-water plumbing is so efficient, or I'd take a cold bath. Maybe I'll jump in Gorham's ornamental fishpond, or a horse trough. No, I'd still want you. And that is why I have to leave. Besides, I need to go see if Daniel is back. And I, ah, need to walk the dog. Don't wait up."

Simone found herself alone. Tonight should have been an evening to celebrate her race win, to count her points and her coins, to rehearse her coming performance. Instead she realized that more money was unnecessary, the success meant little, and the competition meant less.

All she really wanted was Harry.

Chapter Twenty-four

In the morning, Simone was in Harry's arms, and Harry was in rut. Again. Still. He jumped out of bed and grabbed for his robe to hide the evidence. When he'd returned last night, early this morning, she woke up and held her arms out. How could a gentleman refuse? Besides, he was exhausted enough to fall asleep despite the scent of her beside him, her murmurs of content as she snuggled closer, the silk of her skin, the warmth of her body—hell, he hardly slept at all. A few more days, he told himself, and they could be done playacting. He'd pay her the fee, send her wherever she wished, and finally get some rest. A few more days and he'd be insane.

And Gorham was right: He'd be more insane to let her go.

Simone yawned, rubbed her eyes, and asked, "Why are you always running away from me?"

"I'm not—" His mouth puckered up before he could finish the sentence. Lud, was he going to need another sack of sweets before breakfast?

"The dog has to go out again."

Simone looked at the dog, who was snoring at the foot of the bed. Now her mouth puckered.

"Well, he ought to be exercised and the day is going to be too busy for much of that later."

"Nonsense. Today is Sunday, and I doubt anyone in this group will be rushing into the village church." Simone intended to. She needed to ask forgiveness for the sins she had committed, and more for the sins she hadn't committed but wanted to. She would keep sinning, too, if she could get Harry to cooperate.

She did not need to go into the village, Harry told her. Claire and Gorham had a cleric coming to their private chapel at Griffin Woods. They usually attended services at the local church, where Gorham donated enough blunt to make them welcome in the front pew. The villagers were used to seeing Claire and Gorham together, and needed the trade with the manor besides, so no one threw stones or sermons at them. They were not invited to the mayor's house for Sunday dinner, or to the squire's for tea, but otherwise they were fairly well accepted in the neighborhood. "Gorham did not think the village could deal with nine more fast women and fornicators, though, so the vicar is sending his curate here."

"Do you think anyone will attend?"

"If they hope to gain points for Quality, they will. Claire seems to think godliness is worth a guinea or two. I suppose most of the others will go out of duty or habit."

"What of you?" Simone realized she knew little of his thoughts and beliefs. "Do you attend church regularly?"

"The good Lord and I have an understanding. He worries about the hereafter; I do my best here and now. Shall you go?"

"I'd intended to, unless you have other plans for this morning." She stretched, showing her bosom in the sheer nightgown, on purpose. Whatever plans he had could be changed, couldn't they?

He turned away. "I will escort you to the chapel, then, when you are ready."

Now Simone had another sin, blasphemy, to atone for.

The old stone building was a short walk away. It was cold inside, but not as cold as the look on the curate's face when Ruby arrived with her face painted, Sir Chauncey dropped his flask, pregnant Alice wore no ring, and Sandaree wore a gold-flecked sari.

The young man's voice shook; his hands shook—until Gorham put a leather pouch in them. Claire insisted on a hymn, which she sang alone, before allowing the poor curate to rush back to his wife and children and Sunday roast. No, he could not stay to dine with the houseguests. They could hear him thanking God, fervently, on his way out.

After the meal, the women either rested or practiced at the archery range. Claire decided that bows and arrows were suitably decorous for a Sunday, if no one wagered on the contest. No one wagered with her, at any rate.

Again, Sandaree was at a loss. She'd never held a bow and arrow, but neither had Miss Hanson, who refused to learn, saying her fingers were too valuable at the pianoforte to chance a blister. Alice's Lord Comden was teaching her how to hold the bow, which looked more like an excuse to keep his arms around her. Susan Baylor, the ballet dancer, knew the rudiments, but refused to let her protector, Sir Chauncey, improve her form or her aim. He would likely kill them both, she said, since he was already swaying on his feet. Danforth took over as instructor, sneering at the tosspot and at Sandaree, who could not string her bow, had not made the proper responses in church, and would not eat the ham served for luncheon. She was a failure at the tournament, he said out loud, and everyone understood he was not pleased with her in bed, either.

Poor Sandaree was near tears. Simone started to go to her side, but Mr. Anthony got there first. While showing her the basics of the sport, he told her tales of hunting crocodiles with bow and arrow. "Bullets would ricochet, don't you know. Never hit a man-eater, but managed to wound the water several times." He had her smiling again.

Ruby was competent, Maura was clumsy but good-natured about missing the target on her first tries, but Daisy was good. Her father had taught her to hunt rabbits and birds on the farm. Daisy's lover, Captain Entwhistle, made sure Claire's back was turned before he raised his bet with Miss Hanson's banker. Miss Connors, the actress who was to perform that night, was a surprise. She'd been part of a traveling troupe and had learned to shoot an arrow while playing Diana, goddess of the hunt. And while poaching game along the road.

Lord Ellsworth had found a new female companion at the inn, but Claire recognized her as the lass who'd won the archery contest at last year's village fair. She refused to permit the girl to enter the event. She was not one of the original contestants, Claire insisted, so she could not take part now. Ellsworth and his cheat wandered off to the gazebo.

Claire did not bother practicing, which discouraged everyone.

Harry did not come watch. He was busy with correspondence again, Metlock had told Simone, which she took to mean he was conducting government business. She still wished he were beside her.

She was out of form, unfamiliar with the bow that was provided, and wearing a constricting corset. She'd learned from her father, though, and managed to practice while she was a governess, teaching the young girls in her care. Her last employer before the baron was a devotee, and his son, the one who assaulted her and cost her that job, was on his university's archery team. They had a target set up in the garden, which meant she could not let the children play there, and another in the long gallery, for practice at night or in poor weather. Two ancestors' portraits had arrow holes through their foreheads.

Simone had not held a bow since, and took her time learning the one she was given, its pull, its grip, the *thwang* of its taut string. She had not forgotten any of her skill and her aim was still as true. Now all she needed was to remove the tight corset and get Harry to wager some of her money for her. She did not wish to lower her odds by showing just how good she was, so she went to find him after changing into a more comfortable gown without ribbons or lace to catch on the bowstring.

Harry was with Daniel in Lady Gorham's sewing room, according to the disapproving butler. Simone could see why. Daniel was unshaven and his boots were muddy. He looked as if he'd been carousing all night. So did Harry, although his neckcloth was tied better than the spotted kerchief Daniel wore.

"Have you news of Madame Lecroix?" Simone asked when both men rose to their feet at her entrance.

A glance passed between the two blue-eyed Royce relatives. Harry nodded. It was all right to discuss the matter in front of Simone.

She learned that the government did not need the Frenchwoman's confession. They found enough evidence at her house to see her hang, along with two others she named. The traitor Gollup was certainly guilty of shipping guns to France—his confiscated records showed that—but both of them refused to say who had paid for the weapons, who had financed the current plot, or who was to carry out the mayhem they'd planned. Whitehall and the Intelligence Service had not given up, although they were fairly certain the scheme was foiled.

"That's a relief, then."

Both men said, "Amen," and raised their glasses.

Simone wandered around the room while Harry made more notes to give Daniel for posting. Then he sent his cousin off to get some sleep and finally turned to Simone, although he'd been aware of her every step.

"We need to make notes for my performance," she said, as an excuse for interrupting his important work.

"There's time enough, and some of my information keeps changing."

"Hmm." Simone was staring at the portrait of Harriet, Lady Gorham. The severe woman still looked familiar. "Has she aged much?"

"I only saw her once or twice. I have only been in polite society since Lord Royce came back to Town, after all. Even then, the lady was too proud to entertain the earl's son from the wrong side of the blanket." He stood next to Simone, looking at the picture. "I believe her hair has gone gray and she has put on considerable weight since this was painted. I think—yes, I am certain—that one of her teeth has fallen out. She always keeps her mouth closed."

The missing tooth, that was how Simone remembered where she'd seen the woman. And heard her.

Mr. Black raced ahead on their way to the archery range. Sir Chauncey almost shot an arrow into him.

"Who let that fool hold a bow anyway?" Harry muttered. He called the dog to his side and fastened the new collar and lead on him, to keep him close and safe. Then he asked Simone how he should make his own bets. "Do you think you can take first, or should I put my money on you for second place?"

Simone watched Claire take a practice shot. She hit the target, to much applause, but missed the bull's-eye by an inch, despite having a bow of better quality than the ones provided to the others.

"First," Simone said. "I intend to win."

Nine targets were set up, with each woman shooting five arrows. For once, there was no room for cheating, since the distances to the target were exactly equal and everyone could see precisely where each arrow landed. The top six archers were to move to a second round, at a longer distance.

Sandaree, Maura, and Alice were eliminated at the first go-round. The targets were moved. Ruby, Miss Connors, and the ballet dancer fell short. That left Claire, Simone, and Daisy.

This time only one target was set up still farther away. Each woman was given three arrows, feathered differently to identify the archer. They were to shoot one at a time, in turn.

Daisy went first, and missed the center ring of the target. Simone's arrow hit the mark, but not dead center. Claire's did. Ellsworth came back in time to place wagers with the banker. Money changed hands, but Claire was too absorbed in the contest to care. Sir Chauncey fell asleep behind the wagon that held a cask of ale and a pitcher of lemonade, and Danforth and Sir Chauncey's dancer disappeared. The dog barked until Harry tossed him a peppermint. Sandaree stood by the nabob, cheering for Simone.

Gorham did not appear worried. Harry did.

Daisy caught the edge of the center with her second arrow. Captain Entwhistle consoled her. "It's the distance, pet. You could best them all at closer range. Claire must have known that."

Of course she did. She'd seen Daisy hold up a magnifying glass in the chapel when no one was watching.

Simone's second arrow was perfect, edging Claire's a fraction off the center.

Claire was so angry, she told Gorham to step away; his incessant advice made her tense. She missed the center by a finger's width and blamed him. "I told you to stop hovering at my shoulder, dash it."

Daisy's last try was close, but too far away from center to be in contention.

Harry kissed Simone's cheek and handed her her third arrow. "Think of the target as that baron's heart. Or that son of a swine who would have raped you."

Simone's last arrow was so close to her second one that a hair could not have passed between them. So she had three in the bull's-eye ring, with two in the exact center of that. Claire had only one at dead center so far.

Gorham stepped forward to hand Claire the last arrow and give her a kiss for luck the way Harry had done, but she pushed him away. "And make sure that stupid dog doesn't bark. And stop that fool Phipps from snoring and your sacrilegious friends from shouting out odds. How can I concentrate?"

Someone shook Sir Chauncey awake, a servant led the dog away, and the men stopped changing their bets. Gorham held his breath. So did Simone.

Claire's arrow hit Simone's directly at the center—and fell off!

"Another round!" Claire shouted. "I demand another round."

"But you made the rules, Miss Hope," Harry told her. "Three rounds, three arrows for the final set, the best three arrows in the target. In the target," he repeated, "not on the ground." He held his hand out to collect Simone's ten-guinea winner's purse.

Luckily Claire had no arrows left in her quiver.

Lord Gorham introduced the entertainment for the night. In keeping with the Sabbath, Claire had scheduled the more serious, cultural performances. Miss Mary Connors of Drury Lane Theatre was portraying Shakespearean women; Miss Sandaree—"Deuced if I can pronounce the rest of her name"—would demonstrate some of her country's arts; Miss Alice Morrow was going to read from the Bible.

Ellsworth left, along with Lords Caldwell and Bowman. Lord James Danforth looked like he wished he could leave, but since his own mistress, the female he had brought, was going to perform and he had money on the contest, he stayed and scowled. He'd seen enough of melodrama, religion, and heathenish manners.

Mary was a fine actress. She became an affecting Desdemona, a determined Lady Macbeth, a tragic Ophelia.

"Damn if she had to pick the saddest women in all of literature," Sir Chauncey complained, then hiccuped. "I thought this was supposed to be amusing. Those characters all die at the end, don't they?"

Claire tried to hush him. "This is high-toned entertainment, you cork-brained drunk." A servant handed Sir Chauncey a glass of wine, and the bottle. That kept him quiet until Juliet's last speech, at which he started to weep into a large handkerchief.

Simone was impressed, not just because Mary's performance had made a grown man cry. The man was Sir Chauncey, after all, but Mary's acting was far better than Simone's own. All Simone had to do was lean against

Harry's shoulder and smile up at him adoringly. That wasn't acting at all, she feared.

After the applause for Miss Connors ended, Lord Comden helped increasing Alice out of her chair. She padded toward the front of the room, a Bible in her hand. Sir Chauncey groaned.

Alice told him to stubble it, to shut up, which offended Claire.

"Please, we are ladies and gentlemen. At least some of us."

Alice opened the Bible and apologized for being out of season. Then she read the story of another babe, another birth to another surprised mother. Sir Chauncey wept loudly, and Simone felt tears well in her own eyes. Harry handed her his handkerchief.

The story did not take long. Alice did not read all of Luke before shutting the Bible and curtsying to polite applause. She wasn't finished, though. She pulled a deck of cards from her pocket and started to shuffle them in an arc in the air.

Claire leaped to her feet. "Miss Morrow, that is not suitable fare for a Sunday."

Alice kept the cards flying through the air above her head. "Why not? We are all sinners here anyway, trying to pretend we're better than we are. And who are you to talk, with a married man's hand up your skirt and your dugs hanging out like a cow's udders? I may have been raised in a gaming hell, but you were the one who tried to cheat at half the events. If you think that makes you any kind of lady, you are far off the mark. Asides, my mum always said the good Lord had to have a sense of humor. Else why would he create a man? And, Miss Hoity-toity Hope, I am still reading the Bible, only in my own way."

She shuffled the deck again, sifting the pasteboards

into a facedown fan. Then, without looking at the cards, she pulled out three kings. "The magi."

Alice cut the deck, and showed the amazed audience that she had exactly twelve cards in her top hand. "The apostles."

She flipped the deck again and held up the bottom card, a three. "The Trinity."

When she shuffled the cards the next time, the jack of spades was sticking out. "The knave, Judas."

In quick succession, she pulled out a seven, for the day of rest after the creation, and a five, for the books of the Old Testament.

Everyone sat forward on their seats.

"Now, that's more like it!" Sir Chauncey called.

Alice walked toward him and told him to select a card, without looking at it. "The commandments."

He looked. "By George, it is a ten. I'll be damned. Well, I'll be damned anyway, 'cause I've broken more than half of them."

They all applauded, astounded at what they'd seen.

Claire wanted a rematch of the piquet game. Anyone who could handle cards like that, she insisted, must have cheated.

Alice just laughed. She fanned the cards and pretended to study them. Then she pulled one out. "Ah yes, the queen of hearts. The Queen of the Courtesans." She tucked it down her cleavage and curtsied. Comden rushed forward to help her back to her feet.

During the pause everyone wondered how Alice did that, how they could learn, and how many card games they could win if they had her skill. Then Sandaree came forward, wearing her new woolen cape. Two footmen followed her, carrying a folding screen and a large basket to the front of the room.

Sandaree stepped behind the screen while the audience was still marveling at the card tricks, and Lord Comden made much of Alice. Then they all fell silent when Sandaree came out from behind the screen.

Claire gasped. "No, no, no. That is absolutely pagan. Not edifying at all. Not fitting for a Sunday."

"Oh, put a sock in it," Gorham told her, eyes glued to the Indian slave girl.

Sandaree wore her gauze pantaloons, a short vest, and nothing under either but a jewel in her navel. She had bells on her ankles and wrists, no shoes, and a veil hiding the lower part of her face. A gold cord held the veil in place, ending in a tassel that trailed down her nearly bare back. She held a tambourine-like instrument, and began to shake it and beat on it softly while her feet started to move. Her belly moved in a different direction. Her hips moved in five different directions at once.

"Is that possible?" Sir Chauncey asked no one in particular.

"Sshh" came from all sides.

Sandaree lifted a long silk scarf out of the basket and danced with it like a lover, draping it around herself, then sending it swirling in the air to settle over her again, while she kept gyrating and twirling until the tassel flew in circles. She took the veil off her face and let it float down so she could pick it up from the floor, showing that her posterior was as fluid as her front. She replaced the tambourine with tiny finger cymbals so the tempo was sharper, her feet and her muscles moving faster. With a gazellelike leap she vaulted over the basket, pulling out a carved wooden flute. She began to play toward the basket as if she were an Indian snake charmer, only she was the snake, coiling, writhing, swaying. The men were charmed, her captives. The women cooled themselves with their fans.

Again Sandaree danced with her midriff, the jewel flashing, then slower and lower until she concluded with a salaam in front of Lord Danforth's feet.

Ruby wondered out loud, "Do you realize how much money a girl can make like that?"

Miss Hanson wanted to know if Sandaree could teach her to dance that way, if she taught Sandaree to waltz.

The ballet dancer wrinkled her nose and walked out. None of the men did.

"Lud," Mr. Anthony said, "voting for best talent is an impossible task."

Claire did not see why. "This performance was not proper or ladylike. Neither was that card nonsense."

"But a courtesan is supposed to amuse, and damn if I didn't enjoy both of them." Gorham quickly added, "And your singing, of course, my dear."

"What did you think, Harry?" Simone asked.

"I think that was an incredibly erotic dance, and Danforth does not appreciate what he has."

"Look at him, barely telling poor Sandaree how good she was. He almost looks angry that she's half-naked in front of the other men."

"No, he is embarrassed that he's aroused by the dance. A British lord does not show emotion, you know."

A lot of British lords were showing plenty, in their tight trousers and their rush to bring Sandaree a glass of wine, a lemonade, a diamond bracelet if she'd come to their rooms later.

But Mr. Anthony was correct: Judging arias and oranges was not going to be easy. Sleight of hand was no ladylike accomplishment, and heaven knew Sandaree's dance was no debutante's cotillion. Both women had talent and they had both kept the audience entranced. What Simone proposed was just as unlikely to be seen at

Almack's, but she'd keep to her plan, if she could get Harry to help.

She was ready to convince him to go to bed early that night when he said, "I need you."

"You do?" That was just what she wanted to hear. Now she could get him into her bed, for another taste of what he'd shown her before. Then she thought about it. Who wanted a man who was stirred to passion by another woman's seductive dance? Sandaree's performance was suddenly not quite as amusing. "I do not see why every man here is so affected. It was only a dance, after all."

"Only a dance? Claire's voice is only a warble by that standard. But you sound jealous, my love." He lowered his voice. "How can that be, when ours is no more than a business arrangement?"

Was that all he thought of her? An employee? Was that all they had? Simone pounded on his chest, right over where his heart would be, if the bounder had one. "Feelings do not have to make sense. They just are."

Chapter Twenty-five

"I do have feelings, my dear Noma. And I do understand that not everything makes sense. Heaven knows I've had to live with that fact my entire life. Right now I need you, not a woman whose parts revolve as if they're not connected to one another. I'm not saying your friend can't make a man want to drown in the whirlpool her fascinating movements create, but that's what a man does. He feels lust for a beautiful woman doing beautiful things with her body. Hell, that was a mating dance to put a peacock's display to shame. But right now, you are all I want."

Finally! Simone felt like dancing herself, to hear Harry confess his desire. It was no declaration of love—not even of fondness—and no promise of a future after the house party was over, but it was something. Something she wanted.

She knew Harry wanted it, too, although he was full of excuses and evasions. He'd been running from the attraction between them, afraid she'd want more than he was willing to offer. Or afraid he'd want more. If Sandaree's dancing had shown him how foolish it was to waste the time they did have, to deny them both the pleasure, she'd get Sandaree to teach her to charm snakes.

Lust and caring were better than nothing, she decided. If she couldn't have his love, she'd take his lovemaking. Harry's code of honor dictated that he save her for a husband, which he did not intend to be. But how could she go to another man, knowing her heart was lost to Harry? That would be far more dishonest than to wed missing her maidenhead.

Simone supposed Harry's irregular birth fostered his honor and his devotion to the truth. He was baseborn, so he must feel he had to act with nobility to rise above the ridicule, disdain, and shame of his birth. Not that she wished Harry to be less honorable, of course, except now. She took his hand in hers and started to lead him toward the stairs before he could change his mind.

He pulled her in the opposite direction down the hall, toward Gorham's library.

"Aren't we going to our room?"

"Zeus, no. I can't trust myself there."

She wanted to shout out that he could trust her to know what was best for herself, but her disappointment made her ask: "Then we aren't going to . . . ?"

He turned and took her shoulders, looking into her eyes with that blue fire of his stare. "We are going to do what we came for: to do our duty and serve our country. We have to solve a crime, destroy a plot, and make a stir here. This is business, and it has to come before any personal desire. Do you understand?"

She understood he was reminding her of their arrangement. She was paid to act as his mistress. That was all. A pretense, with no emotion, no involvement. He might be stirred by Sandaree's display, but not enough to forget his mission—or her place in it.

"Yes, Harry, I understand."

He rapped loudly on the library door, then opened it

when no one answered. Gorham and Claire were still in the music room, Simone knew, unless they'd left for the late supper Claire always served after the performances. Either way, neither of them could be here in the library.

"Should we be going into the private rooms?"

"What we need is inside." He led her halfway into the room, which was illuminated only by the fire in the hearth and two oil lamps. Harry blew one out, creating more shadows in the long room.

"What am I supposed to do?"

"Wait. Follow my lead. You'll know."

He listened, so she listened, and shortly heard footsteps approaching down the hall. Harry drew her into his arms and pressed his lips to hers. "Now," he murmured. "Act like you're enjoying this."

So she kissed him back and moaned with pleasure and cried, "Oh, Harry." She'd seldom enjoyed anything more.

The butler came in with a tray. He coughed, backed out, and closed the door behind him.

Simone stepped away from Harry. "That was what you brought me here for, to embarrass the poor butler?"

"He's seen worse." Harry's head was cocked, still listening for sounds in the corridor. He took her back into his arms, this time with one of his hands moving down her back, her waist, her backside, pulling her more firmly against his heat and hardness. His other hand was at her breast, feeling her heat and softness.

"Harry!" she said with a squeak. "Someone is coming."

He grinned. "That's the point, sweetings."

Claire and Gorham opened the door, but stopped in the entry when they saw the entwined couple right in front of them. Simone's bright red hair was unmistakable, even in the single lamp's light.

"Dash it, Harry, everyone has the same idea," Gorham

complained while Claire pretended to be studying a nearby bookcase. "I've never seen so many young bucks tugging on their trousers or holding their girlfriends' fans in front of them—or dragging those same women off to dark corners and unoccupied rooms. It was that dance, don't you know. Claire thought she'd try—that is, we are going to discuss the voting and tomorrow's ball. The devil take it, this is my library and I don't have to make excuses. I thought you were using the needlework parlor, anyway."

"My apologies, Gorham. I do appreciate the use of that room for my correspondence, but the portrait of Lady Gorham hangs there. Your wife doesn't approve of us, either. Her sour look is not conducive to romance, is it?"

"Why do you think I took a mistress in the first place? Ah, well, I suppose we ought to see if anyone wants supper. Come, my dear. We are the hosts and should set a better example. Then again, we could see if the gardens are empty."

Claire sent one last sneer in Simone's direction. "You might want to lock the door, Miss Royale. At least pretend to be a proper female."

Simone was blushing like a schoolboy caught stealing apples but she couldn't keep a giggle from escaping. She *was* a proper female who was pretending to be a harlot. Now Claire wanted that feigned doxy to act like a lady, while Harry wanted the lady in her to abandon all modesty and decency. "Thank you. I will. Lock the door, that is."

Harry did it for her when Claire and Gorham left. Then, instead of taking her back into his arms, he gave her a quick kiss on the forehead, crossed the room, and opened the window.

Sir Chauncey Phipps scrambled over the sill. Simone

almost shrieked, but Harry hurried back to put his hand over her mouth. "Sh."

"Do not shush me. Throw that reprobate out!"

Harry pointed to the closed door and whispered, "Lower your voice before someone comes to see what the commotion is about."

She did try for an outraged whisper. "That drunkard is going to ruin everything." Especially her time with Harry now that they were alone again. "Tell him to leave."

"I am sorry, my love, but I can't do that. Chappy is a friend of mine. And one of the best cracksmen in England. A safe breaker, if you will."

"He is a sotted fool!"

Sir Chauncey winked at her. "Excellent disguise, eh? Better than a mustache and dark glasses. No one suspects a souse of anything, and no one watches what they say when he's slumped over a table."

The bald-headed buffoon wasn't staggering for once. He wasn't slurring his words or drooling, and no flask or bottle was in sight. She turned to Harry while Sir Chauncey turned to a certain wall of books. He was sober, a friend, and a thief? Her head was spinning from Harry's kiss; that's why she was so confused. "You say he's a criminal?"

Harry went to help, pushing on a section of the bookcase that swung open to reveal a large wall safe.

"Chappy's no jailbird. Gorham would never invite a felon. He's a sworn knight, elevated for performing heroic service during the war, although no one knows about it. They think Chappy got the knighthood because he paid Prinny's debts to get the recognition. That wasn't the case at all. What he did was steal countless valuable documents for us in France before they threw out all the English. He'd have been sent to the guillotine before he could have a last glass of wine, if the French knew."

"Does Miss Baylor know?"

Sir Chauncey paused in his work to tell Simone, "Susan's a ballet dancer, not an actress. She doesn't have your gumption."

Simone nodded at the compliment.

"She's greedy, though," Sir Chauncey continued. "So she puts up with me. The revulsion she can't hide adds to my character."

The rumpot/patriot was working on the safe with a set of tools he took from a pocket. Simone had a hard time believing what she was seeing or hearing. "So you are here to rob from our host?"

Chappy looked up and grinned. "Bad form, that. We're merely recovering stolen property."

Harry explained it better: "We are taking back what Danforth stole. That way, he can't use the papers to demand money."

"You know that the letters you were looking for are in the safe? Why haven't you had Danforth arrested, then?"

"What, and have the letters and journal be seized for proof of his guilt? That defeats the whole purpose of keeping them away from the scandal sheets and public knowledge. Besides, we still have no proof that Danforth placed the evidence in the safe. He won't talk to me."

"Or me," Simone said, "especially since hearing I have Gypsy blood."

"Or me," Chappy added happily enough. "And I'm not even a whore or a bastard."

Simone looked at Harry to see if he was offended at the reminder of his birth, but he'd gone back to the window. She assumed he was going to close it before the room grew cold, but instead he leaned out and brought in a saddlebag. Daniel Stamfield clambered over the windowsill after it.

"You, too?" Simone remembered to whisper. Heavens, if that butler came back, he'd know something was afoot.

Daniel bowed to Simone, then went to watch Sir Chauncey at work.

"You had this all planned?" Simone asked Harry.

He removed a stack of papers and three books from the saddlebag. "As best we could. I only saw the documents for an instant, so I had Daniel bring extra loose pages and several sizes of journals for the switch. Our package will be as close to the original in appearance as possible."

Chappy had the safe open. They all gathered to look in. Claire saw velvet pouches, leather purses, another strongbox, a set of dueling pistols in a case, plus stacks of guineas and pound notes.

"The entry fees for Claire's contest," Harry explained, "and the prize money."

"Too bad we're such honest folk," Daniel said, reaching over for a parcel of letters tied with string.

Harry saw Simone staring at a diamond necklace by itself in a corner of the safe. "I think Claire would recognize it."

Simone jumped back. "I wasn't thinking of taking it!"

Harry's lips made a grimace. Daniel rubbed the back of his neck.

"Truly, I wouldn't do anything so dishonest!"

Daniel rubbed his ear, and Harry found a peppermint drop in his pocket. "Of course not, my love. You only pretend to be a prostitute. It's not at all the same."

He and Daniel spread the stolen letters out on Gorham's desk, counting the number of pages so they could place the same amount in the fake parcel. The journal was slightly different from any Daniel had brought, but they agreed that Danforth wasn't likely to notice the difference when Gorham handed it to him.

"How will you prove they were his?"

"Gorham will recall who asks for them back, now that I mentioned it to him. But it does not matter if we are wrong about Danforth. The important thing was to collect the blackmail material."

Simone was positive Danforth was guilty. The pompous twit treated Sandaree like a slave, and even struck her. "He should be brought up on charges."

"A duke's son? That won't happen in this lifetime. I daresay he'll face a bit of private retribution, if we have proof."

Daniel flexed his fists. Sir Chauncey studied the sharp tool in his hand. Harry looked grim.

The duke's scoundrel of a son would pay, all right.

Simone wanted to know what they were going to do with the originals. She looked toward the fireplace. "Shall we burn them?"

Harry shook his head. "We are going to take the journal back to its proper owner, and urge her to destroy it. The letters will go to the victims of the extortion attempt, the fools who sent them in the first place. That way, they'll have proof that no one else will hold the letters against them. I hope to God they burn them, once and for all."

He handed the new pile of letters and journal, tied with the old string, to Chappy to return to the safe.

Daniel tucked the originals in the saddlebag and sighed. "I'm wearing a rut in the road to London, I am. Are you sure you won't go this time, Harry? Fidus could be there and back in the wink of an eye."

"You know neither Fidus nor I can be seen in Town yet. Go."

Daniel sighed again on his way toward the window. "I'll be back in time for the ball tomorrow night, Miss Royale. Remember that you promised me a dance."

"I remember. I am looking forward to it."

Daniel grinned, scratched at his armpit, and went out the window.

"May I also request a dance?" Sir Chauncey asked.

"Only if you do not step on my toes."

He laughed. "It's all part of the disguise, my dear. All part of the disguise. But I will try not to tear your skirt. I'll save that for the scornful Miss Baylor. Lud knows I paid for the blasted thing." He followed Daniel out the window.

Harry closed the window, then made certain the wall safe and the books were exactly as they had found them.

"I suppose we're done for the night," Simone said, feeling let down now that the others were gone and the excitement was over.

"Not at all," Harry told her. "We have to be convincing, don't we? And I wouldn't want anyone thinking a quick tumble on the hearth rug was the best I could do. I do have my reputation as a lover to consider, after all."

Simone did not want to think about his reputation or his past conquests. Now, the hearth rug . . .

"And yours," he continued. "Those rakes should know you can hold a man's interest for an entire night." Or a week, a month, a lifetime, but he did not say those words. "Besides, that leather armchair looks deuced comfortable to me."

"You . . . you are going to take a nap in Lord Gorham's library?"

"I have no intention of sleeping, my dear. Will you join me?"

"On the chair?"

"What do you think Claire and Gorham were going to do, read a book?"

"No, he said they were going to discuss plans for the ball. And the voting."

"You believed him?"

"No, I suspected Claire was going to plot a new way to manipulate him to change the point count. Either that or they were going to practice their dancing for the competition tomorrow night."

His lip curled down on one side, then up until he wore a broad smile that showed the dimples Simone adored. "No, that's not what they were going to do. Trust me, my love, that's simply not true."

He drew her over toward the big leather chair, sat, and pulled her across his lap. "But if it's practice we need, shall we dance?"

"On the chair?"

He kissed her protests away.

What a dance it was. All swirls, twirls, whirls; fast and slow and loud and soft. Mostly it was urgent, far more so than the need to win any race, any contest. Simone was dizzy and breathless and giddy—and her feet never touched the ground. She wanted the dance to go on forever, but Harry stopped the music before it was too late to stop. She knew there was more, another kind of crescendo, but this was enough, for now. She doubted there'd ever been a more enthralling waltz, or a more satisfied virgin.

"Oh, Harry."

Oh, hell.

Chapter Twenty-six

Harry slept on the chair in the bedroom. The dog slept with Simone. That's how Harry felt, lower than a stray with a sore mouth. He left before Simone awoke, knowing she'd be too tempting to leave if he didn't go soon. Later she'd be busy getting ready for the ball. He'd be watching to see who took what out of Gorham's safe, after a long, hard ride on Fidus, and a long, cold swim in Gorham's trout stream.

For once, Simone slept late, not surprising after last night in the library. She'd barely made it up the stairs on boneless limbs.

When Metlock told her that Harry had gone riding, she almost scrambled into her habit to join him, but he could be miles away by now, or off on his secret activities. For all she knew, he and his friend Sir Chauncey were robbing the nearest bank.

Sarah came in full of energy and excitement at the coming ball. There was going to be music in the barn for the servants and the tenants, but the wagering among the ladies' maids was more crucial. Whichever mistress won the best-dressed contest, her maid won the betting pool. Sarah was determined to collect the purse.

She brought a breakfast tray so Simone did not have to
go down, to save time.

"Surely it is far too early to begin dressing for tonight,"
Simone protested, wanting to wait for Harry's return, to
spend more time with him.

According to Sarah, many of the women had started
last night, with their hair in papers and clarifying lotions
on their faces. Simone knew her skin already glowed with
the aftermath of Harry's lovemaking, but she couldn't tell
Sarah that, naturally.

She didn't have to speak much, for Sarah told Simone
about all the tricks she had learned from Claire's dresser
while she washed Simone's long hair with various con-
coctions and rinses. She'd also learned a few tricks from
the underbutler.

Simone sat up. "You did what?"

"It was just for practice, Miss Noma. Kisses and a bit
of snuggling, nothing more. I wanted to be sure about becoming a fine lady's maid instead of a fine gent's lady
friend. Begging your pardon, miss, but I'll stay with my
plans, even if they don't pay as much. He smelled of gar-
lic. The second footman's hands were damp, and Lord
Ellsworth's valet kissed like a fish. I didn't care for any
of it. Better that I know now, don't you think?"

"You'll care for it if you like the man better." Simone
smiled on the inside, thinking of Harry's kisses. "But you
are too young. And you might decide to marry instead of
going into service. Then you'll be happy you didn't become bachelor fare."

"But then I'd be at some man's beck and call anyway. I
think I'd do better like my mum, with a living of her own."

Like a housekeeper, or a governess. That was what
Simone wanted, wasn't it? To be independent, not relying
on any man? She wasn't so certain anymore.

Sarah went on while she brushed Simone's hair dry in front of the fire. "And ladies' maids do right well for themselves. Gentlemen are always giving them money to carry messages or deliver gifts, and they get their mistresses's cast-off gowns to sell. Miss Hope's abigail has enough saved to retire on. She doesn't want to go to Cornwall when her mistress leaves here, not at all. She says folk there have no style, and her skills would be wasted. Miss Ruby's maid is almost ready to open her own dress shop, and Miss Hanson's French dresser says she is going to travel if they win tonight. They won't. I bet them all, and the underbutler, that we'll outshine every one of their ladies tonight, and lead at the finish of the contest, too."

"I wish you hadn't wagered so much of your money. I have little chance at the dancing. Harry and I have only danced together a few times."

"Are you too warm so close to the fire, miss?"

"No, I am fine." Her face was red because she'd been thinking of last night's dance.

Sarah clucked her tongue, just as her mother would have. "Master Harry ought to know better."

"But I wanted—"

"Of course you did, but he should have made time for practicing."

Oh. Simone realized they were speaking of two different things. "We'll do the best we can. I've seen Claire dance, and Ruby, and then there's Miss Baylor, who is a natural-born ballerina."

"The wagering in the servants' hall favors Miss Hope, but I put my blunt on you and Master Harry."

"Oh, dear. I hope you do not lose too much."

Sarah smiled. "It's his money anyway. He thinks you can win."

The best thing Sarah learned from the underbutler, who had it from the cellist, was a list of the music to be played that night. And it cost only a kiss or two.

Simone hummed the tunes she knew, and waltzed with the dog, a footstool, and Sandaree, when the Indian girl came to share a luncheon tray. She stayed for a chess game, since neither of them felt like napping, or fussing with their hair and gowns for another few hours.

Simone did go downstairs later, to see if Harry had come back. She thought he'd be closeted with Lord Gorham in the library, watching the safe, but only Sir Chauncey was there, snoring loudly, an empty bottle at his feet.

"A truly inspired disguise," she whispered before backing out of the room.

He winked and went back to snoring.

With no sign of Harry all day, it was finally time to dress. Sarah did her hair up in a new style, long sections of it braided together with strands of rhinestones. Then she gathered the braids to form a glittering coil atop Simone's head, as if she already wore a crown. Small flame-colored curls framed her face and forehead. The curls might have lent a cherubic look, except for the gown that was anything but angelic or innocent.

Simone wore Madame Journet's masterpiece, the black silk gown with the glittering red brilliants on the lace overskirt. The bodice was a bit snug, due to the superb meals at Griffin Manor, but Sarah assured Simone that the tighter fit simply made her breasts look fuller and the décolletage plunge a little deeper. Miss Noma had the figure for it, Sarah swore.

Simone faced the mirror and frowned. "I don't have half the bust Claire does, and the men are doing the voting. You know how they are about big bosoms."

Sarah's own figure was still developing. Half out of

loyalty, and half out of pride in her own work, she said, "Think of Miss Hope as a frigate. She'll get you where you're going, all right. But you're like one of those fancy sloops they race on the Thames, sleek, fast, and exciting just to watch."

Simone felt like a scow with a fresh coat of paint. Whatever made her think she could compete with Claire? The very idea of being on show still terrified her, while Claire was used to the adulation of huge audiences. And even if Simone's gown was lovely, and her hair done in elaborate twists, Claire would still outshine her. That necklace in the safe guaranteed it.

Simone's own neck was bare—and her upper chest, too, the neckline was so low—because Harry's blue sapphire would look dreadful with this gown. She had no other jewelry, not even a locket or a string of pearls.

"Perhaps I should take one of the rhinestone ribbons from my hair."

Sarah screamed at the idea.

Then Harry came in and Simone forgot about her hair, her gown, her bare chest. Here was perfection. Too bad she could not wear him on her sleeve, or change the voting to best-dressed couple. Harry was always the finest-looking man in the room, and not just in her opinion, either. She noticed how every female's eyes followed him around a room. Tonight he was magnificent.

His white satin knee breeches and white clocked stockings delineated every firm muscle, revealing a rider's strength, a fencer's sinew, a woman's dream. His dark tailcoat spread without a wrinkle across broad shoulders, and his sparkling white neckcloth was tied in an intricate knot without being so high that it hid his handsome face. He wore a different stickpin from his usual sapphire tonight, which delighted Simone.

"You put on a ruby to match my gown? How clever."

"No," he said. "I wore the ruby to match this." He held out a velvet pouch that she thought she'd seen in the safe.

She kept her hands at her sides. "But we agreed that I cannot accept such expensive gifts from you."

Harry turned to the maid. "Sarah, I think Metlock needs help in the dressing room. We couldn't get the neckcloth right, and made a mess of things trying."

When Sarah left, tactfully shutting the door behind her, Harry placed the pouch in Simone's hands and folded her fingers around it. "This is not a gift, not exactly, anyway. Think of it as a bonus for last night."

"That's worse! I didn't let you kiss me for the money!"

" 'Let' me? Sweetings, you nearly begged me to kiss you, and more. But I meant the necklace to be a reward for your part in switching the blackmail letters."

"Did Danforth come for them?"

"Not yet. Almost every other chap here did, retrieving some bauble or other for his ladylove to wear tonight. This is a mere token of appreciation. Nothing more. You deserve it."

"It doesn't make me a whore, does it? Taking money for my favors?"

He took the pouch back and opened the drawstrings. "It makes you a sharp-witted woman who did her job well."

Simone still wasn't sure, until she saw the necklace Harry let trail from his fingers. Now she was sure she'd never seen anything more beautiful, more perfect for her gown, unless it was Harry himself.

Diamonds and rubies sparkled like stars on a silver chain. "This must have cost a fortune."

He did not even try to lie. "I meant it to be a loan when I purchased it, to be returned to the jeweler when we returned to London. Like your gown, though, it seems to have been made for you, no matter who first commissioned it. No other woman could ever do it justice. It is yours."

She still did not take the necklace from him. "You had to have known what I'd be wearing when you purchased this. Do you know everything?"

"When I need to. Tonight I need you to be dressed as finely as the other women. No, finer."

"Did you bet on me, too?"

"I tried to tell you, I am betting my life on you. Strangers are invited to Claire's ball tonight, with hordes of raffish gentlemen coming out from Town with their bits of muslin. You will stand out among the entire demimonde."

"Heavens, is that supposed to set me at ease? I am already nervous enough about the dance."

"Come. Let us practice."

"Not in the chair! We'll have no more of your kind of dancing, sir. Sarah will flay us alive if we muss my hair or my gown. I am certain Metlock feels the same about his handiwork."

"They can go to the devil." Harry fastened the necklace around her neck, stood back to admire it, and then started humming one of the newer waltzes. He'd bribed the orchestra conductor. It was the right tune.

It was the right man.

Claire turned purple when she saw Simone, which did not look well with her blue-green ensemble.

"That's my gown! The one I ordered months ago from Madame Journet! She said there was an error and it was lost."

"Surely that is not the same gown." Lord Gorham smoothly stepped between the two women. "You can see how well it fits Miss Royale, pet. It's not your size."

"Are you suggesting I am fat?" Purple turned to puce, which was worse.

"Never, my precious. You are perfect. Your gown is perfect. Remember, we are calling this the Mermaid Ball. You look like a sea nymph."

Claire hadn't told anyone else in the house that the ball was going to have a sea motif. Blue and green silks hung from the walls, with frondlike streamers draped over the windows. Glass bowls with live fish rested on pedestals, and large shells held exotic blooms. A dolphin fountain in the corner spouted punch, and paper dolphins swam from the chandeliers. The only way Claire could match the room better would be if she had a fish tail instead of feet.

Her watered-silk ensemble was exquisite, the colors shifting as she moved. The diamond and emerald neck-lace sat atop her impressive bosom, and more diamonds sparkled in her ears, while pearls crowned her black hair.

"Too much ballast in the bow for a mermaid," Harry whispered. "She'd sink."

So did Simone's hopes. All of the women looked gorgeous.

Sandaree wore a sari of tissue-thin white silk with gold flecks and a wide gold band at the hem. The lustrous fab-ric was wrapped and gathered tight at the waist, then draped to leave one shoulder entirely bare. Sandaree had painted her twining-leaf design on the dusky skin there with gold paint to match the crown of gold leaves she wore. Her dark hair flowed loose down her back, past her waist. She had gold sandals on her feet, and tiny gold bells in her ears.

Ruby was in dark red as always, but tonight her gown's neckline almost met the high waist. A slit in the skirt revealed far more leg than proper, to show white silk stockings embroidered with red roses. Ruby wore long white gloves and a long strand of large pearls. The ruby pendant she always wore hung from her forehead.

Daisy looked like another sea sprite in turquoise satin, with scalloped hem and neck. She carried a fan painted with sea serpents in a turquoise ocean. Captain Entwhistle confessed he'd heard about the ball's theme before they left Town.

Simone glared at Harry. "I thought you knew everything."

"Everything that matters."

Sir Chauncey's ballet dancer's gown had five flounces. She had a frown for him when he staggered into one.

Miss Connors's gown was silver, what there was of it. She had a diamond pendant so large that it filled the exposed vee between her breasts.

"Glass," Harry whispered to Simone. "Her baronet cannot afford the real thing."

Miss Hanson wore white, like a debutante, but of muslin so thin one could see the outline of her legs through the skirt, and so damp it clung to them.

Maura wore a gown with tartan trim. "It's all the rage, don't you know."

Alice wore a tent. That's what she called the expanse of pink fabric needed to cover her stomach. But she looked happiest of all the women, there on Lord Comden's arm. She had no thought of winning the contest, so had no taut nerves.

The voting began. Each gentleman was given a blue card and a pencil to mark his choice of best-dressed mistress for the first round. The women with the three highest scores progressed to the final vote, four if there was a tie.

Everyone speculated that Lord Ellsworth and Mr. Anthony, without their original escorts, could be the deciding factors, if each of the other men voted for his own mistress. Danforth was another question, since he obviously preferred the ballet dancer to Sandaree.

"Hm, I wonder whom I should vote for," Harry teased.

Each man folded his ballot and tossed it into a hat Lord Gorham's butler held—after Sir Chauncey insisted on looking at the hat carefully, to make sure it contained no extra ballots. Gorham would have challenged him to a duel for the slur to his honor if Sir Chauncey wasn't too castaway to be taken seriously.

Twelve gentlemen were choosing between ten women. Some of the men were blinded by affection; some wanted to stay in Gorham's good graces; a few were tired of their mistresses.

The ballots were opened in front of everyone, then laid on a table. Daisy, Alice, and Ruby each got one vote. Sandaree, Claire, and Simone each got three. The others got none. The ballet dancer tossed her empty wineglass at Sir Chauncey, her fan at Danforth, and herself into Lord Ellsworth's arms. Miss Hanson ran back to her room, shivering from her clammy skirts, and Maura cried.

The three finalists were brought to the front of the room, like horses at the starting gate. Gorham's butler began to hand out the ballots, green this time, but Sir Chauncey cleared his throat, belched, and said, "How about if the losing ladies get to vote at this round, too? After all, we're judging the gowns, and no one knows more about fashion than the women."

The men nodded sagely. The women clapped their approval.

Gorham said no. "That isn't in the rules."

"They may be your rules," Mr. Anthony put in, "but it's our money."

"Hear, hear!"

Claire said no. "You gentlemen may not be aware of

the latest styles, but you are wise enough to judge what is most becoming, most pleasing to the eye."

"So are we," Ruby called from across the room. "How many of the swells pick out their own clothes, much less ours?"

Maura said she knew which gown she'd like to have as her own. Daisy and Alice seconded her, although Alice added she'd have to wait to look that good in any one of the frocks.

To her utter chagrin, Claire was overruled by her own guests. The butler ripped the green ballots in half so there were enough to go around. Sandaree put her hands together and gracefully salaamed, first to Lord Danforth, then to Mr. Anthony, and to each woman in turn, while the spectators applauded.

Simone pirouetted, so everyone could see the low back of her gown, and how it clung to her curves. She couldn't help laughing, her pleasure written on her face. Harry blew her a kiss, so she curtsied and blew one back with both hands. She got cheers and smiles.

Claire raised her nose in the air. That part-Gypsy mixed breed, mistress to a notorious bastard, had stolen her gown. The Indian slave girl's costume wasn't even stylish by British standards, or French. Now they were changing Claire's rules and acting like hoydens. Claire refused to look at them, she who had been the toast of London and several small principalities. She tipped her head slightly to Gorham.

He voted for her, as did three other men. Not one woman wrote Claire's name on the ballot. She'd treated them all to her haughty disdain, and cheated them out of a fair chance at the prize money.

Sandaree received six votes altogether, some out of pity for her circumstances.

Noma, who always had a kind word or a smile or an offer to help, who put Claire in her place, received the rest of the votes. She'd won.

The prize this time was a diamond and emerald bracelet, which just happened to match Claire's necklace. The bracelet was worth far more than the ten guineas of the other contests, but Simone accepted it from Lord Gorham with a kiss on his cheek. She would have kissed Claire, too, if the other woman hadn't stalked off to greet her newly arriving guests. Simone was shaking so hard, Harry had to fasten the bracelet on her wrist. He turned it so the emeralds didn't show so much, to clash with her gown. "There, now you look more like a queen. Queen of my heart."

Chapter Twenty-seven

Half the libertines in London drove out for the ball with their ladybirds. Claire invited her friends from the theater and the opera. Gorham invited his acquaintances from the clubs and Parliament. Those who were unmarried, or wished they were, accepted the invitation to what looked like a Cyprian's Ball in a country house. Few of the straitlaced locals attended, scandalized enough by rumors of spies, orgies, and foreigners. In fact, they closed their doors and kept their children inside. None of them wanted their daughters getting seduced, their sons getting ideas.

The Londoners knew about the mermaid theme, unlike the houseguests, and some came in costume. Several men in togas carried tritons; a few women dragged fish tails behind them. One had a small stuffed carp on her head; another's gown was patterned in fish scales. A third appeared to be wearing nothing but net.

There was no receiving line, but a row of servants met the newcomers and directed them to the huge ballroom and the gilt chairs around the edges. Only the ten couples in the contest, it was explained, were to dance the first waltz, all at once. After that, everyone present could raise their hands for their favored couple. The three couples with the most votes got to dance again, one at a time. Three almost-independent judges got to count the raised hands: Lord Ellsworth, Gorham's butler, and a defrocked vicar from London.

Claire and Gorham performed like professionals, or like a lord and a lady. They kept the proper distance apart, looked elegant together, and kept perfect time to the music.

Danforth and Sandaree danced far apart. She knew the steps by now, but needed more guidance than he was giving. So she started to perform her own movements, to his disgust. He roughly grabbed her nearer to stop her from making an exhibit of herself again.

Alice and Comden danced as close as her stomach allowed. They laughed, not paying attention to the tempo or the watchers.

Sir Chauncey and Miss Baylor were erratic. She was graceful; he was disgracefully inebriated. The ballet dancer kept pulling her skirt aside so he did not step on the flounces. He kept staggering into other couples.

Miss Hanson, in a different, drier gown, and the banker would have done well, except he was too fat, too old, too obviously forced into an activity he disliked.

Maura Doyle was too fast and enthusiastic. She and Caldwell performed more of a polka than a dignified waltz.

Ruby and Lord Bowman had danced together for almost a year and could anticipate each other's moves before they were made. They were handsome together, besides. He showed a flair for stylish clothes with padded shoulders, high shirt points, and a ruby in his cravat. She showed her legs.

Neither Daisy nor her partner, Captain Entwhistle, appeared to advantage on a dance floor. She was too used to striding across fields; he was too used to keeping his balance on a heaving deck. They did seem to be enjoying themselves, however, unlike some of the other pairs.

Mary Connors and her baronet danced well, except the actress was too dramatic in her movements. She was used to performing on the stage, with exaggerated motions to be seen from a distance. Up close she looked like a puppet on strings.

Simone and Harry flowed together. He was a masterful dancer and an effortless leader. Simone thought that any female could look good in his arms, and feel good just being there. She laughed aloud, because she had worried, and because she was the one who got to dance with him. He smiled back, and they might have been dancing on the top of mountain, or underwater, for all either cared.

The three finalist couples were Claire and Gorham, Ruby and Bowman, and Simone and Harry. Ruby and Bowman danced first.

"I think we got the most votes," Harry told Simone as they watched the other couple dip and turn.

Simone was doing mathematic calculations. She was still too far behind Claire in point count. If Claire won the dancing contest, Simone's chances of the grand prize were almost nil.

"Don't think about it," Harry told her. "You can't dance and fret at the same time. You'll only look stiff."

"That's silly. Miss Baylor looked graceful even with Sir Chauncey tromping on her feet."

"Not to me, she didn't. Of course I was only looking at you."

"Were you? Really?"

"Well, I did have to watch where we were going, so we could avoid Chappy and the chairs."

"Next time will be easier, with only us on the floor." Which reminded her they'd be alone in front of over a hundred people. "Dear heavens, everyone will be watching us!"

Harry stroked the new pucker between her eyes. "I told you, do not worry or you won't dance as well. Think if all your muscles puckered up like this one."

His touch made more of them tighten, from her belly to her toes.

"You are still too stiff. I should have plied you with wine."

"Then I might fall asleep."

"You wouldn't if I kissed you."

"In front of all these people? Don't you dare!"

He laughed and kissed her wrist, above the glove. Now she felt her bones turn to liquid and her blood grow warm, just as the orchestra started their waltz.

They went round and round, smooth and flowing in wide circles. Her gown swirled and sparkled, and the rhinestones in her hair caught the chandelier's light, so she could see sparks reflected in Harry's blue eyes. She did not look at anything but him, until the spectators pushed closer to the roped-off dance floor. She trusted Harry not to bump them into anyone, but what if the rope's stanchions fell?

"Smile, sweetheart."

"But I want to win, Harry."

"I know you do. But if you don't, I have a surprise for you later."

She smiled, thinking of what it might be. She looked ahead—and tripped.

Harry caught her immediately and swung her around to disguise the misstep as intentional. Then he tipped her back over his arm and kissed her lips before bringing her back upright in another spinning turn, faster and faster, for the climax of their performance.

The applause stirred enough of a breeze to make the chandelier rock. Harry bowed and Simone curtsied to all four sides of the room.

"I think we recovered nicely," Harry said as they started off the dance floor. "We were better than Bowman and Ruby. And we got a louder ovation at the end."

"It was Fordyce. He's in the crowd."

Now Harry almost stumbled. "The one who lived below you at the rooming house, who frightened you?"

"Yes, him."

"Try to keep an eye on him. You can point him out to me as soon as everyone starts watching Claire and Gorham."

"Will he recognize me, do you think?"

"Your mother wouldn't recognize you, my dear. Miss Prunes and Prisms is long gone. Pretend you never saw him before if he does say anything."

Claire and Gorham took their places for their final-round waltz. They had danced together for twelve years. As with Claire's billiards game, practice and repetition made them superb. Like billiards, their waltzing followed the best angles, the proper posture, the surest touch with the cues. It was about as lively as a cue stick, though.

"They're going to win," Simone said. The nearest spectators seemed to be in awe of the majestic couple.

Harry was scanning the crowd for Fordyce, looking where Simone had seen him last. He cursed to himself that no one had found the information he requested about the man's background. His men were still working on it, the latest report had advised. Damn, if he were in London, in charge, he'd already have the man's true name and motive.

He looked back at the dance floor and had to agree that

Gorham and Claire made a classic twosome. They'd win. Harry felt sorry for Simone, who wanted to win so badly. She deserved to, far more than Claire.

Sir Chauncey must have thought so, too. When Claire and Gorham reached where he was standing, he started to fall into a drunken stupor, onto Miss Baylor. She shoved him away, right onto the dancing area, taking the ropes and stanchions down with him. Forced to avoid everything, Gorham quickly turned Claire again, but somehow Sir Chauncey's foot caught the hem of Claire's gown. She fell back, right on her derriere.

This was not a polite London crowd that would have pretended nothing happened. This was a hundred or more libertines and their dolly-mops, women Claire had not invited to her house party because they were not good enough. They weren't pretty enough, talented enough, or rich enough from their trade. They were just honest whores who didn't try to put on the airs and graces of a lady.

They laughed. Loudly. And they laughed more when Gorham tried to help Claire to her feet, but couldn't lift her weight.

Simone and Harry won. Gorham's butler handed her the ten shiny guineas on a silver tray. In the midst of the congratulations and the gentlemen asking for a dance with Miss Royale, Simone asked Harry, "Does that mean I don't get a surprise?"

"It means we have to find Fordyce and find out why he's here."

"I suppose he is here for the same reason everyone else is, to dance and drink, and possibly find a new mistress."

"I doubt it. I never trusted him."

"You know him?"

"No, but Mr. Harris did. Your next dance is with

Daniel, is that right?" When she nodded, he said, "Good. Tell him, circle the room, look for Fordyce. But do not approach the man. He might be dangerous."

"Can you tell me why?"

"Because his name is not Fordyce."

Harry made sure Daniel arrived in time to fend off more would-be suitors for Simone's favors. Noma Royale was suddenly the toast of the demimonde, and everyone wanted to meet her.

Harry went hunting. He also whispered into Sir Chauncey's ear—the one Claire had not boxed when she got to her feet. Sir Chauncey staggered out the ballroom door.

Simone had to describe Fordyce for Daniel, his deep-set eyes and loose jowls. Daniel kept turning her in the dance to look in all directions until she grew dizzy. "Perhaps we'd do better strolling about," she suggested.

They never spotted Fordyce. They did see Claire leave the room, holding a handkerchief to her head. She claimed an indisposition. Her disposition was in dire need of privacy to throw a tantrum of epic proportions.

Daniel did not let anyone approach Simone. "My cousin's particular friend," he told the gentlemen, warning them off.

"You do that very well," Simone told him. "You would make a good brother. Or husband."

Which made Daniel hand her off to Sir Chauncey for his dance with more speed than politeness. Simone was not willing to sacrifice her gown to Chappy's subterfuge, so again suggested a walk during their dance.

He lurched and leaned on her, but gently. They made slow progress, the better to look for Fordyce. If Simone was looking for Harry more than for Fordyce, well, she couldn't help it.

Harry found their quarry first. The oily-haired man who was supposed to be an investor was searching the room himself.

"Lose your ladybird?" Harry asked. "Mine's done a flit now that we've won."

"No, I— Do I know you? You look familiar."

"Daresay you just saw me dance. Good show, eh? The name is Harmon. Harry Harmon."

Fordyce jumped back, before recovering enough to murmur something polite about the dance and his partner.

"Can't say I recall being introduced to you, Mr. . . ."

"Ford." He noticed Harry's grimace. "I say, you are not ill, are you?"

"No. I need a drink, none of that insipid punch the dolphin's spouting. Have you seen it?"

"A profligate waste of good money, like everything else here."

"Quite right. I can see you are a serious gentleman, so please tell me what they are saying in London about some Frenchies trying to overthrow the government and bring the Corsican back. We don't hear much. The woman involved was part of the contest, actually. That's why I'm interested."

"Nothing. I know nothing about any of that." Fordyce, or Ford, hurried off.

Lies. Bitter, arsenic lies.

Harry let him go, but followed at a distance, which was easy enough in the crowded rooms and corridors. He met Simone and Sir Chauncey on the way to the refreshments room.

"Ah, my love, there you are," Harry said, then lowered his voice. "And there he is up ahead. Chappy, you go first."

Sir Chauncey headed for the wine. Harry and Simone accepted more congratulations, more jealous stares and vulgar leers. Harry tucked her arm more firmly in his and led her to the tables of food. Claire had outdone herself, setting up a scene out of Neptune's closet, with huge clamshells as serving dishes filled with lobster patties, oysters, eels in aspic. A mermaid carved in ice stood in the center of the table, surrounded by fruit and cheese cut in fish shapes. Even the wineglasses had fish-tail stems.

They watched Sir Chauncey lurch into Fordyce, then stagger away. Sir Chauncey now had the man's purse; Fordyce now had wine spatters on his neckcloth.

"He has a gun," Chappy reported, after reeling back across the room with a full plate that dripped on everyone he passed.

"And he's talking to Miss Hanson's banker," Simone pointed out. "Do you think there is a connection?"

Whitehall was still looking for the financial backer of Eloise Lecroix's scheming. Who better than a man who ran his own bank? Harry knew the man's name was Spenser and his wife was in Norfolk, but not much else. When Harry'd asked the gentlemen about rumors of sedition, the banker had replied that attempts to overthrow the government were bad for business. He didn't want to talk about it. Both were true. Damn. If Harry hadn't been so distracted by Simone and his frustrated sexual desires, he might have looked further.

Spenser and Fordyce were walking through the French doors to the terrace. "Follow them, Noma, but at a distance. Say you are getting some air while I fill a plate for you. It's too suspicious if Chappy or I bump into him again."

"What if he recognizes me?"

"He won't, and he won't admit it if he does, not when he is using a different name himself. He'll be as upset to see you as you are to see him."

Once outside, Simone pretended to breathe deeply.

She kept looking toward the doors as if waiting for Harry, or another tryst. The two men ignored her, although they did walk a little farther away. They kept arguing in Spanish, which immediately spelled guilt to Simone. Proper gentlemen holding a respectable conversation had no need to hide their words. Fordyce kept looking over his shoulder, so she turned her back on them.

Harry joined her at the railing of the terrace with one plate, one fork, a meal for lovers to share. The two men separated, but Harry had people stationed in the garden to watch where they went. "Could you hear what they were saying?"

"Fordyce wants his money now, worried that he won't get paid with Eloise in jail. Spenser says he'll get it when the job is done. They did mention *el bastardo comman-dante*. I'm sorry, but could that be you?"

Harry couldn't be sure, since there were scores of other officers, some born on the right side of the blanket, who were considered bastards. It did seem likely that Eloise would want to avenge her father's death at the same time as wreaking havoc in the government. It was less likely that she and her cohorts could tie Harry Harmon to Major Harrison.

He knew where Fordyce lived. The man would be arrested as soon as he returned to London, if Daniel brought the message.

Daniel slammed his loaded plate down on the balustrade rail. "Not me. Not again. I ain't going and that's definite. I have my eye on a blonde who—"

He went when Harry explained that more of his hand-picked intelligence officers were less than fifteen minutes away, in Griffin Woods, for just such emergencies. They had riders to carry messages, armed men to keep England safe.

When Daniel returned, the party was louder. Daniel's blonde was draped around the defrocked vicar like a clerical collar. Spenser was in the cardroom. His mistress, Miss Hanson, was sitting at the pianoforte in the music room, entertaining a baritone from the opera.

"Where's Fordyce?" Daniel asked Harry.

"He looked into Gorham's library, according to the footman guarding the safe. Then he asked if I had been here in Richmond the entire time."

"This damned plot is about you?"

"The threads are connected perhaps."

"I say we bash his head in and be done with it."

"Not yet. Besides, a dead man won't give answers. He'll be followed wherever he goes. We have to deal with Spenser first."

"Don't look at me. I won't do it. I told you, I hated acting like a brute, shaking the truth out of prisoners. You get Rex to come interrogate the dirty dish."

Simone was looking from one to the other, wondering what they were talking about. "What does it matter who does the asking? He won't admit he's a traitor anyway."

Harry put another strawberry in her mouth, then wiped the drip of red from her lips.

Daniel sighed and said he'd go.

Daniel's reputation for being one of the army's dreaded Inquisitors preceded him. Spenser refused to go away from the party with the much larger man. So Sir Chauncey spilled his wineglass in the banker's lap. Sopping wet, he had to leave the cardroom.

Daniel had him out in the garden almost before his feet touched the ground, where Harry had two soldiers in uniform waiting behind a wall of shrubs. He and Simone stayed on the terrace.

"Shouldn't you be helping?" she asked.

"What, Harry Harmon dirty his hands with political intrigue? Never."

Daniel came back smiling. "The fellow pulled a knife on me."

Simone rushed out of Harry's arms to turn Daniel's face to the lantern light so she could see he was all right.

He smiled at her concern, but gave her a look of disbelief for doubting his prowess. "It was a little knife." He rubbed his knuckles. "Sorry about your questions, Harry. He won't be answering any time soon. Weak jaw, don't you know. The soldiers are taking him back to their camp."

"That's fine as long as Fordyce doesn't know he's not getting paid for whatever he's hired to do."

"Most likely to kill you," Daniel said cheerfully.

Simone gasped.

Harry frowned at Daniel for frightening her. "He won't get the chance, my dear. I'm here, remember. Thanks to you, everyone in London knows exactly where I am." He pulled her back into his arms and kissed her.

Daniel shook his head and wandered off. "Love. Bah! They better have some of those oysters left. And an opera dancer for dessert."

Chapter Twenty-eight

Many hours later, after showing the crowd that they were still there, and showing the gentlemen that they had no chance with Miss Royale, Harry finally led Simone up to their room.

Dawn was almost breaking, but Simone still wanted to know the surprise.

Harry was ready for sleep. "Now? But you won the dance contest."

"*We* won. Tell me anyway. I was a help tonight, wasn't I? They were speaking Spanish, you know. Not every female could have translated for you."

"You mentioned that before. Twice. Yes, you were invaluable. Spotting Fordyce, overhearing the conversation, knowing Spanish." He rolled over, on his side of the bed, the dog between them. "In fact, if you hadn't sought a new career, we'd never have known Fordyce existed."

"Amazing, isn't it? If I hadn't lost my last position, I never would have met you."

"Amazing." He fluffed up his pillow. "Fate. Luck. Magic. Good night."

She ordered the dog off the bed and rolled close enough to breathe in his ear. "Harry."

He tried to pull the covers over his head, but Simone held on to them. "Very well, you were excellent. And your brother is coming to London. Now go to sleep."

Go to sleep? Simone sat up, pulling all the blankets with her. "What? When? He mustn't know about us!"

Harry sighed and rolled onto his back. "That's why I didn't want to tell you now. You'll worry yourself sick. There was a fire at his school, and the boys were sent home early for the summer holiday. He had no address for you, so the headmaster wrote to Viscount Rexford, Auguste's new guardian. Rex is fetching him to Town, along with the earl and Lady Royce. And Rex's wife and the twins. Your brother will be ensconced in one of the finest homes in London, among people of impeccable reputations now."

"Now?"

"The earl did father an illegitimate son, you know. He was also suspected of tampering with justice once. His wife left him and lived apart for decades. His heir was despised in the army, then became a morose hermit. Rex's wife was accused of murder, but she didn't do it. Oh, and the twins were born a bit early."

"Are you sure it's a good place for my brother?"

"It's far better than the Kensington house, don't you think?"

"What if he finds out? About us."

"He won't. But if he discovers that you were willing to sacrifice yourself to save him from the mills or the mines, he'll be grateful."

Simone thought her brother would be furious that he wasn't the one to make the sacrifice. She had to get him out of London, fast, away from Harry's family, who must know something. Lord Rexford must wonder why he was named guardian, after all. "I can understand about the viscount fetching Auguste, which is very kind of him when my brother could travel by coach to Royce Hall in the country. But to drag his wife and children to London? And Lord and Lady Royce also?"

Which was precisely what he did not wish to discuss, and why he was sleeping as far from Simone and temptation as he could get without falling on the floor. He wished he could lie for once and mention errands in Town, a session of Parliament, plans to renovate Royce House for the next Season, when Daniel's sister was having her come-out. They all might be true, but those were not the reasons the Royce clan was coming to London.

"They are all coming to rescue you, I fear. Daniel felt he had to tell them. The oaf can't even lie in a letter. They have decided that Miss Ryland's reputation will be safer if you stay with them in Grosvenor Square until the countess or Rex's wife can find you a governess position. Perhaps one of them needs a companion."

"That sounds ideal. Why didn't you tell me?"

"Because I still need Noma Royale for a few more days and you'd start acting like a proper female again."

And because he knew what they all expected—nay, what they would demand. Simone was too innocent to realize it, or she did not know the rules that governed polite society. Or else she decided that her sojourn as a doxy meant they no longer applied. He always felt his bastardy kept him from those lofty precincts and the laws that held sway there.

But she was not like his own mother, an opera dancer who was not born to respectable gentility, not educated like a lady, not a blasted Ryland of Cumberland. They were *not* going to let him forget he was a gentleman, despite his tainted birth.

Simone was thinking about how to get Auguste away

from Harry's family. With the winnings she already had, plus her salary from Harry, she did not have to work for a while. "Perhaps Auguste and I can go to Brighton for the summer, or rent a country cottage somewhere."

"You'll be invited to the coast when the family returns there. Your brother will love it. Rex can teach him to sail and ride and fish."

"Will you be there?"

"I went once, for the twins' christenings." That was all he was going to say about the matter. "Now go to sleep. We're going to Richmond tomorrow, and then you have to perform at night."

"I can't win, so why bother?"

"Fine. Then the countess will find you a position. She knows everyone in Town."

Simone did not cherish the idea of proper employment the way she used to, not with a small fortune in sight. Governesses, even ladies' companions, made a pittance in comparison. "I am ahead now, but Claire will win the talent contest. And she'll also take the Quality judging. She looks like a queen, and acts like one, too."

"But you act like a lady."

She put a hand on his chest. "I don't feel like a lady tonight."

He set her hand back on the covers. "Well, you are one. You'll spend a sennight as a courtesan, no more, and it is just an act. An act," he repeated, more for himself than for her.

"No one will know if we stop pretending."

"I will." Lord, he could almost taste her lips, but he imagined his father's disappointment. And the countess's disgust. Even Rex, the half brother he had come to cherish, would be angry. And what of Mrs. Harrison, the woman who had raised him to be better than a bastard, and his own housekeeper, who believed him honorable, if not saintly?

Dammit, they all lived by society's rules, he told himself. He did not. Then he recalled that Simone ought to. He kissed her chastely, briefly, brotherly. And cursed to himself for another hour.

They were a much smaller crowd going to Richmond than originally planned. The banker was gone, of course. His mistress, after learning of his arrest and undergoing an interview with that lummox Daniel Stamfield, packed her bags—and a few of Spenser's—to leave with the visiting baritone. Miss Hanson felt she might as well go, since her pianoforte playing had little chance of winning the talent contest.

Sir Chauncey Phipps's bedeviled ballerina, who had higher odds of earning a few guineas, left after the ball with a wealthy young viscount, a surer bet. Sir Chauncey himself was suffering a morning-after headache that could be relieved only by more of what caused the pain, so he never left Gorham's library.

Alice suffered morning sickness, too, so Lord Comden stayed back with her.

Claire did not wish to visit the maze. Or see any of her guests. Gorham told her Spenser had taken ill, rather than have her suffer the ignominy of another spy or swindler at her house party. Maybe she was right to go to Cornwall, he thought. Even though he hated the idea, the scandals might not reach there. He stayed at Griffin Manor to keep her company.

Harry and Simone rode. The rest drove. Since there'd be no contest at the maze, the men took to betting on whose curricle was faster. Lord James Danforth was so determined to win he took a turn too sharply, struck a

signpost with his rear wheel, and had to pull over to inspect the damage. He blamed Sandaree for distracting
him with her stupid screaming. Lord Ellsworth took her
up in his phaeton, leaving Danforth shouting at his
groom, his horses, the conditions of the road, and the
damned house party.

Harry took a shortcut, he said, through Griffin Woods.
Simone hoped he meant to have a private picnic, or a private tryst. Instead he met an officer in uniform and exchanged a few words she could not hear.

At the maze, Maura and her lover got lost, but everyone could hear her giggling, so shouted directions.
Danforth never showed up. Lord Ellsworth with his cane
and Mr. Anthony with his years argued over who was to
escort Sandaree. Two couples decided to stop at an inn
for ale rather than bother with the exercise. And Ruby and
Lord Bowman got in an argument over his not letting her
handle the ribbons of the curricle he'd bought her.
Everyone heard that, too, so their party was being well
noticed, which suited Harry.

He led Simone into the maze at such speed she was
nearly out of breath when they reached the center. Again
she hoped his haste meant he was eager to get her alone,
but all he did was gather a folded note stuck under a
bench there, and start back out.

"Harry, are you angry with me?"

He was angry with himself. This was a crucial time for
his plans, for the country. Every second he thought about
taking her in his arms, peeling away her clothes, spreading her glorious hair through his fingers, was a second—
hell, it was minutes and hours—he was not concentrating
on his job. He almost sympathized with Danforth.
Besides, today he could not afford to be out of sight of the
company, whether he wished it or not. "Of course I am

not angry at you. Let us stop at that inn the others found.
I am thirsty."

Of course he was angry, Simone decided. Why else
was he so cold and unfriendly? He didn't want her as his
mistress and she'd been too forward. He was foisting her
off on his family because he did not want her as anything
else, either. He didn't trust her with his plans, wouldn't
reveal any of his messages or notes, and hurried to be
done with her company.

She'd failed at winning his affection as surely as she'd
fail at winning the contest.

Claire made the introductions. She had regained her
confidence, with Gorham's help. What could compete
with her singing? Silhouettes? Whichever song or dance
Daisy or Simone could perform? Ha. The ballet might
have been in the running, but that was eliminated now,
along with the harp and the violin. The Shakespeare?
Doubtful. The jig or the card tricks? Never. The nearly
obscene Indian dance? Even the men had to have more
respect for culture than that.

She gave Daisy a wide smile.

While Captain Entwhistle looked on fondly, Daisy
stepped to the front of the music room where she'd placed
a trunk. Claire whispered to Gorham, "Lord, I hope she is
not going to put on a sheet and strike poses of Greek god-
desses or something."

She didn't. Daisy excused her lack of brilliance. She
could sing a little, she explained, and dance a little, even
play wooden pipes, but all without the overwhelming talent of the others. So she did what she did best. Or second
best, she added with a blush and a glance toward the captain, which drew a laugh. She opened the trunk and
brought out an entire layette for Alice's infant: tiny gowns

and caps, swaddling clothes and blankets, bibs and knitted socks so small they might have fit a man's thumb.
Baby things were often plain and serviceable, but these
were smocked and gathered, embroidered with miniature
rosebuds, trimmed with bits of lace and ribbons con-
tributed by half the women. The blanket from the wool
Simone had bought now had a fringed edge, and a bonnet
to match. Alice passed each garment around, while she
wept. So did most of the women, including Claire, who
fondled every little item.

More than one of the men wiped at his eyes, too. A few
had never handled infant wear—or an infant—and marveled at the small size. They all—except for Lord James
Danforth—put a coin in the trunk.

"What kind of entertainment is this?" the duke's son
asked with his usual sneer. "I thought the entertainments
were supposed to be high-toned, not celebrating another
bastard."

Harry tossed another coin into the trunk with a resounding clink.

Then came Ruby's turn. She had intended to sing also,
she confessed. She smiled at Claire and said, "I am not
that big a fool. But I can entertain you, and give you a
memento to take home with you." She gestured toward a
screened enclosure erected at the back of the room, with
oil lamps directing light onto it. "Claire, you come first."

In no time at all, Ruby had Claire's elegant profile cut
out of black paper. She didn't stop at her patrician nose,
but included her plentiful bosom.

Claire handed it to Gorham and pushed him forward.
She wanted the cutout of him to take with her.

"I usually do the gents in a more personal way," Ruby
said with a wink, "if you get my drift."

"Not in my music room, you won't," Claire insisted.

"Anyone who removes his unmentionables will be out of the house and out of the wagering."

So Ruby traced profiles only at first. She was fast and accurate, and laughed while she worked. She added a wineglass held to Sir Chauncey's mouth, put a needle and thread in Daisy's hands.

She refused to do Bowman's silhouette. "I already have one that I'll keep the rest of my life. I'd show it to you gents, but that would ruin your night."

She captured Maura's turned-up nose perfectly, and then Lord Ellsworth's hawklike beak. Alice and Comden posed opposite each other, so she made their lips touch on the paper. Ruby thought she couldn't do Harry or Noma justice in black, not with their vivid coloring, so she got Mr. Black to sit still and cut out the dog's silhouette.

Danforth despised his picture; he claimed his nose was not that high. No one agreed. Sandaree chose not to pose, but Ruby cut a black flower for her, like the henna vines Sandaree painted on her hands. Sandaree bowed and said she would cherish the cutout along with Noma's shawl, gifts from her friends in this foreign land.

For the captain, Ruby put a sailing ship in the background of his profile. For Mr. Anthony, she took away a few of his chins. She cut a bust of Shakespeare for the actress, a racehorse for the baronet. Done with the silhouettes, she took up black page after black page and let her scissors fly while snips of paper fell in a dark blizzard at her feet. She made a chain of paper daisies for Daisy, paper dollies for the baby, a curricle for Bowman, a waltzing couple for Noma.

Even Sir Chauncey stayed awake to watch Ruby work. "Amazing. I've never seen the like." Everyone agreed with that.

Then it was Simone's turn.

She knew Claire intended to sing again that night, so she suggested their hostess perform now, while she arranged her props and clothes. Mr. Anthony said it was only fair that Sandaree have an encore, too, so Simone had enough time to finish her preparations. Sarah waited in the sewing room to help, and Metlock was there with Harry's costume. Harry was still going to be her partner, for tonight, anyway.

When they were ready, Metlock carried a cloth-covered table into the music room, followed by Sarah with a candelabra to place on top. They lowered the room's oil lamps, casting shadows everywhere but at the table, where they placed three chairs, two in front, one behind. Then Harry strode in, wearing a red scarf around his neck, and a red sash around his waist. A sword hung at his side. He had on a white shirt with billowing sleeves, and wore his black hair in disordered waves. He was so handsome, smiled so confidently, that Simone almost forgot the speech she'd prepared. He held his hand out for her to come forward.

She walked into the room, her bracelets tinkling, the hoops in her ears glittering, and her red hair loose down her back. She wore a white drawstring blouse with embroidery at the low neckline, a loose piecework skirt with the bright red petticoat showing beneath the hem.

"What the devil . . . ?" someone asked.

"No devil," she said. "But there are some who consider Gypsy fortune-tellers Satan's servants. I do not. You should not, until you hear what I tell you. First I wish to relate a tale about my mother, who was half Gypsy. She never said she had the Sight, but she twice had a vision of my father drowning. She never let him go near a boat after that, not even a rowboat on the shallowest of lakes. She refused to let him swim or fish from shore. One rainy night he was thrown from his horse and landed in the ditch." She paused for dramatic effect. "He drowned."

A hush fell over the room.

"So cross my palm with silver and I will tell what I see. Who dares to go first?"

Sir Chauncey Phipps did. He handed Simone a coin and she took his hand in hers and closed her eyes. She hummed in a long-drawn note, and the room seemed to resonate with the energy of her concentration. Maura gave a nervous giggle.

"I see you smiling," Simone finally said. "With no drink in sight. You stand tall and steady, totally sober."

"Impossible," someone called out.

Simone ignored the shout and the laughter. "You are in the country with a woman. She is dark-haired and has a pebble in her shoe. No, she has a limp."

Sir Chauncey snatched his hand back. "I know what you are doing. You heard rumors of my past, that's all. Well, that woman is married."

"No, my friend. She is widowed. She is waiting for you in York."

Sir Chauncey looked at Harry. "Truly?"

"Yes."

Sir Chauncey wiped at another tear. "I never thought— That is, I need a drink. The last one I'll have for a while. You say Cornelia is waiting for me?"

Next Simone "saw" Mary Connors, the actress, playing the leading role in a successful new drama at Drury Lane. There'd be no more dreary traveling troupes for her. She described a vision of Maura back in Ireland with Caldwell, surrounded by young horses frolicking on green grass.

"How did you know I was thinking of setting up a racing stud?" Caldwell demanded.

Simone held one finger to her lips. "It's in the blood."

Captain Entwhistle, she predicted, was going to be of-fered command of one of His Majesty's new ships, and he was going to take Daisy with him as his wife, now that peace ruled the seas.

"His wife?" Daisy started crying. "I never hoped for that."

"Why not?" the captain asked after he placed another coin in Simone's hand. "Have to set a good example for my men, don't I?"

Next she described the vision of Mr. Anthony on a ship, too. He was sailing back to India, to warmth and great luxury. He had a woman to keep him company on the long journey, one who knew the country, could con-verse in several dialects, and was familiar with the in-trigues of the princes and their courts.

Mr. Anthony looked toward Sandaree. "Would you care to accompany me, my dear?"

"I should like nothing more, sahib. But my master—"

"There is no slavery in England," Mr. Anthony stated. "Or where this Englishman chooses to go."

"Here, now." Lord James Danforth stepped closer to the table. "I paid a great deal for the wench."

Before Mr. Anthony could leap to his feet, or have a spasm, Simone caught Danforth's sleeve. "Oh, but I see you on a boat, too."

He reluctantly put a coin on the table next to her when someone poked him in the back. "What rot. Everyone knows I have been wanting to purchase Traynor's yacht, as soon as the dibs are in tune."

Simone closed her eyes and hummed. "It is not that kind of boat. Oh, now I see you with a parcel of letters."

"What? I don't know anything about any letters!"

"That is a lie," Harry said from behind Simone. "You

stole them from a certain lady and tried to blackmail some very influential gentlemen."

Simone's audience backed up several feet, away from Danforth and his clenched fists. "I'd call you out for such base accusations, Harmon, but I will not duel with bastards. Or their Gypsy trash."

Simone could see Harry's hand reach for the sword at his side. She put a hand up to stop him and Harry understood. This was neither the time nor the place. He took a deep breath and said, "Good, for I would not accept a challenge from an unscrupulous swine like you. But if the papers are not yours, you will not mind if Gorham throws these in the fire." The marquis held a string-tied sheaf of letters and a journal over the hearth.

Danforth almost dived into the fireplace to rescue the bundle. "Give me that!"

"Of course," Gorham told him, handing over the blank documents.

Captain Entwhistle gave a piercing whistle and shouted, "To arms, men." Two burly sailors raced into the room and bound Danforth's hands. "The navy still needs able-bodied men," the captain told him as the sailors started dragging him out of the room. "They might make you an officer if your father pays 'em enough to keep you out of England. Not on my ship, I swear."

"You cannot do this! Tell them, Gorham. My father is a duke!"

"And he'd rather see you gone for a decade than have the family face a long, sordid trial. That's what his note said, anyway."

Sir Chauncey said Danforth's exit called for another drink, for everyone else.

"Go on, Noma," Ruby urged. "What do you see for me?"

She saw a shop filled with Ruby's artwork, a line of

customers waiting to have their silhouettes made. "I do not see Lord Bowman in the picture," she whispered to Ruby.

Ruby leaned over and whispered back, "Good riddance."

In Simone's vision, Lord Ellsworth was back with his wife. "She is breeding." He gave her an extra coin. "Finally!"

Alice held out a coin. "What do you see for me, Noma, a boy or a girl?"

Simone took Alice's hand and closed her eyes. "A boy."

Harry hid his surprise at Simone's accurate prediction, then reasoned that she had fifty-fifty odds of guessing right.

She was going on: "But you and your son and Lord Comden are on a beautiful tropical island, full of flowers, full of love and happiness. You wear his wedding ring."

"A wedding ring?" Comden sputtered. "I cannot. My father—"

"Is hale and hearty, with many years left before you need to take over his estate. He wishes you to find a wealthy bride, but if you have funds of your own, he cannot force you. I see that Lord Gorham is going to offer you the management of his Jamaican plantation. You and your wife, Alice."

"I am?" Gorham asked.

Simone nodded. "That is what I see."

Alice was crying again, in Comden's arms. "Can we really wed? Our son will be your legal heir?"

Everyone cheered when he said he'd speak to Gorham about the position, and the archbishop for a special license.

"What of me," Gorham wanted to know, "now that my Jamaican property is cared for?"

Simone took his coin and his hand, but reached out for Claire's hand, too. She closed her eyes, feeling Claire's fingers trembling. "I see . . . no, that cannot be right." She paused, hummed, paused again. "All I see is the two of you together right here in this room, Gorham at the pianoforte, Claire ready to sing. You both have gray hair, and a bit more weight."

Gorham shook his head. "My wife will not permit it."

Simone opened her eyes and smiled at him. "Your wife is in Scotland with her butler, her lover, not visiting her relations at all. Her father won't contest anything, not the bank accounts, not the settlements, if you agree not to sue for divorce in Parliament. His entire family would be ruined socially. Lady Gorham will not interfere in your life ever again."

"That cannot be true."

"It is, I heard her say so myself. That is, I saw her say she is not coming home, no matter the cost."

Gorham was ready to send a runner to London that instant, to see if any of what Simone said was true. The man could return before bedtime.

"If this is a joke . . . ," Claire began, her chin quivering. "I know I have not been kind, but to get one's hopes up, that would be too cruel."

"I only tell what I see. Give me your hand again." Simone waited a minute. "Yes, I see you and Gorham here, and a young girl playing a violin. She is a talented musician."

"No!" Claire yelled. "You cannot—"

Simone kept her eyes shut, her clasp on Claire's hand firm. "Your sister's child? No, she must be your cousin's orphaned daughter, the one you were going to care for in Cornwall."

"She'll come here?" She turned to Gorham. "May she?"

"Why not? The girl needs a home of her own, and this place is certainly large enough."

Claire started blubbering, not caring that her face paints ran and her tears spotted the silk gown she wore.

Gorham looked around. "That leaves Harry. What does his future hold?"

Harry? Simone hadn't thought to read his future. When she held his hand, she sometimes imagined him laughing, but nothing more. She couldn't put herself in the picture no matter how she tried. "I might as well."

He gave her a coin and held out his hand. She took it, felt the heat she always did, then a frigid blast of ice. "He's dead! Major Harrison. I see him! Harry, he is dead!!"

Harry went white. "No, you can't know."

"I do know! I see him lying in the road. But, Harry, he is you—"

"My landlord," he quickly told the aghast watchers, taking her in his arms and burying her face against his chest. "That is how Noma met him."

"Isn't Harrison that shadowy chap at Whitehall no one mentions?" someone asked.

"Yes." Everyone knew that much.

"Then we would have heard if he was dead, wouldn't we?"

Which was when a servant rushed in with an urgent message. Major Harrison had been shot.

Now Harry staggered back, almost dropping Simone to the floor. Shot? Harrison was supposed to have a heart attack!

Chapter Twenty-nine

Alice fainted; the actress wrung her hands. Maura giggled nervously, and Daisy started to cry. The men worried about what the world was coming to, with government officials being shot at.

Harry decided he had to go find out more. "My landlord, you know."

Gorham was all for driving to London, too, despite the late hour, to see if he was needed at Parliament, and to check at his town house. He had to know if his wife, her butler, and her belongings were really missing. Comden wanted to go with him, to discuss the Jamaican property, and to purchase a special license. Sir Chauncey thought he might toddle along with the others, and Ellsworth decided he ought to confirm his wife's interesting condition. They'd all be back by midmorning at the latest, for the final competition and settling of debts.

Claire ordered the talent-contest vote also put off to the next day, since tonight was so chaotic.

Three of the men joined Gorham in his coach. Harry rode Fidus. Still dressed in his costume, but with a caped greatcoat thrown over his shoulders and a pistol stuck in his waistband, he looked more like a highwayman than a

Gypsy. He stopped first at the village to drag Daniel out of a barmaid's arms, then rode into the woods, trusting Fidus to avoid hanging branches and fallen logs.

The men he had stationed there were mounted and ready to ride, awaiting his orders. They had more news than the messenger had brought to the manor, although still incomplete. According to their information, Major Harrison was not the only subject of assassination that day. None of the others were successful, thanks to the bodyguards Harry had set in place and the precautions he'd taken.

A firecracker had gone off near the prince regent's carriage. The horses were frightened, but the extra Horse Guards held them under control. The prime minister was fired at; his armed escort shot the man, who was identified as another of Eloise Lecroix's brothers, Jean Casselle. A fire set in the visitors' gallery at Parliament was quickly put out, with no one injured. So was a blaze at the royal exchequer. A female was arrested with a jug of lamp oil. She turned out to be Madame Lecroix's maid.

There was no panic, no run on the banks, no riots in the streets. There was no sign of Fordyce, either. Harry's men never spotted him on the road to London, nor did he return to his watched rooms at Mrs. Olmstead's. The report indicated he had been wounded by Major Harrison's guards. They were special-services officers, trained and ready . . . for him to collapse on the steps. They had fired back, but Fordyce got away.

Harry was furious at himself. He'd thought the plot against the government was foiled with the arrests of Eloise, Gollup, and Spenser. He'd thought Ford, or Fordyce, would be detained, so only his own demise had yet to unfold. He'd thought wrong, dammit. Now a man, a trusted aide, was dead instead of him. How could he live with that on his soul?

Harry set Fidus on the road to London, quickly leaving the three soldiers behind him. While he rode, he thought about the dead man, who had no family, thank goodness, and the live man. Fordyce could not go back to his rooms, nor to any surgeon in London, who would have been warned to report a bullet wound. He hadn't been paid for his filthy work, according to the conversation Simone had overheard. So where would he go?

Alice was put to bed by Maura and Ruby, who decided to stay the night with her, lest she grow more disturbed with Comden gone. In truth, they were all upset and wanted to comfort one another. Who could not be disturbed, with a blackmailer on top of a traitor, and now mayhem in London?

Sandaree was consoled by Mr. Anthony, who moved to Danforth's rooms. Daisy and the captain disappeared together, and the others went up to bed, too.

Simone refused to retire until Harry returned or sent word as he'd promised. How could she sleep not knowing what danger he was in? She put on a warmer gown and went downstairs, where she could hear the door. She kept the dog by her side.

Claire was already in the little-used front parlor, the one she kept for callers she did not wish to entertain for long. Simone almost left when she heard Claire's description of the room, but Claire urged her to stay. She was hoping Gorham would send a message, not about the nastiness in London, but about his nasty wife, and she welcomed the company during her anxious vigil.

Claire dismissed the servants to their beds after they brought tea, since she was quite capable of opening the door herself. There was no reason for anyone else to stay up so late. Or to overhear their conversation.

"How did you know my daughter played the violin?" she demanded as soon as she filled Simone's cup. "Did Harry tell you that, too? Does he have a friend in Cornwall?"

Simone set the cup down. "I do not understand how it works, but I just saw a pretty girl with the instrument in my mind. And Harry did not tell me about her at all, remember? You did. He would never betray a confidence that way."

Claire poured brandy into her own tea. "Why should I believe that? Harry Harmon is a rake and a rogue, a notoriously unreliable combination. I do not see why you trust him at all."

"Harry is the most honorable man I know. Besides, Gorham has been forsaking his marriage vows for a decade, yet you trust him, do you not?"

"I love him. Oh, I see." Claire sipped her fortified tea and looked at Simone. "It is unfortunate when a female falls in love with her protector. Did no one tell you that? It is too easy to have your heart broken. I know. Still, I wish you well. You have done me the biggest favor of my life if you told the truth. I cannot imagine how you knew—I do not believe that Gypsy nonsense one whit; you might as well be reading tea leaves or chicken entrails—but if you are right, I will be the happiest female in all of England. Yes, even if I can never be Gorham's wife."

"Perhaps Lady Gorham will expire soon. It is sinful to wish for another's death, of course, but anything is possible."

"Well, I have been praying for the old bat to choke on a bone any time these past years, so I suppose I won't go to heaven. But tell me, can you see her future?"

"No, not without physical touch. That's how it works.

And no, I have no idea if Gorham is your child's father. Some things must remain secret."

Claire poured another dollop of brandy into her cup. "I'll drink to that."

They both heard the pounding on the front door. Claire rushed out of the parlor to open it, but neither Harry nor Gorham nor a footman in Gorham's livery stood there. Fordyce did, a gun in his right hand, a bloody bandage wrapped around his left shoulder.

The dog growled, and Fordyce told Simone to muzzle him, or he'd shoot. He looked at her. "I know you, don't I?"

She wished she was not wearing a dark gown, with her hair held back in a loose knot. Her appearance was too reminiscent of the boardinghouse. "Of course you know me. You saw me dance, remember?"

Claire was furious that an armed man had dared to shove his way into her home. Worse, he was bleeding onto her carpet. "What do you want?"

"I want Spenser. He has my money."

"Not that I owe you any explanation, but Mr. Spenser was taken away by the authorities after the ball. Something about funding a plot." Claire finally realized that she was most likely confronting the man responsible for carrying out that plot, for shooting a man in London. She fainted.

Fordyce stepped over her and lifted the crystal brandy decanter. He shifted the gun to his left hand, so he could hold the decanter to his lips. "You were at Mrs. Olmstead's. The priggish female in the attics what wouldn't give me the time of day. Miss Simone Ryland, the governess."

"You must be mistaken," she said in French, hoping he'd think she was a foreign *fille de joie*.

"You're no French whore. You're the governess, all right. Mrs. Olmstead said you were smart and educated," he answered in the same language. "No one else has hair that—" Then he realized he'd given himself away, after a decade of speaking English on this accursed island. Not that it mattered. He was a wanted man anyway, if he didn't die of the gunshot.

"I need money. Now."

"There is a fortune in Gorham's safe, the money for the competition."

Fordyce kicked at Claire's skirts and had another swallow of brandy. "I doubt he'd tell his doxy how to open it."

"I have an expensive bracelet upstairs. You might have seen it, the prize in the dance contest. I'll go get it for you."

Claire groaned, but they both ignored her.

"You'd like to go, and raise the servants or fetch a pistol at the same time, I'd warrant."

Those were her precise plans, but she shook her head no.

"I'll go with you, then. And if you scream, you'll never get back downstairs."

Simone looked at Claire, hoping she was waking up enough to sound the alarm.

Fordyce must have had the same thought, for he brought the butt of his gun down on Claire's head.

Simone screamed. She couldn't help it. Fordyce grabbed her, the pistol pressed to her neck. The dog snarled and snapped at Fordyce's leg. He kicked it away, then waited to see if anyone came running. No one did.

"All right. Up we go." He released her, but kept the gun pointed at her back. When he turned to close the parlor door behind them, the dog inside, Simone reached for a vase on a hall table beside the door. She held it over her head, ready to throw.

"You can shoot me," she said, "but everyone will hear.

The servants are not that far away, likely cleaning the music room down the corridor. Some of the gentlemen are playing billiards." She knew Harry would forgive her the lies. "You might get away, but without any money, and they'll go after you. Go now, while you have a chance."

Fordyce was undecided.

Simone heard the dog throwing himself against the parlor door. And something else. Someone was outside, galloping closer. Fordyce heard it, too. He turned toward the front door. Simone brought the vase down on his head just as Harry burst into the house, pistol drawn.

Fordyce staggered, but stayed on his feet. He shook his head and peered at Harry through the water and flowers that dripped down his face. "You! They told me to watch out for you, that you were connected to Harrison. I watched, but you were nothing. A useless drone on your useless society."

"Strange, I do not feel so useless, now that I have a gun."

Fordyce's hand at the back of his head came away bloody. He cursed in French, then turned fast and pulled Simone in front of him. "But I have something you want. What I want is gold. Drop the gun and reach for your purse."

Harry put the gun down carefully. He slowly reached inside his coat—and came out with a knife. He shouted, "Down, Simone," and threw it.

Fordyce's gun went off and shattered an Egyptian burial urn. Then he fell backward.

He stared up at Simone through eyes that were quickly clouding over. "Black eyes. I knew you were that governess."

Claire gasped, holding on to the parlor door frame. Harry pulled his knife out and threw his greatcoat over

Fordyce. Footsteps thundered down the stairs, the dog barked, women screamed, men shouted from outside, servants raced down the hall, and Daniel pounded in from the rear of the house.

And Claire gasped again. "You're a governess?"

Simone wasn't worried that Claire would reveal her secrets—not Claudinia Colthopfer with a hidden daughter. No, she worried that Claire's brains were addled by the blow to her head. Why else was she being so nice? Simone was suddenly courageous and valiant. Harry was instantly a hero. Together, Claire told everyone who would listen, they had saved them all, and Griffin Manor. As if Fordyce had enough bullets to shoot everybody, as if the servants hadn't come running. No matter, Claire ordered champagne for the rescuers, and for the surgeon who put three stitches in her scalp without cutting her hair off.

Simone worried about Harry, too. He never came back that night after the soldiers took Fordyce's body away. He'd held her until the magistrate came, and while she gave her deposition and he gave his. Simone doubted she could have stood up without his arms around her. Then he hugged her tightly, rocking her in his embrace, and said, "Lord, I will never leave you again."

And promptly did.

Chapter Thirty

The men returned at noon. Most of them were jubilant. The plot was foiled, the perpetrators all captured or killed. Gorham's wife had truly decamped, and her father released her funds without an argument. Comden had a special license, and two tickets for passage on a ship. Ellsworth's wife was indeed bearing his child, so he came back to Richmond merely to fetch his things and settle his wagers. Sir Chauncey checked a year's worth of old obituaries and found good news. Not for the deceased, of course, but for his second chance with his first love. He was eager to be on his way, and he was still sober. He'd leave right after the final judging, the presentation of prizes, and the wedding.

Claire was planning a grand celebration for that evening: the crowning of the queen and Alice's marriage. It was to be her last lavish entertainment of this sort. With an impressionable young girl coming to live in the house, she'd no longer be entertaining the demimonde. She was not ashamed of what she was, but neither was she going to let her own daughter experience the fast life. Bad enough the child would have to face the scorn of some in the neighborhood because of Claire's career, but she'd have every other advantage the ward of a marquis could have.

They all gathered first in the Egyptian Room. Everyone was talking about the recent events, making plans, speculating about the contest, laughing at Alice's excitement and Comden's nerves.

Simone was happy for Alice and the others, but had they forgotten what just happened? Men had died, and more might have, so how could anyone care about the foolish contest? Worse, Harry looked exhausted, as well he might, saving the world or whatever it was that he did when he wasn't being a here-and-thereian.

"A bit of work for the regent," he told the others when they asked how he knew so much of the plot. "A chap has to do something to earn his keep, don't you know."

Claire clapped her hands for their attention. First she wanted the men—only ten were left of the original twenty—to vote for the most talented female. She reminded them of all the performers and their varied artistic expressions.

Claire won, to no one's surprise. Simone was so sure of the outcome that she'd traded Gorham the diamond and emerald bracelet for the ten-guinea purse. The bracelet was made for Claire, and her singing deserved it. Claire was so delighted that she kissed Simone's cheek. She was concussed, for sure.

Sandaree came in second, Simone third. That put Claire two points ahead of Simone in the tournament, and bound to win the Quality contest, too. Simone considered the competition over. She'd lost, but that no longer mattered as much.

Claire started to explain the rules for the final judging again, the ladylike aspects to be considered, but Ruby stopped her midsentence. "We are not ladies, Claire, and some of us don't care, so give up. I'm to have a shop of my own, and you're to stay here as Gorham's mistress. Sandaree goes home, and Alice's babe gets a name. Isn't that enough?"

Claire surprised them all by saying, "One of us *is* a lady." She held up her wrist with the bracelet on it. "One of us knows what is the right thing to do and does it. I vote for Miss Noma Royale as real Quality. Raise your hands if you agree with me. The women vote, too."

Every hand went up. Sir Chauncey raised both of his. The vote was unanimous.

Lord Gorham made notations on a tally page. "By my reckoning, that makes Miss Noma Royale the Queen of the Courtesans."

"And maid of honor at my wedding."

"And my good friend."

"My salvation."

"My inspiration."

"Hear, hear."

Simone wept when Lord Gorham handed her ten guineas for the final contest and the thousand-pound grand prize. Then Harry kissed her and placed more money in her lap, from the wagers he'd made on her.

Claire set a circlet of gold on Simone's head. She looked at Harry but whispered to Simone, "May you have one more miracle in your bag of tricks, Your Majesty."

How could Simone be Queen of the Courtesans while she was still a virgin? She could give back the crown and the coins—or she could make love with Harry. The choice was easy. Convincing Harry might be more difficult.

He was already undressed, in the bed, and half-asleep long before Alice's wedding party ended. Claire had filled the ballroom with flowers, musicians, food, and good cheer, all in one afternoon. Simone and Harry left before the dancing, and left a purse for the baby.

Harry claimed exhaustion; Simone claimed the right of the queen. This was their last night at Griffin Manor, and she did not intend to return to London in the same state she'd left it. She doubted she'd see much of Harry at his family's town house or their country property, not with his prickly attitude to them, so this was her final chance to show her love in the age-old way. To the devil with the consequences, she decided. Her reputation could not be ruined any worse, and if she found herself with child, she'd beg Claire for a position as governess to her daughter. Harry would support them, she knew, if she could not; he naturally felt strongly about fathers and their responsibilities. And she'd have part of him to keep forever.

First she had to understand what had happened yesterday with Major Harrison's death. She realized that it was all planned, except the too-final outcome, and that now Harry was free to work at Whitehall as himself. She just did not understand why he could not have told her. "I almost gave the whole thing away, because you did not trust me."

"Others' lives were involved," he answered in a bitter tone. "And you needed to act surprised. This was all because I was sick and tired of wearing disguises, hiding in secret corners, not free to come and go. I never planned my double's death, by Hades, and I will never be rid of that guilt, or what might have happened to you here."

Simone removed her robe as slowly as she could before getting into the wide bed. "But you saved me."

"A man held a gun to your head. I can never forget. I swear, it was the worst moment of my life."

His lips were in a grim line, but not the telltale pucker

of a lie. "Mine, too, when Fordyce shot at you. But what happens now?"

"The family is not at Royce House yet, but you can move in anyway. I have a few details to tidy up at Whitehall. Who is to be in charge of what, with myself as a dilettante volunteer, nothing more. At least I am done with disguises."

He sounded as if he was done pretending to be her lover, too. Simone knew she had to accept that, but not tonight. She inched closer to his side of the bed.

He reached out and touched her unbound hair, spreading it across the pillow. "Tell me, what do you want now that you have won? The prize money will not last forever."

"A good position, I suppose." She touched his legs with one of her own, a better position already.

"You have enough blunt to tempt a bachelor. You could use it as a dowry."

His suggestion was not encouraging to Simone. His heavier breathing was. "Oh, I might save the money for my old age. I could still become a teacher or a companion."

"Which do you prefer?"

"Both. And mistress." She put her hand on his chest and stroked the bare skin there. "You need all three."

"What are you saying, sweetheart?"

"You said you'd never leave me again. I watched. There was none of that grimacing you do when you lie. Will you stay with me?"

"I will still work for the government when they need me, but I could not leave you any more than I could stop breathing. You must know by now that I love you."

"Truly?"

"I do not lie, silly."

"Then I will be whatever you want of me, forever. I love you too much to be happy with another man. I could not let anyone else kiss me, or hold me, or rescue me and my brother. If Claire can live in the shadows, so can I."

He cupped her face in his hands. "But Gorham is the son of a marquis. I am the baseborn son of an opera dancer."

"And I am the product of two misalliances." She kissed his eyelids, and rubbed her hands over his flat nipples. "And Queen of the Courtesans."

"And I am yours to command." His hands moved to her breasts, whose nipples were straining toward him, not flat at all. He sighed at their silky feel, the warmth and the weight. "But you deserve better than a country hideaway. I want more for you."

"What do you want, Harry? Tell me."

First he kissed each breast in turn. Then he said, "I want the world to see your beauty, and your goodness. I want you by my side, forever, the mother of my children. My legitimate children."

"Is that a proposal, Mr. Harmon?"

"It better be, considering that I intend to make love to you tonight." His hand reached down to the hem of her nightgown, and pulled it up so he could stroke her legs, her thighs, and between them.

Simone tried to keep her wits about her, when all she wanted was Harry, wrapped around her. "It's not because your family is coming, pressing you to make an honest woman of me?"

He stopped his hand—and her racing heart. "You are an honest woman. But I want a family of my own—little redheaded girls."

"And blue-eyed boys."

"Simone, they will recognize falsehoods, my sons. All of the Royce males do, in various forms. They will be truth-knowers, like I am. Can you accept that?"

"If you can accept a fortune-teller."

"How do you do that, anyway? I never told you about the violin, or Alice's son."

She shrugged, and pulled the nightgown over her head. "I don't know. I just see things sometimes."

"What do you see when you touch me?" He took her hand in his, against his heart.

Simone shut her eyes. "I see you smiling. You are so happy it brings joy to my heart."

"Then you must be beside me. I never felt such happiness before I met you. I have never been in love, and that is no lie."

After a long kiss, Simone asked, "What do you see when I say I love you?"

"It's Rex who sees colors. I can taste the truth. Your words are as sweet as nectar, the ambrosia of the gods. As sweet as your lips." He kissed them. "As sweet as your beautiful body." He started at her neck and worked his way down. "As sweet as the tiny murmurs you make in pleasure." She murmured. "I could exist on nothing but that honeyed honesty of your love."

"And my dowry."

He had to smile. "We'll save that for our children. I have ample funds of my own, you know. Enough to last forever, like our love. When I say I do, I will. I am yours, only yours. And you are mine."

"Then I see a perfect future for us, my own true love."

BARBARA METZGER
Truly Yours

Alone in the world, Amanda Carville has
no dowry, no reputation left, and no one
who believes her to be innocent of murder,
since she was found holding the gun that
killed her stepfather. Viscount Rexford also
has his troubles. He's scarred by war, and
cursed—or blessed–with the family trait of
knowing the truth when he hears it, and his
success at extracting the truth from military
prisoners has left many doubting his honor
and his methods. When Amanda tells him
she didn't do it, he believes her. Tired of
the truth business, Rex refuses to get
involved...until his heart leaves him
no choice.

BARBARA METZGER
The Hourglass

Coryn, Earl of Ardeth, has spent an eternity in Hell. Fed up, he gambles with the Devil and wins a second chance: if he can find his heart, his soul, and his hourglass in six months, he can return to life. Then he meets Genie, a disgraced water-girl at the Battle of Waterloo. Now, her only hope is this crazy stranger—and she's half-terrified of and half-in-love with the eccentric Earl. Together they have to find his humanity, her social acceptance, and overcome someone bent on destroying their lives.

JO BEVERLEY

LADY BEWARE

For generations, the Cave family has been
marked by scandal, madness, and violence.
But after earning a reputation for bravery in
the army, Horatio Cave, the new Viscount
Darien, has come home to charm London
society and restore the family name. He means
to start with the lovely Lady Thea Debenham.

The magnetism between them is immediate,
but can Thea trust the dark, sexy
"Vile Viscount"? And will Thea's brother
Dare—the most dashing member of the
Company of Rogues—believe that Horatio
does not deserve the cursed Cave reputation?

Praise for the David Slaton Novels

"A must-read for anyone looking for the next great assassin saga."
>—*Kirkus Reviews* on *Assassin's Game*

"The action-filled, high-octane thriller that you have been waiting for. Ward Larsen delivers enough page-turning suspense and globe-spanning action for ten novels."
>—William Martin,
>*New York Times* bestselling author,
>on *Assassin's Silence*

"A superbly written story."
>—Larry Bond,
>*New York Times* bestselling author,
>on *Assassin's Game*

"Slaton is the perfect assassin, and this is the perfect action-adventure thriller."
>—*Booklist* (starred review)
>on *Assassin's Silence*

"A stunning thriller, one that ranks right up there with *The Day of the Jackal*. Frankly, this is the best nail-biting suspense novel I've read in years."
>—Stephen Coonts, *New York Times*
>bestselling author of *The Art of War*,
>on *Assassin's Game*

"Sharp as a dagger and swift as a sudden blow, *Assassin's Game* is a first-rate thriller with a plot that grabs you hard and won't let go."
>—Ralph Peters,
>*New York Times* bestselling author,
>on *Assassin's Game*

ALSO BY WARD LARSEN

* Published by Forge Books

ASSASSIN'S CODE

WARD LARSEN

A TOM DOHERTY ASSOCIATES BOOK
NEW YORK

This is a work of fiction. All of the characters, organizations, and events portrayed in this novel are either products of the author's imagination or are used fictitiously.

ASSASSIN'S CODE

A Forge Book
Published by Tom Doherty Associates
175 Fifth Avenue
New York, NY 10010

www.tor-forge.com

Forge® is a registered trademark of Macmillan Publishing Group, LLC.

ISBN 978-0-7653-8581-9

Our books may be purchased in bulk for promotional, educational, or business use. Please contact your local bookseller or the Macmillan Corporate and Premium Sales Department at 1-800-221-7945, extension 5442, or by email at MacmillanSpecialMarkets@macmillan.com.

First Edition: August 2017
First Mass Market Edition: July 2018

Printed in the United States of America

0 9 8 7 6 5 4 3 2 1

ASSASSIN'S CODE

ONE

To be a day short of one's fifteenth birthday is a characteristically happy time in a young man's life. Considerably less so when there is no chance whatsoever of reaching it.

He was sitting alone in the backseat of a rattletrap Citroën. Malika was in front, and next to her a man named Naseem was driving. He knew why she was in that seat. He would have been there too had their situations been reversed. His identity documents alleged him to be Youssef Aboud, and after six months of use the name almost seemed real. His true name was Jalil, but that, like so much else, had fallen to a distant memory. They'd insisted he use the new identity exclusively, beginning the day he had left home, all throughout his travels, and even after he was established in the safe house in Paris. They'd told him it was a matter of training. If he *became* Youssef Aboud, he would be less inclined to make a mistake under the duress of a roadblock or border crossing.

There had been a great many of those since last summer. His first journey had taken him from Gaza to Syria, and after a month in Raqqa, onward to Turkey and Greece. Then came a surprise detention on the island of Lesbos, and eventually he'd been shipped back to a Turkish refugee camp along the porous Syrian border. It reminded him of the child's game Chutes and Ladders. Three steps forward, two steps back. The second time they put him on a plane to Budapest, where he was interned for nearly a month before being hauled back to Turkey on a bus. It was the southern route that succeeded: Turkey to Macedonia, followed by a leaky boat to Italy, and finally France. It was strange, he thought, how much persistence had been necessary to arrive where he was today—at the most foreseeable of all ends.

"We are nearly there, Youssef," said Malika.

"My name isn't Youssef," he mumbled.

"What?"

"Nothing," replied Jalil, his blank gaze pinned out the window. The day was cold and gray, which seemed predestined. Minutes ago they'd passed a great industrial complex, and Naseem had said something about it being the place where France did its research on nuclear weapons. He might have been trying to lighten the mood, or maybe distract Jalil. There was little chance of either. A second car was trailing behind them, although Jalil couldn't see it. Three men with AK-47s who would go to work in the aftermath. A four-minute delay—long enough for the smoke to clear and the crowds to start gathering.

He shifted in his seat, the vest heavy on his shoulders. They'd made him wear a mock-up around the safe house in recent days, a duplicate item filled with sand. He'd tried to get used to walking with something near a normal motion. Today he wore a thick coat over the vest, the liner removed to make room. It all suited the day perfectly.

As they neared town a light snow began to fall, and for the first time since waking Jalil thought of something other than his fate. He'd not seen snow since he was very young, and he marveled at the flurries of white whisking past his window. He used a button to run down the window, and a few flakes whirled inside.

"What are you doing?" Malika snapped.

"Nothing," he replied. "I only wanted some air."

Silence fell for a time, until Naseem said, "You should pray one last time."

"I will," Jalil lied. He had been praying constantly for the last two days, or so it seemed. They told him it would be easier that way, help him follow the path of Allah and see the light of glory. They were wrong.

"There," said Naseem.

Jalil looked out the window, and he saw a place every bit as foreign as Paris. He had spent nearly a month there, feeling as though he'd arrived on a different planet from the one that held Syria. They had let him go outside only once in that time, two nights ago when they'd taken him to a dreary bar, and made him smoke from a hookah and drink bourbon from a place called Kentucky. He also had a vague memory of an incredibly curvaceous woman, a prostitute he was sure, who told him in Arabic what she would do for him. The others all laughed. Jalil had found her more intimidating than erotic, and when he sent her away she'd called him a homosexual. Then everyone had gone back to the flat and passed out, and in the morning they all cleansed themselves and prayed.

This place was called Grenoble, and it had been a half-day drive from Paris. When they told Jalil this would be his target, he'd researched it on Malika's phone while she slept. It was a midsized town, 150,000 people nestled in the foothills of the French Alps. Roughly the same number of inhabitants as Aleppo today—a city whose prewar population of two million had been on par with Paris itself. So much suffering. The others at the safe house argued constantly about who was to blame for Syria's misery: France, Assad, the United States, Iran. All they could agree on was that someone had to be held accountable.

What does any of that matter now?

Jalil noticed one hand trembling ever so slightly. He gripped the door handle as hard as he could. The car began to slow as they reached the center of town. The city seemed alive. He saw red tram cars gliding over spotless streets, glittering decorations strung across storefronts. There were people all around. No, not people, he corrected—infidels and apostates. He saw smiling women and children, circumspect old men. A group of boys his age were doing tricks on their skateboards. *Which should I kill to most please Allah?* This was the question Malika had told him to focus on once he got out of the car. Such a strange question.

He was again marveling at the snow when a voice drifted in, the words not quite registering. "What?" he said.

"The drop-off point is just ahead," Malika said. "Are you ready?"

He looked at her, thinking how different she looked now. He remembered playing tag with her, when she was a teen and he was just a boy. Malika had never let him catch her the way the other teenagers did. Today she was wearing Western clothing, wedged into pants and a blouse that were too small for her ample figure. Still, as he looked at her exposed hands and face, she reminded him of the pudgy little girl he'd once known. She was even wearing makeup today, although she'd assured him it was only to blend in. Naseem was wearing jeans and a hooded jacket like half the young men in France.

The Citroën pulled to a stop along the busy boulevard.

Malika turned in her seat, and Jalil met her gaze. She looked worried.

"Yes," he said, his voice sounding distant and unfamiliar. "I am ready."

"May Allah be with you." She reached out a hand and he instinctively took it. The trembling was back—no matter how hard he tried, he couldn't make it stop. It occurred to him that this was the first time she'd touched him since the halfway point of today's journey, when they'd stopped on a desolate farm road. She had taken the vest from the trunk and helped him put it on. His hand still shaking, he looked at her with profound embarrassment as a tear streaked down one of his cheeks.

"It's all right," she said comfortingly. "You know how proud your mother will be."

Jalil only nodded. He pulled away, and with a last glance at Malika he got out of the car. He shut the door and began walking away, only to hear a rapping noise from behind. He looked back and saw her banging the window harshly with her knuckles.

Jalil looked at her dumbly, unsure what she was trying to tell him. She rolled down her window and motioned for him to come over. Of course he'd done something wrong. He had always been *that* child, the one who needed correcting.

He went to her window, and after an exasperated glance, Malika took his right hand and reached into his jacket pocket.

"What are you doing?" he asked, anxiously looking over his shoulder.

Her face went stern, and Jalil gasped when she pulled the trigger out of his pocket and set it into his palm. It was the size of a cigarette pack—the kind of wired switch they used in America, he'd been told, to open and close garage doors.

"Did you listen to nothing Naseem told you last night?" Malika said sharply.

Only now did he remember—he'd been instructed to keep his hand on the device at all times once he was out of the car. He saw Naseem lean over and whisper into her ear, and Malika looked at Jalil with something new and terrible in her expression. With her hand over his, she guided the triggering device back into his right pocket. Then she pinched his fingers until the button sank.

He inhaled sharply and his heart stuttered. "Malika! What are you—" He couldn't even finish the question.

Jalil gripped the controller forcefully to keep the button from rising.

"Hold tightly!" she whispered. "Remember, it activates when you *release* the switch!"

He nodded, and felt her hand relax the pressure until he alone was holding the button down. She pulled back, and the window began rising. The last words he heard were from Naseem, a hushed "*Allahu akbar!*"

The car pulled away in an eddy of snow, and he turned toward the crowded shops and sidewalks. There were hundreds of people, grouped in front of store windows, moving on the sidewalks. Jalil took a tentative step, and when he did he heard a tiny metallic noise, then felt something tap his shoe. He looked down and saw a hex nut and two nails on the ground. Near panic, he looked around to see who was watching, the jingle of metal on cobblestone seeming like thunder. No one even glanced his way.

Jalil regulated his breathing, and focused completely on the switch in his pocket. He walked at a deliberate pace, trying to keep the movement of his upper body to a minimum. Trying to ignore the thumping in his chest. The second car would be nearby, three men waiting, sweaty fingers on triggers. Did they feel as he did now? Or was their faith so intense that it precluded any doubts?

His right hand had the switch in a death grip. He imagined his fingers going white from lack of circulation. And there, Jalil realized, was the measure of his life—how long could he keep a simple plastic button pinched between his fingers?

Why had Malika done it this way? Why had she forced him to squeeze the trigger and hold it? He *had* been briefed on one tactical reason to do it that way—if he thought he'd been identified, or if the police were near, he was to hold the switch down as insurance. That way, if he was tackled to the ground or shot, merely letting go guaranteed success. But there had been no threats of exposure, no police nearby. Only now did Jalil understand: Malika didn't trust him. She doubted he would go through with it.

They'd had a long talk last night, and he had expressed reservations. Certainly that was normal. He remembered this morning, when she'd told him his mother had already been given his martyrdom video. *You must honor her today by giving yourself to Allah, Youssef.* She had used the new name to tell him his mother was already mourning his death. How could any son not pay the debt of his mother's grief? Malika had always been clever, the one who everyone knew would go places. And she might have, except that young girls in Palestine had but two possible destinations. One was marriage. The other was where she was at that moment—rushing to a safe house before another martyr was vaporized.

And not just any martyr.

He steeled himself and kept moving. He saw a café with awnings where smartly dressed couples enjoyed coffee and crepes, the smell of burnt sugar and vanilla hanging on the cool air. A clothing store with broad windows advertised the latest fashions. A tram went past with people inside shoulder-to-shoulder, probably as much for the warmth as to get anywhere.

He'd been told to aim for a crowd, and to immerse himself as best he could. There was a small toy store, and he saw children coming and going with their parents. He couldn't do that, although in Syria he'd met men who would, martyrs desperate for horror in their last act on this earth. Maybe Malika was right—maybe he *was* weak.

The snow came heavier, dampening the busy sounds and blurring the brilliant lights. He kept moving. There was a park where an old woman was exercising two dogs. The dogs were chasing one another, tails wagging vigorously. A long line at the Häagen-Dazs shop snaked out across the sidewalk, but that didn't seem right either. He'd always liked ice cream. Certainly more than Kentucky bourbon.

A crowd was gathering near a pavilion where a brass band was preparing to play. Jalil was so engrossed in his search for a target that he didn't see the curb coming. He tripped and went sprawling forward. His left hand flew out of his jacket pocket, trying for balance, but to his credit his sweaty right hand never moved. Someone reached out and grabbed him by the arm to keep him from falling. They succeeded.

Jalil stood straight again, and turned to see a lovely young girl. Her hand was on his right forearm. Only inches from the switch. She was a few years older than he was, and wore a backpack with a baguette sticking out of the top. She smiled and said something in French he didn't understand.

His hand was shaking noticeably now, warm with moisture. He forced his fingers tighter but felt the muscles growing weary. When he straightened to his full height, he heard another tinkle on the pavement. This time it was noticed. He and the girl looked down at the same time. A screw and a few ball bearings rolled into the gutter. She looked up at him and must have seen the sweat on his face, the desperation in his eyes. She looked at the immobilized hand in his pocket. All at once she knew.

They both knew.

Her mouth went wide, and he thought, *Please don't scream. Don't make me do it now.*

And she didn't.

Jalil watched her beautiful young face twist in primal fear. It was awful and frightening. Never in his life had anyone looked at him that way. They stood frozen for a time, seconds that felt like hours. Both stilled to inaction by what he *might* do. His hand began to cramp, and the first twitch came. Muscles no longer under his complete control. It seemed such a simple thing, to hold one's fingers together. Any child could do it. He was squeezing so hard he thought the plastic switch might break. And if it did? What would happen then?

Of course he knew the answer.

"Run!" he whispered hoarsely in English. "Run quickly!"

His words seemed to register. She took one step backward, then turned and bolted away. No one seemed to notice. The world swirled around him as if he were its axis, a flurry of snow and cars and humanity.

His fingers ached.

Tears began streaming again.

He heard the girl scream in the distance.

Then the loud authoritative voice of a man.

Finally, the trembling in his fingers became uncontrollable. He closed his eyes, not wanting to know who or what was near. This was the moment he should have shouted with a martyr's conviction. *Allahu akbar!* The words that came instead were in a level, conversational tone. They were meant for no one in particular. "My name is Jalil."

In the next moment, the boy who had so long ago chased little girls in faraway streets gave his aching hand relief. He let go of the switch.

TWO

It was at six o'clock that evening, four hours after the blast, when the high-speed TGV train carrying Zavier Baland eased smoothly to a stop at the Gare de Grenoble.

Serge Baptiste, a junior man from the local gendarmerie, stood waiting patiently on the platform. His assignment was to collect the senior officer from Paris, and when the doors of the cars slid open he began searching in earnest. Baland would not be in uniform—he had reached a position in the force where such accouterments were no longer necessary—yet Baptiste was sure he would have no trouble recognizing him. He had seen the man's picture more than once, a former colonel from the Paris prefecture who'd gone on to become a rising star in DGSI, the General Directorate for Internal Security. His picture was oft-published, plastered on media sites in both internal and public domains. Conseiller Baland had become something of a poster child for the country's counterterrorism efforts, in part because he got results. But then there was the other part.

Baptiste locked in on a man who stepped from the second car and paused on the platform as if trying to get his bearings. He was average in height and build, his features rather benign, although even from a distance Baptiste saw a bit more of the Mediterranean than a strictly Gallic heritage would imbue. He carried himself in a stiff and upright manner, in the way of a lifelong maître d', and his dark eyes were discreetly active. Baptiste had no doubt—this was the man in the press releases.

He gave a wave, and that was all it took. The two met halfway, and Baptiste said, "Good evening, sir."

"Hardly," Baland replied. "But thank you for being here to meet me. I'm sure Commissaire Valmont has his hands full."

Valmont was Baptiste's superior, head of the local gendarmerie and therefore on-scene commander for the situation. Baptiste guided his charge toward the exit. "Yes sir, things have been very busy. We've secured the perimeter of the attack. My instructions are to take you to the command post straightaway."

"Has it been verified there are no secondary devices?"

"Yes, that was our first priority once the shooters had been dealt with."

"How many were there?"

"Three, sir, aside from the bomber. All had AK-47s and multiple magazines. They waited long enough for the response to begin, then began shooting indiscriminately. Our officers responded, of course, but it took twenty minutes for a special tactics team to arrive and deal with all three."

"Did any of the attackers survive?"

"No."

"Where are we on the casualty count?" the inspector from Paris asked.

"Thirty-three dead and forty-nine wounded. At least five are in critical condition at the hospital."

"Bastards!" Baland spat, more to himself than Baptiste.

"Indeed."

They exited the station, and a patrol car was waiting, another uniformed officer inside serving as driver.

"Tell me," said Baland as the two slid in back together, "where has the command post been set up?"

"At the station, of course."

"In that case, I would like to go to the scene first."

"But Commissaire, my orders are very specific—"

"*If you please,*" Baland interrupted. "It is important for me to see things firsthand."

Baptiste caught the eye of the driver, who shrugged. The car shot ahead toward the center of town.

It was a drive Baland had made too many times. In the falling light he looked out over a midsized city that had until today been largely untouched by the troubles sourced so many thousands of miles away. He recalled his assessment to the interior minister only last week: *Those corners of France unaffected are only waiting their turn.* The minister had concurred.

When they arrived at the scene, Baland saw a perimeter cordoned off by yellow tape, at least half a city block altogether. All around were fire trucks and police cars, and as light snow continued to fall uniformed officers groomed the streets for evidence, everyone wearing gloves and protective footwear as they turned over debris.

The car came to a stop near the controlled entry point, near Place Victor Hugo, and Baland got out and walked straight to the yellow-taped border. He could easily discern the seat of the explosion, a distinctive crater, although it wasn't as deep as some he'd seen. Truck bombs were the worst, leaving what looked like debris-filled swimming pools in the middle of a street. This one was more akin to the hole his daughters had helped him dig in his garden last weekend, into which they'd plugged a sapling chestnut tree. Next to the crater was the twisted frame of a car, its ashen body scorched from a fire that was certainly a secondary effect. It occurred to Baland that the car had absorbed much of the blast, and he wondered why the bomber had stood so close to it in the moment of truth.

Why do any of these men and women do what they do?

Even so blunted, the explosion had blown out the windows of buildings all along the street. Baland saw pockmarks in the façade of a hotel where either shrapnel or 7.62mm semiautomatic rounds had chipped into centuries-old stone. Telltale stains were evident on the nearby sidewalk, already going dark, and Baland saw a number of blanketed bodies. There were also coverlets with markers where smaller bits of biological evidence had been located.

He noticed Baptiste engaged in a conversation with

a sergeant near the entrance—the man was holding something in his gloved hand. Both men looked toward Baland, then approached him together.

"We thought you might like to see this," said Baptiste.

The evidence technician held out his hand to display the remains of a passport. It was ragged, and a hole the size of a one-euro coin had been blown clear through its pages. There were also clear traces of organic matter.

The evidence man offered up a latex glove to Baland, and said, "Would you like to have a look?"

"Certainly not! Bag that right away—we mustn't contaminate any findings."

The chastened policeman slid his find carefully into a bag and walked away.

"Do you think it could be the bomber's?" Baptiste asked.

"Not his real one. If he was carrying it, then it could only be a false lead meant to confuse us."

Baland noticed an ambulance fifty meters away, just outside the cordoned area, where a middle-aged woman was being attended to by an EMT. Baland walked over, and saw that she was being treated for a small wound on one arm. For the first time since arriving he produced his credentials, introducing himself to both the woman and the EMT, before asking, "Why are you only now being treated?"

"I was busy helping," said the woman. "I work at the hotel across the street." He could see her fighting to keep a steady voice. "It was terrible—I've never seen anything like this. There were bodies everywhere."

"You were here when it happened?" Baland asked.

"Yes, I work at the front desk. I was just arriving for my shift."

She was wearing her hotel uniform, but it was filthy, stained with blood and grime. The EMT removed a reddened bandage that had been hastily wrapped, probably something done in the immediate aftermath using a hotel first-aid kit. He cleaned the wound, and was about to apply a fresh bandage when Baland said, "Wait!"

The man looked at him, perplexed, and watched as Baland studied her wound more closely. It was a small gash, no longer than a pencil eraser, but the edges were ragged and inflamed. "Is there something in the wound, perhaps a piece of shrapnel?" he asked, not caring which of the two answered.

The woman said, "Yes, I think I can feel something inside. It's sore, but it can wait. The hospital is besieged with people who need help far more than I do."

The EMT nodded in agreement.

"The skin around the wound," Baland said, this time looking directly at the EMT. "Does it not look more like a burn to you?"

"A burn?"

"I wasn't near any fire," the woman said.

The EMT reasoned, "I agree, it looks inflamed. Infection is always possible, but only a few hours after such an injury I doubt that—"

Baland cut him off by rising and walking away. He

canvassed the aid station, inspected two more patients, then set off briskly toward the car. Halfway there he stopped suddenly, noticing a hex bolt on the sidewalk. Baland bent down and looked at it closely. He didn't try to pick it up.

"What is it?" Baptiste asked, catching up with him.

Baland didn't answer. He stood and looked again at the patients being treated, then regarded the terrible scene inside the tape.

"We must expand our perimeter immediately," Baland said. "Push everything back—another hundred meters in every direction."

"But why?" said Baptiste, looking at the tiny bolt on the ground.

"Just do it!"

THREE

It took less than an hour for Baland to be proved right: traces of some unidentified radiological contaminant were evident. The perimeter was moved back, and then doubled again after consultations with the minister of the interior. The president himself ordered that no resource should be spared in the investigation, and teams of experts were dispatched by air from Paris. The president too used the term "bastards," albeit in private, and gave instructions that he was to be informed of every development.

Of these there arose but one of significance. Within the hour municipal CCTV footage was analyzed, and it took only minutes to isolate the two cars that had been involved. The men with rifles had bundled out of an old Peugeot, and it was right where they'd left it. Specialists had been crawling over that vehicle for hours. More of interest was the car that had delivered the bomber, which turned out to be a dark blue Citroën. Two occupants could clearly be seen in front, and as the video ran everyone saw a nervous young man get out of the backseat and begin to walk away. Then, curiously, the bomber returned to the passenger-side window. The person he conversed with could not be seen clearly, owing to the camera angle, but everyone in the screening room saw what appeared to be an exchange of some kind as their hands met. Then the car departed and the bomber walked away.

The authorities followed up this discovery in the most practical manner. They ignored the bomber for the time being—his was a fait accompli—and focused their efforts on the car and the two individuals inside, who might still be a threat. They followed the Citroën through the footage of two traffic cameras, then lost track when it turned onto a heavily wooded road that ran into the rising Chartreuse Mountains. Cars were immediately dispatched to the area, and after less than an hour the Citroën was discovered abandoned along the side of a small and thickly wooded secondary road. At a glance, the officer who found the car reported one extraordinary bit of evidence inside—a large man wearing jeans and a dark hooded jacket, very possibly of Middle Eastern extraction, who was poised serenely behind the steering wheel. He was quite dead, with a single bullet wound evident on his right temple. More forensic teams were sent in.

Though none of the investigators would ever know it, in those early minutes, as they sat poring over hours-old CCTV footage, the very same cameras were recording the passage of a young woman along Rue Molière. She was heavy, though not obese, and wore clothing that was two sizes larger than necessary. She carried a small bag of groceries, and expressed the same curiosity a hundred other passersby had at the scene before her, even asking one of the officers standing guard at the perimeter what all the fuss was about. She otherwise did not pause before turning in to a nearby block of apartments and disappearing from sight.

She was weary from the exertions of a long and trying day, and by the time she reached the two-person elevator she had gum on her shoe and snow on her shoulders. She trundled down the vacant fourth-floor hallway, and at the halfway point stopped at the door marked 20. Were anyone to inquire, they would find that the small flat was operated as a vacation rental. It had been booked for the next week through an online site, a key provided through the post. Most of the residences in the building were similarly rented out, something the woman had researched thoroughly.

She entered the flat but did not turn on a light, leaving the main room cast in gloom as night took hold. It was the first time she'd been to the place, and she vaguely recalled the online photos: modernist décor, sterile and angular, the only warmth being a few stock photographs of the Alps on one wall. Yet there had been one critical point, and that was where her eyes went. Indeed, it was the reason she'd selected this unit—the view from the fourth-floor window.

She walked carefully across the dim room, barking her shin once on a table and cursing under her breath, until she reached the big window. There she surveyed the scene outside. She saw the perimeter of the blast scene fifty meters away, at least a dozen policemen and investigators milling about. An evidence van and two fire trucks were inside the tape, and a crowd of media—obvious by their shouldered cameras and microphones, and the credentials hanging round their necks—were gathered at an access control point where a hapless junior patrolman ignored their questions. Just behind him was a huddle of what had to be detectives—some likely from the national police, others local. She wished she could hear what they were saying, but in time everything would become clear.

She went to the television, selected a news channel, and set the volume very low. Next she pushed a chair from the dining room table toward the window, staying clear of a shaft of light that leaned in from a nearby streetlight. She sat down thinking she'd chosen well. There was no better place to watch the response unfold.

Earlier she had cursed the bomber, whom she knew to be hapless, for getting too close to a car—it had taken the brunt of the blast in one hemisphere. But now she realized his small error had turned fortuitous. The authorities had expanded the perimeter beyond what she'd expected, and if the blast had carried any farther, the building in which she sat might have been evacuated.

She settled in for the night, putting her bag of groceries on the floor and making sure her phone was turned off. It had been a long day, and her feet hurt from so much walking.

Malika took off her shoes and rubbed her feet,

then pulled out a bag of potato chips and twisted the top off a bottle of Coke. She put her naked feet up on the window box and leaned back, knowing there was not a safer place in all of France.

FOUR

It was the first time the stonemason had ever worked with coral. Porous and light, it had reasonably good strength, and was easier to shape than Virginia granite or the great marble slabs he'd battled in Malta. David Slaton had become something of a connoisseur of the world's stone, although not by choice.

He used the last of his joint mixture—an aggregate of cement, lime, and sand—on the edges of the shell-shaped entryway steps. He stood back with a critical eye, and was satisfied. Slaton began cleaning up, knowing that tomorrow he would have to come back and haul his debris to the nearest dump site, half a mile away. If there was a downside to this job, it had more to do with the local practices than materials. He'd been forced to make every cut by hand because there were no power tools available—and rarely any power if there had been. The raw blocks of coral limestone from the quarry had been delivered via handcart by a man who kept no particular schedule.

And then there was the sun.

If Palawan, in the Philippines, was not on the equator, it had to be within spitting distance. The heat was constant and unrelenting, and today conspired with a cloudless sky to mock Christmas lights that had been strung across the chapel roof two months ago. It was a tiny house of worship, three rows of wood-plank benches on either side of the central aisle, but it was full every Sunday, and the guiding father, an agreeable white-haired man, undertook his mandate with a faith no less ardent than what existed under the domes of St. Peter's.

Slaton had just finished gathering his tools, and was wiping his hands on a rag, when he saw his family a hundred yards distant. They were walking up a dirt path, what passed for a street here, and in no particular hurry. His son was out front—as he invariably was—with Christine herding him to stay on the path.

It was hard to say what gifts or deficiencies his son, not quite two years old, might possess, but he and Christine were unanimous in one regard: Davy had inherited his father's uncommonly sharp eyesight. His son's eyes locked on to him, and his choppy pace quickened. Slaton walked toward them to close the gap. He noticed they were both burnished by the sun, probably more than they should have been, but it was hopeless to expect otherwise living so near zero latitude. Christine's auburn hair had lightened, and her long limbs were reiterated in their son, evident in spite of his residual toddler's pudginess.

They met halfway, and Slaton swept Davy into his arms.

"So did you finish?" she asked.

"Pretty much. I'll come back tomorrow after everything has set, but I think it's good to go."

"Is the owner happy with it?"

Slaton shrugged, but didn't answer.

"David . . . tell me this is a real job."

"Father Michael gives what he can."

"He's not paying you in one of those seashell currencies, is he?"

"Where do you think the fish I've been bringing home every night is coming from? Besides, you're not one to talk. You worked at the clinic every morning this week, and they don't pay a dime . . . or a limpet or a flounder."

"It's not a big deal. Their only real doctor visits every other Saturday—that's not the kind of schedule people get sick on. Anyway, I like keeping a hand in medicine."

"Is your license valid to practice in the Philippines?"

"Probably not. But that skateboarder with a broken arm yesterday didn't ask to see it."

He pulled Davy up onto his shoulders, and got a grunting laugh in return. He seemed to be getting heavier by the day. "I hope you're not implying that I'm a less than adequate provider."

She smiled a smile that warmed Slaton to his depths. She still had that effect on him, even after a year of sailing the Seven Seas. Or at least three of the seven.

She took a long step back and regarded his work. The limestone building was designed as a residence for the father himself, one main room and a shaded lanai in front. "It's good—I like it. Was the arch over the doorway difficult?"

"Not really, a lot of cutting and chipping. It just takes a little time."

"You built it pretty fast."

"Just under a month. But then, I didn't have to worry about plumbing, electric, or insetting windows. And there's definitely no air-conditioning ductwork. It's basically a nicely crafted cave."

"Sort of Flintstones tropical?"

He grinned. "Right—a new architectural style."

Slaton picked up his tool bag, and as he did he saw Christine's humor dissipate a bit too quickly.

"Something wrong?" he asked.

She hesitated, then began swatting at Davy's legs. He kicked back at her, his heels thumping into Slaton's chest. "It's nothing. I'll tell you later."

Slaton straightened and locked eyes with his wife.

"Really," she said, "no big deal. Let's go home."

Home was an Antares 44, a custom-fit catamaran rigged to sail the world. She'd been christened *Windsom II,* after the original boat owned by Christine's father. The new boat was rigged for blue-water cruising with heavy-duty electric winches, an extensive navigation suite, and solar panels.

They put together an early dinner, fish with rice and *kamote,* a local variant of sweet potato. Slaton did the cooking—fish had become his specialty—and while they ate, Christine made a stab at conversation. He typically enjoyed exchanges with his wife. There was something in the manner of her speech, a rich tone with precise elocution, that he found warm and pleasing. He'd mentioned it once, and she had laughed it off, saying he was probably the only man in the world who wished his wife would talk more. But at that moment, some part of it was missing.

Something was bothering her.

They cleaned the table together while Davy pulled out his favorite pastime, a memory game involving paired tiles that could be turned over and matched. Fish, tigers, and elephants, all uncovered two at a time. "He's getting good at that," Slaton said. "He beat me this morning and I was trying."

Christine barely smiled, and he gripped her arm until her eyes met his. She nodded, and chinned toward the cockpit outside. They went above, leaving Davy at the table hunting for a zebra. The deck was warm on his bare feet, and it struck Slaton that *Windsom* had become more of a home than he'd imagined it could be. They instinctively sought out shade, and ended up facing one another near the helm.

"I met a woman at the playground today," Christine said. "She was there with her little boy—he was about Davy's age. I could see she was upset, and I tried to talk to her. Her English wasn't very good, but we got by. Her husband is a fisherman and he's disappeared. She said he rarely stays out overnight, but that he's been gone for three days."

"Where was he fishing?"

Christine told him.

Slaton knew the area. "Those are contested waters.

Have been for a long time. Is anyone searching for him?"

"She reported it to the Coast Guard, but they won't do anything—they're too busy tracking Chinese ships out in the Spratlys. Some of the other fishermen went out to look for him, and one of them spotted his boat."

"Drifting or anchored?"

"Neither. She was tied on to the *Esperanza*."

Slaton straightened in his seat. He looked out over the tranquil waters. They'd been here over a month, long enough to know a little about the local situation. These island chains were ground zero in a far-reaching geopolitical struggle. China, Malaysia, Vietnam, Taiwan, the Philippines—all were laying claims as fast as they could to uninhabited cays and reefs, staking out territory using highly creative means. The simplest route was to pitch a few tents and assign a squad of soldiers to an uninhabited sandbar. China had taken things to a new level, dredging sand and destroying coral reefs to create islands that had never before existed, then populating them with buildings, runways, and troops. Other nations, having fewer resources to work with, had been driving derelict ships onto shoals as markers of sovereign territory. It worked pretty well until the boat began to disintegrate—as was the case with *Esperanza*.

"That old hulk?" he said. "It's in pretty bad shape."

She nodded. "Nobody wanted to go near it."

"Why not? I know there used to be government

soldiers on board, but they pulled out last year because she was falling apart."

"The local rumor is that after the government abandoned ship, a band of smugglers took over—drugs or slavery, depending on who's telling the story."

"And they're still there?"

"Nobody knows. That's why none of the fishermen wanted to go near."

Slaton looked west by northwest. "Thirty nautical?"

"Thirty-six," she corrected.

"I hate to ask . . . but what do you want me to do about it?"

"What do *we* do about it."

He gave her a stern glare. "Give me your take on this woman."

"The wife?"

He nodded.

"She was upset. Her husband was missing, and she's worried to death."

Slaton sensed that his wife had been planning those words very carefully. "We've talked about this for the better part of a year," he said. "I don't get involved in anything unless it takes place far from where we are. You don't *ever* get involved, because that brings Davy into the picture."

"We're just talking about a missing fisherman who—"

"Have you ever seen this woman before?" he cut in.

"No, but what difference does that make?"

"Did she give you her phone number, tell you where she lives?"

"She said something about Villa Grande."

"Five miles away. I guess they don't have playgrounds there."

Her anger flashed. "You're so paranoid!"

"You're damned right I am! It's the only reason I'm still alive. And that's how we've agreed to live—a constant state of paranoia. My past has a way of catching up. The fact that we've gone a year without any problems doesn't put us in the clear."

"So what are you suggesting? That Hezbollah is here in Palawan? Tracking David Slaton, the legendary Israeli assassin, to the other side of the earth?"

He bit down on a reply, and silence ensued. Slaton forced a more conciliatory tone. "I don't like the smell of this," he said. "But if it's important to you . . . I can take a look."

"It's important to the man's wife and son. She's worried her husband might have gone aboard and gotten hurt."

Slaton was already having second thoughts. "If we do this, you and Davy don't go anywhere near that ship."

Christine didn't argue.

"If I see anything I don't like, I leave and we get out of here right away—open ocean."

Slaton saw a half smile.

He didn't return it.

FIVE

To board a ship on the open ocean is never easy, even if the water is only a few feet deep. Slaton did his homework. None of the local fishermen knew about a missing man, but they conceded that if he was from Villa Grande they might not know about it. Slaton found out as much as possible about the derelict ship before pulling anchor in Palawan. *Esperanza* was a World War II–vintage minesweeper, and had been gifted to the Philippines by the U.S. Navy decades earlier. She'd been run aground intentionally in 1999, an ungainly attempt by the government to establish sovereignty over a long-ignored coral atoll.

For years after her grounding, the Philippine Navy did their best to keep the ship in one piece. Steel plates were welded to the deck, lumber used to reinforce catwalks, and at one point someone had installed a generator and window-unit air conditioners, no doubt to shore up the morale of the heat-stricken Philippine Marine contingent who kept watch. The government had thrown in the towel just over a year ago, evacuating their disintegrating outpost, but rumors persisted that smugglers had taken over *Esperanza* in the interim.

Slaton made his approach to *Esperanza* using their inflatable dinghy, a twelve-foot runabout with an outboard motor that would best thirty knots on a calm sea. *Windsom* remained ten miles east, anchored in the lee of a so-far-unclaimed cay.

Slaton traversed the reef at idle, and saw no signs of habitation in the distant hulk. Indeed, in the gathering dusk *Esperanza* cast something of an apocalyptic image. Her hull rested askew on Midnight Reef, ten feet of water on the port side, and the starboard waterline fast against coral formations that were exposed at low tide.

A local news article Slaton had seen maintained that the only inhabitable parts of her structure were a few rooms in the aft superstructure—the bridge, a mess room, and a handful of crew cabins that had been more or less kept up. The Navy had reinforced the ship's port side, starboard being largely unapproachable owing to the shallow reef and heavier seas beyond. On the port beam was a fixed deck ladder reaching ten meters down to the waterline. Slaton saw no fishing dory lashed to the ladder, which was the only functional entrance.

He had surveyed the ship using binoculars from two miles away, and now did it again at a mile. He saw no lights, no laundry pinned on rails, no bags of stinking trash thrown out on deck. Notably, there was also no flag, Philippine or otherwise, flapping from the crooked yardarm.

There was no sign of life at all.

He could think of no stealthy way to approach such a target. Slaton kept scuba gear on *Windsom,* but the currents around the reef were unpredictable, meaning he would have had to drive within half a mile to even consider a swim. On a featureless ocean, that was tantamount to ringing the doorbell. He'd also concluded that waiting until nightfall could prove a disadvantage—he had no night-vision gear, and any drug smugglers on board probably would.

He steered north, along the reef that abutted the ship's starboard side. Breaking waves warned of treacherous shallows, but Slaton could see deeper channels in the reef, evidenced by smooth counter-currents. His inflatable drew only twelve inches of water, less with the engine raised. That was another method he'd used in the past—lift the engine, and a team of commandos paddling in unison could close quickly in virtual silence. As it was, with the wind and currents against him, trying to paddle the last two hundred meters solo would be little more than an endless cardio workout. He decided to use the engine until the last minute, keeping the throttle to a minimum and hoping the breeze would drive the sound out to sea. In the end, Slaton saw but one certainty: If anyone remotely competent was on board the ship, they were going to see him coming. But that wasn't all bad. A naked approach at dusk was obvious, but also unthreatening. It was his best chance to get close. Assuming he could manage that, whatever odds he was up against would begin to swing.

As he came nearer, Slaton got the impression that

the ship's hull was more rust than steel. Her bow was
noticeably high on the reef, and what remained of her
superstructure was in various stages of decay: listing
aerials and davits, deck rails broken, and cables hanging into the sea like vines off a storm-ravaged tree.
The hull looked paper thin, spars and bulkheads
showing through like ribs on an underfed dog; any
load at all in her holds would surely cause seams to
burst. The bow gun emplacement held the remains of
a 40mm Bofors. Once meant to intimidate, the gun
now resembled something from a long-abandoned
museum, its barrel pointed skyward in a final salute.

Twenty meters away, the breeze dropped sharply in
the lee of the ship's hull. He killed the motor and
reached for the paddle. He was wearing old work
clothes—a tattered pair of pants and a sleeveless shirt
stained by mortar—reasoning that an approach to
Esperanza in a black wetsuit and camo would be
needlessly hostile. By the same logic, he'd brought the
smallest weapons from the minor arsenal he kept
under lock and key on *Windsom*—a reliable Beretta
9mm holstered beneath his shirttail, and a Glock 26
on his right ankle. Two spare magazines weighed
down his left hip pocket, ready for a left-handed grab
and reload, and a flashlight big enough to double as
a truncheon filled the back pocket on his nonshoot-
ing side. With his hardware reasonably concealed, he
might appear harmless on first glance—and anyone
Slaton deemed threatening wouldn't get more than
one glance.

The starboard hull loomed high as he approached,

the lowest deck rail five meters above his head. Slaton's dodgy intelligence, a blend of old news articles, hearsay, and local rumors, had so far been spot-on—the starboard side of the ship gave no access to the upper deck. But he did see one possibility. Just beneath the wing of the bridge was a section of hull so rusted it was falling into the sea, and he noted a series of jagged holes that might be used as footholds. He paddled silently closer, his eyes and ears alert. He heard only water lapping against steel and the cry of a distant gull.

He lashed the dinghy by its painter to the base of a broken fitting. Slaton gauged the climb up close and thought it might work. Having brought a rope just in case, he looped it over a shoulder before beginning upward. In less than a minute he was on deck. He secured the rope, which had climbing loops at regular intervals, and fed it down to the dinghy. Ready for a quick departure.

There was still no sign of life, but caution got the better of him. Slaton pulled the Beretta from his waistband as he moved aft. He was on the main deck now, and above him were two upper levels, the highest having once been the bridge—it was rimmed with windows, and catwalks overlooked every part of the ship, the obvious high ground for anyone playing defense.

He stepped carefully, the wisdom of which was proved when one foot began sinking into a rusted section of floor. The problem area was the size of an oven door, and he shifted his weight and leapt silently over it. He immediately rounded a corner and was

ASSASSIN'S CODE | 37

faced with a larger failed section that could only be traversed using a two-by-six plank someone had left in place. The plank took him to the base of the super-structure, and Slaton led with the Beretta through a doorless passageway. He cleared a room where two tattered hammocks were strung between bulkheads and the lone window was nothing more than a web of shattered safety glass. He saw an old generator, mooring lines, and a windlass under repair. The stench was heavy, fetid and rotting, and he quickly climbed a ladder toward the second of the three levels.

The instant his eyes reached the middle floor, he paused and scanned the room at ankle level before ex-posing himself further. He saw nothing worrisome and kept rising. As soon as he cleared the top step, Slaton sensed movement to one side. He whipped the barrel of his gun instinctively, and when the sight settled he saw a wary tiger-striped cat behind it. He lowered the Beretta. The cat looked healthy and plump, and under its front paw was a small dead rat. Slaton half turned to take in the rest of the room, and when he did the cat bolted, taking its kill and disappearing through some unseen passageway.

The light outside was growing dim, and he pulled out his flashlight to inspect a mess hall that hadn't been used as intended for nearly twenty years. He saw an old steel sink, and a makeshift kitchen consisting of a propane stove and a tiny refrigerator. There was no food in sight, but on a table in the center he saw the scattered excrement of some manner of vermin. There were also discarded sheets of plastic, a container of Ziploc bags, and a mechanical scale that could have been taken from a grocery store deli. Trash littered the floor, along with a dusting of what looked like ground tea leaves. He decided smugglers might have replaced the Philippine Navy after all.

He moved toward the stairs that led to the bridge, and was nearly there when a clatter came from above. Slaton trained his weapon on the metal staircase. *The cat?* he wondered. *No, the cat would be finishing its dinner.*

His senses shot to another level, grasping for any sound or motion. All too late, he recognized his error. He'd been too predictable, coming straight up the only staircase. He turned and saw a shadow in the stairwell he'd just risen through. The next thing he saw was the barrel of a machine pistol rising upward.

SIX

Slaton threw himself against a wall as the weapon shattered the silence in full auto, rounds pinging into metal and ricocheting across the room. He felt a strike and a sting of pain in his left thigh. As soon as the burst ended, he curled his hand into the stairwell and fired three unsighted rounds down the path of the rising steps. He heard a thump and a clatter from below, one body and one gun hitting the deck in quick succession. If there was another threat, he knew where it would be.

He vaulted into the stairwell as shots came from above, reverberating like thunder between the gray-steel walls. Slaton returned fire upward this time, suppression to buy precious seconds. Reaching the main deck, he saw the man he'd just hit, unmoving and still. His machine pistol had tumbled toward the doorway that led outside. It would be a useful weapon in this kind of fight, but the idea was killed when a third figure appeared on the threshold. More rounds rained down from above.

Slaton lunged toward the only other way out of the

room, firing four rounds as he leapt shoulder-first into the already-shattered window. The glass gave way and he tumbled onto the outer deck, landing in an awkward roll. He scanned for other attackers as he counted to three, then rose to the window frame, acquired the man just inside the doorway, and sent three rounds toward his head. He waited only long enough to see the man crumple as if his bones had disconnected.

He ducked back down, shouldered to the wall, and ran toward the starboard sidewall where his dinghy was tethered. The Beretta's slide was back, confirming the count in his head—mag empty, no round in the chamber. He dug into his pocket for a spare, and had just reached the corner of the superstructure when two problems arose. A man appeared on the catwalk along the starboard side, his gun lifting toward Slaton. The greater problem was the magazine he pulled from his pocket—the frame was hopelessly bent and he felt the liquid warmth of his own blood.

The sting in my thigh.

Slaton registered a noise from behind, and he saw a man straddling through the window with his gun leveled—no doubt the one who'd been above. That put the count at four, with two down. Manageable, except for the fact that Slaton was looking at a pair of gun barrels from different directions. The man at the window said something. His partner responded. Slaton could discern only that they were speaking French—not one of his better languages.

He stood still, a spent weapon in his hand. With two targets so widely spaced, Slaton knew he could never pull and load his final mag in time. Even if he tried, that one might also be damaged. He had only one remaining advantage.

He had been here before.

In the next two seconds he learned a great deal about the men facing him. Most important, he realized they were not assassins. It had nothing to do with the fact that their shooting had been ineffectual, or that their tactical approach had been flawed. He knew because of what they *weren't* doing right now. Assassins never hesitated.

Never.

The men stared at him with a certain satisfaction—thoughts of payback for their two downed comrades, but also a bit of victory. They were soldiers, in some sense of the word, and so Slaton played along. Completely exposed, and with an unloaded weapon in his hand, he did what any vanquished combatant would do.

He surrendered.

The three men stood together at the corner of *Esperanza*'s superstructure, Slaton at the vertex of a right angle. He was fifteen feet from both men, but most critically, neither of them could see the other. Somewhere over his right shoulder, fifteen feet down, the dinghy bobbed lazily on its line. The man near the door was big, over six feet tall and well over two hundred pounds. Geometry and numbers that were vital.

"I am going to drop my weapon," Slaton said slowly in English.

Neither man responded, but he suspected they

understood. Suspected they'd seen enough Hollywood movies.

With the greatest of care he sent the empty Beretta skittering along the deck toward the man near the door. Slaton dropped the damaged magazine and stood with his empty hands held harmlessly outward. He edged one step back, an almost imperceptible and wholly unthreatening movement. As he did so, he slid his right foot along the outer railing. The Beretta had come to rest halfway toward the big man. It was just short of the two-by-six plank Slaton had crossed earlier. Directly on top of a section of rust the size of an oven door. The big man traversed the plank carefully, his weapon level on Slaton. When he was one step away from the Beretta, and bending down to pick it up, Slaton discreetly hooked the toe of his right boot into the base of an old stanchion.

The floor failed as soon as the big man's knee touched the deck, the section of rusted metal cracking under his weight like ice that was too thin. The fracture spread in an instant and swallowed the man. Slaton was already moving. He launched himself over the *Esperanza*'s starboard rail, pivoting on his right foot while gravity did the rest.

Bullets flew to the spot where he'd been a fraction of a second earlier, carrying out over the sea. Slaton went over the side, disappearing from sight. When the second man reached the rail, he probably expected to find a wounded adversary floundering in the sea. What he saw was a man hanging nearly upside down, one foot hooked into solid metal, and a hand gripping a loop on a climbing rope. In the other hand, a mere eight feet away, was a compact Glock 26.

Slaton never hesitated.

Clearing *Esperanza* for remaining threats took a tense fifteen minutes—Slaton reasoned the risk involved in doing so was preferable to a retreat over open water in a rubber boat. He also hoped to find something to explain who these men were.

There had been no survivors. The big man had ended up thirty feet below deck in what was once a cargo hold. In the beam of his flashlight Slaton saw the body crumpled over a spar, facedown in water. The others had suffered his marksmanship. All four men were cut from a disturbingly similar mold—dark complexions, black hair, and three had beards that were more or less groomed. He searched the habitable areas of the ship but found nothing to explain why four men of Middle Eastern extraction, at least two of whom spoke French, had traveled to the remote reaches of the Pacific to attack him.

His final chore was to search the bodies, or at least the three within reach. On the last man he'd taken, Slaton found his only clue. In the front trouser pocket, amid sticks of gum and a handful of hollow-point bullets, he discovered a memory stick. Intriguing as it was, the significance didn't sink home until he held it to the beam of his flashlight.

What he saw was stunning.

He had come to *Esperanza* in search of a stranded

fisherman. Smugglers would have been his second choice. In his hand was precisely what he'd hoped *not* to find. Indeed, what he feared the most. One word had been printed neatly on the flash drive's plastic case.

SLATON.

SEVEN

The meeting began just before noon in the general director's office of the northern Paris headquarters of DGSI, which, in a somber twist of fate, kept an address in the township of Levallois-Perret—a district that some years ago had been carelessly anointed a "twin city" to Molenbeek, Belgium, Europe's well-documented incubator of Islamic terrorism.

Aside from Baland, in attendance were DGSI director Claude Michelis and Charlotte LeFevre, the head of DGSI's intelligence technologies section. LeFevre was a serious blue-eyed woman whose pants and blouse were always stylish but never pressed, and whose blond hair was anchored firmly by gray roots—in Baland's favorable interpretation, a woman who was trying to keep up appearances, but too hard-working to be consumed by it. She carried the meeting from the outset.

"The radioactive material used in Grenoble has been positively identified as americium-241. Americium is primarily an alpha-particle emitter, with some resulting gamma rays."

"What threat does it pose?" the director asked.

"By some measures this isotope is more radio-active than weapons-grade plutonium, but it's not as bad as it sounds. Alpha radiation doesn't penetrate well. Americium is generally only dangerous to humans if inhaled or ingested. A few contaminated bolts lying in the street are virtually harmless. The other limitation is quantity. Measurements taken on-site suggest the blast contained less than a gram of the material. Put in common terms, I doubt anyone will suffer more than the equivalent of an extra few days of common background radiation."

"So radiation is not a concern," said the director.

"Radiation is always a concern. But this event could have been far worse."

"Where did this americium come from?" asked Michelis.

"Smoke detectors," replied Baland before the expert could answer.

"Yes," said LeFevre, "that *is* the most likely source. Certain types of household smoke detectors contain trace amounts of americium-241—it's used in conjunction with an ionization chamber, a method to recognize smoke. This type of detector has been banned in much of the E.U., but they're commonly available in other countries."

It was an all too common theme, Baland knew—deriving weapons from what was readily available. In the Paris attacks of 2015 the bombers had worn vests packed with TATP, a volatile explosive mixture that could be manufactured from hair dye and nail polish remover.

LeFevre continued, "The amount of material in a single smoke detector is minuscule, three-tenths of a microgram. Spent units can be safely discarded with household trash. Americium is a malleable metal, silver in color, and not soluble. In theory, you could swallow the source from a detector and it would pass right through your body."

"You make it sound harmless."

"Not at all. The explosion in Grenoble generated particles that will ride on the air. If these particles are inhaled, they can establish in the lungs and emit radiation continuously, leading to cell aberrations and cancer."

"All right," said Michelis. "How hard will it be to clean up this disaster?"

"I think we'll make quick work of it. A few blocks of Grenoble will be closed for a month, perhaps two. Mind you, the cleanup will not be absolute—we'll be finding minute pockets of contamination for years to come. But then, I think we can agree that direct injuries from radiation was never the point."

"As a method of terror," Baland concurred, "the damage is complete. Every news report leads with a picture of cleanup crews in full protective gear, and every headline is backed by the radiation symbol. Hospitals in Grenoble are overwhelmed, tourism will disappear at the height of ski season, and radiation film badges will become the latest must-have accessory."

The director nodded, and said, "We've already responded to over two hundred reports of suspicious individuals and packages across France in which radiation was mentioned. All have proved baseless, yet this surge of fear has stretched our resources to the breaking point."

Baland said, "The national police will have to deal with it. Here at DGSI our duty is to ask what comes next. I've been in meetings all morning, and there is no intelligence to suggest a follow-on attack. But then, we didn't see this one coming. We've had too many minor distractions—raiding rooming houses, monitoring gun sales, tracking the movement of suspicious characters. The introduction of nuclear material, even at a low level, is a clear graduation of hostilities."

Michelis said, "ISIS has claimed this attack. I spoke with the president a few hours ago, and he has ordered retaliatory airstrikes. Not that it will make any difference. The problem is what it has always been: Each bomb dropped on a hideout in Raqqa gives them ten new recruits in Saint-Denis. We've been keeping watch lists for years, adding to them exponentially, but we can't keep up. There is simply no way to know which of these Arab cutthroats among us are a danger and which are good citizens. I don't see why . . ." Michelis' voice trailed off. "I'm sorry, Zavier, I shouldn't have said it that way."

LeFevre looked at Baland, who said, "It's all right. I've been known to use worse terms myself. And what you say is true—if we had some way to identify the terrorist element in our midst and intervene, the president would be less inclined to launch air attacks in the Middle East. That, in turn, might dampen the swell of outraged young men. The entire cycle of violence could run in reverse, perhaps even giving way to peace."

"Let's move on," Michelis said. "Have any of the attackers been identified?"

"Not yet, but all appear to be of Mediterranean extraction," LeFevre said, using the new agency term. Ten years ago France's large population of immigrants had sourced largely from North Africa, places like Algeria and Tunisia. The exodus from the war in Syria had forced a broadening.

"Has there been anything new on this car in which the body was found?" the director asked.

LeFevre said, "It's definitely the car that delivered the bomber. We're going over it now for DNA samples and fingerprints. The CCTV video is grainy, but we think the individual at large is a female. We also discerned something interesting in the footage. We can easily see the bomber get out of the car and begin to walk away. Then he returned to the passenger-side window, and this woman can be seen reaching into his jacket pocket. Our analysts believe she was activating the switch on his vest."

"Why on earth would she do that?" the director asked.

"Because she didn't trust him to do it," Baland interjected. He had already studied the video thoroughly and reached the same conclusion.

"Most likely," agreed LeFevre. "A cold move on any number of levels."

"It suggests to me that she also dispatched the driver," said Baland. He got no arguments. "Our lone survivor appears to be one very ruthless woman."

LeFevre said, "We're guessing she switched to a different vehicle. If that's the case, she could be anywhere in France by now. The Swiss and Italian borders are also very near."

With the worst of the news dispensed, everyone agreed to keep looking. Michelis dismissed LeFevre, and once she was gone he turned circumspect and said to Baland, "That was good work in Grenoble, recognizing the chance of a radiological hazard. Going forward we should embed radiological testing in our standard attack response."

Baland waved his hand dismissively. "It has long been on our list. We simply don't have the right equipment at first-responder level."

"One more thing to squeeze out of our budget."

There was a time when Baland would have been surprised by that comment. On reaching the middle ranks in the force, he'd begun to see how preoccupied senior officers were with budgetary issues. He supposed it was the way of things. One step above them in the hierarchy were politicians who viewed law enforcement as nothing more than a cost index. Curiously, as Baland himself reached the higher echelons, he felt a surprising urge to not point out such shortcomings. Advancement had its price.

He said, "I fear the scope of these attacks will continue to escalate."

"More radiological agents?" Michelis asked.

"Perhaps. Or something new . . . biological, chemical. This strike in Grenoble was a simple cell—six individuals. There are thousands of potential jihadists on our watch lists. Even if only a handful go active, it could mean dozens of attacks in the works. Each small in its own right, but collectively . . . it's death by a thousand cuts. I fear we will soon be in the same spiral Israel has found itself in. Policemen on every bus, checkpoints, teaching suspicion to our children."

Michelis nodded. "Where do you think the survivor from this Grenoble cell has gone?"

"She's clearly in hiding, but who can say where. It is always easier to become lost in a big city. Paris would be my first guess, perhaps Lyon or Marseille. It won't be easy to find her—we have one poor image, no identity information."

"We've gone through these motions before. Step up the raids in the Muslim quarters, keep an eye on the mosques." Michelis sighed heavily, then rose from his seat. He walked around his desk and escorted Baland to the door.

Before reaching it, he gripped his protégé's elbow, and they paused side by side. "I should tell you something, Zavier. For five years I have sat behind this desk, and never has it seemed more heavy."

Baland nodded. "These are trying days. But we *will* prevail."

Michelis seemed to study him before saying, "You have a gift—an ability to see around corners, to visualize what will come next."

"It's not so hard. You simply have to put yourself in your enemy's position. Force yourself to think as they do."

Michelis nodded. "Whatever the trick, I want you to keep doing it."

"Of course, sir. And thank you."

When Baland was gone, Michelis started back toward his desk. Halfway across the room he paused at a decorative mirror. He did not like what he saw. He'd once cut a striking figure, but the piercing blue eyes now had bags beneath them, and the regal lines along his cheeks had deepened into channels. His wings of gray hair had thinned and gone to a white that was positively grandfatherly. The strain was showing, and the thought of another year or two dealing with the aftermath of mass shootings and dirty bombs was hardly revitalizing. As Michelis knew better than anyone in France, the struggle against fundamentalist Islam wouldn't end if this crime could be solved, or for that matter the next one. At some point, more likely sooner than later, it would be time for him to pass the baton.

He turned away, sat tentatively behind his desk, and reflected on what his legacy might be. Would he be remembered as the director who let things get out of hand? Or the one who had laid the foundation of victory? At the very least, Michelis prided himself on being a good judge of character, of identifying men and women who could run an effective department. Now, with his career at a sunset, he was quite confident he'd found the right man to carry the battle forward.

EIGHT

"Ow!" Slaton looked down at the bloody needle.

"Don't be a wuss," Christine said as she tied off a suture.

Slaton had been called a great many things in his long career as a Mossad assassin. Never had he been called a "wuss." He was lying naked on their bunk, his left hip high with towels draped across either side of the wound.

"How many stitches?" he asked.

"Only five—a mere scratch by your standards." She applied an antibiotic to the wound and then a professional-grade bandage. Given the tenuousness of their circumstances—not to mention that she was a doctor and he a trained combat medic—they had agreed from the outset that *Windsom*'s medical locker would be stocked comprehensively. She slapped him on the butt to say she was done.

Slaton rotated onto his back, and pulled a sheet up to his waist. "Is that how you treat all your patients?"

"Only the ones who deserve it."

She turned and began putting away supplies. His

doctor was barefoot, her auburn hair askew, and she was wearing a set of loose pajamas. *Windsom* lurched on a wave, and she grabbed the side of a cabinet as a handhold.

They were already under way, six miles removed from their anchorage, and making five knots on a following swell with the autopilot engaged. After leaving *Esperanza,* Slaton had taken an indirect return route to *Windsom*. He bypassed two deserted islands, and gave wide berth to an anchored megayacht—countersurveillance, South Seas style.

Christine had been waiting for him on deck, and when he'd stepped aboard they both felt a wave of relief. A brief reception of kisses and clutching, however, ended abruptly when she saw the blood on his leg. He told her what had transpired, and they'd gotten under way immediately. Slaton pulled *Windsom*'s anchor under the light of a rising moon, and set a course to open water. Christine set up a sick bay.

Davy, at least, had been asleep in his cabin, and they both knew he wouldn't stir until morning. Cruising the oceans was like camping in the sense that circadian rhythms fell in tune with sunrise and sunset. Tonight they would violate that schedule. In three hours *Windsom* would approach busy shipping lanes, meaning someone would have to be on deck. A long night lost to watch shifts and adrenaline.

Christine met his gaze, and he tried to read her. Caring doctor? Angry wife? Protective mother? He saw a bit of them all.

"So there were four of them?" she asked.

"Yes."

"And they attacked you without provocation."

She hadn't phrased it as a question, but he answered anyway. "Yes."

"You don't know who they were?"

"No idea."

"Could they have been smugglers?"

"Definitely not."

Her eyes narrowed. "How do you know that?"

"For one thing, they look Middle Eastern. And they spoke French, which isn't exactly endemic in these waters."

"You talked to them?"

"No, they were communicating with each other during . . . what happened."

Thankfully, Christine didn't ask him to recount the battle.

"And smugglers wouldn't have had this," he said. Slaton reached across the bunk to the bloody trousers she'd cut from his leg ten minutes ago. From a pocket he removed the memory stick and showed her what was written on it. He heard a subtle intake of air before she spoke, her tone strangely hollow.

"Your name."

"My *real* name."

She shut her eyes tightly. "This is all my fault."

"How?"

"You were right," she said. "It was a setup all along. The woman and her son on the playground. If I had just walked away—"

"No! *You* are in no way responsible for this."

She looked at him searchingly.

"The way it worked out—it could have been worse."

"How?"

"They approached you and Davy, but didn't put you in danger."

"If that's your idea of optimism, it's utterly depressing."

Her chin sank to her chest, and Slaton pulled her next to him on the bunk and held her. "This had nothing to do with you," he whispered, stroking his wife's sun-streaked hair. Nothing was said for a time as they both decompressed, the only sound *Windsom*'s twin hulls carving through the sea.

She finally pulled away, a question set in her face. "But I don't understand. If these men came here to attack you . . . then what's that?" She nodded to the memory stick.

Slaton turned it in his hand. "A briefing, probably. A map of where we were anchored, or a diagram of *Esperanza*. Maybe photos of me working at the church, or you and Davy in the park—you've been going there on and off for a couple of weeks."

"Should we see what's on it?"

Slaton considered it, then discarded the stick on the bedside table. He looked at her openly. "Tomorrow. It's been a long day, but we're safe now."

"Are we?"

He cupped the side of her face with a hand, stroked her cheek with his thumb. "Yes, I promise."

Her worry lines finally cracked. First relief, followed by the trace of a smile. Slaton kissed her lightly on the lips. Then again.

On the third she responded, and their tension translated into the physical. Soon Christine was lying next to him on the bed. Soothing hands gripped more firmly, ventured with practiced familiarity. Thirty minutes later both were sleeping soundly, side by side, exhausted in every way.

NINE

The night at sea resolved into the usual challenges. Christine was the first to wake, and took the early shift. Slaton relieved her at 3:00 A.M. in a rising sea. An hour before sunrise, he was still at the helm.

He'd seen only two freighters, both distant. *Windsom* was battering through steady swells, her twin hulls plowing obediently northward. Explosions of spray flew over the rails, more from the windward starboard side, and water slapped over the cockpit in rhythmic sheets. From the protection of a dodger, Slaton programmed a course ten degrees east of what he wanted—given the conditions, he felt it wise to keep the boat angled into the seas.

He trimmed out the jib, confident things wouldn't get worse. After cruising for almost a year now, he was beginning to understand that every sea had its habits—some pleasant, others annoying, a few outright dangerous. *Just like people,* he mused.

He saw a dim light flicker below, and a few minutes later Christine appeared.

"Coffee is brewing," she said. She looked over the seas and the rigging. "A little tight on the main, but not bad."

"I'm trainable."

"Why don't you come below. We should talk before Davy wakes up."

"Right."

Coffee was brewing but not yet in hand. Christine slid into the settee, and Slaton took the seat across from her, still moving gingerly from the wound on his thigh. He pushed the plastic drive across the table. It seemed small and inanimate, which only made it that much more ominous. Slaton watched his wife closely and saw her spirits sink. Whatever comfort they'd stolen last night was lost in an instant.

She picked up the drive as though it were some kind of talisman. "You didn't take a look while I was sleeping?" she asked.

"No. If you want, I can throw it overboard right now." He said nothing more, only waited.

Christine sighed and pulled the family laptop onto the table. As soon as it was up and running, she plugged in the stick. Their first finding was obvious, and not insignificant.

"No access codes or encryption schemes," he said.

"No."

He let her do the navigating, which turned out to be minimal.

"I see only one folder," she said. "Three images."

She looked up at him, and Slaton nodded. She double-clicked.

The first image filled the screen, and Slaton saw a copy of a news article. It appeared to be a screenshot of an online news piece. There was a photo of two men and a caption underneath.

Slaton studied the faces intently. One man was grinning as he received an award, the classic right-hand handshake and coat-hanger smile, the award held jointly by the presenter and awardee. The man receiving the award looked vaguely familiar, but Slaton swept his first impulse aside. *That would be impossible.* He shifted to the man issuing the honor, whom he recognized instantly. It was the president of France. Slaton went back to the other man, and his discomforting thought recurred. The caption at the bottom explained that the award was being issued for meritorious service to the republic. A time and date at the head of the article suggested the picture had been taken three weeks ago. Which made no sense whatsoever.

His concern must have been evident, because Christine asked, "What's wrong, David?"

He met his wife's eyes, but wasn't sure how to answer. "Call up the others."

The next photo came into view—the same man in a policeman's uniform, taken last year if the date could be believed. The photo looked like it might have been sourced from a gendarmerie personnel file. The caption at the bottom introduced him as a newly appointed conseiller to the director of DGSI. Christine navigated to the last image, and a fourteen-year-old news article was presented, the same man again, noticeably younger. This time he was lauded as being the top graduate in the Paris prefecture's spring training class. Slaton couldn't take his eyes from the half-smiling face. He rubbed his chin with a cupped hand, and a coarse grating noise reminded him he hadn't shaved in two days.

"Who is . . . Zavier Baland?" she asked, referencing the name linking all three pictures.

"According to this, he's a fast-rising officer at DGSI. That's France's internal security service."

"Like the FBI?"

"You could think of it like that. They're responsible for counterterrorism."

"Okay," she said cautiously, "but why is this on a memory stick in a killer's pocket . . . with your name on it?"

He let out a long, steady breath, not sure how to answer.

She said, "You told me this was going to be some kind of mission briefing used by the men who came after you."

"That's what I thought it would be. But now I'm seeing another possibility."

Christine waited.

"This was insurance."

"Insurance?"

"Whoever sent these men didn't have a lot of confidence in them. They thought I might survive. So the lead man was given orders to carry this file. If the attack failed, I would find it."

"But a few pictures of a policeman in France? Does that mean anything to you?"

"Actually, yeah, it does. There *is* something special about this guy—something that ties him to me."

"What?"

"I killed him fifteen years ago."

TEN

Baland heard a muted voice behind him, but the words didn't register as he sat at the kitchen table with his morning cup of tea. Then an arm wrapped around his throat.

He smiled, and turned to face his youngest daughter. "I'm sorry, darling. What was it?"

"*Lapins Crétins*! You said you would read it to me before school!" Amélie held out her favorite book. Baland was reaching to pull her into his lap when his wife intervened.

"No, there is no time! Papa will read to you tonight."

Amélie pouted as only a seven-year-old could.

"Yes, tonight," said Baland. "I promise to be home before bedtime."

"You always break your promises," chirped Celine as she came into the kitchen to collect her lunch. At nine years old, she was two years senior and therefore infinitely wiser than her sister.

Baland answered by rising, corralling his older daughter, and kissing her on the head. "Perhaps I should arrest you both. . . . I will take you to work with me and keep you all day."

"Oh please!" said Celine. "Then I will miss that terrible Monsieur Gabard and his boring history lessons!"

"Knowledge of history is essential," admonished Baland. "Do not let one dull old teacher steal your enthusiasm for a worthy subject."

Jacqueline Baland schussed her children toward the door. "Get your jackets, both of you. It will be cold today."

The girls complied, disappearing from the kitchen. When they were gone Jacqueline began clearing dishes. "You shouldn't encourage them when they criticize their teachers."

"You and I have met the man—listening to him is like listening to an old record. He should have retired years ago."

"Say what you want to me, but we must teach the girls respect."

Baland sighed. "Yes, yes . . . you are right."

"I'm going to walk the girls to school."

Baland almost protested, but didn't want to start the argument anew. He considered driving safer for his family: to be near the top ranks of the nation's counterterrorism establishment did not come without a price. Jacqueline, unfortunately, was quintessentially French, and would not permit her joie de vivre to be infringed upon.

"I'll be back in twenty minutes," she said. "Will you still be here?"

"No, I must go in early."

She came up behind him and put her arms across his chest. "You've been working so much lately, darling. The girls miss you. I miss you."

He closed his eyes and put his hands on hers. "I know. I'm sorry, but this business in Grenoble has stirred things up. It will get better soon."

"When you become director?"

He pulled her around and looked at her questioningly. "What makes you say that?"

She shrugged. "A few of the other wives . . . we talk. They've seen your advancement, and there is but one place to go from where you sit."

"You should not discuss such things with your friends."

"Do you deny it? The possibility?"

He smiled and swatted her rump. "I can neither confirm nor deny such information."

She smiled back. "See? You were born for the job."

"On the minuscule chance it does come to pass, I can tell you the job includes cars and bodyguards we will all make use of."

She kissed him on the cheek, went to the next room, and in a flurry of hugs and backpacks and gloves, Jacqueline left with the girls.

The house turned eerily quiet. Baland went to the sink, and as he washed his cup he looked out the window across their wintering garden. Even out of season, everything was trimmed and proper, no thanks to him—he'd hired a gardener who came twice a week to tend to things. He noticed a swing on the play set that was hanging loose on one side, and he wondered how long it had been that way.

He set the cup in a drying rack and tried to think of something else to do. It was no use—he checked his phone and flicked through a sea of new e-mails from work. The phone was secure, or so they told him, and one message in particular held his attention: there had been no progress in identifying the woman they'd seen in the car in Grenoble. He wasn't surprised. The CCTV video had told Baland what he needed to know.

They'd been searching for her for some time, a female organizer, a shadowy young woman who'd been cobbling together local recruits and ISIS infiltrators, and sending them into attacks. Until now she had largely remained under DGSI's radar, but in Grenoble she'd made a mistake. She had also proved herself ruthless enough to depress the switch in the bomber's hand, and later to execute the driver. Perhaps the man had been unreliable or done something to compromise security. Whatever the transgression, she had put a gun to his head and shot him at close range.

Ruthless indeed, Baland thought.

Minutes later he was walking into an iron-gray morning, steering toward DGSI headquarters, which lay slightly over a kilometer from his house. Contradicting the security concerns he expressed to his wife, Baland regularly walked to work himself. Director Michelis had more than once offered to provide a car and protection, to which Baland invariably replied, "Senior officers at DGSI order covert operations—they do not suffer them."

He turned up his collar against a brisk wind and

set out with a purpose. Baland had covered roughly half his morning commute when he diverted into a small grocery store. At the entrance he pulled out a thin pad of Post-it notes, and scribbled a list on the top page: bread, yogurt, and his favorite English tea. He continued writing on the second page, then spent ten minutes with a basket collecting his lunch, checking each item meticulously off his list. At the checkout line, Baland bid the familiar cashier a friendly *"Bonjour"* before giving his scarf a turn around his neck and heading back into the street.

It was ten minutes later, as DGSI's senior conseiller was arriving at his office, that a dark-skinned young woman picked up a basket at the same market and began strolling the aisles. She had a squat build, and was dressed in an ill-fitting dress and thick down jacket. Her wiry black hair was matted with cold rain, and droplets ran down her hooked nose as she shuffled across the weary linoleum floor. She was discriminating in the produce section, checking ten apples before selecting two, but less so in back, where she stocked her basket with *pain au chocolat* and a cheap bottle of table red. She again stalled when selecting tea, going to the back of the shelf for a box of Twining's English Breakfast before moving to the checkout line.

She paid with a prepaid Visa card, trundled outside with a bag in each hand, and walked a circuitous path to a nearby bus stop. There she took a seat on an empty bench, set down her bags, and removed a small piece of yellow paper from one of the shopping bags. She carefully unfolded the three meticulous creases so as not to damage the paper, which had glue on one edge. She read the brief message.

When a bus unexpectedly approached the stop, the woman frowned. She stood smartly, and walked away with her bags in hand. Minutes later she arrived at the small bed-and-breakfast that would be her home for another three hours. Malika locked the door behind her, took a seat at the dining table, and partook of a very nice *pain au chocolat* as she pecked out an encrypted message on her phone.

ELEVEN

For the two men it was a rare event to be in the same building. When their paths did intersect, it was strictly for brief periods, and never on a predetermined schedule. Indeed, their encounters were often no more than chance events, rather like friends bumping into one another at a pub after work. Except the two men were not friends—not really—and there wasn't a pub within a hundred miles of Al-Raqqa, deep in the troubled land that had once been called Syria.

The place had been a small grocery some years ago, evidenced by old advertising posters on the walls, many of them peeling away like dated wallpaper. A few long-empty shelves had been pushed aside to make way for a large rectangular rug, giving the main floor the aura of an arena. A security contingent loitered outside, but only a few trusted men, all of whom kept to the shadows. Neither of the principals carried a mobile phone, and both had arrived on foot. They would depart the same way, with minimal fanfare and in different directions. These maneuvers were not by choice—the leadership of ISIS had simply learned the hard way. A phalanx of black-clad guards, a convoy of vehicles, a stray signal—any of that could be a give-away to the drones. A veritable invitation for an air-strike. Such was the survivalist mind-set these days of the men who administered the Islamic State in Iraq and Syria.

Wael Chadeh was the number-two man in ISIS, answering only to the caliph himself. If the organiza-tion were to embrace a corporate structure, Chadeh would be its chief operations officer. His internal se-curity service, known as the Emni, was responsible for both security within the caliphate and the planning of operations abroad. As a matter of strict religious theory, of course, the Islamic State did not recognize the borders of any country. The caliphate existed not as a nation-state, but rather the very antithesis, a geo-graphic boundary where the only law was the law of God, and where, according to the Prophet, an apoca-lyptic battle would one day take place. Unfortunately, in recent years the caliphate's holdings had shrunk markedly. There were still a few strongholds, but across the Middle East, ISIS was losing ground fast. And when a given territory was lost, the surviving fighters did what they'd always done—they ghosted back into the population to fight another day.

Chadeh had risen through the ranks as a hardened warrior. In the course of battle, he had killed the en-emy in more ways than he'd once thought possible. He had also watched countless men and women around him fall to Western crusaders, their Kurd minions, Shiite militias, Russian bombers, and even a few to Assad's bumbling Alawite army. Chadeh himself had lost two fingers to a piece of shrapnel, carried fragments of a Peshmerga bullet somewhere near his heart, and on occasion had difficulty breathing—he'd been exposed to something terrible in a barrel-bomb attack last year, and his lungs no longer worked as they should. He was rather tall, but had difficulty standing erect, and, in spite of his being only forty-one years old, there was far more salt than pepper in his foot-long beard. Chadeh was a weary soldier in a vicious campaign, and as such, carried a predictably bitter outlook on life.

The man seated next to him on the ornate rug was altogether different. His hands weren't callused, and there was not a trace of grit under his trimmed fingernails. He wore a beard, but at the tender age of twenty-nine it was thin and wispy, offering a far less righteous countenance than what was flaunted by other ISIS leaders. He was well educated, and the few scars on his slightly built frame came not from war, but the usual array of childhood mishaps. His name was Aziz Uday, and, notwithstanding his lack of daring and swagger, he was perhaps the most vital cog in what remained of the broken-down machine that was ISIS.

A native of Oman, Uday had earned a degree from a minor university in England, specializing in computers and information networks. Like many young Arabs thrust suddenly into Western culture, he'd felt disconnected and adrift. So instead of going to Silicon Valley after graduation, where he'd had good job offers, he had answered Allah's call. It had been many generations since a true caliphate had existed, and he viewed it as his duty as a Muslim to serve the Prophet's vision.

Uday's rise had been nothing less than meteoric, and he ended in the senior ranks not by the usual methods—either clever politicking or ghastly brutality—but on the basis of technical proficiency and merit. Even so, his final steps to the top were a matter of being the last man standing: his two predecessors had both perished, one falling victim to an American bomb, and the other executed when it became widely known that he was addicted to homosexual pornography. There were rumors the Americans might have planted the damning pictures on the young man's laptop, but once they were revealed the news spread quickly through the ranks, leaving little recourse but a right good stoning.

In the wake of that scandal, and in spite of his fast-diminishing enthusiasm, Uday had been put in charge of twenty-two of the best technicians in the army of the Prophet. Most were computer and media specialists, but there was also an actress, a poet, and an aspiring electrical engineer. They generated the social media accounts and online journals that were so vital to recruitment, and managed ties to hopeful jihadists who popped up around the globe. Uday's team of keyboard commandos was a classic force multiplier, each man and woman worth a dozen suicide bombers. Because of it, he today had a bigger target on his back than anyone but the caliph himself.

After the briefest of pleasantries, Chadeh got things going. "We held a meeting of the Shura Council yesterday," he said, referring to ISIS's unavoidably fluid leadership cadre. "A great deal has happened in the last two weeks."

"Our success in Europe continues," commented Uday as he stared at a poster of a smiling young boy drinking a Pepsi. The image brought back another era, the Oman of his childhood. He remembered a store very much like this one in his neighborhood in Muscat. He expanded that thought and tried to imagine Chadeh as a child, but there his nostalgic associations faltered. The bearded, dark-eyed warlord next to him defied such extrapolations.

"Yes, Europe is a bright point," agreed Chadeh.

"I was surprised by the inclusion of radiological material in the attack in Grenoble. Was that our doing, or did the cell improvise?"

"It was only low-level material," Chadeh said without answering the question. "We now have a solid report on their response procedures. Surprisingly, the police didn't recognize the complication for many hours. A senior DGSI man had to bring it to everyone's attention hours after the strike."

"Based on the media accounts I've seen, the French are in an uproar. We should expect a heavy-handed response."

"It will die down soon enough," said Chadeh, waving his hand, "just like the others."

"Will it? Route 4 was bombed twice last night."

"Yes, yes . . . I know. Large trucks can no longer pass to make deliveries. Raman tells us our revenues have been cut in half in recent weeks." Chadeh was referring to the nom de guerre of the Egyptian who ran the caliphate's financial dealings—the hapless captain of a ship shot full of holes.

"I can tell you my section is in dire need of diesel to run generators. This brew the locals call fuel is no good—it clogs up the feed lines."

"I have heard quiet words suggesting sabotage," said Chadeh, his tone darkening. "We think someone might be adding sugar to clog the lines."

In a rare demonstration of frustration, Uday said, "Then the problem will soon be corrected—there has not been a shipment of sugar in two weeks." He immediately regretted the comment, although Chadeh seemed to ignore it.

Chadeh said, "The locals are hoarding again, hiding their food from us. We must be more forceful."

"More forceful? We beheaded twelve men this week and stoned four women. At the rate we are going—" Chadeh shot a stern look that cut Uday off. No small part of his rise in the organization came from knowing when to shut up.

The senior man sighed. "You should have seen the meeting yesterday. We sounded like a bunch of old women bantering in the market."

"Was the caliph in attendance?" This, Uday knew, was a delicate subject. The leader of the caliphate rarely engaged in face-to-face meetings any longer, having become increasingly reclusive since a near miss with a drone two months ago, which, according to rumor, had robbed him of the use of his left arm.

"No, he wasn't. But he sent his blessings. The consensus is that recruitment has stagnated—our media campaign must be stepped up."

"I admit, our hit count is down after peaking last summer. The video of the American reporter we burned alive in July garnered over three million views on YouTube. And there was a tremendous bump on Twitter for the photograph of the Yazidi girl being auctioned off as a slave."

"Yes, that one came cheap. She was very attractive, and we saw a spike in young men volunteering in the following weeks. We must leverage such emotions wherever possible. But we need more, something new and inventive."

A fully covered woman appeared with a large plate of dates and figs, and humbly set it in front of the two men. Chadeh scooped up a handful of figs.

"Does the council have any ideas?" Uday asked, trying not to sound tentative. Whatever depraved screenplays were hatched, he would be obliged to be director, producer, and writer.

"How many ways are there to kill a man? We've shot them a hundred at a time, burned them, beheaded them, crucified them." He popped a fig into his mouth, and it made a squishing noise as he bit down, a dribble of juice rolling onto his black-whiskered chin. "There was a suggestion of an acid bath for one of the foreigners—perhaps the Russian pilot we captured. Would there be any technical challenges to such a presentation?"

"Let me think . . ." said Uday, staring at the food.

"Perhaps we could do it slowly. Do you think

viewers would give up on a clip if we dripped the acid, say over ten or twenty minutes? Or would the shock value of simply dumping a barrel over the victim be more sensational?"

Uday realized he had to say something. "Let me research that—the time factor. I will discuss it with our physician. If the prisoner only passes out from pain, the effect of a longer production might be lost."

"Yes, I see your point. That fool Kazbek suggested we search out a wood chipper, but I told him it was out of the question. We cannot be seen as cruel. Besides, where would we find such a thing in the desert? These Chechens, I tell you . . . they have no sense of where virtue ends and barbarism begins."

"None at all."

"But enough of that. Tell me the latest from your section."

Happy to move on, Uday said, "The social media traffic relating to Grenoble is falling off quickly. As far as we can tell, the police have developed no good leads. I have wanted to ask—do *we* know who was responsible?" Uday was rarely briefed on operational specifics, but since his department managed all communications for the caliphate, including external contacts, he could often infer what was going on. Grenoble had taken him by surprise.

"I can tell you we knew of the mission in advance," Chadeh said, but left it at that.

Uday removed a one-page printout from his pocket. "There was a message from Malika this morning."

Chadeh's head snapped up. Uday handed the message across and watched the oil-black eyes rake over it.

Malika was their most important operative in Europe. She ran an agent so secret—code name Argu—that the thread of communication was the only one Uday was not authorized to view. There again, as sole administrator of the ever-changing network, he invariably caught glimpses of the messages. He also knew that any man cunning enough to become the number two of ISIS would suspect he was taking a look.

Chadeh lowered the printout, and said, "Tell me, do we have any cells in France right now that might be considered expendable?"

"Expendable? In what way?"

"A small sacrifice to the authorities."

"Argu again?" Uday asked.

"Yes."

Chadeh had months ago explained that much to Uday. They would occasionally send Malika information regarding small groups or individuals in France, people who were of little practical use to the caliphate. She passed them on to Argu, and soon after, the French authorities would have a minor victory. Uday recognized the ploy for what it was: Argu resided in law enforcement at some level, and Chadeh was trying to fuel his advancement.

"There is a volunteer cell in Saint-Denis," Uday said, as if just now considering it. "The Moroccan brothers—I might have mentioned them last week."

"Yes, I remember your caution. Drug users and criminals, you said, a useless bunch. Do you know where they are?"

"I can find out."

"Very well. Send Malika the address. But stress to her that we are due important information from Argu."

"Very well."

Chadeh's tone turned reflective. "I have to tell you, Aziz, there is a shift in thinking among the council. We have lost a great deal of territory in the last year, and even here in Ragga we have been forced into hiding. Airplanes bomb us until we are frozen in place, and drones see our every move. But the West refuses to fight us directly on the ground. The French in particular are cowards. Our destiny, thanks be to the Prophet, is to engage the crusaders in our land. The council has decided there is but one way to bring them here: We must accelerate our attacks. And there is only one place where we have the assets to do that."

"France?"

"Exactly. But the success of this new strategy will rely heavily on your work."

"My work?"

"Tell me the status of the database project."

Uday blinked, as if changing gears. It was an initiative he'd been ordered to begin last month. "Progress is slow. It hasn't been a high priority, and many of the men and women sent to help me don't last more than a few days. No sooner do I get them trained than they are pulled away to rig booby traps or attend beheadings. We are perhaps fifty percent complete."

"*Fifty percent?* You must move more quickly! I will send over more workers. Would it help to have an increase in funding?"

Uday was stunned. "New hardware is always

useful . . . but I recently put together new spreadsheets for Raman. There *is* no more money."

Chadeh waved his hand as if swatting away a fly. "Perhaps we won't make payroll for our fighters in the eastern provinces next month—it won't be the first time. True believers are happy to fight on the credit of the afterlife."

Uday only nodded, considering the implications of it all. The database project, the information demanded from Argu. Their situation was more desperate than he had realized.

Chadeh rose to leave, and as an apparent afterthought, he asked, "Are you enjoying the girl?"

Uday forced a smile. "Yes, she is . . . very adequate."

"Tell me her name again?"

"Sarah."

"A Christian?"

Uday nodded.

"If you tire of her, I can get a replacement. But as I've told you before, you should consider taking a proper Muslim wife. You are at an age when a man should start a family."

"Yes, I would like to . . . but things are so unsettled right now. The girl will suffice."

Chadeh chuckled. "I'm sure she will. You are fortunate. When I saw her I nearly kept her for myself. Perhaps if you tire of her I will reconsider."

With that Chadeh turned toward the door and was gone. Uday imagined him collecting his bodyguards and vaporizing into the night. He remained on the rug for some time, and it occurred to him that he was always the last to leave such meetings. Each time he seemed to linger a bit longer than the last. Tonight Chadeh's final words had chilled him to the core. *Perhaps if you tire of her I will reconsider.*

Yet that wasn't what kept Uday bolted to the floor.

For the first time ever, he had misinformed a member of the Shura Council. It wasn't something he'd planned—for some reason he had simply blurted out the wrong number. The database project Chadeh had asked about was, in fact, nearly ninety percent complete. A week, two at the most, and everything would be in place. Uday had been staying up most nights to make entries himself, and he regularly diverted staff from projects more critical to the battlefield.

So why did I imply otherwise?

He committed to redoubling his efforts on the database, but at the same time realized that Chadeh's other mandates could not be postponed. Tomorrow he would research the effects of acid on the human body. He would send a dual-themed message to the caliphate's most important agent in France: one granting a sacrificial offering, the other reiterating a demand. Such was a day in the life of the head of the Islamic State Institution for Public Information.

The woman appeared and took away the food tray. She didn't make eye contact with Uday, and never uttered a word. Something about it seemed stifling and unnatural. He stood, walked outside, and was grateful for the purifying wash of sweet desert air.

TWELVE

Somewhere over India, flying through a turbulent and pitch-black night, Slaton heard Christine's voice in his semiconscious head.

"*What now, David?*"

"*It's your decision. The first option is to go to France and get to the bottom of this. I can try to find out why a terrorist I killed fifteen years ago is a senior intelligence officer in DGSI.*"

"*And if it's true?*"

"*Then he's a threat to us.*"

A pause. She knew him well enough not to ask what that meant. "*Would you do it alone?*"

"*I'd ask Israel for help. But the chances are good that they won't go near it.*"

"*Even if they were the ones who ordered you to kill this man in the first place?*"

"*It's complicated.*"

"*No, David, it's insane.*"

"*Agreed. But we can't pretend this isn't happening.*"

"*And the other option? You and I take Davy on the*

high seas, sail as far away as we can? We already did that. We could hardly be more remote than we are today. Whoever is behind this . . . they've found us once. They attacked you."

He remained silent.

"You're going to make me choose, aren't you?"

"I'm sorry. You know it's the only way. . . ."

Slaton's eyes blinked open. He saw a flight attendant passing on his right, a stout drink in her hand and a business-class smile on her face. The air route from a remote island in the Philippines to Israel is both lengthy and indirect. Knowing it would take the best part of a day, he'd upgraded to a sleeper seat and intended to use it. He'd almost succeeded over Myanmar, but was interrupted by a burst of turbulence—mountain wave from the Himalayas.

On the tiny television in front of him he saw a map of southern Asia. A graceful arcing line connected Manila to Tel Aviv, and the airplane symbol was reaching the midpoint. In Manila he'd bought a prepaid phone, and sent a text message to a very private number in Israel. It was worth a try, but he doubted Mossad would help. The current director was a calculating man with a strong aversion to risk. His predecessor, however, who had recruited Slaton and run him for years, was more approachable.

Anton Bloch always did what was best for Israel. He was also responsible for Slaton and Christine being in the situation they were in today. For that reason, he thought Bloch might at least listen.

* * *

Slaton arrived in Tel Aviv at 11:03 the next morning. Customs was uneventful, and his legacy Mossad-issued passport, three years old but not yet expired, held up as expected. He kept two other identities that Mossad knew nothing about, but for the moment overtness was to his advantage. The Mossad item would serve as his calling card.

As if to prove the point, he was not yet out of the terminal building when a familiar profile caught his attention. Just beyond the first baggage turnstile Slaton spotted the distinctively brusque profile of Anton Bloch.

As Bloch began walking away, without a trace of recognition, Slaton thought he discerned a slight hitch in the former Mossad director's gait. He wondered if it was a result of what had happened two years ago. Bloch had taken a bullet to save Christine, and nearly died because of it—which was probably why he was the only person tied to Mossad that Slaton still trusted. Bloch was officially retired, yet invariably kept a hand in things. Watching him walk away, with his heavy stride and brooding form, Slaton remembered Christine's two-word account of the man: *endearingly sullen.*

At a distance, Slaton followed his former boss through a little-used side entrance, and watched him disappear into a sedan parked along the curb. Thirty seconds later he was sitting beside him. Without a word, the driver accelerated into traffic.

As a greeting, Bloch said, "You get more fit every time I see you." His voice was unchanged, a baritone grinder that crushed letters into words.

"I've been working hard. Lots of sun and fresh air. You seem to be holding up." It was true. Limp aside, Bloch looked far more robust than the last time Slaton had seen him. His sturdy build had thinned, and judging by the tan on his nearly bald head, Slaton guessed that he too had been spending time outdoors.

"Miriam has acquired a passion for creating healthy food, and my wayward daughter has finally recognized the relevance of a good education."

"What's she studying?"

"Political science, God help us."

"Maybe she'll follow in her father's footsteps."

Bloch dispensed his signature glare. "You always were one of the few who would goad me."

"I think I've earned it. I'm guessing my passport flagged as designed?"

"Allow an old spymaster a few indulgences, David. But don't worry—when I received your message I was very discreet. Aside from Director Nurin, only one technician, who you will soon meet, is aware of your arrival. The rest of Mossad still thinks what they have long thought—that David Slaton, the legend, paid the ultimate price for his country. There is even a cryptic star in the lobby of the main office that many believe is a memorial to you."

"How uplifting."

"Be thankful—someday it will be true."

Slaton didn't reply.

"Will you tell me what this is about?" Bloch asked.

"I told you in the message—Ali Samir."

"But you said nothing other than the name. You

dealt with Samir a very long time ago—what relevance could he have today?"

"Have you recalled the files on the mission?"

"As you asked, yes."

"Then I'll explain when we can look at them together."

Bloch frowned but did not argue.

"I take it we're not going to Glilot Junction?" Slaton asked, referring to Mossad's new headquarters facility.

Bloch gave a mirthless chuckle. "Certainly not. A nondescript house in a quiet neighborhood is the most hospitality you can expect these days."

"How is the director?"

"Nurin is as ever. He tells me what he wants to tell me, and most of it is the truth—at least, as far as he knows it."

"Is your technician at the safe house?"

"Yes. A very attractive young woman who knows a great deal about computers and nothing about legendary assassins—not unless I ask her to research it. I've told her you are an unimportant nuisance. I also mentioned that you are happily married and will be immune to her charms."

"Was that necessary?"

"You know how my mind works, David—remove every possible complication."

Slaton loosely tracked their progress, and saw that they were heading west toward the coast. The Ayalon Highway gave way to a secondary road somewhere south of Jaffa. The city seemed unchanged, notwithstanding construction barriers that fronted rising sandstone apartment buildings and expanding businesses, all of which spoke of a strong economy. The landscape was endurance itself, arid and dusty, carob and acacia trees battling for moisture among patches of brown dirt. He had not been to Israel in some time—was it two years already?—yet after thirty minutes he felt the connection, the intimate familiarity. Yet while Slaton had spent many years here, his associations were always fleeting, even as a child. A year on the kibbutz, then school in Stockholm. Training sessions in the Negev, followed by a mission in Hamburg. His regular repatriations approached something migratory, a bird finding its way to an agreeable season. All the same, Israel was and would always be his homeland. The place where his journeys began.

The car nosed toward a tall and elegant building, then circled to one side. At a gated parking-garage entrance, the driver entered a code. The door lifted and the car pulled inside, ending at one of four matching elevators. Slaton and Bloch got out, and without a word spoken the car accelerated away. Judging by the other vehicles in the garage—all European, with Italy and Germany well represented—Mossad was not facing budgetary shortfalls.

Proving the point further, the elevator rose to the ninth floor out of a possible ten—penthouses, apparently, were either out of reach or deemed indiscreet—to deposit them at the private entrance of a sprawling condominium. There was an expansive main room, backed by a kitchen that was a sea of black-steel appliances. To either side Slaton saw deep bedrooms through open doors. The furniture and decorative accents were all first class.

"Safe houses were a little more rustic in my day."

"Don't worry, we haven't lost our heads. The place isn't ours—only a loaner from a *sayan* who is unavoidably out of the country for a time."

Sayanim were one of Mossad's long-held advantages—civilians who gave assistance to the Jewish cause, material and expertise, with no questions asked. "How long do you have it?" Slaton asked, staring out a twenty-foot-wide window that offered a stunning view of the sun-bleached Mediterranean.

"Our benefactor is ten months into a twenty-month sentence, a very comfortable lockup in Florida."

Slaton stared at his old boss.

Bloch waved his hand dismissively. "A minor indiscretion involving taxes. I hear he is using the interlude to write a novel."

Slaton heard someone push back a chair in the room to his right.

Bloch leaned toward him and said in a hushed voice, "Talia doesn't know your background . . . you can choose whether to keep it that way."

She materialized from the side room, and did not disappoint. Talia was in her late twenties, tall and rail-thin. Her hair was long and black, framing stunning features and a pair of almond-shaped hazel eyes.

"Talia, I would like you to meet David." The two shook hands, Slaton smiling inwardly as Bloch expanded to Talia, "It's not his real name of course, but he usually answers to it."

"You operational types are always so obtuse," she said, adding a smile that seemed to brighten the room.

"I extracted Talia out of Research Administration for a few days. What she doesn't know about computers is not worth knowing."

She looked appreciatively out the window. "The view is far better than the bunker where they usually have me chained. I might get used to this."

"You shouldn't," Bloch admonished. He turned to Slaton and said, "Talia is a prodigy. She is better at what she does, David, than you are at what you do."

"And what is that?" she asked.

Bloch answered, "David has a very sharp eye and a steady hand. He is a first-class stonemason."

"A stonemason," she repeated.

"I'm not that good, but I do have a passion for it. I recently spent time restoring some sixteenth-century work in Malta—now *there* were some artisans."

"Is that why Anton has brought you here? To build walls?"

Slaton grinned.

"Never mind," she said. "The two of you can have your little secrets."

Bloch, stoic as ever, said, "All will become clear in time. I think we should get to work."

For all the transgression of the Americans, Malika acknowledged their one great contribution to civilization: pizza that was delivered to one's door. It was cheap, involved little effort, and on this night permitted her to avoid the ocean of cameras watching over Paris.

She lifted the cardboard lid and pulled out the last piece, then shoved the empty box across the dining room table in her flat's kitchenette. The meat-covered slice dripped grease onto the table, and as she attacked the pointed end, a message flashed to her secure phone. She tapped the screen and called it up, at the price of an oily stain on the phone's screen. It was a message from Raqqa. She'd been hoping for another, one from the other side of the world. That communication, or soon the absence of it, would have considerable effects on her near-term planning.

She studied the text. It began with an address in Saint-Denis, and ended with threatening language, both to be relayed to Argu. Chadeh was getting impatient for the information he'd been demanding for weeks.

She considered whether to rephrase the message before forwarding it to Baland. As it was, the wording was terse, unyielding, and held a slight suggestion of violence. Seeing nothing she could improve, Malika sent it off into space. She relished making Baland sweat.

She was getting quite good at it.

THIRTEEN

They began in the kitchen, and only when everyone had been issued a coffee cup did Talia lead them to what she referred to as "the command room." A state-of-the-art communications suite had been installed, computers and wires strung in an untidy bird's nest across the *sayan*'s rich hardwood cherry and tanned leather. Talia settled behind the main workstation, and Bloch and Slaton took chairs on either side.

"Please call up the files on Samir," said Slaton.

Talia did, and seconds later a classified Mossad mission report blossomed to the screen.

"It's been a long time," said Slaton, "but as I remember we had no high-res photographs of Samir."

"Things were different fifteen years ago," Bloch remarked. "There were fewer cameras, and our more elusive targets were good at avoiding them. Samir never went through an airport, never got a driver's license or identity card—at least not in his true name."

Slaton said, "I relied on my spotter for the ID."

"Ezekiel," said Bloch.

"Yes. He saw Samir up close during the pre-mission reconnaissance. I'd like to call him in on this."

"I only wish we could. He was killed during a mission in the West Bank three years ago."

As ever, Slaton felt the tiny knife in his gut. It was a sensation he'd not felt in some time, but a regular occurrence through his years with Mossad. "I'm sorry to hear it. Show me what you have then."

"This is the only photo on file," said Talia, tapping out a series of keystrokes.

A foggy image filled the screen. The mission to eliminate Ali Samir had been one of Slaton's first after being designated a *kidon*—a Mossad-trained assassin. He was quietly inserted into Gaza to eliminate the fast-rising Hamas lieutenant, a man held responsible for a string of bombings along the coast. The picture had been taken near a souk as Samir sat on the patio of a teahouse. It was the only image known to exist at the time, and one that Mossad had gone to great lengths to obtain and verify. Six weeks after the photo was taken, from a range of four hundred meters, Slaton had shot him dead at precisely the same table.

Without being asked, Talia zoomed in on Samir, but the face only became more blurred.

"Can it be enhanced?" Slaton asked.

"With time, perhaps marginally. The resolution of the original is very poor. It looks like it came from a security camera or something."

"So it wouldn't be any use for a match?"

"You're referring to facial-recognition software?"

"Yes."

"No, definitely not. The detail is insufficient, and the angle of the shot is awkward."

"All right, David," said Bloch. "I've been exceedingly patient. I'd like to know what this is all about."

Slaton produced the memory stick from his pocket and set it on the desk. Talia inserted it into a port on the computer without remark.

As she managed the new content, following security protocols, Slaton said, "Someone tracked me down in the Philippines." He gave a brief recap of the contrived meeting with Christine at the playground, the ambush on *Esperanza,* and finally recovering the memory stick.

The screen blinked and the three photographs appeared side by side. "They're all apparently taken from news articles," Slaton said. He let Bloch and Talia study them for a time before asking, "You see the problem?"

Talia deferred to Bloch, who finally said, "Surely you are not suggesting that Samir somehow survived."

"I am."

Bloch blew out a snort of exasperation, then referenced the captions of the articles. "And today he is a senior ranking officer at DGSI? Really, David, I have given you a long leash over the years, but this? I think the equatorial sun may have gotten the better of you."

"It's him, Anton."

Sensing the tension, Talia said, "I can verify the authenticity of the news articles."

"Go ahead, but I think you'll find them valid."

Bloch said, "We have only the one picture of Samir

when he was alive. How can you extrapolate that to these other photographs?"

"I'm not," Slaton said. "There's another picture." He looked at Talia, and saw no point in keeping up pretenses about his background. "The sight picture from that day, Ali Samir in my crosshairs—I can see it like it was yesterday."

"But that would mean—"

"Yes," Slaton finished. "I missed."

Bloch rubbed his hand over his chin. "I've gone over the reports from that mission, including the one you filed. Immediately after the shot there was a moment of chaos at the teahouse. At least three witnesses saw Samir go down. In your after-action report you claimed that you didn't get a good look at the results because you were busy breaking down your weapon for egress. Ezekiel had the better view. He was certain you'd scored a hit."

"I saw that much—I remember taking one look through my scope. The bullet struck Samir in the upper chest, left center. I decided against a follow-up because it was a public place and there were too many people moving. I hit him. . . . I *know* that much. But chest shots aren't always fatal."

Bloch shook his head, as if trying to dislodge the idea.

"There is another reason to think he's still alive," said Slaton.

Here the former Mossad director was ahead. "What brought you here today. These men who tried to kill you two days ago were given this memory stick. It means someone else is aware of your link to Samir."

"Obviously."

"Do you understand the leap of faith you are asking me to make, David? If he did survive, how could a terrorist like Samir emigrate to France and join the national police force? Surely they vet their applicants, do background checks."

"Of course," said Slaton. "But a country the size of France—they must hire over a thousand officers each year to the various divisions. Identities can be created or assumed. I've been racking my brain, and I remembered a few things from Samir's mission file. His mother was Algerian—she spoke fluent French, and had spent time in Lyon when she was growing up. We also discovered that Samir had spent a year in Paris with relatives when he was a teen."

"The records are vague on that point," said Bloch, who'd clearly gone over the file himself in the last day. "We never discovered exactly where he went or who he stayed with."

"Even so, the ties were there. Think about it, Anton. If Samir *did* survive our attempt against him— would it not have presented an ideal opportunity for him to be reborn elsewhere?"

Bloch shook his head. "Place a terrorist operative inside a European police force, then wait patiently for him to rise through the ranks? Hamas has never been an organization prone to playing the long game. We've seen them try to recruit individuals who are already established in security organizations . . . but to plant an operative who will take years to become useful? That requires considerable foresight and patience. I dare say, it could come from our own playbook."

"So maybe they're learning. Or maybe this has nothing to do with Hamas at all."

Bloch was silently thoughtful, and Slaton sensed awkward undercurrents. He looked at Talia, and said, "Can you give Anton and me a moment alone?"

"Certainly. My coffee needs refreshing." She got up and left the room.

As soon as Talia was gone, the two men took seats in a pair of heavy chairs that were angled to promote conversation, soft leather creaking beneath them. A well-stocked bookcase dominated the wall behind them, weighty and dense leather-bound volumes, as though knowledge itself would preside over their discussion.

"Will you take this to Nurin?" Slaton asked.

"If you like. But don't expect much. I see no solid evidence of what you suggest, and certainly no compelling reason for Israel to become involved."

"That's what you'll tell him. But what do you believe?"

Bloch steepled his hands under his chin. "Someone is confiding that a rising star in French intelligence bears a resemblance to a Hamas bomb maker long thought dead."

"Which rules out Hamas itself as the source."

"Almost certainly."

"Do you think someone is trying to draw me out? An enemy of Baland who wants me to finish what I started?"

"I can't see it that way. From what you told me,

those men on the derelict ship might have gotten lucky. You were the target then, and I think that will continue to be the case. All this business about Ali Samir, his ghost dangling like a lure—it only exists to move you onto the killer's ground."

"Paris."

"Undoubtedly."

Slaton considered it with his customary detachment. "It could be Samir himself."

"I'm not so sure. If such a senior man at DGSI wanted you dead—he wouldn't have sent the crew you described to the Philippines. The French have units who are far more capable."

Slaton pushed back into the soft leather. It was a good point. He was glad to have Bloch's insight, which was certainly more impartial than his own. "If I go to Paris, set up surveillance—it wouldn't be easy. As Zavier Baland, he's got the entire police force of France on his side. It might be difficult to get near him."

"I'm still not convinced this man *is* Samir," said Bloch, "but for the sake of argument, I'll concede the point. You should consider the alternate scenario. If Baland isn't aware you are coming, and doesn't realize his identity had been blown . . . his guard might be down."

Slaton considered it in silence.

Bloch said, "Of course, David, you realize there is a far easier way to deal with all of this."

"We could send the information through diplomatic channels to France. Let them sort out Baland's background."

"Precisely. You can go back to your boat and your family, and sail away into the sunset."

Slaton gave Bloch a severe look. It was just like the old days. The subtle manipulation. By suggesting the entire matter could be walked away from, he was saying just the opposite. This was the director at his persuasive best, nourishing doubts like so many weeds in a garden, waiting for them to take root. Which told Slaton that at least some of his suspicions about Baland had struck home.

He argued, "But France would ask the same questions you have. They would want hard evidence, of which there is none. The only real proof is an old sight picture in my head. The problem for me is that someone knows I'm out there. They want me to come to France and settle an old score. If I ignore it and try to run, it doesn't mean they'll stop. They found me once, so there's a good chance they can find me again. And next time my family could be put at risk under circumstances I don't control."

"All true," Bloch said, cocking his head in a blatantly noncommittal gesture. "Then again, you always were a perfectionist, David. I think the idea that you might have missed that shot bothers you."

Slaton felt suddenly restless. He got up and paced to the far side of the room. He said, "You realize I have no choice in this."

Bloch nodded. "Knowing you as I do, I would be shocked if you didn't go to Paris to get to the bottom of this."

"So then the question is simple. Will you back me?"

"You know I no longer speak for Mossad. I can take it to the director, but I suspect we both know what his answer will be. There are no visible gains for Israel—only risks. Give me until tomorrow. I've set up a room for you here, and I'll ask Talia to stay the night. She can access everything we've got on file."

Bloch went to the door, pulled his coat from a polished brass hook, and shrugged it onto his wide frame. "When I present this to Nurin, I will emphasize that you are acutely aware of the delicacy of the situation. Having one of our former assassins running around France, seeking out a high-ranking official—it necessitates a high degree of separation. If anything goes wrong, you will be completely on your own."

"I'm used to it."

Bloch cocked his head. "Yes, I suppose you are. I'll have an answer in the morning."

FOURTEEN

Five thousand miles east, in Slaton's distant and deadly wake, an emerging investigation was hitting its stride. The bodies on *Esperanza* had been discovered the previous afternoon by a survey crew who'd visited the old ship to perform an inspection—two months earlier a group of fishermen had reported the hull was leaking fuel and spoiling the nearby reef. The government, in its plodding way, was finally getting around to looking into the matter.

In the fading afternoon light, the crew had circled the ship and seen no sign of fuel oil. The lead man, a conscientious sort, decided to go aboard for a closer look. He'd no sooner reached the main deck than he sensed far greater ills. He smelled the problem before he saw it, and after stumbling across the first body on a catwalk, quite literally, the man had quickly retreated.

The Philippine Coast Guard was alerted by radio, and by midnight four bodies were being removed by officers of the National Bureau of Investigation—the Filipino equivalent of the FBI. Landside investigative forces did their best with little hard evidence, but did get one break right away: From a room key discovered in one man's pocket, they were able to identify the hotel in which the victims had been staying three days earlier. It was quickly determined that the group had booked four nights but, for reasons unknown, stayed only one before ending up dead on a half-sunk wreck in the South China Sea. More headway was made when passports were discovered in the room and all four men were identified as French citizens.

This brought DGSI into play, and the same question was raised on both sides of a nine-hour time-zone divide: Why had four young men from Marseille, who did not appear to be of strictly Gallic heritage, ended up bullet-riddled on a shipwreck in the disputed Spratly Islands?

On the Paris end, the matter was noted by a certain senior officer in the command section. Whatever Conseiller Zavier Baland might have added to the investigation, he kept to himself.

Slaton spent much of that evening looking over Talia's shoulder. He asked her for information on Zavier Baland, and she opened a virtual floodgate. At least, that was the case since the day he'd signed on with the *police nationale*. The last fourteen years of his professional life were an open book, indeed a fairy-tale upward trajectory that was now nearing the apex of France's counterterrorism establishment. Prior to that, however, Baland's life was considerably more opaque, and this was the period on which Slaton asked Talia to concentrate.

"Here is a birth certificate from the official records in Lyon," she said, the document appearing on her screen.

Without asking how she'd acquired it, he said, "Do you think it's legitimate?"

"No way to tell. Birth certificates get lost and have to be replaced. They're notoriously easy to create and alter, and standards vary wildly from country to country—even within countries."

"And driver's licenses and passports are sourced from them."

"Correct."

He took what he could from the document. "Forty-two years old. That would be about right for Samir. The mission briefing I saw fifteen years ago listed him as being twenty-six. We never had an exact birth date because we could never find any official records in his name."

"That's often the case in Gaza, even today." Talia next unearthed a record of Baland's French driver's license. "According to this, his license was first issued when he was nineteen, in Paris. As you know, we suspect Samir may have spent time there as a teen. He could have been trying to establish himself in France even then—if so, a driver's license would be an important step."

"What about school records?"

"Nothing yet. I've been trying to obtain his original application to the national police, which would include the names of the schools he attended. So far I don't have anything."

"You mean there's no record of his application?"

"No . . . I mean I haven't been able to hack into the database. We *are* talking about the French national police, David. There's a good chance I won't be able to break that one—at least not in time for it to be of any use."

"Okay—but we're running out of places to look. What about marriage records?"

"I found that right away. Baland got married seven months after he was hired onto the force."

"What can you tell me about his wife?" Those words had barely escaped Slaton's lips when a wave of guilt washed in. Was this not the very thing he himself was trying to avoid? The question he hoped others would not ask about him? What of Baland's daughters? Should they be vetted as well?

Talia said, "She's French all the way—born and raised in Nice, nothing suspicious in her background."

Slaton was glad Talia had already gone down that path without his asking. Happier yet that it seemed a dead end. He thought again of the briefing he'd had on Ali Samir—Mossad had never learned if the young terrorist in Gaza was married, but the absence of such information was hardly unusual. "Okay, it's almost midnight. Let's give it a rest."

Slaton went to the kitchen and began rummaging through a well-stocked refrigerator. He found two beers, and Talia joined him. They tapped bottles, but neither bothered to toast anything.

They walked out to a balcony with a spectacular view. Front and center was the Mediterranean, a great void that seemed exceptionally settled tonight. On either side the yellow jewels of greater Tel Aviv glittered up and down the coastline. The night air was cool and damp.

"Thanks for your help today," he said.

"It's my job."

"You're good at it."

"How would you know? You're not an information specialist."

"Trust me—I know." He took a long draw, and said, "I want to ask your professional opinion on something . . . but don't feel obligated if you see a conflict of interest."

She looked at him speculatively. "That's a strange way to begin—but go ahead."

"I live with my family on a sailboat. We're about as off-grid as you can get, but apparently someone found us anyway. I'd like to know how."

"Do you have any electronic connection to the outside world?"

"Only one, a satellite internet account. We rarely use it, but occasionally there's no choice when we need information on weather or ports of entry. I set up the account as carefully as I could, and keep up payments using an alias. I thought it was pretty secure."

He gave her a few details about the service, and she responded with a minor excursion on ISPs and cyber-tracking.

"So that was it then," he said.

"Most likely. I can tell you that Mossad has close ties to software technicians in at least one big telecom. Chances are, we're not the first to think of it."

"I'll cancel my service immediately."

"Technology is always a double-edged sword." She recommended a satellite provider he'd never heard of, and gave him tips on how to configure the electronics on *Windsom* for better security.

"Thanks. I'll take your advice."

"My best advice is to remember that there's no sure thing when it comes to communications security . . . not anymore."

"I don't think there ever was."

She hesitated, then said, "You are going to France, aren't you."

"Yes."

"Then I'd like to ask you something, and don't feel obligated to answer if you feel a conflict of interest."

He looked at her and grinned. "Go ahead."

"If it comes down to it . . . would you kill this man to keep your family safe?"

He looked out over the shimmering city and the black sea beyond. "That's not how I look at it. For years now I've tried to *stop* killing to keep them safe. I wish it had stayed that way."

"But since it hasn't?"

"Then I'll do whatever is necessary."

Slaton felt her eyes on him and their gaze intersected along the balcony rail. Talia was stunning in the half-light, her dark hair glimmering and her gaze deeper than the sea beyond. She turned toward the main room, but then paused in his periphery, a vague form in the dim light. Slaton heard a soft brush of fabric as she half turned, and smelled the scent of her perfume. Floral and spice. She said in a hushed tone near his ear, "I hope that someday I can find someone like you. Someone who loves me as much as you do them."

Slaton remained still, his eyes steady on the sea under a calm and moonless sky. He sensed her walking away, heard the sliding door open behind him. A rush of warm inside air spilled out over the balcony. He said, "Talia?"

"Yes?"

"Before I leave tomorrow—I want to know where Baland lives."

FIFTEEN

The raid in Paris came at seven the next morning on an untidy flat along Rue Fontaine. The police used a battering ram on the wooden door, although the frame was so rotted a good kick with a tennis shoe would have done the trick. Twenty armed men in full battle gear stormed through the breach, and they had no trouble overwhelming three sleepy Moroccans and a naked woman of indeterminate origin. Not a single shot was fired.

When the all-clear was given by the tactical team, a contingent of investigators and evidence technicians followed across the shattered threshold. In the lead was DGSI Conseiller Zavier Baland.

It didn't take long to realize that the tip was a valid one, although hardly the coup they'd hoped for. Two Kalashnikovs were found beneath a bed frame, and a shoe box in the closet held six boxes of ammo, two empty magazines for the AKs, and a rusty grenade. The grenade caused a brief stir, and a temporary evacuation, but order was quickly restored when the leader of the bomb squad, brought along for just such contingencies, determined that the grenade was in fact a remarkably accurate novelty item meant for lighting cigarettes—pull the pin, release the lever, and an inviting flame flickered. One computer was confiscated for later analysis, but it had been powered up when they arrived, and on first look contained nothing more threatening than a first-person-shooter video game.

Interviews with neighbors revealed that the group had been renting the place for roughly a year, and that one other young man was an occasional resident. He was quickly identified, and arrested within the hour as he pulled warm baguettes from the oven of a nearby *boulangerie*. The only other find of note was two kilos of midgrade hashish stashed in a dresser drawer. While not the point of the whole affair, the drugs were a welcome find, as they made detention of the suspects that much easier.

By ten o'clock that morning the place had been well turned over, and Baland stood on the sidewalk in front of the building to declare a minor victory over terrorism to a brigade of reporters. He mentioned explosives and weapons at least three times, and let slip that the suspects were likely of Moroccan heritage. He did not bring up the matter of drug trafficking, and deferred when asked if the terrorists had put up a fight. Baland stretched a largely factless briefing into a powerful five-minute sound bite that would lead newscasts across France for the balance of the day.

* * *

When Bloch arrived back at the safe house, in mid-morning, Slaton was in the bedroom packing. He hadn't brought a bag on his journey from the Philippines, wanting as few leads as possible back to Christine. Not surprisingly, Bloch was one step ahead—Slaton had opened the closet door last night to find a selection of bland and unfashionable clothes, all in his size and with commercial labels, along with a tan suitcase. It caused him to remember the former director's words—*remove every possible complication.*

"Nurin wants no part of this folly," Bloch announced.

"No surprise there," Slaton said as he folded the last shirt.

"He won't obstruct if you choose to look into it, but Mossad cannot condone action against French citizens."

"In other words, I'm welcome to hunt down Baland—but if I screw up I'm on my own."

"The clothes in front of you are the end of his support. I'll do my best to intervene if problems arise, but understand that my hands may be tied. Use caution."

"That's your briefing? Be careful?"

Bloch shrugged. "It's not like the good old days."

"Honestly, Anton, I don't remember the good old days being so great." Slaton shut the bag emphatically, tugging the zippers more forcefully than necessary. He looked his old boss in the eye. "There were a lot of times when I felt like I was operating on my own."

Bloch appeared unmoved, but said, "*Strictly* off the record—is there anything else you might need?"

"I've already arranged my travel. Alitalia to Rome, then a connection to Turin. I'll figure out the rest later. My flight leaves in three hours."

"Documents?" Bloch asked.

"I'm good. I'll use the passport I arrived on to get to Italy. After that I'll use another I've kept in reserve."

"Let me guess . . . Swedish?"

Slaton didn't react to Bloch's prescience.

"It always was your most convincing language." He tossed a manila envelope on the bed. "It's the least I could do."

Slaton picked it up, and inside saw a stack of euros and a phone. He checked the phone and found it preloaded with a few contact numbers.

"Does Nurin know you're undermining him?"

"Of course not. Talia requisitioned the phone. The money is my vacation set-aside. Miriam has already informed me that our holiday this spring will be an epicurean tour of Italy experienced from our kitchen."

Slaton nodded. "Thanks."

"Let me emphasize, David—none of this is traceable. Once you walk out that door you are alone."

"Fair enough. But if things progress, there's a chance I might need one last bit of assistance."

"Dare I ask what?"

Slaton told him.

"Surely you jest."

Slaton's steady gaze told Bloch otherwise.

The old spymaster sighed. "I make no promises . . . but what would you need?"

"With any luck, nothing at all. But in a worst-case scenario . . . I was thinking an Arctic Warfare Covert, in the case, with a variable Schmidt and Bender and a full box of ammo. Also a Glock 17, two mags."

Bloch closed his eyes, trying to either remember or forget Slaton's request.

Slaton picked up the suitcase. "That's it then."

"I am in a position to grant you one further advantage. Nurin would never approve of it, but Talia is available—she is still officially on loan, and won't be missed at her regular workplace for the next few days."

"Thanks."

"Don't thank me—it was her idea."

Slaton thought it might be true. He also thought it was an ideal way for Bloch to keep a distant eye on his progress. Without mentioning his suspicions, he walked out and found Talia in the main room.

"Thank you," he said.

She looked at both men in turn, before saying to Slaton, "45 Avenue Pasteur, Courbevoie."

Slaton nodded once, then turned toward the door and was gone.

SIXTEEN

Uday sat facing a computer in the rear annex of an ancient mosque, his fingers weary as he played the keyboard. All around him were cleaning supplies and oil lamps, and against the far wall prayer rugs were piled neatly in a stack. The sweet smell of burning candles saturated the air.

When the results of his latest commands lit the screen, he heaved a frustrated sigh and leaned back in his chair. The server that had been giving them trouble for weeks was still only running at twenty percent capacity. It was hardly surprising—Uday had the unenviable job of keeping the most attacked computer network on earth from crashing.

The first problem was the physical destruction. Bombs were taking out comm nodes with increasing frequency, to the point that he was sure someone in the West had figured out a way to locate and target them. Servers were also being electronically fried, which was probably the work of the Americans—he'd heard that their F-22 fighters had an amazing radar system, and suspected that if the jets flew close enough they might be able to focus enough RF energy on the local systems to do physical damage.

Then there was the electrical grid. It was getting more suspect by the day. The diesel problem he'd discussed yesterday with Chadeh was a primary worry, but at least something they could manage. Last night someone had dropped an airburst bomb of some sort, and what looked like silver Christmas tinsel rained down on a makeshift substation, sending all of Hamat into darkness. The Crusaders at their devious best.

His newest problem, however, might soon make the others pale in comparison. Hacktivists were infecting his media campaigns more quickly than he could track the damage, let alone repair it. Something called Ghost Security had been the first to engage, an army of nameless hackers across the world who never worried about attribution, and who ignored the restrictions legitimate governments placed on electronic chaos. The Anonymous network stepped in after the Paris attacks of 2015, decimating long-established channels for funding and media exposure. Telegram, the encrypted-messaging app they'd so long relied upon, was becoming useless, and replacements were increasingly suspect. Uday had watched their recruiting websites become inundated with eager volunteers this week, only to have the vast majority prove to be ghosts created by online radicals. Last month he'd published an online security guide, telling prospective jihadists which apps to use to avoid detection. Within a week a devastatingly inverse version of the document was sweeping across the web.

Uday had a few decent technicians, including a precious handful who'd had some manner of cyber training. For a time they'd kept ahead of things in a game of electronic Whac-a-Mole, creating new Twitter feeds and messaging sites faster than anyone could wipe them out. But the endgame was increasingly clear—they could never outsmart all the world's hackers. And without the internet to fuel fundamentalist flames, ISIS would quickly degrade to what the West held it to be: an isolated medieval tribe whose only product was brutality.

For Aziz Uday, it was all just another day at his impossible office.

"I have six more men inputting data," said Anisa, the most able programmer on his team, as she arrived from the prayer room. Had the mosque remained active as a place of worship she would not have been allowed inside, at least not in the presence of men. The entire building had been requisitioned some weeks ago, becoming the main data center for ISIS. The resident mullahs had been relocated, with apologies, to nearby mosques.

"How many does that make?" Uday asked.

"Sixteen altogether, and that's our limit—we're out of keyboards."

"How far have we gotten?"

"Ninety-four percent complete with the primary personnel database. Of course, that number is a moving target. We take in new recruits every day, and the raw data often takes weeks to reach us."

Uday nodded. "I suspect some of the paperwork never reaches us at all."

"We are concentrating on entries and not deletions. The files contain at least a thousand martyrs who have moved on to Paradise."

"I don't want to remove anyone—simply annotate their martyrdom. God willing, their profiles might still be useful."

The project had been born last summer out of a request from the Shura Council for the names of those who'd perished in battle over the previous year. Records concerning next of kin—always fertile ground for recruiting brothers and cousins—could not be located, and it was soon discovered that the paperwork had been obliterated by an American bomb some months earlier. After much handwringing, it was Uday who suggested to the council that all records be digitized and placed in an electronic database. It was the kind of thing legitimate governments did.

Uday quickly regretted his suggestion. The council agreed it was a worthy undertaking, but at the same time lamented a lack of wherewithal to purchase more computers or electronic storage. That being the case, ISIS's chief information officer was faced with a mountainous new task: With no increase in either budget or personnel, he was to acquire paperwork on every existing soldier of Allah, every incoming recruit, every vetted foreign contact, and store it in a single, secure electronic database. The project plodded along for half a year. Then, for reasons Uday did not understand, it seemed to find new emphasis in recent weeks, Chadeh inquiring about the status at every meeting. He wondered if it had to do with the new pivot to European operations.

"Did you mention the generators when you spoke with Chadeh?" asked Anisa.

"Wha . . . oh yes," he stuttered, redirecting his thoughts. "But I wouldn't expect miracles."

"Miracles are a thing of God. I pray for no more than a few reliable kilowatt-hours."

"Tell me about our latest videos. Are they finding traction?"

"Better than those of recent months," she said. "The one claiming credit for the Grenoble bombing is circulating particularly well. Not exactly viral, but it has a high rate of being repeated on all platforms."

"Finally a bit of good news," he said.

"I think we should spend more time managing the social media. Committing so many hours to this database is pushing everything else aside."

"We will be done soon, and then we can focus on the rest. It will be a simple matter to update the personnel list once each month—add the new arrivals, annotate who has been martyred and who has deserted." Uday immediately sensed a mistake. Desertion was a taboo topic, something that didn't exist in the caliphate's earthly Paradise.

"The cowards are but a handful," she retorted, "and we should keep their files most accurate of all. Once things have settled, they must be found and punished." Anisa gave Uday a hard look that demanded a response.

"Of course," he said. "But rest assured. If we do not keep up with them, God will hold them accountable."

Anisa seemed satisfied by his logic, and she disappeared into the hallway.

Uday turned back to his screen, and no sooner had he begun typing than a message notification blinked. It was from Malika, a reverse flow in the delicate tributary Uday had built. On brevity alone, he couldn't avoid reading it:

ARGU WILL HAVE RESULTS IN FOUR DAYS

As he dutifully configured the message for relay, Uday wondered what it was all about. He knew Chadeh was demanding something from his well-connected spy, but the details had escaped him. As he hit the send button, Uday was struck by the critical nature of his position. Had he been of a more scheming nature, it would have registered long ago: Every single communication between the Islamic State and its most critical spy in Europe passed through his fingers.

He remembered as a young boy learning about the Persian Royal Road, one of the first mail networks, instituted by Cyrus the Great. In those ancient days it had taken scores of messengers and horses a week to carry a document across the empire. Now instant messaging and e-mail had speeded things to nearly the speed of light, but information still traveled predictable routes.

And trusted messengers were as vital as ever.

It occurred to him that since Malika's agent, Argu,

was so important, it might be wise to set up an emergency means of communication. Thinking Chadeh would agree, Uday took the initiative, typing and encrypting his first message to Malika that had not been dictated from above.

PROVIDE BURNER TO ARGU AND SEND NUMBER
EMERGENCY USE ONLY

He read it through twice, and decided it was good—specific, with no real risk introduced. The moment he sent it, Uday felt a peculiar sensation. His hands seemed almost paralyzed over the keyboard. He pulled them away, balled his hands into fists a few times, and the numbness passed.

He quickly shrugged it off and got back to work.

SEVENTEEN

Slaton was patient in his travels, taking a full day to reach Italy, then another to wend his way to Paris. After a night in Turin, he utilized two trains, two taxis, and a bus, in each case taking every measure to leave as slight a footprint as possible. Although he could not know it, his final leg on a French TGV train was in fact the reverse of the route Zavier Baland had taken to Grenoble six days earlier.

The train pulled into the Gare de Lyon shortly before dinner, and Slaton took a cab to a small but restful hotel overlooking the Seine and the Île de la Grande Jatte, the narrow island that separated Baland's neighborhood in Courbevoie from greater Paris, and so too the headquarters of DGSI. Slaton generally preferred such modest rooming houses over chain hotels whose corporate reservation systems and high traffic levels did nothing to promote the privacy he craved.

He checked in under the name Paul Aranson, in line with his new passport, and as the hotel's agreeable new guest from Sweden he asked specifically for a room overlooking the river. The desk man was happy to oblige, and while waiting for a key Slaton engaged the concierge in a discourse about nearby restaurants and points of interest, not because he was hungry or bored but simply to establish a rapport with a young woman whose services might soon be needed for less conventional requests.

He took in the layout of the lobby, and studied a walking map on the wall that, in spite of its cartoonish appearance, he suspected was quite accurate. He noted roads and transportation hubs, and plotted the main boulevards from Courbevoie by which one could walk across the Seine toward Levallois-Perret.

One of the few details Talia had so far extracted on Baland was his habit of walking to work—he left slightly before eight on most mornings. Wondering how she'd determined this, he decided the most likely scenario was that she'd managed to locate and track his phone. Whatever the source, Slaton took it as fact—he had seen Talia work, and was glad to have her in his corner. Soon, however, a darker answer intervened. Could Mossad have had second thoughts and begun its own surveillance of Baland? He'd seen it time and again over the years, teams from competing agencies tripping over one another, often blowing an important op. *One more possible complication,* he thought.

Slaton was handed a key, and he assured the man at the desk that he didn't need help with his bag, but thanked him all the same. He went past a tiny elevator and climbed a narrow set of stairs to the third floor. The room was comfortable and clean, and the view first-rate, a reaching panorama of the Seine winding its way east under the Pont de Courbevoie. He turned on the phone Bloch had given him, hoping it was secure as promised, and fully expecting that Mossad itself would track him once the device was powered. It was the way of the new world.

He saw one message from Talia. It contained no new background information on Baland, but did provide a detailed schedule of his appointments and meetings that reached into next month. Slaton grinned. *She's got hold of his phone.* It was priceless information. Certainly meetings would be canceled and lunch reservations altered, but the essential fact remained—a leading DGSI officer had been careless.

Slaton studied Baland's calendar. At eight tomorrow morning he saw a staff conference, presumably at the headquarters building since no other location was mentioned. Lunch the next day was at one o'clock with DGSI director Claude Michelis, a place called Le Quinze in the ninth arrondissement. A weekly press conference was set for three that same afternoon. Baland's schedule tonight was clear.

Slaton turned off the phone and began unpacking his bag. Shirts went neatly in the closet, toothbrush by the sink. Trivialities to be sure, but rituals Slaton maintained when acting in his trained capacity. A grasp at normalcy in a role that so consistently precluded it. When everything was put away, he set his plans for the evening. Shower, a change of clothes, seek out a decent dinner in the heart of Paris—some of an assassin's chores were less burdensome than others.

If only Christine and Davy could join me for just a few hours.

That fleeting thought only magnified his frustration. For a year he'd not gone more than a day without seeing them. Now he felt the old darkness closing in, albeit in the City of Light. Safe houses and countersurveillance. False identities and zeroed sight pictures. A brief internal debate ensued. Should he go outside right now and hail a cab? In twenty-four hours, more or less, he could be back in the tranquil South Pacific, the three of them sailing wherever the trade winds blew. But the opposing argument was devastating: How long could that last?

In the end, Slaton was compelled by his greatest strength, and on occasion his greatest weakness: Beholden to precision, he could never allow fate to intervene when control could be had. The answers he needed were clear, and they could only be found in the fabled city outside.

Dinner alone it was.

Afterward he would take a long and watchful stroll, absorbing the lights and fresh air, and making at least one pass down a particular nearby street. Then a thoughtful survey back toward the river, a last check of his phone, and finally a good night's sleep.

All so as to be stationed discreetly in the vicinity of 45 Avenue Pasteur by seven fifteen the next morning.

EIGHTEEN

Breakfast was taken from a neighborhood *boulangerie,* rolls and a tall coffee, and Slaton carried it less than two blocks to reach his destination. He'd scouted the area methodically last night after drawing mental lines between Zavier Baland's home and his office. There were any number of routes Baland might take on his way to work, but one particular intersection seemed a necessity before the options broadened.

There were never absolutes in predictive surveillance. Baland wouldn't walk to work every day. Not when it was raining or when he had a breakfast meeting across town. Not when a sick child had to be taken to a doctor's appointment. A given target's habits often took weeks, even months to establish. That being the case, Slaton was fully prepared for failure. If Baland did not appear before nine this morning, he would go back to his room and contact Talia for updates. Then he would return tomorrow morning a few minutes earlier.

He scouted out positions along Avenue Pasteur, ending at the intersection of the far busier Boulevard

Saint-Denis. By 7:25, with a newspaper and breakfast in hand, he was scanning the busy sidewalks from a bench in the Parc de Bécon, a charming municipal garden that graced the banks of the Seine. He occasionally referenced his phone, even though it was not powered up—it was fast becoming a more typical pastime to stare at a screen than to bury oneself in the terrible truths of *Le Monde*.

With a good line of sight down the length of Avenue Pasteur, Slaton visualized the face he hoped would appear. Instead of the recent pictures, however, he found himself going back fifteen years. The kills came back often enough in his dreams, so he rarely conjured them at will, but the old sight picture was unshakable in his mind: Samir alone at a table, smiling at a pretty waitress. Reading a newspaper and sitting perfectly still. Slaton could almost feel the tension in his finger, the mechanical action and recoil. Then two seconds of chaos. After taking one glimpse at the aftermath through his optic, he'd broken down his gun and egressed. A hit, yes. But had Samir survived?

8:01.

Slaton canvassed the buildings around him. Across the street was a six-by-ten array of apartments, each with two windows, and rows of trellises and planters filled the roof above. On the opposite corner he saw a different kind of roof, full of ductwork and ventilators, and a pharmacy at street level. A building acutely to his right was under construction, a warren of good hides for a shooter, but also busy work crews who were at this hour beginning their day. Slaton admonished himself for getting ahead of things. *One step at a time.*

8:06.

He noticed a man approaching on Avenue Pasteur. The timing was right, as was the height and build. The stride suggested a man in decent shape, about the right age, and on his way to work. Purposeful, but not in a rush. He was wearing an overcoat and carried a small attaché.

At seventy yards Slaton was curious.

At sixty he was interested.

He had exceptional eyesight, and as the man paused at the crosswalk, forty yards away, there was no longer any doubt. He was looking at Ali Samir—alias Zavier Baland.

At that same moment, as Slaton sat watching Baland, a single eye was locked firmly on him through the lens of a small camera. Not seventy yards from where he sat, across Boulevard Saint-Denis, an amorphous figure lay prone on an ill-kept garden rooftop. Soon her method of observation changed: she put down the camera, trading its viewfinder for the magnified scope on a compact rifle.

The watcher had arrived as she had for each of the last three mornings, by way of a fire escape ladder in the back alley. The garden around her was little more than a skeleton of pottery and dirt, a few wistful brown stalks remembering September. It all would be spectacular again in May, but whoever tended it—no doubt one of the tenants in the flats below—had clearly surrendered for the season.

The watcher was virtually invisible as she lay squeezed between rows of wooden planting boxes. She was good at shooting from concealed positions, and had done her share of it. New, however, was the flutter she'd felt in her stomach forty minutes ago. That was when she'd seen the tall man across the street take up a bench with a commanding view of the intersection. There was a second tingle as she'd watched him linger over a newspaper and coffee, yet she told herself it might be nothing at all. The problem was that she'd never set eyes on the man she was looking for—few had, and many of those were no longer of this earth. According to legend, the *kidon* had been killed . . . twice, actually . . . but rumors to the contrary lingered. She had to be sure.

She'd gone to great lengths to flush him out, knowing a better chance might never come. There had still been no word from the men she'd dispatched halfway around the world. Not that she was surprised. The flash drive had been her insurance. If it was the *kidon,* and if he came to Paris seeking Baland, this was where he would start. She knew because this was where *she* would have started. Baland, in all his obstinate predictability, had made his own hunter predictable.

But is that who I'm looking at? Or is it only the hope of so many years?

She'd taken one distant photo, but now she studied his face behind the aiming reticle, the thin cross centered on his head. She shifted to his chest and saw no bulkiness to suggest body armor. *If it was him, why would he bother? He thinks he is the hunter.*

With a glance at her watch, she looked down at a more acute angle. Right on schedule, the soon-to-be chief of DGSI appeared at the corner. Baland paused for traffic, then crossed the street into the park. She watched the man on the bench intently through her Zeiss scope and curled her finger around the trigger. She studied his face intently, but his features gave away little. He *might* be Israeli, but given his fair hair she would have guessed him to be a Swede or a German. Whatever he was, his food wrappers and newspaper went into the trash as Baland passed no more than twenty feet from where he sat.

The man in her viewfinder stood and began walking toward the park. The flutter became a wave. After so many years, could it really be true? Was this the man she'd been looking for? It wasn't a certainty, not one hundred percent. In that moment, however, she decided it was enough. If it *was* the *kidon,* Baland might never reemerge from the park. And if that came to pass—her best chance would be lost.

Her finger began the subtle pressure on the trigger. The man was moving at a casual walking pace, and so she added a small leading correction. More pressure, her finger on the cool metal. The noise from the street below seemed to disappear. Her breathing paused. Then, in the instant before the expected recoil, her view was obliterated.

She pulled back from the scope and saw an aqua-and-white city bus drawing to a stop, its bulky frame ruining her line of sight to the path. She let loose a venomous string of hushed expletives. There was nothing to do but wait. She tried to predict where her target would reappear. After what seemed an interminable pause, the bus finally pulled away. Seeing no one with her naked eye, she used the scope to scan the path until it disappeared beneath a canopy of trees. She saw no one. Her chance was gone.

Malika muttered in Arabic and began breaking down her weapon. She tried to tell herself it might be for the best. She hadn't been completely sure. Ninety-five percent, at best. Yet if it was the *kidon,* might he be reaching for his own weapon at that moment? Perhaps he would be stymied by some similar roadblock. Or he might only be laying the groundwork for tomorrow or the next day. Wasn't that how a professional would go about it?

So many questions.

At that moment, however, Malika was certain of two things. The man she had just seen was an operator. And he was following Zavier Baland.

NINETEEN

Slaton heard the rattle of a bus behind him as he tracked his target into the park. He followed Baland around a long fountain, and then down a tiered garden that stepped toward the river. Baland made no apparent attempt at countersurveillance, and at the river he turned left, aiming, Slaton was sure, for the Pont de Levallois. DGSI headquarters was not yet in sight, but Slaton knew where it was, and the bridge became a necessary funnel. Another opportunity noted.

It all went as expected, and Baland disappeared ten minutes later into the concrete-and-glass fortress that was 84 Rue de Villiers. Slaton continued walking south. He pulled out his phone, and after a turn toward the river placed a call. Talia answered immediately.

"I found him right where we thought he would be."

"That was fast," she said. "What do you think? Could it actually be Samir?"

"It's him."

There was a pause on the Tel Aviv end, then she said, "All right. I should inform Anton before you act."

"I'm not sure I'm going to act."

"What do you mean?"

"None of this feels right to me, Talia. Who's responsible for my being here? Who sent those men and the information on the drive?"

"If you've really found Samir, and he's working at DGSI . . . what difference does it make?"

"Every difference in the world." Slaton reached the Seine and turned along the Left Bank. "I think this is a setup against me. But it's possible Samir is being targeted as well."

"Who would want that?"

"In my case, there must be a hundred suspects. Samir's list is probably longer. The problem is crossreferencing the two—I can't imagine who would come after both of us."

"So what will you do?"

Slaton told her.

"David . . . you can't be serious."

A moment of silence told her he was. He said, "You can inform Anton, but I don't want any interference."

"I'll make sure he understands."

"Have there been any changes to Baland's personal calendar for the next two days? When we last spoke he was set for a one-on-one lunch with the DGSI director tomorrow at a place called Le Quinze."

"Yes, his calendar still shows it."

"Good. If there are any changes, let me know right away. But assuming things remain the same, I want

you to tell Anton to send me the things we discussed." For thirty seconds Slaton provided detailed
instructions—the address of the hotel in which he
was staying, and the precise schedule and means of a
transfer. Then he asked her a technical question.

"Baland's phone?" she said. "Yes, I think I can
manage that."

Slaton explained exactly what he wanted done,
then said, "Thanks, Talia. Send me an update tomorrow morning. I'll call when I'm finished and let you
know how it went."

"What if I don't hear from you?"

"In that case . . . you'll know how it went."

Uday's impure thought came while Sarah was wash-
ing the dishes after lunch. She was wearing a full
robe—such pretenses were necessary for a man in his
position—yet inside their home her head was uncovered, leaving her long raven hair flowing freely over
her back. The robe left much to the imagination, yet
even through the dense fabric he discerned the familiar lines of her slim figure, and saw her graceful
movement as she set clean plates on the counter.
Never had he taken such pleasure in simply watching a woman perform a chore.

Uday could take it no longer.

"Woman!" he bellowed. "Come here. . . . I have
need of you!"

She froze for an instant, then turned and looked at
him, her face the same blank mask he'd seen on the
day she was delivered to him by a squad of Chadeh's

minions. Sarah obeyed. A shuffle of hesitant steps brought her across the room as if floating on air. Uday couldn't take his eyes off her. She stopped short of where he stood, next to the mattress that lay on the floor. Her head fell bowed in supplication, the translucent olive eyes he knew so well pointed at the ground. She spoke in the girlish voice that so weakened him. "How can I please you?"

There was a long pause before she raised her eyes to meet his. Then Sarah lunged at him and tackled him onto the bed. She pushed Uday onto his back, straddled him, and began pounding her fists on his chest. "You are such a bastard!" she tried to say through her laughter.

He made a halfhearted attempt to deflect her blows. "You must show more respect to a man of my exalted position! I am the Bastard in Chief of Daesh Information."

Her assault paused. "Well, here is some information, O high and mighty one . . . you will get nothing until you are nice!"

Uday bucked his hips and Sarah fell to the other side of the bed. He rolled on top of her in a reversal, and was about to start tickling her when he heard a gasp. He went still, and saw a twist of pain in her expression. He immediately rolled away. "I'm sorry, darling—did I hurt you?"

She forged her grimace into a smile, then touched her right forearm. "No, it wasn't you. It's only my arm—it still hurts a bit. I'm sure it will pass."

The thugs who'd delivered her had been rough, injuring her right arm, and even months afterward it bothered her. The day after her arrival it had been severely bruised, but she'd refused to see a doctor—a luxury few could imagine these days.

"I wish you would let me track that man down. I could have him brought before a court and—"

"No, Aziz, you mustn't! It would only bring suspicion. I want nothing to jeopardize what we have."

He touched her arm gently, in the way a sculptor might touch his favorite work.

"There, you see?" she said. "You *can* be nice." It was no longer her girlish voice, but that of the confident woman who'd burst into his life like a second sun.

"You have taken my heart," he said.

"No, not taken. You gave it to me, Aziz. And for that I thank God every day."

He smiled, not considering for a moment that she was referring to a God different from his own. Uday still prayed occasionally, as did she. But when they were together religion was irrelevant; they were like fish from different depths who wanted only to revel in the same sea.

It had begun two months ago, Chadeh's goons delivering her on a cold and rain-swept night. She'd been taken as a spoil of war, a slave from a dwindling Christian neighborhood. They'd marched her into his house by the elbows and forced her onto her knees in front of him. They asked if she was acceptable, and he'd looked down and seen her beaten figure the first time. She was clad from head to toe that night, her burqa sodden and dirty as though she'd been dragged through the mud. In those first moments he had seen neither her face nor her body, only a hunched and filthy form that was curiously still. Not knowing what to do, Uday had thanked the men and told them he was glad to have her. They seemed disappointed, and only later did he realize why—they had hoped he would reject Chadeh's gift, leaving Sarah to them.

Uday sent the men away, but even after they were gone Sarah remained motionless. When his hand touched her elbow to help her rise, she jerked away in fear. Uday had retrieved a blanket, knelt in front of her, and wrapped it around her shoulders. Only then did he lift her veil for the first time. When he did, he was stunned by her beauty. Even more so by the defiance in her eyes. Then Uday had done what seemed the only decent thing—he smiled at Sarah. Her defiance softened ever so slightly.

He gave her hot tea that night, and watched her eat ravenously. He provided her a clean gown to wear and surrendered his bed, sleeping on the couch in his workroom. It continued that way for some time, Uday caring for her. Then, on the seventh day, she had dinner prepared when he arrived home after a long day at work. On the tenth she smiled at one of his feeble jokes. That same week they went outside together for the first time. Sarah followed him to the market, and afterward they stopped for tea. They talked for hours about everything except the war, until an officer of the Hisbah, the caliphate's religious police, ordered Sarah to cover her eyes. She did so immediately, but a furious Uday told the man who he was dealing with and sent him packing. Even so, it was the last time Sarah had gone out in public.

So they carried on in their tiny house, and each day

Uday fell more endeared with Sarah. He also became more frustrated with their situation. They agreed to live in the present—for now she was safe, and that was all that mattered. It was in the fifth week, after a wonderful lamb kebab and a pilfered bottle of wine, that Sarah had come to him late one night. She'd given herself to him willfully, even enthusiastically, and if there was ever any doubt it ended there. The two had become lovers in an increasingly despondent world.

Now they lay together languidly on the old mattress, limbs intertwined, talking with what seemed like an old familiarity. She kissed him and put her head on his chest, and he drank in the scent of jasmine in her hair.

"You were gone for so long today," she said.

"A project at work is keeping me very busy."

"What does it involve?"

He pushed up until he could see her eyes. "There . . . I knew all along you were a spy."

She giggled and buried her face in his shirt. Jasmine again.

"It's actually something I will tell you about," he said. "But only when the time is right."

"I don't want to know anything about the Daesh!"

Uday opened his mouth, but then stifled the words that were rising. He wanted desperately to confide in Sarah—tell her his wild idea that might set them free. But it seemed only a fantasy. After a thoughtful moment, he asked, "You have told no one of our relationship?"

"Not even my mother . . . pray that she is still alive."

"I'm sure she is fine. She must have made it to Jordan. At times I wish you were with her, but if they hadn't detained you as you tried to leave the city . . . I would never have known you."

She maneuvered beside him and kissed him on the lips. Soon they were breathing heavily, her hands fumbling as she unbuttoned his shirt. It all came to an abrupt end when someone pounded on the front door.

Sarah went rigid, and they both looked at the door. More pounding.

"Uday!"

"It's all right," he told her. "Go to the kitchen."

She did, and he fastened a few of his shirt buttons on the way to the door. He opened it to find Anisa. "Uday, you must come quickly!"

"Why?"

Anisa looked past him toward the kitchen, but only for a moment. "I don't know, but Chadeh is furious."

TWENTY

Slaton watched the man from the window of his room, and decided he was quite good. He arrived in a nondescript Fiat, either dark blue or black—it was hard to say in the midwinter gloom. He might have been a *katsa,* a case officer, from the embassy. If Mossad was being particularly cautious, which they probably were, the man might even be unofficial. Whoever he was, he had sent Slaton a text to announce his impending arrival. In a minor stroke of bad luck, all the parking spots in front of the small Courbevoie hotel were occupied. He'd dealt with it well, continuing around the block without the slightest hesitation. On his third lap an ideal spot opened up when a delivery truck pulled away.

From the third-floor window, Slaton watched the man get out. He was dressed precisely in accordance with the instructions sent through Talia: denim pants, dark gray jacket, brown shoes. He was the correct height and build, and while his hair was perhaps a shade too dark, it was cut to the perfect length. A very fresh haircut, Slaton reckoned.

The driver paused on the curb, and casually locked the Fiat's doors using his key fob. After the usual chirp and double flash of the parking lights, he set out in the general direction of the hotel entrance. At that point the man fell out of view from Slaton's perspective, his location a mystery aside from one point of certainty—he had *not* passed under the big green awning to enter the hotel.

Slaton was in the lobby sixty seconds later, where he allowed a passing glance in the wall-length mirror: denim pants, dark gray jacket, brown shoes. He walked outside, went straight to the car, and held out an empty hand as he approached. The Fiat chirped on cue. Slaton opened the small trunk, pulled out a common black roller bag, then dropped the lid shut. He again mimed using a fob, and the car magically locked. He turned back toward the hotel, and on his way to the entrance could not help venturing a guess as to where the driver was holed up. Slaton registered three possibilities: a dark alcove in the building next door, a convenience store window across the street, and a nearby alley. The Mossad man might be hidden in any of them.

Slaton pretended to pocket his keys, then retraced his steps through the lobby and up the stairs to the third floor. He was back in his room three minutes after leaving. He put the suitcase on the bed, unzipped it, and threw back the lid to find a heavy plastic case, sided by a second package encased in bubble wrap. He opened the case and found the component parts of an Arctic Warfare Covert. He assembled the gun and performed a thorough inspection. Satisfied, he broke the weapon back down and reseated each piece into its respective foam notch. Slaton went back to the window and, without so much as a glance outside, he pulled the floral-print drapes closed on one side.

He went back to the plastic case, which had just fit in the roller bag, and set it next to the room's couch. The couch concealed a small fold-out bed, and Slaton pulled off the cushions and partially lifted the folding frame of the bed. This exposed a cavity backing to the wall, into which he placed the case containing the rifle. It was a tight fit, but when everything was put back together, the gun case was completely invisible. The deception would never hold against a committed search, but Slaton had no reason to expect one. More to the point, he was sure the housekeeper would not stumble across it in the course of her daily cleaning. Just to be sure, he used a bathroom towel to dust the floor on either side of the couch, and made sure there was no trash along the floorboards behind it.

Slaton took the second package from the roller bag and removed bubble wrap to reveal a Glock 17 and two spare magazines. He checked the weapon and found the action smooth. He seated a magazine, jacked a round into the chamber, and set the gun on the nightstand. The empty roller bag went quite naturally into the closet next to his tan Mossad-issued suitcase.

Satisfied, he went to the window and looked down at the street. It had been ten minutes. The Fiat was long gone.

* * *

Sitting at the tiny table in her flat in Monceau, Malika read the order to provide Argu with a backup phone. She frowned as she might have for an eviction notice. Until now Baland had been exclusively under her control, and the idea of potentially cutting herself out did not sit well. Still, if she were in Chadeh's position, she would have done the same thing.

Her relationship with the Islamic State had not been born of the usual motivation, which was to say blind religious subservience. She and the caliphate were bound by something nearer an arranged marriage, forced together by circumstances out of either's control, and with the potential for either mutual harmony or ruin.

It had begun five years ago, on the day a rough-edged and dirty teenage girl had departed the hopelessness of Gaza for the only society on earth of greater dysfunction—the wreckage of Syria. Malika hadn't told anyone she was going, including the busy recruiters of ISIS. She had simply traveled alone to the Turkish border, and from there walked south.

The caliphate happily accepted yet another refugee from the back-firing Arab Spring. She was screened by an ISIS officer in the remains of a shattered villa. He asked her if she was a good Muslim, and Malika said that she was. He asked her if she wanted to marry a fighter, and she said that she did. At that point Malika made her one and only request. She would acquiesce to becoming a bride on one condition—she wanted to marry a sniper. The man processing Malika had looked at her oddly, and she expanded that she wanted to marry the man who had killed the most infidels. It was a highly unusual request, but colored in a certain hue of fanaticism. The ISIS recruiter had liked that.

So it was, within two weeks of entering Syria, Malika was wed to a killer. His name was Arwan, 120 pounds of bone and sinew who could hold a gun with the steadiness of a vise, and who was reputed to have sixty-five kills to his credit. He said he was twenty-one, but Malika suspected he was younger than she was, eighteen at best. Yet what he lacked in physical presence, he made up for with an intensity the likes of which Malika had never seen.

In dealing with his new wife, Arwan was neither cruel nor kind—if anything, he seemed monumentally distracted. Not surprising, really, for a young man who should have been in school, but who instead spent his days hiding in cramped spaces and shooting people from great distances. He was rarely home, spending days on end in the field. This in itself Malika took as her first lesson—Arwan, the caliphate's most celebrated living killer, was imbued with an inordinate degree of patience.

But not as much as me, she'd thought.

In the few days when they were together, Malika cooked for Arwan, cleaned whatever room they called home, and when called upon performed as a wife should. After a month she decided it was time for the next step. She told Arwan over breakfast one day that she too knew how to shoot. She said she wanted to learn his craft. He'd laughed at first, but Malika had stared at him long enough, her dark eyes drilling in until he realized she was serious.

That same afternoon, with a rifle in Arwan's hand, they walked away from town in silence—far away, because ammunition was precious, and not to be wasted teaching wives which end of a gun was which. Arwan took up a position and set his example, sending five rounds into a hand-drawn target at fifty meters. Malika did the same to a second. When they walked closer and looked, her grouping was more tight. Malika had beamed. Arwan had stood expressionless. What he did next Malika would remember for the rest of her life.

"Take my hand, Malika."

She looked at him curiously, saw his outstretched hand.

"Take it."

She did so.

"Now squeeze, Malika. Squeeze my hand as hard as you possibly can."

"As hard as I—"

Her words were cut off by a whimper as he crushed her hand in his own. "Do it!" he demanded.

Malika began to respond in kind. Her hand was in agony, but she fought back, cursing his ridiculous game. Bones crushed nerves, and blood vessels bulged. Her anger rose with each new stab of pain. He upped his intensity, and so did she. Malika was a physically strong woman, likely stronger than he was. She knew she was inflicting pain on him, yet his face remained strangely impassive. This angered her further, and she squeezed with every ounce of strength.

She heard cartilage snap, and was sure bones would be next. Arwan's face remained still, no different from when he drank his morning tea. Her own was no doubt chiseled in agony. Then Malika felt the first tears on her cheek.

Finally, she could take it no more. She yanked her hand out of his grasp. Malika stared at this boy she had married. His face remained unchanged, and his voice was calm as he said, "Have you ever killed a man, Malika?"

She didn't answer as she flexed her hand to work out the pain.

"Have you?"

"No."

"Do you want to?"

"Yes!" she said eagerly.

Arwan's eyes narrowed. "Are you prepared to lay in a ditch full of sewage for twenty hours? Can you hold perfectly still while vermin chew your ankles?"

She looked at him blankly.

"There are many kinds of strength, Malika. Find them all, and then you can do something."

With those words, Arwan's second lesson was complete. Others soon followed. From that day in the tawny scrub, shooting under a hot summer sun, their relationship altered. Lessons on killing blunted traditional marital conduct. Husband and wife became teacher and student. It went on that way for three months, until one cool fall evening when an officer had come to her door and informed Malika that she was a widow. She made a point of grieving, and in truth she *was* sad, but less for her and Arwan's joyless future than for the tactical knowledge he had not yet imparted.

Impatient to carry forward with her plan, Malika volunteered for the front lines as a sniper. The commander had laughed. Undeterred, she'd taken the forever young Arwan's rifle and walked to the front lines. She killed two Peshmerga fighters that first day, six within a week. The commander changed his mind. For six months she honed her deadly craft, and by grace of God survived unscathed.

With her bona fides thus established, Malika sought out the highest-level officer who would see her, a colonel named Chadeh. She told him she wanted to go to France. She said she spoke fluent French, which was nearly true, and a bit of English, and that she might be very effective in coordinating attacks on European soil. Chadeh didn't laugh, but he denied her request. He told her she was needed in Syria.

Malika made two more requests to go to France in the following months. Both were rejected by Chadeh, who was rising in the command structure. She did not make a fourth. At that point, Malika took matters into her own hands. One late-spring day, she leaned Arwan's rifle against the wall of a beaten room in Raqqa. Malika had then gathered a few clothes, all the money she had, and started walking toward the Turkish border. When Chadeh heard from her next, in two months' time, it was a phone call from a bistro on Rue de Rivoli.

Malika got up from the table and went to the curtained window. She pulled back the dreary cloth and looked out across the street. The afternoon sky was overwhelmed by heavy clouds, Monceau going grim in winter's pensive half-light. She saw a half-dozen familiar cars parked along the street, and a few new arrivals. The people she saw, if they were spies, did not behave as such. They strolled lazily on the sidewalk or loitered in plain view. What worried her was the chance of others she might not be able to see.

She backed away from the window, and considered a host of new complications. An hour ago she'd seen a news report from the Philippines—she'd been keeping half an eye there. Four Frenchmen of Mediterranean extraction had been found dead under highly suspicious circumstances. The Far East was not a direction in which Chadeh normally looked, yet if he made the connection he might become suspicious. Malika already knew what to say if the matter came up—she would claim to know nothing, and he could hardly prove otherwise. On that ground, she decided she was safe. More maddening was the issue of a backup phone for Argu. Malika decided that was a battle she couldn't win. She went to the door and slipped on her coat.

Twenty minutes later, on a smelly backstreet in Monceau, she purchased a burner at a convenience store. She of course paid cash, and on impulse bought a large bag of crisps and a soda. She covered the two blocks back to her flat quickly, once averting her face from a passing policeman, and later ducking into a used furniture store when a siren approached on a crossing street. Back in her room, she used a pair of scissors to cut the phone out of its infernal plastic packaging. She activated the handset, then recorded the number as a contact in her own phone.

She would include that number in her next message to Raqqa. Until Argu had the device in hand, however, Malika remained in control. She didn't need much more time. Her plan had been years in the making, and this morning—she was increasingly sure—she had finally seen her target. Her first chance to finalize things had slipped away, but it hardly mattered.

Malika knew another chance would arrive very soon.

TWENTY-ONE

Uday located the new command center, and was ushered inside by a guard. The place had been set up only yesterday, in the shell of an ancient Christian church—regardless of faith, houses of worship were generally left untargeted. Inside he found an agitated Chadeh backed by a half-dozen others, most of whom Uday recognized. The mood was less that of a meeting than one of a tribunal.

Chadeh briefly explained the problem, then asked, "When did we send Malika the information on these four men?"

Uday had had the foresight to bring his laptop. He took a seat at a table and was soon referencing his communications log. "I sent her a contact number for the cell in Marseille almost two months ago."

"And now these men end up dead halfway around the world? What was she thinking?"

It was a purely rhetorical question, but with Chadeh hovering behind him, Uday felt an urge to reply. "You believe Malika is responsible for this?" Much of the Shura Council was in attendance, and Uday felt everyone's eyes on him. For lack of a better target, the messenger was being blamed. He felt compelled to keep talking. "I can't say if she ever made contact with these men. The South China Sea is not an area of operations we've discussed with her . . . and I know nothing of any missions there."

"We keep contacts with groups in Indonesia, Malaysia, and Thailand, do we not?"

"We have loose associations, yes, but our footprint in the Philippines is virtually nil. The place where this happened, on a coral reef in the middle of the sea . . . I can think of no reason Malika would have sent recruits there."

"Do we know who was responsible for their deaths?" one of the council members asked.

Chadeh said, "Perhaps they were engaged by a Special Forces unit. The Americans are active in that region."

Uday referenced the most recent press release. "There have been no arrests, but the authorities say evidence leads them to believe that drug smuggling was involved."

"Drugs?" Chadeh repeated. He paced about the room, and his mood seemed to brighten. "Yes," he said, "that makes more sense. These recruits we unearth in Europe are useful, but so many are no more than impressionable criminals. They meet true believers in jail who steer them into our fold, but some give us nothing but trouble."

Uday sensed the crisis ebbing. He said, "If you wish, I can contact Malika and ask if she knows anything about this."

"Yes, a good next step," said Chadeh. "And when you do, tell her to keep up the pressure on Argu. We must have his information by tomorrow."

"Very well."

One of the others said, "Perhaps it is time to tell Uday of our plans. We will soon need his team's expertise." The man who'd spoken was a recognized *hafiz*, meaning he had memorized the entire Quran. An impressive accomplishment, to be sure, but Uday had always been struck by the narrowness of that learning—such men often had no idea how the outside world functioned.

Uday watched Chadeh take a silent poll, before saying, "Leave us and wait outside."

He was happy to comply.

Uday stepped through the great doors of the church, and outside he encountered the same guard who'd let him in. The guard nodded and offered him a cigarette. Uday took one, and without a word between them the two stood side by side in the gathering midday heat. Somewhere in the distance an explosion rang out, but neither flinched. Uday remembered hearing the first blasts of the war, so many years ago. At the time he'd thought it was distant thunder. Now the inverse had taken hold—the last rumble from a storm had been lost on him, and he'd been caught by surprise when rain began sweeping down. *Such strange acclimatizations war brings.*

Five minutes later he was summoned back inside. Only three people remained, Chadeh and two council members. Uday hoped his expression did not betray what he felt—that he would rather be anywhere else at that moment.

Chadeh said, "We are in agreement. As I recently mentioned, attacks in Europe will take on increasing importance in our overall strategy. We will soon launch a broad series of assaults. The skills of your team will be necessary to maximize their effectiveness."

For the next ten minutes Uday listened as the three council members laid bare an audacious plan. Argu would soon provide critical information. When paired with Uday's personnel database, it would be nothing short of a declaration of war. Uday finally understood why his project had found new emphasis.

"Will there be attacks using radiation?" he asked, sensing a connection to Grenoble.

"There are no bounds—we will use whatever can be leveraged. France's weaknesses will soon be laid bare, and an army lies in wait to exploit our advantage."

"Surely you recall how the Americans reacted to 9/11," commented the *hafiz*. "A few thousand dead, and they went straight into Afghanistan—where they remain mired to this day. The French crusaders will take the same course. Hit them hard enough, and they will rush to our ground for the battle of the Apocalypse. When they do, followers of the Prophet from across the world will unite to bring us victory."

Uday stood speechless. He looked at each of the three men in turn, thinking, *Do they not realize what such an escalation will bring?* They looked back at him expectantly, as if waiting for affirmation of their grand scheme. All Uday could say was, "May God be with us."

Those words were instantly echoed around the room.

Baland decided to go home for lunch with his wife. He would normally have walked the entire way, but a light drizzle persuaded him to take the Métro across the river. From there he detoured to intercept his usual path. More than once he'd been reprimanded by his security minders for keeping such predictable habits. It was poor operational security, they said. Baland wished he could tell them how wrong they were.

The signal surprised him when he saw it, understandable since he'd seen it only once before. On the back side of a particular street sign near Boulevard Saint-Denis a circular sticker had been applied, the trendy logo of a surfboard manufacturer. There were a million such decorations across Paris. Part advertisement, part urban graffiti, this one had no doubt been ignored by a thousand passersby that morning. There was a fleeting moment of apprehension, and Baland slowed to take a good look at the sticker as he passed. On its circular edge, at the two o'clock position, a distinct notch had been cut out.

He kept going for another hundred yards, then took out his phone and called his wife. With a heartfelt apology, Baland said that he could not meet her for lunch after all. "Something has come up at work,"

ASSASSIN'S CODE | 151

he explained, and heard disappointment in her voice when she replied, "That's all right, darling. We'll have dinner waiting."

They exchanged a few words about the girls, and agreed to have a date soon. Baland ended the call and pocketed his phone. He pulled out his gloves, put his head down to the drizzle, and walked briskly to the bus stop at Bellini.

TWENTY-TWO

The meeting with Malika was a standing contingency, reserved for either critical situations or when all normal dead drops were thought to have been compromised. Baland didn't like either prospect, but he tried not to speculate on the reason for the summons.

They would make contact at the Palais de Chaillot, where, in June 1940, a smug Adolf Hitler had been famously photographed alongside the Reich's chief architect, Albert Speer. Baland spotted Malika on the very terrace where the Führer had gloated in victory, standing along the stone balustrade with the Eiffel Tower in the background. The plaza today was far busier than it had been then, throngs of tourists taking photographs, street merchants hawking trinkets, and a discreet police contingent roaming the perimeter. Malika had no doubt chosen the place for its highly public nature. Baland disliked it for the very same reason. No tourist would ever recognize him, but he was a relatively high-profile figure in the law-enforcement community, and in any case, there were too many cameras for his liking.

The two made eye contact when he was halfway up the stairs from the Jardins du Trocadéro, and on reaching the terrace he diverted away, implying that she should follow. He went to the entrance of France's national maritime museum, the Musée National de la Marine, and bought a ticket. Without pausing, Baland went inside and began to wander. After ten minutes he took a seat on a bench in a conspicuously unpopular room dedicated to model ships encased in glass. Malika caught up two minutes later, and together they sat in study of a scale crafting of a thirty-four-gun frigate, the work of one Jean-Alain Picard, that had likely not seen so committed a pair of admirers in all its centuries.

"I don't like this," he said straightaway. "Direct meetings are dangerous."

"You have a problem," she replied.

"Believe me when I say I have many problems."

"Not like this. A man was following you this morning."

This caught Baland off guard. He averted his eyes from Monsieur Picard's tiny mast and sails. Up close Malika was as he remembered, although each time he saw her she seemed a bit heavier. Probably the Parisian food, he thought. She was dressed in casual Western clothing, bulky and layered for the season, which only added to her thickened appearance. Her black eyes held his gaze unswervingly, some underlying anger evident as always. During their first encounters in Paris, Baland had thought this was how she regarded the world, but in time he'd come to view it as a resentment reserved for him alone.

"Following me?" he said. "Who?"

"The man who has come to Paris to kill you."

"*What*—" Baland cut himself off, realizing his voice had risen. He looked around to see if anyone had noticed. There were only two other people in the pass-through display room, a young Asian couple distracted by their cameras as they composed shots of every exhibit. "What are you talking about?" he asked in a distinctly lower tone.

Malika produced a photograph, and it took a moment for Baland to comprehend what he was looking at. He recognized his own silhouette on a sidewalk—if he wasn't mistaken, the east side of Boulevard Saint-Denis.

"When was this taken?" he asked.

"This morning." She pointed to a man sitting on a bench in the picture's background. "I think it is the Israeli. The *kidon*."

Baland's suspicion was instantly supplanted by a jolt of fear. Israel had a handful of assassins in its employ, but there was no doubt which one Malika was referring to. "Slaton?" he said in a hesitant voice. "How can you be sure?"

"He followed you to work from Avenue Pasteur. If I'm right, you are lucky to be alive. You should be more careful."

"I am not a spy, I am a policeman."

"You are what you were born to be."

He gave her a severe look. "What makes you think this is him? There are no pictures of the man. I know because you forced me to search his background—and I have the best intelligence assets in France at my disposal. According to the files, the man born as David Slaton died years ago in England."

"And you believe that? Other rumors suggest he met his end more recently in Geneva, although a body was never found."

She waited, but Baland didn't respond.

"That's what I thought," said Malika.

"What do you propose we do about it?"

"There is only one way to deal with such a person."

"You cannot be serious! The risks would be far too—"

"*You* should want him dead more than anyone!" she hissed.

Baland looked at her, and the vehemence in her argument made him understand. "No," he said pensively, the truth beginning to dawn. "Not more than anyone. It was you . . . *you* have brought him here." She averted her gaze, and he knew he was right.

"Yes," she admitted. "But you unwittingly did your part. Do you not recall the other research you performed for me last month?"

Baland thought about it. "The satellite account? The one my technicians tracked to a sailboat in the Philippines?"

"Your technicians are very good. Raqqa came up with the initial lead—they have many helpful sources across the region. Clearly in this case, their information was accurate. See how well we can all work together?"

"That was reckless, girl! Stupid and reckless!"

She looked at him anew, more critically. Baland sat rigid, his gloved hands anchored in his lap.

She said, "Given what he did to you—I'd think you would beg to pull the trigger yourself." When he didn't respond, she added, "You realize what a precarious position you are in. Slaton is here, so the situation must be dealt with, for both our sakes. If you can put him in a certain place, at a certain time—I will finish things."

"What do you propose?"

Malika had clearly given the idea some thought, and what she presented was a surprising blend of caution and practicality. "The important thing is for you to not be predictable until it is done. This man is hunting you, but we must choose his moment. Until then, you can go nowhere you are expected."

"I have to go to work—surely DGSI headquarters is secure."

"Yes, keep your appointments there. But nowhere else . . . and we should create the chance soon."

He nodded, and said, "There might be an opportunity tomorrow." He explained his idea, and she agreed that Slaton might see it as an opening.

"I will visit the place today. If I see any problems, I'll contact you. Otherwise—be ready."

Baland frowned. It seemed a rash plan, even reactionary. But Malika was right on one count—as long as this *kidon* was skulking around Paris, he would have to avoid public engagements, and certainly his family. All at a time when he was striving for normalcy. The idea of requesting a security detail from DGSI crossed his mind, but it exited just as quickly. That would require him to explain why an Israeli assassin was gunning for him, which of course was out of the question.

"All right," he said resignedly. "What other business is there?"

"The raid in Saint-Denis, the Moroccans . . . Raqqa wants to know if it was helpful."

"Yes, that was good. A step in the right direction." The flow of information with Raqqa had long been going in both directions. Baland metered out France's secrets to Malika, doing his best to minimize the damage. In return, he was given information about select ISIS assets in Europe, a means of furthering his advancement at DGSI. Now only one more rung remained on that ladder. He was silent for a time as he considered where to take the conversation. With face-to-face meetings rare, it seemed an ideal time to address the sword hanging over him.

"Where does this end?" he asked in a hushed voice.

"What do you mean?"

"*Merde!* I am not a fool, Malika! If I should become director, we both know that our relationship will become decidedly one-way. What will your handlers want then? Information to sabotage France's every operation against your Islamic State?"

"Certainly not—that would be far too obvious.

Even your internal monitors, blind as they are, would recognize the leak. The sharing must continue in both directions, exactly as we have done."

Baland stared at her. "The men in Raqqa," he said searchingly, "do they understand the leverage you have over me?"

Her face contorted into what might have been a smile, her thick cheeks bulging and lines crinkling around her eyes. "No. They have no idea."

"Do they know who I am?"

Malika shrugged. "If they do, it is not because I told them."

"I've never understood—why have you taken up with them, Malika?"

"I have my reasons."

"Religion?"

She laughed out loud. Leaning closer, she said, "Don't imagine that by eliminating me you can eliminate your problem. These men in Syria might be zealots and barbarians . . . but they are not fools. If they don't know your identity, they could probably figure it out based on the information you've given. They also might uncover our connection. There is no turning back. You can only trust that as long as you are reasonable, we will continue to be so. Our arrangement so far has been mutually beneficial. The only loser is France herself, and what do any of us care about that?"

Baland remained still.

Malika slid a cupped hand onto the bench near his hip. "Take this."

He looked down and saw a cheap phone, white

plastic with a sliding cover. He palmed the device and slid it into his pocket.

"Use it only in an emergency," she said. "It is a direct line to Raqqa. The number is loaded."

"Raqqa? Should I take this as a lack of confidence on your part with regard to hunting Slaton?"

She gave him a withering look. "It wasn't my idea. They consider you an irreplaceable asset."

"Will there be further attacks soon?"

She shrugged. "I would only be guessing. But I can tell you they are getting impatient for the information you promised. It's been over a month."

"Yes, I know. A report like that takes time to research. The department head has assured me it will be on my desk today."

"Deliver it tomorrow morning then, our number-three drop."

"In the morning? But you just told me to—"

"Take a company car if you are worried about your safety! Just make sure you get Slaton to show himself."

Baland looked at her sourly. "He already has once. Perhaps you should have targeted him with something more than a camera lens this morning."

There was a momentary impasse.

He picked up, "This is a complication of your making, and it comes at a very awkward time." Baland studied her openly. "So tell me . . . I know how you found this assassin, but how did you entice him to come here?"

Malika grinned. "That was simplicity itself. I sent him your picture."

An incredulous Baland listened as she recounted what had happened in the Philippines. He remembered the recent request from the Philippine authorities for information on the men. Baland hadn't known what to make of it at the time, but now he saw a perfect fit. "Who were they?" he asked.

"The usual ISIS cannon fodder—a bunch from Marseille whose names were given to me by the Emni. I had a free hand to assign them as I wished. There was a chance they might have done the job, eliminated Slaton themselves. As it turned out, it will be up to us."

Baland looked at her with grudging respect. She was a clever girl. Clever and vengeful. "You took chances in Grenoble," he said.

"What do you mean?"

"I saw you there, on a CCTV capture—you really should be more careful. I watched you reach into the bomber's pocket and activate the switch."

Now it was Malika who sat speechless.

"Who was he? Another of your endless supply of martyrs? Apparently this one was having second thoughts."

Malika opened her mouth, but then stanched what she was about to say. "I told him it was God's will," she replied tersely.

Baland nearly laughed. "And to kill this *kidon*? Will that too be God's will?"

Malika didn't reply. She got up, rounded Monsieur Picard's frigate, and disappeared into the next exhibit.

Baland remained on the bench for some time, thinking about what he'd learned. Events were accelerating, and soon they would reach a point where they could not be stopped. He realized the photograph was still in his hand, and without looking at it he slipped it into the inner pocket of his jacket. Right next to a new phone.

Slaton. That was a complication he had not expected. He looked all around the room, and wondered where the Israeli might be at that moment.

It was like grasping at air.

TWENTY-THREE

Slaton left his room early the next morning, and before sunrise was in the vicinity of Le Quinze with a *café américain* in his hand and a Glock 17 in his pocket. He passed in front of the restaurant only once, regarding the interior layout through its darkened glass windows. He saw a maître d' stand, a cherrywood bar, and tables that were widely spaced—an establishment where discretion was more valued than the number of guests who could be served.

After pausing briefly to review a menu posted near the door, he rounded the block completely. Slaton then moved one street south and did it all again. In an ever-expanding perimeter he noted buildings and walls and pathways, and within twenty minutes he had a mental map more relevant than anything Google could provide. Comfortable with the field of play, he set out back toward his room. He was not yet to the river when his phone trilled. Slaton saw who it was, and picked up. "Good morning, Anton."

"You need to abort this nonsense."

Slaton grinned. "You know what I've always liked

about you, Anton? You're the only person I know whose social skills are more stunted than my own."

"We are not comfortable with this plan."

"Nor am I—but you and Director Nurin have no say in the matter. He chose not to get involved."

"When you asked for weapons, I thought you might act quickly and cleanly. What you presented to Talia is madness."

"I admit," said Slaton, "it's going to take some nuance."

"Nuance? That is hardly your specialty."

"I'll make it work. Are there any changes to Baland's schedule?"

"David—"

"*Are* there any changes?"

"No. According to Talia, nothing that will affect your plans."

"Good. Tell her the timing of the message she sends is critical."

Bloch was silent for a time, and Slaton imagined him laboring to think of valid arguments. What he said in the end was, "All right, then . . . I wish you luck."

We are done!

Those three words, spoken ten minutes ago by his assistant, Anisa, had washed Uday's thoughts onto new and dangerous shores. The database project was complete.

It was Chadeh who had pushed the project over the finish line—he'd kept his word and delivered manpower, twenty individuals of varying capability who'd brought completion virtually overnight. Uday had long ago given up trying to understand the schizophrenic dictates of the Shura Council, but in this case he knew exactly why they'd prioritized the project. A new wave of attacks against France was imminent.

Uday had felt fear before—no one who'd lived in Syria in recent years had not—but this time it settled differently, a cold ballast in the pit of his stomach. The strikes he'd been briefed on yesterday, if they were half as destructive as Chadeh hoped, would kill thousands of civilians. France, likely supported by a coalition of Western powers, to include the United States, would be forced into a ground war. And when they came to eradicate what remained of the caliphate, there would be no half measures. What use were thirty thousand ISIS fighters with small arms, committed as they might be, against a modern army ten times that strength? Apocalypse indeed. The surviving ISIS strongholds would face annihilation.

Uday fought to regain his focus. Only four members of his team remained in the mosque, the rest having been sent home with the job done. In a workroom littered with empty coffee cups and overflowing ashtrays, four sets of eyes fell on Uday. They all knew what had to come next. Under the watchful eye of Anisa, Uday applied an encryption algorithm, then fed the database into the most secure, air-gapped hard drive available. He electronically destroyed the working source files, and saw to it that any temporary memory devices were incinerated in the room's tiny pot stove, the heater that kept everyone warm using the only reliable source of fuel—discarded computer printouts.

The end result could be attested to by everyone present: a complete electronic lockdown of their new database. It contained identity information on every known member of ISIS, both within the caliphate and beyond. Names, addresses, passport numbers. Phone numbers, ages, units of assignment, family ties. That done, Uday looked around and saw four weary but smiling faces.

"You have done well," he told his team, all of whom had worked through the night.

"This is something we have long needed," Anisa added. "We can reference it for unit assignments, payroll records, even notification of next of kin."

Another technician, the newest recruit and therefore the optimist of the bunch, piped in, "This could eventually form the basis for a system of medical records."

Uday nodded, and said something encouraging. His empty gaze, however, seemed to bypass them all. Only he knew the truth. The information they'd gathered would have but one use in the near term, and countless innocent souls in both France and Syria would die because of it.

He looked at Anisa, then around the room. "We have worked very hard for this. I want you all to take the rest of the day off. Enjoy our victory. It will be of enduring help to our caliphate, *inshallah*."

There was no argument. Uday said he would stay a bit longer to shut things down. Anisa was the last to leave, and as she reached the door Uday said,

"Tell the guards outside that security should be increased. This room now holds the our most precious secrets."

A visibly tired Anisa promised that she would.

Moments later Uday was alone. He turned back to his computer, and once more felt the weight inside him, deep and burdensome. With the monitor staring at him in its soulless gray hue, he addressed the keyboard and began to type.

TWENTY-FOUR

The ops briefing that morning had been on Baland's schedule for two days, and because it was entrenched deep within DGSI headquarters he had no reservations about attending. Israeli assassins might be lurking along the shoulders of the Seine or on the boulevards of Courbevoie, but there was certainly no more secure place in Paris than the fortress where he sat drinking tea at five minutes past eight.

This was not to say that Baland hadn't taken precautions since his rendezvous with Malika. He'd slept in his office last night on the surprisingly comfortable couch, something he'd done before while navigating late-night agency crises. Baland had considered telling Jacqueline to take the girls to her sister's in Rouen, but he doubted they were in danger, and the greater distance between them would only add complications. *He* was the one Slaton would be hunting. All the same, he had insisted Jacqueline drive the girls to school today.

His assistant had cleared his schedule for the day,

regrets given to his German Bundespolizei counterpart who'd been penciled in for an evening cocktail at a nearby hotel, and Baland relished the excuse to cancel an afternoon interview with a minor television station. The only outside event he did not alter: his lunch date at Le Quinze with director Claude Michelis.

So prepared, he sipped his Earl Grey and flicked through a newspaper until the director arrived—as was his custom, precisely ten minutes late. The first thing Michelis did was curl a bony finger, drawing Baland to a quiet corner of the conference room.

"Good morning, Director," said Baland.

"Good morning, Zavier. You look well, considering."

"Considering what?"

"That you slept in your office."

Baland's first thought was to wonder how Michelis had found that out. His second was to remind himself that the director was the director for a reason. "This thing in Grenoble," he said on the fly, "it's been bothering me. At least here, if I'm unable to sleep, I can do something productive."

Michelis set a fraternal hand on his shoulder. "This briefing might put us both to sleep, but I suppose it's ground that has to be covered. We weren't prepared for Grenoble, and the president himself has directed me to make radiological threats our top priority."

"A wise decision," Baland found himself saying. A middle-aged woman approached the lectern, and he turned to go back to his seat.

"I'll see you for lunch," said Michelis.

"I look forward to it."

The director was spot-on—the morning's briefings were indeed coma-inducing. Everyone first endured the department's specialist in radiological terrorism, a woman who delivered a lecture on gamma particles and shielding in a flaccid monotone. Next came a bespectacled man who championed a new organizational structure, represented in an unremitting series of Venn diagrams.

Thirty minutes in, Baland stifled a yawn and flicked through the long-awaited report that had reached his desk yesterday afternoon. He'd studied it thoroughly in his office last night, which did nothing to promote sleep. A comprehensive profile of France's vulnerabilities to terrorism, it covered electrical grids, dams, nuclear power plants, and at-risk public venues. Transportation and commerce were given an entire chapter, and Appendix B catalogued armories where conventional weapons and explosives were stored, along with conceivable security weaknesses for each site.

As individual scenarios, much of what he saw was well-trod ground. Taken collectively, however, the information in the two-hundred-page binder in his hands, which was labeled at the highest level of secrecy, was overpowering. It demonstrated profound weaknesses in France's security arrangements, and included the most current threat assessments—susceptibilities to dirty-bomb attacks had even been updated for a dozen high-profile sites. The Eiffel Tower, Versailles, Disneyland Paris—all had been freshly re-examined this week using information gleaned from

Grenoble. There were also a handful of new scenarios, including a hypothesis that a toxic-waste holding pond, located at a chemical factory upriver from Paris, could be breached and diverted into the Seine with catastrophic consequences—only a small car bomb was needed. A computer simulation of a chlorine gas attack inside the Châtelet Métro station was chilling in its body count. In sum, the report was a wake-up call, and would prove invaluable in assembling defensive measures for years to come. *And if such information ended up in the hands of the enemy?* he thought.

That would be utterly devastating.

An increasingly conflicted Baland flicked through the bound pages like a battlefield commander going through a casualty list. Having personally commissioned the study at Malika's insistence, he'd done his best to slow-roll its completion, making at least three changes to his original request. Baland had tried to buy time, hoping for some escape from his situation before the report was delivered. Now, with the document in hand, there seemed little recourse. He would have to send it on to Raqqa.

He imagined redacting select pages, or even entire chapters. That was no more than fantasy, really. Or was it? Baland checked his watch. He had two hours to work with before the delivery. Much of that would be needed to requisition a car, drive to a point near the dead-drop location, then generate a way to be alone without alarming his security detail. He could never sanitize the report in that amount of time. *But what if I only deliver part of it?* he wondered. Malika and her ISIS minders would be furious, complicating things further.

As if that was possible.

Baland decided it might work. He could deliver what they wanted, but in piecemeal fashion, a few choice sections to begin. Enough to convince them of the value of his information. But then he would take a new tack, perhaps demand money for the rest. *Yes,* he thought, *they'll understand that.* He could haggle over a price for days, even weeks. Malika would threaten him, of course, but her handlers in Raqqa would be smitten by the value of his information. They would tell her to tread carefully. In the end, Baland would earn just a little more time. Time to find an escape hatch from his fast-sinking life.

He flicked through the report, wondering which sections to extract. As a senior officer, he would never be challenged about what was going home in his leather attaché. He was leafing through idly when an addendum near the back caught his eye. It had been one of his added requests, an afterthought . . . or so he told himself. Now those thirty-odd pages struck a long-buried chord of interest. He pulled them free from the binder, then added the table of contents from the front. That would whet their appetites, he thought. A terrorist's shopping list.

The removed sections went discreetly into his attaché. Forty pages lighter, the binder was little changed in bulk or appearance. Another speaker arrived at the podium, a liaison from the interior minister's office here to advocate the synergies of interdepartmental cooperation. The very word "bureaucracy" was sourced in French, and it was alive and well in the fortress of Levallois-Perret, and so too, Baland presumed, in the other seats of power: the nearby Ministry of Defense, and the National Gendarmerie on Rue Saint-Didier. The strike in Grenoble had been a seminal moment, standing out among attacks of recent years. It had afflicted the psyche of France herself, and police agencies and counterterrorism forces were responding with predictable myopia. Everyone was sidetracked looking over their collective shoulders for another radiological strike.

Everyone except Zavier Baland, who knew that the next string of attacks, in which he was unassailably complicit, would be very different indeed.

TWENTY-FIVE

Malika made the pickup at a little-used dead-drop location, a soon-to-be-insolvent used book store whose out-of-print volumes collected more dust than customers. Behind a gap in a certain shelf she was surprised to find a thick envelope instead of a digital drive. She made one minor purchase, a yellow-edged study on Charles de Gaulle, and cursed Baland all the way back to her apartment. On arriving she slammed General de Gaulle into the trash bin and removed a sheaf of papers from the envelope.

She shuffled through and found forty pages—two extracted sections, it appeared, of a much larger dossier. Malika slapped the unbound pile onto the table. *What is he playing at now?* Not only had Baland partially fulfilled his mandate, he had done so in the most cumbersome way possible. Malika would be forced to photograph everything, page by page, then transmit the images to Raqqa. She glanced at the clock on the wall. 10:43. There was no way she could do it all now.

She had far more important things to tend to.

* * *

Uday walked hurriedly through a souk, one of the malleable marketplaces that rose each morning amid Raqqa's sandstone squares. He'd spent two hours behind his keyboard, and the heaviness that had enveloped him was gone, replaced by something new—urgency.

The scene all around him was a desperate one. Downtrodden vendors stood by their carts more out of habit than hope. Gone were the bread and spice stalls that had been here only a few years ago. The scent of fried pastries was missing for lack of any way to cook them. An old man sat listlessly on an empty crate that had probably once held chickens. Next to him, tellingly, was the one enterprise on the square that was doing a brisk business—a cart that held all manner of military uniforms. There was no common denominator—desert camo ensembles were interspersed with black special-ops vests, and even a handful of jungle-green patterns had found their way into the mix, albeit at a substantial discount. Uday thought it a perfect representation of the economics of war, displayed on one listing, donkey-driven wagon.

For all the chaos around him, he felt increasingly disengaged from his surroundings. Like the market, his mood had altered, and he was sure it would never be the same again. Dread, anxiety, a compulsion to protect. Uday didn't know the exact moment, but at some point in recent weeks his obsession with jihad had been supplanted by something far more influential. He was hopelessly in love with Sarah.

Because of it, he saw a terrible choice looming.

He paused at a flower stall, thinking it an enigma that after so many years of war people still bought and sold flowers. The stand was run by a smiling teenage girl, and without considering what bombed-out garden they might have come from, Uday pointed to a bouquet that caught his eye. The girl happily pulled the bunch free, and he watched her pluck a few dead leaves from the arrangement.

Uday found himself watching her, and noticed that she occasionally glanced up at the sky. This was a relatively new phenomenon, albeit one with little practical value—the drones were virtually invisible, and fighter-bombers rarely heard or seen before their loads struck home. Even so, like small animals who'd seen too many of their brethren taken by hawks, the survivors invariably found their eyes drawn skyward.

She handed over the bouquet of yellow and red blooms. Uday had no idea what they were. He had never been a man bent to passion, and held little enthusiasm for long walks or lingering dinners. The only time anyone had ever put his name and the word "inspired" in the same sentence, it had involved a coding algorithm. Still, in recent weeks he'd begun to see things in a new light—one whose spectrum at the moment involved yellow and red.

He reached into his pocket for money, but recoiled as if by electric shock when he realized he'd dipped into the wrong one. Uday switched to the other side and retrieved a U.S. twenty-dollar bill—the caliph-ate's fantasy of its own currency had never gained traction. He handed it to the smiling girl behind the cart and didn't wait for his change.

He elbowed through the crowds, trying not to crush the flowers, and on turning the final corner Uday saw his building in the distance. Sarah was on the front steps, using a broom to beat a small rug. Last week he might have felt relief at the sight of her. Today it brought only apprehension. She didn't notice him right away, and he paused to watch her in her chore. Even fully covered, she was the most beautiful thing he had ever seen.

Soon they were inside together, and he presented the flowers. Sarah lifted her *niqab* and he saw a beaming smile. Uday exchanged the flowers for an enthusiastic kiss, and he watched her fill an old plastic bottle with water and begin to insert the flowers. She placed them one by one, delicately and with an occasional turn. When she looked at him again Uday forced a smile, but one that left the rest of his face untouched.

"What is wrong?" she asked, walking over and taking his hand. She was beginning to sense his moods.

He collapsed onto their old couch and she sat down beside him.

"Things are happening so quickly," he said.

Her hands went to his shoulders, and she began squeezing knotted muscles. He felt the tension drain away. "When I first became involved with the movement it seemed virtuous, a struggle that would affirm my beliefs. I thought I could use my expertise to help the caliphate grow, to help common people return to the ways of the Prophet. But now . . ." His words trailed off. "Now I see these leaders for what they are—common men who contort Islam for their own selfish interests. They order others to sacrifice while they bicker about who gets the best villas and vehicles, who deserves the most protection. I hear whisperings that some are even hiding money, saving for the day when everyone must disappear. But the most troubling thing of all"—he turned to look at her—"is that I am in love with my Christian slave. It is strictly forbidden, yet how can what I feel for you be wrong?"

"It's not wrong, Aziz. No more than what I feel for you."

"Our leaders demand strict interpretation of Sharia law. I use my skills to upload videos of beheadings and crucifixions. I can't remember the last time we discussed giving food to the poor, or putting old women in houses. We once did those things. The misery our movement has caused, most of it imparted upon fellow Muslims—I don't see how it can be right."

He looked at her as if searching for answers.

"If you are expecting me to denounce them, to tell you how much I hate the Daesh—I won't do it. They killed my father and brother, and my poor mother suffers. But I forgive them, Aziz. That is how I keep my own faith, and without it I am nothing."

"So you would never rise against them?"

She looked at him questioningly. "If you are asking whether I could raise a hand to harm them— no, not even the caliph himself. But I would sacrifice anything to end the suffering."

"Suffering," he said. "There will soon be much more of that."

"What do you mean?"

He sighed. "I learned yesterday that new strikes are being planned against France. The council are blind—they tell one another that God is on our side, and scheme to lash out at the West like children throwing stones at a pack of wild dogs. Sooner or later, the dogs will turn. But these new attacks—I think there might be a way to stop them."

She looked at him with a confluence of emotions he couldn't read. Pride? Fear? She took his hand, and said, "The choices you make are between you and God, Aziz. No one else can tell you what to do."

"Actually," he said, reaching into his pocket for what would save them, "I have already made my decision. But I had to hear yours. . . ."

Claude Michelis was leaving his final meeting of the day when his phone vibrated with a message. It was from Zavier Baland.

Running late. Can we make lunch 1:30 instead of 1:00?

Michelis sent a reply to say that was fine, and got an immediate response.

Thanks, Chief. I'll call Henri and have him hold our table.

The director sighed and looked at his watch. It was twelve thirty. He hoped it didn't go any later. He was getting hungry.

Michelis' reply did not, in fact, ever reach Baland. For reasons he would never understand, his message terminated in a luxury condominium in Tel Aviv.

Zavier Baland was equally unaware of the hijacked thread. He, however, would realize something had gone very wrong within sixty seconds of arriving at Le Quinze.

TWENTY-SIX

Le Quinze was bustling on the lunch rush, and Baland found the ever-solicitous Henri presiding behind his maître d's podium.

"Good afternoon, Monsieur Baland. Your table is waiting and your guest has already arrived."

"Thank you."

Baland followed Henri through a maze of partitions that was clearly designed to enhance privacy—the reason, along with the food, that the restaurant had risen in popularity with actors, statesmen, and, perhaps most tellingly, a recent influx of wealthy Russian mobsters.

Turning the final corner, Baland was surprised to see someone other than Michelis at his usual white-linened corner table. "I'm sorry," he said, leaning toward Henri, "but I was expecting Director Michelis."

Henri half turned and gave Baland the same look he might have if he'd just been told Bastille Day had been canceled. "But monsieur, I was told very distinctly that—"

"It's all right," interrupted the man at the table in English. "Monsieur Baland doesn't recognize me, but we are in fact old acquaintances."

Baland locked eyes with the man, whose hands were out of sight under the table, and saw a slight nod toward the opposing chair. "Yes," he said hesitantly, keeping with English, "it's all right, Henri."

A relieved Henri disappeared, and Baland settled cautiously into the chair and took stock of the man across from him. He appeared rather tall, and wore a casual jacket and collared shirt. He looked fit and tan, and a pair of unusual gray eyes were keenly active.

"Do you know who I am?" the man asked.

"I have no idea," Baland lied. The photograph Malika had given him was still in his pocket.

"Really? Either way, I'll have to ask you to keep your hands where I can see them."

"Will you not extend me the same courtesy?"

Surprisingly, the assassin did, his hands appearing on the white tablecloth. His eyes drilled Baland, and he nodded as if some great internal question had been answered. "How did you do it?" the man finally asked.

"Do what?" replied Baland.

"Escape Gaza. Settle unnoticed in France."

"I don't know what you are talking about. If—"

"Please, Ali. Let's not waste time."

Baland played his next facial expression with the greatest of care. Gradual understanding, as if old points of fact were connecting. "All right. You have made a mistake, but I think an understandable one."

"Which is?"

"I won't explain without knowing who I am dealing with."

"You're dealing with someone who will gladly kill you for one wrong answer."

Malika preferred rooftops for many reasons. Elevation was always an advantage, particularly in urban areas, where steep angles removed traffic and pedestrians from lines of fire. It also allowed a raptor's view of the surrounding streets and buildings, giving maximum awareness of possible threats and escapes. Today, unfortunately, the rooftop was not her friend.

Her mistake had been arriving late, shortly after noon. She'd wasted too much time in her flat dealing with Baland's partial dossier. She had tried taking photographs of the pages using a proper camera, but had trouble getting acceptable images without a flash. She'd reverted to her phone with mixed results. The test image she'd launched to Raqqa had come back unsent, and for twenty minutes Malika fussed with the phone's settings and resolution controls before successfully transferring a page. Then she had looked at the clock.

She'd arrived at Le Quinze in a rush, but then spent twenty minutes maneuvering onto the roof without being seen. There she'd assembled her weapon of choice, a Remington CSR sniper rifle. Also contained in her three-foot-long cardboard box, the label of which suggested a lighting fixture, was an H&K UMP, a compact semiautomatic in case close work became necessary.

Once in place, Malika had immediately begun watching the entrance of Le Quinze. She would normally have taken time to study the surrounding area. Just as with the rubble warrens of Mosul and Ramadi, angles should have been figured and escape routes mapped. The weather was taking a noticeable turn for the worse—heavy skies held the promise of rain, and the midday light seemed more akin to dusk. The wind was picking up as well, and she wished she'd been able to make estimates of where gusts accelerated between buildings and where eddies seemed to fall.

There hadn't been time for any of that.

Baland's car had arrived right on schedule, at one o'clock, and in those critical moments Malika's watchfulness had gone into overdrive. She'd held her breath as he crossed twenty feet of open ground to reach the restaurant's door, her weapon searching, her finger poised. She was positioned classically as a countersniper—high above the presumed target and looking outward for an assassin. With Baland acting as bait, she had scanned every window across the street, stepped her eyes to each car parked along the curb. Malika waited for the Israeli to appear, confident that if he did, she would see something. A glint, a muzzle flash, even the telltale barrel.

It had now been five minutes since Baland passed through the door. Still nothing had happened. Had she been wrong about Slaton coming here? Might he be nearby, waiting for Baland to come back outside? She decided the answer to both questions was no. He was here, somewhere. But he had found another way.

Which meant the rooftop was a mistake. It was entirely the wrong place to be.

Baland did not flinch, but neither did the man across the table. The gunmetal-gray eyes seemed almost aqueous, enveloping the entire room at once. Baland too was taking in as much as he could. His back was not quite squared to the entrance, and in the periphery, over his right shoulder, he could see people coming and going.

He narrowed his gaze, and said, "I think you might be Israeli—is that it?"

No answer.

Baland produced a slight smile. "Since you called me Ali just now, I know who you *think* I am—Ali Samir. And so you are wondering how a terrorist hunted down by Israel, many years ago now, has been reborn as a senior officer at DGSI." He shifted slightly in his seat to have a better view to his right, never taking his eyes off Slaton. "A searching mind might even imagine that you were the hunter on that fateful day."

Finally a reaction, the eyes regarding him with something distant. *Perhaps a remembrance of my face through a telescopic sight?* he wondered.

"I'll neither confirm nor deny that."

Baland nodded. "Of course. Any other answer would have given me doubt. So I know who you are. Therefore, I will return the favor. I am not Ali Samir," he said, adding a pause to give emphasis to his next words. "I am his identical twin brother."

TWENTY-SEVEN

Slaton's attention faltered on the critical word. *Twin*.

Of all the possibilities, this was one he'd never considered. It did, however, answer the most vexing question: How could a man he killed fifteen years ago still be alive? Unfortunately, Baland's solution, in equal measure bewildering and elegant, sent a tide of new questions streaming into his head.

"Identical twin?" Slaton repeated. "How did you end up here?"

Baland's reply seemed measured. "It was really quite simple, although over the years I have often asked myself that same question. My brother and I were born in Gaza. My mother was Algerian, but had family in France. Gaza was as difficult a place then as it is today. When my mother learned she was pregnant, she told my father she didn't want to raise a family there. He eventually agreed, and they began legal maneuvers to emigrate, applying for French citizenship. The process went favorably, and approval seemed imminent. As they prepared to leave, an unexpected complication arose. Keep in mind—at that time in Gaza there was no such thing as prenatal ultrasounds. I've been told my mother never even saw an obstetrician."

"No one was expecting twins."

"Precisely. When my brother and I were born early, as often happens with multiple births, the problems began. It required alterations to the emigration process. Paperwork had to be rerun, and that took time."

The waiter interrupted to take their drink orders. Baland ordered sparkling water, Slaton coffee. As soon as he was gone, Slaton asked, "When was this?"

Baland's gaze drifted over the room. "I was born in 1977."

"Gaza was still under Israeli military authority."

"Yes. The situation in the Sinai would soon be settled by the Egypt-Israel Peace Treaty, but Gaza was left as ever—a loosely administered territory. When the emigration paperwork finally came through there were mistakes. Approval was granted to leave, but only one child was included. With those papers in hand, my parents decided to send me ahead to France while they sorted through the rest—my aunt, a French citizen, came and took me to Lyon. Two weeks later everything changed. The Israelis undertook a mission against what they called a terrorist stronghold. An errant rocket struck my parents' bedroom. They were both killed instantly." Baland paused. "Errant," he repeated. "That was the word used in the official press release."

"And your brother?"

"He was in a different room and survived the explosion unscathed. Ali was taken in by my father's side of the family. After that . . ." Baland hesitated. "Honestly, you probably know more about him than I do. As far as I know, no serious attempt was ever made to reunite the two of us, in either France or Gaza. There were a few letters back and forth, an occasional phone call. But in the end, everyone simply carried on with what was. Days became weeks, and weeks became a lifetime. I suppose you could say I sit before you today as a product of that never-ending conflict. A victim of fate, as they say."

"Or perhaps a beneficiary."

Baland nodded reflectively. "I have always wondered why I was the one sent ahead. Every day I think about how different things might have been."

"So you've been in France your entire life?"

"Since I was eight weeks old. After my parents were killed, when it was clear I wouldn't go back, my aunt filed paperwork for my citizenship. She decided it would be simpler to claim me as her own child. No questions were raised, and from that point I became a Frenchman in every way. Aside from being the product of parents I never knew, it was all quite legitimate."

Slaton leaned back in his chair to consider Baland's story. It was like something from a classic novel. Twin sons divided at birth into diametrically opposed circumstances. And how different their outcomes had been. All the same, there was more to be explained. "In the last few days I've researched your background. Your rise through the ranks has been remarkable, and you have a curious ability to envision the enemy's next move. It's almost as if you have some kind of . . . how should I say it . . . insider information?"

Baland was about to reply when his face went ashen. His eyes pinned on something to his right.

"What is it?" Slaton asked.

Baland stuttered, then said, "There is a woman, over my right shoulder—" It was the last word he got out before the shooting began.

Slaton spotted her right away. Four tables away, moving quickly—a thick-set young woman in a brown parka. She had a machine pistol, possibly a UMP, tucked tight against her ribs. It was rising in their direction.

Slaton's Glock was available beneath the table—he'd had no idea what to expect from Baland—but he would be dead before he could get it clear and raised into a firing position. He dove to his right as shots came in a fusillade, rounds thundering in as he crashed into an empty table. Slaton reached up and pulled the heavy table over for cover.

The room around him went to madness: sprawling patrons, the clatter of china and silverware hitting the floor. He arced his gun in the direction of the threat, but before he could get a bead, another string of rounds laced into the wall just over his head. Slaton curled his hand around the table, and sprayed fire in the general direction of the woman, keeping his aim high to avert unintended casualties.

The UMP was on full automatic now. Splinters flew from the table in front of him, plaster from the wall behind. Frozen in place, and with the assailant closing in, Slaton prepared to make his stand. He would have one second, maybe less, to acquire the woman and put her down. He set his legs, and was one heartbeat from moving when the report of a third weapon intervened. To his right he saw Baland returning fire from a crouched position.

Then, as quickly as it had all begun, the assault paused. Slaton leapt up, the Glock's barrel searching. There was no sign of the woman, but he saw a splatter of blood on the fabric-covered wall she'd been near. He scanned for other threats, his eyes and barrel sweeping in unison like a radar. He saw nothing to raise an alarm. Then he noticed Baland. The DGSI man had lowered his gun and was staring at Slaton. Which made no tactical sense whatsoever.

Two more shots rang out, muted and distant. The woman's gun, but outside now. In a room paralyzed by fear, Slaton was the first to move. He scrambled to his feet and rushed for the back door. He hit the alley behind the restaurant and immediately turned right—he already knew a left turn would lead to a dead end.

He pocketed his gun at the top of the alley, never slowing as he rounded the corner onto Rue de Clichy. There were no telltale disturbances—no blood on the sidewalk, no shocked passersby looking over their shoulders or backed against walls. Slaton sprinted onward.

He saw his objective fifty meters away: the Place de Clichy Métro station. He flew under the ornate wrought-iron entrance and quick-stepped down the stairs, his eyes reaching ahead. At the mezzanine level he rounded a bastion and arrived at the ticket stile. The crowds were modest, and he used an already-purchased day pass to sail through. Arrows on the wall indicated a split—one platform for the east-west number 2 line, another for the north-south 13. He could see a portion of the eastbound platform, but couldn't tell if a train was present.

A mother hurried past, a young boy following.

There was no time for contemplation. He turned toward the eastbound platform and found a train waiting. By the time he reached the first car the platform was empty. Everyone had boarded and departure was imminent. He didn't see the shooter. Had she already gotten on? It was no more than pure conjecture. A matter of instincts and odds. The door of the car in front of him began to close. Slaton jammed his shoulder in the gap and pushed aboard.

His lungs were heaving, and as the train pulled away his eyes stepped over each rider in the car—sorting faces and body types, whatever was in view. None were the assailant. He never bothered to reference the map near the car's ceiling—the next station was Rome, then Villiers. Slaton had three stops beyond that committed to memory. The car accelerated. The Rome station would appear through the windows in three and a half minutes. He leaned back against a partition and caught his breath, wondering if he'd guessed right.

It was the quickest and most anonymous way to get clear of Le Quinze. Slaton knew because he himself had already run that decision matrix. Cabs, buses, moving on foot—all had drawbacks. He eyed the door that led to the forward cars, but decided against moving. There were too many people here, too much that could go wrong. The safe play was to monitor the platforms at successive stops. If she was on the train, she wouldn't stay for long. Two stops, three at the most. The police weren't fools—they would make the same assumptions he had. They would send alerts to down-line stations, review CCTV footage.

Slaton, however, had a head start on the police. If she was here, he would find her. And if he found her he would get answers. Most prominent: Who else wanted Zavier Baland dead? He edged toward the door and waited for the train to slow. He was beginning to catch his breath.

It would be an hour before Slaton discovered the rest of what had happened. Before he learned what he would have encountered had he gone out the front door of Le Quinze: DGSI director Claude Michelis splayed on the gray sidewalk, his lifeless eyes staring up at a snow-heavy sky.

TWENTY-EIGHT

Malika lurched into her flat cursing under her breath. She dropped her gun on the kitchen table and went straight to the bathroom. In front of the mirror she gingerly pulled her right arm through the sleeve of her coat. Blood covered the shirtsleeve underneath, and she removed that next. It was a new adventure in pain.

"Bastard!" she muttered. *What was Baland thinking?*

She'd never been seriously injured in any operation. Malika had stepped on nails in a warehouse along the Euphrates, and fallen through a rotted roof in Haditha. She'd a spent nearly a year in the worst killing fields on earth and come through virtually unscathed. *Only to be shot in a Michelin Star restaurant in Paris!*

Her shock kept spiraling, the physical and psychological trauma combining into something greater than their sum. The hand of her injured arm trembled, and two fingers had gone numb. Would that pass when the swelling receded? Or was it a handicap she would have to deal with for the rest of her life? She tried to raise her arm to the light for a better look, and a bolt of lightning seemed to strike her shoulder.

She slapped her good hand on the tiled wall.

For twenty minutes she did her best to clean the wound at the sink. Eventually, she could make out the bullet's path—not a clean entry and exit wound, but a ragged tear in the flesh at the top of her outer arm. She tried to take solace that the bullet hadn't struck anything vital, no bones shattered or arteries clipped. She at least wished it had been the other man who'd gotten the better of her, a trained assassin. That she might have expected. But it *had* been Baland—she'd seen it with her own eyes.

It seemed a blur at the time, but now she tried to replay the engagement. She had gotten off a full magazine, that much she knew. Had any of her rounds hit the Israeli? He'd lunged for cover at the outset, but appeared uninjured when she got a clean look at him half hidden behind an overturned table. Then, amazingly, in the moment when she was settling her sight and pulling the trigger, Baland had opened up on *her*. She'd been hit by his first shot, and it sent her reeling, altering the odds instantly. There had been no choice but to run.

She turned on her phone long enough to check for messages. There was nothing from Baland. She sure as hell was going to leave one. They'd agreed he would carry a gun, which was normal for a counterterrorism officer. They had guessed correctly that Slaton would make his attempt at Le Quinze, although being seated at Baland's table was hardly the stealthy approach they'd expected. The plan had been for Malika to take Slaton first, then Michelis if possible. Somewhere in the melee, Baland was to have sent a few poorly aimed shots in her direction.

Their fluid plan had disintegrated quickly. Malika realized that Slaton was inside the restaurant, and Michelis, her secondary target, had not yet arrived. She'd done her best, but the *kidon* spotted her seconds too soon and found cover. How had it all gone so wrong? Thankfully, there had been one stroke of luck at the end—she'd nearly run over Michelis on the sidewalk outside the restaurant. Two quick taps on the trigger, and utter failure gave way to half a victory.

She began to think more positively. Things had gone wildly afield, but Michelis was dead and she had not been captured. Or worse. She turned her phone back off, then went to the room's only window and fingered aside the curtain. She saw nothing suspicious on the street below. Of course there was only one option: She had to keep out of sight and let the coming storm pass. She had just gunned down the director of DGSI and, as far as the French knew, also tried to kill his heir apparent.

Malika had done her best to avoid cameras on her approach to Le Quinze, but these days it was impossible to spot them all. The one-bedroom flat she'd booked the usual way, through a vacation-rental website—false name used and payment wired in advance, no face-to-face contact whatsoever. She ventured outside only when necessary, and typically on the back side of the clock, hoping to avoid encounters with neighbors. As far as she knew, she'd succeeded. Altogether, Malika decided there was no safer place than where she stood right now. She had enough food for a week, two if she went on a diet. The biggest complication—Slaton had escaped.

She went to her suitcase, retrieved gauze and surgical tape—at least she'd had that much foresight—and did her best to bandage the wound. She was able to stop the bleeding, but it hurt like hell.

Once again, her thoughts drifted to the man the world knew as Zavier Baland. He would be at headquarters by now, overseeing the search for an unknown female assailant.

"Idiot!"

With nothing to do but wait, Malika went to a drawer in the kitchenette and retrieved the papers Baland had left at the dead drop that morning. He'd even managed to screw that up, offering only a fraction of what he should have delivered. She was slack-jawed by his audacity, and at first suspected he was angling for money. Now, however, Malika wondered if there might be something more.

She sat at the table gingerly, and her foul mood began to dissipate. She'd spent an hour this morning trying to transfer Baland's information. Now, with more time, she studied the pages in detail. What she saw was a list of prospective targets—and not just any list. It was a detailed itemization of Jewish interests in France—synagogues, community centers, businesses—and the vulnerabilities of each to attack.

Chadeh and his bunch would be tantalized, which

was certainly Baland's intent. Yet she suspected the isolation of Jewish targets would be lost on the leaders of ISIS. They hated the Jews, to be sure, but no more than they hated the world's Christians or Buddhists. Probably less than the apostate Shi'a of Persia. So what then was Baland's game?

Malika set the papers down, then got up and wandered back to the window. She once again pulled back the curtain, and very carefully looked up and down the street.

Slaton saw little more than a silhouette, and it disappeared after only a few seconds. It was all he needed. He had successfully tracked the woman from Le Quinze.

He'd caught a glimpse of her getting off the train at the third stop, Monceau. He had recognized the bulky coat she should have gotten rid of, and even understood why she still wore it—to conceal the UMP underneath. Definitely not a pro. She walked too quickly once she got outside, and he saw by her gait that she was injured. He'd followed her two blocks from the station, and watched her enter the building now before him.

Slaton had checked his watch the instant she'd gone inside. After ninety-eight seconds, a light snapped on in a third-floor window. Ten seconds more than he would have estimated for the third floor, but well within tolerances. And probably further confirmation that she was injured. Since then, he'd twice seen her pull back the curtain to peer out at a gray afternoon. That was another mistake, although Slaton didn't dwell on it. Amateur or not, she was committed. That counted for a great deal.

In a shadowed alcove he switched to a full mag on his Glock, then walked far enough away to be out of sight from the flat's lone window. The neighborhood was residential, and on midafternoon there were only a few other people in sight. Slaton crossed the street and fell in behind a middle-aged woman carrying a shopping bag. As she neared the entrance, he hoped she would turn inside, but she passed the portico without slowing. Seconds later he saw that it didn't matter—the gate giving access to the stairwell was chained open.

He climbed quickly to the third floor, the Glock in hand. There was no one else in the narrow corridor, and he approached the only door that correlated to the geometry he'd seen from the street. Number 14. Slaton backed to the wall next to the door and listened. He heard a few noises from within: a chair scraping across a wooden floor, uneven footsteps. Then a stifled cough, female and husky. Definitely the right flat.

He studied the door: two and a half meters tall, one wide, probably solid-core, with a lock that looked reasonably stout and a frame of average strength. Because it was Paris, there was likely at least one secondary lock on the inside. Altogether, an arrangement that might give way to one well-placed kick. Or one that could take five or even ten. Under some circumstances, not a problem. Very problematic, however, when one was engaging a machine pistol with a handgun.

Slaton considered the window in front. She checked it regularly. If he had the Covert in hand, he could set up shop across the street and finish things cleanly. As it was, it would take at least an hour to retrieve the rifle from across town and get in position. Where might she go in the meantime? A hospital, perhaps, if her injuries were life-threatening. She could leave to seek help from a friend, or even make a rash attempt to depart Paris. No, Slaton decided, he had her cornered now. He couldn't lose that advantage.

As he stood with his back against the thin wall that separated him from a killer, the woman's face was replaced by two others: out of nowhere he thought of Christine and Davy. Slaton closed his eyes. *What the hell am I doing here? This is not my battle.* In the silence of the hallway, his thoughts seemed to recalibrate, like a slate wiped clean. A new option came to mind—a plan more strategic than tactical in nature.

He moved silently to the stairs and stepped quickly down. He crossed the street once more, and took up a vantage point in the recessed entrance of a nameless rooming house. He pulled out his phone and placed a call.

Talia answered right away. "I saw what happened in Paris, David. Are you all right?"

"I'm fine." Before she could get out another word, he said, "I need to talk to Anton right away."

Sixty seconds later Bloch was conferenced in on the call. Judging from the amount of static, Slaton guessed they were at different locations. He said, "Are you following what happened in Paris thirty minutes ago?"

"Yes," replied Bloch, "in a general way."

"Good. I want you to send two *katsas* from the embassy right away." Slaton gave the Monceau address.

"David, nothing has changed. Whatever is occurring there, Mossad cannot be part of—"

"Everything has changed! Tell the director I've tracked down the assailant responsible for this latest attack. I'm standing outside her safe house as we speak."

"What are your intentions?" Bloch asked guardedly.

"Not what they were five minutes ago. You, Nurin, and I need to talk. When he hears what I have to say, he *will* want to get involved."

Bloch went silent.

"Anton, at the very least I've got a known terrorist cornered. It's a street address that would be worth a lot to the French right now. Nurin will understand the value of that—just as you would have when you were in charge. All I'm asking for is a surveillance team to take over the watch."

"All right, I'll see what I can do."

"I'll be in touch after the surveillance team arrives."

Bloch began to ask something else. Slaton ended the call.

* * *

Media outlets swarmed over the scene at Le Quinze. The latest battlefield in France's undeclared war was quickly cordoned off, but distant video shots of the shattered dining area, bathed in rolling flashes of blue light, dominated television and smartphone screens across Europe.

Within the hour, the French minister of the interior, Jacques Roland, delivered an unprepared and emotional statement from a sidewalk near the on-site command center. In terse words he confirmed that DGSI director Claude Michelis had been gunned down in broad daylight, an obvious assassination. Another senior officer of the agency, the much-decorated Zavier Baland, had helped beat back the attack by returning fire and, according to several eye-witnesses, wounding the assailant.

Roland went on to vow that the cowardly attack would only backfire in the end. He assured the world that DGSI would spare no effort in finding the perpetrator, and hinted obliquely that France would be compelled to orchestrate strikes against any terrorist organization held responsible, and in the usual disproportionate manner. The death of the much-respected director would not go unanswered.

When Roland backed away from the microphone, the loudest question shouted was, "Who will take the place of Director Michelis?"

To that the minister looked into the sea of lights and cameras, and mouthed a one-word answer. *Tomorrow.*

TWENTY-NINE

The Mossad team from the embassy, a man and a woman, arrived thirty minutes later. Her name was Neumann, his Feld, and Slaton led them to a bicycle rack around the corner from the building in question.

There the *katsas* arranged themselves not in a triangle with Slaton, but three abreast on the sidewalk. It was a nuance that an untrained would never have noticed, but to Slaton spoke volumes. They had put him on the right, and Feld on the opposite side. If anything went wrong, Slaton had a 270-degree field of fire. Feld held down the same on the opposite side, and their arcs intersected for complete coverage. It had nothing to do with anyone's marksmanship, nor who was in charge, but was simply a practical intersection of geometry and common sense. The kind of precaution that cost nothing, and once in a career might save someone's life.

"There hasn't been any change since I got here," Slaton said. From where they stood all three could see the face of the building in question. Slaton pointed out the particular third-floor window. He otherwise didn't tell them how to do their job. After some deliberation, he gave them the number he'd been using to contact Talia and Bloch. "If something comes up, don't call the embassy and don't call me—only this number."

"All right," said Neumann, who was acting as spokesperson. "Can you tell us who we're watching?"

"I don't have a name. It's a woman, and as far as I know she's alone. The good news is, I don't think she's going anywhere."

"The bad news?"

"She's dangerous, definitely armed, and wounded."

The two Mossad officers exchanged a glance.

"I think you can expect an all-nighter," Slaton added.

Without comment, Feld walked around the corner and disappeared. Neumann smiled amiably for the sake of anyone who might be watching, and said, "Don't know who you are, but you really screwed up my plans tonight."

"Sorry. But believe me when I say, I've been there."

"I'm guessing you have."

They talked for another minute, Slaton describing the inside of the building, as far as he knew it, and taking a few more happy barbs. Then Neumann leaned in and kissed him, first on one cheek, then the other—a French custom virtually mandatory for two friends parting on a residential street in the eighth arrondissement. She walked away jauntily and disappeared around the corner. Slaton went the other way.

He was half a block away when he turned back and looked over the scene. From where he stood neither *katsa* was in sight. His attention was drawn to another building, the one directly across the street from where their suspect was holed up. On appearances that block of apartments was a virtual mirror image of the one they were watching. His eyes held each window from the second floor up, and casually roamed the roofline. He studied angles and lines of sight from a number of those points to the window presently under surveillance. It hadn't come to that—not yet—but he always liked to be prepared. After a minute, he still saw no sign of the two Mossad officers.

Slaton turned away and set out for his room in Courbevoie.

Slaton considered moving to a different hotel, but with no reason to believe his location had been compromised, he decided that the risks in moving—to include carrying a sniper rifle in a roller bag over Paris streets that were teeming with police—far outweighed any benefits.

From his rented bed he turned on the television and followed the coverage of the latest attack. A massive search for a lone female assailant had so far turned up nothing. Slaton happily saw no indication that he was being sought for questioning—he *had* been sitting next to Baland, who according to news reports was one of the assassin's two presumptive targets. The other, of course, was DGSI director Michelis, who'd been shot dead outside the restaurant.

Here Slaton saw further warning flags.

He replayed everything in his mind. Baland's incredible admission of being Ali Samir's twin, then his cool reaction to the attack. Moments before the woman appeared, Slaton remembered suggesting to Baland that his foresight in intelligence matters had verged on prophecy, implying rather obviously that he had a source. Baland had been considering a reply to that very question when he'd astutely picked out the shooter.

Slaton tapped a finger thoughtfully on the remote control in his hand. Finally, he pressed the mute button, turned on his phone, and placed the expected call to Tel Aviv. Talia answered on the first ring.

"Is the surveillance team in place?" she asked.

"Yes, they're in position. Convey my thanks to the director for making that happen."

Another three-way conference began when Bloch said, "Nurin allowed that much, but he is not happy with the risks you are taking."

"Neither am I. When he finds out what I learned, though, I suspect he'll run a new cost-benefit analysis." Slaton covered his entire meeting with Baland, all the way to its inglorious end.

Bloch's first remark was predictable. "Ali Samir had an identical twin?"

"It answers a lot of questions."

"It also means Baland is not the traitor we thought."

"Quite possibly—which makes me glad I didn't shoot first and ask questions later."

"What was your impression of him?"

"Initially he seemed surprised to see me, but once

he realized who I was he didn't seem overly concerned. It was almost as if he was expecting me."

"Am I to take that as an accusation against Mossad?" said Bloch. "I can assure you, David, no one but the director, Talia, and me, knew of your plans."

"No, that's not what I'm suggesting. Talia, have there been any changes to his schedule in the last twenty-four hours?"

"Yes," she said. "I've been watching closely. Baland canceled three appointments today. The only one he kept outside the DGSI building was Le Quinze. It seems fortuitous, does it not?"

"Very much so. And I see other curiosities."

"Such as?" Bloch queried.

"So far I'm not being mentioned in the news reports of this attack. Baland knows who I am. Does it make sense that I show up for lunch, threaten him, and when all hell breaks loose he doesn't even try to bring me in for questioning?"

"A valid point," said Bloch. "What purpose could he have for keeping you in the shadows?"

"I don't know. It's not a stretch to say that Baland might have saved not only his own life, but mine as well. He spotted the attacker before I did, then wounded her before I could get off an accurate shot."

Silence ran until Bloch said, "I will try to convince Nurin to look into this. If Samir did have a twin, as Baland says, then perhaps we can verify it."

"How? You won't find hospital records for that era in Gaza. Chances are, he was delivered by a midwife in his mother's bedroom."

"True. But there might be other ways."

"All right, do what you can."

"What will you do now?" Talia asked.

"I think Baland and I should pick up our conversation where it left off."

"How could you get near him? He'll have an armada of security."

"I'm guessing he'd be willing to meet me again—it's just a matter of arranging it with discretion."

"Any ideas?"

"I'll think of something on the fly."

"All right," said Bloch, "but remember—"

"I know," Slaton cut in, "keep Mossad out of it."

Talia filled the ensuing silence. "There's one other thing we should consider."

"What's that?" Slaton asked.

"Director Michelis has been killed, and Baland is being credited with beating back the attack and wounding the assailant. Very soon, France will have to name a new leader of its counterterrorism force. I think we can safely say who it's going to be."

THIRTY

As both a participant in the recent mayhem and the overseer of the investigation into it, Baland knew the remainder of his day would be spent recounting his story. The first in line to hear it, no surprise, was Minister of the Interior Roland, who had abruptly ended a tête-à-tête with his British counterpart in response to the crisis. They met in Roland's office.

"This is a terrible turn of events," said a clearly shaken Roland. "Claude was a fine man."

"I thought very highly of him," Baland agreed.

"I don't have to tell you, finding this attacker is our top priority. I've been told we've uncovered only one marginal clip from a camera in the Métro. Apparently her head was turned down at the critical moment. There's been considerable internal speculation that this could be the same woman responsible for the bombing in Grenoble."

"I've seen the clip," said Baland. "The quality of the footage isn't good in either case. It's a neat and tidy concept, but in my mind no more than wishful thinking."

"I suppose you're right. Even so, I want your directorate to pursue every angle."

Baland gave the minister a curious look. "You want *my*—"

Roland held up a hand. "Please, Zavier, don't be coy." He got up from his chair and lit a cigarette. Smoking was officially off-limits inside the headquarters building, but no one was going to challenge the minister in his own office. He moved tentatively behind his desk, and said, "Claude came to me only last week—in effect, he handed in his notice."

Baland tried to look surprised, but in truth he'd sensed it for months—a weariness in Michelis, the vacant look in his eyes during staff meetings and the doodling in the margins of signed procurement requests. Perhaps it was the hopelessness of what he was being asked to do. "I hope you told him to reconsider," he said, only realizing afterward how silly it sounded.

"Now . . . I wish I had. But honestly, I didn't try to change his mind. I've felt for some time that DGSI is in need of new vigor, someone with fresh ideas. He put your name in for the job, Zavier. I'll have to run it by the president, who isn't bound by my recommendation, but there's no one better. I think he'll agree."

"I'm honored," said Baland. And he truly was.

"You can't tell me you haven't seen this coming. Aside from your stellar operational record . . . well, I can only be direct . . . you are a Frenchman with Algerian blood. You can mend fences in ways we've never had. I need that. France needs that. These troubles in the Arab world, thousands of miles away, are metastasizing into our society. We've got to put a stop to it, and you are uniquely qualified to take us in that direction. I assume you would accept the position if offered?"

"It would be my duty as a Frenchman."

Roland smiled. "Very well. I will convey the word internally that you are today the interim chief of DGSI. It will take a few days to make things official. We should put together the usual change-of-command ceremony—I think Claude's was on the terrace fronting the Place de la Concorde."

Baland could only nod through his distraction.

Roland asked a few questions about the Le Quinze tragedy, and Baland might have answered them. Then, with a resolute grin, Roland ordered him back to work. Baland didn't remember stepping onto the elevator, nor walking into the leaden afternoon outside the Interior Ministry.

He saw a car and two security men waiting at the curb—something he would have to endure from this point forward. The directorship had long been in the back of his mind, but its sudden arrival seemed disorienting. The question of how and when to tell Jacqueline the good news he sidestepped for the moment.

With his advancement imminent, there was a great deal to consider. He put aside Malika and her controllers in Raqqa, and also the French minister of the interior. In that moment, as he stepped across the broad sidewalk of Rue de Saussaies, one face dominated Baland's thoughts: the *kidon*.

He slipped into the backseat of the car, and felt the smooth acceleration. At the first corner he cracked open the window and a cool breeze rushed inside.

There were two unsmiling men in the front seat, and the one not driving glanced over his shoulder at the slightly open window. If he had security concerns, he kept them to himself.

Baland checked his phone and saw no messages from Malika, not that he would expect any on his government-issued line. There were, however, more than a dozen emails from the office. He slipped the phone back into his pocket without opening any of them. Baland felt increasingly caught between two worlds, and he desperately needed to reconcile that division. On one hand he was about to assume a great responsibility for the republic, a position he'd long viewed as the summit of his ambition. On the other he was funneling information to the very enemy he'd sworn to fight.

The enemy.

By the time the car pulled into the gated parking area at DGSI headquarters, Baland's priorities had been well recalibrated. He opened the door, stepped over a puddle of slush on the curb, and strode into the building that would soon be his.

Darkness fell quickly, and in the deepening shadows the two Mossad *katsas* had settled into offset positions. They watched the window from widely different angles, and one had a view of the back of the building, which was the only other way out. They both noted the peculiarity at the same time.

"What was that?" the lead officer said quietly into her mic.

"I saw it too," came the reply, "but I don't know. I think that's four times now."

"I counted five."

She decided it was a worthy development, and called the number she'd been given. A gravel-edged voice answered in Hebrew. Because it was a voice she'd never heard at the embassy, compounded by the slight delay in transmission, she reasoned she was talking to someone in Tel Aviv. The importance of their op advanced another notch on her mental ledger.

"We saw something strange," she said. "There's dim background light in the apartment, but we've started to see occasional strobes . . . maybe one every minute for the last five minutes."

"Like the flash of a camera?" asked the heavy voice from Israel.

"That's what I was thinking."

"Is it ongoing?"

After a pause, the *katsa* said, "Yes, I just saw another one."

"Have you detected anyone else in the place?"

"Can't say for sure without equipment to look through the walls. But if I were to guess, I'd say no. It's just the woman."

"All right. Keep watching. And we definitely need to know if she leaves."

"If she does, do we follow her?"

A hesitation. "I don't think she has anywhere to go. But yes, if she leaves, stay with her. And be ready—this may be a long night."

THIRTY-ONE

Uday walked purposefully through a maze of darkened buildings. He had received his instructions from an agitated Chadeh two hours earlier: Drop everything and find out what had happened in Paris that afternoon. In particular, the council wanted to know if Malika was involved.

Uday had immediately tried to contact her, but got no response. That hand tied behind his back, he did his best to research things, all along wondering why Chadeh was so concerned. Was he worried that their link to Argu had been compromised? Could the late Director Michelis have possibly been Argu? *No,* Uday thought dismissively. The notion that ISIS might have the director of DGSI in their pocket was unimaginable. Whatever the crisis was, he would learn soon enough.

The building chosen for the meeting had once been a primary school. No child had set foot in the place for years, yet the playground remained intact, and children were encouraged to use it during daylight hours to maintain the image. The school's largest room had seen varied uses over the course of "liberation." For two months it had served as a clinic, then a pullback on the western front caused the staff and patients to be summarily kicked out, and within twenty-four hours it was stocked from floor to ceiling with ammunition and explosives. Once the arsenal became depleted, and as the heathen Kurds came closer, the building was transformed into an ad hoc mess hall for fighters. Then the Kurds had been pushed back a bit, and the food moved closer to the front lines. Tonight, in a fleeting session, the school would find a new use: it would become the seat of the government itself.

Chadeh was waiting expectantly when Uday arrived.

"What news do you have from Paris?" asked the senior man impatiently. He was seated on an ornate carpet atop what looked like a small stage, the kind of platform from which children might present a school play. On the wall behind Chadeh were colorful flowers cut from construction paper, each bearing a child's name. Above them all an outsized poster of the caliph, his finger raised in admonition, glowered down on everyone. Chadeh was bracketed by two men who Uday thought looked vaguely familiar. Had he been more of a politician within the organization, he would have asked for an introduction. As it was . . . the sooner he imparted what he knew, the sooner he could leave.

He said, "According to news reports, DGSI director Michelis has been shot dead by a female assailant. She also made an attempt on another high-ranking officer of the agency."

"Which one?"

Uday checked his notes. "His name is Zavier Baland."

"And Baland was not harmed?"

Uday hesitated only slightly. "No, he was untouched. Apparently he returned fire and wounded the attacker."

"Could it have been Malika?"

"The national police have only released a general description. But based on that . . . yes, it could very well have been her. I tried to contact Malika, as you requested, but she's not responding. If she *was* the attacker, then she's injured . . . or possibly worse." He watched an exchange of glances between the men on the carpet, then asked with an even voice, "May I ask why this is so important?"

After a hushed conversation, Chadeh said, "As you know, Malika has been running an agent named Argu for some time. She has never told us his identity, but we suspect it may be Zavier Baland . . . the man who shot her today."

Uday cocked his head, trying to contain his astonishment. "I see. Yes, a relationship like that—it *would* increase the odds that she was involved."

"There can be no doubt!" one of the other men said acidly.

"Do we have any idea why this has occurred?" Uday asked.

Chadeh frowned, a barely discernible expression amid his wild beard. "That is the question we have all been asking. Allowing that it was Malika, by every account she was the instigator of the attack. Yet she has been running Argu very successfully as an agent. It makes no sense that she would destroy such a valuable asset." After a pause, he said reflectively, "I fear Baland's actions make far more sense—he tried to kill the woman who coerced him into becoming an agent."

Uday, who was not prone to thoughts of conspiracy, was surprised by what came to mind. "It is being suggested in news reports that Baland might succeed Michelis as director. As things stand, Michelis is dead, and you're telling me that Argu is in our pocket. Aside from Malika being injured, is this not an ideal outcome?"

"What are you suggesting? That Malika and Baland conspired in this attack?"

Uday shrugged. "I think we should keep a favorable view. Methods aside, the result seems ideal. Baland is more a hero than ever, and his upward path is clear. The only complication I see involves Malika herself. She is in a perilous position. Assuming she survived, if she were to be captured by the French authorities . . . I dare say she knows enough to destroy Argu. Does she work with anyone else in France, any of our established cells who might render aid?"

"No. Malika only involves others when it suits her. She prefers to operate alone, and does as she wishes. The few times I have tried to steer her . . ." Chadeh left the rest unsaid, then unleashed a string of muttered expletives. "It is always the way with these insolent Palestinians!"

The man to Chadeh's right whispered something in his ear, and the chief of the Emni nodded. "You make a good point." He locked his gaze on Uday. "As God will have it, we may or may not be able to reach

Malika. As you say, there is a chance she will be captured by the police. We must establish a method of contacting Argu directly."

Uday could barely contain himself. "Actually, I only recently instructed Malika to do precisely that . . . it seemed a wise precaution. She has given Argu a single-use phone in case of emergency."

For the first time ever, Uday was sure he saw Chadeh smile. "God be praised! Once again, you prove yourself worthy, Aziz."

Uday said nothing. A reaction probably mistaken for humbleness.

"The time to use it is upon us. You can call Argu directly?"

"Yes—although I doubt he will answer. He surely keeps the phone in a secure place. We will have to wait for him to return our call—it could be a matter of hours, even days."

"Very well. If we don't hear from Malika by tomorrow morning, you must try to reach Argu. We need to hear his version of events, and establish a more permanent method of contact. Be sure he understands his position. He has long been in Malika's grasp, but that control may be lost. You must convince him we have detailed records of the intelligence he has provided—enough that there can be no escape."

Knowing the state of the caliphate's recordkeeping, Uday doubted this was true. Indeed, Argu's very identity remained a matter of some speculation.

"Also," Chadeh continued, "if Malika has survived, order Argu to do what he can to keep her from being arrested. It would be in everyone's best interest."

"Of course," said Uday.

The three men across from him engaged in a whispered discussion, leaving Uday to his private thoughts. In an increasingly common exercise, he tried to push them away. Across the room he heard snippets about God's will and prayer, what seemed compulsory expressions when these men met. There might have been a time, very long ago, when it was authentic. Cursed by a Western education, Uday recognized the group before him all too well from his studies of history. These were men whose true faith had lapsed and mutated, ending in self-aggrandizement. Men who'd become gods unto themselves.

Chadeh dismissed him, and Uday walked outside.

The desert air was like freedom itself. The muscles in his back and neck were clenched, only in part from sitting behind a keyboard all day. As he struck out toward the mosque he referred to as his office, the seditious thoughts invaded again. They were recurring with greater frequency, building each day, planks added to a fast-rising lifeboat that would carry only two people—him and Sarah.

The latest revelation only served as fuel: He and Malika had together been the conduit for all communications with Argu. Now, with Malika at least temporarily out of the picture, Uday was alone. For what might be a very brief window, he was the Islamic State's sole link to its most important agent. A man who was clearly being blackmailed for information. And a man who would soon be the most important law-enforcement officer in the Republic of France.

THIRTY-TWO

"I don't like this," grumbled Mossad director Raymond Nurin. "I don't like any of it."

The debate between Anton Bloch and his successor was a long and spirited one. Nurin had made the crosstown trip to the condo where Bloch and Talia were set up, and with the cool Mediterranean night as a backdrop, the two men diverted their conversation to the balcony. For her part, Talia was happy to adjourn to the communications room.

It was not an overstatement to say that the future of Franco-Israeli relations was at stake. The French had suffered yet another terrorist attack today, and a former Mossad assassin who had inserted himself into things, with Mossad's knowledge if not their endorsement, had apparently tracked the perpetrator to a room in Monceau. For Nurin it was a veritable minefield.

"How sure is Slaton that it's really the attacker in this apartment?" he asked.

"Not one hundred percent," Bloch allowed, "but very close to it."

"Have either of the embassy *katsas* seen her since taking up watch?"

"They've spotted a woman at the window twice, but they have no reference from which to make an ID. Slaton is the only one who's had a good look at her."

Nurin put both hands on the balcony rail, one of them holding a half-spent cigarette. This was a new vice, as far as Bloch knew, and he wrote it off as a response to the stress of the job. He'd never taken up the habit himself, and it seemed a victory of sorts.

A gust of wind swept in from the sea as Nurin asked, "Do we have any idea who she is?"

"None at all. I made a few discreet inquiries, and I'm convinced the French don't know either. There's speculation it could be the woman from the Grenoble attack, but it's nothing more than that."

"And now it appears she's using a flash to take pictures?"

"It's been ongoing for the last hour, strobes that are spaced as if she was photographing . . . something."

"Documents."

"Most likely."

"She's transmitting them."

Bloch nearly smiled. The two men were quite different physically—Nurin being the human equivalent of a blank sheet of paper—yet their minds seemed to process in parallel. *Maybe it comes with the job,* he thought, before saying, "I had a word with Talia about that. She confirmed that to intercept the images would be technically feasible. We could be talking about a landline, Wi-Fi, or a cell signal, but any of those can be captured. The problem is, this woman has been at it for hours."

"Most of her work is already done," Nurin said, completing the thought.

"In all probability. As you know, intercepting signals is a considerable commitment of time and hardware—not the kind of thing we can put together on a moment's notice, particularly on foreign soil."

"So she killed Michelis, tried to kill his successor, then goes back to her safe house, apparently wounded, and begins photographing and sending documents?"

"All measures of conjecture," Bloch allowed, "but yes, that seems to be the case. The question is, what do we do about it?"

"Can there be any question?"

"No, I suppose not. We have to tell the French what we know . . . by whatever means reflects most kindly upon us."

"And therein lies the problem."

"Agreed," said Bloch. "How can we explain that one of our retired assassins just happened to be having lunch with Baland when the shooting broke out, and that he followed this attacker to her safe house?"

"We could tell them where she is without any explanation."

"And they'll raid the place," Bloch said. "But tomorrow, or perhaps the next day—"

Nurin's eyes went skyward. "They'll want to know where our information came from. Without a good answer, Mossad falls under suspicion."

"And not without cause. We *did* know Slaton was going after Baland, and . . ." Bloch hesitated. "I should tell you there was a small measure of assistance."

"Assistance?"

Bloch saw no need to mention the phone or the cash he'd given Slaton, which seemed inconsequential. But his more serious transgression had to be confessed. "Slaton said he might require a weapon or two. I have an old contact who works out of the Paris office."

Nurin's head sank low, until it looked like he was inspecting the rail. "You arranged weapons for him without my consent?"

"Yes."

"And they were delivered using embassy assets?"

"I can assure you it was done discreetly, and the weapons are entirely untraceable."

The director dropped the butt of his cigarette and put a toe to it. He pushed out a long sigh that drifted from the ninth-floor balcony into the night sky. "Is that all?"

"I think it's enough."

"Where is Slaton now?"

"He said he was going to try to reach Baland."

"Reach? As in—"

"*Talk* to him," assured Bloch.

"Why does that not infuse me with confidence?" Nurin replied snarkily, his lips looking as if they'd bit into a lemon. "Slaton has put us in a terrible position."

"Has he? I think he's done us a great service. The

incoming director of DGSI is the secret twin of a long-thought-dispatched and very violent terrorist. I see a great deal of potential in that."

"And a great deal of risk," Nurin countered.

"I admit, it's a difficult call." Bloch pivoted to go back inside. "I'm glad it's not mine to make."

The large man named Didier was attentive as he stood on the sidewalk in front of Zavier Baland's home. He did not return nods to passersby, and watched every car that came up the street, although there was little traffic at this hour. It never escaped his notice when lights came on in the windows across the street, or when raised voices broke the silence, nor was he distracted by the smell of fresh bread from the house behind him. Having been on duty for three hours, he remained alert, disciplined, and kept his eyes moving in a full 360-degree swing. On this night, as it turned out, that wasn't quite enough.

He heard it before he saw the source—a high-pitched whirring noise that reminded him of the robotic vacuum cleaner he'd given his wife for Christmas. The sound was definitely getting louder, closer, yet in spite of his alertness, he saw nothing on the friendly sidewalks around him. Then he looked up, and there was a flash of movement before something struck him on the head.

Didier recoiled, and his hand went instinctively to his sidearm. Everything settled, and he saw what had hit him. It was hovering at eye level only a few feet away. He knew perfectly well what he was looking at—they'd had no end of briefings on the things.

"One, Three," he said into his microphone. Didier was part of a four-man surveillance team. There was one man in the alley behind Baland's house, and the two senior officers were in a white-paneled van fifty meters up the street, staying warm while they monitored the feeds from a pair of cameras.

"Go ahead, Three," said the team leader.

"I've got a—" Didier's words were cut off when the tiny craft jerked to one side. Having had enough, he took a quick step forward and swatted it out of the air like a huge mosquito. It tumbled to the pavement in a clatter of lightweight mechanization, ending near one of Zavier Baland's wintering rosebushes. "I've got a drone," he finished. "The damned thing hit me."

"Is it a threat?"

Didier looked at it. The drone was the size of a Frisbee, and probably weighed less than a can of soda. He knew that far bigger models were available, large enough to carry cameras, fireworks, even riot-inducing banners. Some could ostensibly be modified to carry handguns or small explosive charges, although nobody had crossed that line yet in France. The techs in the office loved their what-if scenarios.

"No, there's no threat. It's a really small one—probably a kid somewhere." Didier scanned the sidewalks and nearby windows for a teen with a controller in his hands. The only person in sight was an old woman walking a schnauzer. The propellers on the drone had gone still, but a tiny green light shone brightly in the center. His training kicked in, and he looked up and down the street, then at the house behind him, thinking, *What better distraction?* He saw nothing suspicious.

"I'll come take a look," said the team leader over the comm link.

Two houses away the back door of the unmarked van swung open, and an athletic man jumped out. He came next to Didier and looked down at the drone.

"Looks harmless enough."

"The damned thing hit me," Didier said a second time. He rubbed the spot on his scalp where it had made contact, but felt no marks.

The leader went closer and poked the drone with the toe of his boot. When he did, both men saw what they hadn't before: Attached to the underside by a metal clip was a folded piece of paper. They exchanged a look, and the leader removed the paper. Holding it by its edges, he carefully unfolded it. In the wash of a streetlight both men saw a message in handwritten English:

FOR ZAVIER BALAND
THANKS FOR THE WARNING
9

The two security men looked all around, this time at not only sidewalks and windows, but also rooftops and alleys.

"Who is Nine?" Didier asked.

"No idea."

They both looked up at the house they were guarding.

"Should we have a look around?" Didier asked.

"No. Stay put and keep your eyes open." The leader walked up the path and knocked on the front door.

THIRTY-THREE

"Do you know who 'Nine' might be?" asked the man in charge of the security detail.

Baland studied the message, and said, "No, it means nothing to me. You're saying it arrived attached to a drone?"

They were together in the study, Baland having excused himself from dinner with his family. Earlier he'd given Jacqueline and the girls a gentle version of what had occurred at Le Quinze. They all took it as well as could be expected, but having armed men now surrounding the house did nothing to lighten the mood. That being the case, when the team leader came to the door, Baland had told them it was a routine check-in, knowing full well it wasn't.

"And you didn't see where it came from?" asked Baland.

"No, I'm afraid not. I didn't want to bother you with this, sir, but the way the message is worded—I thought you might have some insight as to what it meant."

Baland shook his head.

The security man said, "I'll have to pass this up to my commander."

Baland looked at his watch. It was 7:52. The security team was DGSI's own, and the man who would soon be director said, "Whoever sent it must be nearby."

"Probably, although we have been briefed that some of these drones can be programmed to fly preset courses. They go beyond the controlling transmitter's range using GPS."

"Even so, before you call in reinforcements, let's try to deal with this ourselves. You and your men do a quick sweep across the street. Don't disturb anyone unnecessarily—I have to live with these people. Just check the backyards and rooflines. Ask anyone you meet if they've heard or seen anything strange."

"Very well. But I should call in extra personnel to—"

"No," Baland cut in, "that's not necessary. Just leave one man in front, and the rest of you try to figure this out. We're already paying enough overtime tonight. I won't take manpower away from units with better things to do."

"Sir, I really think it would be better if—"

"Be quick about it!" Baland said decisively, and turned away.

The detail's leader didn't argue any further. He used the radio to relay the plan to his team.

Soon Baland was watching it all unfold from his front window. There was a brief huddle with all four men, then one became a fixture on his sidewalk while the others got busy across the street. It gave Baland the chance he needed.

He went to his second-floor study, and from the bottom drawer of his desk he extracted the burner phone he'd taped into a recess. He turned it on, looked at the screen, and was stilled for a moment. There was one unanswered call. Baland shook away his surprise, and was soon quick-stepping downstairs with renewed urgency.

In the kitchen he gave Jacqueline very specific instructions, and he kissed each of his daughters good night. Two minutes later Baland was out the back door. He bypassed the still-broken swing and the finely trimmed hedges, and fast disappeared into a deepening night.

Four minutes after Baland left his home in Courbevoie, a phone rang in Raqqa. So deep was the handset buried in his backpack, Uday almost didn't hear it. When the ring did register, he practically fell off his chair trying to reach it. To begin with, he was surprised that a mobile signal was available—coverage had been acutely unreliable in recent weeks. The second and more unnerving shock, made clear by the special ringtone, was *which* of his phones was receiving the call.

He checked once over his shoulder to make sure he was alone in the room. Satisfied, he swept up his backpack, reached deep inside, and pulled out the special handset he'd begun carrying for just this contingency.

"*Bonjour,*" he said, his range of French expended in a single word.

The caller began rattling away breathlessly in the language, and realizing his error, Uday interrupted with, "Wait! Please . . . is English possible?"

"It is," said the agent named Argu.

"We must be quick," Uday said, again looking back toward the main hall.

"We have sixty-three seconds," said Argu, "or so I've been told."

Uday closed his eyes, feeling stupid. *Think! I must think clearly!*

Argu said, "I saw that you tried to contact me earlier. I assume it has to do with Malika. I don't know what her condition is or where—"

"No!" Uday said, cutting Argu off. His next words seemed to burst forth, as though they'd been held inside him under great pressure. "My name is Aziz Uday, and I am in charge of the Islamic State Institution for Public Information! I wish to defect with a woman, and I can bring valuable information with me!"

Uday thought he might have heard an intake of breath over the line. He wished he'd rehearsed the rest of what he had to say. At the very least, he knew he had the man's attention. But there was still one hurdle to climb. "If you help me," he said with all the conviction he could muster, "I believe your connection to Raqqa can be buried forever."

The silence on the other end of the line was resounding.

THIRTY-FOUR

By nine that evening Le Quinze was predictably cordoned off by yellow tape, investigators going over the
scene to extract every shred of evidence. From a distance Slaton saw evidence vans, camera crews, and
clusters of bystanders. Bright lights had been trailered
in, putting half a block of Paris into daylight. Even
from fifty yards away he could discern the dark stain
on the cobbled terrace, a marker of where Director
Michelis had been gunned down.

Slaton expected Baland to arrive from the direction of his home, and took up his post accordingly.
Much like the previous morning, he spotted him
walking up the sidewalk two blocks away. Slaton
maneuvered to let the DGSI man pass, then fell in
behind him. When Baland was half a block short of
the restaurant, Slaton saw him hesitate on the sidewalk. He took this as a positive sign, and at that point
began a survey of the street.

Urban traffic, Slaton had long ago concluded, is an
eminently predictable thing. Cars and trucks move in
tight clusters, compressed by the effects of traffic

lights, obstacles, and points of congestion. His preference in street craft was to approach an unsuspecting contact at the height of a rush, when noise and motion were at their most distracting. Traffic surges also provided visual and aural screens to any third party who might be watching, and if anything went wrong, the impending break in flow maximized the possible avenues of escape. Each element small in its own right—but Slaton never gave away any advantage.

"Thanks for coming," he said as he approached Baland from the shadow of an old granite wall.

Baland turned and saw him, looking more relieved than startled. "We should go elsewhere," he said straightaway, clearly uncomfortable with their proximity to the investigation.

Another test passed, Slaton thought.

He'd wondered if Baland would even come—Slaton had, after all, gunned down the man's brother—but he suspected they had more common interests than were yet apparent. He led Baland away in silence, two quick turns back toward the Seine, and then down an embankment.

"I came alone," said Baland as they descended a long flight of stone stairs.

"I know."

The river spread out before them, dark and indifferent. Baland looked all around, seeming distracted. "I'm glad I deciphered your message correctly—it was very minimalist. And the drone was most creative."

"It did the job. Although I wasn't sure if you'd come."

"Really?"

Slaton looked at the Frenchman—he could only think of him as such, regardless of where he was born—and reminded himself to not underestimate the man.

"You weren't harmed in the attack?" Baland asked.

"No. And thanks for calling out the threat—you were very astute to see her coming."

"I began my service as a policeman, did I not?"

Slaton gave Baland an inquiring look.

"Ah, yes," said Baland. "Our conversation at the restaurant. Just before it was interrupted I think you mentioned that I seemed to have . . . what was the phrase . . . insider information?"

"Maybe that was harsh. Let's just say you have a great talent for predicting France's misfortunes."

"Actually, you were more correct the first time."

They took up a gently curving path along the Left Bank. Baland's eyes, black in the dim light, studied him with a strange equivalence. "You *are* getting information," Slaton said.

"In a sense. But more problematic is that I am giving it. I am being blackmailed."

"By who?"

"The simple answer would be to say ISIS."

"And the more complicated answer?"

"I will put it like this . . . aside from my failing old mother, there has long been but one person who knows I am the brother of Ali Samir. That person has threatened to expose me unless I regularly supply intelligence to the leadership in Raqqa."

"I see," said Slaton. "For a man in your position, a relationship like that would be a career-ender."

"Prosecutors would no doubt call it treason. If it came to light, I would spend the rest of my life in prison."

"So why are you confessing this to me?"

"We'll get to that—but trust that my reasons are selfish."

Slaton didn't pursue the point. "What kind of information have you been giving them?"

"As little as possible. Yet each week they demand more, and lately they have been making specific requests. Only this morning I gave the operative who runs me certain portions of a highly classified dossier—France's vulnerability to terrorist attacks. Details of our greatest weaknesses are now in the hands of our enemy."

Slaton expelled a long breath. "That's very bad for you."

"Information *has* traveled both ways. I have regularly been given intelligence on second-tier operatives here in France. Small terrorist cells, people to watch for at the immigration counters—dropouts mostly. Men and women who have returned disillusioned from Syria, or malcontents in France who were either denied the ability to travel, or who never had the fortitude to attempt it. Altogether, pawns from the *banlieues* who are sacrificed to advance the caliphate's greater cause."

Slaton understood immediately. "Small victories to aid your rise within DGSI."

"Yes."

"The way you present it . . . it sounds as if this middleman running you, the one who knows of your relationship with Ali Samir, isn't directly under the caliphate's control."

"Correct."

"Who is it?"

"Someone you have met—the woman who attacked us today."

Slaton slowed his pace, then drew to a stop. Baland stopped as well and watched Slaton decipher the code of what he was saying.

"That makes no sense. If she's running you as a valuable agent, why would she show up at Le Quinze and try to kill you?"

Baland gave a half grin. "She didn't," he said, eyeing Slaton directly. "She was there to kill you."

Slaton stood a bit straighter, and his eyes scanned with more than their usual caution. The river flowed steady and slow, and a pair of young men—immigrants from the Middle East, on appearances—strolled harmlessly nearby. He turned back to study a face he'd first seen so many years ago, squared under his reticle on a still and arid morning. It was different now. Fifteen years of aging, to be sure, but an altogether different countenance. A different person.

"Who is she?" he finally asked.

"Her name is Malika."

"Was she sent here by ISIS?"

"I can't say for certain, but on balance . . . I would say not. I suspect Malika spent time in Syria, but she remains an outsider. A sympathizer with parallel aims. She has run a number of small operations in France, enough to earn their trust. Once she had that, she told the leaders in Raqqa that she could recruit a high-level agent within DGSI. I'm quite sure she never gave specifics about who it was or how she could do it. They were of course interested. In time, her results proved her point—all at my expense."

"What is it that she has over you?"

"Think about it, *kidon*. The very same thing that makes her want to kill you. Malika is my niece."

Slaton stared at Baland. "You mean . . . ?"

"Yes. She is the daughter of Ali Samir."

THIRTY-FIVE

The photographs from Malika arrived at the Raqqa mosque in a laborious stream. They were first downloaded one at a time through an encrypted messaging application. Once in hand, each file had to be reconstituted as a document, a process brought to a standstill that afternoon by a local network failure. Having given his team the day off, Uday worked alone until Anisa showed up. It was late that night before everything was sorted.

"Whatever this is," said Anisa, looking through what they'd downloaded, "it appears to be a partial document."

Uday seemed not to hear.

"Is something wrong?" she asked.

"No," he replied too quickly.

They were seated side by side, the room an aqueous yellow in the glow of oil lamps. The electrical grid was down again, and their computers were running on a single generator that had been situated three buildings away, connected using every heavy-gauge extension cord they possessed. They'd learned the hard way that the newest drones could spot a heat signature through walls. In a blackout, any operating generator signified something important to the caliphate, which guaranteed attention from the fighter-bombers.

"Actually, I think you may be right," he said finally. "Chadeh was expecting a larger document." The images had arrived in scattershot bunches, suggesting a logjam in the routing scheme. The fact that anything at all was getting through was a minor victory for the persistence of their network. For Uday, however, the transmission of these new files held a double-edged meaning. Their arrival meant that Malika had survived.

He considered his conversation with Argu earlier. Uday had confirmed what he'd suspected: Malika's agent was Zavier Baland. In their short conversation the two had devised a loose pact. But how might Malika's survival complicate things?

"I don't like how this came through," Anisa said, filling the silence. "Our repeater was piggybacking on mobile towers in Aleppo. This data could have been intercepted."

"Perhaps, but at the moment security is a luxury—we have to take what we can get."

"Has any of this been forwarded to the council?" she asked as she continued to shuffle through the printed pages. "God has truly blessed us. Malika has obtained incredibly valuable information." Uday was sure he heard a hint of feminism in her voice as she carried on, "Here is a diagram of a synagogue in Nice. And a Jewish grocery in Paris."

Uday's gaze narrowed. "Give me that."

Anisa handed over the printouts, and Uday flicked through them. "These are all Jewish interests," he remarked. "Why would Argu send us only this portion?"

"Maybe he hates Jews. Who cares? It is clearly useful."

"The council was expecting more. Are you sure there was no message regarding the rest?"

"Everything Malika sent is in your hands."

He considered it. "Perhaps she is holding back the rest intentionally. We have put a great deal of trust in her."

Anisa glared at him severely. Uday knew she was distilling their discord to a matter of sexism—the inevitable by-product of a society that systematically devalued women. He was happy to let her have the thought, because it deflected attention from the true nature of his worry.

She said, "We should send word to the council to convene an immediate meeting."

An uncomfortable silence weighed in. Uday knew he held every advantage in this room. Anisa worked for him, and women in the Islamic State never challenged men on matters of importance. All the same, he did not want to antagonize her. Not when he was in such a precarious position himself. "You are right," he finally said. "This is truly good news at a time when we could use some."

"Yes . . . we have all been under a great deal of pressure."

"Send a runner to Chadeh and ask him to call a meeting tonight—eleven o'clock."

"Not sooner?"

"No," he hedged, "we still might receive more data. I want to be sure we have everything."

Anisa nodded, then disappeared through the doorway sided by prayer rugs.

Uday waited a full two minutes before going to the threshold. He searched the great hall of the mosque. At the far end he saw the cleaning woman, who came most nights, but Anisa was gone. He returned to his workstation and poised his fingers over the keyboard. The commands he was about to enter were irrevocable—once things were set in motion, there was no turning back.

He took a deep breath, then set to work with a fervor. He had built his trapdoor, or at least conceived of it, in recent days, not sure when or if he would ever be able to use it. Now Uday was glad he'd laid that foundation. Thirty minutes later it was done. He lifted his backpack, looped it over one shoulder, and exited the mosque for the last time into a cold and moonless night.

The more Slaton thought about it, the more it made sense. The woman named Malika was Ali Samir's daughter. It was she who'd sent four men to the Philippines to eliminate him or, failing that, to draw him to Paris. She had been waiting at Le Quinze, knowing Slaton would show himself. Ready to seek revenge against the man who'd killed her father.

Baland stood staring at him, waiting for a reaction. Slaton said, "I saw you for the first time yesterday.

I followed you when you walked to work in the morning. By bringing me to Paris she was putting you at risk."

"Very much so, which speaks to how committed she is to her vengeance."

Slaton watched warily as the Frenchman reached into his pocket. He produced a photograph. "Malika gave me this yesterday afternoon."

Slaton recognized the scene instantly—he was sitting on the bench in Courbevoie. Waiting for Baland. The photo was distant, taken from a high elevation. He remembered surveying the buildings across the street, but doing so with an offensive mind-set. Apparently he hadn't looked closely enough. "I think I've seriously underestimated this woman."

"You would not be the first."

"She came to Le Quinze to kill me."

"Certainly."

"She failed in that, but managed to eliminate Michelis. That clears the way for your advancement."

"She is a clever girl."

Or maybe you're a clever man, Slaton thought. He was struck by the idea that Baland was the winner in everything that had happened. Yet tactically he couldn't find a way to hold him responsible for the outcome—Baland had shot and wounded Malika *before* she'd killed Michelis. If they'd been colluding, that didn't make sense.

They started walking the path again.

"So where do we go from here?" Slaton asked. "You'll soon become director, but you've been compromised. Do you expect me to sit silently and let that happen?"

"Is this a matter of conscience? Or perhaps a nudge from old friends in Tel Aviv?"

"Believe me when I say that Tel Aviv wants very much to stay out of this."

"From what I have heard about Director Nurin . . . I doubt that. Still, there might be a way forward for us all. I'm quite sure Malika has not told anyone in Raqqa of my kinship to Ali Samir." Baland let that sit, allowing Slaton to consider it.

"You regret your aim wasn't better today," Slaton suggested.

"She is my niece by blood alone—I had never set eyes on her until last year. If Malika were out of the picture, a great many of my problems would be solved. It's how I should have handled things when she first started blackmailing me."

"That's very frank."

"Perhaps. But then, if anyone on earth would understand, I'd think it would be you."

"Even with Malika removed, aren't there individuals in the caliphate who could call you out? There's a flow of information that could be linked to you."

"I'm not so sure. A leak could be proven, yes—but France's counterterrorism establishment is a vast machine. There are many possible sources, and a man in my position could do a great deal to ensure that attribution remains clouded."

"You've given this some thought."

Baland's voice went to a shrill whisper. "I have

awakened every night for a year trying to find a way out of this! It's as though I've fallen into quicksand. The more I struggle, the deeper I get."

"So," Slaton said, "if you knew where Malika was right now, at this very moment . . . what would you do?"

Baland eyed him critically. "I would assemble a raid, of course. I'm sure Malika would resist—it is her nature. She might not be a religious woman, but she is a martyr to her sins. She would never be taken alive."

Slaton said nothing. He looked out over the Seine in its timeless drift, ripples and eddies marking movement beneath the surface.

"You know where she is," Baland deduced.

"Am I that bad a poker player?"

"Rather the opposite. You have a special brand of composure. You never lost your nerve in the shooting today—and I noticed that you disappeared immediately afterward. I think you might have caught up with Malika and tracked her from Le Quinze. Followed her to whatever safe house she is using."

Slaton gave a thoughtful nod.

"Is anyone watching her now?"

"Yes."

"Mossad?"

Slaton let silence be his answer.

"Then I'll assume Mossad also knows about my twisted family tree."

The sidewalk ended—the underpass in front of them was under construction, and a detour arrow pointed up a set of stairs toward the street. They stood facing one another, and Baland said, "I want

Malika, but neither you nor Director Nurin has any reason to tell me where she is."

"No, not really."

"Then let me give you one."

For the next ten minutes Slaton listened. At the end, he admitted Baland was right. He had presented Slaton a very good reason for the two of them to work together. An opportunity like none that had ever existed.

THIRTY-SIX

Slaton parted ways with Baland, and as soon as he was alone he sent a text to Talia: He needed an immediate conference call with both Bloch and Mossad director Nurin. Halfway back to his room Slaton got his wish, and he diverted to a riverside overlook to pick up the call.

"Hello, David," Nurin said. It was a voice Slaton had not heard in over a year.

"Director. Is Anton on as well?"

"Yes," Bloch replied in his distinctive voice.

Everyone went through an authentication process for security communications before Nurin said, "We've had discussions about how to handle this situation in Monceau."

"I'm sure you have. Has anything changed there?"

"No, our *katsas* are still outside. We've added some manpower to the surveillance op, three more individuals rotating in. By all accounts, the place remains quiet. I would guess either the woman is sleeping, or her injuries have gotten the better of her."

Slaton didn't comment on that, but said, "I'm

guessing you've decided to hand this matter over to the French?"

"Yes. As much as we prefer to take ownership of such opportunities, in this case our only option is to step away."

"Have you made contact with anyone yet?"

"I just finished briefing our foreign minister. He is trying to contact his French counterpart as we speak. As you know, Mossad prefers to stay in the background whenever—"

"Stop it!" Slaton ordered.

"What?"

"Get on another phone; break this connection if you need to. Do *not* let that call take place until you've heard what I have to say."

"David—" Anton began, only to be cut off.

"If you let that call go through you will miss the greatest intelligence coup since the Stuxnet virus ruined Iran's centrifuges! I am going to hang up now. *Do not* let that information advance through those channels. Call me back when it's done."

Slaton heard one syllable of Nurin's protest before he ended the call.

Uday rushed inside and found Sarah at the stove. She looked up when the door closed and smiled. An expression that vaporized when he said, "We are leaving!"

He went to her and put his hands on her shoulders—not a romantic embrace, but more as if shoring her up.

"What's happened?" she asked.

"I'll explain later. For now you must trust me—we have to get out of Raqqa!"

"All right," she replied in a tenuous tone. "Where are we going?"

"Destinations are unimportant at the moment. The only place we cannot be is here."

Sarah didn't seem surprised. They had talked circles around the idea for days, neither saying it in so many words, but both confiding the hopelessness of their situation. They'd discussed at length his insider's knowledge of the caliphate, and also that his position within it had proved a frightfully tenuous post. Sarah's own fears were far more basic: At any time Chadeh's men could come and take her away as easily as they'd brought her here. To where and what neither of them wanted to imagine.

Now, in a moment, it had all burst from the realm of cautious musings to reality.

"What should I bring?" she asked.

He took a step back and looked at her. "Change to your old abaya. Bring nothing else."

"How will we travel?"

"My brother, Faisal—his truck still runs and he has enough petrol to take us south."

"South? That is a difficult passage."

"Which is why no one will expect it. I know where the checkpoints are—I updated the map for our military commanders only yesterday. If we move quickly, we can be halfway to Damascus before anyone realizes that I . . ." Uday's words caught there, like a dragging anchor finding a rock.

Sarah looked at him expectantly, waiting for the rest. "What have you done, Aziz?"

Doubts washed over him in a great wave, a fear more palpable than any he had felt through years of war. He looked at Sarah and understood why—the risks he was incurring were not his alone. He stood frozen, suddenly overwhelmed.

Sarah saved him. "Yes, Aziz, let's do it! Let's go right now!"

Anisa was running performance scans on the computers in the old mosque. For that reason she was the first to see the attack on their servers. One by one their internal networks were going down. When she finally regained administrative access to one system, she found file after file corrupted. Even their most recent inputs, Uday's newly created personnel database, had become no more than a stew of electronic rubbish.

At first she suspected the Americans, but then Anisa reconsidered, thinking the hacktivists might be at it again. She got on her mobile phone, which was getting a signal through Aleppo, and navigated to a few of their current Facebook and Twitter recruiting accounts. Every feed had been frozen. Whoever had hit them had hit them hard, comprehensively shut down their networks. This gave rise to a new idea. A handful of social media accounts were managed by individuals in her group using smartphones, and a few others by sympathizers across the Middle East and Europe. Looking at a sample of these accounts, she saw normal activity. Which meant the problem was local—only Raqqa had fallen into cyber darkness. She began digging through code, and within minutes found what looked like malicious commands. Anisa was dumbstruck. *An internal problem?*

She then remembered her last conversation with Uday.

He'd been acting strangely for some time, and never had he berated her as he had today. She remembered how he'd hesitated to schedule a meeting with Chadeh and the council. They were a frightening bunch, to be sure, but for Anisa the anarchy under her fingertips was even more so. Something told her that Uday might be late for that meeting. Very late indeed.

And if she was right?

Woman or not, the old buzzards were going to let her inside. If things were as she suspected, they needed to know exactly how much trouble they were in.

Slaton was still waiting for Director Nurin to call back. How long had it been? Ten minutes? Fifteen? His eyes were active as he navigated the busy sidewalks of a commercial district, and his neck was getting sore by the time he reached Courbevoie. He knew the precise whereabouts of the only person in Paris known to be gunning for him, but that very fact—that he *had* been targeted—did wonders to enhance his alertness.

His hotel was within sight when Nurin called back. "Whatever you have, David, I hope it is *very* good."

"I take it you were successful?"

"Yes, the foreign minister is waiting for me to call him back."

"Well done." Slaton began with Baland's admission that his niece had been blackmailing him, and that he'd been surrendering information to ISIS. Slaton ended with, "He wants to eliminate Malika before she's captured."

"That seems risky."

"From his point of view, less of a risk than allowing her to be interrogated. Baland is in a good position to manage any fallout."

Bloch asked, "You're saying this girl, Malika, is not directly under ISIS' control?"

"Baland doesn't think so. He's also convinced that no one in Syria knows about his connection to Ali Samir—and consequently, that Malika is his niece."

"You told Baland you followed her to this safe house?"

"No. He figured that out on his own—but I didn't deny it."

Nurin said, "I am still not seeing any great intelligence value here, David. Why do I have the Israeli foreign minister sitting on his hands?"

"If you go through diplomatic channels, there's no telling which police unit will be ordered to haul Malika in. Baland wants to lead the raid himself."

"And it will end badly for her."

"Almost certainly. But in exchange for her location, he has something to offer. His contact with the Islamic State has always been through Malika, but she recently gave him a backup, a burner phone in case she was compromised as a handler. After the altercation today that seemed to be the case, and Baland got a call a few hours ago. On the Syrian end was a man named Aziz Uday."

A pause, and Nurin said, "I recall that name—he is in their technology and media division?"

"He recently became the number one—Aziz Uday heads the Islamic State Institution for Public Information."

"And you're saying Uday established contact because they were worried Malika was out of the picture?"

"No, that's the interesting part. He wasn't calling on behalf of the Islamic State at all. He wants out."

"Out?" Bloch and Nurin said in near unison.

"He wants to defect, along with a woman. Uday needs help escaping Syria, and he's offered information in exchange."

"What kind of information?" Nurin prompted.

Slaton could not suppress a grin—he envisioned Nurin leaning forward in his chair with a handset clamped to his ear. "I thought you'd be interested. Apparently Uday undertook a project recently to create a new database—a detailed personnel file on every known member of the Islamic State, both at home and abroad. Before he escaped Raqqa, Uday burned his bridges. He destroyed ISIS' only register of that database . . . but not before making one copy for himself."

THIRTY-SEVEN

The search of Raqqa was undertaken with frantic urgency. Doors slammed inward all across town as armed detachments raided apartments and buildings. Nearby farmhouses were next in line, and even fighters had their quarters turned over. In the end, Anisa was proved right. Aziz Uday was nowhere to be found, nor was Sarah, the idolatrous Christian slave he'd been issued.

Anisa sat silently on a case of Turkish motor oil. Chadeh had told her to remain present while the search ran its course, and she watched with increasing apprehension as a look of thunder overtook his already-dark features. One by one, reports filtered in of failure in every quadrant. Chadeh paced the floor of their newest government venue, an automotive garage that had been requisitioned for the night. Tools were scattered about the place, and sawdust carpeted the floor. The air reeked of grease and gasoline. There were three others in attendance—two senior military officers, and a grossly overweight council member who glared at Anisa intensely, weighing, she supposed, either a spontaneous stoning or a roll in the hay. Not sure which would be more unbearable, she simply ignored his stare and said nothing.

Chadeh finally stopped pacing, and asked, "Can we retrieve the personnel information?"

It took a few moments for Anisa to realize he was addressing her, then another beat to get past the implication. By default, she now headed the Islamic State Institution for Public Information. Of course, the promotion would last only until a man could be found, probably one of the technicians she'd trained. Still, she decided to make the best of it.

"I don't know if it is recoverable. It will take days, possibly even weeks, to get things up and running. From what I've seen, this is a malicious attack intended to wipe out data. If it was thorough, the information may never be recovered." Chadeh glowered at her, and she immediately added, "Of course, we could do it all over again . . . create a new database that can be made more secure." Anisa knew, but did not say, that doing so would be a nightmare. The source listings from which they'd compiled the database had been physically destroyed—a matter of security, according to Uday.

Chadeh's iron gaze was unrelenting. "Might Uday have stolen this information?"

She'd already had the same troubling thought. "It is possible . . . yes."

"Which means our enemies might soon have the identity of every member of our army, both inside the caliphate and abroad."

Anisa did not deny it.

"If he did take it," Chadeh asked, "what form would it be in?"

She considered her answer carefully. "It would be possible to transmit it—but I don't think he would have taken that course."

"Why not?"

"Because if Uday is truly defecting, I think he would keep the data in hand in order to bargain for his safety. Certain intelligence agencies would go to great lengths to help him escape with such information. If it were me, I would carry it on a storage device, probably a flash drive." She immediately regretted the reflexive phrasing of this last thought, but Chadeh was too incensed to notice.

The next ten minutes were the longest of Anisa's life. The caliphate's leaders were worried, and justifiably so. Worst of all, her unit was responsible for the debacle. By the time she left the building, she was hoping they actually *would* choose a man to take her place, and the sooner the better.

In the meantime, however, she was given two clear assignments to carry out.

Her second priority: Find out how much damage had been done.

Her first: Locate the traitorous Aziz Uday.

Nurin had interrupted their second call, and Slaton waited for him to call back. He reached his hotel, but not wanting to continue the conversation inside, he took a turn around the block, ending on a quiet residential street. He saw a playground Davy would have enjoyed immensely, and in the wash of a streetlight a pair of old women engaged in a good-natured quarrel. He'd originally thought the decision of whether to get involved in Aziz Uday's defection would be Nurin's to make. Now he realized it was going one rung higher.

His phone rang.

"I need to know more about the deal," Nurin said breathlessly. "Baland wants us to give him Malika, but what exactly is he offering in return?"

"To begin, we get first crack at Uday. He told Baland he's on his way south, toward the Golan Heights. The extraction will be up to us."

"*Golan?*" Nurin remarked. "That is an unusual departure point from Syria."

"Which is why it might be a smart play. I suspect he chose the southern route based on insider knowledge. The caliphate controls only a fraction of the territory it once did. He of all people would know the weaknesses in the perimeter. It's good for us because we can bring him directly into Israel. Uday has done some groundwork for this escape. Before leaving Raqqa, he claims to have sabotaged the caliphate's internal networks: command and control nodes, communications lines. That's going to create a lot of confusion."

"Once the leadership there realizes what he's done, they'll do anything to stop him."

"I'm sure they will," Slaton said. "Whoever takes possession of this database will have more information about ISIS than ISIS itself."

"What is the timetable?"

"Uday is supposed to contact Baland tomorrow to finalize the details of his exfiltration."

Nurin, ever the negotiator, said, "And if we agree to pull him out? What is our payback?"

"Two things. To begin, Baland insists that both Uday and the database, assuming it exists, must be delivered to him."

Nurin protested, "Why would we assume such a risk only to—"

"There's more," Slaton interrupted, doing an about-face on the quiet street to avoid a busy intersection. "He allows that Mossad can copy the data. For many years now Israel has been perfectly happy to sit back and watch Hezbollah, Levant Front, Assad, and the rest beat one another to a pulp. But even if Israel doesn't engage ISIS directly, the value of this database to her allies would be incalculable. The goodwill potential with the Americans alone could put relations in good stead for years."

"Everything you say is true," Nurin responded. "But how can we be sure this list even exists?"

"You can't. But then, what are you really risking? If the database is real, you get a copy and then pass it on to Baland. France will have a list of terrorists to sweep up that will keep them busy for months. If it doesn't exist, you'll have the chief information officer of the Islamic State to interview for a day."

Nurin didn't respond right away, but Slaton could almost hear the directorial wheels turning. He finally said, "Does Baland really believe he can extract himself from this mess he's found himself in?"

"If you put yourself in his position—it might be

worth a shot. Malika is his biggest threat. If we give her to him, and if Uday can be safely retrieved with his information—I think the incoming director of DGSI might have a chance. Better yet, if he does survive, he'll owe a tremendous debt to Mossad."

The silence on the phone told Slaton he'd convinced Nurin. Now he had to convince himself. "But there is one problem," he added.

"What?" Nurin asked.

"Baland's second request—he wants me to bring Uday in. I extract him from Syria and accompany him back to France."

"Why you?"

It was a question Slaton had already asked himself. "I don't know. And I don't like it."

"I can understand your suspicion. You killed the man's brother, and now he wants to put you in harm's way."

"That's pretty much how I see it."

"Then I must know . . . are you a volunteer for this mission?"

Once again, it was something Slaton had been debating. A police car approached along the narrow street, its tires hissing over asphalt wet from recent showers. The car never slowed, and the sound dissipated behind him.

On his long flight from the Pacific, Slaton had considered a great many scenarios, wondering what might lie ahead. Rescuing AWOL Islamic State leaders from Syria had not been among them. Christine would tell him to drop the whole affair and come home, if an Antares catamaran in the South Seas could be referred to as such. In the end, Slaton relented. The information Uday claimed to be carrying could deal a crushing blow to ISIS. Which meant it could save thousands of lives. His hands were tied every bit as much as Director Nurin's. Not for the first time, Slaton found himself dragged into someone else's battle—but a battle he could not avoid in good conscience.

"Arrange for a jet," Slaton said. "I'll be at Le Bourget within the hour."

When the call ended on the Tel Aviv end, Nurin looked at Bloch, who'd been listening in. He said, "How many ways can this all go wrong?"

"I can think of at least a dozen."

Nurin sent the phone he'd been using spinning across a table. "This is all your fault, Anton."

"If you like."

"Unfortunately, the potential positives far outweigh the risks. There was no choice."

"None at all. How will you convince the foreign minister to not call his French counterpart?"

"I'll have to go over his head."

"Yes," Bloch agreed, "I suppose it's the only way." He then changed course. "Slaton is going to need support."

"He'll have it."

"Have you heard anything more from Gaza?"

"You mean our search for evidence to support this mad idea that Baland and Ali Samir are twins?"

Bloch nodded.

"We've only had half a day, but we were able to locate the mother. She lives with her sister and is suffering from advanced dementia. Approaching her would be awkward, to say the least, and I doubt she could tell us much. We looked through the official records for the period, such as they are, but there was nothing useful. Given what we know so far . . . I'd have to say Baland's story is plausible. Malika is Ali Samir's daughter. Baland grew up in France, and he's being blackmailed because of the connection. It all fits perfectly."

Bloch remained silent.

"You think otherwise," Nurin suggested.

"Not necessarily. The facts as we know them fit well. On the other hand, I think we should make every effort to get to the bottom of it."

"What do you suggest?"

"If there is any useful information, it might not be in Gaza. I think there is one place we haven't looked."

THIRTY-EIGHT

That France could not track down a lone female assassin in Paris was an embarrassment to the gendarmerie, a flash point for elected officials, and a source of consternation to the media. On receiving one text message from an unknown number, containing a simple street address, Baland found himself in a position to earn the admiration of them all.

As acting director of DGSI, he had considerable latitude in planning the raid on the flat in Monceau. For a target already proved to be dangerous, the standard response would have been to call in a highly trained tactical team from the national gendarmerie. That, however, would cede control of the outcome, something Baland could not allow. If his judgment was later questioned, he would say time was of the essence, and that they were dealing with but a lone female terrorist.

He commandeered a squad of six well-armed DGSI men, a unit gearing up for an unrelated raid on a Saint-Ouen drug den, and in two unmarked vans they sped through the night toward Monceau. They parked a block away, well out of sight, and Baland ordered his team to wait while he rendezvoused with the lead Mossad officer behind the walls of an adjacent building. The woman had been expecting him, and she assured DGSI's senior officer that the place had been quiet since early evening. Baland thanked her for her help, then asked her to withdraw her surveillance unit.

He dispatched two members of his own squad to reconnoiter the building. They reached the same conclusions the Israelis had. There were two ways into the apartment: the main entrance in front, and a laddered fire escape in back that spanned all three floors. Baland separated one man and ordered him to stand watch at the fire escape, then disappointed him further by seizing his Heckler & Koch UMP submachine gun in exchange for his own more limited 9mm Sig Sauer.

Baland led the raiding party to the third-floor hallway, and when everyone agreed they had identified the right room, the team listened for a full two minutes. Hearing nothing, he signaled the go-ahead, and a man dressed in body armor came forward with a battering ram.

Baland was first through the breach, UMP at the ready. The tension of the moment was quick-lived, and not a shot was fired. The reasons were all too obvious, yet as a matter of procedure the flat was cleared. Within sixty seconds everyone stood at ease with their weapons at their sides. The worn furniture around them and tattered carpet under their feet went completely unnoticed, as did a vaguely sour smell that seemed infused into the air.

With his team beside him, Baland stood dumbfounded, looking helplessly at a ladder in the middle of the room. Eight feet above, at the top-floor unit's ceiling, he saw the cutout frame of a skylight. Or at least where a skylight had once been. The plastic dome had been neatly removed, leaving Baland staring helplessly at a star-filled night sky.

The Israeli Air Force flies hundreds of jets, and the country's Ministry of Foreign Affairs keeps a small airline of its own. Unfortunately, none of those aircraft were in Paris on that cold February night, so when Slaton arrived at Le Bourget Airport it was with instructions to proceed to a fixed-base operator on the east side of the airfield where a chartered Gulfstream was waiting.

The required formalities were undertaken in the flight department lounge. Slaton showed his forged passport to a young woman who'd been expecting him, signed two cursory documents, and without further ritual was led through a set of doors. Fifty yards of red carpet runner later he ascended the stairs of a sleek business jet. Every facet of the experience was smooth and well-practiced, and thirteen minutes after arriving at the FBO, Slaton was airborne. He sat alone in an oversized leather chair, six others going empty around him. Aside from two pilots on the flight deck, there was but one other person on board,

262 | WARD LARSEN

a pleasant flight attendant who showed a keen interest in his wine preference.

It all required a mental shifting of gears, but that
was something Slaton had grown accustomed to over
the years. How many times had he surveilled a bomber's den by day, then spent an evening tipping cock-
tails with diplomats on an embassy terrace? Mirroring
his thoughts of two days ago, he wished there were
some way to share these better moments with Christine and Davy.

"A Bordeaux perhaps?" the young woman asked,
interrupting his musings.

It took no more than a smile, and the stemware on
the teak table beside him came half full.

"How long is the flight to Tel Aviv?" he asked

"Three hours and fifty-two minutes," replied the
flight attendant, who was certainly French, and
who'd introduced herself as Nicolette.

"That's very precise."

"Our clientele generally appreciate attention to detail."

"I assure you, none more than I do."

Ten minutes later Nicolette delivered a worthy
Chateaubriand to go with his Bordeaux. She made an
attempt at conversation, but he clearly had a lot on
his mind, and she tactfully retreated behind the curtain of her galley. Slaton put the steak under his knife
thinking about Aziz Uday and Zavier Baland and
ISIS databases, but by the time he was done, with the
lights of the Côte d'Azur passing beneath the wing,
he had pushed it all aside. Nicolette removed his

empty plate, and he looked down at the void that was the Mediterranean.

Slaton wondered what the best season was for cruising these waters. Fall, he guessed, after the human tide of August had receded, but before the Scandinavians came running from winter. October, perhaps. Eight months from now. He conjured a map in his mind and plotted a tentative passage from the Philippines. A run through the Malacca Strait, to begin, then across the southern Bay of Bengal. A watchful approach through the Red Sea and Suez Canal. Then, finally . . . the sleepy Mediterranean in all its warmth and red-tiled charm.

Eight months.

Slaton reclined in the chair, and minutes later was sound asleep. It was not a consequence of the heavy meal or the wine, nor even the high cabin altitude. By resting now, he was preparing for the next day—a day, he was sure, that would put him in far less civilized conditions.

Anisa took control in the besieged Raqqa mosque that same night. Her first orders reflected a slight inversion of Chadeh's instructions. They had to get a functional communications network up and running. Only when that was done could frontline units be instructed to search for Aziz Uday.

The first application to regain usefulness was an old version of FireChat, a wireless mesh network that required no internet connections. The messaging system was cumbersome and slow, and had gone unused for months, which was probably why it had been left untouched in the system-wide meltdown—what she increasingly saw as an act of sabotage by Uday.

Unfortunately, FireChat did not reach beyond Raqqa. If Uday had indeed run, he was likely farther afield. Anisa decided to employ one of their little-used high-power radios from the tallest rooftop in town. The German-made units were reliable, but came with one serious drawback—they acted like an electronic beacon to the eavesdroppers in the sky.

For a time Anisa was happy she'd been put in charge of things, but that sense of empowerment ebbed when Chadeh arrived and began watching her every move. The caliphate's military chief was still seething, and he paced from one workstation to another—helpless to act himself, and not realizing the distraction his glowering presence was creating. Even less helpful were the four men dressed in black he'd brought along, all heavily armed and standing by the door.

And so it was, when the first useful information arrived, Anisa felt a massive wave of relief. A technician at the back of the room—a woman, she noted proudly—announced, "I have a message from the checkpoint near Suluk! They say Uday was seen running through the village. A squad is searching for him now."

Chadeh ordered superfluously, "Tell them to find him! Stop at nothing!" He rushed to his security detail and whispered sharp instructions. Two of the men disappeared, sprinting out the door. Anisa was sure they'd been told to round up a battalion and join the hunt in Suluk, which was north of Raqqa near the dangerous Turkish border.

Everyone waited nervously for the next ten minutes, at which point another technician said, "I have another sighting. . . ." A long pause, then, "It's in Hajin."

This brought pause. Hajin was east, almost to the old Iraqi border.

A confused Chadeh hovered behind the young man. "One of them must be mistaken," he said. This time he shouted his orders for everyone to hear, and one of the guards at the door ran off, having been dispatched to assemble a squad and get to Hajin as quickly as possible.

Anisa fired off a message to Suluk asking for an update. Strangely, she got a reply almost immediately. SEARCH STILL IN PROGRESS.

For fifteen minutes everyone waited. Then a third sighting was reported, this by an oil field security detachment outside Dayr az Zawr. Chadeh looked at the lone guard remaining at the door. He did not send the man running. Every spare soldier in Raqqa was already en route to the first two sightings.

Anisa felt an uneasy squirm in her gut. She sent a request for updates to both Suluk and Hajin. The replies were immediate and identical. SEARCH STILL IN PROGRESS.

Her innards went to full-blown seizure. *Uday . . . he has done this*. She sat frozen in place, a burqa-clad statue, as she wondered how to tell Chadeh they were busy chasing ghosts.

THIRTY-NINE

Uday and Sarah were, at that moment, in the back-seat of his brother Faisal's road-beaten Toyota Land Cruiser. The SUV had once been registered as a cab, in a time when people had money in their pockets and places to go, and Faisal kept his lighted taxi sign in the trunk and an expired permit sticker in the window on the odd chance he could make a few dollars. The license plate had expired too, but it was one of the few positives of living in Syria these days that things like vehicle registrations and licenses were universally ignored.

The roads south of Raqqa were in abysmal condition: a lack of upkeep, heavy military convoys, and the odd roadside bomb had conspired to turn remote highways into ribbons of black rubble. The Toyota's headlights bounced an uneven path through the pitch-black desert. They'd advanced ninety miles in four hours, which Faisal claimed as a victory, and were now pressing deep into the lawless expanses of what had once been the Homs Governorate of Syria. On the far horizon Uday saw a group of small buildings, a few with windows glowing dimly from whatever fuel sources remained: oil lamps, generators, candles.

Faisal slowed further as the road degraded to little more than a camel path through the desert. The chassis groaned on every pothole, and he muttered complaints about the damage being done to his longtime means of employment. Uday was silently pleased. His rushed research had so far proved accurate—they'd not encountered a single checkpoint since leaving Raqqa.

"What is that?" Sarah asked, pointing ahead.

Everyone went rigid as two massive shadows materialized out of the night. They were just off the roadbed fifty yards ahead, twin mechanical goliaths. Soon the figures resolved in the headlights, and they all stared at the bizarre sight—in the middle of the open desert, a pair of huge bulldozers.

"At least they are working on the roads," said Faisal.

"No," Uday said, having the benefit of insider knowledge. He remembered requisitioning parts for these very machines—and he knew precisely why they were here. "The caliphate does not use such equipment to build. Remember, we are near Palmyra."

Palmyra. There was no need to say more.

Uday stared out the window and was happy for the darkness. He had no desire to see beyond the machines. To see what he'd been complicit in destroying. Uday had produced countless videos for the caliphate, uploaded thousands of photographs. Many were grotesque and inhumane, bordering on sadistic. Yet it was the images from Palmyra that he'd found strangely haunting, perhaps because they represented something more fundamental—not attacks on bound and helpless humans, but an assault on civilization itself.

He remembered as a schoolboy learning the ancient legends. Hadrian, Tiberius, Solomon—all had walked these same sands over the millennia, visited the same oasis crossroad. The Islamic State had come as well. They did not control Palmyra any longer, but there had been more than one occupation at the height of the caliphate's reach. Today its fighters were gone, some no doubt having melded into the local populace. At the crest of its domination, however, ISIS had made its terrible mark.

Uday remembered editing videos to put their work on display. Palmyra, one of the world's most revered archaeological sites, had been declared idolatrous by the caliph. Its ancient stone theater was used as a backdrop for executions, a video Uday himself had uploaded for the world to see. Orders were eventually given to raze every "totem of idolatry." Structures that had withstood thousands of years of weather and earthquakes and invasions became little more than targets to a cult of religious fanatics who attacked them with dynamite and heavy equipment. Men whose education was drawn entirely from one book, and whose teachers slanted its words into a blueprint for an apocalypse, brought ruin as best they could.

Uday's hand tensed over the door handle as he watched the great machines slide past his window. Clearly they had been idle since the Islamic State's pullback. Even so, as the caliphate steadily lost control of territory, he'd heard Chadeh discuss new tactics. Among them—returning teams of infiltrators to places like this, a desperate effort to prove their continued relevance.

He felt a peculiar sensation come over him. "Stop!" Uday shouted.

Faisal stomped on the brakes, and the Toyota skidded to a halt. "What is wrong?"

Uday stared at the nearest bulldozer, only a few yards away. He tried to remember what the mechanic had asked him for over a year ago. *What was it?*

"Aziz?" Sarah asked haltingly.

Finally he remembered. "Give me a rag," he said.

"A rag?" replied Faisal. "But what—"

Uday shot his brother a hard look. Faisal reached beneath his seat and produced a stained piece of cloth. Uday took it, opened the door, and walked to the first of the big machines.

It was painted desert tan, a Russian-built behemoth that had been abandoned by fleeing government forces early in the conflict. The caliphate had claimed the earthmovers as a spoil of war, but for nearly a year they had sat idle on the shores of what was then called Lake Assad. In time, the caliph had seen a need and ordered them put into service. Uday was given a list of spare parts to obtain online.

Now he circled the great machine like a bird circling its prey, sharp-eyed and purposeful. Searching for an opening. He thought he saw what he wanted in a recess of the engine bay. Uday went to work using the rag, but quickly realized that his hands weren't strong enough. He spotted a large wrench on the floor of the driver's compartment. The wrench's span wasn't big enough to grip the housing, so he turned it into a hammer, battering the thick plastic blow after blow. It finally came loose and fell to the dirt, oil spewing onto the ground from a broken line. With his method in place, he had the second bulldozer disabled in less than a minute.

Uday stood back when he was done, completely out of breath. The sleeves of his robe were stained black as he stood back and regarded his work. The two engine oil filters he had ordered from St. Petersburg, necessary for the machines to run, were lying on the ground, their plastic cases shattered and fabric filter rings crushed. Oil oozed from the portals on both engines, dripping down the great treads and turning the sand beneath them black. Leaching back into the very desert from which it might have been extracted.

"*Aziz?*" Sarah's voice, wrapped in caution.

He turned to see her standing outside the SUV, a guarded expression on her face.

"Are you all right?" she asked.

He dropped the wrench into the dirt, and found himself smiling. "Yes, darling. I am better than I have been in a very long time."

FORTY

The Gulfstream floated gracefully out of a clear starlit sky, and shortly after three that morning began its final approach to Palmachim Air Base, south of Tel Aviv. Slaton saw the blackness of the Mediterranean sweep past the window, followed by runway lights, and finally a rush of concrete before the tires kissed the earth—arriving within inches of the place and two minutes of the time that Nicolette had promised so many hours ago. That degree of exactitude and sureness, he knew, was about to come to an end.

The jet taxied hurriedly to a quiet corner of the airfield, and when it stopped he saw a long car in the shadow of a hangar. *Bloch or Nurin?* he wondered. The answer was fast in coming.

"Hello, Anton," Slaton said, sliding into the limo's backseat.

"The director sends his regrets," Bloch replied. "He's rather busy."

"I can imagine."

"A great deal has happened since you left France."

"You could have sent a message—I'm sure the airplane was capable."

"I thought it better to let you get some sleep on the flight."

"Is it going to be that kind of night?"

Bloch gave a wistful sigh. "I think it is what I have come to cherish most about retirement—eight hours of uninterrupted sleep every night."

"Except tonight."

"We heard from Baland. The raid was a failure—the girl wasn't there."

Slaton's gaze turned critical. "Did I make a mistake? Was it the wrong apartment?"

"Don't worry—your instincts for the dark arts remain as reliable as ever. She was definitely there, and stayed for a time. The French recovered trace evidence of gunshot residue. There was also blood in the bathroom, along with some skin and hair that is being analyzed for DNA."

"I doubt they'll find any matches."

"I would stake my dubious reputation against it."

"So how did we lose track of her?"

"The *katsas* missed an exit, and obviously she became suspicious. There was a skylight in the roof, and she very conveniently kept a ladder in the flat. The roof in back is very near a neighboring building, and from there half the rooftops in Monceau come into play. I'm sure it was a planned contingency on her part."

"I missed it too. The mistake is on me as much as anyone."

"Now is not the time for recriminations. This

woman, Malika, *was* there for a time. I think the response might have been quicker if Baland hadn't insisted on leading the assault himself."

"I'll bet he's disappointed."

"He used a far stronger word—Nurin talked to him directly. The French have gone back to searching, but she's gone to ground again. Another safe house, I would imagine. As far as anyone can tell, she's working alone."

"It will be awkward for Baland if she's taken into custody."

"Undoubtedly. But that is not our problem."

The limo was already to the freeway, accelerating quickly on a nearly empty road. The city around them was in a deep sleep. Slaton asked, "Has Baland heard from Uday about the details of this exfiltration?"

"Not yet, but we expect contact soon . . . assuming he is still alive."

"Do you have reason to believe otherwise?"

Bloch said, "The Americans run the best signals intelligence in Syria, and we asked them to pass along immediately anything relating to Aziz Uday. It didn't take long. They isolated radio traffic and messages implying that the caliphate is looking for him— looking very hard."

"That's good—it supports the version of events Baland has given us. It means Uday really has defected."

"That is our view as well. The Americans also mentioned that they've recorded an 'event' on certain internal servers within Raqqa. Virtually all ISIS comm networks appear to be either down or degraded."

Slaton considered it. "So their wizard really did throw a wrench in his machine to cover his departure."

"It would appear so."

"I think I like this guy."

"Good, because very soon you may be hauling him out of Syria on your back."

While Anisa rushed from one workstation to another coordinating the search for Uday, Chadeh convened a meeting with two other men in a quiet corner of the mosque. She watched them discreetly, noticing that they'd taken with them printouts of the information Malika had sent earlier. There was a hushed argument, and the men gestured at different pages. Finally, Chadeh led the group back toward Anisa.

She held her breath as they approached.

"We have come to a decision," he said. "This information Argu has sent us—it is useful. Unfortunately, any value will be lost if Uday manages to reach the West. We must initiate the first wave of attacks immediately."

"Attacks?" Anisa repeated.

"We must strike these targets before the authorities are alerted. Use any cells or individuals in France who can be contacted."

"But the database has been—"

"Enough!" Chadeh said, cutting her off with a slashing motion of his hand. "Your glorious database has proved a failure in the worst way. Surely other methods remain to contact our recruits in Europe."

She thought about it. "There might still be paper files in the trash cans—unless Uday has seen to those as well."

"Yes, that's good. I can order commanders to spread the word among frontline units. Many of those from Europe will have contact numbers for friends and family members."

Anisa nodded, conceding that Chadeh had a point. They were going back to square one, but it might be possible to muster a small force quickly. "How many teams will we need?" she asked.

Chadeh handed over the printout, and she saw certain paragraphs circled. "We have identified seven targets to be attacked, God willing."

"So be it. I will work through the night. By tomorrow afternoon the orders will be sent."

"No. You are to have this done by morning. That is not God's will—it is mine."

The Toyota was an hour beyond Palmyra when its headlights illuminated a fork in the road.

"Which road should I take?" Faisal asked.

"Have you seen any route numbers?" Uday asked.

"Road signs?" Faisal laughed. "You are not in England anymore, my brother."

Uday tried to recall the route he'd traced with his finger over a map on a computer screen. He knew the caliphate still ran one roving checkpoint in this area, but he couldn't remember exactly where it was supposed to be today. "Steer left," he said, "away from Damascus."

A straight line would have given a three-hundred-mile run from Raqqa to the Golan Heights, but his chosen route was necessarily longer to avoid villages and known trouble spots. The ground they'd traversed so far had until recently been controlled by the Islamic State—although "control" was a strong word anywhere in Syria these days. Map or not, Uday knew they were at the limits of the caliphate's reach. Soon they would be crossing sparsely populated desert, and any encounters there would likely be with a local tribe, the sort who were happy to take a "transit tax." Less likely, but of greater risk, was to run into Hezbollah or a squad of Assad's thugs. The risks down any road here were measurable, although not much different from what Bedouin had faced since the days of Christ: tribal mistrust, difficult terrain, and a place where lines on maps were meaningless.

"Are you sure we have enough petrol?" Uday asked.

Faisal, who rarely had a care, flapped his hand in the air. "I am sure we can reach Nawa. There I will find more . . . have no worries. My brother is a big man, nearly a member of the Shura Council." He chuckled, and when he looked in the mirror Uday and Sarah both smiled at him. As soon as Faisal looked away, Uday's humor dissipated.

He said, "You realize that you can never go back to Raqqa."

"Yes, I know," Faisal replied, echoing their earlier conversation. He was a bachelor who'd moved to the city on Uday's coattails, and seeing the limitations of driving a cab, he had done well administering a food-distribution center under the caliphate's banner. In

Nawa, Faisal would have to find something new. But then, he always did. The brothers had been raised on the tan shores of the Gulf of Oman, and from there launched into the world. They kept in touch with their extended family, cousins mostly, who asked guarded questions about what the brothers were doing in Syria. Uday was sure Faisal would be welcomed back in Muscat if it came to that. He, however, had his sights set farther west.

Uday's ardor for the caliphate had long ago been beaten down by the brutality of the regime. It was his feelings for Sarah, however, that had put the idea of desertion into his mind. Once that choice was made, he'd tried to consider every consequence. He could think of only two people in Raqqa who might suffer reprisals for his defection. Both were in the car with him now.

He felt Sarah take his hand, and when he met her gaze Uday didn't like what he saw—a woman trying to be brave.

"It's all right," he said. "I have planned everything."

"How can we get across the Israeli border?" she asked in a hushed voice as the SUV groaned over deep ruts.

"I am making arrangements. If we can safely reach Nawa, I have friends there who will give us shelter for a day or two—Druze who are not aligned with the government." The Golan had a well-earned reputation as an independent region, a place where tribal alignments were more fluid than in other governorates. Certain groups there even favored Israel, and the seemingly endless war in Syria had driven growing numbers across the border to apply for Israeli citizenship. It was dangerous territory, to be sure, but laced with an air of opportunity. "A man is going to come. He will guide us across the border."

"But we are talking about Israel. They watch the Golan closely, and the U.N. keeps a buffer zone. How can we get through such defenses?"

"That is the beauty of it. The man who is coming to lead us out—he is Israeli. He will take us to safety."

Sarah nodded thoughtfully, and he thought he might have seen a softening in her expression. Then all at once it went to stone. "Look!"

He followed her gaze through the front windshield. Two heavy trucks were blockading the road ahead. Both flew the black flag of the Islamic State.

FORTY-ONE

To his mild surprise, Slaton was not delivered to Mossad headquarters. The car traveled north along the coast highway to Haifa, followed by an easterly turn into darkening hills. In a few hours the sun would rise, and Slaton knew perfectly well what would be beneath it: Mount Meron, with its uneven green cliffs presiding over the smooth Sea of Galilee. He was familiar with these hills, having spent time here as a teen. Indeed, these were the grounds where he had learned to stalk and shoot small game, innocently honing skills that would one day be leveraged by Mossad to a very different end. Soon after they'd turned away from the coast, Bloch told Slaton what he already knew: This would be the staging point for an extraction op across the Golan Heights.

Civilization disappeared behind them like an apparition, and when the car reached the safe house, there was not another light in sight. Bloch and Slaton got out, and under a dome of stars they set out along a curving gravel path. When the track straightened, Slaton saw a modest house at the end backed by a large detached shed. Halfway up the straightaway, two men materialized from the siding, Uzis slung across their chests. Everyone nodded cordially—or at least as cordially as was possible under such circumstances. Two minutes later they entered the house.

The three men who were waiting inside reminded Slaton of himself not so many years ago. Young and fit, each with the kind of stony gaze that wasn't a product of mere training.

Bloch introduced them to Slaton from left to right. "Aaron, Tal, and Matai. They know who you are."

Handshakes were exchanged all around. Aaron was tall and leanly built with a tight professional haircut, Tal dark and intense. Matai, with shaggy black hair and a careless smile, looked as though he ought to be teaching college English—causing Slaton to suspect he was the most dangerous of the bunch.

Aaron, obviously in charge of the unit, led everyone to another room and began a briefing. "We're extracting two individuals from Syria across the Golan border. Is that still the big picture?"

"For now, yes," Slaton said.

"Can I ask where this information is coming from?"

Before Slaton could respond, Bloch said, "No."

Aaron frowned.

Slaton intervened, "I've met the source who's in direct contact with our defectors."

"And you trust him or her?"

"Absolutely not. When I go into harm's way, I never trust anyone who's not standing next to me."

Aaron's expression brightened. "You really are him," he said. "The one we all thought was dead."

Slaton didn't reply. Aaron didn't pursue it. They diverted to a room full of guns, explosives, body armor, and comm gear. Slaton gave a low whistle. "You guys are serious about this."

"About staying alive? You're damned straight." For five minutes Aaron briefed everyone on what was available.

Slaton once more shifted gears: Chateaubriand and Bordeaux had given way to full magazines and flash-bang grenades. At the end, he had only one question. "How will we move?"

"I was hoping you'd ask that."

Aaron led Slaton and Bloch outside, then down a dirt path to the shed. It was too small to be called a barn, but big enough to contain a vehicle or two. Aaron took a grip on a large swinging door, pulled it open, and tugged a hanging cord to snap on a light. Slaton stood looking at four large ATVs. They were painted in a desert camo pattern and tricked out for weapons carriage.

"Nicely done," he said.

"The Syrian side of the border goes mostly to desert, so we decided staying off-road was to our advantage. I figure these are good for a twenty-mile penetration. If the retrieval is deeper than that, we might have to revisit the concept."

Each of the ATVs had two seats, and the tactical math did not escape Slaton. Four of them, two people to extract—even if one of the ATVs had a mechanical failure or was damaged, everyone had a seat. It was exactly how he would have planned it.

He asked, "Have our border patrols been alerted to this op?"

"No," answered Bloch. "In order to maintain secrecy, we've decided to wait and see which sectors will be in play. We'll notify only those checkpoints that have a need to know, and even then at the last minute. We've coordinated with the IDF to cancel any roving patrols scheduled for our crossing window. You'll have drones overhead for the entire mission, and the operators are already busy logging the current positions of Syrian border units. There hasn't been much activity in recent months. The Golan is a relatively quiet frontier compared to the rest of Syria, and the government has cut patrols to a bare minimum."

"Tunnels?" Slaton asked. He knew Hezbollah had dug extensive networks along the border with Lebanon.

"None that we know of—and we probably *would* know."

Tal came out of the house and called Aaron inside, leaving Bloch and Slaton alone near the shed.

"Okay," said Slaton, "so all we need now is someone to rescue. Which means a call from Baland."

"It would appear so. Hopefully our man Uday has made his way south."

They began walking back to the house. Halfway there, Slaton paused on the dirt path, and said, "I'll catch up with you in a minute."

Bloch kept going without question.

Slaton turned a lazy half circle, sensing again what had struck him earlier. Familiarity. The hills and dry air, the brush of a night breeze across scrubland. Sweet nocturnal scents that would soon be beaten into submission by the sun. At his feet were clumps of weeds he'd seen before, some native species he remembered pulling from vegetable gardens long ago.

The land around him wasn't the only bit of déjà vu. The shed, the house, the hard men he'd just met—that was a homecoming of another kind. Sometime in the next twenty-four hours he would be part of a special-ops team crossing a very unfriendly border. It wasn't what had been on his radar when he'd left Palawan.

Or was it?

How many times had he put the old ways behind him, only to find himself drawn back in? At some point he had to wonder if it was a fundamental flaw in his character. Some magnetism to that ferrous life built on adrenaline and danger, even violence. *No,* he argued internally, *I'm not setting out to kill anyone tomorrow. I'm here to rescue a man with information that might save lives. Even Christine would approve of that.*

That was what he told himself. Again and again.

He looked into the still-lit shed. Near the combat-rigged ATVs he saw a toddler's tricycle, a happy Red Rover with an oversized front wheel. Next to that, a plastic Hula-Hoop and a ball. In years past he would have viewed such objects as no more than visual clutter. Now, gladly, he understood their importance. Perhaps all too clearly. The incompatibility of his two existences, which he'd hoped would lessen over time, seemed more distinct than ever.

Slaton drew deeply on the sweet-scented air. He went to the shed, jerked the cord to turn out the light, and dragged the big door shut. By the time he reached the house his thoughts had recoupled. Get this done, and in twenty-four hours he could be on his way back to join his family. And the more time he spent with them, he reasoned, the more places like this would become a distant memory.

There were four guards at the checkpoint, and even in the wash of the headlights Uday could discern long beards and dusty clothing. All were clad in black, and each man carried a rifle, although not in a threatening manner. They stared at the oncoming Toyota SUV as if it had arrived from outer space.

"What should we do?" Faisal asked. His hand was on the gearshift lever, the engine idling.

"Be calm," instructed Uday. "Put your hands where they can be seen, and let me do the talking."

The Toyota came to a stop, and one of the men approached the driver's-side window with a flashlight in hand. The beam paused at Faisal's open window, then shifted to the backseat and bounced back and forth between Uday and Sarah. The soldier's face was dirty and scarred, and a sudden smile put a set of rotted teeth on display.

"Welcome, and God be praised. We expected you earlier."

Uday felt Sarah's stare, but ignored it. "We were delayed. You have what we require?"

The guard waved, and two of his companions approached. One was struggling under the weight of two jerry cans, and based on the effort he was expending they were certainly full. The other man carried a wicker basket.

"Faisal," said Uday, "unlock your petrol door."

Faisal's left hand went down to the floorboard, and they all heard a faint clunk as the fuel door opened. The man carrying the cans unscrewed the cap and began fueling the Toyota.

The second guard came to the window. He pulled an expensive-looking phone from the basket and handed it through to Uday. He then provided three large water bottles, followed by a package of flatbread and carved meat. "You have done well," said Uday. "It will not be forgotten. Tell me your names, brother."

The man who seemed to be in charge spouted off four names, and Uday looked at him intently as if trying to remember them.

The leader said, "We have heard nothing from headquarters since your message—that was many hours ago."

"I know," Uday replied. "The Americans have once again blocked our radio and phone networks."

"One day the crusaders will set foot in our caliphate . . . then we will teach them something."

"The end of days is imminent, God willing."

"Is there anything else you need?"

"No," Uday replied. "And don't bother calling for instructions. The network won't be available until well after daybreak. You and your men should stand down for the night, get some rest."

"They will be most grateful."

The man doing the refueling finished, and he carried away the empty cans.

The leader waved his hand, and one of his men mounted the truck on the left, started it, and backed out of the road to create a passage.

Uday said, "We must continue south from here, toward Nawa. Do you have any information on government patrols?"

"*Nawa*?" the man repeated.

"I cannot discuss specifics, but trust me when I say our mission is a vital one. You know this area, and anything you can do to aid our safe passage would be a great help."

"The government has been busy elsewhere in recent weeks. Hezbollah are staying close to Damascus. Whatever you do, keep to the roads—the Bedouin have been getting nasty, but they rarely leave the desert. I suggest Route 110, then after Bawidan there is a rough road. It will take you southwest to Nawa. This time of year it should be in good condition—your vehicle will have no trouble."

Uday thanked the man, and implied that Chadeh himself would be informed of his helpfulness. Faisal soon had them under way, the Toyota's headlights once again bouncing aimlessly over tawny desert scrub.

"That was very clever," Sarah remarked.

"Clever means nothing until we are safe."

"Still . . . I am impressed."

"Until a few hours ago I headed the Institution for

Public Information. You know what they say—information is power."

Uday looked down and regarded the phone they'd given him. It was a satellite device—probably the only one the unit had been issued. He turned it on to find the battery fully charged. They really *had* made an effort. He quickly obtained a signal, and after a deep breath, Uday began typing numbers. His finger hesitated over the green send button. He realized it was the middle of the night in Paris. His finger slipped away.

As tempting as it was, the call could wait. Uday wanted Zavier Baland to be wide awake when the final arrangements were made.

FORTY-TWO

For the balance of that morning, Baland guided the hunt for Malika from his old office in DGSI headquarters—decorum had never been a strong suit, but even he realized it would be poor form to appropriate Michelis' suite before his funeral played out. Because it was a small room, analysts cycled in two at a time. Presently he was facing a captain from the national gendarmerie, who was the forensics lead at the flat in Monceau, and a woman from his own command center.

"Do we have any fingerprints yet?" Baland asked the evidence man from behind a desk that seemed suddenly inadequate.

"More than we'd like," said the captain. "At least twenty discrete sets."

Baland raised an eyebrow.

"The place has been rented out weekly for the last year, so it's not really surprising. Based on the condition of the prints, and the fact that one set consistently overlays others on high-use surfaces—things like tap handles and doorknobs—we think we've distinguished the ones that belong to our suspect."

"Let me guess," Baland ventured. "They don't match anything in our databases?"

"I'm afraid not, which seems inconceivable when one considers that we have fingerprints on two hundred and ten million people. We're not sure how this woman arrived in France, but it obviously wasn't through any official point of entry."

"Are you suggesting she's not one of our home-grown insurrectionists?"

The captain, who exuded the manner of a typical Parisian, did not answer right away. Baland knew that a great number of his countrymen, even those in the law-enforcement community, still grappled with the idea that sons and daughters of the republic could be every bit as violent as the hordes of refugees who'd been flooding in.

"We will cover every possibility," the man finally said, "including that she could be an undocumented resident of France. A DNA analysis is ongoing—we should have the results soon."

Baland steepled his hands under his chin. "The very fact that she left hair and blood evidence behind tells me she's confident we won't find a match. All the same, keep at it." His head turned inquiringly to the woman from the command center. The beaten look on her face told Baland all he needed to know, but as acting director he felt compelled to go through the motions.

She said, "We checked the rental documents for the

flat, but it's a stone wall—everything was done on-line using untraceable funds. In the field we've had the usual sightings, but all have so far proved to be false leads. I expect that will continue until we get a better photograph of our assailant. We've interviewed at least a hundred taxi drivers, and checked CCTV footage from every public transportation hub within two kilometers of the flat. The woman has simply disappeared."

Baland nodded thoughtfully, then gave his analysts the best pep talk he could muster. At the end, he said, "And make sure everyone understands that new leads are to be sent straight to me." The tone of these last words was nothing less than a warning, and having installed that in their minds, he sent the two back to their respective grindstones.

Alone in his office, Baland leaned back in his chair. He clasped his hands behind his neck, stared up at the ceiling, and wondered how the hell he was going to find Malika. The first idea that came to mind was something near fantasy: He could slip quietly out of the building, walk across town to the next scheduled dead drop, and leave her a message. It *could* actually work, assuming she was still mobile and willing to venture outside. He could tell her he was sabotaging the search for her, and insist on a meeting. Unfortunately, she was very likely harboring reservations at that moment, due in no small part to the fact that he'd shot her during their last meeting. On top of that, he himself was frozen in place. He'd already been forced to explain to the head of DGSI internal security why he'd slipped out of his house last night, giving the lame excuse of "a little fresh air" to gloss over the truth—that he'd ditched his protection detail in order to rendezvous with an assassin.

He regretted not pressing Malika in previous meetings about who she associated with in Paris. Certainly there were others in her orbit, evidenced by five bodies recovered from the Grenoble attack. Too late, Baland realized he should have deployed a DGSI team to track her quietly. He had long considered it, but always discarded the idea, fearful of how Malika would react if she spotted any kind of surveillance.

He pushed away his recriminations, knowing they were only a distraction. Malika could be anywhere in France right now, injured and angry. She knew enough about Baland to ruin him.

And worst of all?

She might understand the direction in which his aim had been off at Le Quinze.

He was ruminating on it all when a call came through on his private phone. He didn't recognize the number, and felt a surge of anticipation. He picked up and instantly recognized the voice of Aziz Uday.

At the same time that Baland was taking a call from Syria, a handful of other phones around France were making parallel connections.

In a shoe repair shop in the Reuilly, nestled comfortably along the Right Bank, the proprietor's son listened in silence as his orders from Raqqa, expected for months, finally came through. He was to round up his partner and undertake an assault on a Jewish grocery store a short distance up the river. Far across town, an out-of-work waiter in Montparnasse was cashing his unemployment check when he received an encrypted text message: he was to activate the cell he commanded, assemble the suitcase bomb they'd been working on, and deliver it without delay to a nearby Jewish community center.

For the leadership of ISIS, the process was not without snags. When a burner phone in the glove box of a taxi in Toulon went unanswered, a backup recruit across town had to be contacted to get things moving. An aspiring martyr in Bordeaux, who they'd hoped would steer the cement truck he drove for work into a bagel shop, had changed his mind, or more accurately his religion, having taken up with a stunning Catholic girl in recent months. It was discovered that a cell leader in Caen had been sent to prison, a wrathful young man whose anger was no doubt cresting at that moment, but whose usefulness to the caliphate could only be banked.

In the end, however, Chadeh had his wish. Seven cells, each consisting of between two and six individuals, began preparing for assaults on targets across France. All were to take place in the coming forty-eight hours.

FORTY-THREE

With "what" and "how" settled, the Mossad team in the foothills of the Golan Heights waited through the predawn hours to finalize "where" and "when." Bloch took the call they were waiting for at eleven thirty that morning. Everyone at the safe house stood watching as the former head of Mossad was briefed by Zavier Baland. The conversation lasted less than two minutes. Slaton had a vision of Baland on a balcony, or perhaps the roof of the DGSI building, doing his best to stay out of sight and talk in hushed tones. It was a testament to the circuitous nature of modern communications that Aziz Uday, the once-removed source of the information, was less than a two-hour drive from where they stood.

"So far so good," said Bloch after ending the call. He walked to the kitchen table, which had been taken over by a large topographical map. The map was already peppered with information: borders had been highlighted, Syrian army outposts marked in red, and potential corridors of ingress and egress were charted like so many deep-water channels through treacherous shoals. "Our defectors expect to be in Nawa by dusk."

Aaron cracked open a water bottle and set the cap on Nawa for reference.

"They plan to leave town on foot at midnight, and move due west," Bloch continued. "By one o'clock tomorrow morning they should be at least two kilometers clear of Nawa, and from there they want to forward exact coordinates by phone."

"Phones can be tracked," Aaron said. "We should prearrange a geographic point—an old barn or a derelict pump house."

"We are not talking about professionals," Bloch countered.

"We'll make it work," Slaton interjected.

Aaron asked, "Are we still extracting two subjects?"

"Yes, your primary objective is a man named Uday. We've also agreed to bring out a woman on his request."

Aaron again. "Do we know why he included her in the deal?"

Slaton liked this question, and had been about to ask it himself. A relationship between the two might affect either's behavior during the op.

"No," said Bloch, "but we should assume she's his girlfriend—he was quite insistent that she be included."

"Nawa is twelve kilometers into Syria," said Aaron, plotting on the map. "If we stage near the border, and run over open desert—it'll take between twenty and thirty minutes to get there."

Slaton said, "Maybe less if we can find goat trails or old army roads."

"Army roads?" Tal inquired.

"When we kept the Golan Heights after the Six-Day War, the Syrian regime didn't like it. For years afterward they ran military exercises up and down the border. It was no more than saber-rattling, but their corps of engineers put down a pretty extensive network of unimproved roads. They're no longer maintained because the government has far bigger problems than Israel these days. But the roads are still there."

Aaron said, "Point noted. Now that we know where we're going, we should get fresh drone pictures. If any of these roads look clear and usable, we'll take advantage."

There was no dissent, and soon everyone had new assignments: Slaton and Aaron were responsible for mission planning, Bloch concentrated on intel, and Tal and Matai were assigned to equipment prep.

With everyone busy, Slaton buttonholed Bloch. "Did Uday mention the database?" he asked.

"Yes, he says he's carrying it."

"We need to tell the others about it."

Bloch gave him a severe look.

Slaton stood his ground. "I've been on too many missions where things were kept from me. I can tell you unequivocally—secrets do not promote success."

Bloch relented. "All right, we will tell everyone Uday is carrying valuable information—make it a primary objective, if you want. But we can't divulge the nature of the data."

Slaton decided it was a reasonable compromise. "All right. So let's get to work."

Slaton went to the big map, and found himself alone for a time. Once again, it seemed all too familiar. Brown and tan topographic information, threat markers, coordinate grids. There were a lot of moving parts to this mission, and they would hopefully be held together by the binds of training, knowledge, and even chutzpah. All the same, Slaton knew better than anyone the most important determiner of success.

Luck.

FORTY-FOUR

Uday's plan went wrong minutes after they reached Nawa. It was a warm midafternoon, and Faisal slowed the weary Toyota on the outskirts of town. Enduring rows of olive groves gave way to a sleepy collage of low earth-tone buildings. They were one- and two-story affairs mostly, flat roofs topped by dish antennae, and in the gaps between the homes tough-looking trees sprouted desperately from the hard earth, their scant foliage offering little in the way of shade. Faisal veered onto a road that led to the heart of town, jogging left and right in an increasingly urban setting. That was when the trouble began.

A turn around a sharp corner revealed a checkpoint.

"Look!" said Faisal.

A hundred yards ahead, four men stood casually around a truck. They seemed interested in the approaching Toyota, but hardly alert. All wore uniforms, yet no two seemed to match; one wore a helmet, another a beret, and two had different-colored kaffiyehs wrapped around their heads. It was the flag flying from the truck that cemented who they were—a yellow standard with green script, the first letter of "Allah" reaching up to grasp an assault rifle. This was Hezbollah, the self-proclaimed Army of God.

"Turn around!" Uday ordered.

"It's too late; they have seen us! If I turn away they will only become suspicious."

Uday knew his brother was right. On either side of the road were homes with walled courtyards. There were no side streets or driveways into which they could divert. They were trapped, and worse yet, none of them had papers. On Faisal's suggestion, they'd discarded their ISIS-issued identity cards in the desert hours ago, everyone agreeing there was more danger than value in keeping them. Now they faced a genuine roadblock, one Uday had not prearranged.

"We will talk our way through," said Sarah.

"No, talk is not enough," Faisal countered. "Quickly, give me all your money!" He pulled a wad of bills from his pocket—fortunately Syrian pounds and Turkish lira, and not the Islamic State's failed gold dinar.

Sarah's pockets were empty, and Uday pulled out a meager handful of Syrian pounds. He handed them to Faisal realizing he should have brought more—the first obvious flaw in his rushed escape plan.

Fifty yards from the checkpoint, Uday saw a fifth soldier. By then every set of eyes was on the approaching SUV. The two in the center brandished their weapons threateningly, and a third raised his hand in a classic halt signal. The Toyota slowed, and

Uday saw Faisal slip the money into the small leather folder that had once held his credentials for driving a taxi. His brother had done this before.

The traffic cop, who was evidently in charge, approached Faisal's open window. Up close his uniform was dusted in brown, so too his untrimmed beard and ragged hair. A commander who'd been in the field for some time.

"Papers," he said, no rising inflection to denote a question. He held out a hand, and said, "Tell me where you have come from."

"Damascus," said Faisal, handing over the leather folder.

The man looked inside, paused a beat, then said, "Damascus? You took a very indirect path."

Faisal shrugged. "I am afraid I got lost."

Uday didn't like the trajectory of things. He gripped Sarah's hand, and felt her squeeze back. He couldn't read the man's reaction to the cash, but he noticed that the folder was still in his hand. He'd also not shown it to the men behind him. *Is that important?* Uday wondered. A feeling of helplessness overwhelmed him, and for the first time he regretted getting Sarah involved. He should have taken a less perilous escape route. He should have brought more cash.

"You are from Raqqa," said the officer accusingly. His eyes were on something on the windshield, and Uday realized it was the old taxi sticker. It had been issued by the Syrian government, and was probably coded for a particular city.

"The vehicle is from Raqqa, yes," said Faisal. "But we are from—"

The man cut him off with a wave, and those behind him tensed perceptibly. The leader gave a signal, and one of the men who'd been standing back came forward with a mirror mounted on a stick. He began to inspect the undercarriage.

The man in charge shifted to the back window, bent down, and stared at Uday, then Sarah. He circled to the rear of the SUV.

"This is not good," Sarah whispered.

"I know," said Uday. He quickly pulled out the sat phone. A voice call was out of the question, so he pecked out an urgent message to Baland. He was about to put the phone back in his pocket when Sarah said, "Give it to me!"

He gave her a cautious sideways stare.

"Give it to me, Aziz!"

The harshness of her tone surprised him, but with the men busy searching, he slid the handset across the seat. He watched Sarah tap the screen a few times, then slip it into the folds of her abaya.

Before Uday could ask what she was doing, the leader came back to Faisal's window, and said, "Open the tailgate."

Faisal reached for the remote unlocking latch.

"No!" the man shouted. "Get out and do it yourself."

Faisal got out warily and went to the back. The Hezbollah squad stood back as he unlocked the tailgate and swung it open. The leader ordered him to uncover the compartment beneath the floor. Faisal did so, and when no explosions resulted, the leader closed in, pushed him aside, and performed an inspection.

Uday knew there was nothing incriminating in the vehicle—they themselves were the contraband.

The leader shut the tailgate and came back to Uday's window. "Get out!" he ordered. "We are taking you for further questioning!"

Before Uday could protest, Sarah said in a loud voice, "Enough of this! Does Hezbollah have nothing better to do than accost innocent travelers? We have come to Nawa to see my sister. You should let us pass!"

The leader seemed put off by her tone, but only for a moment. He yanked open the rear door, dragged Uday out, and sent him stumbling across the dirt siding. He ended up next to Faisal. The man reached for Sarah, but she saw it coming and exited the opposite door, doing what little she could to keep control of the situation. Uday had never seen this side of her—nor had he ever been more proud.

Sarah walked around the car to face the commander. With a look of defiance on her exquisite face, she said, "Where are you taking us?"

He replied by slapping her on the cheek, then pushing her toward Uday. It wasn't a forceful shove, but Sarah seemed to lose her balance and went tumbling against an old cobbled wall. She let out a yelp as she struck the wall, and came to rest in a heap.

In a move he would later reflect on as chivalrous, if grossly inadvisable, Uday lunged at the commander. Two soldiers seized him by the arms, and one sank a rifle butt deep into his ribs. Uday grunted and doubled over in pain. When he finally lifted his head again, he met Sarah's gaze. He saw that she was all right. She then gave Uday an almost imperceptible nod.

The technician in him tried to decipher what she was saying, and his best guess was: *The phone is still on.*

He was only half wrong. The phone *was* still on.

But that wasn't what she was trying to tell him.

FORTY-FIVE

Slaton had few recollections of his father, who had died when he was a boy. One of his sayings, however, he remembered well: *Dreams are forward-looking. Nightmares only relive your past.*

Slaton was looking down on himself as he played the memory game with Davy, the two taking turns uncovering tiles stamped with pairs of animals. Giraffes, lions, zebras. The field of play was tremendous, an array consuming the entire table in *Windsom*'s salon, at least a thousand pieces. Davy seemed unbothered by the complexity—on the contrary, he was unstoppable, unearthing matching pair after matching pair as fast as his tiny hands could collect them. As the array dwindled, Slaton got his chances, and on every opportunity he turned over the same tile—the one with Ali Samir's picture. Try as he might, a match never came. At the end Davy had run the board, and Slaton was left staring at two tiles. He turned over the one with Samir's picture. Then he turned over the other and found it blank. . . .

"*David!*"

A distant voice.

"David!"

Slaton blinked his eyes open. Anton Bloch was standing above his bunk, a look of concern etched on his face—even more than usual.

"Yeah . . . what's wrong?"

"We have a problem."

It was requisite, Slaton had always thought, that to become director of Mossad one must have a penchant for understatement. What they had was far more than a "problem."

The team gathered in the kitchen around their mission map. Bloch aside, the others looked much the way Slaton felt—fuzzy and sleep-interrupted. With the mission scheduled to begin just after midnight, they'd all expected to sleep into the evening. It wasn't an easy thing to do, given both the violation of circadian rhythms and the nature of the mission. Bloch had been prepared, providing no-go pills for each member of the team—essentially a high-dose ration of Ambien. All four of them partook, and it did the job. Now they'd all been awakened out of a hard sleep, but yawning and shoulder-scratching aside, no one asked for a go pill. That too was an option in any special-ops pharmacy, but it was hardly necessary. They were about to breach one of the most heavily guarded borders on earth, and thereafter engage Israel's most hated and persistent enemy. That was enough to get everyone jacked up.

"It happened less than an hour ago," said Bloch.

"Uday was taken into custody by Hezbollah." His grimace seemed to deepen, spreading across his face as if by some tectonic process.

"Hezbollah?" Slaton remarked. "Are you sure?"

"Nearly so, and it's not a surprise. As you're all aware, Hezbollah has long been aligned with Syria's Ba'athist government. They've helped fuel the civil war by contributing thousands of fighters. In recent months, some units have taken up patrols along the border with Israel, freeing up government troops to deploy elsewhere."

"That complicates things," Slaton remarked.

"Welcome back to our little corner of the world."

"Where did this happen?" Aaron asked.

"They made it to Nawa, but were picked up at a checkpoint."

"How do we know?"

"The satellite phone—Uday fired off a short message as they were being taken into custody. Thankfully, Baland called us right away. We were able to capture and isolate the signal. We discerned a muted female voice for about twenty minutes, then the connection was terminated. We think it was the girl, judging by the audio, so Uday must have given her the handset. Apparently her name is Sarah."

"Do we know if she still has the phone?"

"Unknown. She might have ended the call for tactical reasons, or perhaps the battery was getting low."

"Or someone searched her and found it," Slaton suggested.

"Very possibly. Talia is working on it. As long as the phone remains turned on, with some battery power, she thinks she can track it—not continuously, but an occasional ping that can be triangulated."

Aaron said, "Even if we know where the phone is, we can't be sure that's where *they* are."

"True," Slaton seconded. "And we can't be sure they're all together."

"I agree," said Bloch, "there are serious gaps in our understanding of the situation. I can tell you we've been monitoring communications channels closely. There has so far been no increase in message traffic to the outpost in Nawa. To me that implies they were taken by a local crew—I doubt they even realize who they've got."

Aaron exchanged a look with Tal and Matai. "And who *do* they have?"

Bloch didn't even glance at Slaton—he could no longer sidestep the question. "The principal we are trying to rescue . . . his full name is Aziz Uday."

After a pause, Aaron said, "ISIS . . . a leadership position."

"Correct. Aziz Uday is, or I should say *was,* the head of the Islamic State's information and technology section. For reasons that are not yet clear, he wishes to defect."

Someone cursed in Hebrew, before Aaron said, "Okay. That means the longer we wait, the greater the chance that Hezbollah will find out who they've got. Looks to me like we either gear up and go at sundown . . ."

"Or we don't go at all," Slaton finished.

Slaton exchanged a look with each of the other

three. There was never any hesitation. "Smash and grab?" he said.

"Smash and grab," Aaron replied.

"Fair enough." Slaton readdressed the map. "So let's try to figure out where they are."

FORTY-SIX

Their hostages were, as verified by a Predator drone that was loitering four miles overhead, somewhere inside a sprawling two-story villa on the outskirts of Nawa.

"At least that's where the phone is," Aaron remarked.

Bloch gave an overview. "We've been watching the villa continuously for the last hour. There are three vehicles in front, all military, two guards outside. The good news is that we know this place, and it correlates to our situation. Hezbollah has been using this villa for months as a base for a regular contingent that rotates in and out of town."

"And the bad news?" Tal asked, knowing like any good operator that was coming as well.

"There are usually close to twenty men in these units. We also believe the villa serves as their armory—they'll have no shortage of guns or ammo."

Before anyone could grumble, Slaton said, "Having weapons available isn't the same as having them in hand. As long as they aren't expecting us, we'll have a brief window when we can work quietly."

"Reinforcements?" Aaron asked.

"The nearest Hezbollah unit we know about is thirty kilometers away. There are government units closer, including a remote outpost five kilometers away, north along the border. A contingent roughly the same size."

"That gives us fifteen minutes after any alarm is raised," Slaton said.

Bloch turned taciturn. "And here I should remind you of something. Each of you knows the importance of this mission. Director Nurin—on the instructions of the one man above him—has given strict orders. This is *not* a strike against either the Syrian government or Hezbollah. If you come under attack, you are authorized to return fire. But remember—the objective is to bring three individuals to safety with the least amount of collateral damage."

"Three?" Slaton was the first to remark. "I thought we were bringing out Uday and a woman."

"Yes, as did I. In going over the feed from the phone, however, we've identified a third person working with them. It is only conjecture based on captured audio, but it may be Uday's brother. Whoever it is, if this man helped them flee Raqqa, he would be at dire risk if left behind. I think we have an obligation to include him. Plan to bring back three—if it turns out to be two, all the better."

Bloch waited, and no one protested. "Good." He looked pointedly at Slaton, and then Aaron. "If things get difficult, it is essential that you prioritize. Uday *must* be extracted. The girl and this other man are of secondary importance—do not risk his safety for them."

"I think that's a mistake," said Slaton.

"Why?"

"Because Uday himself is a secondary objective."

Slaton stared at Bloch, but not as intensely as did the other three.

Aaron, speaking for Tal and Matai, said, "Whatever you two are talking about, I think we have a damned good need to know."

Bloch nodded. "Yes, David and I have already discussed this. You should all know that Uday claims to be carrying some *very* valuable information."

Matai asked, "As in papers or a computer?"

"Possibly, but we don't know for sure. It's most likely an electronic file carried on a memory device. I can't divulge anything about what these files contain—but trust me when I say it is vital we obtain them."

Aaron suggested, "Any of them might be carrying it."

"Or for that matter," added Slaton, "it could be sitting in that building on the desk of a Hezbollah captain."

"I agree, these are all possibilities. Hopefully once we have Uday, he can tell us."

The team was wide awake.

"All right," said Slaton, "three hours until dusk. Let's do this."

Everyone began their private preparations. Soldiers

everywhere had their rituals: weapons checked and loaded, holsters tight, batteries charged. Lucky charms pocketed and "last letters" placed in footlockers. When Slaton finished with his gear, he found himself trying to remember his parting words to Christine. *I love you both*—that was what he *should* have said, but he remembered something less profound. Something along the lines of, *I'll be back before you know it*. At the time it had seemed enough.

He walked outside, pulled the phone Bloch had issued him from his pocket, and studied it thoughtfully. He dialed Talia, and she picked up right away.

"Hello, David."

"Hi."

"I've still got a good ping on Uday's sat phone," she said.

"Good . . . although that's not why I'm calling."

Slaton hesitated there, until she said, "Are you okay?"

"Yeah, I'm good. I just have a favor to ask."

"Sure, what can I do for you?"

"Remember when I told you about the satellite connection on my boat?"

"Yes."

"Did you track it down?"

A hesitation.

"It's okay," he added.

"Yes, Anton thought we should know where your wife was."

"He was right. Do you still have a lock on it?"

"No, I haven't been following it . . . but I'm pretty sure I could find it again if I tried."

"Try."

"Why?" she asked.

"I want you to send a message for me." He gave her a specific address.

"Okay. What do you want me to say?"

"Nothing out of the ordinary. Tell them I miss them, and that I'll be home soon. And mention to my wife that I was thinking we should cruise the Med this fall."

"Okay, I can do that. Anything else?"

"No, I think that about covers it. Thanks."

FORTY-SEVEN

The Golan Heights was born as a volcanic plateau, a great table of inner earth rising above the Sea of Galilee and the Jordan River. Dozens of volcanic cones give evidence of its creation, and the resulting basalt plain stretches eastward deep into Syria. On flat and relatively featureless terrain, the forests of past eras have been replaced by scrub and low-lying brush, and in a few quarters beaten into farmland. It is a place with little cover, hardpan surfaces, and has long been sparsely populated. For Slaton's team, it was a topography that translated directly into one word—"speed."

The ATVs had been purchased as stock models, but their recreational lineage ended there. Engine performance had been boosted, and on a decent road they could eclipse seventy miles an hour. Thin steel decks had been added front and rear for carrying gear. The tires were special run-flat variants, and light armor had been welded over vital points on the engine. The exhaust system was sound-suppressed, and rerouted to minimize IR signature. For tonight's mission, which demanded speed over unimproved terrain, optional roll cages had been installed. The vehicles were staged forward on an Army flatbed, and unloaded within a mile of the border as dusk was taking its grip.

At that point, Slaton and the others got a final update from the drone before making their dash into Syria. The planned route avoided not only Hezbollah outposts and minefields, but all known inhabited structures. Farmhouses, villages, and even storage sheds were kept two hundred yards distant.

The Golan Heights border was established by the U.N. in 1974. Erring on the side of caution, two lines of demarcation were drawn—to the west was a boundary designated "Alpha," and to the east "Bravo." The buffer zone between them had been monitored by U.N. troops ever since.

"The sector we're going through is watched by Fijians," said Aaron. "They're actually pretty good, as far as U.N. troops go, but I found what looks like a useful gap."

"Okay," said Slaton, as he quietly watched the others. Matai was triple-checking his weapons, and he saw Tal rolling his neck as if warming up for a big game.

Aaron continued, "Once we get across Bravo there are a few farms, but most are fallow this time of year. Outside that, the terrain will be rough."

"Then you should lead," Slaton said. "You've got the most time in one of these seats."

"Right—so let's do this."

* * *

They departed in loose formation into a moonless night. Slaton was impressed by the quietness of the ATVs, especially at high throttle settings. Everyone wore night-vision goggles, necessary to avoid the thicker stands of vegetation and hidden wadis. Each man also wore comm gear, although as quiet as the ATVs were, talking was impossible as they bounded over the rock-hard landscape.

The buffer zone was quickly behind them, and Slaton followed Aaron's lead as they skirted groves of mature olive trees and grainfields waiting patiently for spring. They stopped twice in the first ten minutes, once to let two cars pass on a crossing road, and again when Aaron spotted two young boys walking on a distant path. Slaton wished they could have waited until the early-morning hours, when most people would be asleep, but their hand had been forced.

Thirty cautious minutes later they reached the outskirts of Nawa. Aaron slowed the convoy as the first habitations came into view, and they parked half a mile clear in a dense stand of brush. All four men rendezvoused at the top of a gentle hill, Aaron and Slaton in the center, Tal and Matai on the flanks. Everyone was alert for the slightest deviation in sound or movement.

Slaton said over the tactical frequency, "Drone updates?"

Bloch responded immediately, and in less than his

usual forceful tone—even thirty miles away, he too sensed a need for quiet. "No change. The phone is still giving a signal from the targeted building, twelve hundred meters from your present position. I see no police or patrols in your quadrant. One vehicle checkpoint remains on the north side of town."

"Okay," Slaton said, "that's as good as we're going to get."

They struck out in tight formation, Tal and Matai keeping wide, and Slaton taking the point. They trotted low through the scrub with MP7s—everyone's assault weapon of choice—poised and ready. Tal also carried a short-barrel shotgun on his shoulder in case the need arose for close-quarters work. Slaton veered away from a home that was ablaze with light, and on reaching the first street they shouldered to a wall but kept moving, pausing only occasionally in shadows to look and listen.

The town was quiet but alive. Music flowed from some unseen window, and a few cars could be heard in the heart of town. The scents were there as well, a tang of cooking meat on one brush of wind, the stench of a backed-up sewer on the next. The sensory static of civilization. Five minutes later they saw their objective: the once-grand villa that had been commandeered by Hezbollah and transformed into a militia outpost.

The team had spent hours studying the place, two stories of earthen brick and barrel tile. They'd memorized the shape of the courtyard wall, the location of every door and window, and had a good idea of the interior floor plan. Now everyone saw it all firsthand. The villa's windows were mostly lit, and at that moment there was no one outside. Everyone's ears strained for sounds. The occasional distant voice interrupted the night, but in every case the tones were calm and conversational. They all heard a chair get pushed back across a tile floor somewhere inside. There was still no moon, and aside from the splash of a streetlight on the southern edge, the exterior looked dark and impenetrable.

Aaron looked at Slaton, and whispered, "Looks a lot different from our daytime, God's-eye reconnaissance view."

"I know," Slaton replied. "But then it always does, doesn't it?"

Uday was alone in the small interrogation room. He was sure Sarah and Faisal were nearby, probably in a similar space—one door, no windows, a small table that separated two chairs. He'd been questioned by an officer for nearly an hour, and had no doubt the others were being asked the same questions. *Where are you from? How do you know one another? Why are you traveling to Nawa?*

Thankfully they'd had the foresight to go over it once, on a long stretch of road after Palmyra. The story of a hired driver and a young couple running away from Damascus to escape a forced marriage. It was plausible, but Uday didn't delude himself—their one-play act, no matter how well performed, would only buy time. Up to this point, things had been relatively civil. Uday, unfortunately, had been in charge of videography for ISIS—more than almost anyone on earth, he knew the depths to which interrogations could sink. He also knew where they inevitably ended, countless pixelated images of butchery burned into his mind. There was actually some small comfort in knowing the endgame. Very soon, he, Sarah, and Faisal would encounter men who were far less reasonable. Men who were better interrogators than they were liars.

That he had not already been transferred to a more secure facility he took as a minor victory. His greatest fear was that he and Sarah would be separated. For that Uday had no plan, and he knew they would use it against him. He wondered what had come of the phone—he'd seen Sarah conceal it in her gown. The militiamen would have searched her by now, but that was an image Uday didn't want to dwell on. He tried to remember whether there had been anything incriminating on the handset. He'd used it only to call Baland, but the device had been given to him by a frontline ISIS squad. What might they have installed? Verses from the Quran? Pictures of the caliph? He should have taken the time to sanitize the phone's memory, just as he'd always done to equipment acquired by his division in Raqqa. How far away that seemed now.

He was regretting yet another mistake, hunched forward with his head in his hands, when the door burst open. Uday saw a Hezbollah officer he'd not seen before, backed by two guards.

"Aziz Uday," he said.

Uday felt a tightening in his chest, and his hands

squeezed his thighs. He'd thought they might identify him, but not so quickly. "I don't know that name."

The officer, who was significantly older than the previous interrogator, only scowled. "Take him!"

The two men rushed to Uday and each grabbed an arm. They lifted him to his feet, and although he didn't try to fight, his legs seemed unresponsive. "Sarah!" he said hoarsely.

There was no reply.

He was dragged down a hallway, his feet trailing behind him, then out into the night across a dirt parking apron. A big SUV was waiting twenty yards away, both doors on the right side open invitingly. He got his feet beneath him and tried to see inside, hoping against hope to find Sarah already there. Then, quite unexpectedly, the man on his left suddenly released his grip.

Uday twisted in that direction as the other man kept going. But only for an instant. All at once the second guard let go as well. Uday stumbled momentarily, then got his balance and stood straight. The second man crumpled to the ground like a bag of wet sand. Unsure what was happening, he looked back at the first guard. He was on the ground as well, silent and motionless, with a small round smudge on his forehead. Something dark was pooling beneath him on the ground. In the same instant that these facts were coalescing in Uday's muddled brain, the limo began to disintegrate before his eyes. The front windshield burst outward, glass spraying into the sky. A man slumped from the driver's seat and fell to the dirt. He too remained still.

A breathless Uday saw two dark figures approaching. They were thickly built and moving fast. Their weapons swept rhythmically, side to side, and both wore night-vision gear on their heads. His nontactical brain could hardly keep up, but a vague hope arose.

One of the figures spoke. "Aziz Uday?"

Uday nodded.

"Come with us! We are here to take you to Israel!"

FORTY-EIGHT

Slaton had spoken to Uday in English. This had been one of their easier pre-mission decisions—Bloch had gleaned through research that Uday had attended school in England.

"Let's go!" Slaton ordered.

Uday seemed hesitant, and didn't respond right away. This too was expected. Because he was a technician, this was likely his first combat exposure. He was overwhelmed by the rapid-fire sequence of violent sensory inputs. When Slaton grabbed his arm, Uday tried to pull away. The stonemason's grip wasn't to be broken.

"No!" Uday pleaded. "We must get Sarah and my brother!"

"We'll take care of it," Slaton insisted. His tone was hushed. Other than one shattered windshield, no alarm had been raised, their sound-suppressed weapons working as advertised. He began pulling Uday across the dirt lot. Aaron backed away with them, his head sweeping left and right in search of threats.

"You have the personnel data?" Slaton asked.

"No, that's what I'm trying to tell you! It's on a memory stick—Sarah has it!"

Slaton didn't stop moving, but forced Uday's eyes to his own. "Which room is she in?"

"I don't know. We were separated. But they've discovered who I am—they were going to take me elsewhere."

Slaton keyed his mic. "*The girl has the data,*" he transmitted. "*Find her fast. The third man too if you see him—it's Uday's brother!*"

Tal and Matai acknowledged, and Slaton watched two hulking figures dash with guns raised through the doorway Uday had just exited. Slaton planted Uday behind a solid courtyard wall, and in the same moment he heard the muted mechanical clanks of suppressed MP7 fire, staggered in controlled semi-automatic groupings.

"Stay with him!" Slaton ordered Aaron, and didn't wait for a response before sprinting toward the entrance. Then on the radio, "*One's coming in support, same door!*"

He burst through the entrance with his weapon ready. Down a long hall he saw two bodies down, both enemy. The end of stealth was imminent. Tal emerged from a doorway pulling a woman by the elbow. He directed her eyes toward Slaton, who was nearest the exit, and gave the woman a slap on the ass that would have made a horse bolt. Slaton held out his hand like he was asking her to dance, and she sprinted toward him. Slaton had just touched her hand when he saw flashes of motion at the top of the hall.

He trained his MP7 there and saw two hostiles

with rifles, but Tal was in his line of fire. At that same moment Matai burst from another room with a man in tow. There was shouting and flailing, a flurry of moving bodies. Slaton had no shot, so he used his body to shield the woman and shoved her outside. The instant they cleared the doorway Slaton heard an exchange of fire—unsuppressed rounds now mixed with the clank of the MP7s.

With the woman clear of the hallway, Slaton pivoted against the doorjamb. He trained his weapon down the hall, ready to give supporting fire. He saw Tal already moving. Another Hezbollah man was on the ground, motionless. Also on the floor was the man Matai had been trying to rescue. Matai was on one knee, and Slaton heard his report on the comm link. *"This is Three. The brother took two rounds, one in the head. He's done."*

"All right, egress!" Slaton ordered, leaving regrets for later.

Tal and Matai ran toward him, keeping to one side to leave Slaton a clear line of fire. Their tactical awareness proved invaluable seconds later when two more green-clad figures appeared at the end of the hall, both brandishing weapons. Slaton dropped the one in front with two quick shots, then the second with a single tap.

The instant Tal and Matai hit the doorway, voices rose from the connecting hallway, frantic shouting in Arabic. Slaton extracted a flash-bang grenade and tossed it toward the intersection. He didn't wait to see the results, but heard it go off as he sprinted away. Tal and Matai were already ahead with the girl.

They all ran across the courtyard to the wall where Aaron was protecting Uday. Slaton was the last to arrive, but before anyone could speak, the sound of an engine rattled the night. A big truck somewhere nearby.

"We must get Faisal!" Uday shouted.

"He's dead," Slaton said. It was a cruel but necessary reply—not because it was the truth, but for the shock it would induce on Uday. A stunned captive was always easier to handle.

Slaton heard Aaron coordinating with Bloch on the comm link. They were discussing the best egress route. He turned to Sarah. "You have the memory stick?"

She stared at him, and he wondered if she spoke English.

"Do you have—"

"No!" she said suddenly.

Slaton felt a clench in his gut. "Did they take it from you?"

"No—I knew they would. So I hid it."

"Hid it? Where?"

Sarah told him in heavily accented English.

Slaton keyed his mic. "*One here! Everybody hold on—we've got a problem!*"

The hurried meeting convened two minutes later between the chassis of two rusted-out cars in a scrapyard. Tal and Matai watched the perimeter while Slaton and Aaron hunkered low with Uday and Sarah.

"It was the place where they stopped us," she said.

Slaton pulled out a map and a flashlight, doing his best to not let the light spill from their hide. They all heard shouting in the distance, but according to Aaron, who spoke fluent Arabic, their adversaries seemed stalled in confusion.

Sarah dragged her finger along a road on the map. "Here—this road." Her finger stopped. "This first square—they stopped our truck there. When we got out, a man pushed me, and I fell down easily. There was a wall. I hid the stick under a loose stone."

Slaton looked at Aaron. "The location checks—we first picked up the phone's signal in that square."

Aaron looked out into the night. "Two hundred meters from here, back through town."

Slaton took only seconds to make his call. "I'll go. Sarah will have to come to show me the exact spot. You three take Uday to the ATVs, then circle west." Slaton tapped a spot on the map outside town near a minor wadi. "We'll meet back up there."

Aaron stared at Slaton, but didn't argue. The logic was clear. They would try to get the memory stick, but if Slaton and Sarah failed, the others would at least bring out Uday. A partial victory, but a victory all the same.

"Do you want to take Tal?" Aaron asked.

"No, just the two of us. Less conspicuous that way."

Everyone heard more shouting in the distance, and the big diesel they'd heard earlier began moving. The response was organizing.

"Not much time," Aaron said. "In twenty minutes

this place will be crawling. We'll try to create some distractions and draw them in a different direction."

Slaton looked at Sarah. "Can you do this for us?"

She locked eyes with Uday for a moment, then nodded. "Yes."

Slaton eyed her briefly, and saw one problem. "You'd better hide that." He pointed to the front of her abaya. Somewhere in all the running and pushing, a necklace with a Christian cross had worked its way free at her neckline. Sarah tucked it back in, but not before kissing it once. Slaton hoped she'd added a prayer with the kiss.

"All right, then," he said. "Let's go!"

FORTY-NINE

Slaton led Sarah down a narrow street. He knew where the square was, having studied the town's layout in preparation, and was sure he could find it without referencing the map. Bursts of gunfire sounded behind them, north of town, punctuated by the occasional explosion. The sporadic nature of the exchanges suggested that Aaron and the others were so far having success keeping the Hezbollah fighters, and any government troops who'd joined them, tactically off balance.

Sarah was doing well, moving quickly but not in a way that would draw attention. A learned skill, he supposed, for a Christian girl growing up in the Islamic State. Rounding a corner, he saw a pair of men in the distance; both were armed and running north. Slaton kept Sarah, who was dressed conveniently as a local, between him and the two soldiers. One of them might have glanced their way, but soon both disappeared behind a building.

The square came into view, and Slaton guided

Sarah into a shadowed corner. "Is this the place?" he asked.

"Yes. There, at the far end—the low wall."

Slaton looked and saw the wall at the far end of a wide open square. He also saw a new problem—ten or twelve civilians milling about precisely where she'd pointed. He saw two rifles, but it wasn't a military unit in any sense of the word.

"Who are they?" she asked.

"Probably locals. They heard the gunfire and they're wondering what's going on."

Slaton lifted his weapon and sighted it on the group.

"You can't just shoot them!" Sarah protested.

"I'm only looking." Slaton stepped his reticle through the crowd one by one. He saw two AKs, and an old man carrying what looked like a scimitar. *Great,* he thought, *we successfully engage Hezbollah, only to get beat down by a freaking neighborhood watch.*

He said, "Could you find it quickly?"

"Yes, I think I know the exact place."

"So if I fire a few rounds in that direction, get them to scatter for a minute or two . . . could you retrieve it?"

"But you might hit someone by accident."

Slaton took his eye away from the scope, and said in a level tone, "I don't hit things by accident."

"You can't know that—there are children out there."

Slaton tried not to roll his eyes. "Look, I really am a pretty good shot. Now get ready to—"

"No, there is a better way!"

Before Slaton could respond, Sarah turned and dashed into the square.

He backed into the shadows, cursed, and trained his gun on one of the men who was holding an AK. His finger poised on the trigger.

Halfway to the crowd, Sarah began shouting as she ran. Whatever she said, it was in Arabic, a rudimentary language for Slaton. He caught a few words, but missed the meaning. Soon every set of eyes in the crowd was on her. Slaton watched a mother grab a young teen and haul him off by the wrist. A young woman was next, and soon it became a stampede. Twenty seconds later the square was completely empty. He watched Sarah kneel near the base of the wall, and used his scope to scan for threats as she ran back toward him.

She skidded to a stop in front of him no more than a minute after she'd gone. Sarah held out her open hand, and in it was a white memory stick.

"Okay," he said, "that was good." Slaton took the stick and pocketed it. When Sarah turned to go, he said, "What did you say to them?"

She smiled. "Only the truth. I shouted that the Israelis were invading."

The rendezvous west of town almost went well. Using his NVGs, Slaton spotted Aaron and the others in the shallow wadi. Uday had apparently been given a short course in driving an ATV, because the fourth vehicle, the one Slaton had been driving, was parked with the others in a stand of brush fifty yards away.

They gathered in the wadi's natural recess, and Slaton told everyone they'd recovered the data. Aaron briefed the egress plan. It all took no more than thirty seconds—but that was thirty seconds too long.

The first burst sent everyone to their bellies in the natural trench, and soon heavy fire was raining in all around. Slaton pushed Sarah's head low. The incoming barrage was coming from their left flank. Aaron ventured a look with his goggles, and had no trouble identifying the source.

"There's a Hilux stopped on the road," he said, referring to the Toyota truck that was a favorite of militias and warlords across the world. "Looks like it's mounted with a fifty-cal."

"Range?" Slaton asked.

"Twelve hundred, maybe a little less."

Rounds pinged off nearby rocks. "The gunner's not bad."

"Unfortunately."

Both men looked at the ATVs. It would take thirty seconds to reach them over open ground, twice that to mount up and get clear.

"Do you think he's seen them?" Slaton asked.

Before Aaron could answer, one of the ATVs rocked under a hit, the seat bursting in a cloud of fabric and foam.

"Yeah, maybe so," said Aaron. "I'm not sure where this guy came from. We pulled the bulk of the force north of town."

"I expect they're all headed our way now." Slaton peered up over the ledge and spotted the technical. "The driver was smart to park so far away. At a thousand-plus meters our MPs are worthless. All they have to do is keep us pinned down and wait for help."

"We brought one long gun," Aaron said.

Slaton looked at Matai's ATV where an HTR 2000 Barak was mounted. He exchanged a look with Aaron, who said, "You're the shooter."

"Right."

Slaton began moving. He crawled the first ten yards, but the ATVs were on relatively high ground. He jumped up and made a dash for the weapon. There was a brief lull as the gunner adjusted his aim; then rounds began pounding the desert all around. Tiny explosions of dirt and stone filled the air, and stands of brush got shredded. Slaton lunged for the rifle, pulled it free, then sprinted back and literally dove into the wadi. Back in cover, he instantly began moving perpendicularly, away from the others. The best shooting platform he could find was a flat stone shelf at the edge of a rise. The telescopic sight was made for night work, and he had no trouble acquiring the gunman on the Toyota's high bed. The man was partially masked by an armor plate, but his head was clearly visible. That was all Slaton needed.

The earth was still exploding to his right, but Slaton tuned it out. He felt the familiar calm settle. His breathing slowed, his muscles relaxed. In the green glow of the scope he registered smoke coming from hot-barreled .50-cal. Slaton used it to estimate windage. Old equations came into play, bullet drop and crosswind corrections. Tried-and-tested rules he'd used countless times before.

In places like Gaza.

On targets like Ali Samir.

He began the slow pressure on the trigger, not squeezing for an instantaneous shot, but giving the rifle a say in the matter, a steady window in which it could do its work. The gun kicked, and Slaton quickly reestablished his target in the scope. He found the Hilux, then the .50-cal. There was no longer anyone behind it. A hit, most likely, but he really didn't care. The incoming fire had stopped, and no one else was taking up the gun mount. For the next two minutes that was all that mattered.

He pulled away from the sight, and with his naked eye he saw two trucks coming up the road behind the Hilux. They roared right past the Toyota, never hesitating.

"Go, go, go!" Slaton shouted.

Aaron was already prodding their charges toward the ATVs, while Tal and Matai covered the rear. Small-arms fire began crackling in the distance. Suddenly a grenade exploded fifty yards away, on an angle toward town. Slaton reckoned it had been delivered by either Tal or Matai—not a strike against the enemy, who were well out of range, but an effort to confuse them and avert their eyes. A little fog of war.

The trucks were getting closer, and all at once they stopped and men began pouring out of each. Whether they were Hezbollah militants or government troops was immaterial. Within seconds they all began shooting from a range of two hundred yards.

Slaton and the others had covered barely half the distance to the ATVs when the fusillade began. At first there were only stray rounds, hunting and rang-ing, but soon the barrage began to thicken and gain focus. Something slapped Slaton hard on the back, and he realized there was no one around him—he'd taken a round in his vest. He regained his balance and ran directly behind Sarah, hoping to shield her. A scream from behind caused him to stop and look back. He saw Tal rolling on the ground. Slaton reversed and helped him to his feet. Tal was bloodied and grimacing, but his legs started churning again. By the time they reached the ATVs, Slaton was dragging Tal along, a strong hand under his armpit. The first RPG hit, erupting a shower of dirt.

Aaron had already done a damage assessment on their vehicles. "One bike took a hit! The others look operable!"

The very contingency they'd considered ahead of time.

Everyone mounted up, Aaron and Matai each with one of their subjects, and the injured Tal quite literally riding shotgun next to Slaton. In a loose line they rocketed out into open desert, drawing a fresh hail of gunfire. Soon the barrage began to lessen as magazines ran empty. Two minutes later they were out of range.

Aaron throttled up and took a straight-line course back to Israel.

Speed was life.

FIFTY

Gabrielle Baland was sleepy, and trying to stay awake through her favorite television novella, when she heard an insistent knock on her door. She blinked and ran a hand across her thinning pewter hair. She wasn't expecting anyone, certainly not at this hour, but all the same she rose to answer it.

She looked at her door and was surprised by how far away it seemed. What would once have been a few effortless steps had become something of a project. Gabrielle crossed the flowered carpet as quickly as her seventy-six years allowed, shuffling past walls full of framed memories, and using counters and chairs as handholds. She lived in a pensioner's flat, one bedroom and a kitchen centered on a small main room, a few fusty pieces of furniture that would certainly outlast her.

On reaching the threshold, she propped herself straight using a cane from the hat rack—her arthritis medication had run out, and her knees were acting up. That thought in her head, she opened the door hoping to see the delivery boy from the pharmacy.

Instead, Gabrielle encountered an unfamiliar woman of about forty. She was dark-haired and tall, and smiled in a most engaging manner.

"Madame Baland?" the woman queried in flawless and pleasing French.

"That's right."

"My name is Jeanne Arnette. I was a friend of your son's many years ago."

"My son?"

"Why yes, Zavier."

The woman seemed attentive when Gabrielle said, "Oh, yes . . . my Zavier. Have you heard from him?" she asked hopefully.

Jeanne Arnette gave her a curious look. "Actually, no—I was hoping to locate him through you."

Gabrielle shrugged, and her mouth went to an upturned U. "I'm sorry, but I can't really tell you much. He's become a very important man in Paris, or so they tell me. I haven't seen him in years."

The woman standing outside her door seemed to deflate a bit, and said, "I'm sorry, madame. I myself have not seen him since we were children, but a mutual friend mentioned that you lived here and . . . well, I thought it might be fun to catch up with Zavier. I hope there was not a falling-out between you?"

Gabrielle sighed. "I suppose you could call it that." She heard voices on her television chattering in the background. It occurred to her that her show had become very boring. "Would you like a cup of coffee?"

The woman smiled. "Why yes, that would be very nice, thank you."

* * *

Baland sat alone in his office. He was staring at the far wall, where a map of the Middle East hung crookedly—it had been dislodged earlier that day when he'd taken down a photograph of his daughters. There was a better map in Michelis's office, so he'd left the old one where it was. Oddly, it struck him that the blue and brown cartography seemed more true now that it was off-kilter.

It was well within Baland's mandate to request a satellite feed from Syria. If he was lucky, and the orbital gods were with him, he might be able to watch the mission in Nawa play out in real time. The problem was that he couldn't make such a request without an explanation. The truth, of course, was out of the question—that he had dispatched an Israeli assassin to collect an ISIS defector who knew far too much about the incoming director of DGSI.

So Baland sat in his office and waited. Waited while somewhere in a cold and faraway desert events took place that would shape his future. *How has it come to this?* he wondered. His fifteen-year career, once seemingly destined for the stars, was wobbling on the precipice of failure. *No,* he thought, *not failure.* If his secrets were divulged, it would be nothing short of treason. A lifetime in prison. *How does a man explain something like that to his daughters?*

The girls were increasingly in his thoughts, as was Jacqueline. Their marriage hadn't been perfect, but who could claim that? He'd had a good run: challenging job, steady pay, good family life. All put at risk the day Malika had come into his life. As if that weren't enough, she'd brought Slaton to Paris, who in turn had introduced Mossad into the equation. And there it was, he thought. Everything come full circle—Israel. The country responsible for murdering his parents so many years ago was again his tormentor. Malika and Uday, even the *kidon*—Baland could deal with all of them. But how could he conceal his catalogue of deceits when an entire country was involved?

He pushed away from his desk and padded over to the map. He stared at the small brown strip of land between the Mediterranean and the Dead Sea, birthplace of so many of the great religions. Hanging tilted on his wall, it looked terribly insignificant. And perhaps it was.

He circled his desk, trying to re-form his scattershot thoughts. It was like trying to put back together an exploded grenade. With a trace of discomfort, that imagery stayed with Baland a bit longer than it should have.

The team paused for a detailed accounting of injuries at the first stop, which came immediately after they crossed the Bravo line into the U.N. buffer zone. Tal had taken a round in his right arm. He was in moderate pain, but the bleeding was under control. Slaton and Aaron had suffered damage to their vests but, tomorrow's bruises aside, had come through unscathed. Uday and Sarah had escaped with no more than scrapes and contusions, and for him one minor shrapnel puncture in his hip. Uday also complained of sore ribs, which he attributed to taking a rifle butt to the stomach earlier in the day. Matai was miraculously untouched.

The moon had risen in the east, looking down with equal benevolence on the land of the Jews, the land of the Shi'a, and, somewhere far to the north, what remained of the Islamic caliphate. The team got back under way at a more sensible pace, and when they arrived at the safe house Bloch was there to greet them. At his side were an emergency-room physician and his assistant, both of whom immediately went to work on Tal.

"Mossad keeps a medical team on staff now?" Slaton asked as he dismounted, watching them lead Tal away to the safe house.

"They're contractors," Bloch said. "One of Nurin's more practical initiatives."

"That's one point of view," Slaton said flatly. He shrugged off his vest, lifted his shirt, and inspected the damage in the ATV's side mirror. He saw a large red welt on his back. A roll of his right shoulder guaranteed pain tomorrow. He made a more deliberate inspection, and was happy to find no other injuries. He'd seen it before—operators so deep in the grip of adrenaline they didn't recognize serious wounds until they collapsed in the debrief.

On the way back to the safe house Slaton encountered Aaron and Matai, and the usual salt-edged post-firefight banter ensued. Aaron good-naturedly accused the legendary sniper of doing nothing more than laying down cover fire, while Matai mumbled something about boots and quicksand. Slaton took it all in the spirit in which it was intended, and gave back in good measure.

He caught back up with Bloch, and found him talking to Uday in the main room. Sarah was standing to the side looking shell-shocked. Slaton walked over to her with all the calmness he could muster. Their relationship to this point had involved a good deal of shouting and pushing—nothing short of abuse under any other circumstances.

"Are you all right?" he asked.

"Yes," she said, adding a less than convincing smile. "Thank you for helping us."

He returned her smile. "You did well. It was quick thinking to hide the data stick, and you were clever in getting it back."

She shrugged. "I've been living under the Daesh for over a year now. One learns how to get by."

Slaton nodded. "I'm sorry about Faisal."

Her brow furrowed back to despair, and the resulting lines seemed more etched than they should have been in such a youthful face. "It wasn't your fault," she said. "I know what would have happened to us all if you hadn't come."

"Did you leave family behind in Raqqa?"

"No, my father and brother . . ." The lines grew ever deeper. "I have only my mother now. I pray she is in Jordan. As you know, we are Christians," she added, as if that explained something. Tragically, it did.

"Well . . . you're safe now."

Uday and Bloch came closer.

"You have the memory device?" Bloch asked.

Slaton retrieved it from his pocket and held it out in an open palm. Everyone stared.

Contained within the little plastic stick was an invaluable roster of terrorists. Information that would soon be leveraged by Western intelligence agencies to decimate ISIS and its networks. There was likely no more valuable ounce of plastic and circuitry in all the world.

Slaton held it out as if it were a stick of dynamite.

Bloch took it in hand very much the same way.

FIFTY-ONE

With the strike orders from Raqqa disseminated, pockets of activity took place across France.

A cell of three students in Toulon, who'd been given a suicide vest months ago along with two semi-automatic weapons, arranged to meet by simple text message. In the corner of a charming café they sipped their last espresso before Paradise and discussed how best to attack the headquarters of a popular Jewish newspaper. A pair of unemployed cousins from Paris' eighteenth arrondissement cloistered themselves in their grandmother's basement, where they retrieved and loaded two hidden handguns for an attack on a kosher grocery store. The best technicians of the bunch, a crew of four North Africans who'd been schooled by an expert on how to cook explosives and build a truck bomb, coordinated among themselves by coded phrases via e-mail. Having stockpiled material for over a year as they waited their chance, their orders were to destroy the largest synagogue in Lille.

After considerable trial and error, all seven of

Chadeh's groups made final preparations before assaulting their assigned targets. In a mélange of hastily produced suicide videos, magazine loading, and prayer, all set about their duties in earnest, this a consequence of the closing words of their directive from Raqqa: It would please God most if they could expedite their martyrdom.

Slaton didn't let Uday and Sarah out of his sight. As detainees went they were cooperative, even eager, delighted to give everything they knew about the Islamic State. Director Nurin conceded reluctantly that the pair had to be surrendered to France, but his instructions were clear: Mossad was to make the most of every second the two were in hand.

A pair of senior Mossad interrogators arrived at the safe house and began interviewing Uday and Sarah separately. With considerable foresight, the man talking to Uday supplied an aerial photograph of Raqqa, along with a black Sharpie, and for nearly an hour the former head of the Islamic State Institution for Public Information circled points of interest—meeting places, safe houses, and the mosque where ISIS' computers were at that moment housed—like a tourist planning a holiday.

Liking how things were going, Mossad took its time feeding and clothing their two guests. That leisurely pace ended when a new message from Nurin arrived: Baland had been advised of the mission's success, and was impatient to get Uday and Sarah on French soil.

Bloch copied the flash drive before giving it back to Uday, and transport was arranged to Palmachim Air Base. During the drive, Slaton took a call from Nurin, who explained how he wanted things handled. Slaton would accompany their charges back to Paris, and deliver them to Baland with a message. After that, Slaton's involvement in the affair would be at an end. With more than a few doubts, Slaton acquiesced.

When no more excuses could be manufactured, the same Gulfstream that had brought Slaton from Paris departed on the reciprocal journey. Not surprisingly, they were still in the company of Nurin's interrogators. Under Slaton's watchful eye, the gentle inquisition was kept alive on the flight to Paris, until an exhausted Uday fell asleep somewhere over Italy. This was not unexpected, and as Uday got his first rest in days, the pilot was quietly asked by one of the Mossad men to take a brief tour of Spain, adding another two hours to the journey in the hope that their interviews might carry on just a bit longer.

As the Gulfstream chartered by Mossad wheeled above the Pyrenees, Anton Bloch was preparing to go home after an all-night shift—the kind of schedule he had not endured since his own tenure as director. His role in the odyssey terminated at Mossad's Glilot Junction complex. There he signed off on a mission report, ensuring its authenticity, and also took the time to inquire about Tal—the surgery on his injured arm was complete, with a favorable prognosis for full recovery. Bloch quite literally had one foot out the main office door when someone called his name from behind. He turned to see Talia tracking after him.

"We have a problem, sir!"

Bloch took a deep breath, then let it out in a controlled manner. *How many times have I heard those words?* He looked around and, noting a few early risers in the lobby, continued outside to the courtyard before asking, "What kind of problem?"

"The *katsa* from Paris reported in two hours ago—the one who interviewed Gabrielle Baland."

He frowned. "Two hours ago? And I am only now hearing about it?"

"Based on her report, I wanted to check on a few things." She explained what Zavier Baland's mother had said in the interview, then presented Bloch with a printout. "This took some effort, but we dug it out. It's the passenger manifest from a flight—Air France from Paris to Cairo."

He took the paper in hand. "And why is this important?"

"Check the date."

Bloch did so: *September 15, 2002.* He blinked as he stared at the paper, trying to catch up with what Talia was implying. A most implausible theory began rising in his mind. "This is not definitive in any way," he said in a low voice.

Talia, seeming unsure if Bloch was saying this to himself or to her, said, "No. But if there is even a *remote* possibility—"

He held up a hand to cut her off.

"Go home quickly and pack a bag!"

"Let me guess—warm clothes?"

"Yes."

Within the hour Bloch and Talia were boarding a second chartered jet, the pilots having filed a flight plan to Paris that would be flown in a far more direct manner than the previous sortie. As the jet's wheels began rolling across the tarmac, Bloch hung up his phone after a lengthy call. There had been no chance to go home and pack his own bag.

On the opposite side of Tel Aviv, Mossad director Raymond Nurin stuffed a tie in his pocket, ignored the bent collar on his shirt, and bypassed the dormant coffeepot in his kitchen as he strode to the front door. The limo waiting outside in the soft predawn had a perfectly good mirror in which he could make himself presentable, and there was a bottomless pot of coffee in his office. He would likely need both before the day was done. Having been awakened and briefed by Bloch on this new development, he reckoned that at some point today he would be faced with a very uncomfortable decision. One that would likely necessitate a meeting with the prime minister himself.

FIFTY-TWO

Slaton looked out the Gulfstream's window as they approached Le Bourget Airport. It was nearly noon in Paris, and the weather was horrendous. The captain had announced before beginning the descent that a severe storm was rolling in from the North Sea, and that the ride would be turbulent. The airplane bucked and twisted through the sky on their final approach. Even after the wheels touched down, Slaton felt crosswinds buffeting the airframe, and rain reduced visibility out the window to no more than a few hundred feet.

The jet came to a stop on a quiet corner of the airfield, its engines winding down in relief. Once the turbines fell still, the prevailing sound came from a pulsing, wind-driven rain that was peppering the aircraft's hull. The crew provided umbrellas, but they were useless against the deluge. Slaton sloshed across the tarmac beside Uday and Sarah, and they were met by a four-person entourage—to his trained eye, a competent security contingent. Zavier Baland was not among them. Without so much as a cursory customs inspection, France's newest three arrivals were ushered into the first of two cars, and without hesitation the driver launched into a street that looked like a river.

Slaton was happy to have crossed the first hurdle—he would not have been surprised if the security team had turned him around and sent him packing, back to the Gulfstream for a return trip to Israel. They were on Baland's turf now, Uday and Sarah effectively in DGSI's custody. Yet Slaton was still being included. Better yet, he'd not yet been frisked—he was still carrying the H&K VP9 he'd been issued for last night's mission. It was an undeniable comfort in the face of one thought he couldn't shake—that Baland's life would become much more simple if the limo in which the three of them were riding went not to Levallois-Perret, but to a quiet ditch in the countryside.

Traffic slowed as they reached Boulevard Périphérique. An exhausted Sarah appeared to be sleeping—her eyes were shut and her head lolled against the far window. Never one to squander an opportunity, Slaton said to Uday, "I'm guessing you know who we're going to see."

Uday looked at Slaton uncomfortably. "Until recently I could only speculate on Argu's identity—Malika never told us. But Chadeh recently confessed to me that he believes Argu is Zavier Baland, the man who will soon oversee DGSI."

Slaton gave no response.

"What will he want from me?" Uday asked as he stared into the gloom.

"The personnel list, of course. And more privately . . . perhaps a signal that you won't betray him."

Uday's gaze remained outside.

"I'm only giving you fair warning. Baland helped you escape the caliphate, but he's also done great harm to his country. It might prove a difficult secret to keep."

"But not impossible," Uday suggested. "Chadeh suspected Baland, but I doubt many others were aware of it."

"Maybe you should tell him that. I'm guessing Baland will want to speak with you privately. You should think about it now . . . how you want to handle your relationship."

"I only want to live in peace with Sarah."

"I hope that works out for you," Slaton said. "But your own history isn't exactly pristine. You were a senior commander in ISIS."

Uday sank deeper into his seat. "Do you think Baland and I might reach an accord?"

"No business of mine. But if you're asking my advice, I'd say you have a lot to bargain with. Not only are you giving him the personnel file, but you undertook a digital slash-and-burn campaign before you left."

"I must also tell him about the new wave of attacks that are imminent. They are based on information he recently gave the caliphate."

This was news to Slaton, and he looked at Uday curiously.

"I explained everything to the Mossad man who was questioning me."

"Okay, that's good," Slaton said, deciding that Bloch could fill him in later. He reached into his pocket and pulled out the glossy photo of Raqqa on which Uday had circled the mosque. "You could also give Baland this."

Uday took the photo in hand. "What will he do with it?"

"Do you really have to ask?"

There was a lengthy pause. The rain became a torrent, the car's wipers overwhelmed at their highest speed.

Slaton said, "I've been wondering about this agent who recruited Baland—Malika. What do you know about her?"

"I was told she was a black widow who traveled to France of her own accord."

Slaton was familiar with the term "black widow": the wife of a fighter who'd been martyred to the cause.

Uday went on, "She said she had a way to force information from a high-ranking French official."

"What was in it for her? Did she ask for money?"

"Not really. There were a few transfers, but mostly for operational expenses."

"Operational?"

"Malika has become very important in Europe. Her work went far beyond Argu. For example, she organized the recent bombing in Grenoble."

"*She* was responsible for Grenoble?"

"Yes. She herself recruited the martyr for that operation." A sad smile creased his lips. "Malika knows the persuasiveness of God."

Slaton weighed whether to tell Uday the truth—
that Malika was less a disciple of God than a vengeful
daughter. He decided that secret wasn't his to give, and
in doing so he felt an unexpected wave of relief. The
fates of Baland and Uday were increasingly intertwined, yet Slaton was fast becoming an outsider. The
mystery of Ali Samir had been solved, and the terrorist's daughter, who'd lured him here, was being hunted
down. Very soon, he would be on his way back to the
South Pacific.

He looked outside, and in the distance saw the
modernist edifice of DGSI coming into view—panels
of reflective glass in a concrete frame, all blurred by
sheets of rain. There were two guards in the front
seat, and Slaton saw the one on the passenger side, a
thickset dapper man, murmur something into his
collar-mounted microphone. He guessed the man
was talking to the lead car, which was blazing a path
fifty yards ahead.

In that moment Slaton felt an old and trusted caution. Not imminent danger, but an approaching boundary. In two minutes he would be inside one of the
most secure facilities in France, effectively in Baland's
hands. At that point, Slaton would lose control.

Sarah seemed to rouse from her slumber. He turned
to her and Uday, and silently mouthed to each, *It's
okay.* Both looked at him curiously as he edged forward in the seat. He unzipped the front of his jacket,
and set his feet firmly on the floorboards.

"Turn left at the next street!" Slaton ordered. His
command was reinforced by the H&K, which appeared between the two headrests. The barrel was

steady on Dapper's temple. The driver could see it clearly in the mirror.

"Hands where I can see them!"

The dapper guard placed his hands on the dash. The driver, professional that he was, already had both on the wheel. "If either of you talk into your microphones, I *will* kill you!" His eyes were fixed on Dapper. "Take the next left turn!"

As expected, Slaton saw two sets of darting eyes. The driver complied, and the lead car disappeared the instant they rounded the corner. Slaton realized he would only have seconds to work with. "Faster!" he ordered. "Take the next right!"

The driver again did as asked. As soon as they rounded the second turn, Slaton looked back. There was no sign of the lead car. His eyes held the panorama of what was around them. Relatively busy streets on midday, a combination of businesses and apartment blocks. It would have to do.

"Stop!"

"What are you doing?" Uday asked.

"Don't worry."

The car came to a halt.

"Put it in park, turn the engine off!"

The driver did so.

"Keys!" Slaton held out his empty left hand.

The driver finally spoke. "Our orders are to—"

Slaton whipped his left elbow into the driver's head, the H&K remaining steady on his partner. It was a sturdy blow, but only an attention-getter. The keys dropped into his hand. He saw a mobile phone on the seat next to Dapper.

"Give me the phone!" he said. "Very carefully."

The man frowned, but complied. Slaton wanted to take their guns, but there wasn't time to do it safely. The second car had to be closing in.

With his eyes locked on the guards, he reached for the door handle and began backing outside. He said to Uday, "I'm going to shut down this phone. Tell Baland I'll turn it back on in exactly one hour. He will call me."

Uday said he understood.

Once outside, Slaton held the H&K more discreetly, tight against his chest in the open fold of his jacket. He locked eyes very briefly with both Uday and Sarah. "Good luck to you both."

Neither responded, but everyone in the car was watching Slaton as he darted behind a parked delivery truck a few steps away.

As soon as he was out of sight, the two men in front threw open their doors and bustled out to the curb. Their hands went into their jackets, gripping their weapons but not drawing them. They ran to the delivery truck, but in no time were spinning circles on the sidewalk, their eyes scanning helplessly.

A sudden metallic clatter on the limo's hood drew everyone's attention, and one of the men drew his gun and trained it instinctively on the source. His weapon came back down just as quickly. Caught on a stilled wiper blade, the plastic fob and metal key hung limply on the rain-splattered windshield.

FIFTY-THREE

Perhaps the scar would be minimal, Malika thought as she studied her wound in the dim light of a naked bulb. Working by the reflection of a broken mirror, she changed the dressing for the third time. Just as she was finishing, the sound of a siren rose outside.

From the tiny slatted vent that served as her window she looked out across the rain-wet streets of Clichy-sous-Bois. She saw nothing unusual, which was to say she saw tenements and smoking street grills and countless young men loitering in packs. Hearing a siren here was like hearing a seagull at the beach. Malika turned away not even waiting for the sound to fade. If Baland had found her, he would never be so overt.

The room was little more than an attic, a no-questions-asked hideaway above a taxi garage in one of the most distressed banlieues of eastern Paris. The garage was owned by a grizzled old Tunisian whose son was in prison—according to the French for trafficking guns, according to the old man for having parents from Africa. The attic was always open to friends of the caliphate, particularly those taking flight from the flics. For more than a year now, Malika had been a frequent flyer.

She retrieved the dog-eared newspaper the old man had slipped under her door, and noted it was today's issue. There was an article on page 2 about the continuing search for Claude Michelis' assailant. The police expressed boundless confidence, this in spite of little new evidence. She crumpled the newspaper and fed it into her pot stove—she was running out of fuel, and the damp, drafty room made her yearn for the desert.

She settled on the bed, the mattress folding around her like a taco, and began eating from a tin of cookies. They were sickeningly sweet, but she kept at it. Lately she seemed hungry all the time, and she wondered if she might be getting diabetes. It wasn't easy, keeping the weight on. Her youthful metabolism fought to rid her of every calorie, but so far she'd managed. The worst had been putting on fifty pounds to begin with, a binge she'd begun in Gaza two years ago.

It had been surprisingly effectual. Who from her old village would recognize her now? The anonymity her new shape permitted her was even more useful than she'd imagined. With her drab dress, poor hygiene, and tangled hair, she was invisible on the streets of Paris, and on the better avenues given a wide berth. Her redoubtably surly nature only amplified her isolation. Men ignored her, women tilted up their noses. All precisely as she wanted.

She wondered how long it would take to reverse

the process. Six months? A year? She didn't like the idea of plastic surgery, but her hooked nose ought to be dealt with, and a bit of dental work seemed inevitable. All the better when the time came to disappear. She had enough money for it—she'd been skimming ISIS operational funds for over a year now. It wasn't any great amount, but that was also by design—large accounts would only draw attention. She'd set aside enough to live on. Two years, maybe three. Enough to be reborn once her raison d'être was fulfilled.

Her thoughts turned to Slaton. She had necessarily bunkered up for the last day and a half, letting her wound heal while the police spun their wheels. But she couldn't wait forever. Her plan, years in the making, was tantalizingly close to success. There was an excellent chance that he was still in Paris. If so, it was time to finish the job.

And Malika knew exactly where to start.

Baland was caught off balance by Slaton's disappearance, but tried not to lose his advantage. He spent a full thirty minutes with Uday and his girlfriend, asking the most pertinent questions, before ushering them out of the office—it was nearly time to make a phone call to an assassin.

He had used the more spacious director's suite for the meeting, even if wasn't officially his, for the gravitas it conveyed. Once he was alone, Baland strolled to the wet bar in the corner. He picked up a decanter of amber liquid and held it to the light, then removed the top and drew in the aroma. The scent brought recognition: a nice double-malt Scotch Michelis had been particularly fond of.

He wondered what had spooked Slaton. A number of answers came to mind, but none were more than speculation. He supposed such men had overdeveloped cautionary instincts. Baland considered putting in an order to triangulate the call he was about to make, but decided against it. He remained in a delicate position, and wanted no chance of the conversation being recorded.

Standing pensively at the bar, he used his private phone to place the call at the prescribed time. Slaton answered right away.

"I'm not tracing your phone," Baland said straightaway.

"It's not my phone. And I didn't think you would."

Baland pulled a tumbler from the shelf, and from a full ice bucket he began distractedly transferring ice cubes one by one. The clinking sound must have carried over the phone, because Slaton said, "I thought you were a good Muslim."

Baland poured a brace. "*Voilà!* You now know the full catalogue of my secrets."

"Why don't I believe that?"

Baland tipped back the glass once. The Scotch really was good. "Uday and I had a long conversation."

"Good. Have you reached an accord?"

"We are in general agreement. His past aside, he has done France a great service. The caliphate is reeling, and will soon be more so. He tells us that new attacks have been ordered on French soil, but with his help we may be able to forestall the worst of it. We are treating his arrival as a straightforward defection, the details of which will remain clouded. Uday and I have agreed it is in our mutual best interest to keep my relationship with the caliphate quiet."

"I hope you can keep it that way—but that's between the two of you."

"Is it?" Baland asked. "You know as much about me as anyone."

"I have no interest in you or your past dealings."

"And Mossad?"

"What about them?"

Baland thumped his glass down firmly, a rattle of wet ice. "I am not a fool! Mossad had sole custody of Uday for fifteen hours. Don't tell me he wasn't interrogated!"

"He was."

"So you see my dilemma. Director Nurin will someday try to leverage my misfortune for the good of Israel."

"Probably. In his shoes, wouldn't you do the same thing?"

Baland didn't reply.

"Look, it's very likely that someday you *will* hear from Mossad. But we're talking about Israel, not some band of organized criminals masquerading as a religious movement. Israel and France keep largely parallel interests. I'm sure that in your new capacity you'll someday come across information that might reflect poorly upon Israel. A scheming mind might even expect you to search for it . . . as insurance, one might say."

Baland's eyes narrowed. "You really have cut the cord, *kidon*."

"I've had strong differences with Mossad in recent years . . . but Israel will always be my homeland. What I'm saying is that arrangements can be made. Deals can be forged."

"Can they?"

"Trust me—Director Nurin revels in them."

"So he will keep my little secret for a price? Why should I believe it?"

"From what I can see, you don't have much choice." Slaton paused before adding, "But as a display of goodwill, the director wants me to pass along that Israel will not share the ISIS personnel database for one week. That should give you time to vet the list and act accordingly. In return, Nurin asks that you restrict the dissemination of what you find during that period to France and her former colonies."

"In other words, he doesn't want me to tell the Americans."

"Like I said, Nurin is a deal maker. Israel could benefit greatly from passing this information to certain allies. I'm only the messenger, but it does seem like they deserve something for the risks they've taken."

"And you, David? What of the risks you have taken?"

"Irrelevant. My part here is done."

"What about Malika? She's still out there." Baland let that settle for a few beats. "She brought you here, and has already tried to kill you once. Can you and your family be safe while she remains at large?"

The silence this time was extended, and Baland

found himself envisioning the fluid gray eyes he'd seen at Le Quinze.

"What do you know about my family?" Slaton said in a level tone.

Baland knew he'd hit his mark. He poured a second brace and wandered to the wide window that provided the director's office a reaching view of Levallois-Perret. "You have a wife and a son very far from here. I know because Malika asked for my help in tracking down a certain satellite account in the middle of the Pacific. Only recently did I realize who it involved."

"So we both have good reason to be rid of Malika. But you have the police forces of an entire nation at your disposal."

"And you are the kind of man who leaves little to chance. If the two of us pooled our abilities . . . certainly Malika would never escape. She is the last problem we both face."

"What do you propose?" Slaton asked.

"First that we find a way to lure her out. Then the two of us can devise a strategy to finalize things." Slaton said nothing, which Baland took for assent. He continued, "I think Uday might be of use in finding her. He has long served as Malika's go-between—chances are, he has more information than he realizes. I've procured rooms for Uday and Sarah at The Peninsula. They will remain under heavy guard, but I think at this stage in our relationship it would be useful to treat them more as guests than detainees."

"A few nights in a five-star suite? That sounds like something right out of Director Nurin's playbook."

"I will take that as a compliment. This afternoon I must extract everything possible from Uday regarding these new attacks—it is my duty to make that the priority. I will also be in touch with the Defense Ministry regarding a certain mosque in Raqqa. But later, I think, we should convene a more quiet conversation. Let's meet tonight at seven, in the lobby of The Peninsula. Uday and Sarah will join us. If we can together find a way to deal with Malika, everyone will be better off."

"All right, I'll be there. But there's one thing you should understand very clearly."

Baland stood staring at the building's forecourt far below. The blue, white, and red tricolor snapped rigid on its pole. "And what might that be?"

"That glass you're looking through is not as thick as it ought to be."

Baland stiffened.

The connection went dead, and his eyes darted between distant buildings. He saw people milling about the streets and in the windows of nearby office complexes. The tree-lined Boulevard du Château was thick with parked cars, as was the distant Hôpital Américain. He stood rooted in place, his basal instincts in seizure as he awaited a tiny projectile to penetrate the glass. Then his policeman's brain took hold and convinced him otherwise. Baland slowly took the phone from his ear.

"No," he whispered to himself. "Malika might do it that way. But you won't because you have no reason."

* * *

Eight hundred yards distant, Slaton backed out of a nook between cement columns in a fourth-floor parking garage. He headed straight for the stairs, pocketing his most recent purchase, a small but powerful set of binoculars. He turned off the phone he'd stolen from Baland's guard, removed its SIM card and then its battery. On the way to street level he dropped one piece in the trash bins of three successive floors. His Mossad-issued phone remained off as well—he'd been carrying it too long for continuous use.

Slaton hit the sidewalk in full stride and turned west. Choppy gusts and a sheeting rain lashed his dark blue windbreaker, and his hair was soon matted and disheveled. The jacket was a thin item, purchased one year ago for use on *Windsom* during tropical rain showers—little use against a tempestuous North Sea squall. As he made turn after turn, carefully checking the streets around him, the irony did not escape Slaton: At that moment, the South Seas could not have seemed farther away.

Far outside of the City of Light, and three miles aloft, the chartered jet carrying Bloch and Talia suffered through a holding pattern thirty miles south of Le Bourget Airport. A line of storms was passing over the airfield, and the pilots, in a decision Bloch thought conservative, had decided to wait things out.

"We need to land now!" he complained to the flight attendant.

"I've passed along your concerns to the pilots," the

young man said, "but they tell me the weather is too severe at the moment. It is a matter of safety."

Bloch was about to argue the point when Talia touched his hand and raised a finger, as if to say, *Wait a minute*. As soon as the flight attendant had gone, she said in a hushed tone, "I know we're not supposed to do this, but we must be holding at a low altitude . . . it works." She waved her phone at him. "We have a signal."

Without even looking to see where the flight attendant was, Bloch took out his own phone and turned it on. He had three bars of reception. Better yet, the Gulfstream didn't appear to be falling out of the sky.

"Thank God!" said Bloch. Slaton's number was already loaded, and he immediately placed the call. It ended in frustration ten seconds later.

"He must have turned his phone off!"

Talia looked crestfallen. "I'm sure he's only being cautious."

Bloch didn't reply, but he knew she was right—for someone in Slaton's position, it was a perfectly reasonable act. Only hours later would they realize how regrettable such precautions could be.

FIFTY-FOUR

The woman walking her bichon frise under an umbrella took no notice of the man, nor did the small tour group rolling amoeba-like toward the Arc de Triomphe. He meandered up Avenue Kléber at six forty-five that evening with little conviction in his stride and an aimlessness in his path. With his head under the hood of a light jacket, he seemed almost bewildered, taking a number of sudden turns, but always ending up back on Avenue Kléber. Anyone watching would have written him off as a disoriented tourist—this part of town was full of them on the best of days, and the inclement weather had imposed itself on everyone. Perhaps an American expecting a travel-brochure Paris of lights and riverside strolls, but who'd instead been subjected to the vagaries of a freak storm.

It was curious, Slaton had always thought, how something as simple as rain could revise tradecraft. It brought coats and hats into play, and countless upturned umbrellas. People who hadn't exercised in years darted across sidewalks and leapt over puddles.

Electronics—things like earbuds and radios and cameras—could be shorted out by the moisture, and their performance was invariably degraded by reduced visibility and increased background noise. Conversely, electronics were easier to hide under raincoats and hoods. Taken together, it was an all-new gallery of advantages and disadvantages waiting to be employed on either side of the game—offense or defense.

Right now, Slaton was strictly defending.

For nearly an hour, in an ever-shrinking pattern, he had walked the surrounding area taking in sights and sounds and smells. Noisy transportation hubs and silent bank guards. Fresh-baked cake in patisseries and garbage in the bins behind them. Every sensation seemed to heighten as he neared his objective—the hotel named The Peninsula.

Slaton still couldn't say what had alerted his instincts in the car. Something Baland had said? Or Uday? The continued elusiveness of Malika? There was no clear answer, only an edge of caution he hadn't sensed in a very long time. An edge of caution he invariably trusted.

He'd so far seen nothing out of place on his approach to the hotel. If anyone was following Slaton, they either were very good, or had a large team in support. He'd kept his phone turned off, but there were still ways one could be tracked—CCTV cameras, for one. His countermeasures were rudimentary at best, and in this new age of comprehensive urban surveillance, walking the streets of Paris was akin to walking across a Hollywood movie set.

He saw The Peninsula in the distance at 6:54. One could hardly miss it. The hotel was as grand a façade as existed in Paris, a mix of classic and contemporary themes in an imperishably opportune location. Within easy walking distance were the Champs-Élysées and the Arc de Triomphe, the latter encircled by Place Charles-de-Gaulle, the most famous roundabout in all Europe.

Slaton kept to the opposite side of Avenue Kléber, the leafless trees along the boulevard giving nominal cover. Like the weather, the seasons too had their say in tradecraft. The hotel entrance came into view, and right away Slaton didn't like what he saw. A black limousine was parked on the street directly in front, and on the sidewalk next to it stood Uday and Sarah. They were talking with a thickly built bald man in a loose-fitting overcoat. The man had security written all over him. Slaton watched closely, and after an extended conversation, Uday and Sarah were ushered into the car.

Because the windows were tinted, and because rain and gloom were cloaking the fast-fading light, he couldn't tell if anyone else was inside the car. He scanned the sidewalks and hotel entrance, but saw no sign of Baland. He also saw no other guards, which seemed incomprehensible given Uday's importance. The bald man closed the door, and began looking up and down the street expectantly.

Looking for me, Slaton thought.

He checked his watch. 7:02.

He turned into the recesses of an alcove. It was a quiet space, and what he saw on the inset door told him all he needed to know: the name of a small bank, along with a FERMÉ sign, guaranteed that the alcove was his until nine o'clock the next morning.

7:05.

From the shadows he watched the bald man take out a mobile phone and place a call. Slaton's suspicion escalated another notch. Baland had proposed a meeting at the hotel, yet Uday and Sarah were about to leave. It all felt wrong. He watched the bald man walk away with the phone still to his ear. He strode under the steel-and-glass awning fronting the hotel, passed between twin stone lions, and disappeared into the lobby.

Slaton began moving again. His first inclination was to go straight to the limo and talk to Uday, but a flash of motion behind the tinted driver's window convinced him otherwise. There was at least one other man.

He crossed the street three cars behind the limo. Keeping his head down, which was quite natural in the rain, he retraced the bald man's path into the hotel. Once inside, Slaton scanned the expansive and finely trimmed lobby. He spotted him in a quiet corner, still talking on his phone. Slaton pulled back the hood of his jacket and walked directly toward him. He was larger up close, at least six foot three, and the buttons of his suit strained across his chest with every move. When he saw Slaton coming, the man pocketed his phone and raised a hand as if hailing a cab.

Slaton's gray eyes were expressionless, and he was the first to speak when they merged. "Where is Baland?" His tone was no more than curious, the inflection inquiring.

"Conseiller Baland has sent a car. Your meeting must take place at headquarters."

"Headquarters," Slaton repeated, appearing relieved. "All right, but I'll need to use the toilet." Immediately behind them was a hallway, two clearly marked restrooms at the end. When Slaton took his first step in that direction, the bald man seized his arm. Slaton allowed it for an instant, long enough for the grip to go firm. He felt thick fingers clamping his biceps, as he knew they would, and creating a distinct pivot point. He then subtly leaned away, which unsettled the big man's balance, effectively drawing him from the lobby into the narrow confines of the hallway.

The bald man opened his mouth as if to say something.

At that precise moment, Slaton rotated and slammed an elbow into his clean-shaven temple. It was a targeted blow, but not quite sufficient. The guard tipped against the marble-tiled wall like a felled tree, but he remained upright on wobbling knees. Slaton put a hand over his crown, jerked his head away, then slammed it into the stone. The man instantly went slack and crumpled to the floor.

Slaton first checked to see if anyone had noticed. Confident he was in the clear, he dragged the man deeper into the recesses of the hall. Between twin doors labeled for men and women, he saw what looked like a service closet. Slaton tested the handle and found it unlocked. Inside were bathroom supplies: a broom, a mop . . . and five seconds later, one thoroughly unconscious Frenchman. Slaton already knew which pocket to search. He retrieved the bald man's phone, then quietly closed the door. Walking calmly back to the lobby, he thumbed to find the call log and tapped on the most recent.

Baland answered in French.

"What the hell is going on?" Slaton replied.

A pause. "Where is—"

"Tell me what's going on!"

"I sent a car to bring you to headquarters with Uday and Sarah. We have to discuss—"

"Why isn't Uday being protected?" Slaton broke in. "He's a valuable asset, and the men you put on him are not DGSI. They're amateurs."

Another pause. The call suddenly ended. Slaton stood staring at the phone. Seconds later a flourish of motion caught his eye. Outside, movement near the car.

The driver had gotten out. He looked agitated and alert as he stood at the street-side door. With two open palms he gave a "stay right there" gesture to Uday and Sarah in the backseat. Slaton expected the man to come running inside to help his partner. Instead, he rounded the rear of the limo and set off down the street on a dead run.

In a terrible rush, Slaton suddenly understood. "No . . . *no*!"

He sprinted toward the entrance, but far too late. He'd barely cleared the hotel's front doors when the bomb went off.

FIFTY-FIVE

Slaton was hurled to the ground by the blast, glass raining down all around him. The sound was deafening, and he lay stunned for a time. He blinked his eyes open and struggled to his knees, trying to get his bearings in a cloud of smoke and dust.

He should have heard screams and car alarms, but for a time there was only the crash of a relentless cymbal, a pounding in his head. He willed himself to his feet, encouraged that he succeeded, and did a quick personal inventory. Shards of glass and debris carpeted the marble around him, but he could find only a few minor scratches. One sleeve on his jacket was torn, but he saw no blood beneath.

The smell hit him next, a chemical, sulfuric tang, along with the first hints of burning flesh. He turned his attention outward and saw vortices of dust curling through the air, obscuring the world beyond and muting the surviving streetlights. The rain was still coming, already cleansing, and as the smoke and dust dissipated, Slaton noticed what was directly in front of him: a full-scale carving of a sitting lion, its stone head on the ground at his feet. By pure chance, the sculpture had absorbed the blast in his direction, a tiny cone of protection in the sphere of destructive energy.

Far less fortunate were Uday and Sarah.

Only moments ago he'd seen them in the limo. The car was barely recognizable, a twisted heap of metal. A massive crater marked ground zero, and bits of burning debris were strewn across the boulevard. Slaton saw bodies on the distant sidewalk, some writhing, others ominously still. Dozens of passing cars had been stilled in the street. He saw a policeman giving aid to a survivor as he talked on his mobile. Sirens were rising in the distance. The emergency response here, so close to the signature landmarks of Paris, would be quick and overwhelming.

Slaton walked unsteadily toward the street, his legs barely compliant. He stepped over leg-thick tree branches that were smoldering like spent matchsticks. Two blocks away he realized the guard's phone was still in his hand. He crossed the street easily—traffic had seized, no movement in either direction—and sent the phone spinning into the back of an open-bed truck that was filled with construction refuse.

Slaton turned up the opposite sidewalk. One by one his senses came back online, and he gradually picked up his pace. The sirens behind him seemed to fuse into a single wail. As if Paris itself was crying for help.

The first of Chadeh's attacks occurred, by sheer chance, only minutes after the bombing at The Peninsula. Two young men walked into a kosher grocery store in Reuilly, removed handguns from beneath their long raincoats, and began firing indiscriminately. A clerk and a manager were the first killed, and six customers perished in the aisles. A quick-thinking stock clerk, a young girl of Moroccan extraction who was in fact a Muslim, ushered the three remaining customers out the back door. Seeing the place empty, the terrorists inadvisably emptied their magazines, taking out windows and a wine display before venturing outside. Whatever luck they enjoyed to that point ended abruptly when they encountered the wrong off-duty policeman, an officer from a special weapons and tactics team who was a champion marksman, and who happened to be carrying his service weapon. Four bullets, all in one direction, ended the affair.

Before news of the crime even reached a police dispatcher, the second attack commenced in Toulon. Three young men rushed a newspaper office, only to be stymied by a heavy lock on the front door. Two carried semiautomatic weapons, and the third wore a suicide vest under his bulky jacket. A frantic debate ensued about whether the bomb might breach the steel door, and as the three shouted among themselves, fate intervened once again. This time it was in favor of ISIS.

A small bus carrying a group of Jewish students from a nearby college, there to take a tour of the newspaper's offices, parked directly outside the entrance. The driver of the bus saw what was happening, but all too late, and one of the terrorists shot him in the head. The bomber ran onto the bus, and with a scream of "*Allahu akbar!*" he pressed the switch that snuffed out thirteen young lives. The only mercy for France was that his collaborators were among them.

Baland held a news conference within the hour in the media room of DGSI headquarters. He confirmed that seven people were dead in the bombing at The Peninsula, including both occupants of the car carrying the explosives. Twelve bystanders had been injured. He assured frazzled Parisians, as verified by new first-responder protocol, that no radioactive material had been involved. He also addressed attacks in Reuilly and Toulon, before pivoting to his most delicate briefing point.

In an announcement that had been preapproved by his superior, the minister of the interior, he warned that reliable intelligence suggested further attacks might be imminent. In a confident tone, Baland promised his countrymen that security agencies across northern Europe were working tirelessly to interdict any planned strikes, and that no one in his section would rest until every plot had been stopped.

In the final segment of his briefing, Baland acknowledged that the Islamic State was almost certainly responsible for the day's mayhem. He also let slip that the woman being sought for the murder of Director Claude Michelis, whose ties to ISIS had been proved, was being studied as a suspect in the bombing at The Peninsula. This last comment took much of France's leadership by surprise, not the least of whom was a flummoxed minister of the interior, and would generate considerable debate that evening in official halls around Paris. In that moment, however, fixed steadfastly under the strobes of so many cameras, the director-select was certainty itself, and few doubted him in light of his past prescience on matters of terrorism.

Baland preempted any questions by leaving the podium abruptly, but he did lob one afterthought within range of the microphone bouquet.

"Expect no changes to the ceremony the day after tomorrow. I will take command of this department from the Place des Invalides at nine o'clock Saturday morning. The cowards can do nothing to stop that." His jaw resolute and his stride determined, Zavier Baland left the media room with the air of a man on a mission.

Slaton approached his room carefully.

With heightened senses, he looked up and down the hall, seeking the slightest deviation. He pulled the H&K before moving inside, and cleared the small room in seconds. His bed had been made and clean towels were racked in the bathroom. The only addition he noted was a mint on his pillow. With nothing obviously amiss, he went to his suitcase. He'd left it on the dresser, the two halves shelled open to put all his possessions on display—a veritable invitation.

He pulled his phone from his pocket and turned it on. It vibrated to announce a message, but he ignored that momentarily to call up a photo of the suitcase he'd taken earlier. In the image he compared three specific markers to what was before him now: a bent collar on one shirt, the orientation of his tooth-brush, and a half-buried sock that lined up perfectly with the top left side of the case. Had anyone gone through his things, no matter how carefully, they could never have reconfigured all three in precisely the same manner. The suitcase looked exactly like the picture.

Slaton set his gun on the dresser.

Has caution got the better of me? he wondered. The answer was fast in coming. *Certainly not.* The acting director of DGSI had just tried to lure him into an explosive-laden car. Then there was Malika, who'd brought him to Paris with but one aim. Caution was paramount.

His ears had stopped ringing from the blast, and his only injury of note was a minor laceration on the back of one hand. He went to the bathroom mirror. His hair was wet and disheveled, and his shirt had a tattered sleeve and blood on one cuff. Slaton began unbuttoning his shirt, and he was reaching for the shower handle when he remembered the message. He pulled it up and saw that it was from Bloch: CALL IMMEDIATELY.

The connection went right through, and when Bloch answered, Slaton said, "I'm okay."

A pause, then, "Why wouldn't you be?"

"You haven't heard about the bombing?"

"*Bombing?* I've been traveling—what's happened?"

Slaton gave Bloch the bad news.

"Dear God . . . Uday and Sarah, you're sure they were in the car?"

"Positive. I was supposed to be with them, but when it became clear that wasn't going to happen, someone settled for two out of three."

"Baland."

Slaton was momentarily put off. "Yes . . . but I would have expected you to say Malika."

"Something has come up on our end—I'll explain later. How do you know it was Baland?"

"He arranged the meeting, and I was talking to him right before the blast. He hung up on me when he realized I wasn't going to get in the car. Seconds later, the driver ran away and the bomb went off. It was a complete setup."

"Apparently so. But a man in his position will have no trouble blaming others." Bloch almost said something else, but his voice seemed to cut out. Slaton thought he heard Talia whispering in the background. Bloch said, "Apparently there is more. A second attack has occurred in Paris, and another in Toulon."

Slaton blew out a long, steady breath. "Okay, so where do we go from here?"

"Israel's Paris embassy. As I said, we have new information. It is imperative that we talk in a secure place."

Slaton pulled the phone slightly away from his ear. "You're *here*? In Paris?"

"I told you, I've been traveling. Talia is with me. What I have to tell you will reinforce what Baland has just done. Thirty minutes?"

Slaton hesitated as he tried to make sense of things. It was hopeless. "All right. Thirty minutes."

"And be very careful, David. You are now a marked man."

Slaton ended the call with Bloch's final words pounding in his head.

He was still in front of the mirror. The smell of the blast clung to his clothing, a tainted blend of smoke and death. He turned on the tap and leaned into the basin, scrubbing his hands and pulling water onto his face. After toweling down and changing into fresh clothes, he wedged the H&K back into his rear waistband, covered by the loose tail of his shirt. The steel frame felt hard on the small of his back—cold, bulky, and undeniably reassuring. He surveyed the room: a suitcase full of clothing, a few toiletries in the bathroom, an empty roller bag in the closet. The Arctic Warfare Covert remained hidden in the frame of the folding bed, along with the Glock.

Bloch was right. One moment of madness at The Peninsula had changed everything. That hail of glass and steel served as a private declaration of war. Baland had tried to kill him. Slaton didn't understand why, but he would find out soon. He considered whether Baland would order the police of France to hunt him down, as he'd already done with Malika. Given the day's chaos, it would be simple to drum up a justification for his arrest.

Still, Slaton saw problems with an all-out manhunt. Unlike Malika, who was tied to ISIS, Slaton had Israel in his corner. Reluctant as they might be, Bloch and Nurin would not stand in silence if he were declared an enemy of France. He reasoned that Baland *would* try to kill him—but he would do so under the radar. All while trying to stamp down a new string of ISIS attacks.

He began to view things more positively: in the coming days DGSI would be monumentally distracted, battling ISIS on its home ground. That gave Slaton a narrow window in which to operate.

He looked all around and made decisions.

Does Baland know about this room? Probably not. But he would uncover it soon enough. Slaton gave it a day, no more than two.

Should I take everything or leave it in place? He looked around, saw nothing that couldn't be replaced, and decided to leave it all where it was. When Slaton locked the door behind him seconds later, he had no way of knowing how vital that decision would be.

FIFTY-SIX

Baland met the recently elected president of France for the second time at 11:34 that evening. The leader of the republic looked weary as he wandered the room shaking hands and gathering the latest information. France was under siege, and while there had been an executive briefing an hour ago, the president evidently felt a need to visit the command center—a show of support for the troops, if thirty technicians and senior officers could be referred to as such.

When he reached Baland, the balding and thickly built president said in his famous baritone, "I have great confidence in you and your department, Zavier."

"Thank you, sir. We will not rest until France is secure."

Baland felt a supportive hand on his shoulder, and could not deny a brief jolt of exhilaration. *How far I have come,* he thought. The hand pulled away, and after a few words to the woman next in line, the president excused himself, Baland was sure, to retire to his private suite in the adjacent wing of the Élysée Palace.

The room regained its momentum, everyone going back to keyboards and phone calls. A third attack had only recently been interdicted: A suspicious young man seen loitering outside a Jewish community center in Montparnasse had been confronted by a pair of policemen. He'd tried to run, but was quickly caught, and within the hour an unarmed suitcase bomb was uncovered in a nearby apartment, along with two other suspects. All in all, a noteworthy victory for good police work.

Baland was increasingly struck by the dichotomy of his position. His mission for the last fifteen years had been to stop this very kind of thing, and he'd taken to it wholeheartedly. He'd earned the trust of coworkers and had a family to protect. But now? Now he had personally given the enemy a target list that was playing out before his eyes. *If this had to happen,* he thought, *at least it is happening to the Jews. They will never be my countrymen.*

But how many more attacks would there be? He began doodling on a scratchpad the names of possible targets from the report he'd given Malika. He came up with almost thirty that had not yet been struck, but certainly there were more. He'd already seen a preliminary download of the personnel list brought out by Uday, and those numbers were staggering: over three hundred individuals and small cells across France, and half again as many in nearby Belgium. He supposed there was some mathematical model to calculate the permutations. The more critical estimate, however, was far more simple. *How long until it is all brought back to me?*

He'd been lucky so far. The exclusivity of Jewish targets had not been an absolute, thanks to the bombing at The Peninsula that he himself had coordinated. Baland had intended that most of his problems would be resolved in one cataclysmic moment. The men he'd hired for the job were no more than thugs, and he'd expected they would perish in the blast. Both had unfortunately survived, and one was already in custody—unconscious, but expected to recover. One more loose end in his fast-fraying existence. All thanks to one man.

Slaton . . .

Baland's errant thoughts were interrupted when an Air Force colonel stepped to the front of the room. He began a briefing on a mission under way from a forward air base in Turkey, and Baland listened with great interest. He was suppressing an urge to ask the colonel for targeting details when Charlotte LeFevre, who would soon head up *his* technology division, rushed into the room and made a beeline for him.

"Sir, I have news on another case."

"Not now," said Baland, as he decided to engage the colonel privately after the briefing. "What we are doing here takes absolute priority."

"But this is very unusual," LeFevre said.

Baland felt her insistence as she stood by his shoulder. "Does it relate to this woman who tried to kill me? Or one of the recent attacks?"

"Actually, both."

He finally gave LeFevre his undivided attention.

She handed over a report titled "Lab Analysis,"

along with a case number. "What is this?" he asked, waving the paper at her.

"The lab report on the woman who killed Director Michelis. We recovered DNA material from the apartment she was using as a safe house."

Baland looked at the bottom of the page. "This says there was no match to any of our databases."

"Which was true when the report was drafted."

He looked at the date. "That was only yesterday."

LeFevre produced a second lab analysis. "This is a report on the remains of the bomber from Grenoble. It also had no match in our database."

Baland's impatience got the better of him, and he barked, "Tell me what you're trying to say!"

"These two samples have an unusually high degree of commonality. We think it very likely they are brother and sister."

FIFTY-SEVEN

The Israeli embassy was situated on Rue Rabelais, for Slaton conveniently located in the nearby eighth arrondissement. By no coincidence, it was but three streets removed from the Élysée Palace, where, at that moment, the leadership of France was reacting to a terrorist assault of unprecedented scope.

Slaton arrived in a taxi, and was dropped at the embassy's front entrance in the middle of a downpour. He had no trouble being admitted to the building—Neumann, the lead *katsa* he'd met outside Malika's flat two night ago, was waiting to collect him.

She greeted him cheerfully, and said, "I hope whatever we're doing tonight will turn out better than our last adventure."

"If that's an apology, it's not necessary. We all underestimated her."

She escorted Slaton around a stanchion, and they bypassed the security station under the watchful eyes of three screeners. Slaton had not been here in years, and he saw that major renovations had taken place. The most obvious improvements related to security: Upholstered office dividers had been re-placed by a maze of ill-disguised steel barriers, block-ing access to the consulate's more sensitive areas, and the new windows fronting the street looked thick and multilayered. There were also more cameras than in a Vegas casino, and no effort was made to hide them.

He followed Neumann through winding corridors, finally ending in a wing whose splendid trimmings suggested something beyond analysts' offices and visa queues. Portraits of former ambassadors lined the hallway above gilded Louis Quinze furnishings, and in a central rotunda was a fine oil rendering of the Old City of Jerusalem. Neumann turned in to a well-equipped conference room, undoubtedly the ambas-sador's domain on better days. Bloch and Talia were waiting on one side of a long table. Bloch looked weary—retirement had clearly insulated him from grueling workdays. Talia, on the other hand, appeared ready for a dinner date. Their eyes settled on him, and for a fleeting moment Slaton wondered how he must appear. *Probably like I've just come from a bombing,* he thought.

Neumann closed the door, but she remained in the room and took a seat, meaning she'd been cleared in on Bloch's "new information." As was the tendency in operational settings, the greetings were perfunc-tory, and Bloch set the course.

"Regrettably, the French police have confirmed your assessment, David—Uday and Sarah are dead."

"Have they questioned the guard or the driver who ran off?"

"The driver has disappeared, and the man discovered in the service closet hasn't regained consciousness. Apparently you were a bit too enthusiastic in your efforts—not for the first time, I might add."

Slaton didn't apologize. "Will he survive?"

"The doctors think there is a good chance."

"Has either man been identified?"

"No, but the French are certain the one in the hospital is not DGSI."

"They were amateurs," Slaton said.

"Very possibly, but for the moment it is a dead end. We have more important concerns. In our interviews with Uday, we learned that Baland provided a secret DGSI report to ISIS documenting France's susceptibilities to terrorism."

"Baland mentioned it to me."

"I suspect he did not tell you the entire story. Baland apparently provided only a small part of the greater report. What he gave up was telling—it exclusively involved Jewish interests in France."

"*What?*"

"In the last few hours it's already begun to happen. Attacks in Toulon, Montparnasse, and Reuilly, and only moments ago a Jewish museum in Montmartre. ISIS is wasting no time. I would imagine they see Baland's information as perishable, given Uday's defection, meaning they will strike as many of these targets as possible in the coming days."

Slaton sat in silence. Baland had indeed held back on him.

"That is not the most troubling news," Bloch continued. He looked to Neumann, who picked up.

"I recently paid a visit to Gabrielle Baland," she said.

Slaton's eyes narrowed as he tried to associate the name. He drew a blank. "Is that Baland's wife?"

"His mother—it was relatively easy to track her down. She's a widow in her late seventies, lives in Lyon. I went to see Madame Baland, explaining that I was a friend of Zavier's from school days who wanted to catch up with him. She said she hasn't seen her son in years."

"Was there a falling-out?"

"Very much so. She knew he was living in Paris, and that he held an important position. But they are completely estranged. No birthday cards, holiday visits, or phone calls—no contact of any kind."

All at once Slaton thought he saw where this was going. "You said she hasn't seen him in years. Let me guess . . . fifteen?"

Neumann nodded.

Talia said, "We recorded their conversation. You should hear it firsthand."

She addressed a laptop on the table, and soon muted voices captured by a hidden microphone began playing. Talia turned the screen so they could all see it, providing an English translation of the conversation.

Neumann: "I am sorry to hear that you and Zavier had a split. How long ago was it?"

Mme Baland: "Twelve years? No, fifteen I think. It seems like a lifetime."

Neumann: "I don't wish to pry, but was there some event that precipitated your estrangement?"

Mme Baland: "*There was never difficulty between Zavier and I. But the troubles began right after he returned from Egypt.*"

Neumann: "*Egypt? Was he there on holiday?*"

Mme Baland: "*I never knew. He left very suddenly, and when he returned . . . I sensed a change in him. I saw Zavier only twice before he left Lyon, and even then we barely spoke. I asked him what had happened, but he wouldn't tell me. He was simply a different man.*"

Neumann: "*A different man. You say that with conviction, as if—*"

Mme Baland: "*Would you care for more tea, dear?*"

Talia stopped the recording.

Neumann said, "From that point she no longer wanted to talk about her son. I didn't feel like I could press any harder."

"There is more," Bloch added. "Talia was able to extract a record of his travel. On September 15, 2002, Zavier Baland traveled from Paris to Cairo on Air France. He returned five days later."

Talia said, "It matches perfectly. When he returned, Baland became estranged from the one person in France who knew him well."

Neumann added, "I learned little more from the interview that night, but as I was leaving his mother turned very cautious. I think she knows what happened. In those critical days so many years ago, her son left her forever and was replaced by . . . something else."

The room went silent, and Slaton saw three sets of eyes on him. Each was convinced.

"We went back and searched where we could," said Bloch. "Baland moved to Paris one week after returning from Cairo. We tracked down his first landlord, and ascertained that he changed his address with a number of government agencies. One month later he applied for a position with the national police force, and was hired soon after."

Slaton stared at Bloch, trying to wrap his mind around it. "You're telling me the man I shot in Gaza fifteen years ago was the *real* Zavier Baland?"

"It would appear so," said Bloch. "You might recall, the mission you undertook to kill Samir was weeks in the making. There must have been a leak—we've had our share. When Samir realized we were coming after him, he somehow convinced Baland to travel to Gaza, by way of Egypt, and traded places with him on the morning when you were waiting. Effectively, your marksmanship helped him escape Gaza and take up a new life."

A profound silence descended on the room.

Talia broke it with, "And if all of this is true . . . it means the terrorist Ali Samir recently sent information to ISIS regarding Jewish targets in France. Information that is being acted on as we speak."

"And in just over twenty-four hours," Bloch added, "he will become the new director of DGSI."

FIFTY-EIGHT

Baland walked back into DGSI headquarters, having taken leave from the ongoing hunt at Élysée Palace. He made a few inquiries downstairs, ensuring that everyone knew he would be in his old office—even if his thoughts had slipped from the search, he could not ignore it completely.

He sank heavily behind his desk, and made no attempt to check his messages. In the guise of Zavier Baland, Ali Samir sat alone reflecting deeply on what LeFevre had just told him. *They are brother and sister.*

No words had ever affected him so profoundly.

Jalil, he reflected. *My only son.*

He had never known the boy—never even seen him, in fact. His wife had been pregnant when he'd escaped Gaza, and she'd given birth two weeks after attending the funeral he had so artfully arranged.

No, he corrected, *I have seen him once.*

That mental image stormed into his head. The CCTV video of the bombing in Grenoble. He remembered watching Jalil walk back to the car. Remembered seeing his sister press the button to activate his suicide vest. It seemed a singularly callous act . . . but had he not done much the same to his own twin brother? Perhaps. Malika, however, had been explicitly cruel. Not only had she killed Jalil, but in her final actions she had demonstrated a complete lack of faith in him.

She probably had her reasons. Jalil had been raised by his mother, no doubt made into a lamb. But Malika—she was something else. *She is every bit as ruthless as I am,* Baland thought, more with disbelief than pride. He'd had no hand in her upbringing, at least not in any proper way. He had been too busy constructing bombs to be a father, a talent he'd resurrected today at The Peninsula.

Yet still she is like me.

The door to his office suddenly opened, and Baland stirred back to the present. He recognized a man named Trevant, who was in charge of building security.

"Pardon, Monsieur Director," Trevant said, prematurely using the title. "I thought you were at the Élysée command center. I have come to update the security keypads. If you wish me to come back later—"

"No, not at all," Baland said, waving him in. There were two secure fixtures in the room, a small wall safe and one drawer in the heavy desk. Both had locks necessitating a fingerprint scan and a four-digit code to gain access.

Trevant said, "I have already reprogrammed the units in the director's suite with your fingerprint, and

I cleared the old code. You may create a new one whenever you wish."

"Yes, I remember how to do it." Baland watched the man connect a small electronic device to the wall safe. "You are working late tonight, Trevant."

"Not at all, sir. I work two of these shifts every week."

Baland should have known that . . . the keepers of DGSI security worked in the dead of night. *How much more have I missed?* He felt a darkness come over him, something he'd not felt in a very long time. He looked at the computer screen beside him and saw e-mails piling up in his in-box. Some would have seemed important a month ago. He pushed away from his desk and watched the man work.

"Tell me, do you have children, Trevant?"

A hesitation. "Of course, sir. Two boys."

"Are they good?"

Trevant laughed uneasily. "As good as any, I suppose. One of them wants to be a policeman, but the other . . . he finds a bit of trouble."

"What kind of trouble?"

Trevant paused in his task. He smiled awkwardly at the man who was so many steps above him. "He stays out too late, I think, and has difficulty holding a job. But Luc will straighten out—he has never been arrested or anything like that. I look after him, and someday, God willing, he will look after me."

After an uncomfortable silence, Trevant went back to his lock. A series of beeps punctuated the stillness, and he said, "*Voilà!* You have two days in which to move any secure items to your new office."

"Yes . . . thank you."

Trevant was gone minutes later, and Baland reached down and opened the secure drawer in his desk. It was full from front to back with files. Only one interested him—directly at the head, the all-important binder. He extracted the same section he had earlier, and paired it with Uday's addition. With well-manicured fingertips he neatly squared it all on the blotter in front of him. Forty printed pages, and on top of that the well-traveled memory stick. The same information Chadeh had held for a brief time in Raqqa.

"Is this what it has come to?" he whispered.

He'd had a good run in France and nearly succeeded. Nearly carved out a respectable life. But now, with all that was happening around him, it was folly to think his secret would not be exposed. Since the day Malika had first cornered him on the Pont Neuf, he'd known this day would come. Baland had postponed the reckoning to the best of his ability, but with each passing day his options seemed to narrow. He was like a juggler who'd gone beyond his comfort level. Too many knives in the air. He might silence Slaton, but how many others in Mossad knew the truth? So, too, a handful of zealots in Raqqa. And of course there was Malika. He could never contain a secret so widely dispersed.

He felt an old fury rise from deep within. Malika, his fratricidal daughter, had been instrumental in his ruin. But she was not its source. That went undeniably further back. To a childhood spent in dusty streets cleaning up after violence, and so many years thereafter making others do the same. It all rushed back in a torrent of hate. Just when he'd thought they were out of his life forever, the old oppressors had returned to seize him by the throat. The directorship. Jacqueline and the girls. A mostly honest career. All would soon be lost to the tormentors of so many generations of his people.

The Jews.

I never really escaped, he thought. *We have only come full circle.*

The man who'd tried not to be Ali Samir for so very long regarded the information in front of him. If nothing else, the last fifteen years had granted him opportunity—a chance to hurt them in Europe more than anyone since Hitler. He flicked through the pages and saw endless opportunity. Chadeh's first wave of attacks had to be nearing its end, and with Uday having ruined ISIS' comm networks, no others would be ordered soon. Baland, however, was in a perfect position to pick up where Chadeh left off.

His longtime constraint—his sense of duty to France—had effectively been displaced. It occurred to him that he would first have to claim the directorship, but that would happen just over a day from now. After that, he could order attacks against Jews with one hand, and mismanage the French response with the other. For a week, maybe two, he would have free rein in running both sides of the campaign. Baland thought back across history and wondered if there was any precedent. A war in which one man commanded both armies.

He inserted the memory stick into the computer at

the side of his desk. The old hatred burned brighter as the screen flickered to life. The execution of his plan might have to wait another day, but the planning could begin immediately.

The only question was where to begin.

FIFTY-NINE

"The only question is where does this end?" said Bloch from his chair in the embassy conference room. "In just over twenty-four hours a ceremony will be held in which Ali Samir takes charge of DGSI."

Slaton said, "That can't be allowed to happen."

"Certainly not."

Talia said, "What I don't understand is the motivation. Baland, or Samir, or whatever we call him—what is he after?"

"A point worth considering," said Bloch.

"You know what's really mind-bending?" Slaton offered. "I don't think Malika realizes who he is. She believes she's been running an op on her uncle, when all this time—"

"My God!" Talia blurted. "It's actually her father."

Bloch said, "It explains why she has been so ruthless. To her, Baland is a traitor to the cause her father died for."

"That makes sense," Slaton agreed. "But it brings up something else. Aside from being blackmailed by Malika, Samir has been playing by the rules since putting his brother under my gun sight. For fifteen years he's been a model policeman. Could he really have waited this patiently for a chance to strike against Israel? And in such an indirect way? In Gaza, Samir never attacked France or Western interests. He was at war with Israel, plain and simple."

"What are you suggesting?" Bloch queried. "That he has become a responsible citizen?"

"The way he sacrificed his brother—I don't think it started out that way. But by everything we know, he's been on the level since he came to France. He's got a wife and two daughters. Give any man an opportunity for a positive, productive life, even one who starts out as a reprehensible terrorist . . . he just might take it."

Silence prevailed, until Talia said, "If we give this information to the French, what will they do?"

"Actually," Bloch said, "I have already discussed that option with Director Nurin. Our evidence is compelling, but it is not overwhelming. Baland will fight it. He'll say the idea of an alternate identity is as absurd as it sounds. Remember, he is not without influence. He has already eliminated two of his most damning witnesses, and as we speak there is no evidence to link him to the deaths of Uday and Sarah. If he can eliminate Malika before she is interrogated, and perhaps the two men he involved in the bombing—he might survive with his reputation intact."

"And he'll know it was Israel who threw him under the bus."

"Director Nurin used a more crass phrase, but his conclusion was the same." Bloch steepled his hands on the conference table before locking his gaze on Slaton. "The government of Israel has taken a narrow view of this situation. Our duty above all else is to protect Jewish interests. If Ali Samir is reborn as the head of French counterterrorism, the damage he could inflict, both here and in Israel . . . it is incalculable."

"But *would* he go back to his old ways?" Slaton asked.

"That is the unanswerable question. We are talking about a man who only hours ago received a long list of willing jihadists. Men and women awaiting the call to duty."

Bloch leveled his most severe gaze. "Nurin has made his decision. Ali Samir must be stopped, and we cannot be certain the French will take timely action."

Slaton looked at Bloch, then Talia. "Are you saying what I think you're saying?"

Bloch said, "I realize you are no longer employed by Mossad, David . . . but yes. The new director of DGSI must be targeted. The potential for damage outweighs any risks."

"Not counting the risks taken by me."

Bloch frowned. "You should know that a second *kidon* is en route, in case you decline."

Slaton stared at his old boss. He stood and crossed the room to a nicely stocked wet bar. Pulling a water bottle from a bucket of ice, he twisted off the cap and tipped it back once. "When am I to kill him? Thirty hours from now? The ceremony when he takes command?"

"I shouldn't tell you your business, but it seems the

obvious opportunity. You already have the right weapon."

Slaton felt strangely at ease. He was beholden to neither Israel nor France. He considered the reprehensible things Ali Samir had done during his time in Gaza. He considered the straight road the man had driven since. Then he remembered The Peninsula, and Uday and Sarah. He avoided dwelling on the discomforting intersections between Samir's life course and his own. Finally, he thought about Christine, and what advice she would give him. Unequivocally, he knew what that would be.

"No," he said. "I won't do it. I'm sure your other *kidon* is as good a shot as I am."

"I doubt that very much . . . but I'll inform the director of your decision."

Slaton had never before turned a mission down, and while he felt no obligation to Mossad, his duty to Israel did leave room for regrets. The divergence he'd faced for so long was rearing up again. Duty to his family versus duty to his homeland.

Bloch said something to Talia, but Slaton was so engrossed in his inward thoughts it didn't register. She began working her laptop as Bloch said, "There is one other thing you should know before you leave."

He beckoned Slaton behind Talia so they could all view her screen. Slaton saw a black-and-white video of a woman peering through a small rectangular window. He couldn't see her face, but he instantly recognized her by nothing more than body profile and the way she moved—he had followed Malika for some time after the shooting at Le Quinze.

"Where was this footage taken?"

"Not *was*," said Bloch. "This is a real-time feed."

"You know where she is? Right now?"

"Yes. We've known for the last—" Bloch checked his watch. "—six hours. It was only recently, however, that we realized *who* she was."

Bloch got up and walked to the room's only window. There he drew back an unusually thick slat—Slaton suspected the window covering itself was some manner of electronic baffle against eavesdropping, augmenting the bulletproof glass. He followed and looked over Bloch's shoulder.

"Across the street," said Bloch, "the building on the left. You can see a series of five narrow windows, no more than vents really, along the second floor. The center window is directly across the street from our main entrance." He let the slat fall.

Slaton gave him a questioning look.

Bloch explained, "The violence France is experiencing is not without precedent. We have long understood that our Paris embassy is a target. We keep excellent surveillance inside the building, of course, but one of our brighter technicians reviewed the security plan and suggested monitoring the surrounding area. A small team was brought in for a visit, people very much like you—tactically oriented, one might say. We asked them where they would set up shop if they wanted to surveil, or perhaps even target our facility. The window I just showed you was everyone's first choice. Until three months ago, the entire second floor of that building was a warehouse for a small technology company. When the company was bought out, the space fell vacant, and we took the liberty of installing a few cameras. There are others in adjacent buildings, and one or two on nearby rooftops."

"That bright technician is going places," Slaton said.

"I told her the same thing."

Slaton looked at Talia, who appeared uncomfortable. "It was only common sense," she said.

Slaton pulled the slat back a second time, and studied the lay of the surrounding area. Fragmented thoughts rushed through his mind, one by one falling into an intriguing pattern, like ten pieces from ten different puzzles joining miraculously. He challenged what was brewing in his head from every conceivable angle, and he did see flaws. Every plan had them. But the risks were far outweighed by opportunity.

Bloch said, "We've been watching her very closely. So far there is no sign she's carrying a weapon."

"She has one . . . something small," Slaton said almost to himself. He kept looking outside, transfixed not by the scene, but by an idea.

"If you like," said Bloch, "we can arrange a departure for you through the back entrance. You can fade away unseen very easily. On the other hand, I assume you are carrying the handgun we provided. If you would like a silencer in order to—"

"I've changed my mind," said Slaton. "I'll take out Baland at the ceremony."

Talia and Bloch looked at one another, then at Slaton.

He dropped the slat, and said, "But I do it my way."

Bloch knew better than to argue. "What can we do to help?"

Slaton actually grinned as he looked at Bloch. "To begin . . . I'd like you to come out on the sidewalk with me and have a cigarette."

The former director of Mossad was rarely surprised, but clearly Slaton had got the better of him. "Neither of us smoke," Bloch said.

"True. But Malika doesn't know that."

SIXTY

To drop a thousand-pound bomb from miles in the air is an undeniable act of brute force. To employ such a weapon with maximum effectiveness, however, requires a certain degree of artistry, particularly when four of them are to arrive at the same point in a span of two seconds.

The artisans that night were two French Air Force pilots who'd been tasked to fly their Dassault Rafale fighters from an air base in Turkey, where they had been forward-deployed, into the arid skies above Syria. The tasking order had arrived unexpectedly—the most important ones always did—and appeared sourced from the highest levels. A high-value target had been identified in Raqqa. It was an unusual mission from the outset—the target was a well-known mosque, which would normally have been off-limits. That being the case, the pilots undertook their preflight planning with the greatest of care.

The first variable, they realized, was that the walls of a house of worship would not be fortified like those of a military facility. Surveillance footage confirmed

that there was but one level to the mosque, no base-
ments or upper floors to complicate their equations.
The blast was to be optimized to destroy equipment,
electronics apparently, although any personnel inside
were considered fair game. There was the usual concern for civilian casualties in surrounding buildings,
but no specific limitations had been placed on the
strike. This told the pilots two things: Whatever lay
inside was important, and someone was very certain
of their intelligence. Taken altogether, the pilots agreed
that a payload of four one-thousand-pounders was
just the thing.

The mission began smoothly, and the Rafales were
eight miles distant when the target came into view on
their weapons displays. Gliding through the black void
of night four miles aloft, the pilots set a shallow dive
with their jets arranged in an offset wedge formation,
roughly half a mile apart. They hit their "pickle"
buttons almost simultaneously, and for eighteen seconds the four bombs guided and glided toward their
target. They ran as two sets of two, the lead bomb in
each pair 650 milliseconds ahead of its partner. All
that was straightforward, like four batted balls heading for the same fence in a ballpark, notwithstanding
that their inertial and GPS guidance packages would
cause them to converge on one particular seat.

Greater nuance lay in the fusing. The leading
bombs—they had been dropped in pairs to protect
against a lone failure—were fitted with delay contact
fuses. Fifty milliseconds after penetrating the outer
wall, which would place them well within the void of
the main building, the bombs would unleash their

fury. The trailing projectiles operated on an entirely different principle. They would guide initially to a point slightly beyond the first pair, and assuming they survived the shrapnel and debris sent up by their predecessors, which was highly likely, radar altimeters would begin a brief countdown. Ten meters above the ground, and centered on the original blasts, firing signals would be cued and airbursts initiated. Quite literally, explosions on top of explosions.

That was exactly how it all happened. The former mosque in Raqqa, and present home of the Islamic State Institution for Public Information, was obliterated in less time than it took to tie a shoe.

The most unforeseen consequence—fortuitous or not, depending on one's perspective—began ninety seconds before the first bomb arrived, when a man walked out of the targeted building. The caliph of the Islamic State was two streets removed from ground zero when the blasts struck home, and he was knocked flat on his ass by the concussive wave. As a stunned but uninjured caliph was picked up by his security detail, everyone had a good idea what had just happened. No one mentioned the irony of what stood between them and the mosque: Shielding them from the explosions was the neighborhood's oldest and most stalwart building, an Armenian Catholic church.

Less fortunate were those inside the mosque, including the entirety of the governing Shura Council. They had gathered at the mosque for a briefing on their faltering computer networks, and chief among them was ISIS' beleaguered military commander. Unlike the caliph, Wael Chadeh never knew what hit him.

SIXTY-ONE

The hard rain had gone to drizzle, but the wind refused to yield. Slaton and Bloch stood hunched on the sidewalk in front of the embassy, illuminated in the wash of a subdued streetlight. Their collars were turned up and the wind was at their backs. A pack of Marlboros had been donated by a security screener, a matronly woman who was happy to rescue the visiting contingent from an unnamed sister agency in Tel Aviv who professed a dire need for nicotine.

"It's been a long time since I've done fieldwork," Bloch groused, putting the cigarette between his meaty lips.

"It comes back fast," said Slaton.

"Remind me why I am standing in the rain at one thirty in the morning." Bloch took a long draw, and immediately stifled a cough.

"Because I need a decent night's sleep."

Bloch stared at him a few beats, and in the interval a cab rushed past and splashed mud onto his black Oxfords. "You know, I've made my living getting into people's heads. I'm good at sensing motivations, predicting what men and women will do in given situations—so good that they made me director of Mossad. I must tell you, David, over the years . . . you have vexed me more than any of our enemies."

"I'll take that as a compliment. Chances are, it's why I'm still around." He paused before expanding on why they were outside. "I want Malika to know I'm still here. I want her to stay awake all night watching this front door. While she does, I'll be inside getting some much-needed sleep."

"And in the morning you will be sharp and she will be fatigued? Do you really need such an advantage to eliminate her? We have a live video feed on this woman—constant eyes on an unsuspecting target. I know it is your rule to seize every advantage, but this seems extreme even by your standards."

Slaton looked at Bloch, and could not contain a grin. "I appreciate your confidence in my talents for the dark arts. But there's more to it than that—I'll explain later. For now, I have two requests. I'm going to need a fresh phone. And tomorrow I want some help. You said Nurin had sent another *kidon*, in case I balked at the job."

"Yes."

"Is he here in Paris?"

Bloch smiled this time, enjoying a small victory. "*She* is in the neighborhood."

Slaton smiled back. He'd helped train two female shooters in his time with the service. They'd been among the steadiest he'd worked with. "Perfect. I may need her assistance."

The former director dropped his cigarette on the

ground before reaching its end, and snuffed it out with a toe. "Approved. But whatever game you are playing, David, remember . . . Israel is to be kept at a distance."

"You can tell Director Nurin the feeling is mutual."

A gust of wind whipped up the urban valley, and Bloch looked skyward. "Is there anything else?" he asked, irritation back on display.

"No, you should go inside now. Nobody stands out in the rain after their smoke is done. I'll catch up with you in a minute."

Bloch disappeared through the front entrance.

Slaton kept his free hand in his pocket, a perfectly natural stance on a cold and rainy night. The true reason was more purposeful. Talia was monitoring the room across the street on the live feed. While they'd still seen no evidence of a weapon, if Malika suddenly produced one and raised it to the window, Slaton had to know immediately. Warning would arrive as a vibration to the phone in his hand.

He never looked directly at the window in question, but he knew exactly where it was. Indeed, it was the focal point of geometry running through his head. Angles and distances to every curb, trash can, and parked car, and one wintering urban sapling, particular attention given to what would still be here in the morning.

He looked up and down the street, a few last mental snapshots captured, then took his final draw. Slaton had never been a smoker, but like many things he was not genuinely interested in, it kept a place in his repertoire. He knew how to operate bar-code scanners in stores, how to run a jackhammer, how to bus a restaurant table. He could drive a front-end loader, and knew that hotel vans typically departed lobbies at the top of every hour with drivers who didn't give a damn whether you were a guest when you tipped in advance. Smoking was core curriculum, and he could carry it off like a pack-a-day regular.

He looked up at a mist that swirled down through the streetlight's aura and brushed against his face. The moisture felt good, almost cleansing. He tried once more to imagine why his plan wouldn't work. Like Bloch, he too was a student of human habits and motivations, although Slaton's view was more narrow than most—he took things only as far as necessary to put a specific vital organ under a gun sight for the necessary few seconds. Physical vulnerability—that was his customary endgame.

Tomorrow, however, was going to be altogether different.

Fifty yards away, at the window across the street, Malika watched the man in the dark jacket intently. Even through the darkness and rain, she could tell it was the *kidon*—this was the third time she had seen him.

At the moment he was in an extremely vulnerable position. She hadn't expected that. He appeared relaxed, pacing casually back and forth across the same few yards of concrete. When his cigarette reached its end, he didn't light a second. Probably because of the rain.

Within seconds of flicking away the stub, he turned back inside, and Malika watched him disappear into the glowing warmth of the embassy lobby. She checked her watch and noted the time. Then she settled back, took a deep breath, and got as comfortable as she could on the cold concrete floor.

SIXTY-TWO

Six hours later Slaton walked out of the embassy into an indifferent morning. The wind and rain were fading, trying to hold on, as the sun hid behind the clouds. He carried a small attaché borrowed from the former chargé d'affaires, a man whose current status at the embassy was indeterminate, which told Slaton he was certainly Mossad. The attaché was quite empty, but it advanced the image he was after—a man on the move who had business at hand.

Slaton had gone no more than ten paces on the puddled sidewalk when he put his new Mossad-issued phone to his ear as if answering a call. He stopped abruptly, the way people did for calls of such importance that walking at the same time was inadvisable. He meandered back and forth on the same square of cement for a full two minutes, then pocketed the phone and resumed his westerly trek.

He kept a casual pace, and acted out a simple countersurveillance routine along the way. He arrived at his hotel some thirty minutes later, damp and disheveled and self-assured. At the front desk Monsieur

Aranson of Sweden engaged the concierge in a brief back-and-forth about the weather, and she asked if he was enjoying his stay. He assured her that he very much was, thank you, and bid her a pleasant good morning before rambling across the lobby and disappearing into the rising stairwell.

As soon as he was out of sight, Slaton broke into a vertical run, taking the steps three at a time. Inside his third-floor room seconds later, he quickly retrieved the Arctic Warfare Covert from its hiding place, and also the Glock 17. He set the Glock on a table and removed a small screwdriver from his pocket—another acquisition from the embassy. With a deftness that would have impressed any surgeon, Slaton broke down the gun, removed the firing pin, and had the Glock reassembled in less than a minute. The screwdriver and pin went into his pocket. He palmed a full magazine into the weapon, then racked the slide to charge a round into the chamber.

The handgun he placed in the attaché, and that went unlocked onto a midlevel closet shelf. He went to the room's large main window, outside of which was an exterior fire escape, and unlatched the window lock, then nudged the frame ajar a fraction of an inch. He carried the roller bag with the sniper rifle to the door, then paused to study the room. Struck by one imperfection, he went back and repositioned one of the two upholstered sitting chairs, pushing it against the wall by the window at a forty-five-degree angle. Returning to the door, he again looked over the room and was satisfied.

Slaton shouldered into the hall with the roller bag

in hand. He locked the door behind him and made his way to the stairwell. Before reaching the lobby, he diverted into a rough-edged hall and walked a weaving passage through the service corridor—he had learned on the day he arrived that it led to a back door. Luck was with him, and he encountered no hotel staff along the way.

He exited into the alley behind the hotel. It was open on either end of the block, but instead of turning Slaton held a straight line to the service entrance of the opposing building. Having observed the place for days, he knew that back door was unlocked during business hours, and that it accessed a hallway where the establishment's toilets were located. Seconds later he emerged into the hub of a busy café. Patrons gathered around bistro tables, taking espressos and croissants. The line at the counter was three deep. No one gave a second glance to the casual, athletic man carrying a suitcase who left unhurriedly through the front door, hailed a taxi, and disappeared into the rush on Boulevard Saint-Denis.

After spending most of the night crafting attacks against Jewish interests across Europe, an exhausted Baland reported for work the following morning to learn the status of the ongoing battles.

At the Élysée command center the mood had brightened. Only one new attack had been reported overnight, giving hope that the worst was behind them. Also to the positive, the mosque in Raqqa had been bombed hours ago, and the initial battle-damage assessment confirmed that the place had been flattened. There were no apparent survivors, and ISIS message traffic had fallen off precipitously. A few analysts went so far as to suggest that elements of the caliphate's leadership could have been inside. Such claims were maddeningly difficult to verify, and the degree of the victory would take weeks to ascertain, but clearly Uday's information had been accurate.

The buoyant mood in the command center faded just after nine o'clock that morning when a senior officer from Baland's cyber unit delivered sobering news. From the trove of Uday's personnel list, certain phone numbers had been given special scrutiny, and a day-old message was uncovered. Overnight, the encryption had been cracked, revealing a grave directive: A cell of four young men in Lille had been instructed to assemble a truck bomb, which they'd been preparing for months, and obliterate the city's main synagogue.

The Élysée command center went into action, every element of France's police and intelligence establishments focused as one. Within thirty minutes signals intelligence had pinpointed the receiving address, and an oversized assault team launched a raid on a small home in Roubaix. What they found was alarming: four unmade beds, signs of a hasty departure, and residue from a sizable stash of explosives. Worse yet, in a small attached garage they discovered a laboratory, precursor chemicals, and tracks where a heavy vehicle—a work truck, according to neighbors—had recently departed over a sodden driveway. The working estimate was that the crew were carrying enough explosives to level a city block.

With a fair understanding of the weapon, as well as the target, authorities placed Lille and the surrounding townships under virtual martial law. Incredibly, nothing was found. The cell of four men, along with a truck carrying over a hundred pounds of TATP, had simply disappeared. Orders were given for the net to be widened.

In a private thought, Baland suspected they were chasing the last of Chadeh's attacks, and he would eventually be proved correct. In that moment, however, as he sat quietly in a chair at the back of the room, he silently cheered the cell on, hoping they succeeded spectacularly. With a strange new detachment he watched people around him, men and women he'd once considered his countrymen, as they worked frantically to avert the strike. He observed their procedures in the way a chemistry student might critique a peer's laboratory demonstration—seeking faults in the process.

As it turned out, the joint team in the Élysée command center had it mostly right. They were looking for the right people and the right weapon—but in altogether the wrong place.

SIXTY-THREE

The essential reason the cell could not be found was that its commander, a transplanted Egyptian, was clinically psychotic. He had arrived in France as a student five years earlier, but dropped out of school and overstayed his visa. He'd quickly fallen in with a group of three other young men in Lille, each a societal orphan in his own right, and risen to become their de facto leader. A group of lost boys, they were precisely the kind of castaways targeted by jihadi recruiters. Once established in the fold of ISIS, however, they proved an unusually patient bunch, plotting their bombing for the best part of a year.

It was only recently that the leader's mood swings had begun. On good days he was a man of thoughtfulness and some cunning who could steal a truckload of fertilizer from a farm without it being missed. On others he claimed to have lengthy conversations with God. Yesterday he'd been drifting toward the latter persona when the order had come through: They were to immediately cobble together their bomb and attack a synagogue in Lille.

The group had always known it might happen this way, a sudden call to action. It was the leader who balked first. He told the others that men in Raqqa should not dictate what target they struck or when. There was general agreement at first, but as they all watched the news it became clear that a broad wave of attacks was indeed being unleashed against France. French authorities had gone into a martial tizzy, and when it became clear that one strike had been interrupted by police, the cell in Lille realized that if they didn't act quickly their chance might be lost. The three underlings deferred to their leader, and in a moment of divine inspiration, he gave them the good news. God had told him what they needed to do.

They worked throughout the night, taking advantage of the horrendous weather conditions, and by early the next morning everything was in place.

In keeping with his promise to minimize Israel's involvement, Slaton had not used embassy computers to plan his assassination. He did, however, need internet access in order to begin his preparations.

He began at a midgrade hotel, where he made an inquiry about reserving a banquet room for a corporate event in the coming summer. Halfway through the sales pitch, he expressed a need to check dates on his calendar, but claimed to be stymied by a dead mobile phone. The corporate sales agent, a smiling middle-aged woman whose English was flawless, graciously granted him access to the hotel's business center. Slaton asked for fifteen minutes, and she discreetly disappeared.

He worked quickly, and had no trouble learning that the change-of-command ceremony for the General Directorate for Internal Security was to be presided over by the minister of the interior, and would take place the next morning at nine o'clock sharp on the forecourt plaza of the Place des Invalides.

This last element surprised but did not disappoint Slaton. He would have expected such a shadowed organization as DGSI to change leadership behind closed doors. Indeed, more purist intelligence agencies, the likes of Mossad and MI6, had for generations gone to great lengths to conceal the identities of their senior officers. Slaton had expected DGSI to take something of a middle ground—a low-key gathering of families and friends, along with the upward-aspiring heads of agency divisions, all shrouded within a headquarters conference room. As it turned out, DGSI's custom was for a modest outdoor affair, and the recent attacks seemed not to have changed anyone's thinking. Baland himself was on record as saying, "The bastards won't keep us from living our lives in the open."

Which only made the assassin's job that much easier.

The ceremony was to be staged in the shadows of Les Invalides, the grand collection of museums and monuments that was testament to the French fighting will. As a backdrop Baland would have Napoléon's tomb, the enduring standard of the glory of France. Tomorrow's event would be a modest affair, no brass band or troops in formation. An honor guard, perhaps, and a handful of dignitaries with nothing better on their calendars. Regrettably, the number of family and friends in attendance would be markedly lower than at the last handover, since the outgoing director's camp would be preparing for his funeral. As put by one officer in a press release, "It will be a wedding with one side of the church empty."

Even so, Slaton expected a solid security effort in light of the recent attacks.

He departed the hotel discreetly, avoiding further contact with the sales associate, and was lost in thought as he turned toward the river. When he had snatched Uday out of Syria two days ago, he'd had the benefit of state support. Drones, satellites, manpower, all the necessary equipment. This would be a very different kind of op.

In essence, Slaton was undertaking a political assassination. The embassy had provided a phone and a weapon that were clean, and a contact number for their backup assassin—a woman who lived as deeply in the black as Slaton ever had. Otherwise, he was very much on his own.

The plan crystallizing in his head was going to change that.

SIXTY-FOUR

The terrorist cell from Lille was exposed, rather surprisingly, not by the legions of police and military who were swarming across northern France, but by a marine mechanic who'd been called in to investigate—at double-time wages—a forty-six-foot Bertram cabin cruiser that had begun taking on water in the storm.

The boat lay moored in the municipal basin along the Chenal de Gravelines, just west of Dunkirk, and the alarm had been raised by the owner of a neighboring yacht who'd ventured to the piers at the height of the maelstrom to check on his own boat. The man wasn't much of a sailor in his own right, so when he saw the problem he did what he always did—he called Viktor Foulon.

Foulon was at his kitchen table, settling down behind a bowl of hot cereal, when his mobile phone trilled. His first inclination was to ignore the call, but at a glance he saw who it was. He sighed and picked up.

"Monsieur Dumas, what can I do for you on this lovely day?"

"Viktor, you must come to the harbor at once!"

Viktor looked out the window. He saw pelting rain and a black sky. "Is there a problem with *Cassandra*?" he asked. *Cassandra* was Dumas' old eighty-five-foot Feadship, which without Foulon's regular attentions would no longer be afloat. He nearly made a living off the old barge, which had decayed to the point that it was more a floating cocktail patio than a seagoing vessel. Which was fine with Foulon, since Dumas had more money than sense.

"No, it is not my boat," said Dumas. "The Bertram next to her is listing badly. I think she may go down."

Foulon knew the boat, but had never met her owner. "Do you know whose boat it is?" he asked.

"I can't recall his name, but he's one of those financial managers from Paris—I had a martini with him once on *Cassandra*."

A financial manager, thought Foulon. *A possibility.* A gust of wind caused his roof to creak. "All right," he said despairingly, "I'll come have a look."

"Very well. If you need me I'll be at the café on the quay." Dumas rang off.

Café on the quay. Foulon cursed and let his breakfast go cold on the table.

Suspecting a faulty bilge pump, he retrieved his toolbox, then donned his heavy slicker for the walk to the harbor. The wind had been howling all night, and rain was still sheeting up and down the coast. If it had been anyone but *Cassandra*'s owner, his longtime financial anchor, Foulon would have told them to go to hell.

Arriving at the dockmaster's office ten minutes later, he was more wet than dry, and the hair under his loose hood was tousled, like that of a child whose favorite aunt had rubbed his head. He explained to the man on duty, old Bernard, that there might be an emergency. Foulon was given a key to the vessel without question. Back out in the rain, he headed up Pier 3 to the deep-water slips at the end and found the boat in question. She was named *Formidable*, but at that moment she was hardly living up to it—standing by her transom, Foulon saw a list to port that must have exceeded ten degrees. He also noticed that her bilge pumps were working furiously, steady streams of water spewing from fittings above the waterline. Not good.

As he stepped onto her off-kilter deck, the next thing he noticed was that he didn't need the key—the sliding door to the main salon was already wide open. Foulon came under shelter, and with the driving rain no longer pounding his oilskin, he pulled back his hood. As soon as he did, he registered what sounded like a hushed argument inside the cabin. The tone was sharp, but the language made no sense to him. He walked into the main salon to find three dark-skinned men who looked more surprised than he was.

Foulon blinked away the rain, and right away saw a number of peculiarities. On the settee nearby was a big suitcase, its flap hanging open, full of what looked like white clay. On the dining table he saw snarls of wiring and colored tape and batteries. The three men were all on their knees, and between them was what could only be described as a small crater. The floor of the boat had been breached, and a jagged meter-wide hole was edged in soot—undoubtedly the reason *Formidable* was sinking. Then Foulon saw the most disturbing sight: on the floor just beyond the hole, what was left of a fourth man, his body ripped to shreds in a pool of blood.

"*Merde!* What the devil is going on here?" Foulon demanded.

To anyone who did not know Foulon, what happened in the next twenty seconds might have seemed chaotic and unexpected. In fact, it was an outburst thirty years in the making. Viktor Foulon's true talent had nothing to do with either bilge pumps or wrenches. Having spent eight years in the French Foreign Legion, he had killed more men than he cared to remember in the darkened jungles of Congo and Ivory Coast. After leaving the service, he'd earned a solid reputation as a brawler in the watering holes of Gravelines, and as any local policeman would attest, Foulon was a volatile handful when he was drunk. What most did not realize was that he was far more dangerous when sober.

It did not harm the ex-legionnaire's prospects that he stood six feet five inches tall, or that his 260 pounds were cut from a template that might have patterned the marine diesels he worked on. The three men facing him were altogether different. In terms of size they were neither slight nor stalwart, simply the other ninety percent, and while Foulon couldn't know it, none of them had any combat experience. Ironically, it was the only one with any kind of training—two months in a jihadist camp in southern Libya—who made the first mistake. The smallest of the three, he lunged toward a shelf.

Foulon's eyes reached the shelf before the man's hands, and he instantly recognized the dull-black machine pistol. As he realized that he too needed a weapon, and probably in a hurry, it occurred to Foulon that he was already holding one.

He swung his toolbox in a giant arc. It was a professional-grade item, red and rectangular, built of high-tensile steel. Inside were fifty pounds of hammers and wrenches and bolts. The box picked up speed through 180 degrees of rotation, and arrived, catastrophically, at the skull of the man fumbling with the safety on his machine pistol. Foulon immediately reversed the motion, stepped forward, and began waylaying everything in his path like a wrecking ball gone amok.

Shelves shattered and light fixtures exploded. Men screamed and blood splattered walls. A set of cabinet doors disintegrated, and the rack of radios inside was pulverized, sparks spraying outward like a miniature fireworks display. After seven or eight great swipes— Foulon wasn't counting—he stopped and evaluated the situation. Panting like a winded bull, he saw one man on the floor with a crushed skull, certainly dead. Another was out cold, and the third lay moaning and incoherent—he had a very crooked arm, and had ended up sprawled across the already-dead fourth man. Gray smoke curled through the cabin in an acrid cloud of burning insulation.

Foulon dropped his dented toolbox and ran up the pier to the dockmaster's office. "We need the police!" he shouted as he burst through the door.

A surprised Bernard actually chuckled. "You're joking, right?" He pointed across the channel. On the opposite wharf Foulon saw six police cars and two military vehicles.

"What the hell is going on?" he asked.

Bernard's eyes fell to Foulon's heaving chest, and he said, "Maybe you should tell me."

Foulon looked down and saw that his shirt was covered in blood—as far as he knew, not his own. He explained what had just happened.

With forty years on the docks, Bernard was not the excitable type, yet by the time Foulon finished his story the dockmaster's face had gone ashen. "Were they Middle Eastern?" he asked.

It was Foulon's turn to be taken aback. "How did you know that?"

"Because four thousand policemen have been scouring the north of France for them. Haven't you seen the news?"

Foulon said he had not. He rarely watched television, and never in the morning. He vaguely remembered seeing something about terrorists on the muted television at the bar last night, but he hadn't really paid attention. Bertrand filled him in.

As Foulon listened, he felt a bit of relief. He'd long been on a first-name basis with the harbor police, thanks to a string of minor indiscretions. Now he was sure he'd killed at least one man. But he hadn't been drinking, and if the four men on *Formidable* had been up to no good, he might be all right. So Foulon got a favorable version of things straight in his head, and he told Bernard again to make the phone call. He waited nervously for the police to arrive.

He need not have worried. By that evening's news cycle, Viktor Foulon, ex-legionnaire, marine mechanic, and saloon wrecker of some repute, would be recognized far and wide as a hero of the French Republic.

The news from the coast reached Élysée Palace within minutes of the police arriving on scene.

"We've found them!" announced the national police liaison. "The four men from Lille have been stopped in their tracks—they were trying to steal a pleasure boat in Gravelines."

The president of France, a steaming espresso in front of him, had just found his way back to the command center. "Who caught them—national or local gendarmes?"

"Actually," said the liaison, "it seems they encountered a local man. He's a marine mechanic, and apparently an ex-legionnaire. He took matters into his own hands. Two of the four are dead, and one is unconscious."

The presidential brow furrowed, and he seemed about to say something, but then only cocked his head to encourage the liaison to continue.

"Explosive disposal teams are working the scene. They estimate they're dealing with over a hundred kilograms of TATP along with the associated hardware. Apparently an initiator charge went off prematurely and blew a hole in the bottom of the boat. It began to sink, which is presumably why someone called in the mechanic."

The army chief of staff snorted in exasperation. "Incredible! We are dealing with imbeciles!"

"Perhaps," said the president. "But committed imbeciles have harmed us far too often. The important thing is that the plot has been interrupted."

The liaison said, "We found a map on the boat that suggests they were targeting a cruise ship in Le Havre. We've long been worried about that kind of thing. Should we stand down our search in the north? Our forces are stretched very thin at the moment."

"Do we have information on any other possible strikes?"

"No, Mr. President. We of course will remain watchful, and continue to monitor communications out of Syria. But this episode exhausts our current intelligence—we know of no other cells that have been activated."

The president considered it, then looked around the room, and said, "Where the hell has Baland gone?"

The intelligence chief said, "I believe he returned to DGSI to check on things there."

The president shrugged and took a sip of his espresso. "Very well," he said. "Stand down your search."

SIXTY-FIVE

It was midmorning when Slaton exited a taxi two blocks from Invalides. The rain had finally abated, and as soon as the cab was gone he crossed the street to an inexpensive hostel. He'd been steered to the place by Neumann, who had occasion to know such recesses of the city, and she assured him it would meet his two main requirements: vacant single rooms and a willingness to operate on a cash basis.

Slaton purchased lodging for one night, and the proprietor, a man with wild hair and a deeply grooved face, explained that the room would not be available for another two hours. He also said that if Monsieur so desired, he could leave his bag in the locked closet behind the desk. Slaton accepted enthusiastically, no hesitation to suggest that the case might hold something valuable. Fifteen minutes later he was walking unencumbered across the storied grounds of Invalides.

There was never a question of where to start. He took his phone from his pocket and called up a very accurate mapping program he'd downloaded. It was designed for agricultural use—in particular, the application of pesticides—but inherent in the platform was the one thing Slaton needed: precision.

He began on the stone terrace where the ceremony was to take place, and was forced to estimate the spot where the interior minister would tomorrow shake Baland's hand, or perhaps put a banner over his shoulder—whatever pomp fit the circumstance. This put him in the middle of a half acre of stone pavers, Arcane limestone if he wasn't mistaken, that spread artfully back toward the museums. In front of him the terrace ended abruptly, bordered by an empty moat that was guarded by rows of inert cannons. Slaton marked the location and elevation of the spot where he stood, then set out on his search.

He walked the surrounding gardens, up the Esplanade des Invalides and toward the river. At the Quay d'Orsay, with the Seine spreading before him, he checked his phone and saw a range of 562 meters. He marked the spot as a border, then moved west, canvassing rows of apartments along Rue Fabert, and taking a lingering look up Rue de Grenelle. A few of the buildings there caught his eye, and he marked them on his electronic map. He spent a full thirty minutes on his survey, along the way standing amid groups of tourists—always in abundance here—and snapping a few photos for later reference.

He initially discounted the idea of using the eastern border along Rue de Constantine—the street was home to any number of embassies, Canada and Great Britain among them, which implied added layers of security. Then, in a burst of inspiration, he doubled back for a second look. His idea coalesced as he stood in the skeletal shadow of a hand-sculpted, wintering horse chestnut tree.

Slaton stared at the Colombian embassy, or more accurately its placeholder. It was a narrow three-story affair wedged on an urban triangle, shouldered tightly between a slightly taller residential building and a small branch bank. More intriguing was what Slaton saw on the front door, and along the high façade above.

He went closer and read the notice posted on the door in French, Spanish, and English:

THE EMBASSY OF COLOMBIA IS CURRENTLY CLOSED FOR RENOVATIONS. LIMITED SERVICES ARE AVAILABLE AT OUR TEMPORARY ANNEX AT 45 RUE DUROC. WE APOLOGIZE FOR ANY INCONVENIENCE.

He looked up at a scaffolding and saw two workers busy refurbishing a cornice. The outer stone edifice had been pulled and rebuilt, this obvious to Slaton by mortar joints that were a near match in color to original sections, but without the telling stains of the urban wear. He knew a good deal about Lutetian limestone, also known as "Paris stone," which for centuries had been cut from the quarries of Oise, north of the capital, and shipped conveniently downriver. In recent years the rock had become fashionable, and it was shipped in great quantity around the globe to enhance terraces in Dubai and mansions in Hollywood. Having worked with it, Slaton knew the stone had unique characteristics: it was easy to cut, durable to the elements, and available in a wide array of colors. So as he stared up now at a major rebuild, clearly in its final stages, his curiosity was piqued.

"It looks good," he called up in American-accented English.

One of the men kept working, but the other, a hirsute fireplug of a man, smiled amiably.

"Is the stone from Oise?" Slaton prodded.

"Of course," said the stocky man. "You know Paris stone?"

"I've worked with it a few times in the States. Once to build a patio for a mansion, and at another site a small concert pavilion. I like it better than the Italian stone, easier to work with."

The man began climbing down a ladder, and when he reached street level, he said, "*Italian* stone?" The words came through puckered lips, as if he'd tasted something sour. "No one uses that rubble here."

"I didn't mean to interrupt your work."

"We are almost done for the day." He wiped his hand on a tarp that was hanging across the scaffolding. "The mortar will have to set before we finish the last section—after the weekend, I think."

Slaton looked up and saw a few remaining gaps in the long cornice. "It looks like you've been at it for some time."

"Three months. The weight-bearing wall behind the cornice had cracks, and the only option was to replace the top three meters, a big job."

"What was the original thickness?"

The man smiled. "You do know your stone. The original wall was over two meters thick."

"Two meters?"

"The man who first commissioned it would accept nothing less."

"Who was that?" Slaton asked.

"Napoléon."

Slaton stared. "As in . . . Bonaparte?"

"Is there another?"

Not here, Slaton thought, before saying, "How thick is the new wall?"

"Just under half a meter. The committee for . . . how do you say it . . . *authenticité architecturale.* They insist on perfection to the eye, but cannot raise enough money for honesty to the original structure."

"Believe me when I say, it happens everywhere. I had the same problem in Malta. Let me guess—there's a void between the outer wall and the existing interior walls."

"*Certainement.* But who will ever know but us?"

Slaton smiled.

The Frenchman gave him an overview of the project, and pointed to various repairs in the building's façade. Slaton asked a few knowledgeable questions, and complimented him on his workmanship. The mason suggested agreeably, and not without a bit of pride, "Come, let me show you. As a brother mason, you would be most interested." He started up the ladder with a beckoning wave. His partner, who Slaton suspected did not speak English, showed no interest whatsoever.

Without hesitation, Slaton stepped on the first rung and began climbing.

SIXTY-SIX

Twenty minutes later Slaton walked away from the unfinished Colombian embassy with his sniper's mind in overdrive. His tour of the walls under repair had been comprehensive and enlightening, and he had thanked his guide unreservedly as he and his partner began packing up their tools for the day.

Slaton walked quickly, details falling into place one at a time. The outline taking shape in his head was not yet complete, and one variable would be beyond his control. Yet if he could make it all coalesce, each of his objectives would be met.

His first stop was a home-improvement store, where he purchased a powerful hammer drill, a variety of drill bits, an extension cord, and a pair of workman's coveralls. In another section he found a diamond-edged cutting tool and a large suction cup. Nearing the checkout line, he added a heavy canvas sack. Once he'd paid, in cash, his purchases went into the canvas bag. On the way back to the hostel, he detoured into a narrow alley bordering a construction site, sought out the filthiest puddle available, and dropped the new coveralls in the middle. He stepped on them a few times for good measure, then picked up the wad of wet cloth. He twisted the coveralls once to squeeze out the excess water, then stuffed them back in his bag.

He arrived at the hostel ten minutes later, and was told that his room had opened up. The desk man retrieved the roller bag containing a rifle from the storage closet. Slaton knew he hadn't ventured a look inside. He knew because there were no awkward stares when he handed it over or, for that matter, no police standing in wait.

He climbed quickly to a second-floor room, and found a predictably Spartan affair. Slaton didn't bother with even the most basic security inspection. He removed the coveralls and the drill from the canvas bag, then refilled it with the case containing an Arctic Warfare Covert. The bathroom was a community arrangement down the hall, but there was a clean towel on the shelf in his room. Slaton made it less so when he used it to scrub the worst of the mud from the wrinkled coveralls. He slipped them on, damp and dirty, directly over his clothing, and transferred a few smudges from the mud-soiled towel onto his hands and face. He left the empty roller bag in the room, took the drill case in one hand, and heaved the bag containing the rifle over his other shoulder. He quick-stepped down the stairs, and diverted toward a side exit that bypassed the front desk. When he reached the street Slaton checked his watch. He had been inside the hostel nine and a half minutes.

The hostel was soon lost behind him. It was a

building he would never set foot in again, joining a lengthy list of deliberately avoided addresses scattered across the world.

Slaton set out directly for Invalides. He was right on schedule.

SIXTY-SEVEN

The temperature dropped markedly, and Slaton's breath was pluming in front of him when he reached Invalides. The scaffolding in front of the Colombian embassy was vacant, just as the mason had said it would be. It was Friday afternoon, and with new mortar setting and a weekend pending, Slaton was confident the jobsite would be vacant for days.

He set down his equipment at the base of the scaffold, and began sorting through it as any tradesman would to start a job. The extension cord he plugged into a ground-level receptacle before heaving the coil upward over the top of the scaffold like a commando tossing a grappling hook—a surprisingly transferable skill.

With the weather improving, the streets and courtyards in front of the museum complex had become busier. He saw couples meandering, and guided groups who paused to take pictures. None of them seemed to notice the tall workman in coveralls who shouldered a heavy bag, climbed a ladder to the top of a scaffold, and disappeared into a building under repair.

The opening through which Slaton passed was four feet high and half that in width, and he crouched to pass through to the dead space behind. The entrance was clearly temporary, meant to allow work crews to address the new wall from within, and a tarp had been strung across it to keep out the rain. The space behind the new frontage formed a narrow corridor, roughly one yard in width and five feet high, with buttresses every few yards for support. Updated electric and heating conduits were already being run through what was effectively a new utility pathway.

Slaton had seen the passageway from the outside during his visit with the mason, but now, as he stood inside, he recognized his first mistake. The still-overcast skies left the interior extremely dark. Slaton wished he'd purchased a flashlight, but after folding back the tarp he decided the problem was manageable.

The primary modification necessary was to drill two holes in the half-meter-thick exterior wall. Having worked with Paris stone before, he knew it was feasible, but also that it would take considerable effort. He began with a new mortar joint four feet from the entrance. Mortar being easier to penetrate than stone, the initial one-inch hole took a mere twenty minutes. He then paused to study the more exacting work.

Slaton went back outside and took in the forecourt of Invalides, and also the view across the park, in particular where Rue de Grenelle strayed into the city.

His angles had to be as precise as possible. He went back inside and began drilling the second hole, slightly to one side and at a marginally different angle from the first. Once the drill was through, he pulled the bit and peered outside. It was like looking through a soda straw, but he liked what he saw.

He set to the greater task of crafting two custom slots. The drill hummed in the narrow confines of the passage, and mortar dust and stone chips flew for another hour. The muted sun was halfway to the horizon by the time he had the portals he wanted, along with three broken bits, an overheated drill, and two very numb hands.

He set the drill aside, withdrew the component parts of the rifle from its case, and assembled the weapon. He looked left and right down the dim passageway, and at one end he noticed a pair of stone slabs. They were no doubt leftover blocks from the construction of the wall, each probably weighing a hundred pounds. He slid them one at a time across the floor, then stacked one on top of the other, just behind the larger of the two holes he'd fashioned. Slaton ensured the arrangement was solid, then set the sniper rifle on top. The barrel fit neatly into the gap, the tip three inches short of the outer opening. The slot was six inches in height, and between two and three inches in width, tapering outward near the top so the view of the scope would not be obstructed.

He settled into a sitting position on the floor—the width of the passage didn't allow him to lie prone—and trained the weapon on a statue near the plaza.

At 120 meters the statue's head looked like a giant playground ball through the magnified scope. He scanned left and right, up and down, and made sure the focal point of tomorrow's ceremony could be sighted with room for adjustments. The Covert had a bipod stand, and Slaton noted that one leg was lower than the other, the stone base being uneven. He also realized that if he widened the base of the hole slightly, the barrel of the rifle could be retained farther into the recess with no loss of functionality.

The modifications took less than ten minutes, and after a second trial with the rifle he decided his shooting stand was complete. He went to work on the second aperture, which was far more simple, the only alteration being to increase the bore to a smooth three-inch diameter. That done, he checked his angles one last time. Satisfied, Slaton searched the floor and picked up a few loose scraps of stone. By trial and error, he found one that could be used to seal the larger of the two fissures. He went outside and gauged the appearance. From the exterior, the signs of his work were nearly invisible. He left the smaller hole open, but decided to add one more fragment to disguise the larger opening. As his skilled hands worked the chip into place, it occurred to him that he had arrived at a bizarre intersection of his two domains. Creating and destroying at the same time.

He pushed his equipment deep into the passageway, and emerged into a gathering dusk. Slaton pulled the tarp closed behind him. He climbed down to street level, pulled the ladder away, and slid it neatly between the wall and the scaffolding. Removing the last external sign of his presence, he unplugged the extension cord, draped the coiled loops over one shoulder, and was soon walking down the Esplanade des Invalides toward a rain-swollen Seine.

SIXTY-EIGHT

Baland sat alone in the director's private conference room. Since Slaton's phone call yesterday, his new office, with its panoramic view of the city, had summarily lost its appeal. The conference room was part of the suite, but with four solid walls. To make his isolation complete, Baland had given his receptionist firm instructions to shunt any calls that were not from the interior minister.

As had been the case for hours, Baland concentrated completely on the papers in front of him. He worked feverishly, shuffling files and scribbling notes, inputting the names and numbers of terrorist recruits into his personal phone. Though he remained one day removed from ascension to the directorship, his first formal order was already on the books: Find Malika. The more informal, and provocative, version had been a loose suggestion to district captains at the daily briefing: *Shoot her on sight*. Such specificity was worth a try, but he doubted it would be carried through in that manner. Ethicists and lawyers invariably got in the way—the kinds of curbs that, as Ali Samir, he had never had to deal with in Gaza.

They'd also been hunting Slaton. He had discarded the phone he'd used to contact Baland, and they'd had no luck discovering how he'd entered France. Baland wanted very much to deal with him now, a window of opportunity that was certainly closing. The Jews, the Islamic State, Malika. Someone was going to spill his identity—it was only a matter of who and when. Given the current state of affairs, his original estimate of a week or more was likely optimistic. He now allowed no more than a few days. At that point, it would be time to disappear.

He'd sorted through the list of ISIS operatives effortlessly on his computer, segregating those who lived in either France or Belgium. Baland was astounded to find the names of fourteen hundred men and women. He allowed the data itself no more than a ninety percent accuracy. Contact information would be invalid for some recruits, and a few had probably already found their way to the eastern battle, a one-way ticket to Ankara followed by a bus to the Syrian border. Even so, Baland was sure he was looking at a thousand willing attackers in the cities around him.

A veritable army.

Many of the files had photographs to go with backgrounds, and a good number listed weapons in the given recruit's possession. He flicked from face to face and saw a gallery of rogues. Some had to be college students, while others were certainly criminals. The bold had kitchen knives, the brazen stolen guns, the educated closets full of TATP. Baland studied their unrepentant gazes, and saw the scars of hard lives. Among them, in perhaps one young face in twenty, he recognized what he wanted more than anything. It was an attribute he had long ago learned to discern— the already-dead eyes of eager martyrs.

All were now his.

A message blinked to his mobile. Baland scanned it quickly. Something about a boat having been discovered in Gravelines. In a reversal of roles that was gaining momentum, he viewed the news in an all-new light. *Something to keep the gendarmerie busy in the countryside.* He pushed the phone aside.

Work faster.

From the vulnerability report he had extracted twenty-seven primary targets, and forty-two he labeled as secondary. Baland would spend every available minute tonight pairing recruits with targets. After that he would get a few hours' sleep before the ceremony at Invalides. There was no way out of that, and he had to admit, a part of him wanted to attend. An hour or two to bask briefly in what might have been. It would also serve to fuel his new legend. He imagined photographs of the event going viral in the coming weeks, situated under a banner headline: "New DGSI Chief a Traitor."

His alternate life would soon be gone, reverting to the original. The cruelest irony of all: It was the Jews who were forcing him to again become Ali Samir. For that they would pay dearly. He decided to try to spend a few hours with Jacqueline and the girls before abandoning them. It was more than he'd given his pregnant wife and Malika fifteen years ago.

If only I had known . . .

He expected to send the first commands tomorrow night—the larger cells would need time to plan. With any luck, the primary strikes would occur by midweek. Even if only half succeeded, he would be orchestrating the greatest blow against the Zionists of Europe in generations.

Another message blinked to his phone. Baland nudged the handset farther away on the table. As he did so, an earlier thought returned. *Too many knives in the air.*

Slaton made two stops before reaching his room. The first was a small grocery store, where he purchased corn syrup, cocoa, and food dye. The second was an internet café on the edge of Clichy.

In his survey of Invalides he had taken a number of pictures of the surrounding grounds, both interior and exterior shots of the wall under repair, and also a telling photo of the hide where the Covert lay in place. Using a wireless link, he connected the smartphone Bloch had given him to a machine that printed photographs. He transferred seven images, and waited patiently as they spit one by one into a trough. The quality was first-rate, and he collected the hard-stock pictures and placed them in his pocket. A check of his watch confirmed that he was comfortably ahead of schedule.

From a trash can he scavenged three discarded sheets of printer paper, all of which had weak images on one side—an ink cartridge gone dry. The back sides, however, were quite clean.

Outside the café, a lone waiter ran a few tables beneath an awning. Slaton took a vacant seat, ordered a white coffee, and asked the waiter if he might borrow a pen. The waiter was an older man, proper and deferential, and Slaton envisioned him working tables at more storied establishments in years gone by. And yes, of course he had an extra pen.

Slaton's coffee came quickly, and he set to work. From memory he drew a sketch of the Colombian embassy and the grounds of Invalides. To further reinforce things, he drew a dashed line between the two critical points. Alongside that he made a note: 138.2 meters. Satisfied with the first draft, he folded the paper neatly and nested it with the photographs in his pocket.

When he could think of nothing else, Slaton pulled out his phone, dialed Air France, and said to a welcoming reservation agent, "I'd like to book a ticket. Munich to Manila, one-way . . ."

Five minutes later he checked his watch, drained the last of his coffee, and set out toward his room in Courbevoie. As a temporary residence, it had proved comfortable and pleasant, far more so than the hostel he'd just vacated in a rush. Even so, it was an address that would soon be condemened to the same terminal list: *Places to which I can never return.*

SIXTY-NINE

Malika was in Slaton's room, sitting in the chair by the window, when she heard someone approach in the hallway outside. The footfalls were heavy, definitely a man's. She lifted the weapon she'd found in the attaché. It seemed only fitting to use his own weapon, although hers was at her side beneath her folded jacket.

She heard the lock tumbler click, saw the door swing open. Then the most satisfying moment—the look on his face when he saw her. Malika knew what any hunter knew: the most unsuspecting prey was the one that came to you.

"Be very still!" she ordered. Malika said it in English. It wasn't her best language, but it was likely the only one they shared.

Slaton said nothing, but he did as she asked. His lean frame stood frozen, hands loose by his sides.

"Away from the door . . . slowly."

He complied.

It was the first time she'd seen him up close. He was attractive in a way, bigger and more powerfully built than she'd noticed from a distance. Yet what struck her most were his eyes. They were an unusual shade of gray, and in them she saw . . . *what?* Not what she should have seen. No concern or calculation. Not even confidence. His gaze was simply empty, like a window that was somehow both clear and opaque.

"Turn around," she said. "Pull the jacket over your head . . . but keep the sleeves on your wrists." He again complied, removing the jacket as he would a T-shirt, but leaving the sleeves bunched over his outstretched wrists. Malika saw the expected weapon in his waistband. She got up and crossed the room carefully. Very, very slowly, she reached out and removed the handgun. Malika tossed it on the chair she'd been using. The door was still ajar, and she kicked it closed with her heel.

Standing two steps away, she weighed whether to search him for other weapons. She knew he was physically superior, and the concept of holding a gun against such a man's spine or throat, then trying to frisk him with a free hand—that was pure Hollywood. In close proximity, he could turn the tables in a fraction of a second. She decided to keep things as they were—her barrel trained on him with a wary eye, at a range where they both knew she couldn't miss.

"Drop the jacket," she said. "Then move away."

Again he did as she asked. The jacket fell to the floor, and he sidestepped away from the door. Never averting her eyes, Malika bent down and picked up the jacket. She rifled through the pockets, and found a handful of photographs and a folded sheet of paper. Slaton was still facing away, and her eyes flicked back and forth between the stationary assassin and the images. She unfolded the paper, then smoothed it with her free hand on the table next to her. Malika saw a hand-drawn diagram that made perfect sense. The two of them were, after all, cast from the same mold.

"I thought so," she said to his back. "Where is this?"

He spoke for the first time. "Where would you do it?"

Her thick cheeks broke into a half smile he couldn't see. "Invalides, tomorrow morning."

Slaton said nothing.

"If I didn't find you at the embassy, I was going to look there next. I knew you wouldn't rest until you'd killed Baland."

"Baland? Not at all. I've come to kill your father, Ali Samir."

Malika felt her blood rise. The pain came rushing back. How many times as a young girl had she cried herself to sleep? How many times had she dreamt of this moment? Her father's killer squarely under her sight. "So you learned that much . . . that I am the daughter of Ali Samir. Good. Then you understand why I am here. But before you die, I will grant you a small mercy. The man you are hunting here in Paris is not who you think. He is my father's twin."

Very slowly, the assassin turned to face her. Malika's hand tensed on the trigger, but he came no closer, made no threatening moves.

He said, "I understand perfectly. The two were born in Gaza. Their parents—your grandparents—had intended to immigrate to France. But they weren't expecting twins. New paperwork had to be run. The man who became Zavier Baland was sent ahead. Then your grandparents were killed by an errant Israeli rocket. Your father, Ali Samir, was doomed to remain in Gaza. I know all about that."

Malika only stared at him, her hand rigid, her finger poised.

"But there's a part *you* don't understand," he continued. "On September 15, 2002, the real Zavier Baland traveled on an Air France flight from Paris to Cairo. It was a meeting arranged by your father—created because he knew I was hunting him. He understood that sooner or later I, or someone like me, would succeed. He fed Mossad information about where he would be on a certain day, at a certain time. A teahouse in Gaza. When I lined him up in my sight that day, there was no question in my mind who I was shooting—Ali Samir, unrepentant bomber of women and children. That was exactly what your father wanted me to think. . . ." His voice trailed off, as if inviting her to think about it.

And Malika did think. *He is trying to talk his way out of a bad situation. He is desperate, weaving an impossible story.* Yet she couldn't shake one image . . .

Gloves.

She had met her uncle face-to-face on only five occasions since arriving in France, and in every case Zavier Baland had worn gloves. She'd noticed, but written it off as no more than an eccentricity. Now, however, a distant memory intruded. When she was four, perhaps five years old, her father had come home one day with a burn on the back of one hand. Malika could still remember her mother dressing the wound. Years later, when she was old enough to understand who he was and what he did, her father had explained. He told her the scar was a badge of honor, caused by some manner of bomb-cooking gone wrong. Now it acquired an all-new relevance: As far as she knew, that scar on his right hand was the only physical difference between the two brothers.

Slaton went on, "Yes, you're beginning to see it. Your father traded places with his brother, Malika. *He* was the one on the return flight to Paris the next day."

Her eyes narrowed, but her shooting hand was set in stone.

"A friend of mine recently talked to Gabrielle Baland," he continued, "the woman who raised Zavier. She said her son was a changed man after he returned from that trip. He moved to Paris immediately afterward and the two became estranged."

Malika began shaking her head, as if to dislodge the growing madness.

"It's true," he said. "But then, maybe deep down you suspected it all along. Your father abandoned his family to steal his brother's life in France. He left you and your pregnant mother by yourselves, let you think he was dead. Now he's issued orders to hunt you down. You . . . his daughter."

Malika wanted to argue, but she felt as if she'd lost

the capacity to speak. Her world narrowed and she focused completely on the notch above her weapon. She tried to hold it steady on the figure in front of her.

"I'm not here to kill Zavier Baland. That's already been done. I'm here to do what *you* brought me here to do. I'm going to kill your father, and this time I won't miss." He took a step forward. "Now that you know the truth about him . . . I suspect it's what you might want as well. He'll never let you rest, Malika. You know too many of his secrets."

"Stop!" Her arm locked straight.

He was five paces away, but still coming at her. She pulled the trigger. The gun clicked but didn't fire. In a flash Malika slammed her left palm into the butt of the magazine, racked in a new round, and squeezed the trigger a second time. The result was the same. She stood stunned, confused. Slaton had gone motionless two steps away. He didn't look surprised or angry or murderous. The gray eyes remained blank, no sign of intent or emotion. She tried to make sense of it all—the failing gun, his reaction to it. Malika was never able to complete that thought, because in the next instant the window beside her exploded.

In a blur she saw Slaton drop, hitting the floor like a sack of gravel. She dove away from the window and crashed into a wall. Rounds burst in at a high rate of fire, peppering the room. Glass rained to the floor, and a picture on the far side of the room was knocked from the wall. Malika looked at Slaton. A smear of red stained his neck, and blood was fast pooling beneath him. The gray eyes were empty as ever, only now focused to infinity.

The incoming fire didn't relent.

Her own gun was on the chair across the room, as was the one she'd taken from Slaton. Both were small-caliber. Whoever was outside had vastly superior firepower. She looked at the door—it was still cracked open.

Bullets streamed in, fractions of a second apart, thumping into wood and plaster, ripping apart fabric. Then, all at once, a pause. The killer was either finished or changing magazines. Either way, it was her chance. With a hard look at the door, she stood, lunged over the dead assassin, and threw herself into the hallway.

SEVENTY

The hotel's proprietor and both housekeepers heard the commotion, but none of them recognized it for what it was. The maintenance man, however, a middle-aged immigrant from North Africa who'd done a stint in the Moroccan Army, recognized the sound of gunfire.

He was unclogging a toilet on the second floor when the first shots rang out, and he called the police right away using his mobile. When the shooting ended as abruptly as it had begun, his curiosity was piqued. The action, he thought, seemed to be taking place one floor above, although he knew from experience that sourcing such staccato sounds could be difficult. He cautiously took the service stairwell to the third floor, and right away noticed that the door to number 14 was ajar. Everything seemed quiet, and with nothing more than a plunger in his hand, he moved guardedly down the hall and peered inside.

What he saw was perplexing. The room was a wreck. Both windows seemed to have shattered inward, leaving glass strewn across the carpet. There were holes in the walls, and the floor was covered by stuffing from a chair that seemed to have exploded. The other big chair looked untouched, and on it he saw a folded jacket and two handguns. There was no one in the room, but he did see one sign of human habitation—on the central floor a dark red stain that could only be blood.

The gendarmes arrived within minutes, and their first determination was clear-cut: Whatever battle had come to the small boutique hotel in Courbevoie, it had run its course. The building was secure. With everyone on edge given the recent spate of attacks, the assault on Room 14 was immediately stamped as having possible terrorist involvement. Evidence technicians were quick to arrive, and their initial findings sent straight to the DGSI command center.

Charlotte LeFevre—who had been on duty for forty-eight hours—was the first to see the results. Based on the preliminary report, she ordered the immediate acquisition of CCTV footage for the area around the hotel. She soon found what she was after. LeFevre copied the best image from the video, and forwarded it to the detectives on scene, along with a question. They reply came almost immediately. She rushed two floors up to the director's suite.

Baland's receptionist tried to turn her away, but LeFevre was adamant. She waited breathlessly while her arrival was announced, shifting her weight from one foot to the other as she stared at the heavy door.

She thought she might have heard a desk drawer slide shut. Finally, Baland appeared at the threshold of his office.

"Yes, Charlotte, what is it?" he said, gesturing for her to come inside.

LeFevre followed the director-designate toward one side of the room, and they settled into large chairs. She covered the essentials of what had happened. "Our people have been interviewing the hotel staff, and when I heard their description of the man who'd rented the room, I began going over CCTV footage." She slid the photograph onto the desk. "This was captured by a camera across the street minutes before the shooting started. I remembered the description you gave me of the man who brought Uday in—the one you thought might be responsible for the bombing at The Peninsula."

Baland looked at the picture. "Yes," he agreed, "I think that might be him."

"Three hotel employees confirmed it—he's been staying in this room for the last few days. There's also footage of a woman—I think it's the one we've been after, the one responsible for Director Michelis' death." LeFevre waited for a reaction from Baland, but saw little. "She can be seen leaving the scene of this shooting one minute after it was called in."

Baland seemed to consider it all. "Did you say there was blood on the floor of the room?"

"Yes. The teams are recovering samples as we speak."

"But this woman didn't appear injured?"

"Nothing obvious. If anyone was wounded, they managed to escape. I've alerted hospitals to watch for gunshot victims seeking treatment."

"Yes, very good."

LeFevre went over other initiatives she'd ordered in the burgeoning investigation, all quite standard, and Baland nodded his agreement. She thought he seemed distracted, and, hoping to draw him out, she asked, "Have you heard anything new from the Defense Ministry on this boat in Gravelines?"

"Gravelines . . . no, nothing of importance. One more crisis averted. Let's get back to finding these two."

"Of course, sir," said a deflated LeFevre. The eagerness of the chase she felt was apparently not shared by her soon-to-be boss.

She was nearly to the door when Baland forestalled her departure with, "Tell me something, Charlotte . . . is LeFevre your maiden name?"

A bewildered LeFevre turned back around. "Well . . . yes, sir, it is."

"But you are married."

"Of course. I kept my maiden name for professional reasons. My husband's name is Weiss."

"Ah, yes. I remember now. I met him at the New Year's party—Avrim. And you have two boys?"

"That's right," she said, thinking the trajectory of the conversation odd. "Eight and ten."

"If you don't mind my asking . . . do you raise them in the Jewish faith?"

"We do, yes. We attend Temple Beth Israel every Saturday. Why do you ask?"

Baland smiled a smile that was benevolence itself. "Temple Beth Israel—yes, I know exactly where that is. Isn't it wonderful how people of different faiths can live together so agreeably in France? Always remember that, Charlotte—it's what we're fighting for."

She nodded.

"Keep up the good work."

LeFevre took this as her cue to leave. Once in the outer office, with the door closed behind her, she looked at Baland's receptionist, a sprightly older woman, and mouthed the words, *Is he all right?*

The woman smiled understandingly, and whispered back, "He's been under a great deal of stress lately."

LeFevre started back to the command center, thinking, *Aren't we all.*

On the other side of the door, Zavier Baland walked to the far side of the room. He stood motionless in front of the great window, taking in the evening landscape of Rue de Villiers and Paris beyond.

SEVENTY-ONE

It was a morning made for a ceremony. The air was crisp and the skies clear, an apology for the preceding days. A steady breeze had the tricolor fluttering smartly on its staff in front of the majestic dome at Hôtel des Invalides.

The improved weather had extracted pent-up crowds, but few grasped the substance of the ceremony being assembled on the museum's forecourt plaza. Most of the tourists who paused in their languid strolls thought it might have something to do with Napoléon, whose body lay interred nearby. Parisians enjoying their weekend expressed a passing interest, but they'd seen such affairs before. Least attentive of all were pairs of young lovers strolling the Seine, who cast barely a glance, their fuzzy heads swimming with remembrances of the previous night's wine and ardor.

Jacques Roland, minister of the interior, stood officiously at the podium while a dozen department heads mingled behind him. A hundred chairs had been brought in for an audience, but at five minutes before nine only half were full. Most of those who'd come were department personnel, along with a few upward-aspiring commanders from the various regional divisions.

The man at the center of it all, Zavier Baland, was not disappointed in the turnout. In truth he found it encouraging, a sign that the bulk of the country's counterterrorism forces were exhausted, taking time off to sleep and catch up with their families after the long shifts of recent days. For the same reason, media coverage of the ceremony was virtually nonexistent—a pair of junior reporters from competing dailies had shown up to go through the motions.

Baland saw Jacqueline in the front row, but the girls had gone off to their regular Saturday language lesson. He and Jacqueline had argued about that, but Baland prevailed, insisting that their daughters' education took a higher priority. In the moments after the matter was settled, it occurred to Baland that the decision might well be his last involvement in their lives.

He would issue his orders to attack the Jews of France later today. When the ceremony ended, he would attend a luncheon at headquarters—there was no avoiding it, since he *was* the guest of honor—but he had otherwise cleared his calendar. At four o'clock the first burst message was set to be transmitted. He'd done his best to pair trigger-ready cells with targets appropriate for their weapons. Others, those individuals with more intent than means, he decided to keep in reserve for a second wave. A month from now, perhaps two—however long it took for France to let her guard down again.

Baland accepted that a percentage of the strikes would fail. He would be issuing the orders without forewarning, and he knew that no soldiers, even committed jihadists, liked being sent into action on short notice. On the other hand, many had been awaiting the call, some for years. Even by his most pessimistic estimate, he was confident that dozens of Jewish targets would be struck in the coming days. The police forces of France, already fatigued and scattered across the country, would be caught flat-footed by the scale of the new offensive.

The voice of the protocol officer interrupted his calculations. "Three minutes, everyone."

Baland began edging toward the podium, where Roland was pulling notes from his pocket—no doubt his prepared remarks.

"Monsieur Director!"

The title sounded strange, but Baland's attention was snagged by the voice. He half turned to see Charlotte LeFevre approaching. Or as he now thought of her, Charlotte Weiss.

"I know there isn't much time, sir, but you asked to see the hourly as soon as it was available."

"We only have a moment," he said. "Is there anything new on this business in Courbevoie?"

"There is one peculiarity. The blood we recovered from the carpet in the room—it wasn't blood at all."

He looked at her curiously. "What was it then?"

LeFevre referenced her phone. "Corn syrup, cocoa,

and red food dye. Simple, but very convincing. I'm not sure what to make of it."

Baland said nothing. The protocol officer looked pointedly at LeFevre, and said, "One minute."

She backed away, saying, "We can discuss it further after the ceremony." She scurried away and took a seat in the back row.

Baland heard someone whisper his name, and saw Roland beckoning him closer to the podium. He had been instructed to stand at the minister's right shoulder for the duration of his remarks, which were to last roughly fifteen minutes. Baland edged closer and stood very still, trying to make sense of what LeFevre had just told him.

Roland began to speak. It was on the last word of his morning welcome, with the sun reflecting off Napoléon's golden dome, that the bullet crashed into Zavier Baland's skull.

Everyone heard the shot, followed by a distinct echo.

LeFevre saw Baland go down, and a frantic scramble of bodies ensued. Someone tackled Roland to the ground and covered him protectively. On realizing what had happened, most simply ran. A few took cover behind statues, and a handful of others, likely men and women with military experience, jumped into the empty moat surrounding the plaza—the best foxhole in all Paris.

LeFevre flew into action. She was the first to reach Baland's side, and therefore the first to see it was hopeless. The bullet had struck above his left ear, and the damage was catastrophic. His eyes were locked in a forever gaze into a faultless morning sky.

LeFevre looked all around, and saw chaos in every quarter. She had no idea where the shot had come from.

SEVENTY-TWO

The principals were bundled away in armored limousines. When five minutes passed without further gunfire, a response began to organize on the stone plaza. Because LeFevre was dressed as a civilian, she flashed her senior DGSI credentials to every uniform in sight. She was soon the on-scene commander.

The mystery regarding the source of the shot was quickly resolved. A nearby policeman who'd been doing his job—looking outward from the ceremony and not watching it—reported seeing a small puff of smoke, and perhaps a muzzle flash, from a spot above the scaffolding that fronted the Colombian embassy. By the time his story reached LeFevre, fifteen minutes had passed since the shooting, and an armored vehicle with a tactical response team was just arriving. The team had been on alert for forty-eight hours, but there was no weariness or lack of urgency in anyone's step as they fanned into position. LeFevre briefed the commander, and they quickly pinpointed the shooter's hide above the embassy entrance. An assault squad of four men was dispatched, and sixty seconds after they scaled the platform and disappeared behind the high wall, the leader waved an all-clear signal.

The commander and LeFevre were next up, making use of a ladder that was resting against the scaffolding. Thirty feet above the sidewalk they followed the squad leader inside a narrow gap behind the exterior wall. Everyone looked down at the body of a thickset young woman. She was resting facedown, one arm bent awkwardly under her torso, and her opposing shoulder was still pressed against the butt of a rifle. There was a gaping wound on her temple. Perhaps out of habit, one of the tactical men said something about calling an ambulance.

Another member of the squad emerged from deep in the crawlspace, and said, "There are tools in back, including a big masonry drill."

The commander acknowledged the information, then looked at LeFevre.

She knelt down and took the liberty of half rolling the body. One side of the woman's head was destroyed, but her face, dark-skinned and with a prominent curving nose, was relatively undamaged. LeFevre was quite sure she was looking at the fugitive they'd been after, the woman who'd shot Director Michelis.

She tried to put together the sequence of what had happened, but saw only half an answer. Then she noticed the commander and his squad leader inspecting something near the wall. LeFevre got up and joined them.

"What is it?" she asked.

The commander pointed to the rifle, which was trained outward through a vertical slot. "I would say this is your assassin. Her weapon lines up perfectly with where the director was standing. Ballistics will easily confirm it."

"I can see that much. But who shot *her*? One of ours?"

He cocked his head. "If any policeman did this, they would have taken credit by now." The commander gave her a circumspect look. "Tell me—how many shots did you hear?"

"Only one . . . although, I do remember a very distinct echo."

The commander exchanged a glance with his senior subordinate. "Check into it," he said.

The man nodded and disappeared.

"Check into what?" LeFevre asked.

The commander leaned down and looked through a second hole in the wall. It was far smaller than the first, and very near where the body was resting.

"Do you think she drilled these holes?" LeFevre asked.

"Most likely."

"Was the smaller one a mistake? Maybe drilled at the wrong angle?"

The commander stifled a response. He stood and gestured for LeFevre to have a look through the smaller aperture. She knelt down a second time, and found herself peering through a circular hollow the diameter of a soda can. It gave a pinhole view across the terrace of Invalides, then down the length of Rue de Grenelle, where traffic ran oblivious to the nearby tragedy.

"I don't see anything," said LeFevre.

"Neither do I. But I think we should have a closer look."

It took less than an hour to discover the second shooter's perch.

The tactical team commander picked out the building with remarkable acuity. During a long walk up Rue de Grenelle, and with regular glances over his shoulder, he had paused suddenly where the road made a slight bend. Beyond that, Invalides would no longer be in sight. Directly in front of them stood a tall residential complex.

Forensic teams were brought in quickly and swarmed through the building. Operating under the commander's guiding principle, they began searching residences that had a line of sight to the distant embassy. Of particular interest was a vacant unit that had recently gone up for sale. How the killer had gained access to the home would be thrashed out later, but there was no denying what everyone saw within seconds of going inside. A perfectly round hole, roughly ten inches in diameter, had been cut from an east-facing window—the circle of glass removed was on the floor beneath, still attached to a suction cup. Across the room, a chair had been pulled up to the granite kitchen island. It was here that the most definitive evidence was discovered—a technician confirmed traces of gunshot residue on the stylish green granite.

LeFevre stood next to the commander as technicians began going over the place. She said, "So this is it—he was here."

"I'm convinced," the commander replied. He turned to face her. "You just said 'he.' What makes you think it was a man?"

"An educated guess," she hedged.

The commander didn't belabor the point. He looked around the kitchen floor. "I don't see a casing. It's all very professional."

Looking into the distance, LeFevre recognized the reverse view of what she'd seen through the tiny hole in the embassy wall—the building in which they were standing would have been somewhere in that urban picture. Then she remembered something else. "The echo I heard. It wasn't an echo at all. He shot her right after she killed Baland."

The commander nodded. "Almost instantaneously. With his scope trained on the smaller opening in the wall, his field of view would easily have included the larger one. He would have seen the muzzle flash of her shot. I'd guess his bullet arrived about four seconds later. Three if he was very good. At that point, she would have been looking through her own scope to confirm her shot." He left the rest unsaid. "It's a classic countersniper kill."

"Countersniper," she repeated rhetorically. LeFevre looked searchingly across the park. "How far away is that?"

"Seven hundred and eighty-one meters."

She looked at him incredulously.

He patted his tactical vest. "We carry laser range finders—I took a quick shot."

"But that opening we saw . . . you're telling me he put a bullet through a tennis-ball can from almost half a mile away. I don't see how anyone could do that."

"Anyone? Certainly not. But there are a few who might. In truth, he got a little lucky. I saw marks on the inner walls of your 'tennis-ball can.' The bullet grazed the stone and ricocheted. Judging by the assassin's wound, I would say the round tumbled the last half meter. At that point it hardly mattered. The velocity was sufficient, and the round was heading through a tunnel to a target only inches away."

LeFevre's gaze fixed on the distant Colombian embassy. She could barely see the front door, let alone the tiny aperture. She heaved out a sigh. "What else?"

The commander regarded the distant building. "I see one other thing that suggests a professional—although it's quite circumstantial."

LeFevre only waited for an explanation.

"You see . . . he didn't take a follow-up shot. It would have been quite easy to do. From here the shooter had no way to see his target. He knew where she was and how to reach her, but there was no way to tell if she was struck by the first round."

"So why didn't he shoot again?"

"I've been wondering that myself, and can think of only one reason." He turned to face her. "Whoever your man is—he is very confident in his abilities."

SEVENTY-THREE

Windsom swung lazily on her anchor in a halfhearted trade wind. She was laid up in the lee of a half-moon cove, a nameless spit of sand somewhere north of Papua. The sea shimmered in the early light, shades of blue on the surface reflecting what lay beneath— the dark shadows of coral heads twenty feet down, lighter shades speaking of a bleached-sand bottom.

Christine secured Davy's life jacket and lowered him into the runabout.

"Birds!" he said eagerly, pointing to the island.

"Not now," she said. "We'll go ashore later."

The two of them had explored the cay yesterday. They'd found two palm trees and a few stands of grass between them. A certain species of tern had taken to nesting on the high ground, battling a certain species of crab for real estate above the tide line. Davy had enjoyed walking among the birds, who seemed to have no fear of humans.

This morning, however, they had a different destination. Probably the *only* other destination within a hundred miles.

Her name was *Mistral,* and she'd arrived four days ago. Neighbors for as long as their respective anchors held. The Smiths were from New Zealand, a couple slightly older than her and David. They had a nine-year-old girl named Nina, who was getting along famously with Davy.

"Nina?" Davy asked as Christine navigated the hundred yards to *Mistral.*

"Yes, Nina!"

Davy bounced happily on the wooden seat. Play dates on the high sea were a rare event, and for that reason the children's age difference fell to irrelevance. John and Linda were already on deck, coffee in hand. Their Beneteau 55 was longer than *Windsom,* a handsome boat but without the utilitarian width of a catamaran.

"Good morning!" Christine hailed as she idled the runabout toward a boarding ladder and tied on.

"Good morning," said John. He helped Davy up the ladder. "Coffee's on."

"Sounds wonderful." Once aboard, Christine exchanged a hug with the adults, and watched as Nina collected Davy and took him below. She'd known these people for only a few days, but they already seemed like family—a familiarity brought on, she knew, by their shared isolation.

"Dinner at my place tonight?" Christine asked.

"By all means," Linda said. "What can I bring?"

"How about a few of those lobster John's been snagging?"

"Done."

They chatted for a time, John his usual gregarious

self—a seemingly universal Kiwi trait, in Christine's experience. Linda, however, was more subdued, and by the time John went below to feed the children, Christine was feeling uneasy.

"Is something wrong?" she asked once they were alone.

"Well . . . I hope not. But there's something you should know. Remember a few days ago, when you asked to use our internet for a search on that man your husband was meeting in Paris?"

Christine nodded cautiously. Her self-imposed communications blackout on *Windsom* had been driving her to distraction, and at the time David had been gone for a week with no word. When she'd met the Smiths and seen *Mistral*'s first-rate satellite suite, she hadn't been able to hold back. She explained that her own service was being dodgy, and that David had gone to Paris to meet someone named Zavier Baland. She wanted to learn more about the man.

With Linda at her side, Christine had searched the online news services. She discovered that the man David thought he'd killed so many years ago was not only still alive and working as a counterterrorism officer, but had also beaten back an assassination attempt the day before. He'd wounded his attacker in the process. Christine's world had gone into free fall until the last paragraph of the article, where she learned the attacker had been female. Later, as she regained her bearings back on *Windsom*, she found herself wondering how many people could be gunning for the man. Might Mossad have assigned someone besides David to the job? There were no clear answers, and since that time she'd soldiered on in the face of two uncomfortable certainties: David was unaccounted for, and Baland remained unharmed.

"Yes, I remember what we found," Christine said, her words seeming distant.

"Have you heard from your husband?"

"No . . . why do you ask?"

"I did another search this morning. There have been a number of terrorist attacks in France in recent days. The man you asked about, Baland. He was killed—shot dead by a sniper Saturday morning in Paris. Nearly two days ago now."

All Christine could manage in reply was, "A sniper, you say?"

"Yes. But the good news is, the assailant was also killed."

"Oh . . . I see." Christine was trying to construct a sentence, something about whether the attacker's identity had been released, when a distant sound intervened.

They both looked to the far end of the atoll and saw a seaplane approaching. The rumble of its engine rose slowly, but soon overpowered every other sound as it came directly overhead. The aircraft was red with a white stripe, set on top of long white pontoons. It looked tiny against the endless blue sky. Passing directly over *Windsom*, the aircraft banked to its left in a wide half circle and began easing down toward the protected waters of the lagoon.

"Could that be David?" Linda asked.

Christine didn't have an answer. Her eyes were riveted to the little seaplane as its floats kissed the azure water, and then a trail of white spray erupted as it settled on the lagoon. As the craft steered toward the tiny beach, she realized one of two people was going to step off. Either Anton Bloch or her husband. If it was Bloch, it could mean only one thing.

The engine clattered to a rough idle as the aircraft nosed to the shoreline. Strangely, Christine found herself overtaken by a sense of ease. She saw two figures inside, one obviously the pilot. One of Davy's infectious chuckles rose from below. Her heartbeat, her breathing—everything seemed to go on hold until a tall, athletic figure stepped out on a pontoon and jumped ashore.

Christine breathed again.

"Yeah," she said, "that's David. He always did know how to make an entrance."

She took the runabout to the beach to collect her husband, leaving Davy on *Mistral* with the Smiths— he was playing contentedly with Nina, and Christine suspected a private moment with his father might be needed.

The seaplane was already churning its way back to deeper water. David stood on the shoreline, his shoes in one hand and a plastic bag in the other. Christine never slowed and nearly ran him down with the dinghy, the outboard kicking up behind as it hit the sand bottom. She leapt out of the boat, and he dropped what he was holding and took her in his arms.

Neither said anything for a time. They simply held each other, a salve for the hardships they'd both endured in recent days. David finally pushed away, and said, "Where's Davy?"

"On *Mistral* with—"

"Who are they?" he said in a clipped tone.

Christine only stared at him.

He closed his eyes. She saw the tension drain out of him like a sponge released from a grip, taking its true shape and pulling in air. He drew her close again and buried his face in her hair. "I'm sorry," he whispered in her ear.

"It's all right. I know it's hard to turn off that switch."

They fell quiet again, simply happy to be close. Eventually she took his hand and led him to the only furniture on the island—a downed trunk from an old palm tree that had either fallen or been washed ashore. They sat in the building heat, the sun on their backs.

He said, "I tried to get a message through a few days ago."

"I didn't get it. I kept everything turned off like we agreed. How did you even know where we were?"

"Our security needs a little tweaking. We can talk about that later."

"Our new neighbors have a good comm system. I got the news just a few minutes ago," she said. "Baland was killed."

"Was he?"

Christine eyed him with a narrow gaze. She remembered Linda mentioning the time of the attack, and she did the time-zone math. "It happened forty-two hours ago." The words came out almost like an accusation.

"I didn't pull the trigger. At least, not on him. The way it all went down . . . it was complicated."

An awkward silence ensued. "Okay," she said. "We can leave it at that—if that's what you want."

He pulled in a deep breath, then let it out slowly. "No, we should talk about it. I want you to know everything."

He went day by day, giving particular attention to the endgame. He explained how he'd confronted Malika in his room, and how with the help of another *kidon* he staged his own death. He told her how the other *kidon,* whose name he had never even learned, provided a second long-range weapon. Then the setup at Invalides, and the two final shots.

When he stopped talking, Christine thought about it for a time. "So you arranged both their deaths."

"Yes."

"I understand your reasons . . . but why did you do it in such a roundabout way? I mean, I hate how I'm thinking, but wouldn't it have been easier to simply shoot her when she was in your room, then assassinate Baland the next day?"

"Separately, yes. But it's important to think forward. Consider the consequences. If I'd killed Malika in my room, I would have had a body to deal with. If her death was discovered, I'd have ended up as the prime suspect in her killing. The hotel staff would have had no trouble describing me, and that would have made it hard to get near Baland the next day. On top of all that, if I'd been the one to assassinate Baland—every policeman in France would be after me right now. And they'd keep looking for a very long time."

With a troubling adeptness, Christine saw his logic. "The way it worked out, Baland's killer has been identified. And she's dead."

He nodded. "It's the woman they've been looking for—the one who already tried to kill him once. I heard they even have her DNA to match. Not much there to investigate."

"And as to who might have killed *her*?"

"Someone killed an assassin two seconds too late. If a policeman had done it, they'd give him a medal. Honestly, I doubt the French will be paying overtime to figure that one out. They'll go through the motions, but as we speak . . . it's probably halfway to being a cold case."

She looked at him uncomfortably. "That's all very . . . efficient."

He looked away. "That's never how it feels. The world is an ever-changing place. At any given time, in the circumstances of a particular moment . . . I do what's necessary. Nothing more, nothing less."

The seaplane began its takeoff run over the glass-smooth lagoon, its engine violating the silence and scattering terns across the island. The big pontoons lifted, and the aircraft levitated, slow and ungainly as it clawed into the sky. Soon it was no more than a speck on the southern horizon.

"Do you think it will help?" she asked.

"What?"

"That Baland, or whoever he is, is dead?"

"Maybe . . . a little. But others will take his place. Just like ISIS will find a new set of so-called leaders."

"The ones who let God take responsibility for their crimes?"

"That's nothing new. People have been killing in the name of religion for thousands of years. And not just Islam."

"It seems so irrational."

"It's like throwing knives at a sunset."

Christine didn't like the darkness she felt building. "I think you'll like our new neighbors," she said.

"Kiwis?"

"How'd you know?"

He pointed toward *Mistral* and she saw the New Zealand flag astern. "Right. Your legendary powers of observation."

"How's my boy?"

"One week smarter."

"Wish I could say that." He got up and strolled toward the water's edge. "I was thinking about heading west, maybe the Med this fall. What do you think?"

"I think the Med's a long way from here. But I like Italian food." She noticed the package next to his shoes in the sand. "Bring me some lingerie?"

"Wouldn't do you justice."

"Clever answer, Slaton."

He retrieved the bag and showed her a set of oversized LEGO bricks. "I got it at the airport in Manila."

"He'll love it."

"I like that memory game, but I think we're all ready for something new."

"I think you're tired of losing, so you're changing the game."

"Maybe so."

She got up and stepped toward the runabout. "Okay, I think it's time for some introductions. Oh, and we're having lobster tonight—assuming you and John are reasonably proficient hunter-gatherers."

Together they pushed the little boat into deep water. Christine vaulted aboard, but watched David hesitate. "What's wrong?"

Standing shin-deep in the Pacific, he said, "I worry sometimes . . . about Davy."

"Davy's fine. We're doing the best we can, and today that's pretty good."

"I know, but . . . what if he ends up being like me?"

The question was like a loaded gun. Christine saw right away that he wanted to take it back. She looked at him curiously, and almost hedged with, *In what way?* What she said was, "I hope he turns out just like you."

After a moment, Slaton grinned. "Clever answer, Doctor."

ACKNOWLEDGMENTS

I would like to express my deepest appreciation to those who helped with *Assassin's Code*.

As always, thanks to my editor, Bob Gleason, for telling me what to fix, but allowing me to fix it. Your rich imagination and in-depth knowledge, not to mention your apocalyptic predilections, offer the perfect sounding board for ideas.

The staff at Tor were instrumental as ever, including Linda Quinton, Elayne Becker, and Emily Mullen. And of course, thanks to the inimitable Tom Doherty for what you have built on Flatiron's 14th.

All appreciation to my agent, Susan Gleason, for your unfailing enthusiasm, dedication, and, of course, the wine. You have been, and will remain, essential.

I also would like to thank Ileen Maisel and Lawrence Elman at Amber Entertainment for their ceaseless efforts to bring this series to the big screen. Along the same lines, executive producers Bob and Patricia Gussin. The finish line, we all hope, is near.

I certainly could never have completed this book without the steady support of my wife and children.

For the eighth time, and with no less enthusiasm than the first, thank you.

Finally, I would like to recognize those on the receiving end of my stories. This series could never have become what it is without the support, feedback, and word-of-mouth recommendations of so many readers. From the bottom of my heart, thank you all for helping me bring Slaton to life.

Read on for a preview of

ASSASSIN'S
RUN

WARD LARSEN

*Available in August 2018
from Tom Doherty Associates*

A Forge Book

ONE

It was just as well Pyotr Ivanovic didn't realize he was about to die. As a man who comprehensively enjoyed a good meal, his last on this earth would be free of any misgivings regarding his soon-to-be-issued digestif.

He glanced out the starboard window at a night-shrouded sea, the occasional breaker highlighted in dim moonlight. Lovely as the panorama was, it was far less compelling than what rested before him on the white-linened table. His new chef had outdone himself tonight. The steak before Ivanovic was a choice cut, thirty ounces of grain-fed beef flown in from Australia and seared to perfection. Against that, the potatoes Lyonnais were but an afterthought, the haricots verts no more than garnish. The bottle of Bordeaux, he allowed, did the steak justice, one of the best from his extensive shipboard collection. Thankfully, the new man had learned quickly. Ivanovic did not count calories. He courted them openly, throwing himself upon the culinary altar of any chef who could do them well. Tonight's meal, as it turned out, was more special than most. It was a celebration of sorts, marking the beginning of the most ambitious undertaking of his career.

Which made it very ambitious indeed.

The head of his security detail came through the salon door, bringing a gust of wind with him. October had arrived full force on the Tyrrhenian Sea, the opening volley of winter's campaign. Ivanovic looked up in annoyance, but he knew there was no use in berating the man—that was life at sea.

The ship was called *Cassandra*—ship because no vessel 190 feet long could be referred to as a boat, and *Cassandra* as a prod at his late mother. He still laughed inwardly at that: the ship had already been around the world once, while her namesake, as far as he knew, had never in her life traveled more than ten miles from the miserable Ukrainian village in which she'd been born.

The yacht had been built to his demanding specifications by a man who, if not the finest marine architect in Greece, was certainly the most expensive. The mahogany planking beneath his feet was inlaid with gold trim, and every fitting and furnishing was of the highest quality. Marble floors and columns predominated, so much weight that the poor architect had warned the boat might capsize. Another three million had allayed the man's worries, something to do with stabilizers and ballast to keep the ship upright, and causing Ivanovic to jest that her keel had been laid not in lead but gold. Ultimately, however, he had what he wanted—not a refuge for the odd vacation, but rather a stage, a platform from which all manner of business and pleasure might be consummated.

His thickset security chief padded across the salon. He was dressed in his usual ill-fitting suit, and his only visible accessory—sourced not from Gucci or Hermès, but rather Beretta—bulged obviously beneath a wrinkled lapel. The man handed over a communications printout. "This just arrived," he said in Russian.

Ivanovic took a ten-page printout in hand and removed his reading glasses from a pocket. "Is the loading complete?" he asked.

"Yes. The ship will sail shortly after midnight from Sebastopol."

Ivanovic skimmed the report, which contained an official manifest purporting what was being carried and where it was being taken. He chuckled at the creativity involved, and with some effort extracted the few truths. The destination was listed as Mumbai, which covered things nicely. *Argos*, a ship his new subsidiary had acquired only last month, was to leave Crimea for the Black Sea, then run a gentle slalom through the Bosporus Straits, followed by a left turn into open water. There she would disappear into the Mediterranean's river of commerce.

"Bring me any new updates," Ivanovic said dismissively.

His security man disappeared and he readdressed his steak, his eyes still scanning the paperwork page by page. He was remorseless in his attack, his hands sawing hunks of flesh and plugging them into his mouth. At the other end of the twelve-foot table a young woman sat ignored, but that was nothing new. It had long been Ivanovic's custom to work through dinner—he'd always felt he was at his best behind a good meal, his senses at their most heightened.

"You are not eating," he said distractedly, his eyes pinned on a cargo manifest.

Ursula, the new blonde from a tiny village in Siberia, twirled her fork through a salad.

"It is too much for me," she replied.

He measured a lewd reply, but the sport of it escaped him. He was already growing tired of this one. She was young and rail thin, eyes as blue and empty as a cloudless midday sky. She'd spent the day shopping on the island of Capri, now three miles off the starboard beam. Ivanovic had no doubt she'd spent every dollar of the ten thousand he'd allotted. What had to be a new dress clung like shrink wrap, and the bracelet flopping on one of her wrists looked like a diamond-studded handcuff.

"When will we leave for Saint-Tropez?" she asked.

Ivanovic ignored the question, sensing a bit of negotiating capital for later use in his suite.

He finished his steak, and with barely a pause the cook appeared with a massive crème brûlée in one hand and a torch in the other. In a flourish of culinary stagecraft, the cook lit his flame and soon had the topping caramelized into a crust that looked positively volcanic.

Ten minutes later, his great belly full, Ivanovic stepped out onto the wide aft deck, which doubled as a helipad, and prepared his customary cigar. Fighting a brisk wind, he managed to light it, and stood in survey of his surroundings. In the distance Capri rose from the sea, and a string of amber to the east outlined the Amalfi Coast.

Earlier today, viewing the harbor of Capri, he'd seen one other ship in *Cassandra*'s league. Ivanovic had checked the ship's registry, and was surprised to find that it wasn't owned by a Russian, but rather a Greek. *Probably that bastard marine architect*, he mused. Twenty years ago it would have been a Saudi, before that a Brit. Today, however, across the Med, the competition was largely between the oligarchs. Men who wore their wealth as a badge in the face of invariably humble beginnings.

Ivanovic himself was a case in point. The son of a Ukrainian pig farmer, he had always known he was destined for more than his muck-booted elder. How *much* more had surprised even him. He'd walked out of the foothills of the Carpathians at fifteen, and within two years found himself in Moscow doing small favors for third-tier mobsters. In time, the grade of both his dealings and the crooks he associated with rose in parallel. And now the bar had risen one last time. To a point that could go no higher.

He heard footsteps behind him, and turned to see his security man again.

"Is there something new?" Ivanovic asked.

"No sir. I just wanted to mention . . . I think it might be safer inside."

"You worry too much."

The security man, whose name was Pavel, and who was the closest thing Ivanovic had to a friend, nearly said something. Instead he stood down.

Ivanovic said, "They tell me Abramovich's new ship will be nearly a hundred meters."

Pavel shrugged. "I wouldn't know."

"A hundred meters. That's a very round number—someone should do it."

Pavel eyed Ivanovic's cigar, clearly calculating how much longer it had to burn. Ivanovic went to the starboard rail as a wayward cloud blotted out the moon. He pulled a long draw on his Cohiba, then flicked a bit of ash into the wind-driven water below.

From a distance, the sinewy young man looking through his scope saw a fragment of white-hot ash flutter down to the sea. The burning cigar itself was bright, like a beacon atop the rotund lighthouse that was Pyotr Ivanovic. He saw another man on deck, yet had no trouble distinguishing which of the two to target. The Ukrainian stood out in any crowd, his height and girth at the limits of human potential.

The shooter was still getting used to the new scope, a synthetic hybrid of optical and infrared imagery, and he was pleasantly surprised. Technology in armaments had never been a Russian strength—manufacturers there had long leaned toward simplicity and robustness. The picture before him was unusually sharp, if a bit undermagnified.

The story behind his equipment had been explained to him by a pair of engineers, this in itself a departure from long-held practices. They told him the scope was not a Russian design, but had in fact been "acquired" from America's leading edge research facility, the Sandia

National Laboratories. This was nothing new. Russia had long ago stopped trying to keep pace with the West, realizing it was far more economical to let them do the expensive research, development, and testing, then simply steal the results. It had been going on for decades, going back to the Cold War. In those heady days, virtually every new American airplane was followed within a few years by a curiously similar Soviet twin. A time lag had been unavoidable then, Soviet developers forced to work largely from photographs, which necessitated considerable guesswork and reverse engineering. Now the internet age had simplified things greatly—today Russia simply hacked into computers and filched proven blueprints, shortening the "time to shelf" considerably.

The assassin checked the scope's calibration one last time, then verified the synchronization. It was the first time he'd used this system in the field—even his practice had been limited to tightly controlled simulations. The rifle was at least familiar, which gave a degree of confidence. Best of all, his level of personal risk on this mission was less than on any he'd ever undertaken.

A gust of wind brushed the shooter's cheek. On any other day it would have got his attention, but tonight he ignored it entirely. His finger began to press the trigger and his breathing slowed, the habits of eight years taking hold. It couldn't hurt. Finally, in what could only be termed a playful impulse, he jerked his finger through the final half inch of travel.

The big gun answered, bucking once and belching a tongue of flame. All as expected. The bulky suppressor helped, but there was no dampening the supersonic round. The killer resettled the scope for what seemed an interminable amount of time. He was almost ready to admit a miss when Ivanovic jerked violently.

He saw the Russian's head slam forward on a neck carrying its last neural transmissions to the limbs below. His massive body seemed to hesitate for a moment, like a felled tree deciding which way to drop. Then he cartwheeled over the ship's rail and into the sea.

The splash was momentous.

It was all the confirmation the killer needed. Job done, he tidied up his gear, surveyed carefully his course of egress, and blended into the night.